4 A.M. Until 4 P.M.
By
Tricia Lomax & Maura Farrar

ISBN: 978-0-9559905-5-7

Maura's dedications.

This book is dedicated to my beautiful friend and co-author Tricia Lomax.

To my three children, Daniel, Mathew, Lucy and to David. To my parents Lilian and Joseph Gallagher and to all my sisters and brothers and to my grandparents and great grandparents for finding and understanding about all our beginnings. And finally, but not least I dedicate this book to myself, Maura Farrar.

Tricia's dedications.

For Maura - This journey with you has been awesome, amazing and a huge part of my life, this book is a testament to all and everything and is something very special. Thank you.

Especially to my husband John - who has caught me before I have fallen and flown by my side when I reach for the sky. And for Jasper our best friend.
To my parents who gave birth to my creativity, especially my mum who I will share this books success, she deserves it.
To Jenny and Matthew, special niece and nephew. My sister Janet (the best in the world) and brother in law Stephen.
To all my friends who have supported my writing.

To Tony our editor and Janet our proofreader, we couldn't have done it without you.

INTRODUCTION

This book engages mind and body, with its narrative and beautiful, visual imagery of the landscape, which is located in an English, un-commercialised, seaside town.

The elements of the land and sea form part of the novels structure, which permeates throughout the book and is as fundamental to the characters lives as are their emotions and intentions and interactions amongst others as well as between themselves.

The moon is considered a female force, an element of nature and the tides are lead by her and consequently it is she who determines the sea's moods, whether they are savage and brutal, or gentle and calm.
The story shifts between past and present, fact and fiction.

The two central character's Anna and Jo meet at dawn on a coastal cliff path, after a sonic boom has woken them both from sleep. This 'bang' ricochets and has a ripple effect, not only on these two women, but also the other main characters that witness their 'meeting' and become drawn into their worlds.

The story vacillates between several story lines – all uniquely intertwined by Anna and Jo's exploration to find happiness and identity.
Anna's quest to understand herself, is her self discovery in the writing of her book 'Fermanagh House', where she begins to fathom the consequences of the life she has lead.

Jo has fled from her own past and disconnected from her world, to live a life of anonymity and seclusion in a beach hut. As a result of the 'bang', Jo is inadvertently carried on a tidal wave that moves and courses and shifts her, out of her disappearance and disassociation.

The imaginative mystery, becomes a multi-layered riddle, wherein the lives of the characters are each given room to lap in and out of one another, creating windows that lead into dreams and reality as if everything is in some way connected.

Like life some elements of the plot are supposed to remain indecipherable.

This book enriches the reader with depth and understanding of these people and the extraordinary impact they have on each other.

This is not a single story, but several or more stories each being spun concurrently.

The repercussions of the 'bang' in these peoples lives is significant and fundamentally changes their own journey, as each individual experiences the turning tide within themselves.

Part 1

THE CLOCK

Wednesday 14th June - South London.

Like the proverbial cat and mouse, his toying, his indecisive pushing and playing around the madness of himself, captures him. He lifts his glass and draws a large measure of the ruby liquid, allowing it to arrest his tongue and coat his taste buds with rich tannin. He pauses for thought, knowing that eventually his eyes will become mesmerised, with nothing to displace them.
The two missing clues from the morning paper knock on the extremities of his conscience and he briefly allows their entry.
4 Down – Music of the night (----o-------) (12)
His mind runs through the list of composers, he knows the answer is elsewhere.
11 Across – This is not only applicable to Latin teachers! (2,4,8)
He smiles knowingly, however complex the conundrum set before him – he is not outwitted by its master.

Glancing toward the coffee table, with its pile of daily papers, his eyes catch the front-page headline of the latest celebrity revelations –

SEX ROMP 'Ménage à Trois' YARDLEY TELLS ALL.

He picks up the tabloid and speed-reads the article, turning to the inside pages he continues. He envies with greed, Yardley's exploits with the two women and for all the world, how he wishes it had been him. And how he would have written the piece, describing in detail, the erotica and how the women had begged him for it. There can be in his opinion, no greater accolade, than to have ones name and photograph, attributed to sexual prowess, for the entire world to see.

He lifts his glass and drinks again.

Dropping the paper back down, he selects his dictionary
for inspiration and flicks the pages at random, for an
answer to the clues. Eventually after much thought and
with triumphant aplomb, he tops up his glass and fills in
the answer to 11 across, INLOCOPARENTIS. Satisfied
now with just one clue left, he directs his attention to the
letter.

He reflects momentarily on how he had found her and a
shaft of steeliness bores through him; she had challenged
his determination, after his initial investigations proved
unsatisfactory. Her disappearance was just that, no one
seemed to know of her whereabouts, although it didn't
help because during his recovery he thought little of her,
the scar she had left him with, took months to heal. He
had lost lots of blood and the resulting weakness gave
him a listless depression, he felt old, frail and closed
himself off from the world. His few known associates
drifted away, after their enquiries of him were snubbed;
he preferred a solitary existence and detested their
inquisition into his accident. Eventually to his relief, they
withdrew and let him be.

In pursuit of her, it didn't help asking questions, months
after she had gone. With salubrious sobriety, he
relinquished his procrastinations and hired a private
detective. The costs were prolific but he found his sense
of well being amplified, by what he set out to do, he had
a sense of purpose. He intended to find her.
With this new directive he opened his door to the world.

Each day now he walks a little further, picks up a daily
newspaper and buys fresh food to eat. It was a few
months past the first anniversary of his estrangement
from her, that he received the news. She is living,
accompanied by a dog, in a wooden cabin at the seaside
town of Fenton, on the east coast of Yorkshire. She is
again out of touch and out of his reach; the distance
between them makes his quest more alluring.

In his fantasies alone with her, she is his to play with. He can undress her in his mind; he can make her do anything. He loves it when she goes down and rides above him but as her momentum quickens he fights and wrestles with himself. This un-acquiesced release drives him to hatred, as he calls out 'you fucking bitch' over and over again. On the rare occasions, when his fraught actions, earn him a feeble and unsatisfactory orgasm, he weeps, his hardly spent force adds to the furnace within and his spitefulness towards her grows. He cannot ejaculate her from his mind. The pulsing erection that is his core and central to him does not mirror his physical ability and because of this he seeks revenge. She holds his manhood, holds his penis and therefore he will not let go.

From early adolescence he had striven for control with women. At the age of fifteen he had bequeathed himself, his unworldly, innocence had been snatched away as he surrendered to the sexual demands of Judith, thirty years his senior. She promised to teach him everything there was to know and in doing so, she determined his needs and left him in pursuit of women. Thereon after, his goal, his ambition was to take back the control he had lost, to become the master of himself. And throughout his life, in his social circle, he searched for his own power and autonomy over women. Until he had found 'her' he was enveloped by women, seduced and trapped and unable to dictate the relationship; somehow it harked back to when he was fifteen and powerless and doing something he did and yet did not want to do. And then at last with 'her' she was ambivalent to his advances, the seduction came from him, she didn't trap or enslave him, she opened a platonic platform of space to share and for him to just be himself.

This earnest and beguiling premise set the rules and he basked in the glory of it. But as the fledgling inside her blossomed and she sought to spread her wings and fly, she found her capacity of assured independence to flee the nest and fend for herself. And she was no longer under his protection, no longer held within the confines of his nest and demands and somehow he had to hold her, he had to clip those wings and pin her to the ground. He would not, nor could not let her go.

With the testing and pushing of boundaries, their relationship changed, the open, sunny aspect that shone out, transformed to a depth of darkness that tormented and tortured his soul.

Wednesday 21st June – Fenton, East Yorkshire.

Jo is jolted awake from a deep dream, as if from a sudden bang; she lifts her head from the pillow, to hear and meet with silence. She waits tentatively, hoping and praying, that no one is prowling around, trying to get into the hut. Jason is unusually restless, alert and is whining at the bottom of the steps, he too has been disturbed by something. This adds to her fears and she slides beneath the sheets in an attempt to hide.

At the exact same moment, Anna too is wide-awake. The loud boom she hears shakes everything inside the caravan. She sits up and listens. She can hear nothing now, no more booms or shaking. Carefully she pushes away her covers and swings her legs over her bed to get up and then checks on her son, Adam. To her surprise, he is still sleeping, arms akimbo. 'That's good!'

The night has been hot and sticky, removing covers, tossing and turning to try and cool down. Jo unfurls herself and peeps out from inside this cocoon and decides to get up. She goes down the stairs, and gathers her wash things together, to head down to the beach for an early swim and bathe. After putting on her t-shirt, shorts and sandals she takes a bag, containing sponge, soap and shampoo; and adds a water bottle, an apple and a handful of biscuits for Jason and sets off.

After slipping on her trousers, jacket and flip-flops, Anna collects the spare caravan keys, kept in the clothes cupboard for emergencies. 'Right, I need to see what's been going on, what's happened.' She glances across the caravan, to double check on the boy before leaving. The keys are hung up on the hook by the door, the spare torch is on the sideboard – Adam will be safe for a little while. For a moment she stands on the threshold of her caravan, listening before leaving it.

What strikes her as she hovers on her doorstep is the silence. Anna hears the regular breathing from her son but feels something isn't quite as it should be.

Their caravan is run by the clock, it has to be, what with their comings and goings but now she notices something. The clock no longer ticks out the time. A chill runs down her spine as she gazes at the clock. At 4 a.m. the hands have stopped - Dawn!

After closing the door, she listens for the drop of the catch and then continues down the two steps from the caravan. The campsite is quiet and dark. There are no lights on in any of the other vans, which surprises her. Surely someone else must have heard the loud boom, which has shaken Anna and her caravan. But there is nothing.

The air is warm and sultry, the sky and land are hidden by mist, which drapes and covers the stars and moon, as well as creeping along the ground. She switches on her torch, which lights up the path, as she walks towards the road, which leads away from the campsite, towards the beach. Anna knows her way around the site but as she makes her way through it, she is surprised at the normality of her surroundings. It makes her stop and ask herself, has she dreamt the sound, is this a dream too, or is she really on the path, which leads towards the beach? A path she walks most days with her son. She begins to feel disorientated, unsure now, of whether she is awake, or asleep.

On leaving the hut, Jo hears the distant sea rushing in and out, and the light as it penetrates through the darkness, gives life to the vegetation all around. She goes down the steps, walks around the stone path and then as her feet brush through the grassy undergrowth, along the hedges, she feels the damp dew on her legs and continues down through the tiny trail. With Jason following, she ambles along between the bushes, alongside the fruit trees and then climbs through the gap in the stone wall. Gingerly picking her way through, avoiding the nettles, weaving in and out around the thicket and eventually coming out at the bottom of the hill, not far from the footpath to the beach. There is still another piece of grassland to cross, before she joins the public footpath, Jason stops and sniffs before running to catch up.

The footpath set along the cliff top, provides a panoramic view of the coast, a rugged vista, and a white grey mass of rocks, dropping down into the foaming sea. She decides to take the path heading towards the nearest beach, stopping at the bench half way along, to sit and enjoy the early morning, the light coming upon this new day.

The path to the right is quite tricky, it runs along the cliff edge and is difficult at the best of times; this coastline suffers from severe erosion, especially on this stretch of cliffs – warning notices, testify to this along the route. The bench is her favourite stopping place, a hidden corner, just off the path, a good place to sit, daydream and absorb the sounds of the sea, listen to the gulls and during daytime, the far distant people and holidaymakers down on the beach. She sits and watches as Jason burrows, snuffling his way in and out of the long grass.

The diffused light of early dawn now filters through the morning haze, as Anna turns off the torch and continues down the beach path. The earth smells new and refreshed, after the exhausting heat of the night. The daisies and buttercups, that begin to show through the ground mist, are still curled up in their protected sleep. The spangles of dew, still hang untouched, suspended in the crisscross patterns, along the spider's webs.

As Jo sits on the bench, she hears a sound, disturbing her rhythm of meditative thoughtfulness, of swishing footsteps coming her way. She can see from a distance, the figure of a woman, head down, walking along and wonders who it can be.

Anna makes her way along the path, as the light of morning begins to grow. She is startled to hear, the low deep bark of a dog and doesn't see the animal straight away but as she passes a clump of rhododendron bushes, a black Labrador stands in the grass, as if to bar her way. She is taken aback, by seeing the dog so early on, when she believes she is alone.

Jason darts out and bounces across to welcome her, his tail wagging; he jumps up to say hello. Anna is startled by his sudden intrusion and is unsure, stopping in her tracks, unable to move on. Jo gets up from the bench and the woman notices her. "Here, Jase." Jo calls out and walks towards her. "It's ok, he's friendly, he won't hurt you, he's just saying hello." "I was a bit startled that's all." The woman in front of her looks a bit bohemian, Anna thinks to herself.

Anna looks up from Jason and their eyes lock together, there is an instant recognition. Anna is a bit uneasy, as she experiences the long, unbroken, steady gaze. Anna's grey, blue eyes reveal a sensitive smile, an honest open look; Jo is captivated and captured by her presence. She feels she has met this stranger, her good friend, some time ago and holds onto this moment, she wants to invite and keep and not let go.

"I'm going down to the beach; I'll walk along with you if you like."
Anna pats the dog and they begin walking, Jason following on behind.

"What brings you out so early?"

"The bang, did you hear it? That's why I'm up at this time, I couldn't get back to sleep, it really shook my caravan, did it happen to you?" Jo stops walking and looks at her. "Yes, I was disturbed in my sleep by something and woke up." "Thank God, I thought I must be hearing things, so." Anna continues, "Why haven't others also heard it? Why aren't they here now, investigating it?" "I don't know, I can't imagine what it could have been."

Anna is surprised and confused, as if this woman knows her already, by how she looks and how she speaks to her. But Anna has never met this strange woman before. "I'm going to have a swim, I usually do most days." Jo coaxes her, "Are you coming?"

A dip in the sea, Anna reflects, as she walks by the woman's side to the beach. The thought and prospect makes her surge with joy and pleasure but there is also some trepidation edged with fear, which tingles along her spine.

Soon they reach the top of the three flights of steep steps, which lead to the beach and continue chatting, discussing the bang, neither reaching any conclusion, as to what it might have been.

Anna doesn't feel uncomfortable, as she walks along with the woman and her dog. "Where do you live?" Anna asks. It dawning on her, that if the woman comes here most days, then she must live in the area somewhere close. And why does she have a bath in the sea? "I live back there. In the opposite direction of the way you came, in a beach hut." "God." Anna exclaims, not intending to utter her thoughts aloud but she does. "That's different." "Yes, it is." "So what do you do then?" "I make things. I make things from the bits I pick up from the beach, from driftwood, from whatever strikes me as being interesting, different and useful!"

Anna is silenced by this woman's explanation of her life.
As they continue to walk, she wonders what it would
feel like to live in so small a space and tells herself, the
sea dip makes sense, you wouldn't have a bath or toilet,
probably in a beach hut.

As they round the corner, the sea stretches out in front of
them. Anna watches, as the rays of sunlight, spill
through the hazy blue sky and fall on to the small crests
of the waves, which ebb away. She gazes as the sunlight
on the crests of the surf, appear to fragment and collapse,
like shattered glass and fall back into the sand and sea, to
be reabsorbed. The softness and paleness of the blue sea
and sky are still merged together, after being bound by
their night's embrace. Reluctantly, each element begins
to separate, to allow the other to emerge. Sighing at the
loveliness of the scene, she follows the woman, dream
like. On reaching the sand, both women take off their
shoes.

The long expanse of beach is empty. There isn't that
much sand yet, as the sea has only just gone on the turn.
The tide gently laps in and out, leaving its curved outline
of dampness, tracing the edges of the water. Jason takes
off with a dash and leaps over the brimming waves,
down the beach, sniffing, searching and chasing along.

Jo turns to look at this person beside her, for a fleeting
moment, looking empty and adrift. She want to take this
moment, this person and fill her to the brim, to pour into
her, this water, this ocean, and touch and cascade
through the waves and let it wash in and wash out,
cleansing both of them right now. Deja vu. Remember
me, remember you?

Jo drops her bag on the sand and asks, "I'm going in are
you coming?" She takes off her shorts and t-shirt and
dashes towards the edge of the sea. Once in and over the

initial shock of the cool water, she turns and sees the
woman sitting down, looking out to sea and shouts.
"Come on it's fantastic." Anna hears the woman call her
and she tries to answer, call back, "Not yet." but she
hasn't heard and continues to swim out further.

Jo dives into the increasing wave of water. The feeling
of total bare skin, unhampered by clothing, never ceases
to amaze her, the melding as one with the sea, it is
breathtakingly brilliant, a wondrous experience.

Anna turns to the rocks to undress, she is unable to back
out now, but why has she talked herself into this
situation, she could have said no. 'Oh fucking hell.'
Anna thinks, as she finally takes off her jacket and pants
and pulls her nightdress over her head.

Walking into the sea she gasps and catches her breath, as
the water reaches her knees and splashes against her
thighs. The sharp coldness has woken her and makes her
feel alive. Anna feels she will explode, if she doesn't
surrender to the sea and be absorbed, so she too begins to
swim.

Suddenly Jo hears a splash from behind and there she is,
shrieking, as her breath is taken by the cold, she covers
her breasts and ducks down beneath the water.

They both adjust to the temperature and begin to swim
further out into the deeper water. Jo is unaccustomed to
swimming with another person. Arriving at the sea so
early, she always has the luxury of the ocean to herself.
However, today is so different, swimming alongside this
woman. To notice her flesh, her fullness, floating,
bobbing, with hers, it is beautiful, sensuous and quite
magical. Jo becomes drawn towards her, with an intense
desire to reach out and touch, to connect to her and
become one with her in the sea. Her face seems
transformed and has such vibrancy and life, and is so

different from their earlier encounter on the cliff top; she seems so happy and alive. Jo reads this as an invitation, as this moment in time is special and meant to be. Anna is heady with life, intoxicated with the sensation of her physical self, in the presence of this woman. It has been a long time, since she felt so alive, so real, so in touch and in tune with herself and the reality and feeling of herself and life and Anna tingles with the sensation of it.

Looking around for the woman, Anna sees her rising from the sea, her long, curly, dark hair, like tendrils clinging to her head and her breasts, large and full and heavy. The sea swirls around the women and Anna aches, feeling such a surge, a heady force, rising within her. It is crazy and Anna wants to hold her, to feel the woman and embrace her.

Jo lifts her arms up from the sea and as the water drips from her fingertips, she wipes her face and Anna makes her way towards her. Jo leans her head back; to squeeze her dripping hair and her breasts almost touch Anna. She ducks down again, under the water, behind her and in front of her and then Anna is shocked, as the woman catches her from beneath.

Jo swims over and under her and closes in from behind and tentatively puts her hands and arms underneath her, to support her, at the same time kicking her legs, to pull her with her. After the initial shock and surprise Anna relaxes and gives herself and allows her body to be supported by the woman. Anna is enjoying this experience and gaining confidence and laughingly pushes the woman away and then swims closer, only this time she is above, face to face, looking down at her. Jo begins sinking and taking in seawater and after coughing and spluttering, she swims away and then turns, grinning back and they laugh together.

Anna kisses her gently on the temple and they embrace. Their embrace seems to last for eternity and Anna closes her eyes, being dazzled by the sunlight, which shimmers and sparkles on the surface of the sea.

Stella wakes as the dawn breaks, she stirs and turns and looks outside to the changing sky. The chair is comfy and she feels safer here rather than her bedroom. Her feelings of sadness have diffused a little and she stands to stretch herself from her sitting position. Remembering the night, she is glad now that Charles decided to leave and go home. And yet why is it, she wonders, that she always needed to shout out to him, to return and stay until the morning? The inner turmoil of wanting and not wanting him rises within her once more.

It was well past midnight when Charles had left and her fitful dozing in the chair since has caused her mind to somersault her ideas of him. Why Charles? What are we about? She is conscious of her discontentment and wishes now that she had taken herself to bed. She is aware that she meets with the vulnerable part of the man, hidden beneath the loud persona, that most people recognise. How had she fallen for this meek and almost weak person, knowing as she does his darker aspects? He drinks from her and sucks out her sympathy, sorrow and pity, to the point almost, that she feels herself to be given up and dried out like the sand. She feels a chill in the air coming from the window and draws her dressing gown tightly to her body, feeling sad again as she looks and hears the sound of the sea outside.

Stella acknowledges her need to get away from Fenton for a while, to put some distance between them. She would arrange a business trip to France, to refresh and gain a sense of perspective about her life. She knows that staying around here feeling as she does, will drag her down. She needs to stretch herself – and have a sense of belonging to the wider world, not just be another part of the parochial ambitions of this seaside town. Yes, she will make arrangements with her French contacts and have a trip over there.

Leaning over to the telescope, she catches the end and pulls it to her eyes, to enjoy the dawn breaking over the horizon, as it begins to cast its light across the bay. Peering through the lens, she can see the faint glinting light, as it sweeps along the waves. Holding it with anticipation and expectancy, she hopes that it will fuse out completely in one moment, in one huge, cascading flash of light. This is a special time, an offering up and reenergizing of the land and sea, from darkness to light. She swings the telescope nearer inland to the beach and notices its magnificent stretch of unblemished sand and the faint ripple of sea washing itself in and out again. As she moves the scope to the right she stops and holds it tightly. There are footsteps leading to the edge of the water, firm indentations in the sand. Following these impressions, she finds at their source a pile of clothes and shoes. Leading off from the garments are tiny footprints and she deduces that they belong to a dog, as they are dotted about at random.

Her eyes return to the mound of belongings and she raises the lens and tracks the footsteps towards the sea. It takes a few moments before she catches them in her sight. At first she makes herself double check and as she does so, she gasps, drawing in her breath, she can hardly believe what she sees. She holds the telescope hard and is aware that she is shaking, the task of holding the lens so that it stays steady is difficult and she can feel her hand trembling. Regaining herself, she takes in the sight of two women, as they reach out and embrace each other. As the seawater runs from their hair and down their naked bodies, she is taken by their natural, sensuous, gestures, as they hold each other gently and intimately. Stella turns the lens slowly, to zoom in closer to the women, she wants to find out more, she wants to be a part of their discovery, she wants to climb inside their embrace and feel their fingers on her own skin, and she wants to be the centre, the core of their explorations.

Suddenly the spell is broken. Jo hears Jason barking and running towards the sand bank below the cliffs, she can just see the back of a man retreating and climbing up, heading through the long grass, towards the cliff top. Has this person been watching us and if so for how long? It is time to come out of the sea. She is soon followed by the women, whose name she does not know.

"My name's Jo, what's yours?"

"Anna, it's Anna." she replies.

They walk away from the sea, up the beach to where their clothes are on the rocks.

"I'm going to take a shower to wash the salt water off?" Jo tells her.

Anna is already hastily dressing, the material of her clothing covering up her nakedness and returning Anna to her sense of self.

"I won't be a moment." Jo goes over to the beach showers, soaps and showers herself quickly, and then returns to put on her clothes over her wet skin.

Anna is waiting silently.

"Would you like to walk along the beach?"

"No, I'd better get back for Adam, my son."

Jo needs to do her usual early morning searching and hunting for pieces of driftwood and various treasures, left by the outgoing night tide.

"I will have to be getting back to my caravan." Anna continues.

They each say goodbye and Anna walks slowly away from the beach.

'Fucking hell.' Anna says to herself, 'Where did all that come from?' But inside she feels thrilled and alive and wide awake.

Anna doesn't see the man edge away from his position above the beach as she rounds the corner, to return up the steep steps and back along the path to reach her caravan.

Jo turns her attention to the sand and its offerings of the day. Some days are better than others; she has days where she finds so much, that she can hardly manage to carry it all back up to the hut and sometimes needs a second trip down. Today her mind strays back to swimming in the sea with Anna and reliving the experience, the beauty and joy of it and yet she feels a haunting, a past recollection that she doesn't want to remember.

Jo picks up several whole shells, some interesting coloured pebbles and a green and red fishing float knotted with plastic line, this will be amazing on one of her beach boats, it is a really good find. She begins to feel hungry and reaches inside her bag for the apple and hands out some biscuits to Jason who is at her side. She returns back along past the shower and fills her water bottle at the tap and takes a drink, refilling it, before setting off back to the hut for breakfast, her clothes are dry now from the heat of her body.

Anna's head somersaults as she walks away from the woman and the experience she's had. 'What was it?' Anna tries to make sense of her emotions. 'Why had she been so tuned in and turned on by this woman? Why had it felt so natural, so flowing, as if it all belonged and fitted into place? When really it didn't, it couldn't, how could it?' Anna hadn't known the woman. She tries to shake off the feelings, which tumble in and out of her mind, whilst her stomach fills with butterflies.

Arriving back at the caravan, the thrill of the experience on the beach has left her and she is disconnected from the reality of what happened. Now it is too far removed from her – no longer touching her senses but pushed behind in the background of her mind, her thoughts, whilst she gets on with another day with her son. Now this is real, Adam is a reality. She unlocks the caravan door and goes in. Passing the clock, she again notices its silence. It is still 4 a.m. the same time she had left in the early hours.

Anna wants to crawl back into her bed. It invites her with its turned back duvet and crumpled pillows, but as much as she longs to get in, she begins the process of taking the duvet off, the pillows, sheets and then lifting up the end of the foldaway bed, she puts it away until night time. After folding the bedding and putting it on the small seat under the window, she decides to make a pot of tea. She fills the kettle with water from the butt and lights the gas stove. It is stuffy in the caravan, so she unlocks the door and opens it, fastening it back. After hanging up the deckchair striped door curtains, she mashes herself a pot of tea. Sitting on the seat opposite Adam's bed she glances across at her son, she feels a little guilty, even though he is still sleeping. He has short fair, cropped hair and looks older than his years. Although fourteen, her son has learning difficulties, which means he behaves and thinks like a much younger child of seven or eight years old. Anna loves him but he is hard work and a huge responsibility.

On returning to the hut, Jo's first instinct is to head on up the stairs, back to bed, she needs to forget and remember both at the same time. She needs to bury her head and sink beneath the covers, to return to the nighttime, to a dreamless sleep, to rest and return to a clear day, leaving the nightmare, the ghosts behind. 'It's never over,' she thinks, no matter where she decides to hide and run, like in her dreams when she's gasping for breath, the chaser is not far behind. 'GO AWAY, LEAVE ME ALONE' She doesn't want to know anyone, she thought she was safe here, hidden in this hut, a runaway in isolation, just here on her own with Jason living simply day by day. Jo feels angry at life at the world at people, and doesn't need anyone. She fiddles with her sandal strap and it doesn't undo with ease, so she tears and rips at it, until it gives and shoots off her foot, she vents her frustration and hurls it across the floor, Jason watches on cowering. Not this anger again, she is engulfed and wants to lash out, to scream and shout. She decides to make some tea. To light the stove today when it's hot, seems a mad idea but she starts to do it anyway. It's as if she's an automaton, going through motions she knows, to pass through this space in time. She quickly knots the paper and puts the sticks on top, in the belly of the stove and lights it, adding more wood as the fire grows. She fills the kettle from the water tap and gets her mug ready and stands and stares out of the window, out into the ocean, fixating her eyes to the cascading waves and it's only when the whistling kettle several minutes later, unlocks them, that she returns back to the moment and registers to herself that she has just lost another piece of time!

Tiredness sweeps over her, as she pours the boiling water into the mug. Jason peers at her from the doorway and she beckons him over with a hug of love.
Jo bends down to pat and stroke him, "It's not you Jase," She says, as she nuzzles him and wants to cry. He tells her that he's hungry with his soft whine. "Ok. Then, let's eat and then we'll sleep."

After putting the pan on the stove she pour in milk and a little water left from the kettle, adds oatmeal, sugar and salt to make porridge and stands and stirs it, so that it doesn't stick. When the porridge is ready, she fills Jason's bowl with dried dog food and hers with the hot oats. She sits down at the table, they both eat their food, Jason greedily gulfing his down, Jo eats hers slowly, blowing the spoon to cool it. Jason finishes and sits next to her, looking up, waiting for his share.

"I'll save you some," She tells him and sure enough she will, as nothing gets wasted here. After the tea and porridge, she puts the pots to soak in the sink and shuts off the air to the stove.

"Let's go back to sleep now Jase."

Jo goes up the steps to her bedroom and takes off her clothes and crawls under the sheet, to the comforting safety and warmth and closes her eyes. She surrenders to the usual shakiness and holds tightly to the covers, waiting for sleep to take her.

Much later she wakes up with a sigh, turns and stretches and opens herself to the day. She dresses and goes down the steps and quizzically glance at the sink filled with pots and remembers the meal of porridge, a vague recollection of a swim and her mind in a curious way, merges a memory of the past in time. Somehow reality gets lost in a vision and this moment begins this day.

Looking around the hut, a claustrophobic feeling, of being trapped and hemmed in, within the confines of such a small space, beckons her outside, into a wide-open space. This place of hers, usually gives her a sense of protection and safety, yet she feels scared now to go outside. Her sense of calm and centeredness, within her new world, has abandoned her. Jason watches over, sensing her unease and creeps across the floor and licks her legs, she turns and sits reluctantly in her comfy armchair; he flops down at her feet. As she sits, she hears the train rushing along its track in the distance, an

aircraft flying above leaves behind its thunderous hum.
Jo glances around for a moment and registers the jobs
that have to be done but somehow she cannot motivate
herself to get up and start any of them, a feeling of
exhaustion creeps through her, a sleepy cotton wool
feeling demands that she should lie down and submit to
its hypnotic state. She feels the tears welling up inside
and a deep, deep, wanting to let it out, to cry and cry,
why?

Jo thought she had found this place of heaven, away
from her past, a brand new start, a definitive new
beginning. Her meeting with Anna earlier has nudged
her inner being, her core, her soul and triggered
emotions that she thought she had run away from. No
wonder her sense of safety seems to have deserted her.
She must find a way to cope and live with this, and come
to terms with her past and heal herself, care for her
wounded inner child and adult self, to recognise what
was and what is now, her future.

Jo reflects and remembers her writing journals, so many
words, written over years of her life, bundled together in
a plastic carrier bag, bound and stuck together with tape,
looking like a large suffocating head, a metaphor for her
own. She knows that she must un-stick and remove the
tape and plastic bag and let it breathe, give it life, open
the pages up and honour those words, those years of life
and wake herself up and live.

Jo eases herself out of the comfort of the chair and
returns up to her bedroom to open the trunk. She unlocks
the lid; looks inside and stare face to face with the black
plastic head. She lifts out its heavy weight and cradles it
in her arms, like holding a fragile baby, careful not to
drop it and then places it on the bed. She takes a small
end of the sticky tape and pulls it; bit-by-bit peeling it
off, she unwraps the bag, finally having to find some
strength to rip and pull away the last layers, to tear away

the ageing plastic, as if finding a paper doll inside. It's at this point, as she pushes and pulls away the remaining remnants of plastic, that she feels as though she's assisting the giving birth of a raw and vulnerable entity; her initial action of strength subdues to a gentle tenderness, almost protective and so careful as the contents splurge out. After a wait and the final push of a few stubborn and stuck diaries of the afterbirth, she touches and picks up, hold in her hands, this being that has been hidden and in its womb for such a long period of time.

Her hands glide, ruffle, sift and push aside, postcards, notelets, photos, coloured pages, bundles of papers stapled together, diaries, drawings, all creased and folded and dated over many, many, years of time.

These papers hold a life story, memories, reflections and day-to-day happenings of her life. It feels like time now to remember, to look, to read, and to find courage somehow, to open this world up, make sense of it and yes remember. She carefully turns over, leafs through and starts to collate and put them into date order, trying to do this without seeing the words written is quite difficult, already she's pulling back, not wanting to remember, to know what's in here.

The words are jumping out, screaming at her, glaring and knowing, leaping into her eyes. How difficult to re-own these thoughts and accounts of her life, they are so far removed from the here and now, this simple, reclusive and unworldly existence in this hut. This is her reason for being here, she had to run away and hide, from fear of being haunted and hunted, from the daily agony of pain, anguish and suffering. It can't happen again, she has to remain separate, safe and alone. Jo turns over a photograph and hardly recognise the person that she sees. Who is she? Those far away eyes, lost and unreachable, come back from wherever you went. The

same long, heavy, curly hair, the sad expression behind
the smiling face. She decides with an urgency that brings
her back in focus, to have her hair cut short. Jason
sensing her shift in energy, comes bounding up the stairs
and with a bang, bang, wag of his tail, eases and
stretches out full length, after an exaggerated yawn and
full shake, he makes his way towards her, bringing
purpose to the day.

Jo decides to organise what time is left of it, and get on.
She make a mental list of things to buy whilst going
downstairs and gathers her rucksack and sets off into
town, leaving Jason behind in the garden.

Scrambling up the track to the roadside, her mind is
preoccupied, the tape of her life, rewinding, playing and
fast-forwarding to now. Her continual analysis and self-
scrutiny, a dark shadow floating by, the papers of earlier
flashing in front of her mind, the same questions
haunting her since arriving here.
'Did I have a choice? Did I have to disappear? Could I
return? Was it all a dream? Why?'
Her answers are, 'No, I had to disappear, I didn't have a
choice.'
'Oh, if only it had been just a dream, and now a new
question arrives, would I want to return if I could?'
Her own answer surprises her, 'No. I feel happy here and
mostly at peace during the daytime, I can feel joy and
laugh, that's enough.'
With a sense of purpose now, she adds to her list of
shopping items, rice, pasta and extra milk. She relishes
already her return and immersion into working at the hut,
with all that that entails, so stocking up on the essentials
will equip her with enough, to keep going for a good few
days. She gains an extra hour for meandering around the
shops, whilst waiting for an appointment at the
hairdressers; they can fit her in for a trim, if she comes
back in an hour. So she calls at the charity shops and
picks up a couple of t shirts and a weighty Peruvian

jumper, that seems a real bargain for only £5, great forward planning for the coming winter. She peruses the book shelves and is tempted by a couple of titles but decides on a whim to buy In Search of Lost Time, Vol I by Marcel Proust, his great themes - time and memory, love and loss, art and the artistic vocation. This seems like an appropriate book for today.

Sitting down in front of the mirror at the hairdressers is a challenge, what style, how short, the forthcoming dread of the new look, the meaningless chitchat and small talk from the girl. Jo manages to look beyond the mirror, hoping she has given a decent description of how she wants her hair to look. She offers her the following - short and choppy, so that she can easily manage it after swimming in the sea; she is reasonably pleased with the result and knows that when she has roughed it up a bit, it will look better. She soon realises how beneficial it is to keep it like this, with the constraints of living in the hut. She is glad to return and realises that she is suddenly famished and sets to making a meal.

A single blackbird's note penetrates the early morning
air as Anna finishes off her mug of tea. The beauty and
poignancy fills her with such a sense of loss and sadness,
'what is it?' she wonders.

"Is it time to get up mam?" Adam asks, drawing her
back into her sense of daily life.

"Yes." Anna replies as she rises and begins to prepare
his breakfast of cereals.

"Do you want some toast?" She asks, re-filling the kettle
for another cup of tea and lights the grill to make toast.
Adam sits up in bed, his short hair sticking up at all
angles, his blue eyes begin to clear and focus after his
sleep. "Out of bed, come on, or you'll have your
breakfast all over your sleeping bag and you won't like
that."

He unzips his sleeping bag and pulls his long sturdy bare
legs out of it.

Anna hands him his food.

"Shorts or trousers today?"

"Shorts mam."

She goes into the kitchen and takes a pair of blue shorts
from a black plastic sack kept under the bunk bed,
hidden away in the kitchen behind the curtains.

The caravan is old fashioned and well over thirty years
old and has a higgledy-piggledy layout but it has worked
over the years for Anna, her husband and their three
children.

"Can I go out as soon as I'm dressed mam?"

"No, 9 o'clock is our rule remember, we don't go out
until nine."

Her son will want a time check every ten minutes, to
know how much longer he has to wait before he can go
out of the caravan, to play with his friends around the
camp site. The caravan and campsite have been a
blessing for Adam, it has meant that he can go out, as
he's grown older, to play with the other children and be
safe.

After throwing the first lot of toast into the bin because it has burnt, Anna puts two fresh slices of bread under the grill and watches until they turn golden brown on both sides.

"Do you want peanut butter on it?"

"Yes."

Adam is sitting with his blue shorts at the side of him.

"Shorts on first please."

Adam grumbles as he usually does when asked to dress but because he is at the coast and wants to play out, he doesn't put up his usual fuss and Anna holds his plate whilst he steps into his shorts. She puts his navy t-shirt and black socks on the floor.

"Right, when you've finished your toast I want you to get dressed. Put some deodorant on too Adam."

Returning to the kitchen, she takes the burnt toast from under the grill and replaces it with two new slices and fills the kettle again, to wash up last night's pots and the breakfast dishes. Anna butters her toast and takes it with her tea into the living room.

"How much longer mam before I can go out?"

Anna gazes at the clock, it is still at 4 a.m. for a moment she remembers what happened.

"Mam?" Adam interrupts her thoughts.

"I don't know, I don't know what time it is. We'll wait until Big Billy comes to empty the bins and then we'll ask him for the time. It's about 9 ish when he comes around isn't it?"

"No it's not, it's later, that's not fair." Adam stomps. "You said I could play out at nine."

"Chill out mate, you can read your jokes out for me while you're waiting."

Anna opens the large front window and immediately feels the through draft, between the open caravan door and window. Adam reels off his usual list of knock, knock, jokes as she folds up his bedding and puts it with her duvet and collects the breakfast pots to wash. After filling the kitchen sink with water, she starts to feed the dishes into the sink and calls out.

"Your jobs, Adam."

Adam takes out the pee bucket and empties it in the toilets, then rinses it under the tap outside. He hands Anna back the bucket as she passes the water but to fill. "When you've emptied the slop bucket you can go find Big Billy. But come back first and tell me what time it is because the clock's broken. Wash your hands as well," Anna reminds him.

Adam pops into the caravan briefly, to tell her it is 9 o'clock and she reminds him to be back at 12.30 for dinner, Adam flees before his mum delays his freedom longer. 'I bet it's not 9 o'clock anyway,' she thinks to herself.

Sweeping through the living room and kitchen floors Anna hears the daily activities of the campsite as it wakes to a new day. The elderly people call good morning to one another, dogs bark to be taken out for their walks, cars set off on their journeys to markets and car boot sales and early morning excursions to other areas on the coast, or into the Wolds. The rhythm of the day has begun, even if the clock has stopped ticking, to mark out the beat of the passing of time.

Anna collects the black sack of dirty washing, a packet of soap powder, 50p and makes her way to the campsite washhouse. She doesn't need to lock the door. The washhouse consists of four, huge, white, sinks and an old round cylinder boiler, which takes a 50p, and an old-fashioned mangle and dolly tub. The hot water, half fills, two sinks and she puts in the darks and lights, the soap powder and then tops them up with cold water. She begins to lift and drop the dirty clothes, pounding the fabric as she gazes out through the window onto the campsite. An old man is mowing around his caravan and trimming already neatly trimmed borders. Anna fills up the empty sinks, beside her two full ones with cold water, to rinse the clothes. The cold, splashing, sparkling clear water reminds her briefly of the experience she had with Jo in the sea. She remembers how exhilarated she'd felt and how wonderful the feeling and connection with life had been, but as she turns off the cold water taps and transfers the hot clothes to the clear, cold, water and watches as it grows cloudy, she feels foolish and wrong, ashamed in a way with what happened. Anna turns the mangle, as one by one, she feeds the washing between its rollers, to squeeze out the water, into the old grey dolly tub beneath it. It never hits the tub, it always goes on the floor, whichever way she moves it. Anna is soaked and as she puts the clean clothes back into the black sack, she wonders about the woman and her thoughts about their early morning swim. 'Probably,' Anna thinks, 'she hasn't even recalled any of it. What good would it do anyway to think about such things? It isn't real, not really. It isn't connected to daily life, which everyone lives.'

As the dampness of the wash water, seeps through to her skin, she lifts up the dolly tub and empties the dull, milky, white water, down the big sink and swills it out, then rinses all four sinks, before taking the washing to peg out on the line in front of the caravan. She hangs the remainder on the clotheshorse by the door. Putting a few pegs on it, to stop the washing from blowing off. Going indoors she puts the kettle on to make tea and think about what to do for dinner. Her son had called back for drinks and jam sandwiches earlier but he'd want his meal in an hour or so. Sipping her tea, she knows she'll have to do a bit of weeding around the front of the caravan sometime, as well as go into town to buy a few bits and pieces. Adam would go with her, if she promised him a visit to Mad Micks, or the £1 shop. Anna accepts the financial frugality of her life and circumstances and even consider herself well off in comparison to her mum, who'd had nothing with eight children to raise.

Anna's back tingles as she closes her eyes and hears the sea, smells and tastes the saltiness of it; she smiles and bites her bottom lip. 'Jobs to do, no time for dawdling.'

Adam eats his beans on toast and tells her about the two
dogs he'd taken for a walk. She listens and makes a short
shopping list.
"Right Adam, what do we need?"
"Bread." Adam offers.
"Milk." Anna adds.
"Biscuits and crisps and pop."
"We'll see."
Anna puts the dishes into the sink before collecting her
handbag and shopping bag to go into town.
"Can I lock the door?" Adam asks.
"Yes" Anna says handing him the keys.
"Which way do you want to go, the donkey track way or
through the houses?"
Adam isn't bothered.
"We'll come back via the donkey track." Anna decides
as they set off through the streets, a ten-minute walk into
the town centre.
Anna picks out the holidaymakers as they head towards
the centre. Holidaymakers wear different clothes.
Brighter colours than the local people and new,
especially the working class families who stay at the big
campsites. The young lads wear all the brand names and
hats and hoodies and the girls, short skirts and low cut
tops and shoes they can't walk in. The middle classes
don't visit in high season; they are usually around at the
beginning of the year or in autumn.
Walking along the front, they pass the large spacious
hotels, boarding houses, 'apartments' and holiday
cottages, Anna always thinks, out of season this would
be a perfect place to come alone for a few months to
write a book.

Jo unpacks her shopping and fills her rice and pasta jars to the top and puts her milk in the place that she calls the fridge; this is next to the sink in the kitchen area of the hut underneath a large stone slab, which she uses as a worktop. Holding up this slab are two stone pillars and at the bottom, a flag floor, that continues across the kitchen and into the living area. She's built into this space a shelf, mainly used for storing vegetables, salads and juices; underneath on the flags she puts milk, cheese, bacon and eggs. She has strung a wire across the front and hung a curtain; she managed to find a red and white gingham remnant in one of the charity shops, and this makes a perfect screen for hiding the contents behind and looks really good. Jo prepares a hasty meal of bread and cheese and remembers the hours of hand sewing the edges and the top; it was worth the time spent.

The kitchen area is quite small and compact; it's about 10ft x 10ft square and joins onto the living room. In this space there is the sink and fridge and a large old wooden cupboard, which she uses for tinned and dry foodstuffs and hopefully preserves of jams and chutneys, if all in the garden grows well. She also has plenty of shelving for pots and storage jars, plus lots of hooks for hanging utensils and pans. Opposite the sink she has an old rectangular table and two chairs, she takes her plate and sits down. When she bought this furniture from the junk shop, she intended to buy just one chair, but the chap wouldn't accept a lower price, he said.
"What am I going to do with an odd chair?"
So she ended up with the two and always favours the seat facing the living area, she made a cushion for it, with the bit left over from the gingham curtain. It has taken her quite a long time gathering pots and jars and various kitchenwares from the car boots and flea markets around town, she finds it a pleasure to cook now.

During the summer season she mainly makes cold meals, salads and barbequed food, cooked in the garden. She tends not to use the stove for cooking on, as it becomes too hot inside. Also the time and effort spent gathering wood is a daily job, even in summer, because during the winter when she needs the stove on every day, it uses a huge amount. So Jo likes to stockpile the summer wood for the winter. She has a covered area at the rear of the hut next to the improvised outdoor shower, where she keeps it to dry out.

When Jo bought the hut just over two years ago, the place was so overgrown with vegetation and trees that she struggled to find the door. It was one of the first jobs that she had to do, clear the weeds and heavily prune back the trees, to the side of the hut. This wood and the dead wood on the ground, kept her fuelled up for the first winter. She has since continued to cut back the trees to the rear garden. There is still plenty of work to be done. The fruit trees, further down beyond the paths, last year produced a fine crop of apples. She wrapped the ripe and unblemished ones in newspaper and put them in a wooden chest, for use during the winter. Jo's hoping this year that the plum trees that she pruned back hard in the spring, bear fruit later on in September. She has just enjoyed the last of the rhubarb, that she stewed in a large batch and has eaten it with yoghurt and honey. There is nothing like picking food from the garden and enjoying it at the table the same day.

Now that she is becoming more organised, she will put a table out on the roadside, in the inlet by the lay by, with any extra produce throughout the year and sell it. She's made an honesty box and a sign with a list of prices for the various fruits and vegetables and this money will help towards buying more seeds and her own shopping. There is a tiny glasshouse that was damaged when she first arrived. Jo managed to repair it and has put in a few tomato plants and peppers that she's trying to grow for the first time. She also has a small vegetable patch that she dug over in February during a dry spell and has planted out over the weeks with potatoes, cabbages, carrots, lettuce, radish and spring onions. These are the main crops with a few others popped in here and there to fill up the space.

Jo is certainly a lot fitter and healthier since coming here to live. Every day is filled with energetic activities, either walking down to the beach, or working in the garden. She hopes to eat as much as she can from the garden produce and has bought lots of bottling jars for making jams and chutneys this year. As well as the produce from the garden there are hedgerow pickings to be had, with her favourite fruits, blackberries and bilberries. She hopes also to make wine when she gets equipped for the job, using elderflowers, dandelions and elderberries, and intends to plant rows of gooseberry and blackcurrant bushes and also some strawberries for next year. Lots and lots of plans of things to do. Life here is simple and it is very satisfying after a hard days work, to sit in the comfy armchair, with Jason at her side, just resting together quietly with a book to read.

Life is so different now compared to how it was when she arrived. She was lethargic, stuck and aimless, without energy and spent her days staring into space. One day was like the next, feeling desperate, cold and senseless, total inertia, a dark space in time, her hiding place was certainly that, a big, black hole, going nowhere.

Jo can't tell you how long she stayed in this meaningless, frightening, endless, demoralising existence. Surviving wasn't really an instinct, fending for herself was not a reality, looking back her condition could have deteriorated badly, as no one around here knew her and people who did know her, wouldn't have known her whereabouts, or if she was ok. She definitely, even in this awful state, could not go back. There was no feeling of future, no looking forward and no going back.

Time stood still and was irrelevant, she just couldn't go on, couldn't get up, couldn't eat, and wasn't functioning in any sense at all.

Jo really doesn't know what might have happened, had it continued in this way, and yet she does know, she doesn't think she would be here now, had it not been for a whining sound at the door one morning. The whining continued and eventually she went to see what it was, she just wanted the noise to stop, for it to go away and it didn't. When she opened the door and looked down, there was a dog, a black labrador pushing forward towards her, desperately trying to come inside. In her bleary and weary, bleak condition, she just let him in and sat down again.

The dog looked rakishly thin and unkempt; he just flopped down on the rug beside her. She could tell by its lifeless eyes, that it had almost given up; somehow they recognised each other's neglect and despair and made a connection to help each other. Jo found a grain of strength and stood up from the chair. She looked around this dingy, grimy, hut and saw it, as if for the first time and couldn't remember when she last ate and felt her own wasting and hunger and the desperate situation hit her. She had nothing, except for a tin of tuna and as she pressed the can opener down and slowly turned the key, it was the catalyst to move her, to help her find a way forward, to keep them alive, and with that she found Jason and her life began.

Writing a book however isn't a luxury Anna can indulge in. It takes all her time to keep up with her homeopathic studies and taking care of her children. Anyway, Anna considers, who would want to read what she wrote and what could she write about?

Walking around Mad Mick's she tells herself not to buy useless ornaments, which end up being put in cupboards, or given to charity shops. Adam stands at the counter with a huge gob stopper.
"It's 50p mam."
After paying they walk across the road into the £1 shop. Anna spots a beautiful, blue, floral notebook. It is large an A4. She still has the notebook in her hand as she pays for Adam's gun set.
The girl at the till looks at her holding the book and asks, "Do you want that?"
She is about to give it to Adam to put back, when she changes her mind and gives the girl another £1.
"Go on then."
As they stroll back to the caravan site, Adam sucks happily on his gob stopper, taking it out of his mouth frequently, to give her an update on its colour and to talk. Her son loves talking. It doesn't matter much to him what the conversation is about, he just enjoys chatting and company. Walking up the donkey track to the site, Adam collects handfuls of grass, to feed to the donkeys in the field. He calls out and the donkeys plod slowly up to him. He is not timid of them, as their long, pink tongues, wrap around the blades of grass. After wiping his hands down his blue shorts, he sucks purposefully on his gob stopper, satisfied with his work.
On reaching the campsite Adam asks.
"Can I go to Callum's to show him my gun set mam?"
"Go on then, but you know what time tea is don't you?"
Adam disappears without listening to her instructions, as she turns towards their caravan. 'Cup of tea,' Anna decides, as she puts the few bits and pieces away she's bought. After filling the kettle she puts the oven on.

Baked potatoes she decides for tea. Taking the bowl
from the sink, she puts the two large potatoes in with a
clean scourer and takes the bowl to the cold-water tap
outside to clean them, then puts them in the oven to
bake. Grated cheese and tomatoes, she decides for the
filling.

Sitting down with her pot of tea, Anna takes the book
she's bought out of the plastic bag. It is nice. Opening
the book, she strokes its empty, white pages, so much
possibility, and so much space to say so many things.
Calmness fills her, a soft contentment.

Later that evening Adam tells his doctor, doctor, jokes
from his book, it has almost become a traditional way
now to end their day, in bed with a hot water bottle and a
cup of drinking chocolate. Anna is unable to fall asleep
because he continues to call out from the opposite side of
the room, "Knock, knock, mam, doctor,
doctor......mam."
She continues to respond, until the last traces of light
have gone and it is too dark for him to read anymore.
"Goodnight Adam."
"Goodnight mam."
"I love you."
"I love you too."

Anna wakes whilst it is still dark, she has dreamt about
her father Patrick McGee, who died three years ago. She
misses him. The dream had been so strange. It was about
her father as a young man, a slim, dapper, red haired,
Irish man.
"A mad Irish man." Her mother had often called him and
Anna knows that to be true. She had seen her father's
rages. and the seething explosion of his quick temper.
She had watched as her mother yelped, like a frightened
dog, cowering at her father's violence. Anna cries as she
remembers her mother's fear and shame, at what he had
done to her mother. It had made Anna feel ashamed too,

she had felt her father's belt and hand as a child and had been put in her place and knew the consequences of stepping out of it. She wants to forget these thoughts and memories and leave them behind. Her father had died, a frail elderly man in his 80's, not this young dapper man she has dreamt about and who she remembers from her childhood. Her father had had a difficult and bad childhood. Being abandoned by both of his parents as a boy and being brought up by a reluctant grandmother and the orphanage.

He had come to England when he was eighteen to seek his fortune in America; Blackpool, Preston and Leeds were as far as he got. Anna knew her father's only sister, Aunt Bridget but that was it.

As a child of nine she had gone with her mother, father and two older and two younger sisters to Ireland, to Enniskillen in county Fermanagh, to visit her father's grandmother. The home had been a small farm near loch Irne. She remembers the dark looming doorway of the barn and the black dog barking and pulling on its chain in the doorway. The visit had been the only one her father had ever made back to Ireland. It was the last time he saw his grandmother and aunts. Whilst he was there he got drunk and rode a cycle backward and went swimming in the loch. He tried to climb into or out of a window; Anna has forgotten which, naked.

Anna remembers walking down a long green shady lane, with her father's cousin Jim and him telling them, that there were leprechauns and fairies all over the place and about a boy who climbed up a tree and fell and died and Jim saying to Anna.
"How would you like that dying at your age?"
Anna was aware that this comparison Jim was making, was to shut her up, because she'd tripped on some roots of a tree and a branch had gashed her leg. She still has the scar, a tiny teardrop shape. Anna doesn't really know

anything about her father's early life, or about Ireland, not really. She has always considered herself a Yorkshire woman through and through but she also feels and has an inner sense of the unknown history of her fathers and consequently her descendents who were Irish. As a child she had hated that connection, had been ashamed of being a child from a working class, Anglo Irish, catholic family. You could never be you, yourself, your identity had to be as a part of a big family. In Anna's early days, larger families were more common but there was also stigma attached to being one of eight children, as if you were somehow taking too much space up on the earth. "Oh yes," Anna would get, "You're one of the McGee's aren't you?"

Closing her eyes she returns to her dreams, they are no longer about her father but about herself, a different self, a woman who she wants to be, someone who believes in herself.

In her dream Anna gets out of a taxi and walks into a G.P's practise and asks the receptionist if she can see Doctor Gallagher. The receptionist asks Anna her name she gives it confidently.
"I'm not here as a patient, I'm here to see and speak to Doctor Gallagher, I'm your new homeopath, I'm expected."
"Come through." The woman opens the door, which leads out of the reception area and practise rooms.
"Doctor Gallagher." the woman says as she opens a consulting room door and allows Anna to pass.
"It's Anna McGee, our new homeopath."
Something is wrong. Anna knows that the doctor should be a woman; instead it is a middle aged, grey haired man. He rises from his seat and glowers disapprovingly at her, but holds out his hand to shake hers. 'This is wrong,' Anna thinks, as she extends her hand to the man in front of her.

"Is it time to get up yet mam?" Adam calls out.

Anna emerges from her sleepy dream and asks her son to wait for half an hour, until it becomes a little lighter. Her day has begun again, she lays with the tip of her head out of her covers, warm, safe and peaceful, savouring the few moments of stillness and quietness before she has to get up. She closes her eyes and begins to doze.

"Mam?"

The sun is fighting to gain entry into the hut, this early
morning of June, via the gaps in the curtains where they
don't quite meet. After a few moments of tossing and
turning and remembering the night, with its habitual
broken patterns of sleep, Jo stretches and unfurls to a
new, beautiful day. Her decision not to attempt to find
the world of sleep once again is made as she leans across
to the window and tugs the curtain to one side, to let
more of the strong sunshine in. She can hear the sound of
the sea; the birds busy in the garden and puts her head
back under the sheets, to inhale the musty smell of the
nighttime. This intimate scent of hers, built up over days
and days from her naked body, is like a drug and quite
intoxicating and makes this upstairs bedroom, although a
private space, feel like merging with another human
being. To wash the sheet and cover becomes almost a
ritual, the timing has to be just right. She needs to hold
on to this scent awhile longer, the battle with hygiene
losing out again. After saying goodbye to this soft
comfort, this sinking holding protective cocoon, with a
promise to return, she pulls back the duvet, puts on her
clothes and descends the stairs.

"Hellos, ellos, Jase."
Jason yawns and stretches and pads across, brushing his
waggy tail against her bare legs. Jo feeds him first and
notices that his dog food is getting low; she makes a
mental note, to cycle to the pet shop in town, sometime
soon. It took a long time before both of them gained
strength and body weight, as she looks down at him
now, she smiles at what they have both achieved, the bad
times seem over at last. They only ate a little at first;
Jason wolfed down his food, whilst it took her longer to
gain an appetite but now she relishes her meals and eats
hungrily with enjoyment. Most days her stomach is a
reminder to stop work, as time passes quickly when
she's engrossed in something.

Jo pours fresh orange and helps herself to oatcakes and spreads them with butter and tree honey. In the corner of the sitting room she notices the bag containing the beach finds, that she dropped there some days ago. There is plenty of work to get on with. She needs to do several jobs in the garden first and then she can look through the beach finds later and decide what to make.

Outside she checks around the vegetable patch and pulls out the weeds, and notices with delight that the squash that she planted are filling out nicely and should be ready to eat during August. She's been enjoying lighting a barbeque on the dry evenings – she made this with an old oven shelf rack, supported by a pile of bricks. The squash will roast nicely on that, and with a bowl of couscous, it will be lovely. She's able to boil eggs and potatoes when she has finished cooking her meal of an evening, to eat cold the next day. Jo fills the watering can, from one of my many water butts and waters the tomatoes and peppers in the glasshouse and the window boxes filled with herbs. This is a daily job and is essential to do it early on and sometimes on hot days, late in the evening also. The plants in here are thriving, she's had tomatoes daily, since the beginning of June and with the lettuce, spring onions, potatoes and herbs they have been the base ingredients for a good meal. Jo does more general tidying around the beds and throws the lot onto the compost heap. After cutting back some of the long grass around the fruit trees, she notices one or two dead branches in the cherry tree and decides to prune them out. The small branches are good for the barbeque. The larger ones she adds to the woodpile for the stove. She stops regularly to have drinks of water and then carries on; Jason ambles around the garden and returns often to find out what she is doing. Her skin has become acclimatised to the sunshine, with spending so much time outside; it's a wonderful feeling, the heat from the sun, as it warms her body through her clothing.

This is such a secluded place because it is private land and off the public footpath, so there are never any passers by, just the two of them living alone. It was only after clearing away the overgrown jungle of vegetation, when she was stronger and capable of the work, that she realised the size of the plot. At first she wasn't sure what to do with the ground; it has just evolved over the last couple of years. At first planting and hoping and finding out what was successful, she is still surprised when things flourish and grow and often disappointed when a seedling gets eaten by slugs or just dies. Pondering this last train of thought, her mind turns in on itself and she begins to feel quite morose and recognises the onset of inertia and gloom. Death and dying. Death and dying. Stop. Stop. Come on move on come on. Her body feels a prickle of moisture, followed by a chill, so she decides to take a shower, to refresh and cleanse these thoughts away. This is one of her many survival techniques, she's learnt along the way, slowly and surely, with practise, she's found them to be a good first aid kit for her psyche, since coming here.

The hut, although having running cold water from an underground spring, doesn't have a bathroom, or even an inside toilet. Jo discovered after clearing the climbing ivy at the rear of the hut, an old outhouse, with a covered concrete paved area about 4ft square at the side. She didn't have any ideas for this space in the first year here, so just left it alone. In the outhouse to her surprise, she found an earth closet. She doesn't recall this mentioned in the details for the place. Maybe because it was so overgrown it hadn't been spotted. After cleaning it out and scrubbing and bleaching the seat she had a toilet. After each use she shovels on some earth and then when the container underneath is full, she adds it to the compost heap in the garden. In her urgency to run away, she wasn't put off by the fact that the hut didn't have a bathroom or toilet, she was struck by its location and the guide price. She couldn't afford to use up much money for a home, as she didn't have a clue as to what she was going to do, or if she could generate any income or not. At that time she wasn't in any condition to find work. She was on the run and just wanted to hide away. Its sanitary offerings were irrelevant, her mind was all over the place, the hut came up for auction, was affordable on her budget and when the hammer came down she had the winning bid.

In the first year she struggled with everything, looking back now it seems a blur; she know that she didn't look after herself very well. Although she did lots of clearing the ground outside, the hut both inside and out required lots of attention, it really was run down and neglected. She didn't have the time or desire for a bathing routine, she supposed she never even noticed herself at all. She just existed, was alive but didn't really feel alive.

Occasionally she would go down to the beach late on and take a swim and gradually opened her eyes to the surroundings. It was only after Jason arrived, that she began to spend a lot of time, working, mending and cleaning as best she could, to try and make the place habitable. The windows were the first big job that she tackled, they had been raining in, because the putty had crumbled and fallen out in places and the paint was peeling off everywhere. She raked out the old putty and re puttied them. Then scraped off all the old paint on the inside and out, sanded and primed them and painted them sky blue. She scraped and rubbed down the old door and painted that to match, she removed all the old ingrained paint on the brass handle and keyhole, and this took ages but was worth it, Jo began to notice her filthy clothes; her hair a tangled up knotted mess, and longed to take a bath in hot soapy water. She became aware of the aches in her joints, especially her sore back and hurting arms and legs; she was physically coming back to life. Mentally she was waking up and noticing where she was and her feelings started to return. Tugging at branches that flicked back and hit her hurt, she stopped trying to tug on them even harder, fighting them. She just gave in and felt the pain, the pain hitting her body, although she couldn't cry, she knew changes were taking place within her.

One day she had gone on a visit into town to collect some food items. The junk shop on the edge of town has lots of bit and pieces on the pavement, so she stopped to take a look. Propped up was a bicycle with a ticket on for £30 and she looked it over, wheeled it around, it was in fairly decent condition.
The shop owner who she now knows as Bob, called out from inside the shop, "Get on it love, and see what you think, it's not my sort of thing but I thought I'd stick it outside, maybe someone might want it, it's not your modern thing but it goes".

So she sat on and cycled around the car park, the saddle needed adjusting for the height, but apart from that it was perfect so she bought it. It even has a basket at the front for carrying things in, which is really useful for collecting shopping. A few days later she was wandering around the back of the hut and had a flash of an idea. She remembered a huge, square, plastic tank, that had been outside the junk shop near the bike and thought if somehow she could put it up on top of the roof of the covered area next to the outhouse, she could make it into a summer shower. She could collect rainwater in it from the hut roof and rig up a shower hose from it, she knew this would be great to use after gardening or working on the hut, very basic but ideal during the summer. She had been using the shower on the beach, on the days she spent collecting driftwood etc, but to rig a shower at the hut would be brilliant if it worked. So she returned to the shop and asked about the tank.

"You're back are you love?" said Bob.
Jo asked him about the tank and checked it for any holes.

"It's an old cold water header tank, there won't be any leaks in that, a fiver love and it's yours."
For £5 it was worth the risk, if it didn't work she could always use it for collecting rainwater in the garden. She asked him how much to deliver it.
"Where to love?"

Jo told him she was living down the road, by the side of the lay by, at the beach hut.
"Bloody hell love, you never, that old run down wreck, well seen as you bought the bike, I'll drop it down for nowt. Say tomorrow early morning how's that, names Bob, by the way."
"Thanks, that's great tomorrow morning then." She quickly replied.
She didn't want to inform him of her name. So she handed him the money, jumped on the bike and rode into town. She's bought several things since at a reasonable price and never hangs around to chat and when he's dropped things off at the hut, he's said hello to Jason and dashed off.

Anyhow she managed to lift the tank onto the roof of the outhouse and diverted the guttering from the hut into the top of it, instead of the water butt. She bought a length of plastic hose and fittings and fitted it through a hole near the top, where a pipe must have been. She pushed it right through, so that it almost reached the bottom of the tank and then hung the remaining length of tubing on to a hook half way up the side wall. It was not until weeks later, after days of heavy rainfall before she could test the shower out. When she first tried it, she was so delighted that it actually worked, and the water was running out of the end she was swinging, before she realised she was using up the precious water. She has learnt to stick her finger partly over the end whilst wetting her body, and then returns the hose to the hook; soap herself all over and then quickly washes it off, using as little water as possible. The tank holds gallons of water but after a prolonged dry spell it runs out, so she's learnt to be pretty frugal with it. She also put a plastic cover on the top, to help keep the water clean.

After her quick shower she returns inside and goes upstairs to change her clothes, she doesn't have a huge array of clothing, what she has she's bought from the local charity shops. The only possessions she brought on her arrival, were the clothes she was wearing, denim jeans, t shirt and fleece jumper, a Gore-Tex jacket, walking boots on her feet and a rucksack containing the black, plastic bag of journals, her bank card, passport, £50 and loose change, the key for the hut, an ordnance survey map of this area, a packet of biscuits and a bottle of water. She had never been to this part of the country before, that was the reason why she had chosen it, especially its secluded location. She knew no one around this area; it would be the last place anyone could imagine her to live.

She resists the temptation to lie down on top of the crumpled covers and rest, she knows that if she does, she will find it hard to get started on her jobs and end up lazing around and achieve nothing. So she changes into a fresh t-shirt and shorts and returns downstairs feeling hungry and prepares something to eat. She opens a can of tuna and adds it to a few cold, cooked potatoes and boiled eggs. She arranges lettuce and sliced tomatoes on a plate and spoons plenty of the tuna mixture on top. She bought a crusty cob yesterday at the local bakers and butters two slices to go with it. She'll have the quiche that she bought also for her meal tonight, with more of the salad and tuna. The bakery is ideal, especially when it's raining and she can't cook outside. They sell pasties and cold pizzas, these are tasty and filling and reasonably priced too, if she knows that she's going to cook on the barbeque, she calls at Martins the butchers and buys a chicken leg or sausages. She pours a glass of fruit juice and takes the meal outside. Looking out to sea she is reminded of the treasures collected from the beach and looks forward to starting working with them.

Jason sits waiting for a few titbits; she puts to one side some egg, potatoes and tuna for his dog dish and gives it to him after she has eaten hers. She sits for a few minutes and gathers her thoughts before returning inside. She has been making boats and painting pebbles for the last few months. The idea came after walking on the beach and finding several pieces of driftwood that she collected with the intention of burning them on the barbeque. On arriving back at the hut, she held one of the pieces and wondered where it originated from, a boat, a shipwreck, someone's home, this tiny piece of wood had its own history, how long had it been washing around the sea? There were old, rusty nails that had bled their browny, orange stain, what had it been attached to? She was taken by its shape like the hull of a ship and its strange beauty; with tiny holes washed through to the other side by the sea. After placing it upright on the stone wall to dry out, she didn't feel that she could burn it. She imagined this piece of timber sailing across the sea, with its own brightly coloured sails, gaily riding the crests of the waves, chopping in and out of the troughs, and out to sea to new horizons.

Days later she cycled into town and returned with a pair of white, heavy cotton trousers, from the reduced rail in the charity shop and a length of wooden dowelling and a tub of PVA glue from the DIY shop. Also a ball of string, a set of brushes and a selection of acrylic paint from the £1 shop. She had to return again, when she needed a few eyelet hooks and a bradawl tool, to make the holes in the boat for the masts.

This first boat 'Joanne 42' turned out to be full of character – with the starboard face of a whale and lots of interesting knots, its worn away shape, buoyant and strong. It had a small doubled up piece of plastic struck in, with an old flat-headed nail, inferring an anchor at the port side. The width of the boat about 18". The main mast 19" with sails at both sides and rigging, enabling both sails to work independently of each other. At the head of the main mast, a small sail flapping down. She cut out the sails from the cotton trousers and carefully turned and sew an edge around each one and then painted them with PVA glue a couple of times to stiffen them, before brushing on a diluted aquamarine blue paint. Finally finishing them with an embroidered green stitching, 'Joanne' in the bottom and '42' in the top corner of the foresail. She then used the eyelet catches screwed into the hull, to slip the rigging lines through. She was so impressed with the start of the fleet and continued creating lots of different sized crafts, with an array of coloured sails. She has quite a collection now and has also painted and varnished interesting shaped pebbles that will make unusual paperweights, or doorstops.

Now that the holidaymakers are flocking into town, she has decided to set up a stall with them on, together with any excess fruits and veg and hopefully will make a small income from it. She can foresee the coming winter months, when not actively working in the garden, making more boats and also painting canvases using oil paints, for sale next year. She tends to work outside at the garden table, if the weather permits and it's warm enough; otherwise she has a tiny workroom just off the sitting room. It's a narrow room with a window looking out to the front garden, although it's adequate with a workbench down one side, she prefers to be looking out to the sea.

Today is lovely for working outside; it is warm and not too much wind to hamper her. So she takes her last haul of treasure and places it on the table and begins to play around, selecting the boats, discarding some odd shapes onto the reject pile. She has ideas for these oddments, to make into kitchen signs with hooks, or garden shed signs, or other bits and bobs. The fishing float she salvaged from the beach, she will incorporate into the hull of a large boat, and this will be quite impressive when it's finished. She loves working with her hands, fiddling and gluing, painting and screwing and sewing the sails. It is time consuming but the enormous pleasure she gets from making them, is very satisfying at the end of the day. Tomorrow she should have enough stock to set up her stall.

Anna opens her eyes to respond to her son but can't
focus on his questions or his face.
"Ok. Adam, just let me surface."

So her time is up again but the dreams of her father as a
young man and of being a homeopath, with the belief
and confidence to walk into a G.P's practice and
announce herself boldly, remain in her mind. The dreams
have begun a process, something that she hasn't allowed
to come to the forefront of her mind, let alone her life
before. It is the possibility of having some impact and
input into the creation of her life and destiny. To step off
the wheel she had stumbled onto as a young child and to
fashion aspects of herself into who and whatever she
wants to be. She has been and become, everything she
was supposed to. She has achieved her working-class
destiny and fulfilled her ordained role in life. She has
been a dutiful, obedient, daughter. As a child she adored
her mother and would have done anything for her, to
please her, to be of use and service.

After coming away from the 2nd world war as a young
girl from a large working-class family, her mother knew
all about usefulness. Anna's role in the family was to be
both of use and of service. That niche had become her
place and as time passed throughout the days of her
childhood Anna accepted the halter, which had been
placed on her. Before it, she had had some of her father's
mad Irish instinct and spirit about her; she was a bit of a
tomboy. She had told her mother she intended to travel
to India, her mother said she couldn't. Anna didn't
answer her mother back, it wasn't allowed, you couldn't
dictate to your mum, what you intended to do with your
life.
"You'll get married and fall on like I did." Her mother
would tell her.

In the meantime Anna worked in her mother's service,
made beds, washed up, went shopping, swept the stairs

and cleaned the bedrooms out on Sunday, after Mass, with her sister. Anna and her sisters had to work in the family home in order for it to function. Her dad would talk about bundles of sticks being hard to break but single sticks could be easily broken. When she was young she wanted to be a policewoman but everyone said she wouldn't grow tall enough. They were right; her full height had been 5 feet 2 inches. Not 5 foot 2 eyes of blue, but 5 foot 2 small, skinny, specky and spotty and invisible. Somewhere she read that if you became a librarian you couldn't get married. When she could read the full title of her favourite book, Ammelia Jane her heart surged with pride. When Miss Grady began reading at story time, Family From One End Street at the end of the school day, Anna was captivated, English literature made sense, had purposeful meaning and for Anna it was like opening a door, to not one new world but many. She had found a key, a very special one, which unlocked her from her inherited destiny.

Through her early years she grew more and more absorbed in reading books and stepping out of her world of chores into different places. Reading wasn't something Anna could do too much of, or too openly, as a girl. Books were considered a luxury and a bit of a waste of time. Jobs didn't get done, when you were sat with a book in your hand.
Anna 'seeing her boyfriend' ran parallel with her discovering literature. She couldn't remember when she started 'seeing her boyfriend' but it was an accepted part of daily life. When the girls had gone to their beds at night, they would all go to 'see their boyfriends'. If Anna hadn't actually started the game straight away and tried to talk to one of her sisters, she would get, "Shut up I'm seeing my boy friend."
When you went to 'see your boyfriend' anything could happen. Usually Anna put herself in the role of being the ugly female, who after an awful lot of rejection, torture, humiliation and various highlights of bodice ripping,

would become accepted. This became a safe and private place to play and act out her grown up life, which was an unsafe, unknown place. Her future grown-up life would be what ever her Mum and Dad told her it would be, so she wasn't sure what to expect.

After leaving school she would work in a small office, after she'd spent the year before learning shorthand and typing. That's where the problems began, she knew she wouldn't end up in an office typing, she'd told her Dad she didn't want to learn to type. He had been saddened by her response. She would, he told her; end up like her mother as a cleaner, if that's what she wanted. She looked at her Mum as her father spoke, about ending up like her but Anna's mother didn't say anything. She couldn't spend her life sitting behind a desk typing. The prospect made Anna feel as if she were being suffocated and she just wanted to break free. She told her father it didn't matter what she did.

Later that day Anna and Adam set off for a picnic on the beach.

Sharing cheese sandwiches and a bottle of juice, they sit on the sand resting against the rocks, eating their dinner. After his food Adam runs off trying to join in with the groups of children scattered around the beach. She watches her son running around trying to engage with other children. She sits back after putting the crisp packets and extra bottle of water into her bag, so her little patch is tidy. This beach Anna ponders, doesn't feel like the same place she had spent time with the strange woman. The scene now in front of her is of a long, wide, expanse of sand, the sea far away with people swimming and squealing children, who are either jumping the waves or plunging in. Gazing out to sea, it is so utterly blue, that she can scarcely make out where the sky and sea separate. The sky is a soft, hazy blue in the sunshine and the warm air is so different from the coolness of that dawn morning. Now the warm softness surrounds Anna, breathing gently across her back and face as she rests and leans back, closing her eyes.

Jo chooses to rise early with the birds and get on. She is full of enthusiastic energy and bounces around the hut. This aura of energy is almost palpable, swishing around and with the sun shining it spurs her on. She checks her workroom with glee and an anxious anticipation, after all these are her boats, her pebbles and soon they will be for sale. The fleet propped against each other, there are about thirty in total, well thirty precisely, she has counted them several times and knows each one intimately, she has held them in her hands and given each scrap of wood a new life. This sailing fleet with their blue, green, yellow, orange, red and pink billowing sails look brilliant and together with the pebbles she's certain they will sell themselves to the passing public.

The pricing is a difficult matter; she knows that in a trendy shop in a London suburb they would fetch a substantial amount. However here in this coastal town she knows that she will have to price them fairly low, if she is to have a constant turnaround. She enjoys making them and needs to sell them on quickly. She hasn't any overheads as such, no stall fee; the table will be on her land – a small inlet at the side of the lay by, on the roadside above the hut. The materials she uses are beach finds and a bit of material, string and glue, so any money she makes will be mostly profit. Alongside some surplus garden fruits and vegetables she thinks she will do ok. She knows that once she starts selling the stock, she will be even more enthusiastic to make more and allocate extra time for doing this.

After a quick breakfast of muesli and a glass of fruit juice, she packs the boats and pebbles carefully into plastic bags. She double bags the pebbles because they weigh heavy and she doesn't want the bags to split. She has a folding wallpaper pasting table, a car boot buy, although fairly light, it is large enough and with a handle isn't too difficult to carry up the track to the roadside. So she sets off with the table and stool, she decides it will be best to have something to sit on, rather than standing around all day. At the roadside there are very few cars passing by, it is still too early for people setting off to work or arriving as day-trippers. Jo returns and waters around the garden and picks a few lettuce, spring onions, and tomatoes and takes them inside the hut. She separates what she needs and puts the rest in a box and takes it up to the stall with the honesty box. She is thankful that people have put money in after taking the produce and it is still in the box at the end of the day. Jason follows her up and down again to the hut, busily sniffing and stopping and then running along side.

Jo is undecided as to whether or not to return to the hut for lunch, or take it with her. Her decision is made with the early heat from the sun, it is going to be a very hot day and she doesn't fancy eating a warm lunch, so she will nip back later. She prepares a pasta salad and leaves it in the fridge. Then after brushing her teeth and going to the loo, she has a quick all over wash. She decides it will be wonderful at the end of the long hot day, to go down to the beach when it is quiet and have a swim to freshen up. She puts in her bag a water bottle and an apple and also the book 'In search of lost time' that she hasn't yet started to read; she imagines she will have plenty of reading time during the day. With this and a pocket full of £1 coins and change, she ferries up the bags of pebbles and boats. Back at the stall she sets out several boats in different sizes and some of the pebbles on to the table. She has plenty over to replenish as the day progresses. Jo realises she hasn't thought about a sign for the boats. She's got one for the garden produce, albeit a small one, but not one for the nautical display. She will have to make one for the next day of selling. Anyway, she will see how it goes today.

Jason is quite happy to settle down once everything is set up. Occasionally he gets up and has a sniff around and takes a drink from his water bowl then lies back down again. He is very good and never goes off into the road; he knows his boundary and stays close by. Jo sits down, attempting to read the first chapter of the book, but she can't concentrate, her mind is held like a huge intake of breath, waiting for the first passers by. It will be a good idea to have the stall when the local car boot is on, as it is just down the road in one of the large farmer's fields. There will be lots and lots of people walking by then. The car boots are held fortnightly and the next one will be in a week's time.

Jo soon realises how tiring it is to be doing nothing, just sitting around, it reminds her of the first months at the hut, sitting aimlessly, waiting and wondering, however now she is filled with a hopeful anticipation, full of promise, unlike before. When the traffic begins to build up and slow down, the passengers and drivers appear interested and curious as their heads turn for another look at the stall. Maybe they will return for a walk later on in the day, or stop by on their way home.

After awhile the walkers and cyclists arrive, most of them stop and take a look and are complimentary about the crafts. Jo is elated on her first sale, the largest boat with yellow sails; the lady who buys it comments on her newly painted bathroom and says that it will be perfect to sit on the shelf of her pine cabinet. So with a £12 start Jo is really chuffed. During the morning she sells two large pebbles and four other boats, making a grand total so far of £50. She is tremendously happy with that. Also she clears most of the lettuce and tomatoes and that amounts to a few pounds also, a good morning's work. She is filled with an inner pride and joy and is ready for lunch, so she ties Jason to a nearby bush and dashes back to collect fresh cold water and food.

Returning to the stall and shortly before she reaches the top of the track she hears a voice, that of a boy talking to

Jason. Jo hurries and finds him leant down stroking and tickling Jason.

When he catches sight of Jo he jumps up saying, "Is this your dog?"

"Yes."

"What's he called?"

"Jason."

As the boy carries on stroking Jason he begins his questioning.

"Are these boats yours? Did you make them? How much are they? Can you put them in water? Will they sink?" and on and on he continues asking, "Can I take Jason for a walk?"

Jo is unsure about the boy, for his age and size he makes the impression of a much younger child.

"Maybe not now, because it's a bit too hot today and he's happy just lying in the shade."

"Have you got a pirate ship?"

"No, I haven't done a pirate ship; I only have the coloured sailing boats."

"Will you be doing a pirate ship?"

"I'll have to think about making one."

Suddenly his attention is taken and off he goes.

As the day drifts on, Jo wishes she had brought her straw hat, as the sun is scorching down. She is looking forward to her swim later to refresh and cool down; she knows Jason will be too; it has been a long hot day. By the end of the afternoon she has sold three large pebbles and six small ones, three large boats, five medium boats and four small ones making a total value of £120, wow that's so pleasing. Along with the produce it is nearly £185 not bad for a day. Jo soon packs the remaining stock and returns to the hut, this time it is quicker carrying things down the track, especially with the knowledge of success. It is lovely to be back inside, away from the strong sunshine and sit awhile in the armchair before sorting everything out.

"The tide will be coming in soon Adam." Anna tells her son as she begins to gather their belongings.

"No, I haven't finished yet. I'm not going back, not yet."

"Five minutes Adam, and then were off. We'll buy an ice lolly when we get to the top if you're good." Anna bribes.

Anna begins to walk towards the slip, which leads away from the beach and calls, "Adam, ice cream?"

Her son comes panting up besides her, his fair face, pink and freckled with the sun and traces of sweat on his forehead and nose.

"We'll call and get some shopping." She explains to her son as they walk away from the beach along the promenade.

Huge elaborate sandcastles with watercourses have been abandoned, as people begin leaving the beach, because the tide is coming in. Due to the little coves along the coastline some parts of the beach can be cut off by the tide, so you have to be aware of the tide turning.

Anna shops between the two supermarkets and small stores to buy their food. Adam will eat most things, so she tries to keep their food fairly healthy. She buy's an iceberg lettuce, tomatoes and a piece of cheese, which has been reduced.

"We'll buy some eggs from the little shop near Mad Micks." Anna tells him.

As always before they arrive back at the caravan Adam wants to go off and spend a bit of time with his friend.

"Six o'clock." Anna reminds him as she watches her son saunter towards his friend's caravan.

His friend's van has electricity unlike Anna's, so he is able to watch the children's programmes, play with their dog and scrounge food, which means he won't eat all of his tea.

Anna's feelings sink as she unlocks the caravan door and puts the few groceries away. She fills the kettle from the water butt and runs a few new potatoes under the cold-water tap outside, slices them and puts three eggs in to boil. She will save one of the eggs for Adam's egg mayonnaise sandwiches. She pours the hot water into her pot and makes tea.

Opening the window she remembers the blue note book she's bought and gets it out of the cupboard as well as a pen. 'Give up,' Anna thinks, 'who are you kidding?' A part of her says 'drink your tea and then prepare the evening meal.' The other part says 'no write, write something anything, just don't sit here waiting to serve up a poor mans salad.' Anna sips her hot tea as a way of distracting herself. 'OK what can I call it. I don't know, I don't know, focus think. Not some shitty, crappy, title but something strong and noble! You wish! OK. OK.' Tiring of her critical self, 'shut up now, because I'm not going to listen to you.'

The eggs, Anna saves them and the new potatoes just it time.

Drinking her tea Anna returns to her writing.
'Anna Magee, Enniskillen House, Homeopath in Practise. No they all sound corny and shitty as if they came from an old woman's magazine or cheap paperback romances.' She wants it to be refined, sophisticated, sleek and smooth and all those things that she is not. She hasn't considered a rough structure and a working synopsis as she opens her blue notebook. Names come to her but she dismisses them as quickly because they also sound corny and old fashioned. She is about to close her notebook, when an idea strikes her. 'I don't have to keep a title I use now, nor do I have to keep the names I use now.' This thought, these prospects free her. The fact that she has nothing to lose one way of another, means she can just play with ideas and mess

about. 'No one needs to see it, so it is all right, OK. Fermanagh House,' Anna names her book. Anna, John and Maya will also be people in her book. 'To start how can she start?' She will begin it how it was in her dream. She would get out of the taxi and go to Fermanagh House, the name of the doctor's practise.

One day Anna decides she will go back to Enniskillen and reacquaint herself with the place and people and then she will be able to put the right things in her book. Anna begins to write.

FERMANAGH HOUSE

Anna Magee paid the taxi driver and took her case from him outside Fermanagh House. Maya Gallagher had sent Anna the details and Anna had found the journey from Yorkshire to Enniskillen remarkably easy. Anna's things would be arriving on the Thursday so Anna had enough to see her through until then. Fermanagh House was a large double fronted detached house with bay windows and a solid looking white front door at the side of which on the wall were the brass plates with the names of the three doctors John Doherty and Maya Gallagher and Michael Gallagher..
....

"Mam, mam."
"What?"
"You said be back at six for tea mam."
Anna looks at her son and down at the blue book she's been writing in. Time has moved on so quickly.
"I'll go out again." Adam offers.
"No you won't. Go wash your hands and then I'll dish up tea."
Anna rinses the lettuce leaves, cuts the eggs, tomatoes and grates a little of the cheese to spoon over the new potatoes. Adam returns to share the simple salad with a

piece of crusty bread. She knows if her son leaves now, she won't get him back until it is almost dark and that's too stressful, wondering where he is and will he be safe and where would she begin looking for him. Keeping him in now with the promise of a cup of drinking chocolate, the sweets that she's hidden, a hot water bottle and knock, knock, jokes is a nightly routine. She clears the dishes, puts the kettle on to wash up and make the hot chocolate, whilst he plays on the floor with his toys. She refills the kettle for the hot water bottles and makes up the beds before it gets dark.

"Let's play snakes and ladders a bit." She suggests to distract him.

Anna often wonders how lovely it would be to go out for an evening stroll, to walk up to the farm or down to the beach at the end of their day, instead of having to distract her son, until it became too dark for him to play out. Adam would jump at the suggestion of an evening stroll but it wouldn't be enough for him, he would either run away, or kick out to be allowed to go with his friends. She had tried it again and again and it always ended up the same way, the results never changed.

Eventually her son settles and falls asleep, Anna feels shattered.

The pages she has written in the book have been closed and Anna is back in her real world. Tired and alone she knows the following day will be filled with the same repetitive routine, with little if anything to alter it. As she drifts off to sleep, outside the rain begins to drip, drop on the caravan roof. She wonders what the woman is doing. Sleeping? Out walking maybe with her dog. The tide will be in, so the beach isn't a possibility. Anna feels she would like to see the woman again, no matter how briefly, just to confirm and reassure herself that what had happened really had. The clock still shows 4 a.m. and even with a new battery hasn't worked since. 'Since when?' She'd found an old watch with a broken strap in a charity shop for a new timepiece, as she felt unable to bring herself to buy another proper clock, so now the old one remains set at 4 a.m.

Anna's heart is pounding when she wakes up and she remembers her dream. She had been face to face with the man in her book, John Doherty. She tries to blink his eyes out of her mind. 'What in God's name is she doing with herself?' Anna asks. 'Get a grip and come back into reality.' She has felt this pull, ever since the day when the bang had awoken her and she had met Jo.

What Anna now decides she wants to do, is close it all off completely, so it no longer exists. 'Does it exist?' Close the stupid book too, just close everything. Close her eyes, her mind, her thoughts, herself, so no one and nothing can see her. The piercing eyes of the man in her book and now in her dreams disturb her; she can't cope with the scrutiny, in her imagination, or in her dreams. Her own cowardice as she lay alone in her caravan makes her sad. She stopped looking at herself many years ago, too many years ago to remember. Now she can't bear looking at what she has become. Looking at her reflection in the mirror used to feel so disappointing for her. Now she feels that she has caught up emotionally with what she knows and sees visually, when she sees her reflection. She has spent so many years of her life longing for those looks, which never came and now even in her imagination she can't bear them.

The gaze of John Doherty has re-connected Anna to that long, deep, empty, lonely space, inside her soul, which she has shut up and closed off from in order too survive. To be cut off and disconnected is the only way she can exist. The woman and the man in her book have reminded her of this and she closes her eyes and weeps. In Anna's mind the phrase returns to her again, 'and I longed for those looks, which never never came.' She doesn't want the man in the book to look at her; she wants to return to sleep. To return to oblivion and her sweet, silent, warm dreams of darkness, where her soul always finds peace and rest in.

The rain falls faster and heavier on the caravan. It washes away the dust of the hot summer day. Far away there is thunder but not here near the caravan. The thunder and lightening are far away out at sea.

As dawn begins to emerge she wakes unrefreshed and tired but unable to return to sleep. The air is cooler than it has been and she is thankful for that. She rises from her bed and slips on her tracksuit bottoms, jacket and shoes. Putting the spare caravan key into her jacket pocket, she takes the torch and begins to make her way towards the path, which leads her to the beach. She doesn't need the torch, because the light of dawn is gently filtering through the mist of the early morning and giving enough light to let her find her way. The ground is soddened from the night's downpour. Her feet squash through the mudded grass, until she reaches the beach footpath, which is more solid going. Her heart races as she slowly approaches the place where she had earlier seen the woman. As she rounds the corner to where the bench is, she sees someone, she is absolutely certain of it her heart leaps with excitement. Quickening her pace until she reaches the spot where the bench is, she carries on ahead towards the beach path, to catch up with the woman and her dog. Reaching a small thicket of trees, wet leaves touch her face and she stops. She has passed through this thicket many times, just as she had when she and the woman went to the beach, but now something stops her from continuing the journey through the thicket. She wipes the wetness off her face from the leaves and turns around to go back home to her caravan; she suddenly doesn't feel safe or sure. She walks as quickly as she can back to the campsite and feels relieved when she catches a glimpse of the caravans. She hurries as best she can, her progress being hampered by the muddy grass. Before going inside she kicks off her sodden shoes, to rinse some of the mud off her legs and feet from the cold-water tap. Throwing her muddy shoes underneath the caravan she unlocks the door and goes inside. Taking an old towel she wipes her feet and legs down after slipping off her trousers. After taking off her jacket she climbs back into bed, snuggling deep down beneath the covers, with her head hidden, safe, warm and cosy.

Next morning Anna surfaces, it is daylight.
"Mam can I go down to the beach with Callum and Callum's mum today?"
Adam asks from inside his sleeping bag.
"Let's get up and dressed first."
Adam is full of life and energy and his pace never slackens except when he is asleep.
"Did Callum's mum say you could?"
"Yes."
"Alright then, you could take those crisps and some apples with you for a snack."
"Yes."
So her day is set.
"I want you to go and take the things for the snack to Callum's mum and I want to know what time you're going to be home. Not until 9 o'clock." Anna pre-empts Adam's next question.
"Oh."
"Just chill out a bit and we'll find your nice shorts and yellow t-shirt, and on Sunday we might have a walk down to the car boot sale. See if we can find any wellies or second hand stools because we've only two left and we could do with a couple more."

Anna decides to clean the caravan windows and wash the nets and weed and dig over the patch at the front of the caravan whilst Adam is down on the beach.

"3 o'clock mam I'll be back." Adam calls to his mum through the caravan door.

"Wait a bit Adam." Anna manages to call before he runs off.

"A pound each for ice-cream. And no cigs."

Adam turns around and smiles his cheeky smile. She smiles too at her son who is so happy and full of life and sunshine. So much expectation, his endless optimism, never ceases to amaze her.

Without Adam to entertain or worry about she races through her jobs, which she has set herself. The lace curtains look better after their wash. Shirley in the caravan next door had passed them on. She shakes and dusts down the grey top curtains. She would like something more fresh and summery but the grey velour will have to serve for the time being. Anna polishes the wooden surfaces of the caravan, the two wardrobes and the old sideboard, which is built into the side.

At 1.30 she has done all she needs to do. They will have beans on toast for tea. The following day she can do the washing and that would free her up for the car boot sale on Sunday.

After a cheese sandwich and a mug of tea she decides to have a little stroll. She makes her way again to where she and the woman had first met. Anna doesn't expect to see the woman; she just has a sense of being draw to the spot. Sitting on the simple wooden bench she sighs, finding it difficult to sit down and relax. She has spent so much of her time, her life on the go and on the move. To simply sit in the moment feels uneasy and wrong. People walk passed with their dogs, some on leads, some not, young and old, men, women and families. She feels alone, isolated, here on the bench. Her mum would have loved the caravan Anna contemplates.

Rising from the bench, unaware of the beauty in front of her she returns to her caravan. The strange feeling has stayed with her since the experience with the woman. It has left her more confused than she has felt for a long time. She has learnt to switch herself off and now she is somehow in the process of a thaw. This prospect isn't an experience she either wants or welcomes. She has unplugged herself from her life with due cause.

Adam would return in an hour, so she decides to sort clothes for the following day to wash. She likes to keep up with her washing because Adam needs a change of clean clothes at least twice a day, especially when it rains because he loves to jump around in the muddy grass and get filthy. Her mother had died before any of her children had come along. This saddens her because neither her mother, nor her children, ever met each other. She misses that warm, safe, relationship of family life. Anna's children had granddad McGee and his second wife Bessie but it wasn't the same. The children had loved their granddad but only saw him when Anna took them to visit, or on the few occasions her father came to visit her. She could count on her hands the times her father actually came to visit her. Bessie, her father's second wife, would say, "He's not coming to visit you lot, just the grandchildren," she would tell Patrick's son or daughter when she called. "He's not bothered about visiting you." Somehow that used to make Bessie feel better and dampened down her anger and jealousy and mortification of sharing her second husband with so many people.

Anna puts the kettle on and pours the beans into a pan in preparation for Adam's return home. She misses her family. The closeness as a child and young woman had been so located and safe. She feels alone now and isolated from her family, and knows fundamentally she can never return, never go back to how it was, to what they had, too much has happened between them for that. Anna waits.

Jo decides this morning after breakfast to walk into town. She needs to buy Jason dried dog food as it's running low and will only last two or three days more at most. Also she has another idea for the boats, to add a finishing touch, a bit of extra character. She thought of it last night whilst sitting and reflecting before going to bed. To make an anchor for the boats by threading a piece of fishing line through a lump of lead shot and feeding it into the hull. If she presses a brass washer into the side of the boat and drill a hole through with the bradawl, she can push line through and knot it. The lead anchor can then be pulled up and down using the line.

Jo has a commission to complete of a large boat with red sails, with 'Stella 30' stitched in green across its main sail. If she makes an anchor with the lead shot and finishes the boat with it, she's sure it will look great. So she'll call into the fishing shop down by the harbour before collecting Jason's food. She has only walked to the harbour a couple of times since living here and that was late in the evening when most people had left. But she remembers the fishing tackle shop because it had a large plastic fisherman wearing waders standing outside, holding a rod, and reeling in a flapping fish. In the window display were lots of colourful floats, different sea rods and reels, and fishing net draped at the sides with seashells and pebbles on the window ledge. She will be able to purchase the fishing line and hopefully pieces of lead shot there. She needs also a loaf of bread and two slices of roast ham from Martins butchers, to eat later in the day with mango chutney and salad.

With the intention of having a well-earned treat at lunchtime of fish and chips, she picks up her rucksack and Jason's lead and sets off. The weather again today is another hot and sunny one, lovely for walking and enjoying the sea. "Come on Jase, this way". Down the steps and through the path, heading towards the cliff top footpath and down the steep steps to the beach. The harbour is at the far end, away from the sandy beaches near the Brigg. They pass the beach shops selling ice cream and candyfloss. On the paved area adjacent to these, are round drum containers, filled with buckets and spades, kites and footballs. Propped against these, blown up to shoulder height, are rubber dinghies and paddles. Dry suits hang on a rail, with surfboards piled up at the side. Various beach tents and windbreaks and mats rolled up, a brightly coloured scene. Surveying the expanse of beach to either end of the coastline, her eyes take in a picture postcard snapshot. Images of children, chasing each other and squealing, of digging in the sand, adults helping and taking part, deckchairs and beach towels, of kites in flight. Held in enclaves and huddled in segregated areas with blots of sand separating the groups apart. Interspersed and breaking up the image like the undoing of a spell is a dog racing and interfering or a child running with a bucket and tripping and then in tears back to the huddle again of mum. And far out on the horizon, freight ships appears, motionless, set in time. Where the sand meets the sea with a gentle lapping, there are children paddling and splashing and into the deeper water further out, swimmers heads are dotted about. Jo is struck by the number of people, the mass and whirl of activity, each group living in their own worlds, yet joined together as a whole picture of life here in this place.

Jo is tempted to turn around and retreat back to the hut and to solitude where it feels safe. But as she looks around she realises that she is virtually invisible almost here amongst everyone, she really doesn't stand out at all. She is not a part of their picture; she is an outsider, just her and Jason in their own little world. No one has tried to enter, to interrupt, or break in to their space, so she carries on around the bend, past the café, where people sit outside having drinks and breakfasts, chatting away. The bacon smells lovely, it fuels her appetite and then on past the deckchair attendant in his little hut, reading his paper oblivious to the world. Meandering in and out of tiny people, either shying and hiding away from Jason, or eager and reaching out trying to touch and stroke him. Walking on through pushchairs and infants and dad's proudly swaggering from side to side with toddler on top, and then on past the public toilets and the mini golf. Then the benches, seating arms folded guests looking out to sea. Along past children looking down through the railings, holding tight, aware of the deep drop down to the beach. Towards the kiddies roundabout and carousel, the music tinkling and playing along. Passing carriers of candyfloss and bags full of picnics, swimwear and towels, marching to find ownership of their place in the sand. The beach huts for hire at £8 per day, openly showing their contents, the kettles and cups on a tray. Looking up past the cabins she can see the old town and the road passing through, the cars full of more people, today is a busy day. On and on the pavement until finally reaching the harbour, the cobbled slope stretching down to the beach ahead.

Jo's heart lifts at the sight of the fisherman standing outside the fishing tackle shop; she ties Jason's lead to a post outside and enters in. The shop is empty and when the doorbell chimes as it shuts - out pops an elderly man to serve. She asks to have a look at some heavy fishing line and likes the yellowy, green reel he shows her. Then she questions the man regarding the lead shot, he rummages about at the back of the store and returns with a few different sizes. Amazingly, Jo is so delighted when he shows her one with a hole at the top, it looks like a small weight about 1" in size and will be absolutely right for what she needs it for. So she buys ten of these along with the reel and has a last browse around before leaving. The pet shop for Jason's food is situated near the edge of town, so she plans to collect it on her return. Although she realises that she would have been better coming for it on her bike, as it's quite heavy to carry, so she decides to get a small amount, to put him on for a

few days. Jason is panting, waiting in the heat so she
takes him down the cobbled landing to the sea edge. She
stops to look at the old fishing boats leaning on their
sides, rusty, with tell tale signs of life on the sea,
saltwater damaged paint and well worn decks, but with a
beauty and a strange offering of comfort as they sit here
randomly along the wall side. Jo unleashes Jason and off
he bounds into the waters edge and then jumps across
into the sea. She finds a place along the wall to sit
awhile, giving Jason time for a swim to cool down.
Eventually Jason looks to find her and she calls him,
with a majestic shake he returns and drops to the ground.
Jo tells him it's time to go for fish and chips; he will love
his share of these. As she gathers her rucksack and
checks for money, a young man in his twenties appears
by her side. He has a heavy green rucksack on his back
and is carrying a bottle of water. Jo notices his dirty feet
inside his sandals and sunburnt legs below his shorts and
wearing a short sleeved, checked shirt, on his upper
body, and tied around his waist a navy blue fleece jacket.
He is unshaven with rather unkempt shoulder length hair
curling around his ears.
He announces "Your dog was looking at me from over
there." and then proceeds to bend down and stroke Jason
asking his name.
On his arm just above his wrist is a thick line of dried
red blood from a recent cut, he must have just left it, and
the skin around the cut has an angry raised weal. She
mentions Jason's name and the man continues to stoke
and pat him whilst he glances up at her, his eyes have a
watery, glassy stare. It's as though he is intimating a
stronger friendship with his over familiarity to Jason and
the knowing look that he is giving her.
Jo feels quite uneasy and doesn't offer any more
information and then as suddenly as he appeared he
jumps back up and with a backward lingering look says,
"See you later Jason." with an affirmative nod, whilst
pulling forward the shoulder straps on his rucksack to
adjust its weight and then walks off.

Jo watches to see which direction he takes, as he moves off up the cobbled landing and when he reaches the top her view is obscured by the passing of a vehicle. So she waits a few minutes and then sets off and makes her way on up the steps towards the town centre. There are quite a few fish and chip shops in the town. She decides on calling at the one on the main street that is always busy, waiting outside her appetite grows with the wafting smell of salt and vinegar and the vats of deep-fried battered fish and fresh potato chips. She orders Jason to wait outside and pays for the food and sprinkle lots of vinegar and salt on them to eat outside. She finds a bench to sit at and eat, there is nothing quite like eating fish and chips with one's fingers, the fiercely hot fish, the puffing and blowing, taking in big mouthfuls at a time. It is such a long time since she has eaten this wonderful meal, before she devours the lot; she has the constant nudge from Jason as a reminder to leave him some. She is pleasantly full and still there is plenty left for him along with some crisp batter too. Jo makes Jason wait whilst the food cools some more, she doesn't want him to burn himself in his eager greediness.

When they have both finished they call at the shops for the bread and ham and then walk along and call at the pet shop. Jo buys just enough to carry in her rucksack, she will return on her bike for more in a few days time. Jason's food is always bulked out with the extras from her meals, so his dried food lasts longer for that. With their shopping achieved and nothing else left to do she decides to take the road back down through the town to the beach and up the cliff top path, as it will be a much more pleasant walk than on the pavements and crossing the roads, negotiating passing cars.

They slowly drift back down to the promenade and walk past the beach huts and shops and cross over to the steep cliff steps. It is a nice way to keep fit along with the gardening and Jason loves this way too. Once back up on

the top cliff path Jo makes a stop at the bench and sits
down. She doesn't want to sit too long, otherwise the
ham and bread will not stay fresh. However it's almost
impossible to pass this bench without stopping because
of the amazing views looking out to sea. She hasn't been
sat very long gazing out across the ocean, when she
hears footsteps coming up the steps, she turns towards
them and recognises the figure of the man from earlier,
down at the cobbled landing. He looks to where they are
sitting and draws nearer towards the bench and sits down
next to her.
"Hello again, you two." he says as he bends down to
stroke Jason who is asleep.
Jason wakes with a start.
"Were just going now, so you can have the bench."
He laughs and says, "Thanks, you don't have to go you
know, you can stay and talk."
"No we really do have to go now, come on Jason."

Jo definitely doesn't want to stay and talk, she doesn't
want to get to know this person, she wants to return
swiftly back to the hut. She walks off quickly calling
Jason, who seems to want to stay in the attentive
company of this man.
"Come on Jason, here, come on were going."

Jo reaches the turning off from the public path and
glances back and sees the black outline of Jason running
to catch up. She is unnerved when she sees the man
stand up from the bench and look in her direction; she
was hoping he wouldn't notice the route that she is about
to take. And yet she can't go back in his direction, back
to the beach, or take the public pathway along the cliff
top, she has to go towards the hut. She hurries along,
urging Jason to keep up, she wants to reach the safety of
the hut as soon as she can and just hopes the man doesn't
decide to follow. She is quite breathless when she
unlocks the door and throws her rucksack off. She enters
the workroom and leans against the workbench and

waits, checking for every sound, in fear of hearing footsteps outside.

Jo doesn't know how long she stands but feels unable to move and it isn't until she feels the numbness in her arm, from where she has been leaning, that she has to straighten up and move from the spot, where she has been glued for a very long time. She is quite shaken and wants the day to end, but worries about how she will get through the night. The darkness ahead is what she is afraid of.

It's nighttime now, the light of today is fading and the interior of the hut is getting darker and she doesn't want to end up stumbling around looking for the torch, so she decides to light the storm lanterns and candles. She doesn't feel like going up to bed just yet, even though she feels quite tired, she knows that once she lays down her mind will begin its regurgitation of the past and await its nightmares of the night and a disturbed and troubled sleep. She turns up the wicks and tops up the lamps with paraffin and lights two, one she leaves on the table and the other she sits on top of the stove, she decides not to bother with the candles. The lamps cast strange shadows and flicker into life, after giving off their initial burst of grey smoke and settle down. She sits and wishes that she had a bottle of wine to drink, it would be lovely to crack open a bottle of red and take time sipping and enjoying the slow drift into a drowsy numbed out state. However she doesn't have one, so she will have to savour and enjoy one another night. It is the desire to escape from her thoughts of this moment, to hide away from her inner voices and the tap, tap, of past conversations and haunts.

Jo decides to listen to the radio. She bought this digital radio last Christmas, as a treat. It was an expensive purchase at around £50, however she wanted one that would perform well and would be strong and last a good long time. She needed to hear music and peoples voices, to hear life outside that was safe and impersonal. She has always loved music and the radio, especially classical music. She tunes in also to other stations, depending on her mood of the day and mainly listens on an evening after the day's work has been done and she can sit and relax in silence, enjoying escaping to another place. Tonight as she tunes in to the different stations she cannot find one that matches her mood and spends a few minutes switching from one to the other. So turning off the radio she looks at Jason, who has been asleep curled up on his bed for a good while. He is a comforting sight, she watches as his body gently gives and heaves in and out with his breath, far away in doggy dreamland where ever that is. She knows that with him she is safe here on her own. Yet after today she has a constant urge to turn around and check for a presence behind her and she does so again. How silly in this darkness, when the entry of anyone would soon bring Jason out of his sleep. Rationally she knows that no other person is in here and yet her body is on high alert and ready in waiting just in case. She tells herself again that they are cut off and apart from the town, so why would anyone come past. The land is well away from the public path and road so they are safe. It is so difficult to look back and remember what was.

A feeling of sadness and grief fills her now. The dark corners here are a stark reminder of how far she's come and what was before. She doesn't want to snap out of her memories right now, to jump up and suddenly change tack, maybe because of the night and how hard it might be to find something to concentrate her mind on. But also she feels strong enough inside to let it just be, whatever, to allow it to float through and why not, she doesn't have to hide from herself anymore. So she's glad to welcome herself to herself and although it feels scary, she acknowledges that yes she is ok. Her body affirms these thoughts with a generous sigh and surrenders, relaxing into the chair. She was for many years at the mercy of a man who was obsessed by her. Over many years his threatening actions and menacing phone calls drove her to where she is today. 'Is he here, has he found me?' She asks herself these questions as she sits. His breath blowing in her neck, just behind her ear, she can feel. Her body tightens in expectation of the sudden grab and her readiness for the ensuing struggle that will come for sure. The never knowing when or where, surely she is too far away now, no more, no more. She has to reassure herself, 'yes you are safe now, the destruction is part of another world gone by, it is over.' With these thoughts she blows out the lamp on the stove and says goodnight to Jason and takes the other lamp upstairs to the bedroom. She crawls under the duvet and with the last blow she is in complete darkness and glad for the safety of the bed and buries her head and inhales the sweet aroma of her own skin.

It is awhile later before she notices the drops of rain falling down on the roof, how long has it been raining she wonders. She pulls the duvet up and around her for warmth, as the temperature falls. Now that the leaks are mended in the hut, the windows and a couple of places in the corners of the roof due to the blocked gutters, it is a nice cosy place to be when it's raining outside. Although she longs for sleep, she drifts and listens to the roar of the sea and the patter, patter of rain and hears in the far distance the sound of thunder, followed by a crack of lightening. She tries to sleep but her body is tense and stiff. She stretches out and hears the rain falling heavy now, much faster and feels quite chilly and gets out of bed and finds a blanket, that she keeps folded on the chair in the corner of the room and puts it on top of the duvet and crawls back inside.

Inside the dream she enters as if through a tunnel, she's sucked in and unable to stop. Through this black hole she travels lightly and floats and gathers speed. She cannot slow down and is being pushed from behind. And then with eyes seeing through darkness, she see him and knows that she has to get out, away from this tunnel, now filled with terror, but she cannot get out, there is no way out, she can't breathe anymore, and gasps and tries to take in air, but there isn't any and this person behind is taking her and pushing her down, she is being swallowed up and sucked in and is disappearing. She is no more. Awake. Awake. Bolting upright. Breathe, trying to breathe, 'where am I?' The darkness is still here, she is still in darkness, 'where am I?' Breathe, Breathe.

A crack of distant thunder and then the rain, she is covered in sweat and feels shaky and lays in wait for the daylight to return. After what seems like hours she drops off back to sleep and when she wakes up the rain has stopped.

It is cool now around the hut and she longs for a mug of tea. So she puts on a pair of bottoms and a top and goes downstairs and lights the stove. She will make a big teapot of tea and fry eggs for breakfast; and have a few cold potatoes to cook with them and along with fresh orange this will be a good start for the day. She chats along to Jason waiting for the stove to heat up and the kettle to boil. Wandering into the workroom she looks out of the window at the damp grass outside and hopes that the day for the car boot will be a fine one. She's soon fiddling about with brushes and paints, dipping and mixing colours for the sails of boats that are works in progress, so they will be ready for the next stall. The whistle of the kettle reminds her to stop and she puts the brush into a glass of water and returns to brew tea and put the frying pan on for the potatoes and eggs.

Once the breakfast is done she leaves the stove to die out, as the sun is starting to break through the early morning mist and the hut will soon warm up. She won't have to water the garden today and the nights rain will have filled up the shower tank. She does three eggs, two for her and one for Jason and shares the potatoes between them. She puts his share on top of his dried food and he wolfs it down. She plates up her breakfast and pours a glass of orange juice and takes it to the table to eat and cuts a thick slice of brown bread and butters it.

Sitting and eating she reflects on the night. In the early days here she would have retreated into a day of unease and melancholy and sat doing nothing, and unable to eat. Now she knows how important, whatever the night, to look after herself and be strong. It will pass, the night, it does pass, the night, and she has survived and is stronger for this. This breakfast is important and she eats everything and helps herself to two big mugs of tea. Then with the remaining water she fills the bowl at the sink and washes up. She also has a small camping gas burner for use when she doesn't want to light the stove, for boiling the kettle and heating a pan. But even now in summer it is fulfilling to light the stove and feel its gentle heat around the hut, so occasionally like today this is what she does. After washing up she decides to change her sheets and goes upstairs and gathers together the pillowcase, sheet and duvet cover and dirty towel and underwear and then puts in the t towel from the washing up. Opening the door she lets Jason into the garden and brings the bike from the back of the hut and fills the cycle basket with the dirty washing.

After a quick wash and toilet she cycles up into town to the launderette, she fills the washing machine and puts in a packet of soap powder and £1 coins and leaves it to complete its wash. This gives her time to do the shopping. She calls at the health food shop for sunflower seeds, walnuts, sultanas and a bottle of olive oil. She adds a couple of carob bars to the basket and after paying, packs them into the rucksack. She calls at Martins for half a pound of pork and leek sausages for her evening meal. It seems quieter today around town, the rain and dampness early on has deterred people from going down to the beach, they wait to see what the weather will be like later on. Back at the launderette she doesn't have to wait too long before the washing is done. She puts the damp washing into a plastic bag and then into the basket, it is heavy now and won't quite fit. So she has to take a careful ride home to avoid the bag dropping off onto the road and also too it is difficult to stay balanced with the excess weight at the front. When she gets back to the lay by at the top of the road, she is relieved to dismount and walk down to the hut with the rucksack and bag of wet washing and then return back for the bike. She pegs the sheet and duvet cover and the other bits on the line and feels satisfied with the mornings work. The sun is coming out and today is going to be ok after all.

Anna waits for her son to return back from his day out. She feels tired and wants to rest but dare not nod off in case he comes back and finds her asleep and runs away again. She puts away her notebook but the nagging thoughts still remain as she waits. Remembering the man in her book leaves her feeling unsettled and disturbed. Why is she afraid of looking into his face? Why is looking into his eyes so disquieting? Anna closes her eyes because she doesn't want to see the man again. What is it that she doesn't want to see? She isn't sure. Is it the man looking at her? Or is it her looking at him? Anna can't decide and really doesn't want to. What is it she doesn't want the man to see when he looks at her? Herself. Anna doesn't want the man to see her because she doesn't want to see herself. When you look into the eyes of another what you're really doing is looking back at yourself. Anna has spent so long not looking into anyone's eyes. She can't cope with the scrutiny of another's gaze because she feels judged, unworthy and invisible. Anna has worked out that if she can remain invisible, then no one is able to tell her what she already knows about herself. Anna feels flat and disappointed when her son returns.

He asks Anna if he can have tea with Callum.

"Yes." she tells him, "But no later than 7 o'clock."

She puts a tea plate on top of the pan of beans; they will do for breakfast. She takes the blue note book and places it on the table in front of her. 'How can I be afraid of something that I am in the process of creating?' Anna is undecided as to whether or not to continue with the Fermanagh House book. 'I don't have to be myself in the story. I can't write about myself, I don't want to be me. I don't want to be a woman who doesn't have the courage to take a long, slow look, to scrutinize a man at leisure, like the man in the book.' The man has taken over; he is dominating Anna with his long, innocent, stare. 'I'll feel better tomorrow,' Anna reassures herself as she returns the book to its drawer and in the morning I'll get started on the washing.

Anna makes up the beds and puts the kettle on for the hot water bottles; they will be nice later to snuggle up to. Time seems to be dragging and she is happy when Adam returns home at 7.30 to fill in the empty space of his absence. She could live alone, she wouldn't mind that but it is the space inside herself that Anna doesn't want to live in.

As Adam begins his knock, knock, jokes followed by his doctor, doctor, ones she relaxes and finds peace and contentment in the warmth of her bed and the company of her son and falls asleep.
Except for their breathing in the caravan, it is silent. No rhythm of the clock ticking out time. The tick of the little wristwatch can barely be heard.

The tide has turned and now beats hard against the rocks. The wetness of the sea seeps through into the earth, slaking its thirst after the heat of the day but destroying most of the life, which grows within its path. As the swollen sea continues to throw itself against the rocks and cliffs, a soft, wispy haze begins to gather and drifts across the ground covering everything. The woman in her bed sleeps, her dog dozes as the sea near the beach hut splashes and slaps against the cliffs. The land rests as does its people but there are some who do not rest but wander about through the mist and shadows. Some are of this world but many are not.

Anna calls out in her sleep but no one listens or responds to her and in the morning when she wakes she will have forgotten her dreams. She sleeps in her safe, warm, cosy bed, her body and mind, recharging itself for the next day's routine.

After breakfast Anna completes all her chores. The weather is fine so she knows her washing will be dry by lunchtime. She has given Adam money to go to the supermarket to buy bread and milk. It takes him over an hour to return.

"Adam, if you want us to go to the car boot sale tomorrow, you need to come back when I ask you, not mess about at Callum's and then decide to return."

"Sorry mam."

She had known that her son would go to Callum's first, so why is she chiding him for doing what she knew he'd do? Because, it would be nice just once, for him to do something straightforward, and Anna surprises herself by adding, something normal. Adam does his best. He struggles with his boundaries and she knows it could be so much worse than how it is. Anna tells him to come back for 12.30 and she will make a picnic to eat outside with Callum. Adam brightens up and goes off to find his mate.

Anna grates what is left of the cheese and butters slices of bread and makes the boys sandwiches. She finds packets of crisps, which she's hidden from her son and two apples. She cleans out two water bottles to put orange juice in, and adds a few plain digestives. She has also hidden a tube of fruit pastels, which she splits in half and leaves the carrier bag with the picnic in on the kitchen table.

'So,' Anna reflects, 'I don't have any jobs to do in the caravan.' Outside the grass where it reaches the flags needs trimming but she decides to save that and washing the outside of the caravan for another time. A slack time, when Adam is bored and his friend has gone off for the day without him. She makes herself a pot of tea as she waits for her son to return for his picnic and looks around. The caravan is old and a bit shabby but clean and comfortable, serviceable, for hers and her children's needs and uses. It doesn't have running water but there is

the cold-water tap just outside the door and a shower
block with toilets so they manage. Electricity would be
useful and make life a lot easier and more comfortable
but it isn't really a necessity Anna convinces herself. Her
husband had said no to having electricity connected.
"It wasn't worth it," he'd said and she hadn't argued.

The boys come panting into the caravan and Adam is
soddoned. They have been having a water fight. After
giving her son a clean dry t-shirt and their lunch, the
boys set off to their den to play pirates. Anna eats her
cheese sandwiches and finishes her pot of tea and then
gets up and closes the door but doesn't lock it in case her
son returns.

Opening the large front window she again surveys the
caravan and breathes in the fresh air. She takes out the
blue note book and a pen and sits on the seat beneath the
open window. Her washing is blowing on the line as she
glances up. Opening the blue book Anna begins.

*Greeting Anna was a small vestibule with a door facing
her and one immediately to her right. Anna turned the
handle of the door to her right. The room Anna entered
was large with low-beamed ceilings and a dark wood
fireplace. Three further doors were facing Anna, which
led off to other rooms...*

Anna sees Adam from her spot in the window returning.
Closing the book she also closes her thoughts and puts
the notebook away for some other time. Her son tells her
the travel arrangements for the next day's car boot sale.
Callum's mum is going to give them a lift to the car
booty but then she will be going on to Thornby, so Anna
and Adam will have to make their own way back to the
campsite.

Sitting in the back of Callum's mum's car at 9 o'clock
on Sunday morning is an experience Anna could give a

miss. Adam and Callum are in the back of the car giddy
with excitement, whilst in the front seat Callum's baby
sister Cara howls because she wants to be free from her
baby seat. As Anna tumbles out of the car with the boys
Callum's mum gets the buggy out of the boot and straps
the baby in to more screams.

"Tell Callum's mum thank you." Anna prompts her son,
"And tell Callum you'll see him later."

Anna half leads, half pulls Adam away from Callum
calling, "Thank you again." and keeps out of the way of
the Stewards as she does so, as they guide the cars into
the field line by line.

Anna tells Adam at the outset, "If you get lost meet me
here."

She emphasises, "Next to the hot dog burger van."

Her son is ready for off.

"Adam." Anna repeats herself, this time catching his
chin to bring his face in line with hers, so she can repeat
her instructions and make sure he is listening.

For a brief moment he looks directly into her eyes and
then his gaze wanders.

"Adam."

"What?"

"Where did I say to meet?" Adam looks around, there is
too much stimulation for him to be able to settle or
focus.

"Where?" Anna repeats so that he has lodged her
instructions in his brain.

"Hot dogs."

"Right." Anna relaxes. "Now if we get separated we
know where to wait and find each other."

Adam remains close to her for the first few stalls but
when he sees something that distracts him and takes his
fancy, he completely forgets his mum and wanders off in
his own world, to look at a collection of fantastic
samurai swords.

Anna only finds one stall at the car boot sale, which are
selling stools but they are just too expensive to even

consider. She is disappointed but continues on her rounds, picking up a couple of naked action men for 50p, a kite and a tennis racket to keep her son busy. All her goods fit into the carrier bag she's brought. She knows Adam will have enjoyed the day and spent five times over the £1.50p she gave him. Anna walks to the hot dog stall but he isn't there. After standing, waiting for him, she sets off to trawl the car boot sale to look for him. When she eventually finds him he has a large bag of sweets in one hand and in the other he is flicking a lighter.

"Can I have that lighter for the caravan." Anna lies to her son.

"That's what I bought it for." Adam beams.

Anna takes the lighter from him and makes a mental note to drop it in the first bin she passes.

"It's time to start making tracks back Adam."

Anna shows him the goodies she's bought and explains how he can sort out his action men clothes when he gets back later, so he and Callum can play. Adam chatters as they leave the car boot field and follow other people, who are also on foot, walking back towards the town centre.

The traffic begins to filter back towards the town centre away from the car boot. The bargain hunters are returning slowly in their cars as queues build up. Jo decides to eat her lunch, before the walkers pass by the stall, on their way back from the boot fair. Quite a few had expressed interest when they had stopped by earlier this morning. She is hoping for a few sales and a busy period, before everything quietens down later this afternoon. She has not sold as much this week, but even so it has already been successful. The garden signs have turned out to be a good seller. Although a cheap item, they are much quicker to make than the boats, so she's pleased about that. At the same time, she's conscious of a cloud floating through her mind, casting a shadow over her optimism and joy, her pleasure in living. This haunting feeling is still with her after the encounter with the man the other day. She feels rather jumpy and on high alert and not her calm self that she has become accustomed to, these past few months. Her hunger seems to abate as her preoccupation; and fascination with this man, takes her mind off to a faraway place. She picks up and holds a pebble, trying to connect and find an anchor, to something that is real. Breaking into this internal space, she vaguely senses people approaching from the roadside and hears voices that seem far away. Turning around she look beyond the group of people coming towards the stall and her eyes fall upon a woman and a boy. A part of her holds a recognition with these two people. They are from some other world, some other time and place, faraway and almost forgotten.

"Go on mam." Adam tries to persuade Anna.
"Let's go look at the boats and see if she's done a pirate ship yet, go on mam."
"I said I'd think about it Adam. I didn't say I would go and buy a boat."
"Look mam." Adam points his finger to an offshoot just beyond the lay by; "You can see her stall it's just down there."

Anna sees people gathered around the stall but is unable to see if the woman is there. Maybe she won't be there, Anna tries to tell herself by way of reassurance, but what does she need reassurance for, nothing happened. They had a brief experience, nothing more. The boy hurries across and Anna slows down almost to a standstill.

"Have you got a pirate ship today? Have you made one yet? It will have to have some cannons on, so that it is a pirate ship." Turning around Adam calls out, "Mam, come on look, mam."

As Anna levels up with the stall she sees the back of a woman's head, who has short hair. 'Thank God,' Anna cries inside. 'Thank God. Thank God. Thank God.' She is safe, the woman isn't here, there are just customers milling around the stall, looking at the woman's goods. The bright colours of the sails on the boats stand out so vividly, that she feels compelled to go closer to the stall, to look at them and touch them. As Anna lifts one of the small boats with a blue sail, the woman who has been leaning across the stall straightens up and turns around. Her heart leaps, as she comes face to face with the woman she had swam with in the sea.

"Hello." is all Anna can summon up.

The woman looks through her and makes Anna's heart drop. Anna recognises the look the woman passes her. It is a look, which says I don't know you do I. Anna, feels crushed and wants to run away as if she's done something wrong. She feels ashamed of her invisibility before this woman, as if they had never met and they hadn't shared those quiet moments. 'How can she have forgotten,' Anna almost cries? When Anna recovers she looks about for Adam and to her horror sees him talking to the woman.
"Can you make me a pirate ship, because I want one?" the boy asks.

Jo vaguely hears herself reply, "Yes, I could make one for you."

"But I want a really big one, bigger than these boats, because it's a pirate ship."

"Well I have lots more pieces of wood, much bigger, that you could choose from down at my hut, where I live."

"Mam, come and look." the boy interrupts.

"You can draw a picture for me of your pirate ship and I can make it from that."

Anna wants to run away but this isn't possible, she can't run off and leave Adam. She manages to catch his eye, and hopes he will come to her, but he doesn't and actually calls for her to come and join him.

"Mam." Adam calls, "Come and talk to Jo she says she can make me a pirate boat."

Anna walks towards her son and the woman, in the hope of encouraging him to come away and just let this awful experience come to an end. Anna glances at the woman briefly now as she talks to her son.

"They don't have a pirate ship Adam, so we'd better get off now, come on please."

"No mam. Jo says if I draw a picture of what I want she'll make me the pirate ship."

"Adam." Anna pleads.

"Please mam, I really want one."

"Ok." Anna surrenders.

Anna turns off now and focuses her gaze and attention on Adam.

"How much would it cost?" Anna asks.

"I charge around £10 or £12 for the large boats and commissioned ones."

"Please mam."

"I could have it for my birthday gift."

Anna relents.

"I have to draw a picture and then we can take it to Jo's beach hut and I can pick some wood to make it."

"Ok. Adam, we'll do that."

Jo nods by way of an agreement and Anna leads her son away down the cycle path, away from the woman and her stall. Adam is excited as he leaves the stall, with instructions to return on Tuesday with his drawings, whilst Anna is filled with regret and disappointment.

The woman. 'If I could only run and hide,' Jo tells herself, because of the woman appearing again, reminding her of a long time ago, a part of her past almost forgotten.

"Come on Jase, come on let's go."

She packs up the stall and returns to the hut and takes her stock and puts it in the workroom, back on the bench. She places her day's takings, in the old earthenware pot, on the top shelf in the kitchen. Then kicks off her sandals and pads around the hut barefoot trying to settle to something. She should feed Jason and herself, however she doesn't feel ready to eat just yet. Her mind is preoccupied and churns over and over. How can she expect to live here and not encounter different people, especially now that she has started selling her wares by the roadside? How naïve and silly, to think that she could keep herself away from humanity and contact with others, Jason nudges her leg and looks up in anticipation. "Ok Jase you can have your dinner."
Jo fills his dog dish with food and puts it down on the floor.
"Here you go then."

With Jason content at his food bowl she ascends the stairs to the bedroom and lies down on top of the bed on her back, looking up at the wooden beams. She remembers a poem and wonders if she still has it filed away with her journals. She stands up and goes across to the lid of the trunk and opens it, staring back at her is her pile of notebooks, papers, and photos. They are still mixed up and in no particular order. She lifts some of them out of the trunk to take a look through, in search of the poem that she hopes to find. She remembers that it was written on a postcard and starts to look amongst the jumbled papers. She notices cards written by a hand that was once hers and quickly turns them over. Then she finds it.

METAMORPHOSIS:

I remember the glory of being
lifted up – high so high -
Pushing, struggling, floundering through
the air with all my limbs quivering
akimbo with excitement and rage –
The lights – white and yellow shivering and
shimmering, swimming in and out of my
vision – the sounds startling and
stunning and whizzing past my ears –
Held high – held aloft –
Held in the air – held another sacrifice –
Held another validation and confirmation –
Held another human life
And now, today, I remember
the strong sure arms I surrender to for the
Great laying down –
Still as reverently and gently as that
first lifting up but oh, not the same –
This time it is a surrender – a giving up
and a giving in.
This time I fall through sound, past light
and time – the drop is gentle but swift
and I have no time to grasp and strive and
gasp for life or light or sound or reality.
Oh, the letting go the letting go,
the great laying downs, the giving ups
and giving ins and letting goes –
done with so much ease but such profound
reluctance.

She picks it up and returns to bed. As she lay on her back, she re reads the card and then presses it, words facing down onto her breasts. The giving in and letting goes, done with so much ease but such profound reluctance. 'Oh yes, yes it was a letting go. What happened, where did you go, my friend, my love? That soft warm space where I lay my head, I needed you back then, remember why and when.' Turning sideways, she takes hold of the pillow and feels the woman's arms wrapped around her, how lovely to sink into her belly and drift into a deep sleep. She finds no dreams in this restful, peaceful, place, her body surrenders and gives in, the drop is gentle and swift through this light, until darkness and waking later to light once again. A beautiful awakening, stirring slowly and blinking into sunshine, how long has she slept, how many hours have past? She stays for a while and rests and takes time to slip out of this place to the day.

Going down to the kitchen, she notices there are no dishes from the previous evening and Jason whines to be let out. She opens the door for him and begins to prepare breakfast for them both.

Anna walks away from the meeting with the woman at her stall. Her hair has changed but Anna still recognised her. Adam is happy and bubbling away with what he wants to put on the boat. He has to have guns, "Cannons probably." he tells her. Walking into the town centre she listens to her son but feels bereft. Not one look of recognition or validation of who she is, or what they had shared. Inside Anna is lost, disconnected from her sense of reality and location; she has unhooked herself and is just drifting. She feels an overwhelming desire to hide, to run away from everything and everyone and just vanish.

On returning to the caravan Anna gets paper and coloured pencils for Adam to draw his boat. "If were to take it tomorrow you'd best get started on it now." Anna tells her son. "You can go out after your dinner."

As he does his drawings Anna begins to scrub a few new potatoes and puts them on to boil. They will have an earlier dinner today. She puts the few slices of bacon beneath the grill on a low light and melts a knob of butter in the frying pan, to gently fry the two tomatoes. Whilst waiting for the food to cook she looks at her son's drawing. In front of him is a picture of a pirate ship. The huge banana shape has a skull and cross bones on it and all down the side are guns poking out from holes.
"It's lovely." Anna tells him.
"Will she like it mum?" Adam asks, "Will Jo like it?"
"I'm sure she will."
"I want the sails to be dark purple, not black." Adam enthuses.
Anna drains the potatoes and adds a knob of butter, before sharing them with the bacon and cooked tomatoes. She eats her food slowly, the new potatoes smell and taste of the earth. The bacon is salty and more'ish, the tomatoes juicy. After her meal Anna is content and sits on the seat beneath the window,

considering what to do next. Adam goes out to play with his friends, even if Callum hasn't returned; he will find someone to play with.

Anna rises to clear the table, rinse the pots and pans. The day is hers now, so why doesn't she want it? Why doesn't she embrace it and revel inside it. She feels like an automaton, with no inner part of herself remaining. She understands that her only use is to be serviceable, she has no other part or function, and she isn't anything anymore. She has never been herself, because she hasn't known herself anyway. She has become a woman of use and service, to be brought in and put away when not needed. Anna is impudent; she can't function, or enjoy life, when she isn't involved in being of use or of service.

In days gone by she would have had a busy and happy life, fulfilling other people's needs. That would have satisfied her too, being retained, the old, faithful retainer. 'Fuck that,' Anna chastises herself. But inside she knows the 'Fuck' doesn't come from her heart. Anna has no value in herself, no worth, therefore it follows she is worthless. That's the bottom line really, because she cannot get much lower than that can she? She's lost the knack of life, of living. It has been knocked out of her by her upbringing, by the dutiful nuns and holy priests and later, later on, by him. Anna is at a loss as to what she can do. What does she want to do? She doesn't know. Yes she does, a bit. She wants to reach down, deep inside herself and haul herself out, to begin again, to wipe away her years of usefulness and conditioning – of her purposeful, meaningfulness and to start again from the beginning. To feel the reality of herself – every inch, piece by piece, to blossom, to grow, to become whole. To look in pride at herself in the mirror and to return the steady gaze back. To accept who she is and to create who she wants to become. 'Bollocks,' Anna thinks. She isn't anything but she is a realist and a pragmatist.

She goes to the drawer and takes out her blue note book and pen. Gazing out of the front window, Anna begins. If I can't be who I am or don't know who I want to be, then I can make her be and do what she wants, what she needs to be, to fulfil herself and at least give her, her life. I will make this Anna live. She will know how to live her life for herself, to be purposeful by being herself.

"You have a busy day" Maya reminded Anna. Anna looked at Maya and both women grinned at each other. "It's exciting isn't it" Anna said. "Isn't it just" Maya confirmed. "Time to go" Maya told Anna.....................................

Anna flicks through the sheaves of paper, in awe of how much she has written. Several hours have passed since she picked up her pen. Closing her book, she spots Adam chasing around the caravans she calls him. He dashes across.

"Is it tea time now mam?"
"Yes, come in now and put some clothes on your action man, whilst I finish your tea."
Anna opens a tin of macaroni and puts bread under the grill to toast. When the macaroni is hot she grates a little cheese on it before serving it up to her son. He has been playing hard and is tired. Anna puts her blue note book away in the drawer and makes up their beds. She isn't looking forward to going to see the woman with Adam tomorrow, but is less anxious because for whatever reason or motive, the woman didn't acknowledge her. 'Join the club,' Anna tells herself.

As Anna drifts off to sleep she begins to wonder and isn't sure anymore, if her experience at the beach had actually happened, or was it all just in her head. Had she dreamt it – imagined it and does it matter now? The moment has gone, it is in the past and no longer connects to her life now.

The next day is lovely as Anna walks with Adam to the beach hut, "You've got your drawings haven't you?" Anna asks her son as she locks the caravan door. "Yes." Adam replies, he has his drawings and is excited and happy at the thought of meeting up with Jo.

Anna is resigned now at the prospect as they walk towards the path, which leads from the town centre, towards where the woman had held her stall in the lay by.

'Why did I put myself under pressure from the woman yesterday at the car boot fair? Stella 30, her own name she asked for embellished on the sail.' Jo hasn't encountered anyone for a long time, with such a firm presence of mind and determination to get just what she wants. She had zoomed right in, through to the front of the others around the stall and with such directness, as if dismissing everyone else in a flash. Jo had on display her own boat 'JOANNA 42' at the back of the stall as a showpiece and she had asked to take a look at it. Jo had offered it to her and told her that it was her own boat and not for sale. She had a business like air and wanted to know how much it would cost, to make one similar. Jo had said around £12 - £14. She was unlike most of the people who had passed the stall, the holidaymakers, casually dressed in brightly coloured clothing. She was wearing a navy suit and a white blouse unbuttoned at the neck. Her hair, shoulder length, golden brown and wavy and her eyes bight and intense and her skin fresh and glowing with a healthy ruddy complexion.

"Could you have it ready on Tuesday?" she had asked. Jo had found herself saying, "Yes." too readily without thinking too much, as her eyes fixed upon hers.
She had then proceeded to elaborate on how she wanted the boat and finished by asking where Jo worked so that she could collect it.
"Right then Joanne I'll see you Tuesday." She had said.
"Jo, my names Jo."
"Tuesday then Jo bye." She'd answered with a quizzical look.
Hence the reason that Jo feels under pressure, not just with having to complete a boat today from scratch but also having her collect it in person tomorrow. Jo is annoyed with herself, for offering the woman a glimpse into her personal space and doesn't feel comfortable about it. It's so much easier making the boats from her ideas, without any constraints as to how they turn out. But having someone else's design to work around is hard

work and quite unnerving, wanting to get it just right. It is rather an odd experience to be honest, to feel this pressure, living the life she does now, that has no time constraints or personal connection with people. She goes outside to the pile of driftwood, to find a striking piece of timber. In a strange way she still feels captured by her as she recalls her soft and gentle accent and her penetrating eyes. As if a thread, an umbilical connection, has woven itself around the two of them, and joined them together 'STELLA 30 – JOANNA 42'. 'How many people pass us, like ships in the night, before we decided to drop anchor and ride out the storm?' As she looks through the driftwood she eventually discovers Stella, a well formed, heavy, typical boat shaped piece of hull. Washed in she imagines from some tropical island in the sun, after travelling around the worlds oceans, until breaking on the shore of Fenton to be discovered by Joanne 42. Jo takes the wood and cuts two pieces of dowelling for the masts and using a bradawl, she makes the holes and glues them in. Taking some white material she cuts two triangular sails, one larger than the other and stitches a hem around each one.

Although quite time consuming, the process is almost meditative and hypnotic and allows daydreams to slip in and out with each thread of the needle. She sees flesh, pink and soft and rounded, arms entwined, gentle lips licking and kissing and caressing and feels sexual stirrings that she hasn't felt for what seems like a lifetime. She changes the cotton thread to red and emblazons STELLA 30 into the bottom corner of the main sail. In her dreamland now she is swimming with the woman, she swims over and under her and closes in from behind her, and tentatively puts her hands and arms underneath her and supports her, at the same time kicking her legs to pull her with her. She paints the finished sails with diluted PVA glue on both sides, to stiffen the cotton fabric and leaves them to dry in the sunshine. She swims away and then turns grinning back to her and they laugh together and she kisses her gently on the temple and then they embrace.

Later Jo washes out the brush and mixes some dark green acrylic paint with water and strokes this over the sails. With just the rigging to finish, she uses lengths of string and winds it around the tops of the masts and through each sail, and then brushes them with PVA glue. With the added touch of fishing line and lead shot for the anchor, several hours later Stella 30 is complete, and Jo is pleased and satisfied with her work. She steps out of dreamland, adjusts her eyes to the daylight and returns inside for lunch. She grates two carrots and sprinkles them with sunflower seeds, sultanas and redskin peanuts and adds a dollop of oil. On the plate she adds tomatoes, lettuce and a piece of cheese and takes time out to enjoy the meal. In quiet reflection, she sits outside under the branches of the old cherry tree. 'Stay careful and protect yourself,' she repeats this mantra, over and over again. 'Stay careful and protect yourself Jo.'

The next day is beautiful, full of sunshine; she pours a glass of orange juice and a dish of cereal, after feeding Jason and takes it into the garden to eat. She has lots to do today and needs to go into town later for fresh milk and bread and spend time doing jobs in the garden. She hopes that Stella will call early to collect her boat and also the boy with his pictures for the pirate ship, so that she can get on. After breakfast she has a quick wash and begins work in the garden. In the vegetable patch, the beans need tying in around their stakes, they will be ready soon, how lovely, fresh green beans to add to her diet, wonderful. Also she needs to cut down the grassy areas which are beginning to get out of hand, she usually manages with a pair of shears but it is such a slow job and quite often she gives up before finishing it, however she needs to make headway with this, otherwise she will be looking for a goat! She soon has the beans secured with bits of twine and clears the vegetable patch of weeds and starts on the grass.

When Jason jumps up and begins to bark, Jo stands up
stretching backwards, with hands on her hips, hoping to
ease her aching back, 'no wonder I soon give this job
up,' she thinks to herself. Looking up the track to the
road, she notices the head of Stella bobbing in and out of
the bushes. So she puts down the shears and pops inside
to wash her hands.

"Hello, Jo are you there?" Stella shouts.
"Yes I'm coming, I'm just washing my hands."
She is casually dressed to day, wearing jeans, trainers
and a pink, short-sleeved polo shirt and she smiles as Jo
greets her outside.
"This is a surprise I never knew that this hut existed, it's
so secluded isn't it?"
"Yes it is very private and out of the way of the town."
"Have I interrupted you from your work?"
"I have been tidying the garden, I'm glad to have a break
and to stand up, it's back breaking sometimes, but I
enjoy it."
"I'll just go and get your boat." Jo adds, breaking away
and returning inside the hut.

Leaving the lay by, Adam leads Anna towards a gate,
almost hidden by large hawthorn bushes, he pushes it
open and Anna follows. A rough, grass track, weaves in
and out of the bushes and she begins to wonder whether
Adam has got it right. Have they taken the right path?
Anna isn't sure now because the path seems to be
leading nowhere and there isn't a beach hut to be seen.

Eventually he calls out, "It's here, I've found it."
As Anna rounds another corner, in front of her, hidden
by bushes and trees, is a hut. She can just make it out
beneath all the cover of green.
"It's here mam."
Anna sighs and is grateful to have found the beach hut at
last. The hut in front of her is made of heavy wood and
the door and window frames have been painted blue.

Beneath the window frames there are window boxes, full and overflowing with various herbs. She recognises sage, rosemary, sprigs of mint and basil.

Jason runs off again, barking up the track as he hears someone else coming. The dog spots Adam and it jumps up to greet him, licking his face as Adam nuzzles and pats him – both are happy to see each other. Anna follows them towards the beach hut, the dog now running on ahead. As Anna turns the corner to follow Adam and the dog, she hears women's voices.

"Wow, she's lovely, thank you." Stella takes hold of the boat and inspects it in great detail.
"I really like how you have done it, well done you; you have put a lot of work into it." Stella says adding. "I absolutely love it but I wonder if you could maybe whitewash the wood and paint the number on the side of it as well, obviously I will pay you extra if you can do this."
"Yes I can, but it will take time to dry, so you won't be able to take it with you now."
"Oh that's fine, maybe you could bring it to my house, if that's ok?"
"Where do you live?"
"Cliff Top Road, number 4 the next road up from the beach, you'll easily find it."

Adam bursts through the bushes with great speed and interrupts their conversation. "Here Jo I've brought the picture of my pirate ship." As Anna comes closer, she watches as Adam tries to push his pictures into Jo's hands.

She hears Jo say, "I'll call tomorrow then." The visitor holds on to Jo's arm.
"Lovely I'll see you at my place then at 7 o'clock."

Anna watches as Jo changes her attention to Adam as her visitor begins to walk away. Anna briefly glances at the other woman as she passes her. She is beautiful with long golden, glossy hair. Anna is struck by her youthfulness and healthy glow. The green eyes, which glance briefly at her as she passes, are hypnotic and seductive. Anna feels a pull towards this woman, but she doesn't speak to her and Anna notices the beginnings of a smile on the woman's lips, as she walks away absorbed in herself and her thoughts.

'7 o'clock,' Jo ponders to herself as Stella leaves, 'why 7 o'clock?' and then realises that she will probably be at work during the day.

"Right." Anna hears Jo say to Adam "Let's see what you've got here."
Adam hands her his pictures and she unrolls them and begins to examine them. Jo briefly glances up and nods slightly, then returns to Adam and his pictures.

Jo and Adam stand by a table, which has Adam's drawings on. The spot is well shaded by a cherry tree and will be cool and comfortable on hot summer days. Near the cherry tree is a workbench and at the other side is a small greenhouse with tomatoes growing and a turned over patch, where the tops of onions, potatoes and carrots grow, lush and green in the earth. This woman Anna thinks, has worked out her life. From what Anna can see of the vegetables and herbs, she must be fairly self sufficient, with her crop of homegrown vegetables. Adam and Jo leave their spot by the table and go further around the side of the hut, to where she stores her driftwood, so Adam can choose his piece. Anna waits for them to return.

"The Purple Pearl I want to call it," she hears Adam tell Jo. "And I want purple sails not black ones."

Adam negotiates with Jo as to how many sails they will have and whether Adam wants a plank for his ship.

The blue front door is slightly open and Anna can see a large, brown leather armchair, it looks battered but comfortable. It has a throw in blues, greens and terracotta. She can also see a black, cast iron stove and two rugs on the floor. Anna is impressed with the brief glimpse of the interior of the woman's hut and of her life outside it. The other woman, the visitor is beautiful Anna thinks, as she turns away from the hut, disappointed in herself and Jo. How can she have forgotten, she hasn't, she's just not interested. It meant nothing to her, otherwise how can she not acknowledge it. Anna is brought back from her thoughts as Adam and Jo join her.

"Could Adam go to the Army shop in the town and see if they have any cannons or something which we can use as cannons for his ship." Jo asks Anna.
"Yes we can do that."
"It would be good, if you could perhaps let me have them before the weekend. If you can find any, Adam."

Anna isn't aware that she is staring at the woman but she is. Jo asks her, "Is that alright?"
Anna returns to herself and says, "Yes we'll go and have a look." Turning Anna calls to Adam as he plays with the dog, "Come on then Adam, we'd better start making tracks."
Adam hugs the dog and they say goodbye, before leaving the garden, returning to the grass track, to go back into the town centre. Anna is filled with such a profound sense of disappointment. In her mind she keeps seeing the image of the beautiful woman and her soft slow smile and she feels invisible, as these two women appear to have an understanding which Anna is on the outside of. Adam is thrilled with the prospects of the 'Purple Pearl'.

As they walk back into the town centre, Adam continues his excited chattering of what he wants and doesn't want on his pirate ship. They stand outside the Army shop, 'Mountcross & Son', both of them gazing into the window. There aren't any miniature cannons in the window display and she hadn't really expected to see any. "Come on. We'd better go inside and ask the man if he's got any little cannons or maybe he will have something which we can use."

Walking into the shop, Anna is struck with how dark and dingy the place is. It is very much a masculine kind of place. There are glass counters along each side of the room, one facing the other. Beneath both counters, within the glass cases, are allsorts of army memorabilia. There are medals, pictures, photos, buttons and the kind of stuff she finds in Adam's trouser pockets before washing them. There are ex army jackets hung up around the shop, a pile of green, army jumpers and green, army shirts. Anna looks in the linings of the jackets and on the lapels of the shirts and jumpers, to find men's names, written neatly inside them. They have belonged to soldiers, before being washed and put on public sale.

Turning around, Malcolm glances at the woman, as they approach the counter, he strokes back his dark, greasy hair; and waits for Anna or the boy to speak. Anna hesitates for a moment before beginning, feeling uncomfortable, as she looks at the white, pasty-faced man. Anna wants to leave, to walk out of the shop, but she knows she needs the cannons, so she asks.

"Were looking for something like little cannons to put on a pirate ship that's being made." Anna makes a box shape with her hands, "It's about this tall and this wide." The man looks intrigued. Anna watches as the man runs his chubby fingers, through his dark, lank hair, as it falls down across his face. He seems to spot something that he is looking for and slides back the glass panel, lifting a brass bullet case out from beneath the counter.

"I've got three of these, old bullet cases."

The man gathers the other two bullet cases from beneath the counter and puts all three into the palm of his hand. The slim, long, pointed cases would make good cannons, Anna thinks. The pointed ends could protrude on the outside of the boat, whilst the rounded ends would be inside. Anna lifts one of the bullet cases from the man's hands to examine it.

"£2 each."

Anna is torn, she wants Adam to have his boat but these bullet cases are taking the price up to nearer £15, rather than the ceiling of £10, which is Anna's limit.

"Alright." she tells the man, whilst looking at Adam and says.

"This really is it."

As the woman and boy leave the shop, Malcolm still feels the sensation of the woman's touch on his hand, choosing one of the larger bullet cases from further down the cabinet, Malcolm rolls it backwards and forwards between the palms of his hands, the cold metal warming up as he does so, giving Malcolm a feeling of satisfaction.

Adam is beside himself wanting to take the bullet cases directly back to Jo. "No, she has work to do on the boat before she can put your cannons on, so let's give her a bit of space and time and we'll return Friday as we arranged."

Adam carries his bullet cases back to the caravan proud of his trophies and wants to take them to show Callum. In the end Anna has to concede.

"Ok, then, but you have to come back with them as soon as you've shown them to Callum – agreed?"

"Yes mam I will." Adam squeezes the cases in his fist
before dashing away.
"Come back for dinner."

She decides to keep dinner simple, beans on toast and an
apple and banana to finish. Whilst opening the can of
beans and pouring them into a pan, she reflects on what
happened with Jo, as Adam likes to call her. The golden
haired, green-eyed woman was so lovely, radiant,
beautiful and young! She would have no chance in
comparison to a woman like that, comparison with what?
To become a friend of Jo's maybe. Why should she want
that, when it is evident to Anna now, that Jo moves in
elegant and sophisticated circles? Anna knows
instinctively, when she briefly met the woman at Jo's
that she is all that Anna is not, all that she could never
be. Anna doesn't reach the point in her self-analysis, to
wonder whether the beautiful, golden haired woman,
would actually be someone who Anna would want to be.
Anna is certain she doesn't want to be herself. As her
mind turns these thoughts around, Adam runs in hot and
busy with a guilty expression on his face. "Show me the
gun cases." Anna asks.
"A boy took them off me."
Anna turns off the beans and puts the toast on Adam's
plate.
"Come on, show me where?"
Adam drops his head.
"Let's go."

Walking towards Callum's caravan, Anna asks him if
he's either given them to Callum, or sold them to him.
Adam merely continues to walk with her in silence, with
his head bowed. As they arrive at Callum's, Adam waits
at the back of the caravan.
"Come on."
"No. I'm not going in."

Tapping on the door, Anna can hear the children inside eating their meal – the clattering of cutlery on pottery and the aroma of pizza, wafts through the open door. "I'm sorry to interrupt your meal," Anna says to Callum's mum "But Adam's left his bullet cases here and we've to take them down to the lady who's making his boat today." Anna exaggerates, but needs must.

"Just a minute."

Anna listens; she hears the voices of Callum and his mum debating.

She catches, "Adam said...."

Callum's mum returns to the door.

"Callum said Adam has swapped the cases for a set of toy guns."

"No, I'm sorry, he's not allowed to."

The women stare at one another. "I'll get the guns." Anna says turning away.

Adam vanishes.

"Adam." Anna bellows at the top of her voice.

She shouts three times and spots Big Billy standing in front of Adam, who makes him, turn around and return to his mum. Anna recognises the look on his face as he walks towards her. His mouth is tight and turned down, his shoulders and head bowed. Adam appears to be passive but Anna knows he is mortified.

"I need the guns Adam."

"No you're not having them."

"Ok, then we'll go and tell Jo you don't want the boat." This enrages him. "No, No." He shouts. "You do that and I'll. ...And I'll."

"What Adam? You'll do what?"

"I'll fuck you up and flip you."

"Will you?"

"Yes."

"Then I'll take you home and you won't play with Callum or swap guns or do anything else again."

"Fuck you."

"Callum's mum wants his guns now. We have to go and give them back."

Adam passes his mother, dipping under the caravan to retrieve the two, black plastic guns. Anna holds out her hand and her son slaps them down hard.

"I'll do your dinner when I come back."

"Fuck you." Adam walks away in the direction of the town centre.

Anna returns to Callum's caravan and swaps back the bullet cases for the two guns. Back at her own caravan she hides the bullets inside the boxes, underneath the seats of the caravan. She checks their supplies; they need bread, cereal and something for the next few days. She puts a plate on the pan of beans and butters the two pieces of toast and leaves them in a lunch bag, beneath the step, in case Adam returns before her. After closing the window she takes her bags, locks the caravan and chooses the route through the streets to the town centre. She is used to the abuse she receives from her son; she knows that later when he returns home, he will be sorry. The abuse makes Anna feel sick, deep inside her, she is aware too of monitoring the confrontations which happen with him; if he is ever thwarted from what he wants or doesn't. Anna is careful, she is aware of what her son is capable of when he is angry. The temper tantrums of a teenage boy his size have no comparison to those of a toddler. The only things they share are the impulsiveness, the unwillingness to reason and the rage, the wild, blind rage.

Jo sets off to Stella's house, she notices a chill in the air
and wishes that she had put on a fleece before she'd
cycled away. The atmosphere has a heavy dankness
floating through it; maybe rain is on the way. She has the
boat safely wrapped in newspaper and plastic bag, so it
won't come to any harm. What a determined and
confident character Stella is, she doesn't feel she has a
choice about delivering the boat to her house today,
when she had pressed Jo with her request at the hut on
Tuesday, she had found herself again, saying yes to her.

Stella's address is on Cliff Top Road, number 4, just up
from the beach, the next road up. 7 o'clock she had
stipulated, in her prompt tone of voice. Jo didn't think to
tell her that she doesn't own a clock, or even a watch,
she never needs one living here, and doesn't run her life
by the hands of a timepiece, there is no point. So she
hasn't a clue as to what time it is right now, she has fed
Jason and decided to eat on her return. If she isn't around
when Jo arrives, then she will call back another day, or
Stella can pop to the hut to collect it. Jo begins to
question her decision to take the boat, when she realises
that a thick sea fret is heading inland and taking a lot of
the daylight out. She doesn't have any lights for the bike,
having never needed to cycle in the dark. 'It looks like
your pushing the bike back on the pavements,' she
reprimands herself, if this weather keeps up. She finds
herself pedalling on and on chuntering to herself, the
sensible thing would be to turn back, but before long she
is nearing the town centre, so she carries on.

She cycles to the roundabout and turns off down through
the main street of the old town and then past the hotels
and B & B's, the next turning left, hopefully should be
Cliff Top Road. Stella's house number 4 is the second
house on the right overlooking the sea. The building, a
three-storey end town house, is painted white and very
smart in exceptional condition. The sash windows look
to have been replaced with new hardwood ones and the

original door has a feature, oval leaded window, with a fishing boat in. 'No wonder she likes my boats,' Jo thinks to herself. Lifting the latch on the metal gate and easing the bike through, she props it against the wall. She holds the doorknocker, a polished brass seashell and gives it a couple of bangs. She listens for footsteps behind the door and cannot hear anything at all, maybe she isn't in she wonders, and decides to give it another few knocks before leaving. As she turns to reach for the handlebars of the bike, she hears movement inside and catches a reflection through the leaded glass, coming towards the door. Stella opens it wearing a fluffy, blue bathrobe and flip-flops whilst drying her hair with a pink towel.

"Oh my God, what time is it?" are her first words, her head on one side looking up at Jo, whilst rubbing her hair.
"I'm sorry, I don't know, I don't know what the time is, sorry, maybe I should go."
"No, no come on in; please take your shoes off though." Stella tells Jo as she disappears off into one of the rooms.

Jo takes her sandals off and notices her grimy feet, dirty from the dust of cycling here. She's not used to worrying about such things; the hut doesn't abide by these laws. Her life doesn't revolve around clean feet, what with Jason and going in and out of the garden, trailing in muck all day. She gives the stone floors a good sweep now and again when it really needs it.

Stella comes back into the hallway, "It's 6.15." she informs Jo, with a puzzled look.
"Oh so sorry, it's just that I don't have a watch, or a clock for that matter, so I guessed really when to set off, I'm sorry if I've caught you at an inconvenient time." Stella takes a surreptitious look at Jo's feet and then meets her eyes full on.

"Oh it's ok, you're lucky to have caught me in this early, I've been down on the beach surfing, and came back early because of the weather, I have a spare watch by the way if you need one."

Stella surveys Jo's appearance, and concludes that she looks the needy sort, unable to afford a watch.

"Thanks but I don't need one normally, I don't run my life by the clock, I don't have to keep to times for anything, except for today obviously."

Stella begins to walk away again, through the doorway to the left of the hall, whilst carrying on talking, seeming to not take in what Jo has just said.

"Come through, I'll show you round the place in a bit."

She goes to the wine rack in the corner of the room and pulls out a bottle of red and salutes Jo with it.

"Would you like to pass me two glasses from the shelf behind you?" she asks.

Jo is taken by surprise, firstly by Stella offering to show her around the house and secondly with the assumption that she would share a glass of wine with her, she hardly knows her! This woman definitely isn't slow in coming forward, she takes life head on, the next minute the corkscrew is in the bottle and with a hefty yank comes the pop and then the glug, glug, she begins pouring the wine into the large glasses. Jo smells the deep, spicy aroma coming off the top and actually can't wait to taste it; it has been such a long time since she has had wine of any description. This is good stuff.

"That's better." Stella says after taking a long lingering mouthful.

The kitchen like the frontage of the house is in top condition, someone, her presumably, has designed it, white cabinets stretch around the walls, incorporating several steel appliances, the cooker is huge, with four small rings and a large centre one, and a griddle looking thing at the other side. Her fridge has double doors and is huge. She has a coffee machine and a juicer, food processor and a food mixer. The whole kitchen could be used for catering purposes it has everything.

"Did you notice the leaded glass in the door, with the boat, that's what attracted me to your stall the other day; I thought it would be perfect for the house?"

"Yes, I did, it looks original, is it?"

"Yes, it dates from the 1700's I had to have it restored because the old lead had given way, but it was well worth it, it just makes the entrance look great don't you think?"

"Absolutely, it's good that you wanted to restore it, I should imagine many have disappeared over the years, people just getting rid of them for new UPVC doors."

"Have you brought my boat?" Stella asks.

Jo realises that she has left it in the basket carrier of the bike. "Oh, yes I'll just go and get it; it's in the carrier on my bike." She puts down her glass on the glossy work surface and goes back outside to get the bag.

When she returns she notices her wine glass has been topped up and Stella is well down her glass, she likes her drink. She is busy opening cupboards and putting spices and cooking pots onto the worktop.

"Just help yourself to more wine, I have to prepare a curry for later and I need to get started on it if you don't mind." She says this whilst reading the back of a packet without looking up.

Jo doesn't feel that she can suddenly leave, and feels strangely included in this space and relatively at ease, considering she hardly knows Stella. Stella begins chopping and frying onions and then grinding spices and adding these to the pan and then some chicken pieces. She places all of this into a casserole dish and pours in coconut milk and tomatoes, it smells absolutely wonderful, and the kitchen is filled with the heady, sweet aroma of curry.

"Now then, come on I'll show you round."

Jo puts down her glass and follows her, through the door to the right. "It was in a bad state when I bought it, an elderly couple lived here and they had to go into a nursing home. It had stood empty for a few years before it went up for sale. I don't think it had been touched since the day they had moved in, all the old features were still in it".

Jo glances around the huge room, and out of the window looking out to sea, what an amazing view. She utters the same words. "What an amazing view, what a huge room, it's so light and airy." "I decided to knock the wall down between two rooms and make this large living room, I have kept the original cornicing, doors and cupboards and fireplace. The fireplace had a gas fire in it which I removed because I wanted an open fire, and it works well with the cast iron surround."

The room has a contemporary layout with a large red leather corner settee and a square pouffe to match. An oblong coffee table sits on top of a rug. The floorboards have been sanded and stained, but the main attractive features, apart from the obvious view of the sea, are the walls. She has framed paintings on every wall; it is like being in an art gallery. Stella notices Jo's eyes as they travel up and down and across the pictures and remains quiet. "I thought you would like my art collection," she says after waiting for Jo's attention to return to her. "I'll just go and get our glasses, whilst you have a better look, feel free."

She leaves the room and Jo steadily makes her way around each wall, hardly aware of the rain beating down on the windows. She is in awe of this room, some of the large canvases are so engaging, and she doesn't want to look away; there are oil and acrylic paintings of different styles. A few seaside themes, but mainly unusual artworks, Jo wonders where she has picked them up from; no two seem to be by the same artist. She must have collected them over a long period of time. Jo is particularly attracted and experiences an affinity with a smallish canvas that is unframed. It is set in amongst some of the larger pictures and she nearly misses it. It is of a church stained glass window and is rather beautiful and simple. Jo is so transfixed and unaware of Stella, leaning by the doorjamb with glasses in hand, observing her. She is now wearing brown linen pants, t bar sandals and a multi coloured blouse, her hair an uncombed fluffy mess. How long has she been watching? It is when Jo turns around that she looks across and smiles, offering her a full wine glass. 'I mustn't drink anymore,' Jo thinks to herself; she can feel the effects of the wine already and wishes that she had eaten before she set out. She still has to ride the bike home, although looking at the rain beating down on the window, pushing it more likely; she is going to get soaked. The smell from the curry permeates through the kitchen and Jo is starting to feel quite peckish. No sooner has she thought this, than Stella breaks away and comes back with a dish of Bombay mix.

"Help yourself."

Stella picks up a handful and starts to munch. She begins to talk and munch at the same time, explaining about her art collection, buying off the Internet and picking up paintings on her travels around the country and France. She then gives Jo a virtual tour of the ones she loves the most and offers up the history and background of some of the artists.

"I'll eventually work my way around all the walls of the house, I just love collecting them, I can't stop, come on I'll show you upstairs, the other room down here is just my office."

This time they go up a wide staircase, to a large open landing, with three doors leading off. The central room they enter first has an armchair and a gable window with a telescope stood in front of it. The walls are lined with bookshelves and full to bursting with novels and art books.

"This is my chill out room, especially in winter when the sea is grey and angry and I can read or sit and watch the storms outside. In the summer months I'm usually surfing when I get time, or working mostly, so I don't come up here much then, unless I can't sleep".

The weather up here is more apparent, the rain is sheeting down and it's impossible to see the sea.

"Wait until you see the best room in the house, come on?" Stella asks Jo to follow her into the next room.
"Wow." Jo is lost for words, what a mega bathroom.
"I wanted something really special in here; it took me ages to decide on this."
It is a huge wet room, in the corner the shower; with jets fixed at intervals on the two walls and a massive showerhead at the top.
"You can have the shower coming out of the walls, or the top, or both if you fancy a real blasting, it's a real wakeup on a morning."
A bidet, toilet and washbasin are fixed into the wall without any pipe work showing, is so clean and neat. Jo's mind harks back home to the hut and the outside toilet, 'what would she think?' she wonders. And then the wow factor, the curved spa bath, sunk into the floor, with a tiled ledge around it, in fact the whole room is tiled, both the walls and the floor, with the floor sloping slightly into the shower corner. The tiles are a subtle sea blue and the suite white, perfect, really lovely. Jo takes this scene in and doesn't feel the slightest bit envious of her house, she knows that it's absolutely marvellous but she is completely happy with the hut, some people would probably need convincing but she is actually happy living in it and truly content.
"It is lovely, it really is."
"Oh God, am I showing off, sorry Jo, I'm just so thrilled with it now that it's finally finished and any chance I get I want to show it off, so forgive me."

"No need to at all, I've enjoyed you showing it to me, so thanks."
"Come on let's go finish our drinks." Stella says.

Returning downstairs, the curry aroma is emanating strongly from the kitchen, Jo hasn't had a curry since she can't remember, and feels ravenous. "Now where can I put you?" Stella's says as she picks the boat up and lifts it, twirling it around, as if to find a place for it. "I'll decide later, I am delighted with it Jo, I may even have another one made, anyway." Stella's sentence is interrupted by the opening of the front door and a beating down of heavy footsteps on the doormat.

"Hello, it's me, are you there, got bloody wet through on the 10th hole and gave up, Stell?"
Are the words from the person entering the house. The man behind the voice strides into the kitchen whilst still talking.
"Oh, so who else do I share the pleasure with this evening?"
"Oh, no I'm just on my way home; I shall have to be setting off now."
"Where have you parked, I didn't notice a car outside?" the man asks.
"I came on my bike."
"It's absolutely shocking weather out there, surely you aren't hoping to cycle in that?" The man retorts.
"Yes, I will be ok." Jo says whilst thinking the opposite, but doesn't have any choice.
Stella interjects "Stay, have some food with us, have you eaten, is that ok by you Charles, the rain will probably ease off later?"
"Sure the more the merrier, you know me Stella".
Charles shakes Jo's hand and adds. "Charles pleased to meet you dear and you, what's your name seeing as we haven't been introduced?"
"It's Jo Charles, sorry, I should have said, so how about it, are you ok to have curry with us?" Stella asks.

With the relaxing effect of the red wine and the tempting
offer of this wonderful curry, to Jo's own astonishment
she finds herself saying, "Are you sure, that's kind of
you, although I do feel as though I am intruding on your
evening?"
"No not at all, it's always nice to meet a new face in this
town, what do you say Stell". Charles's eyes are intent
upon Jo's, he looks her up and down, averting his eyes
as he looks at her feet.

Charles is a large stocky man, with a head of thick grey
hair, blue eyes and a red ruddy complexion, Jo guesses at
being around his mid fifties. Wearing a pair of chinos
and a blue and white checked shirt and brogues on his
feet.
Stella goes to get a clean wine glass and asks Charles.
"Red or white Charles?"
"I'll have what you two ladies are having, the curry
smells good, I'm rather hungry, I only had a quick bite at
the clubhouse so I'm ready for it." Charles replies.
Stella finds another bottle of red and opens it, she then
pours Charles's glass, her own and moves forward to top
up Jo's.
"No I'm fine thanks."
"Oh go on, have another." She insists.
Jo puts the glass forward telling herself that this is
definitely the last one.
"Go on into the living room, the curry isn't ready yet."
Stella suggests.

Charles and Stella sit on one side of the settee, Jo on the
other; the Bombay mix from earlier is still on the coffee
table and Charles grabs a handful and pours some into
his mouth. Stella begins a conversation with Charles
about a property that she has viewed this morning. He
replies, that it is new on the market and he will be going
to take a look during the week.
"Sorry for talking business Jo." Stella apologizes as she
realises that Jo is left out of their conversations.

"No it's ok, carry on."

"Jo lives near Woodend Farm, down at the beach hut Charles, she has made me a boat." Stella says as she returns to the kitchen and comes back with Stella 30 in her hands. "What do you think Charles, I don't know where to put it yet, maybe in the upstairs room or maybe even here on the window ledge, what do you think Charles, do you like it?"

Charles lets out a chortle, "Jo, I'm sure this will be just the beginning knowing Stella like I do, this will be the start of a whole fleet." Charles stops laughing. "The hut, well, well, that one went on the quiet, sold by auction, I found out when it was too late, I believe it was advertised on the internet, well done you, in a bit of a bad state though, have you managed to tidy it up?"

"Yes, I have thanks, it took me some time but it's fine now."

"Good girl, it has been the weather for it, we have had a splendid year this year; I've been on the greens most weeks, I've tried to get Stella interested, haven't I Stell?" Stella leaves the room saying. "It's not the sport for me Charles, anyway I'll leave you two to chat, whilst I put the rice on and the samosas."

Charles begins talking at length about property and the market and the impact of housing prices and their effect on the town and about local people being forced out by people buying holiday homes and second properties.

"There's no end to it, one has to feel sorry for the young people today, but business is business and I must say it's booming for us."

Stella shouts from the kitchen "Supper's ready Charles, Jo."

Again Stella is quick to fill our glasses again.

"No more for me if that's ok, I've had plenty thanks."

"Positive, you can have another if you want."

"No, I'm fine honestly." Jo says, already aware that what she has already drunk has made her feel quite wobbly and lightheaded.

"Well just help yourself if you change your mind."

The meal itself is an absolute feast. They all help themselves to the rice and curry and seconds too, with the samosas and mango chutney to finish it off it's perfect. Charles and Stella top up their glasses as they eat. After the meal Stella piles the dishes into the dishwasher and puts the coffee maker on and then we all return to the living room. Jo is conscious of the rain as it still hammers down on the windows and makes up her mind to go straight after the coffee. Although the meal has been gorgeous, she is beginning to regret not setting off earlier, and doesn't fancy getting absolutely drowned and the thought of this starts to make her want to giggle. Stella returns to the kitchen to collect the cups and coffee and even chocolate mints to have with it. Charles begins another long tale that he had overheard at the golf club this morning and has them both laughing.

"Well I really must be going."
"No you can't set off in this, it's like stair rods coming down out there." Charles retorts.
"I'll be ok, it won't take me long."
Charles looks down into his wine glass and mutters.
"Well I suppose I've had one two many to give you a lift, I had a couple of beers at the clubhouse earlier too, how about we ring for a taxi?"
"No need for that, stay the night, leave in the morning when it's daylight." Stella announces.
Jo is quite taken aback at her offer and generosity; after all she doesn't really know her.

"That's it then sorted, settle down Jo, here have a top up." Charles leans over the coffee table to fill Jo's glass. Jo begins wondering if they are a couple, an unlikely one at that she thinks, with the age difference between them.
"I was going to walk it Stella, but how about it, if Jo's staying, what's another one?" Charles cheekily asks.

"Oh Charles, what are you like, go on then." Stella says hardly surprised.

Jo is in an uncomfortable situation, she hardly feels that she can insist on going home and also she can't think of a reason to excuse herself either. So with that she settles to the idea that she is here for the night.

After coffees and chocolates Stella rises from the settee and strides over to the corner and turns on the speakers and the room fills with the sound and sexy voice of Janey Bekson. Stella turns around and begins to dance her way back across the room, her shirt lifting up as her arms rise and her linen pants float outwards. She seems without inhibitions and completely wrapped up inside the music enjoying herself, 'what a woman,' Jo thinks.

"Come on you two." Stella motions, encouraging Charles and Jo to dance.
Charles doesn't hesitate, he just stands up and begins to move around – not in the same easy fashion as Stella, more halting and stiff, but nonetheless without restraint. They cavort and laugh and make passing hand connections with each other, enjoying the music.
 "Come on Jo?" they both ask.
Jo feels more awkward sitting watching them, so without much hesitation, she too is floating, weaving around the room and dancing with them. With the help of the wine Jo is in the moment and enjoying this space alongside them. They are happy with her presence on the floor and it isn't long before their arms are locked into each other's in a circle holding on, wrapped together. The warm tactile intimacy from the three of them emanates through their skins and leaks out, filling the room. It is as if they have known each other for a whole lifetime, not the brief exchanges they have shared so far this evening. As Stella breaks away to change the music, Charles catches Jo quickly by the hand and pulls her towards him, his chest close to hers and then before she can think

or detach herself, he pushes her away and dances alone. This is a fast moving experience and Jo's reactions are blocked and pushed down, as everything is moving so quickly and she can't keep up with what she wants or doesn't want to do, she is being swept along with the giddy, heady, whirl of it all. Her body is alive and feels sexually turned on by these two people; she is being teased and tested and welcomed into their net, it will be much later before she realises how entrapped she has become. They continue dancing like this for a long time, the tempo and rhythm dictating their movements, fast or slow Jo is having a good time. Charles is the first one to sit down.

"Oh that's me I'm buggered Stell, I'm going to sit this one out." His shirt is damp and he has beads of sweat on his rosy red face. He checks the wine bottle and announces that he is going to find another one, and leaves the room.

As the music changes to the sounds of Juliet Delphin – My Lovely Friend - Stella tiptoes towards Jo and in a theatrical gesture, as if playing the lead from a musical track, she takes Jo by both hands and starts dancing and lilting gracefully around the room taking Jo with her. Jo has entered another realm, another world. This space so engaging and captivating, she wants more; the spell finally breaks when Charles steps back into the room. Stella finishes her last act with a warm embrace; she touches Jo's cheek with her hand and trails it through her hair and slowly down her back before finally breaking away.
"Top up girls."
"Not for me, thanks." Jo answers.
Stella announces, "Back in a minute." and she disappears out of the room.
Jo is aware of her hot, sticky, body and needs a drink of water. The wine and curry combined with the dancing have given her a real thirst.

"I need a glass of water Charles, if you don't mind I'll just go and get one from the kitchen."
"Water, don't touch the stuff myself, go on, don't fill one for me though."
In the kitchen Jo tries to get hold of her senses, she presses her face to the cold steel of the fridge and then runs the cold tap, hoping to grasp what is going on here. She cups her hands under it and greedily drinks mouthfuls of the cold water. It is good to be here on her own quenching her thirst; she decides that she will set off home.

"Jo, I have a surprise for you, come on?" Stella appears inside the doorway and then disappears.
Jo turns off the tap and leaves the kitchen. Stella's voice beckons her from the top of the stairs. "Jo come on up". Jo hesitates and wants to take her leave and go home.
"Come on you'll love it." Stella shouts down the stairs.

Jo slowly mounts the steps and feels her decision to leave fading away, in the grip yet again of this situation. Stella's voice is coming from the bathroom. Jo enters the room and sees the spa bath full to the brim with bubbles, a haze of heat frothing off the top.
"Just for you, go on feel free, I just knew you would like it." Stella says with a huge smile on her face. "There is a bath towel on the rail, I'll leave you too it." Stella then passes Jo by the door way and goes down stairs.
'What do I do now?' Jo thinks to herself, her hope of leaving vanishing instantly. She admits the chance to have a bath wins her over, she hasn't had one since arriving at the hut and this is incredible, she cannot turn the offer down. So she takes off her clothes and gently dips her foot into the water and steps into the glorious, huge bathtub. There is a shelf to sit on and she leans back, resting her neck on the edge of the tub, as the water laps around her breasts and the bubbles froth up into her face. 'Oh this is something else, heavenly,' she could stay here forever soaking in this water. Her head

starts to drift away as she closes her eyes and sinks down into the water. She doesn't know how long she has been bathing, when the sound of footsteps and then the splash of water wakes her from dozing.

"Hi I thought that I would join you, I need to freshen up after the dancing." Stella says, as if having a casual conversation in the street.

She has brought two glasses and a bottle with her, and puts it on the edge of the bath beside her. "Hi, are you enjoying the bath?"

"Yes it's lovely, thank you."

She reaches the bottle and starts to pour two glasses of wine.

"Oh not for me, thanks, I don't want another glass, if that's ok".

"This is a fantastic Beaujolais you must try it." Stella insists.

"No, thanks honestly I have had enough tonight, I don't often drink so I've had enough."

Jo considers getting out of the bath, dressing and leaving, however she feels self-conscious about her nakedness in front of Stella, her young and beautiful body, against her own naked 42-year-old self. So she holds out the option and hopes that Stella decides to get out before her. Stella fills her own glass and begins to take sips of the wine and then rests the glass on the ledge. She seems settled here and totally unselfconscious.

"I'm so glad that you came tonight, it's been great fun meeting you." Stella says continuing "Don't mind Charles he's ok really, you'll get used to him after a while. Sure you don't want a taste of this Beaujolais, just a small one."

"Just a small one and then that's it, I have had enough, thank you." I reply to give myself some thinking time about this situation.

The wine is lovely. It's almost as if Jo has slipped into a time warp, so familiar, and beginning to feel so natural and easy, the raindrops and everything outside is another world away. Like being sucked down into a vacuum, a deep and inner sanctum, and an experience that seeps into every orifice.

"Enjoy yourself Jo, have fun." Stella leans across and picks up some bubbles and places them on the end of Jo's nose.

'Am I enjoying this, am I having fun?' Jo's mind cannot work through these ideas; her whole being is locked out. It's as if her choices have been taken away from her, at each step of the way this evening her actions have been pre-empted by Stella; she has outwitted her every movement. Jo has entered into a complex game and in her fresh and raw state she didn't see it coming, was not prepared for it, and yet her own premonitions correct, why had she arrived with barriers down and not protected herself? Did she hope and want for this to happen? This all too familiar ground that she left behind long ago, is back again. She takes sips of wine whilst thinking, unable to answer Stella's questions and keeps her body submerged under the water. She looks across to the doorway and notices Charles's figure; he is furtively staring in from the far edge of the door. When their eyes connect he moves away quickly. Jo submerges herself completely underneath the water, wanting to wash away, to drown and disconnect herself right here and now from this moment.

The first thing Jo is aware of as she opens her eyes, is having a raging thirst, her mouth and throat is so dry. She is unable to comprehend her whereabouts; she needs a drink of water urgently. As her eyes take in the strange bedroom, she wonders where she is and how on earth did she get here. She raises her head and looks around the room, large and spacious and not her own, lavender walls and a pink door, huge antique wardrobes and drawers with an array of colourful scarves hanging on the knobs. Turning sideways groggily, she is aware of a person lying next to her; she can see the grey, tousled hair of Charles, facing the other way. She slips out of the bed and looks around for her clothes but can't find them and decides to check out the bathroom and get a drink of water. Taking a long gulp of water she sees her clothes on the floor in a heap and puts them on. There are three wine glasses and an empty bottle on the bath edge and a rim of scum around the bath, discarded towels also on the floor. It is dark outside. Her head throbs and she feels queasy and tiptoes downstairs and puts on her sandals still inside the doorway. The door is locked and she gently turns the key and leaves the house. Her bike is propped up and waiting, the rain has stopped and the path and vegetation has a wet glossy cover, she lifts the latch on the gate and mounts her bike for home.

Cycling on the pavements she is helped along by the streetlights. The road uphill seems like climbing a mountain, as she puffs and pants in the eerie silence, there is no sign of life, no cars around or people at this early hour, just a ghost town to hurry through. Jo is glad when she reaches the roundabout and then on to the main road, where she speeds up on the flatter ground. On entering the gate by the lay by, she is glad to be home, her legs are soaked from the bushes. When she reaches the hut Jason hurries to the door and is so pleased to see her, he is anxious and she can tell he has been fretting being left here alone. She lets him into the garden to relieve himself and fusses and praises him for being good. Jo drinks cold water from the tap and takes off her wet sandals; give Jason a handful of biscuits and goes upstairs to bed.

She peels off her damp clothes and discards them on the bedroom chair. Her body so unused to the after effects of alcohol feels clammy and heavy, as the hangover pounds her head and makes her stomach churn. She lifts the duvet and crawls underneath it and lies down hoping that this will help, she lies still not wanting to turn over but comfort is not easy to attain. Jo wishes for sleep to take and rescue her, hold and steady her and kiss her goodnight. She tries to drift and dream and stay away from flashbacks of the night and hopes to remain safe and soar, amongst the pink dreamscapes far above and away. The early light sometimes fills the room with brilliant brightness, and she tries to avert her eyes, at other times underneath the covers, it is dark and cold as hours slip by. She manages much later to go downstairs and feed Jason a meal and make a pot of tea with sugar in and return back to bed. The splash of sweet tea hits her stomach and assimilates it in her senses, expecting the dry taste of red wine, it takes awhile to accept and want for more. After finishing the tea she retreats under the duvet again and dips in and out of sleep.

The dreamscape this time is no longer pink and safe but dark and black and haunting. She wanders in and out of rooms looking to find someone, but there is no one so she runs faster and faster opening closed doors, her eyes searching into the corners and still there is no one there. She is alone. And then later as she continues to search feeling tired and out of breath, she senses someone behind her, chasing her, she hears his breath in her ear, and feels it on the back of her neck, so she hurries faster and faster to get away, she dare not look back, she has to get away. She panics now as her feet gather speed and she notices that she is no longer moving forward, she is being sucked backwards and the person behind is reaching out to grab her. And then later, the black cloud all around, above and behind her engulfs and takes her breath away, it is suffocating her; she is fighting for breath, for air. And then later, she struggles and fights this blackness one last time and finally wakes up with a sudden jolt, startled and gasping and wondering where on earth she is, her body is covered in sweat. She enters in and out of these nightmares, tossing and turning trying to run away. When she wanders the rooms again she opens the door to a bedroom and is glad when someone is there, she is no longer alone. But her pleasure is soon eroded, when the two people sitting up in bed smile at her and throw back the covers, the woman is squeezing her large breasts with both hands, and the man is holding his penis and wanking it, looking at her and then back to his hand, as she turns to leave, the door is gone and this room is all there is and she cannot get out.

Charles drives home after leaving Stella's house, in his jade green jaguar car. As it pulls up to the automatic, double, wrought iron gates, he sinks back into the comfort of his leather seat and waits whilst the gates open slowly and silently. The engine purrs quietly and Charles reflects on his good luck, his mantra of being in the right place at the right time, it has paid off yet again. Charles holds onto his fortuitousness and allows a smile to settle over himself, secretly satisfied and emboldened by his position. Even his own deep and hidden secret that he carries around within himself doesn't trade off these good feelings and cannot mar the moment. As always when he arrives home, he enjoys the impressive sight of the double fronted mansion house and his 4 X 4 parked in front on the shingle driveway. This sweet feeling of contentment with himself and the world remains, as he drives passed the large sign 'THE MANOR HOUSE' to the right of the driveway as the gates close behind him.

He parks his vehicle at the rear of the house, locks it with his security key and makes his way to the hall doorway. The door to the house is locked and Charles opens it. Taking off his jacket, he hangs it on a hook on the hallstand at the entrance to the hallway. He gives his usual brisk brush with his feet on the rush mat and strides through to the kitchen, his leather shoes making noisy footsteps as he walks the tiled floor. Charles needs a coffee. The last couple of nights of heavy drinking have left him with a slight headache and he needs a rousing wake up, in order to get on with his busy day.

Time wasting and living a sedentary lifestyle, are not a part of Charles's makeup, he abhors sitting down during the day when there is work to be done. Usually this entails travelling to and fro from properties and often other parts of the country and sometimes when a timely situation arises, to Europe. Eastern Europe is opening up and there are deals to be done and time is of the essence for Charles. A slight irritation runs through him as he crosses the hallway to the kitchen for the morning paper, to discover it isn't where he insists it should be. "Damn", he says loudly to himself. Taking a clean mug to the coffee maker he pours out the dark, thick liquid, just short of the top, he opens the fridge for the cream jug and adds a couple of thick splodges, then stirs it with a spoon. After putting the mug on the marble worktop, he searches around for the newspaper. His irritation grows with impatience as he enters the hallway and shouts out, "Margaret where the hell are you, give me one guess where you have put it?"

Charles walks towards the other doors as Margaret leans over the oak banister and peers down.

"Put what Charles?"

"The paper, the bloody paper woman, it's not on the table." Charles voice rises with impatience.

"It hasn't been delivered yet Charles and it's nice to know that you are home, I need to talk to you about Abby."

"Oh what the hell's she been up to this time; you know darling that you can handle her, she doesn't always have to come to daddy when things go wrong. You know how busy I am at the moment, I have a lot to deal with, and for all I know, I could be off again at the drop of a hat, you know how Giles is, we have a business to run after all and I can't spend my time running around after your daughter. I know, I know, you don't have to say it, she looks up to me, well if she even started to do that, she would pack this fancy idea of hers in and sort out a university placement and mix with a better sort and then maybe we wouldn't have this drama week in, week out." Charles rants.

"Charles darling try not to upset yourself, I'm sure she will work things out, like she said after her gap year she will decide what she wants to do and she hasn't yet."

"Gap year, well I'll tell you about a gap year." Charles answers and is interrupted suddenly as Abby joins her mother on the landing and looks down.

"Hi Charles, don't worry, I don't know what mummy has been saying but everything's alright, nice to see you by the way, where were you last night?" Abby chips in. Charles feeling slightly uncomfortable by her comment answers. "Hello darling, come on down and tell me all about it, I'm having a coffee would you like one?" he asks trying to change the subject quickly.

As Abby descends the stairs, Charles looks up lovingly and tells her. "Work, work, work, you know the story, busy busy, anyhow come on, you haven't seen the paper today have you, your mother seems to think it hasn't been delivered yet but you know how confused she gets sometimes."

"Oh daddy, must you say that, anyhow I've lots to tell you, the thing is daddy I have a plan, well I have an idea, you will approve I'm sure. There is a fantastic course starting at York Uni, so if I could move out of the flat to a bed-sit, or anything daddy in Thornby, I can commute by train and it will be a fresh start, you know how you have been wanting me to decide what I want to do, well I have and it's perfect, so daddy what do you say?"

Charles looks at Abby as always in wonderment – her orange hair, a tangled unruly mess, her petite frame, a girl, not yet a full and rounded woman – dressed in a multitude of colours. Calf length, black leather boots with a small heel and pointed toes, dark green tights disappearing beneath a short, skin-tight, woollen skirt, tan coloured with a rubbed up and worn texture. And then layers of tops, each one peeping out from underneath the one above, a coral pink silk shirt, a blue and green t shirt and a fine mesh, almost lacy black top. Various strings of beads and chains adorn her neck and a bag slung over her shoulder, no doubt containing her ever-present mobile phone – her contact with her 'world'. How can he say no to her, how can he ever refuse this girl, his daughter, oh how he wished. This is his only failure, his deepest regret, the inability to father and yet how she adores him. The pleading way she gives her gentle shrug, as her green eyes pierce knowingly through his heart, teasing and wanting him, she needs his strong, manful handling. Especially, considering the ineptitude and indecisiveness of her mother, propelling her towards him during the ups and downs, as she wrestles with her young life.

"Abby what is it this time, what is the course – it is time you made a decision and stuck to it?"
"It is a three year textile design under graduate course and I have applied, so what do you say, can I move to Thornby?"
"Why don't we wait and see and assess the situation when you are accepted on the course, if that is it Abby, what you really want to do and it's not just another idea that falls by the wayside when your love life takes another turn. I'm so pleased Abby that it's over with him and you are focusing on your future at last, remember what I said, I will not support you if you mess around with the wrong crowd and I don't want to see you with him ever again. So now that we have got that settled my lovely, how about a coffee". Charles turns and takes his mug from the worktop and drinks.

Abby's phone startles Charles with its piercing ring and feeling unable to listen to another girly conversation he takes his coffee mug into his office. He sits down in the swivel chair and sips his drink; Abby's conversation has thrown him off his intentions for the day and as hard as he tries to distance himself from her, the more difficult it becomes. Abby knows how to manipulate him in a way no other person can. How can he be sure, that her relationship with this person is over? Charles takes the last drag of coffee and turns his thoughts to last night with Jo, another surprise – she too has the ability to reach inside of him and test him, unwillingly, her naked body full and rounded with the shape and curves of a woman, not that of a young girl, developing and growing. Abby's transcendence has not happened yet, is

she waiting for the right man to take her and fill her. If
only he thinks, this is his longing, his wanting, last night
as he looked on at Jo naked and vulnerable, he knew she
was there for the taking and yet that's it he couldn't, he
never could, this is his failing. Oh, if only he could.
Charles reaches down and slides open the desk drawer
and lifts out the bottle of scotch and hastily twists the top
and pours a good measure into his whisky tumbler on the
desk. He puts the glass to his mouth and sips the fiery
spirit and takes pleasure and comfort as it hits his throat.

"Oh Charles darling, sorry to disturb you, I'm going into
town shopping, is there anything you would like for
lunch?" Margaret asks as she pops her head around the
office door.
"I'm going out, work to do, I'll be back this evening, late
probably, so I won't be eating here." Charles tersely
answers.
"Bye then darling don't work too hard." Margaret calls
as she disappears down the hallway.

Charles's answer to his inner failure as always, is to find
a solution through success and outward achievements, to
be a formidable businessman at the forefront of town. To
be always one step ahead of the competition, to never
rest and allow the field to catch up. His thoughts return
again to the previous evening and the meeting with Jo
and the good fortune of that. Jo has ownership of the
land adjacent to Woodend Farm and befriending her,
might one day prove to be a winner. Rumour has it on
the grapevine that Rushton's from Woodend are thinking
of selling up and with his hand in glove connections
amongst members of the planning office, it might just be
beneficial to win her over. If the farmland is given
planning consent for residential build, then it would be a
potential goldmine and a sweep for him, if he could nail
it down with all concerned, through the back door so to
speak before word gets out, ears to the ground Charlie
boy. The whisky has the desired effect and without

dwelling on other things he decides to collect a paper in town and gather his thoughts over lunch at The Sailors Arms.

As day fades to nighttime, Jo becomes trapped in her
bed, unable to feel safe to wander around; she dare not
even go and make another pot of tea. She hears Jason
snoring at the bottom of the stairs and waits for dawn to
break, for light to enter in, to wake herself from this dark
place, to reacquaint her mind and body with the hut and
her life here. Much later she is woken from dreams by
Jason who is barking to be let out, she can tell he is
desperate, so she goes downstairs and opens the door for
him. Daylight has arrived but the day is wet and it's
raining quite heavily outside. She fills the kettle in need
of a mug of tea and returns upstairs to put on her clothes.
Back downstairs she sits for a long time, drinking
another mug of tea and stares out of the window at the
rain, just watching and waiting. Eventually she musters
her energy and gets up from the chair and decides to try
and wash away the demons of the night. She undresses
and takes her shampoo and soap outside and stands in
the rain to wet her skin and hair. She then goes to the
shower and soaps her body all over and lifts the hose and
lets the water pour over her head to rinse the soapsuds
away.

Anna feels better with herself as she walks through the streets, passing people who live on the coast or holidaymakers. She needs usual stuff, bread, milk and a few potatoes. Anna walks around the frozen food shop and picks up a pizza for a £1 and fresh Swedish meatballs, which she can put with pasta or spaghetti. She adds six eggs to make an omelette for Friday's dinner. Anna sits on a bench outside the war memorial park with her shopping. She can manage now, go back to the caravan and cope. Start again anew with Adam. It doesn't do to harbour ill will or grudges. She has to put it behind her and not take everything personal or to heart. She has to keep herself going for as long as possible.

The toast and water left for Adam have gone when she returns. So he's been back, Anna fills her kettle and lights the stove. The caravan hasn't got a fridge so she puts the pizza on a little shelf beneath the bunk bed in the kitchen. After putting away her basic groceries she sits on the seat beneath the window.

Rising, Anna decides to open it and let clean fresh air flow through. For a brief moment, as she opens her window, Anna remembers the day her eldest sister died. It was before the dawn broke. Her sister's body laid little more than a skeleton, with her head thrown back and mouth gaping. All life gone, ravaged by the cancer, which gripped her and hauled her into it, until it was too late and she was lost, absorbed and consumed by it. Anna's aunt had also been with her sister at the moment of her passing; she had gone to the window by the side of her sister's bed and opened it. Her aunt had said, "We have to set the soul free; we have to let it leave." And Jane's soul did leave her poor, damaged, broken body. Anna was glad when it was done. Watching her sister, die the slow destructive death, tore Anna to pieces. By the end her sister couldn't eat and every sips of water she tried to take came back instantly, so she was parched as well as starving. Anna had held her sisters hand, she had become reduced to the shrivelled body of a tiny bird, whose heart barely beat, – Anna was even more conscious, of the strong and steady rhythm of the beat, which ticked out the time of her own life. Anna knew as she held that tiny hand, it was the last time, she would be with her sister. Anna's sister died in the early hours of the morning, their father had tried to hang on to his eldest child. As life left her, Anna's father breathed his life back into his daughter and momentarily she returned to consciousness and her unfocused gaze fell on to her father, "You should have let me go." Jane, admonished her father. 'Where Jane?' Anna often asks herself as the years pass by. Anna now knew that in the dying 'you' went somewhere. Where? 'Away' is all Anna can think, away from the awful nightmare of the endless drawn out drama of dying, no not of the dying but of the awful experience of living, in the agony of life, not death.

Death was the place where Anna's sister had wanted to go. She had not wanted to remain alive in this world, she had wanted to leave it, because her life had become agony and death was her only salvation from life. Anna's sister had been so alive it had seemed impossible that she should die. Anna remembers how her sister would collect her washing from the outside clothesline, fold it over and smooth it down and place it on the airer to finish off. Then she would take a draw from her cigarette and Anna would watch as the smoke rose and dropped and mingled through the shafts of sunlight with the particles of dust, which spun and danced in the air. The soothing, rhythm of her sisters actions, as she carried out her chores, fascinated Anna, mesmerised her almost.

It is all over now, their life. Anna and her family's lives are finished, their childhood gone, where? Anna is bereft. How could it, how did it all happen. It had all seemed so real, permanent, solid, firm and fixed in this world and now it has slipped away and disappeared like mercury. Wiped off the face of the earth. Where is the

continuity, the permanence, and the forever stuff, which
Anna had been brought up in? She had been born into
something huge, strong and solid. Where did it all go
Jane? You should know. Now you're dead, you should
know about everything. So tell me? No you can't can
you, because like the past, like our safe, solid, childhood
you're not here anymore are you? You're dead you're
gone forever. I don't want it to go – to leave. I want to
return and belong and be a part of that safe place. The
past is safe, secure and I know it. No fear, no surprises.
Not to grow old or sick or die. Not to be afraid or scared
but to live, like a dream, to keep returning to it again and
again. But you had a miserable childhood, you've
forgotten that haven't you? Anna rises from her seat and
sighs.

The evening meal would be beans on toast. Anna is
stalled but doesn't want to tidy or clean the caravan;
she's had enough of that for the day. So what Anna asks
herself? Anna knows if she had brought her homeopathic
homework or books, Adam would have been bored and
she would have been stopping and starting and never
getting anything done. She wishes she had brought a
simple material medica or miasm book to read up on.
With those she could just pick out remedies and read up
on them. It would have been a more useful occupation,
rather than sitting in the caravan twiddling her thumbs.
The notebook Anna remembers. I'll do that she decides.
Opening the book at where she had left off Anna begins
to write.

**Turning around John Doherty lifted his cup and took
a brief sip before raising his gaze towards Anna. The
eyes still drew Anna with their intense precise
address. They seemed to question her she felt. Anna
didn't drop her gaze this time because she wanted to
examine what the feeling she was experiencing was
and how it felt. Anna wanted to know what it was
that this man had which sent people around him**

scurrying away or feeling subservient, as Mary appeared to be. How was she feeling, Anna asked herself? Shocked a bit Anna realised, a bit stunned by the intensity of his gaze – almost stare Anna concluded. Was he aware of it Anna wondered – seriously wondered? Trying to understand that Anna felt she needed to work it out. Why Anna asked herself? Anna sipped her tea but decided not to try and make conversation with John Doherty. Anna wanted to know where she stood in this practise and had no intentions of beginning a pattern of behaviour with this man, which she then couldn't change because it was set. Anna wouldn't trap herself in that snare she had walked away from a man who had reduced her to nothing and she wouldn't go back to that place again not with anyone not again.

Anna closes her book and puts it in the drawer of the sideboard. Lighting the grill, she takes the plate off the beans and lights the gas under them.
"Go and wash you hands and face." Anna tells her son. Adam obeys his mother and sits at the table as she spoons out his beans and places another piece of toast at the side of his plate. He is back then, it is over. Whilst her son eats she makes up his bed and pulls the curtain slightly and puts his knock, knock joke book on her son's pillow. After finishing his tea she rinses the dishes and folds up the table and makes up her own bed. Anna is grateful to be locking up her caravan tonight and climbs into bed with its comfortable hot water bottle and hot chocolate. After finishing her drink she begins to settle down for the night. Anna listens as the rain begins to fall heavily on the caravan. She hears her son's breathing as she drifts off to sleep. Anna welcomes the sleep. The tide is on the turn and she can hears its roaring power as it rolls and smashes against the rocks in the distance.

The next morning, Anna tells her son as she washes up
the dishes and tidies up her bedding. "We'll go into
Thornby today."
"Can we go to the £1 shop?"
"Only if you're really good."
Anna makes a few jam sandwiches and pours juice into
the water bottle and takes the sack and locks up the door.
"Come on." Anna tells her son, "let's have a good day."
The day is wide open and clear, except for a few strands
of clouds, thin and wispy, higher up in the sky. They
climb on the bus and sit at the back. Anna makes sure
that they sit on the side where they are able to see the
view. She leans her head back and waits for the bus to
set off. These are Anna's moments, moments she
snatches, before she has to monitor and watch and
supervise her son. She can relax and enjoy the journey to
Thornby along the coast road. Anna catches glimpses of
the wide-open bay and the blueness of the sea is
beautiful to look at.

Thornby is busy, filled with holidaymakers and day-
trippers.
"We'll go around the charity shops first Adam."

They set off around the town. One by one they work
through each shop and finish off with a tour around the
Pound Land shop. Adam goes straight to the counter to
ask if they have any 'key rings' or 'wallets' Adam
always asks the same questions in all of the shops. Anna
finds a pretty floral shirt for £2.79. It is nearly new and
looks like it might fit her. With plain black trousers and
maybe a white vest top underneath, it would look nice,
open and casual, simple and summery. She could wear it
to take the bullet cases to Jo's. She buys it and puts the
two skirts back that she has picked up.
"£1 shop then Adam."
"How much can I have mum?"
 "Two pounds."

Anna likes pound shops; they are plain, simple and
straightforward. She saunters around looking at the
candles, paper and books. She picks up a rose candle,
remembering its significance, it is said that lighting a
rose candle attracts the spirit of young girls. Anna
doesn't particular want to attract the spirits of young
female ghosts but she loves the scent and smell of real
roses. She chooses perfume and goes to look for Adam.
He has a large packet of sweets and a black, plastic gun
set.
"When we've paid Adam, we'll go and find a fish shop
and have dinner."
It costs nearly £3 for fish and chips, so Anna buys one
lot and a portion of mushy peas. Adam wants to buy pop
but she reminds him that they have some. Finding a
bench near Fleetwood's supermarket, they sit down.
Anna splits the fish and chips in two and pours half the
mushy peas on to Adam's chips. Munching on their
dinner, the hot fish, is succulent and melts as they eat it,
they dip their chips into the mushy peas and enjoy their
meal. Anna sits back and drinks her juice satisfied.
"Come on." She tells her son as she screws her fish and
chip paper up and throws it into the bin.

They make their way down to the front where the small
fun fair is.
"One ride." Anna says.
The music of the fair ground bangs out the old songs,
which Anna remembers from her days at fairgrounds,
she went to with her sister. The Equals 'baby come back'
playing reminds her of the speedway. Anna would sit on
the outside bike because Nettie was nervous, excited and
afraid of being thrown off the ride. She would often
stretch her arm out to support her sister, as little by little
she began to slip down sideways off her bike.
"What do you want to go on?"
"The dodgems."

Anna watches as her son goes around and around
squealing with pleasure and joy, excited at the
exhilaration of the ride.
"Mam can I go on again?"
"We have to go now, we need to go and catch our bus
back home. You can have 20p to put in the claw
machine, to see if you can win a Homer Simpson."
She holds out the 20p, Adam would prefer another ride
on the dodgems but is pragmatic enough, not to lose the
money. He puts his coin into the machine but doesn't
win the toy.
"When we get to the frozen food shop, near the bus stop,
we'll call in and buy an ice cream lolly."

The day has turned out reasonably well Anna thinks, as
Adam licks his chocolate ice-lolly, as they wait for their
bus to go home.

That night Anna dreams again of John Doherty, the male
character in her notebook. This time he is smiling at her.
The smile is gentle and draws Anna closer into his face.
His eyes are heavy and hooded now, not blazing in front
of her but seductive and Anna wants more. As she leans
closer to him, he lowers his head. Her heart races as she
expects him to kiss her on the mouth but instead he lifts
his face up, so she can see his eyes and whispers words
into her ear. Anna can't hear what he is saying; he is
speaking low, almost a whisper. She catches the lilt of
his Irish accent; it brings back the voice of her father.
"I'll fuck you, you bitch." Anna gasps at John Doherty's
obscenities and moves backwards away from him. She is
falling, her heart races with fear now not anticipation,
and then she wakes, grateful to be out of the dream. Her
head, forehead, neck, back and chest are wet with sweat.
She sits up in bed to get her bearings and wipes the
perspiration away. "God that was scary." Anna thinks.

It is too dark to get up and there is a chill in the caravan,
which always creeps up, in the early hours of the

morning. The dream has disturbed and unsettled her. Her
sense of ease with playing at writing has gone. Anna
feels unable to control this male character she has
created, he seems to exist now on his own. 'This is
creepy, I don't like it and if this is how it's going to be,
I'll get rid of Mr, Dr,' Anna corrects herself, 'Doherty.'
Eventually she returns to sleep and the dream doesn't
return to trouble her.

She is thankful the dream seems to have left her and over
the course of the next few days, whenever she has free
time, she doesn't go into the drawer to take out the
notebook.

On Friday morning, Anna has a complete body wash in
the sink and puts on her white, t-shirt vest and the new
floral blouse she bought from the charity shop. Of course
it is raining, but it can't be helped. The grass and bushes
on the track to the woman's hut will be damp and wet;
she will have to wear her waterproof coat.

Adam had left the caravan just after 9 o'clock to go and
see Callum, to make up with him after the guns and
bullet case swap. Anna puts the bullet cases in her bag
and is ready to go. She locks up the caravan and goes to
find him. He answers Callum's door.
"Please mam can I stay with Callum, his dad's going to
take us fishing a bit later, please mam?" Adam pleads.
"Were supposed to be taking the bullet cases to Jo's."
Anna reminds him.
"She won't mind if you just go mam please."
"Is Callum's mum there?"
"Hang on." Adam goes back inside and is replaced by
Callum's mother.
"It's alright, he can come with us."
"If you're sure?"
"Yes, he'll be fine."
"He doesn't have a line."
"That's ok we have a spare and a net so we'll manage."

"Ok, thanks, see you later Adam." Anna calls out.

Anna walks away from the caravan feeling a bit put out. She doesn't really fancy the idea of going to this woman's place alone, as Adam has been the one since the beach experience, who did all the talking. 'How hard can it be?' Anna asks herself, as she begins the walk to the lay by and then onto the beach hut. She feels weary in the miserable weather; her feet are already soaking before she gets there.

The walk through the streets and houses along the tarmac paths are boring and dull, Adam would have brightened the journey, with his endless chatter about nothing and his stories about the gangster battles and fights he and Callum share.
Just as Anna passes through the gate, where the hawthorn bushes are, she spots a tall man walking towards her. This is unusual, because basically the only place the path leads to is Jo's beach hut. The man stops. He is dressed in a black, long length coat with his collar turned up; his head is bent down against the rain. Anna isn't sure what to do. The man steps aside into the longer wet grass and waves her forward and through. Anna is relieved and mumbles thanks.

The blue front door of Jo's hut is shut but she can hear the dog inside barking. She must be out or she'd come to the door, to stop Jason barking. Anna walks around to the back of the hut, she hears what sounds like a gushing stream of water and sees what it actually is as she turns the corner. Some kind of contraption, which acts like a shower and beneath it Jo is standing. She is wiping the water from her face and squeezing her hair.

As Jo begins to squeeze out her hair and put the end of the shower hose back on its hook, she notices through the corner of her eye a figure and quickly double checks, to see that she has not imagined it. It's Anna coming towards her, Jo looks beyond her to see if Adam is with her, and is glad to see that she is alone.

Anna watches as Jo turns around and on her back and hips and shoulders are large blue bruises. The sight shocks Anna.

Anna's face shows a look of concern and worry and as her arm reaches out to touch Jo gently, she asks, "My god Jo, what's happened to you? Did you fall?"
"What do you mean?"
Anna takes Jo gently by the shoulders, "What's happened? Your back it's covered in bruises and looks really painful and sore."

Jo now understands, what she felt out here in the rain and in the shower, she thought it was just the cold water hitting her skin, she must have hurt it last night, but she cannot remember how.

"What has happened?" Anna asks quietly again as she gently runs her hand down and across Jo's back "Arnica, Jo, you need some Arnica for that, it will help."
As Anna looks up, the woman she had seen at Jo's hut the last time she visited, is watching them. She is standing a little way off. Anna notices the look on the woman's face, it is almost a glare and as she reaches for the towel to cover Jo, the woman disappears as quickly and quietly as she had appeared.
Anna finds the towel quickly, as if disturbed by something and places it around Jo's shoulders. Jo suddenly feels quite vulnerable and doesn't know what to say to Anna, as she waits for an explanation.
"Come on let's go inside."
Indoors Jo tries to regain herself.
"I'll just go and put some clothes on."
Jo hurries upstairs and calls to Anna. "Sit down, stay, I won't be long, I'll just get dressed."

The room is simple and comfortable. The black stove has not been lit but Anna can imagine how warm and cosy the hut would feel on a cold, blustery day.

In the security of the bedroom, Jo tries to glance backwards over her shoulder to look at her skin, without a mirror she is only able to see a few marks, however when she touches it she can feel the painful areas and winces and wonders, but immediately switches off and gets dressed.

She returns downstairs wearing jeans and a pale blue t-shirt, her hair is wet and spiky.
"Gosh, I feel so hungry have you eaten?" Jo asks Anna.
"No I haven't."
"Would you like to share some soup with me?"
"That would be lovely, thank you."
"It's carrot and orange soup, I made it the other day."
"That sounds nice."
Jo lights the camp stove near the sink and empties the contents of a preserving jar into a pan and stirs it with a wooden spoon. Whilst the soup heats up on a low light she places two bowls on the table and the breadboard with crusty bread. The waft of the carrot soup fills the air and soon it is ready to pour into the dishes.
"Thank you." Anna says, as Jo beckons her to the table.

Anna is pleased with the invitation to share a meal and in spite of her confusion with Jo's seemingly blowing hot and cold in her temperament, decides she wants to stay. It feels as if the gulf, which separated them after their meeting on the beach, has been filled just a little. Anna feels comfortable now, as she had done when they first met at dawn.
They both sit and slowly eat the soup, dunking big chunks of the bread and butter in. The pleasure of eating is paramount and silence is set, neither starting up a conversation.

This is a treat for Anna, she is relaxed and comfortable and this place with Jo is effortless to be in. Anna is happy being served the beautiful, orange coloured, carrot soup with a piece of crusty bread. It tastes earthy and hot and comforting. The women glance often at each other as they share their meal.

Outside it is still raining but indoors Anna feels warm and comfortable and at ease.
In this parallel world that Jo visits right now, she inhabits a place where the woman sits, a soft cushion, the strong sure arms she surrender to, for the great laying down.

"Jo, are you ok?" Anna asks, breaking into Jo's disassociation.
"Yes thanks, I'm ok." Jo replies whilst looking up into Anna's blue eyes.
"Thanks that was lovely."
"I'll show you my work room later and you can see the work I've done on Adam's pirate ship."
Anna remembers the bullet cases and takes them out of her bag, "this is what Adam has chosen for the cannons."

Jo remembers the reason for Anna's visit today.
"Yes they will be great." Jo examines the cases and holds them up.
"It was the man in the Army shop who suggested them."
"Come through to my workroom and I will show you the boat so far."

Inside the workroom there is a workbench down one side of the small room and a window, which faces the front of the hut.
"You really do have everything here." Anna likes this secure, self-sufficient world Jo has created.

Jo shows Anna the wood and cork she is using to make the boat.

"I'm going to use an empty cotton reel and paint it black and make a hook, probably out of a piece of an old coat hanger and use string to tie on a piece of lead shot to make an anchor." Jo holds the three bullet cases in her hand and puts them next to the pieces of wood she has prepared for the ship.

"The bullet cases will look great".

Anna is pleased with the boat, the 'Purple Pearl', she knows it will end up quite remarkable and Adam will be happy with his pirate ship. Anna looks around the workroom, it is filled with different shapes and colours of driftwood, as well as logs and branches and boxes full of all sorts of odds and ends. On the bench are the large masts and sails waiting to be glued and sewn.

"I can make three holes and put the bullets through, so that they stick out of one side, and on the other use a flat piece of wood to stick out for 'the plank', that should look really good. Do you think Adam will like it when it's finished? Where is he by the way?"

"He has gone with his friend fishing, so he couldn't come with the bullet cases, but yes he'll like it, he will think that it's great."

"How about we arrange for Adam to see it, say next Tuesday, that should give me enough time to finish it."

"That'll be fine, I'll drop you off some Arnica tomorrow for your back, you need to take it as soon as possible for it to help. It will help with the bruises."

Jo feels tempted to refuse this offer and suggest that she is ok and doesn't need it, however she doesn't want to reject Anna's kindness and concern. "That's kind of you, are you sure?"

"Of course I don't mind, but I will just bob in quickly, as I won't have much time, but I don't mind honestly." Anna adds. "And thank you so much for the soup; it was lovely, thank you. I'll have to be going now, so I will call first thing in the morning."

"Ok then, I will carry on working on the pirate ship, now that I have the cannons for it, so that's good and I will see you tomorrow then."

"Well I'll get off then so see you, bye."

"Bye and thank you." Jo sees her to the door.

Anna leaves and makes her way back along the wet, winding path, and through the damp bushes. Her feet are sodden when she arrives back at the caravan so she takes off her shoes and dries her feet, then fills the kettle to make herself a pot of tea. She isn't sure what time Adam will be home for dinner, so she decides to drink her tea and then think about preparing a meal. She decides on tuna pasta bake with bolognaise sauce, so she cooks the pasta and pours in the tomato sauce and mixes in the can of tuna then puts it in the oven on a low light. Anna enjoys her tea and reflects on what happened at Jo's. She feels relieved now that they have caught up on their early relationship. Anna remembers her promise of Arnica and takes it out of her small kit of remedies. She takes one of her small plastic envelopes from the box and pours in four Arnica 30c tablets. She slips the plastic envelope into her bag for the following day.

Later after they have eaten, she walks with Adam down the donkey track to the park. Adam plays on the roundabout and when two small children jump on, he grabs a hold of the handle and runs around, spinning the children faster and faster, until they squeal with delight and he is hot, red and flustered. After running around again Anna calls to him to come for a walk on the beach. The tide is in and the waves are high. The sea smashes against the rocks and where it meets the turn of the current, the waves smack against it and the sea flings itself high in the air, to crash back down again into the sea. The roar of the sea is the loudest she has ever heard it. Three young children stand at the end of the little slip, which leads into the sea and scream, as the waves reach and drench them. The experience delights and thrills them and Anna takes Adam away so he can't join the children in their dangerous pursuit, of daring the waves to see who will get the wettest. They walk up the steep hill back to the town centre. Straggling holidaymakers are making their way back to their campsites and day-trippers to their cars, coaches or the railway station. The shops are shut but the pubs and restaurants are opening. Anna smells the aroma of the fish and chip shop as they pass.

Jo's attention turns to doing more work on the pirate ship, she is very pleased with Anna and Adam's find of the bullet cases for the cannons. She finds a screwdriver and makes the holes for the cannons to fit through. And then presses the cases in and glues them into place. Now that these are fixed through the hull, she needs to tidy the centre of the boat and decides to carve up more cork into flat pieces to glue across the deck, this will add buoyancy and encase the bullet cases so that they will look more like cannons sticking out. This is a fiddly job measuring and cutting the cork, as each piece is a different size. When this is finished she leaves the glue to dry before painting it all black.

She is aware that Jason hasn't had much attention these past few days and feels the need to take him for a walk, so she get his lead, puts on her coat and sets off down the paths to the cliff top. The rain is starting to ease off slightly and the sky is a little brighter than the greyness of earlier, so they shouldn't get too wet. She walks and stops to chat to Jason as they head along towards the cliff. They take the path to the right along the difficult route for a change. This way is tricky but she decides today it will be ok. Jason has a natural tendency to sense his footings and never stalls or stumbles as he ambles quickly along, he enjoys this walk and he is happy today. The sound of the sea crashing into the rocks below and the seagulls shrieking and soaring above and then gliding to perch on a shelf in the cliff, adds to the pleasure of the walk. Further along she notices another landslip, a fresh terracotta crater that has left its brown heap down on the beach. The cliff edge is encroaching nearer towards this path; she ponders the thought of how long before the jaws of the land eater, take this ground she is standing on.

Eventually her hunger leads her back towards home and she cooks dried pasta, add olives, tomatoes, potatoes, boiled eggs and sprigs of fresh mint. She devours a large bowl full, along with chunks of dried out, buttered crusty bread, followed by a pot of tea. After feeding Jason she decides to return to work on the pirate ship. She sinks some brass washers near to the cannons for added effect and paints the hull with black acrylic paint. She paints white, skull and crossbones on the large mainsail and mixes up blues and red paints to find the shade of purple that is deep and daunting for the sails. When these are painted there is no more work that she can do, until everything is dry, so she leaves the ship and tinkers about with the smaller boats. It's nice to be working away and getting on again. She switches on the radio to a classical music station and enjoys the evening, continuing until the light finally ebbs away and she has to stop and go to bed.

The next day the rain has stopped and the sky is blue
with a few scattered white clouds, although not as warm
as it has been, it is a good day outside. Jo tends the
vegetable patch and takes lettuce, carrots, tomatoes and
potatoes up to the roadside with the honesty box. During
the morning she hears voices coming down the path and
awaits the arrival of Anna and Adam.

Adam is excited to be going back to Jo's. Anna warns
him as they approach the blue painted door. "No
messing, no rooting or touching stuff agreed?"
"Yea, yea." Adam agrees happily not interested in what
his mother is telling him, his excitement growing as he
hears the dog barking.
Adam runs the last few yards shouting "Jo, Jo." In full
steam he dashes across to Jason to pat and play with him.

Anna arrives looking slightly stressed, unlike yesterday
fully at ease and relaxed with herself. "Adam, careful
with Jason, don't get him too excited, Adam."
Adam jumps up and runs inside the hut shouting and is
into everything. "Where is it Jo, my pirate ship?"
"The Arnica Jo, if you take one now and then another
one in the morning and evening, I've given you four to
take, they should help you."
Jo takes the remedies and puts them into her pocket.
"Thanks very much, I will take them, thank you."
"Adam come here, it's Jo's hut, you can't just run
around and go where you please."
Adam seeming not to listen, dashes to the staircase and
goes up the steps two at a time and looks around the
bedroom.
"Come down now." Anna demands "Now Adam."
"Is it up here Jo?" Adam shouts down.
"Come down here Adam, now."
Adam appears at the top of the stairs looking sheepish
aware now of his impetuousness and then saunters down
the stairs smiling and talking ten to the dozen.
"Down now, Adam."

"I can show you your pirate ship but it's not finished yet Adam."

With that he descends the stairs.

"Is that your bedroom?"

"Yes it is my bedroom Adam."

Anna scolds Adam again, reminding him not to go into people's houses and going off to where he wants.

"Were not staying." Anna informs me, as Adam begins lifting lids and opening boxes.

"Adam, what did I say?"

Anna decides they are leaving. Adam is out of control and she needs to get him out of the way. Jo's hut has too many interesting nooks and crannies for Adam to keep calm and not to touch things.

"Come on I'll show you the ship and see if you like it." Jo intervenes.

She takes them into the workroom and shows Adam the 'Purple Pearl'.

"Well then what do you think?"

Adam suddenly lost for words just stares at the boat.

"Mam."

"Go on then Adam, tell Jo what you think of the ship."

"It's brilliant, when can I have it?"

"I will have it ready on Tuesday for you if you want to come and collect it."

"Yes we can do that, we can call then on Tuesday, say thank you to Jo Adam."

"Thanks Jo." He says as Jason appears and nudges his legs. Adam reaches down and follows Jason outside.

"We have to go into town now, so we will call on Tuesday for the boat." Anna turns to leave.

"Adam come on we have to go now, say goodbye to Jo."

"Bye Jo."

Anna leads her son away and up the path from the hut.

"Come on now Adam."

Anna is cross and angry as she walks quickly away from Jo's, 'What is the point?' Anna asks herself, as bit-by-bit her anger dissipates.

"What did we talk about Adam just before we went into Jo's?"
"Sorry mam."
There is no point. It's always the same, why did she think it would be any different.

As Adam undresses for bed she hears something click in Adam's trousers as he throws them on the floor. "What's that?" Anna asks.
"Oh nothing just my key?"
"Show me."
"Where did you get this from?"
Adam looks down.
"Where?"
"You got it from Jo's didn't you?" Adam remains quiet.
"You can take it back yourself." Anna tells him.
"No I won't."
Anna goes into the kitchen to undress and puts the key in her bag. "She's going to think were right idiots isn't she?"

Jo rises early, having hardly slept at all last night, her
back although feeling easier now had kept her awake.
She was unable to sleep on it and had to lie on her
stomach, listening to the rain dropping on the roof
above. There is a chill inside today and she decides to
light the stove to make porridge, the rain is still pouring
outside, the sky is grey and bleak and the ground outside
is wet and uninviting. She will spend the day inside,
working on the boats and pebbles; she needs to finish off
the pirate ship, so that it is ready for Tuesday. She adds
sultanas and sprinkles cinnamon and a spoonful of honey
to the porridge and makes a drink. After the filling meal
she sits down in the chair and enjoys another mug of hot
tea. She picks off the bookshelf a copy of Freya King's
art and turns the pages, their intense vivid colours fill her
imagination and she feels inspired to paint and makes a
mental note to call at Mad Mick's, to buy some art
materials, next time she goes into town. She drifts and
settles in the chair, feeling the warmth from the stove
and the porridge heavy in her stomach. Jason has
returned quickly from the garden and is happy resting on
his bed dozing too.

Adam is in bed too, he isn't listening, or interested in
what his mam has to say. For Adam the key experience
is over and he's forgotten.

Next morning Anna puts more Arnica tablets into
another small plastic envelope and begins her journey
back to Jo's. Anna is upset and cross with Adam in spite
of her understanding and her acceptance of his
disabilities. Understanding and accepting is one thing but
being on continual call and loosing her sense of
perspective, are not experiences she can control. The
chains of living with a mentally disabled child aren't
simple, neat or ordered but mad, wild and out of control.

Adam makes his way to Callum's as Anna locks up the caravan, she calls out to remind him to be back for half past twelve.

Anna weaves through the damp undergrowth, thinking about her journey, since she and Adam arrived at the coast.

Time passes and when Jason's ears prick up and he barks, Jo wonders what has alerted him. Shortly after someone knocks at the door with a short, sharp, urgency. This brings her to her feet and she opens the door slightly.

"Open up Jo, I'm getting bloody soaked out here." The large stocky figure of Charles, dripping wet in his Barbour coat stands in the doorway.
 "Oh hello, what are you doing here?" Jo blurts out.
"Come on Jo let me in for God's sake, I thought you might like to have lunch at the Sailor with Stella and I, it's the usual roast and they have the best pint in town, what do you say, I'll wait whilst you get ready." Charles orders.
"No sorry I can't come today, thank you anyway, sorry." Jo replies still holding the door to.
"Oh come on you will enjoy it, Stella's looking forward to seeing you again, we didn't get chance to say cheerio the other day, you left so early." Charles says as he waits for Jo to open the door. He isn't taking no for an answer. Jason is picking up the tension between them and is becoming agitated.
"No I said I can't sorry, I can't come out with you." Jo reiterates.
"Look Jo, I've reserved a table for 12 o'clock, come on, what's to stop you?" Charles asks losing his patience; he pushes the door against Jo and reaches out to touch her shoulder.
"Look I've said I can't come, so please can you go."

"No need to be like that, its lunch that's all, a good meal in great company, come on." Charles reaches further and strokes Jo with his hand, she winces as he touches her sore back and she pulls away from him.

Jason begins barking again and Jo's attention is taken now to the garden path as he runs towards it.

The sound of raised voices stops Anna's contemplations; she is surprised as she makes her way towards the front door. There appears to be some kind of dispute going on between Jo and a man. Anna watches as he catches hold of Jo by the shoulder and she winces and pulls away from him, he looks angry. As she steps closer to the door, the pair turn around.

Looking ahead Jo can see Anna coming down the path. "I have a friend calling to see me, she is here now, so if you don't mind, you will have to go." Jo is thankful of Anna's timely arrival.

Charles quickly backs off. "Well another time then, don't forget though, lunch at the Sailor, see you later." Charles steps back and walks away, unused to taking no for an answer. The man looks at Anna and almost growls at her as he goes past.
"Is everything alright?" Anna asks.
Jo is a bit dazed but stands back to allow Anna to step indoors.
"I've brought your key."
Jo holds the key in her hand and looks outside, glad to see the back of Charles receding in the distance.
"Are you here to collect the pirate ship, I'm afraid its not quite ready yet?"
"No I'm not, I've come to return your key, I'm sorry Adam took it the other day, he does things like that, I didn't realise until it fell out of his pocket that evening."
"It's the key for the trunk in my bedroom; I hadn't noticed it missing, thank you for bringing it back."

Closing her hand around the key Jo takes it up the flight
of stairs to the bedroom.
"I noticed," Anna begins as Jo returns downstairs "Your
back and shoulder still seem to be tender."
"Yes, they are, the Arnica has helped a bit thanks but I
didn't sleep well last night, it's still sore."
"I've brought more Arnica with me, if you like I could
put it in some oil if you have some and massage it into
your back, that will help it".
"Thank you that's kind of you, would you like a pot of
tea first, I have the stove on and can soon make some,
and take off your coat to dry."
"That would be lovely, it's not a nice day out there, the
stove makes the room so cosy doesn't it."
"Yes it does, sit down whilst I make some tea."

Jo takes the teapot and pours the tealeaves out into the
bin and rinses it, then fills the kettle with water to boil.
She notices Anna leafing through a book peacefully, at
home and seeming quite content, 'stay here my friend,
stay with me;' Jo thinks how lovely that would be. When
the kettle boils she pours the water and scolds the
tealeaves and waits for it to mash. She takes two mugs
from the drainer and adds milk from the fridge, and
wishes for the first time that she had another armchair
for both of them. 'I will get one,' she thinks, as she sees
into a future time, of them sitting, chatting and drinking
tea together, content.

"Who was that man, what did he want?"
Jo begins to tell her. "The other night I cycled over in the
rain to Stella's, a woman from Fenton who
commissioned a boat, she asked me to take it to her
house. I went in the evening and she invited me to stay
because of the rain. I had too much to drink and I stayed
for a curry with her and the man that you have just seen
leaving. I shouldn't have drunk as much as I did; I got
carried away with the wine. Stella ran a bath for me and
I don't remember after that what happened. In the early

hours of the morning I woke up and found myself in bed next to Charles, - that man, feeling hung over I left and came home. So you see when I showered the other day, I hadn't been aware of the bruises on my back, I was just getting over a hangover."

"God Jo, you can't remember?"

"No I can't, Charles was here asking me out for lunch today, I'm so glad you called, I didn't want to go."

"Jo you must be careful, you know out here all alone."

"I know, I'm so glad that I have Jason here with me."

Anna looks worried and concerned and sips her tea deep in thought. "Do you have some oil, would you like me to take a look at your back?"

"Yes I have some olive oil, will that be ok?"

"Yes that's fine, could you get it and an old bowl or basin?"

Jo finds the bottle of olive oil and a terracotta dish.

Anna takes the Arnica tablet from the plastic wallet and with the back of a spoon crushes the tablet in the dish and adds the olive oil and blends the remedy and oil together. "If you take off your shirt, I'll apply the oil to your back and shoulders it really will help, but you need to lie down on something."

"We can go upstairs to my bedroom and I can lie on my bed."

"Yes that would be best it will be more comfortable for you."

They go upstairs with the bowl of oil. Jo removes her top and lay face down on the bed. With her fingers, Anna takes some oil and gently puts it on Jo's back, slowly and carefully and very lightly, stroking it on. Jo winces a little at first and then arches her back as Anna continues to rub the oil into Jo's back and shoulders. Anna feels Jo's shoulders begin to fall and relax under her rhythmic, gentle, massage.

As Jo begins to relax, she succumbs to Anna's touch and the slow strokes of her fingertips massaging her skin.

The experience reconnects Anna physically to Jo and the sensuality and tenderness fills her with warmth, openness and acceptance. Anna rubs what is left of the oil into her hands and looks at Jo. It is enough for now, although she feels, senses, that there could be more between them. Anna can feel the openness, release and suppleness and receptiveness in Jo's body as she works in the oil and Arnica into her skin. 'Not yet though, not yet,' Anna thinks.

This experience makes Jo want to heave and cry and sob, she cannot let this show, cannot let this happen here and now. Her senses are waking and her body is making connections, it's like the inner messages to her brain are struggling with the correct responses and she needs Anna to stop, but cannot tell her. Jo drifts away from her, into a safer place inside her head and travels deeper and deeper, to forget.

"Jo, are you ok, do you want me to stop, is that enough?" Anna calls out.
"Jo."
Jo's mind tries to find its voice to respond, but it takes time, she is unable to at first.
"Jo."
"Yes that's fine, thanks, I'll put my t shirt back on."
Anna stops her stroking and takes the bowl. "I'll go back downstairs and wait for you."
"Ok." Jo needs time to regain herself, so she takes a few moments to compose herself and pulls her t-shirt over her head and ruffles her hair.

Returning downstairs, Jo feels heady and drowsy and sits down in the chair. Anna talks to Jo, but she doesn't quite take in her words.
"Can I see the ship?"

"Gosh, I feel tired."
"The Arnica should help Jo."
"Thanks."
Later the women get up and walk into the workroom.
The boat is on the workbench and already resembles a
pirate ship. Its body is two pieces of black wood, with a
plank sticking out and cannons on the other side and a
cotton reel anchor and two magnificent purple sails.

"It's wonderful, you're very clever." Anna smiles.
"Thank you, I'm glad he'll like it."
 "I'd better go now, I've told Adam to be back for twelve
so I'd better go."
"Yes ok."
Anna looks at Jo and she returns her long steady gaze.
"Until Tuesday then. Sorry again about the key and don't
forget to apply a little more oil into your shoulders
before you go to bed."
"Yes, thanks, bye."
"Goodbye Jo."

Anna walks slowly away now, her thoughts clarifying the further she gets from Jo's hut. The few days' left before Tuesday will pass and until then she will keep busy. Adam will be pleased when he sees the ship and she feels happy at the prospect of seeing Jo again. The time in-between, will allow Anna space to think and reflect about her feelings for Jo. How do I feel Anna asks herself?

Jo is grateful Anna decides to leave; she needs space to be, to think and rest. Her mind and body still quietly anaesthetized once more, how many more times can this happen. She could never have imagined, living here, away from people, that entirely innocent connections with Charles, Stella and Anna would get close and invade her boundaries so quickly? Jo sits knowing that this state she's in right now is due to her relationships with these three people. Someone mentioned years ago to her, that it doesn't matter where a person goes to live they cannot escape unresolved issues, that these will come back to haunt and repeat, again and again, until the person has learnt from them and has changed. Sitting here she knows that she did run away and try to hide, from her past, from people who had hurt her. She truly believed that she would be free to live, to forget and start again. 'Don't beat yourself up. Don't do that to yourself,' She repeats this mantra over and over. 'Be kind and gentle, let it go.' So where to now? What happens next? It doesn't help not being able to remember the evening with Charles and Stella and the marks on her back, how did she get those? Maybe she slipped in the bath, that would explain them, and waking up next to Charles, did anything happen between them? Her vagina doesn't feel that it has been penetrated; there is no soreness or bruising around it. And where did Stella sleep, where was she that night? Questions and more questions without answers, she supposes she will have to wait and see what transpires with these people. She can protect herself and make sure her boundaries stand strong and sure from now on. She doesn't have to give herself again, she is about to say unwillingly, however she did, albeit under the influence of a large amount of wine, surely she is wiser from the experience, she won't drink in their company again. And Anna, gentle Anna, like her long lost friend, a reflection from the past, emerging and melding through quantum time, leaping out to touch and be with her. 'Let's hold on to what matters, who we are, let's reach out sometimes and share each other.' She is so glad of the sudden bang of the dawn that drew them together, 'there are no accidents, we are walking the path already there before us, where will it lead and how far will it go?' Internal reflections, the unknown, 'some people never stop to think and find themselves, but what a deep and delicious place to travel, to pause and ponder, to digress and wander, and to wonder at the beauty found within. To try and accept oneself with all its shadows and surface with a smile, hoping that the path laid out before us, for all its transgressions and imperfections is worthy and worthwhile, however long it may be.'

Breaking through her ruminations, Jo hears a smashing, cracking, torrential downpour, hitting the panes of glass; again and again the rain lashes down. In this strange dreamy place that she inhabits, in this other land of hers, she answers to another voice and gathers herself up. She finds loose change and puts on her waterproof coat and wellingtons and locks the door behind her, telling Jason she won't be long.

She sets off down the path, through the trees and across the fields and on into town. She must be mad in this weather, however she is on a mission and walks steadily, head down, bracing herself against the rain sheeting down. Her trousers are soon wet through and the water is dripping down into her boots, wetting her socks, but still she presses on. Up through the main street, intent on her destination, to the church. There are few people along the way, one or two quickly nipping in and out of the shops. The road is fairly busy with cars ferrying and collecting people, keeping them out of the rain. At the far edge of town she arrives at the small 12th century church; she walks around the side to the old oak door and stands inside the canopy where it is dry. She turns the huge, round iron handle to the right and hears a welcoming click; it's open much to her surprise. Closing the door behind her, she removes her coat and quickly shakes and hangs it over the end of a wooden chair by the entrance to drip. She stands still and lets her eyes traverse the interior of the church. It's the first time that she has been inside; and has often wondered what it would be like. It is dark and eerily quiet despite the heavy rain. It's as if the rain has suddenly stopped. There are tiny stained glass windows down the two sides and it's hard to make out their pictures in the faint light. There are pews at both sides and the pulpit is on the right at the front, beyond that there is a font and some more pews, probably for the choir.

Jo steps forward and moves slowly around the church. It is a lovely simple sanctuary, peaceful and cool, but not chilly and austere. There is a box containing tall slim white candles placed on a stone plinth, she takes one and lights it and places it on a holder and puts her coins in the box at the side. She watches and gazes into the flame, as the smoky wick flickers, into a golden yellow light. Jo stands transfixed and feels the warmth and lets her eyes enter into a journey through time, away and far above this space, travelling upward and out to meet and sing with the angels. When the candle starts to pop she averts her eyes and chooses a pew to sit down on and rest. The pew is harsh and hard and wooden. It is not comfort that she is here for, she needs to be a part of this energy, to connect and feel it on her skin, to let it soak down upon and inside of her, to affirm her essence and say thank you for being alive on this earth. Time remains still and she allows the minutes to stretch, in order to stay here for a long time, no harm can come upon her here, she is safe and protected, taken care of and needs this support right now. It is like entering a big bubble and being secure in its outer, flimsy skin, where nothing can penetrate through. Inside this skin, a golden, eternal energy of light permeates and absorbs through her central core, filling her with beauty and peace. She will return, she can return and with this affirmation she rises and departs to the outer world, so real and sometimes grey and dark, the sunshine is lost for now, but that too will return.

She puts her wet coat back on and sets off on the soggy journey back home. The rain still falls and at the door Jason is waiting, pleased to see her again. She takes off her coat, trousers and socks and hangs them over the kitchen chair and puts it near the stove. She adds a large log to the stove and fills the kettle to make tea. After dashing upstairs for a t-shirt and jogging bottoms she decides to cook eggs and have them with buttered bread. She puts three into the pan to poach. It is dark inside, so different from the last weeks of sunshine.

After the food she goes through to the workroom and starts work on the boats, to finish off the pirate ship for Adam, is her priority, and then she can while away the hours on whatever takes her fancy. When the 'Purple Pearl' is finally finished she holds it up and turns it around, 'wow, yes,' Adam will be pleased, it has turned out really well. She feels happy, her trip into town to the church has helped regain her sense of perspective and even though the rain still pours outside, her disposition is happy, she is alive.

It is cosy and she is content to work away as time slips by, eventually the ensuing darkness and tiredness takes hold and she sits down in the armchair, with a mug of milky, hot chocolate. The aroma of the scolded milk still lingers in the air as she rests. Later she cooks a pan of pasta and adds a few black olives, tomatoes, garlic and a sprinkling of pine nuts for the evening meal. Jason makes short work of the leftovers, mixed in with his dried food. Jo lets him into the garden and remains inside, there is no point getting wet again. When he returns she adds another log to the stove and turns down the air vent and retires early to bed. She lies down and nestles under the duvet and soon fades into a deep and heavy sleep.

Waking the next day, she hears the rain pounding heavily on the roof and remains covered and hidden under the warmth and snuggle of the duvet, waiting for the moment when her body decides to turn on its side and get up. Sometimes it is difficult, especially today and to stretch the moment, to linger longer in the confines of this special private space, is almost a battle of wills. Cherishing this, whilst knowing that she can't or wouldn't want to stay here all day, but how long does one take before rising, this quandary is the moment when her body decides for her and up she gets. 'As wonderful and lovely as some things are, we cannot keep them forever, is it that we don't allow them to, or if we did would the glow, the appetite subside?' Thoughts, how they ruminate inside, questioning and wondering, plenty of time here on her own to ponder decisions and choices. She quickly puts on her t-shirt and bottoms and goes downstairs to Jason's morning welcome. She opens the front of the stove and adds pieces of firewood to the few remaining embers and opens the air vent to bring the stove to life. And fills the kettle with water, she decides to make porridge today. She pours milk into a pan and a couple of spoonfuls of oatmeal and places it at the side of the kettle and chats away to Jason as she goes about their breakfasts, setting the table and getting his food ready, returning to the pan to stir it. A large pot of tea and porridge with sultanas and honey stirred in is a welcoming start to the day.

Today Anna and Adam will be calling to collect the 'Purple Pearl', so Jo plans to work on the boats and pebbles. She wonders whether they will call early or later on in the day. Looking outside, the rain is pelting down, they will be soaked by the time they arrive, so she will keep the stove going for them, they might like to stay for a pot of tea before setting back. After breakfast she refills the kettle and lets Jason out into the garden and makes a quick dash round the back of the hut to the toilet; this is one of the times, when it's wet or cold that she envies other people and their luxury bathrooms and inside loo. The kettle is whistling when she returns, it takes a couple of kettlefuls to provide enough water for a decent wash. She washes as best she can with the flannel and soap, then towels herself in front of the stove and is soon dry. Then returns upstairs for a pair of clean knickers and puts her clothes back on. She pops a few pairs of dirty pants into the bowl of water to soak, to rinse out later and dry in the kitchen during the day.

For lunch she decides to make a chilli and cook it on top of the stove. She peels an onion and adds carrots, tomatoes, garlic, mushrooms, potatoes, a can of kidney beans, a handful of walnuts and slices of chorizo to a large stockpot. Adding a couple of teaspoons of chilli powder, salt and pepper, cumin, cocoa powder and cold water to cover, replaces the lid and pops it on top of the stove to slowly cook. The meal will provide a good lunch for two days and she can easily heat it up again on the camping stove if she doesn't have the wood burner lit tomorrow.

With the meal prepared, she goes into the workroom and sets about painting the larger pebbles, remembering to stir the chilli pot occasionally; the hot, spicy aroma, wafting through is a reminder. As the morning progresses and Anna and Adam haven't arrived she begins to wonder if they might not come, the rain is still pouring down heavily. She wishes that she had some corn chips in her stock cupboard to eat with the chilli, but as she hasn't she cuts up the last of the bread and places it on top of the stove to heat through. Jo ladles the meal from the pot into a large bowl and quickly rescues the bread as it begins to burn. The smell of toast and the deep, sticky, chilli, soon stirs her taste buds and with a puffing and blowing she eagerly sets to with a spoon. Lovely, wholesome, hearty, tasty food, it's good to produce a simple meal so easily.

After lunch she returns to the workroom and messes around with ideas, using paper and pencil and decides that tomorrow she will go into town and buy art materials; paints, canvases and brushes and make a start on a painting. She will hang the paintings in the hut, it will add interest to the walls and hopefully, she might be able to sell them alongside the boats and pebbles. As the afternoon progresses and still no sign of Anna she decides that the rain has prevented her from coming. She doesn't blame her, especially with Adam; it wouldn't be much fun both of them getting drenched through. The rain too is making Jo feel rather hemmed in, after spending all day again inside, so whatever happens tomorrow she will go into town. She needs to buy bread and milk and other food items and also have a look around for some painting equipment.

As early evening draws in she makes tea and has the last of the cheese with a few crackers and listens to the radio. The news bulletin mentions heavy flooding and parts of the country cut off, without mains water, the weather forecasting more rain and flooding for the next few days and not much change beyond that. Without a TV here, the world outside seems far away, another reality altogether, no vivid pictures of events unfolding before her eyes; it is like being detached and living in a land removed from everyone else. Yet tonight with the rain still coming down, it is building a bridge, a connection to that other reality and bringing it to life, making it real, and linking it to here at the hut. When the newsreader departs to the music, she is glad to hear the sounds and turns up the volume to drown out the rain, the news has spoiled the feeling of comfort that she had.

She hopes that the sun will be shining tomorrow.

Anna has arranged to meet Adam before going on to Jo's to collect the ship, she walks along the cliff top footpath to the bench to wait for him, because he knows a quicker way to Jo's without going out of the town centre and through the gate at the side of the lay by. The path seems much longer to day and closed in, with the long, lush, green growths of bushes and trees and wild flowers. The sky is heavy too and overcast and the atmosphere feels oppressive and is weighing Anna down. There is no air. Anna finds herself inhaling deeper and deeper to have enough oxygen to breath. She no longer feels free.

Arriving at the bench she is unable to rest, she paces up and down in the muggy atmosphere. Time seems to hang and Anna hopes she won't have to wait too long. Sitting briefly on the bench Anna gazes at the view, the sea, a sad, sombre, leaden blue and the sky now growing darker with grey clouds, which gather across it.

Now there is practically no air to breathe. Anna is aware too she will need to take shelter if the storm breaks before Adam arrives – she can't leave until he does. The heavy drops of rain began to drip, drop, plop on Anna and gradually fall faster and faster. Anna gets up from the bench and makes her way to the small thicket just beyond the seat.

Standing just underneath the shelter of the trees on the edge of the thicket, Anna continues to wait. Turning her back away from the thicket, she stands facing forwards, watching along the footpath for him to arrive. The rain beats harder now on the leaves which shelter Anna, nudging her further into the thicket for cover.

Anna almost stumbles as she backs herself beneath the tree and gently rests her head against its solid trunk; she inhales the earthy smells of the freshly washed air from the ground and through the trees and leaves. She draws

in the sweet, intoxicating, gentle and peaceful
atmosphere as she leans back against the tree.

Anna begins to close her eyes as the man leaps forward
and grabs her, around her throat with one hand and
covers her mouth with the other. The black-gloved hands
drag Anna backwards into the denser part of the thicket.
She cannot breathe she is unable to move. She isn't
aware that she is grabbing a hold of and pulling at the
hands, tearing at them, trying to prise his hold off her
and twisting her body around to free herself from his
grip. Anna is petrified, shocked and stunned to her core
as the man pulls her down to the ground. His face now is
close up in front of her, hissing and spitting words at
Anna, obscenities, which she can't hear or understand.
Her mind now drowning deeper into a dark, black,
paralysed state.

Get up, she keeps telling herself, get up, but as she tries
to pull herself free, away from him, the man puts his
weight across Anna and holds her down on the wet
grass. "Shut up," Anna hears him, "Shut up or I'll kill
you."
He now holds the long, shining, steel blade in front of
her face, "Shut up or I'll kill you now." The man starts
ripping and pulling at Anna's skirt and grabs hold of her
knickers and begins to drag them down. He holds the
knife in front of her face until he forces himself inside
her. His body covers and suffocates her, as he pushes
harder and harder inside, ripping at her as he does so.

Anna tries to scream but the sound won't come out –
nothing will come out of her. The pain as he bangs and
bangs against her is unbearable and she begins to choke,
for want of air and freedom from this animal above her.
The darkness inside her begins to rise up in Anna until
all there is, is blackness, a heavy, dense, enveloping
darkness, which is suffocating her.

When Anna comes too she is curled up on the grass. She feels the rain still splashing on her. Is he still here? She dare not move, or look to begin with, until sensing that he is gone, and then Anna slowly uncurls herself and sits up.

What if people come? She has to get up she needs to get away. Anna stumbles to her feet. Trying to walk, she falls and looking down Anna spots her knickers wrapped around her ankles. She removes them and screws them up. Around her there is nothing, no one. Anna doesn't want anyone to see her like this. Her body hurts. Her back is in so much pain. She feels as if the man has put the knife up inside her and twisted it, cutting her and lacerating her, the pain burns and is deep inside her.

Anna scuttles away from the spot where the man has raped her, past the bench and back to the track, which leads to her caravan site. She walks as quickly as her battered body and stunned mind allow her. To get home, back to her caravan is all she wants, to be inside, to be safe.

Anna fumbles in her jacket pocket and finds her caravan keys and opens the door and stumbles inside quickly, closing the door behind her. Anna takes a deep breath and then begins to strip off her clothes and puts them in a black plastic bag to throw away. She fills the sink with cold water from the water butt and takes the wet flannel and puts soap on it and washes her mouth, face, hands and arms and rinses the flannel and washes her breasts and belly and then rinses it again to wash her body where he had entered and violated her. Anna swills the water away and rinses the sink. After drying herself she puts the flannel, towel and soap into the black bag and ties it up and throws it in the corner. After putting on her nightgown and dressing gown Anna begins to brush her hair. Filling the kettle from the water left in the butt she

makes a pot of tea and fills her hot water bottle and sits
on the seat beneath the large window.

The rain beats harder and harder on the caravan as she
clings on to her hot water bottle.

Anna nearly jumps out of her skin when the caravan
door opens and Adam walks in.
"Thank God" Anna tells her son.
"I'm sorry mam."
"It's alright." She says sharing her tea with him.
"Callum's mum said to stay until the rain stopped. I
wanted to come and meet you mam but I couldn't."
"It's alright, it's alright were safe now."

Anna finds dry clothes for her son and makes him
change. She puts on her shoes and refills the water butt.

Returning indoors Anna tells him, "Were going to stay in
for the rest of today now Adam."

After locking the caravan door and closes the blind in the
kitchen, she makes more drinks and a hot water bottle
each to warm them up. Adam plays on the floor with his
action men and she watches him whilst looking out of
the front window.

It pours down for the rest of that day and Anna only
finds peace curled up in her bed with another hot water
bottle, knowing that here she and her son are both safe.
Here no one can hurt them.

The ache in the small of her back eases with the hot
water bottle and she smears jell between her legs to
sooth the soreness and the sharp burning, aching pains,
deep inside her where he has put his filthy self. Anna
listens as the rain beats against the caravan and a low
wind moans against it as she closes her eyes. "I know

you," the voice whispers. "I know you, I know who you
are."

Darkness engulfs and overwhelms Anna as she falls
deeper and deeper into her terrifying nightmare, unable
to escape the heavy dark face next to hers. Anna listens
now to the obscenities and can understand them as they
pour out of his mouth. She tries to fall backwards away
from his closeness, wanting to escape the nightmare of
his oppressive weight but she is trapped.

The following day after breakfast Anna begins to clean
and tidy the caravan up. "Adam." Anna calls her son
before he escapes to his friends.
"What?"
"I want you to come back at 12 o clock. Listen to me."
Anna says holding her sons face so he will focus and
listen to what she wants him to hear. "Were going to the
beach to have a picnic."
"Ok." Adam beams at his mum, his huge open smile
warms the coldness of Anna's thoughts.
Anna returns the smile, still amazed at what power her
son's innocence has. "Right, off you go then."

Anna spends her time sorting out the caravan because
after their beach picnic she will be returning back to the
city with her son. She won't tell him about their return
until it's time to lock up the caravan when they set off to
the beach. Anna opens the window and then washes and
rinses out their clothes to leave on the clotheshorse. She
takes the black plastic sack to the skip parked further
away from her caravan. Making a neat pile on the small
seat, Anna covers their bedding with a plaid travel rug
and plumps up the cushions before sweeping and dusting
the sitting room.
Anna makes ham sandwiches and puts apples, crisps,
chocolate biscuits and four small cartons of fresh orange,
as well as Adam's bottle of water into a bag. She puts
the kettle and pan on for hot water and checks in her

store cupboard to see what tins are left. She removes the lid and washes the drops and clogged sauce off the neck of the tomato ketchup bottle and returns it to her store cupboard. She makes peanut butter sandwiches with the remaining bread and butter for Adam's return. The milk will be finished off with a few more pots of tea. Anna pours the scolding water from the pan into the bowl and half from the kettle and tops it up with cold water. By 11 o' clock the caravan is in order. Anna closes the kitchen blind and checks all of the windows, making sure that their catches are fastened down. 'All done.' Anna thinks as she sits on the seat in front of the window. 'Just this window to close and to fasten.' Anna tells herself as she looks out.

So here they are then. She cannot bring herself to think about what happened to her yesterday. This is too much for her to cope with. She will have to apologise to Jo about not turning up, for letting her down, but maybe because of the rain she wouldn't have expected them to call. What would she say to explain her absence? She would tell Jo the truth, that she had waited, but Adam hadn't turned up, so she'd returned to the caravan to wait for him and the rest of the day it had rained so they had stayed indoors. Jo would understand.

Anna stands up when she sees Adam weaving through the caravans on his return. He will be unhappy when she tells him about going home after the picnic but that's how it has to be. Anna closes and fastens the front window and hands her son the bag with his peanut butter sandwiches and carton of orange juice in.

"Right sweet heart. After we have had our picnic on the beach we'll have to start making tracks back."
"No." Adam says.
Anna coaxes him out of the caravan and after emptying the slops bucket and rinsing out her pot, she tells her son.
"Say goodbye until next time, to the caravan."

Adam is angry, upset and refuses to say his goodbyes but Anna knows unless he does he won't settle. The goodbyes are a closure, which Adam needs each time he leaves. She checks around the caravan, it is fine ready to be closed up. Anna picks up the little steps from outside and places them on the kitchen floor whilst Adam stands next to the cold-water tap eating his sandwiches.

"It's not fair." he exclaims as Anna finally pulls the caravan door too and locks it.

"Say goodbye."

"Goodbye." Adam spits out unhappily because he is being forced to leave his haven of freedom.

As Adam sets off to walk towards the beach path Anna calls, "No, we'll go through the town centre today Adam, we can pop into Mad Mick's and buy you some sweets and get an ice lolly."

"Can I have a pack of four ice cream lollies mum?"

"We'll see, we'll see, no promises."

Anna looks forward to returning to the city. There she can lose herself among the hustle and bustle of her busy daily life. He won't be there, Anna hopes. She will come back here, she has to return but not yet, she isn't ready yet, too much, too many things have happened. Anna needs space and time to think, reflect and to decide. 'Decide on what?' She isn't sure, not yet, it is too soon. But Anna knows in the end she will decide what to do. Anna has no choice but she does have time.

After a night of tossing and turning, waking to more rain Jo decides to have a quick breakfast. Afterwards she puts on her waterproof coat and wellies and with rucksack she braces herself against the wind and rain, setting off into town. She needs to focus on being productive, to actively engage with her ideas for the paintings; the weather will be what it is regardless, so no point dwelling on the negative. Walking head on into the wind, she convinces herself it's a good idea and looks forward to what she will return with. Once in the town centre's shops, she is happy that she has come. It is good to think about shopping and calling at different places for food items. She gets the heavy things first and puts them in the bottom of the rucksack. She buys bread, milk, a pasty, sausages, cold meat and cheese, enough to last a few days. Then goes to the £1 shop and Mad Mick's to buy the painting materials. She chooses a selection of brushes, a sketchpad, a box of oil paints and two small canvases and manages to fit these into the top of the rucksack.

On the way back the drains along the roads and pavements struggle to cope with the deluge of water running into them. Each time a car passes, it hits the water and surges up and splashes her from head to foot. Passing the homes with gardens along the way, she notices many with inches of standing water and hurries along. When at last she reaches the road out of town and towards the hut, she reflects on the weather forecast and hopes that they have got it wrong and dryer weather is on its way.

By the time she arrives at the hut, she is so relieved to be back and removes her coat and wellies to dry off. "It's no fun today out there." She tells Jason as she rubs herself with the towel. After unpacking the rucksack and putting the art materials in the workroom and food away she feels hungry and takes the pasty from the bag; she shakes it out onto a plate, it is all broken from the weight of the other things on top of it. Jason waits eagerly for his share. The short pastry is filling and packed with vegetables, it is well seasoned, tasty and still quite warm. She finishes with an apple and a drink of fruit juice. She will heat the chilli tonight, left over from yesterday and have it with corn chips that she remembered to buy in town.

Jo finds herself again captivated by the rain as she stares out of the window. As each new droplet hits the pane, it slides down and merges with other raindrops and joins the rivulets of water at the bottom of the sill. A mesmerizing process as her eyes look again to the top of the glass, to follow the next raindrop down, up and down, transfixed and hooked, she looks up and down again and again. Eventually she draws herself away with difficulty, her eyes wanting to attach themselves like glue to the never ending drops of liquid running down.

She turns her attention to the new paints and finds a flat piece of wood to mix the colours on and enjoys the gooey, thick splodges as she plays around mixing them together and then testing them out on the paper, thinning the paint by adding a little turpentine to the mixture. The messing around gives her ideas and inspiration and soon she is planning several pictures. Firstly she needs to sketch out on paper before putting any paint on the canvases.

As the day draws out, the daylight disappears and she has to stop and abandon painting for another day. So regretfully she turns her attention to heating food and making a pot of tea, still aware of the murky weather outside. The night is soon upon them and it's not long before she has to light the lamps, it's hard to image the sunshine and summer that was here not too long ago.

Sitting down in the chair with Jason at her side, she reflects and wonders if Anna and Adam will come tomorrow to collect the ship, she hopes so.

Leaning to the side of the chair, to pick up her book, she realises that she has taken it up to the bedroom; and is debating as to whether to go upstairs and get it, when Jason's ears prick up and he begins to growl. "What's wrong Jase?" Jo asks him, as he leaps up from his resting position. He races across to the doorway barking, jumping up and down frantically. She tries to listen between his barks to find out what has disturbed him. "Jason quiet." Jo shouts to no avail, as he continues his fervent jumping and barking. Something, somebody must be outside, but who or what? She goes across to the windows to check and looks out of the side window she cannot see anyone and quickly dashes to the other windows, surely there must be someone around, Jason is still barking ferociously; he knows that there is something outside the hut. Jo decides to let him out. He darts around the side of the hut to where the shower is. She can hear him scurrying around the back, by the trees, searching out whatever it is that has disturbed him. She follows him. In the flash of a second she is certain that she has seen someone, running around the edge of the garden, up towards the path to the road. 'Where is Jason?' "Jason, Jason." Jo shouts out, and then whistles. She can hear rustling around the back of the hut but dare not go and check. Waiting for him, she can hear footsteps disappearing up the path and the voice of a person shouting is nullified by his barking. This carries on for quite some time, whilst whoever it is reaches the road at the top and Jason's barking finally stops. 'Who the hell was that?' Jason returns as if grinning from ear to ear panting and gasping with his tongue hanging out. "Who was it Jase? Come on let's go inside."

Inside she cannot settle down, the intruder outside is still snooping around in her mind. Jason goes straight to his water bowl and takes in large gulps of water. 'Thank

God you were here Jason,' Jo thinks. 'But who was it?' She is unable to forget the incident and sits down. She is agitated, pacing around the hut, avoiding standing in front of the windows, wishing that she had curtains to pull across and wondering if the person will come back.

Eventually she cannot stand the feeling any longer, and is too scared to stay, she decides to leave the hut and puts on her coat, takes the torch and with Jason sets off; she has to get away.

Once on the path through the trees she cannot find solace in her actions, leaving the hut now fills her with fear, she feels too scared to carry on, but even more frightened to go back, she stands rigid and stuck, as she listens for footsteps. 'What now? What do I do now?' She stands and waits, Jason beside her wondering, what on earths going on. Hearing a rustle in the bushes behind her, she moves on quickly, with ears pricked listening to distinguish what it might be. Jason hurries off in front and Jo calls him back to stay close, as they carry on down through the dark, dense, foliage. She has to switch on the torch and keep it shining on the ground in case anyone spots it from afar. Their progress slows as they walk through the open field, she can hear the rushing sound of the sea and curses it, as it blocks out other sounds around. If another person is following she won't be able to hear. But Jason should, he did at the hut, 'so they will be all right,' she tries to convince herself. She walks on not really knowing where she is heading; she just knows that she doesn't want to be back at the hut, isolated in the dark. She carries on.

Jo now chastises herself for walking out, she should have stayed and gone to bed, that would have been the best idea. She is a fool; she would have been all right with Jason watching out. Yet she feels unable to return, the person might come back and be hanging around, snooping about, waiting and watching out for her.

Soon she is on the path to the bench and decides to sit
for a while. As she sits and thinks her mind starts to
churn and make sense of what's happened.

Her mind returns and rewinds the tape of the past. Could
it possible be, no it couldn't, the man that she ran away
from, maybe he has tracked her down and knows that
she is here, alone in this hut. Maybe he has found her.
Surely he can't have, how could he. NO, NO, NO.' How
will she know who it was, what would bring someone
out here watching her. She feels so fucking angry, what
if it was him. She wants to smash everything in sight.
She wants to smash this fucking bench and put her fist
through it, it is irritating the fuck out of her and she
wants to explode and shout, just fucking shut up, shut
up, just stop it. She can't get rid of this anger; it is
uncontrollable and bigger than she is. She wants to bang
her head against a wall, so hard that she can't think
anymore, she wants to hit it and hit it, so that it hurts so
much and then she can stop thinking. She smashes her
fist and hits out so that it hurts. She can't stand this
anymore it is eating her up. She doesn't know what to do
with it anymore, how does she make it go away? She
stands up and with Jason's lead in her hand she lashes
out and hits the wooden bench. Fucking leave me alone,
she rants and raves, over and over, hitting and hitting,
again and again.

Jason cowers down and creeps further away and then his
rough barking stops her and she turns around. Jason runs
off through the thicket.

Possessed with inhuman strength, as if her body has
taken on the might of a wild animal, she waits for its
prey, ready to launch and spring up and attack for its kill,
and enjoy the taste of the juices, as the ravages of anger
abate.

Looking down on herself from above, she moves away and walks on. Distancing herself, she leaves her former skin behind. Like a shadow fading away, the edges blurring and disappearing.

When the dawn breaks, she returns exhausted back to the hut and notices her hands and arms are raw, bleeding and sore. She fills the kettle and puts it on the camping stove to boil and washes herself in a bowl of warm water and makes a pot of tea. Jason is warily watching her then goes and lies on his bed. She is thirsty and parched and desperate for a drink. After pouring the rest of the hot water into a bowl she refills the kettle. Then gently sips her tea and adds a spoonful of sugar; she needs comfort, sweetness and warmth. When the water is ready she strips of her clothes, carefully washing her body all over and towels it dry. She puts the dirty clothing into the bowl when she's finished, to soak and transcends the staircase to put on fresh clean clothes. She washes out the items in the bowl then rinses them in clean cold water and hangs them on the backs of the chairs to dry. Afterwards she pours another mug of tea and sits down and rests, thinking of nothing, nothing at all.

Part 2

THE BEACH HUT

Jason's barking interrupts Jo's sleep. She groggily opens her eyes and listens, waiting and hoping for silence, but Jason's frantic climbing up and down the bottom stairs stirs her and in her dozy state she realises something is very wrong. "Ok Jase, I'm coming." Jo shouts and leaves her bed to find out what the problem is.

The room is dark and she tentatively reaches out to the bedside cabinet for the torch. Switching on its light she is conscious of a strange sound and wonders where it is coming from. Her gaze follows the torchlight down the stairs and the startled worried eyes of Jason meet hers as he creeps up the steps. Her concern for Jason prevents her from taking in the scene below. She tries to reassure him and feels the terror creeping in her voice. She's unable to take in the shocking sight, of dark, lapping water, touching the bottom steps and further away the whole floor appears to be covered in murky, black water.

Several ideas rush into her mind at once, maybe there is a leak in the roof, or has a window been left open, or the tap, did she leave the tap on? 'Oh my God, Oh no, what's happened?' Jo stares in disbelief and then tentatively descends the steps. When she reaches the bottom, she treads gingerly and dips her foot into the water and steps down to discover how deep it is. She can see something floating and sticking up out of the water. When her foot finally touches the floor she looks down and flashes the torch to see how far up her leg the water is. Jason behind her is whining and she cannot console him, the level is lapping just below her knee. 'Fucking hell, what's happened?' She cannot think, nor act; she doesn't know what to do and shines the torch towards the sink to check the tap, although she already knows that this is not the result of a dripping tap. The problem is beyond and outside the hut that's for certain. The rain is pouring down outside. Her body begins to shiver and tremble as she stands naked getting cold and her eyes take in the huge scale of the problem.

Jo decides to return upstairs and wait it out, she can't think of anything else to do, surely there's no way the water can rise up to the bedroom. "Come on Jase, come on up you go." She encourages Jason to climb the rest of the stairs and pushes his bottom from behind. Jason being a creature of habit always sleeps downstairs on his bed and hardly ever comes up to the bedroom, so he is reluctant. "You can't go back down there, Jase, go on up you go." She climbs into bed and pulls the duvet over, as her body shivers and shakes, she can't control it. She tightens her muscles to stop the movements and then lets go; this has the effect of increasing the twitching and trembling. What a nightmare, she wants to wake up and hope this hasn't happened; yet she knows that this isn't a dream, it is real, and the hut is flooded knee deep downstairs.

Jo spends the rest of the night, hoping and praying that the water will recede and turns angry with hate at the rain, which is still falling outside. 'Please stop,' she pleads into the darkness. As time expands to eternity she lies in wait for the dawn and daylight, to look again downstairs and test the level of the water. She worries with trepidation and fear, still shaky and cold. Jason at the side of her bed is nervous and also awake, unable to settle.

Eventually dawn begins to break through the dreadful darkness and she goes downstairs to test the water, her eyes take in with disbelief the sight before her. The force of the water has dislodged the chairs; she can only see the table. Black soot is leaking and spreading sludge from the belly of the stove. Floating on top of the water are pages from books and a rug and Jason's bed has ended up wedged across the workroom doorway. She can't bear to look, to see anymore of her worldly goods, her only possessions, her home here ruined and destroyed. Standing once again in the water that still reaches her knees, she senses something different now, not just the daylight, but the silence – she stands and listens for the noise, the sound of the rain, it's gone, there is an eerie silence, a still quiet deadness here in the hut.

She realises now standing here, her predicament for both of them – they will have to remain here until the water level drops. The weight of the water pressing on the door surely will make it impossible to open, and also outside of here it will be deep too. If she did try to open the door, it could let more water in. She wonders where the nearest dry land will be for Jason. Maybe she could get out via a window and help him through and then wade through with water, with Jason swimming by her side. She dismisses this as too risky and decides to wait it out, at least for a time anyway.

Returning to the bedroom she puts on warm clothing, at least they're safe up here. This time she sits with Jason at her side, stroking his black woolly coat for comfort and reassurance. The bleak and worrying situation leaves her in shock and she sits in a trance unable to muster any useful strategy. She is yanked backwards to other frightening and troubled times, as if her whole body has suddenly been sucked down into a black hole and is disappearing – losing her ability to think or feel, just a dull deadness, blanking out her mind. She remains so very still, hardly breathing and unable to move, to protect herself, to be invisible. If no one sees her or knows she is here, then they can't get her. Her body ready on high alert just in case, her psychic awareness her only antenna, looking and sensing for danger. Her ears picking out and checking every sound in the silence for the intruder, hoping and praying that she is safe and cannot be attacked from behind. The back of her neck is rigid and tingling, waiting and ready for the whisper and his breath to touch it. She cannot move, cannot speak. She sits and waits, still aware of the murky water lapping down below.

Daylight recedes to darkness and her growing physical discomfort of wanting to urinate forces her to move. She takes the torch again and steps down the stairs, the water although now receding is still just below her knee. The agony of holding her bladder which is at bursting point gives, she cannot hold on any longer, and is reduced to letting go. As her bladder slowly trickles and then gushes out, her eyes fill with tears and like a small child she starts to cry. The warm urine running down her legs feels curiously comforting, so glad for this letting go. She looks back and worries for Jason, he too must be desperate to go out – somehow she has got to find a way. "Stay there, Jason wait." She wades across the floor, swishing through the water towards the window, the jumpy torchlight flashing ahead. She reaches it and repeats her command, Jason is whining from his position on the stairs. She unhooks the catch and pushes the window out; the torchlight picks up the floodwater against the side of the hut. Flashing the torch further away, the same scene is lit, of water, water everywhere. She returns to the stairs and tries to console him. There is nothing she can do, but wait for the water to recede.

Much later when Jason wets himself on the bedroom floor she tell him it's ok, and she's glad, he is absolutely desperate and sorry. "It's ok Jase, it's ok." As nighttime advances they doze on and off until the light begins to filter again inside the hut. Thankfully, the water has dropped to a few inches now and she goes and tries the door, to her dismay it has swelled with the water and won't budge, she pulls at the handle frantically to no avail, she feels weak and frail, her energy is sapped and she gives up.

Anna unlocks the caravan door and hauls in the trolley full of groceries she's brought and takes off the sack she has on her back, filled with clothes and paper and the second hand book she's bought. Mark, Anna's eldest son, follows in behind her and pulls the door to.

"I'll unpack, and then I'll make something to eat."
"Right." Mark replies and takes out his pouch of tobacco and cigarette papers to roll himself a cigarette.

Mark is eighteen years old and in between bed sits and hostels. He is a master at destruction, mostly directed at himself, but he is pretty good too at creating chaos and trouble and confusion whenever he can and with whom ever he chooses.

Anna begins to unpack the groceries and opens the door and puts out the little steps. After rinsing out the water butt she fills it and then the kettle. As the water boils for tea she finishes putting her things away. Mark leans against the open door smoking, paying lip service to his mother's request for him not to smoke indoors.

Anna lights the oven and puts the cheese and onion quiche in to heat, "We'll have a tin of new potatoes with it." Anna tells her son as she pours out the boiling water to make their pots of tea.
"Right." is her son's response as he flicks his tab end onto the grass.

After the meal, Anna stacks the pots on the side next to the sink; she is too tired to do more. It is early autumn and the nights are drawing in and Anna knows she must make the beds before the blackness of nightfalls.

Anna senses the weight of her son's boredom, as she lay warm and exhausted in her bed. She hopes he will be too tired to go out, in the early hours on the prowl, but she feels too tired to stay awake to see if he does.

Mark hears his mother's breathing and knows he is safe to open the large front window, underneath where his mother has made his bed, to have a smoke. He draws in the smoke from his cigarette and pokes his head out of the window. 'What the fuck am I going to do here?' He hates this fucking place and always has, even when he was a boy and would come here with the family. The whole place is dead, dead and dull and boring and she had given him his talking too before they caught the train. 'This is going to be so fucking boring,' Mark tells himself as he takes his final drag and flicks his cigarette end out of the window.

Closing the window Mark settles into his sleeping bag. He is tired and it is warm and dark so he might as well sleep if he can.

As they sleep another shower begins to splash and splat against the caravan. A wind has risen and the night grows cold and dark as the clouds cover and darken the autumn sky.

Margaret wakes with a start and squashes her pillow
with her left hand as she lay on her side, in order to read
the bedside clock. The illuminated digits display 4:00.

She closes her eyes to pull herself back once again into
the arms of sleep but is unable to drift back off; she
senses that she is here on her own. She turns over onto
her left side to seek her answer, yes, he isn't here.
Charles is missing. Margaret is used to her husband's
insomnia and inability to sleep the night through. He is
always wandering the house and whatever else she never
knows. So it is no surprise that she finds herself alone in
bed. She enjoys sleep and always regards it as part of her
beauty treatment, she always manages eight hours and
can always fall back to sleep, in spite of Charles's
frequent tossing and turning and getting up.

She listens to the heavy downpour of rain hitting the
window and wants to escape, let her mind digress and
fill with fantastical fantasies, she wants to take these
back inside her dreams and escape into a wonderland,
another world completely. She feels happy to wallow
and enter into her imagination as her eyes close. She
abandons herself behind their dark black shutters.

The warmth of the bed underneath her and the duvet
covering her body cocoons her and heightens her
movements. She rolls onto her back and notices as she
strokes her naked legs across the sheet how sensuous it
feels. She continues to spread and stretch and stroke her
left leg and then her right and as she does so, slides her
arms beneath the duvet to explore her body. She enjoys
the languid, fingertip touch and sweeping as she draws
her hands across her large breasts that sag heavily at
each side. She cups and lifts each one in turn and pushes
it towards her centre, 'I am a curvaceous woman'.
Letting her right hand travel further down, she stops as
her finger finds her tiny belly button and then the
curving swell of her stomach.

She continues with her right hand and as her fingers meet the soft cushion of hair she quickly draws back to ease her left breast that is trapped between her side and then with left hand on right breast she gently strokes and pulls at her erect nipple. Again and down again. As she returns her right hand down, she squeezes and cups her buttocks and eases her legs wider apart, to allow the tops of her legs to open.

With fingers eager, she finds her moist and open vaginal lips and strokes the soft top of her clitoris, she wants to find an easy rhythm that will excite her, that will bring her to the edge of her climax and yet not allow herself to come. She has time now and there is no need to rush, she doesn't want a quick and urgent satisfaction, she wants to give herself what she needs, she is a woman after all.

In Jo's paralysed state she is incapable of action, too much has happened recently, that she feels a shadow of her former self. Her aliveness has disappeared and she has difficulty remembering who that other self was, the self that engaged passionately with living and suffused with energy, could tackle almost anything. She is desperately trying to connect and find that person inside of her, to help her find a way out of this troubled mess – the appalling state of the hut and the mental turbulence that has resurfaced and reminds her of her former life before she came here. What can she do? Her coping strategies seem to have left her and death looms all around. Her body feels full of the murky waters, it is stagnant and the pool no longer glistens and is clear and fresh. The salty taste and tang of the sea that crystallized and cleansed her has vanished to some other land. She is treading the stilted marshes, stuck and sucked into the deep, cloggy and sinking mud. The damp, earthy, musty smell, permeates and enters her pores and that is what her tongue finds as it licks across her lips. This place is contaminating her and she must get out, where to, where can she go?

"Come on Jase, let's get out of here," Willing herself up from the step she wades across to the window and lifts up the catch and pushes the pane out. She squeezes through the gap and Jason whines and barks to remind her not to leave him. "Don't worry Jase you're coming too," She tells him as she stands in the wet mud outside. "Come on then, up you get," She urges him to the ledge of the window. Jason puts both front paws onto the ledge and she lean inside to grab his backend and pull him through. After a couple of goes she succeeds and Jason joins her and with a leap into the air and a brisk shake he splashes through the water relieved to be back outside.

Jo surveys the scene and her heart sinks, what was her vegetable garden is no longer, the healthy, green foliage, of only days ago, is now a mushy inedible mess. In the greenhouse there are a few red tomatoes on the plants, but she knows that they will soon start to rot with too much water in the pots. She opens the squeaky door and helps herself to a couple of handfuls. Jason returns and reminds her of his hunger and his missed meals, she realises that his dried food will probably be somewhere immersed under the water in the kitchen and she tries to think what she can give him. She needs to get back inside and find something for both of them. This is more difficult, trying to step over the herbs in the window box. The few extra inches she has to stretch across, means finding some extra inner strength. After landing with a splash she looks around the kitchen and scans her memory for the foodstuffs she keeps on the highest shelves. She knows that there are jars of dried fruits and nuts and a few tins, although there is not much she can do with those. Also she keeps a container of biscuits and crackers, these should be ok.

Treading carefully through the water in the kitchen, her feet become tangled up in the floating debris and sludgy mud and again a sense of despair rises within her. She looks on the higher shelves and finds glass jars and tins that are ok and selects a can of tuna, the can opener and a bowl from the kitchen drainer, and pours the contents into it and then adds a large handful of biscuits and crackers from the tin, these will do for Jason. She takes another bowl and fills it with dried fruits, nuts and biscuits. Satisfied with finding a meal at least, she gathers the bowls and climbs back out through the window again. Jason can hardly wait for her to struggle outside; he is desperately hungry and jumps up to the bowls as she picks them up from the window ledge. "Here you go then Jase." He wolfs his food down in a few seconds and looks up for more. Jo slowly eats hers although without the same relish, her mind is too disturbed to feel hungry, she manages the nuts and fruits and some of the biscuits and gives the rest to Jason. 'Well that's a start,' She thinks and then decides she must go down through the garden and towards the beach to check and see the extent of the flooding.

Apart from the obvious clinging debris, around the base of the bushes and trees and the mud under foot, the land looks the same, the swaying branches and the green expanse of leaves above show no signs of the past flood. The heavy bunches of apples, pears and plums hold out hope that all is not lost. The growing roar of the sea is a pleasant and welcoming sound, increasing as they wind their way down the paths towards the cliff top, the seagulls soaring in the sky above, screech and dip towards the land. Jo notices as she looks around, beyond the main channel of flooding, where the water is still a few inches deep, there are areas further away from this that have escaped and are green and lush and untouched by the mud and debris. She wonders if the hut is the only dwelling to have been affected.

As they turn and meet the path along the cliff top she is amazed by what she sees, there are two, huge, fresh, dark terracotta chunks of earth at the edge where the land has slipped down and taken part of the footpath with it. As she ventures hesitantly and carefully towards it, she can see down on the beach where the land has dumped itself in a heap at the bottom. The tide below is quietly receding and few people are on the sand. She issues words of caution to Jason and is filled with a fleeting sense of relief as he stands by her side. After many minutes of standing and staring down the crevice and looking at the mound of earth below, they walk on towards the bench. Approaching the thicket, there are two bollards and red tape blocking the footpath and she wonders as she peers through the bushes, if more of the cliff has succumbed to the might of the flood. Unable to go any further she turns around and they make their way back home.

Retracing their steps past the cliff erosion, Jo stops once more.

"Thank you, thank you." these words she utters to whoever is her guide out there, looking over and protecting her. Feeling sheltered and in the arms of her saviour, they slowly make their way back. The rain subsides now and the heavy, dark skies lift and crack apart slightly as shafts of light begin to break through, so too her inner barometer shifts from darkness to light. Her feet absorb the strong, sure, welcome energy, from the ground beneath them and draw it up through her legs, which propels her forward with a newfound strength. The exhilarating elation that comes from surviving a near miss, a catastrophe side stepped, of escaping disaster and death, or being party too it, lifts and raises her up and out of body, to the lighter clouds above. Her head and body are soaring and know that whatever happened she's survived and is still here, alive and real and part of this earth and belongs.

The treading through mud and thick, matted, clogged up grass, draws her back down from the skies above and to the earth and she makes her way home. "We'll be ok Jase, we're all right, we can do it, can make everything ok again, we've done it before, we'll be ok."

Back at the hut, she again tries to push the door to open it. Although it has swollen, she can see that if she scrapes away some of the debris and mud, then it just might shift. So she goes to the back of the hut where she keep the garden tools and finds the spade and begins shovelling up the slurry and dislodged rubble around the front of the door and chucks it to one side. Eventually there is enough clear space to push the handle and door once more, after several attempts at jiggling and pushing; she manages to open it. 'Well that's something,'

Inside the hut she's able to survey the damage and the extent of the clean up necessary, to regain order and habitability for both of them. The sight before her is overwhelming, she doesn't know where to begin, and she just knows that it is going to take a huge amount of time, probably more than she can give on her own. Just the task of getting rid of the sludge and flood damaged belongings fills her with dread, where can she take it, to get rid of it? And where do she begin?

The first job Jo decides upon is to search the shelves and cupboards and discard anything that has been contaminated with the floodwaters and then put the rest that's ok up on the higher shelves. Hopefully there will be something to salvage and keep. She soon realises the difficulty she is faced with, when she is soon covered in black, filthy mud. How on earth, when everything is sorted is she going to clean this place? She pushes the thought out of her mind, believing it to be unhelpful and negative and not productive to the task in hand and carries on. Because of the difficulty of soiling the jars and tins etc with dirty hands, she has to keep filling a bucket with fresh water to clean herself during the process.

After a few hours of toiling away, she takes outside the rubbish and water damaged goods, in the hope of seeing progress in her efforts. She is saddened to loose the rugs and armchair, her thoughts to try and clean them soon give way when she dips the rug into clean water and she can see that the fibres are completely black and will never wash out. The kitchen chairs and table should be ok when they dry out, she will be able to sand and paint them, so she lifts the chairs up onto the tabletop to dry. She is sorry to see pages of her books covering the floor, washed out from the bottom shelves of the bookcase and decides to leave the floor until last, as it is still covered in sludgy water and will be a huge task in itself. The packets of dried foods and powders have washed into the flood water and she is so glad that she's used lots of glass storage jars for most of the food stuffs and these are ok, so she puts them on the higher cupboard shelves.

Making her way into the workroom she is shocked by what she sees. The lone survivor is Adam's 'Purple Pearl – Pirate Ship' lolling on its side on the bench. She is instantly irritated for leaving her stock of paints and brushes on the lower shelf of the bench near the floor, along with the finished pebbles and boats. The little coloured boats are no longer sea worthy but have capsized and sank to the bottom of their sea. The gaily-colourful flotilla that greeted her upon entry into here is gone and the purple sails of the pirate ship upon the bench looms eerily out, a stark reminder of what has happened. She cannot bear to look anymore and retreats back into the living room.

Jo knows that everything upstairs is ok and feels tempted to rush upstairs and away from this murky mess, but realises that if she does she will dirty the bedroom, so there is no point, so she presses on. She hasn't a clue as to what time it is but the message sent from her stomach tells her that it is hungry and needs to eat. She is aware too of Jason, who is spending his time outside, occasionally coming in to see that she is still here - he will need food. His dried food has been washed into the water and she knows that she will have to make a trip into town to replenish their food stocks. She looks herself up and down and knows that she cannot go into town in this filthy mess. So she fills another bucket of water and tries to clean her hands, arms and face, and covers herself up with a coat and boots. Fortunately she keeps her money on a high shelf and takes some along with the bag hung up in the doorway. She will have to walk into town, her bike although dirty should survive once cleaned off and oiled, but she hasn't time to do that just yet.

After calling for Jason from lower down the garden she sets off and takes the route up to the top road and struggles through the bushes, matted with debris then pushes her way through the gate at the top. Walking into town along the road there is further evidence of the flood; lots of patches of gravel and silt and some of the edges of the road have been washed away. Further along to the Junk Shop, she notices the usual outdoor display of bric-a-brac has been removed and there is a skip parked up in the car park, full of old cupboards, chairs and clutter. And then along down past the housing estate, with furniture piled up in the front gardens and sandbags placed by the doors. Gosh, she's not the only one then, she feels relieved almost by this thought. She quickly goes to the Pet Shop and buys dried food and biscuits for Jason and then calls at the Supermarket, to buy a pint of milk, a sandwich, a packet of biscuits and a cake and cereal bars. With a full and heavy load she returns home.

She is ravenous now and soon eats the sandwich and a hefty wedge of the cake and gives Jason a large bowl of dried food, which he wolfs down greedily. "Now what Jase, what's next?" He wags his dirty tail, happy and oblivious to the dire situation they are both in. "It can't get any worse than this surely, Jase, can it?" Jo chats to him as she glances around and decides on what next to clean. She's aware that she will have to have a shower and clean herself as best she can before it becomes too dark. Jason will have to sleep on the bottom step tonight. She can't allow him upstairs again, because his coat is covered in dirt. She starts the slow, laborious process, of shovelling the sludge from inside the doorway; the hut although drying out a bit, is beginning to smell rather foul.

Soon daylight turns to dusk and she is deflated by the small area that she's cleared of mud, what a mammoth task this is going to be. She must take a shower and clean herself up before going to bed. The problem is how does she keep her feet dry and clean? When everywhere is caked in mud. She undresses and takes soap and her wellies to the shower and stands underneath the trickle of water coming out of the hose and showers as best she can. Although the water manages to wash a patch of the floor, the surrounding area is thick with mud. So she stands for a moment to let the water run off her body and then steps into the wellies and goes back inside. She fills the kettle and lights the camping stove to make a well-earned pot of tea. She has done enough for today and recognises that she needs to conserve energy, to be able to tackle the clean up. So she cuts another piece of cake and opens the packet of biscuits to enjoy with the tea and then settles down for the night.

During the early hours, she is again woken by the sound of heavy, pounding rain hitting the roof, this noise is no longer comforting, she is not cocooned and safe, curled up and snuggled in the warmth of her cosy bed. She is floating on a life raft, being washed around the shore, conscious of the depth of water all around, lapping and soaking and seeping through her skin. Her body is tired and hurting, the rain rods, fierce and relentless, jabbing and soaking her soft and flabby limbs. The blown up raft, tipping and swaying with the rush of the waves is hurtling and churning, as she tries to hold on. How much longer can she endure this hellish nightmare, how much longer can her hands grasp the ropes of the rubber dinghy, when they are red, raw and encrusted with salt. Then she is unable to grip and hold on for her life, she is upturned, drowning and sinking and being pulled down through the surf, desperate for breath. As the current tosses and turns and swishes her around, she opens her eyes and there are bubbles rising up through the water before her and she is being sucked down and down. And then with a panic and a jolt she wakes up, fighting for breath, yanking off the duvet, to take in a huge, lungful of air. Her hair is stuck to her head and she is covered in sweat, and then she is cold and shaky and pulls back the duvet to keep warm.

Later as she slips again into dreamland, she is laying against the towering cliffs, battered, bruised and bleeding, with salt stinging her open wounds. She can hear the squawking sound of the seagulls, excitedly landing at her side, hopping and flapping and waiting for her disintegration and their next meal. She can hear the rush of the tide coming closer; as she opens her eyes she sees water through sandy crystals, getting ready to wash her away. She awakes once again, as the water laps around her and the rain above is still pelting down. This time she cannot turn over and return to the myriad of dreams.

However bleak it sounds out there she needs to get up and begin again the process of cleaning up. She dresses in yesterday's dirty clothing and goes downstairs and greets Jason, praising him for sleeping on the step. She starts by filling the kettle and makes a hot drink; after giving Jason his food, she munches a couple of cereal bars. Luckily although it is raining hard, there is no sign of any water, coming in through the doorway. "Let's hope the rain stops Jase."

The daunting task ahead of her seems almost impossible today, when it's raining outside. It's no good going in and out of the hut with the slurry, because that will bring more mud inside. After contemplation, she decides the best thing to do, is to start in the furthest corner of the hut, away from the door. If she can clean this, she will feel that she has achieved something and at least part of the hut will be habitable. So with this in mind, she begins with the shovel, scraping and then brushing the dirt into a bucket and then pouring it near the doorway. After working away, she is able to see the stone flag floor underneath and is staggered by how deep the flood level has been. The watermark on the wall is level with the second step of the staircase. She carries on shovelling and moving the sludge, until the mound near the front of the hut declares a halt, this will need to be taken outside before she can add anymore. Although she has worked hard and achieved a clear corner, there is a mammoth task ahead.

Jo is aware of her hunger and again at the state of her appearance, she is filthy all over, her hands are black. She will have to walk into town to the shops for something to eat. The rain is still pouring, so she takes a bar of soap outside and washes herself as best she can. The cold rainwater, icy against her skin, startles and shocks and takes her breath away, so she quickly rubs on the soap and cleans off as much of the dirt as she can and then dashes back inside to dry off. She is frozen. There is no point in using a towel to dry herself, as there is nowhere for it to dry. So she shakes and jumps up and down, willing her skin to warm up and dry. Jo finds dry, clean clothes and puts on a warm, fleece top, and feels a bit better. She can now go into town and buy something to eat. She is so hungry now, the work has been hard and energy sapping, she needs something substantial inside her stomach to satisfy her. "Come on Jase, we'll go for some fish and chips today."

Walking into town, she can already taste the salt and vinegar and the crunchy batter and flaky fish. The thought of the food propels her in the direction of the town centre. Jason waits outside as she buys fish and chips with mushy peas and a bread cake. She takes this to one of the tables outside, under cover of the large awning. The food tastes like one of the nicest meals of her life, she is so thankful for the readiness, each mouthful filling a void, so hot and direct, entering, satisfying and warming her up. After the lunch she calls at the bakers and buys a pasty, bread rolls, a tub of pasta salad and also a carrot salad and then bobs into Martins butchers and gets two slices of cooked roast beef; she can make sandwiches tomorrow with this. These purchases will keep her going for a couple of days. On the way home, she realises that she needs a packet of cereal for breakfast, so instead of walking all the way

back to the health food shop, she calls into the
supermarket, on the outskirts of town and buys a box,
plus another pint of milk.

With her rucksack full, she is satisfied that if the rain
clears up, she can make good progress in the days ahead.
Walking along the main road she curses, when spray
from the traffic soaks her legs and Jason's coat. Nearing
the lay-by, she notices a parked car by the gate and
wonders who it belongs to. As she gets closer she
recognises it as Stella's vehicle. Her heart skips a beat
and as she opens the gate, her feeling of optimism
subsides, when she sees rivulets of water, again running
down the path. 'Oh no, not again, please no.' Her boots
sink and squelch, as she steps in and out of the mud and
heaves herself forward. Jason runs off ahead, pleased to
be away from the traffic. Walking towards the front
door, she spots Stella, coming around from the far side
of the hut.

"My God, Jo, are you alright? When I looked through
the window and saw the state of everything, I was
beginning to get really worried when you weren't here,
how awful, are you ok?" she asks.
"Well yes, I am, were ok aren't we Jason. I just wish it
would stop raining, it's coming down the path again like
a stream."
"The forecast isn't good; I think it's going to carry on for
the rest of this week, I'm sorry to tell you."
"I'll just put my shopping inside; you had better not
come in because the floor is a real mess."

Jo opens the door and the mound of cloying mud lies
before them. Seeing the sight through Stella's eyes, she
too is shocked by the scene.

"Oh Jo, what an absolute mess, look at it, what's that
pile of earth doing there?"

"It's the mud from the floor, I couldn't take it outside because of the rain, I'll have to wait for it to stop, before I can put it on the garden."

"Oh Jo, you can't stay here, you can't live here in this, you'll never clear all this up on your own, especially in this weather."

"I will be ok when the weather picks up; it's just not helping with the rain still coming down."

"You can't stay here, how can you cook and eat and keep clean?"

"I have an outdoor shower round the back of the hut and I managed to wash today in the rain."

"You are joking, showering outside in this weather, you're kidding me. You are serious aren't you, my God Jo, you're unbelievable, you must be mad."

"Not really, if it hadn't been for the flood I would be fine and clean and cooking on the stove and warm here."

"What are you going to do?"

"I'll just have to hope that the rain stops and I can clean the hut up and get back to normal, my vegetable garden has been destroyed so I'll have to buy food from the shops which is a shame, but these things happen, we'll be ok."

"No Jo, you can't stay here in this, it's impossible."

"I don't have an option do I? So that's it, I'm here, this is my home, and I'll sort it out somehow."

"Look I'll try and see what I can do, in the meantime if you need to have a bath or a shower, you are welcome to use mine, that's the least I can do."

"Oh your ok, there's no need, I will be ok honestly."

"There's no way I could stand being here for an hour, it doesn't bear thinking about, I know were all different, but bloody hell Jo, you can't possibly think you can clean this place up on your own, it's never going to dry out." Stella's words hit hard and a touch of realism strikes a cord of truth and hurts.

"You might be right but this if all that I've got, so I have to try and keep on trying." Jo says more quietly this time.

"Look Jo, leave it with me, I'll sort something out, I'll make a few phone calls and see what I can do."

"It's ok Stella there's no need to put yourself out, I'll manage somehow."

"What's all this about being a martyr for God's sake, give me your phone number and then I can ring you later."

"I haven't."

"Don't tell, me you haven't got a phone either."

"No I don't have a need for one here."

"Everyone has a phone, what about in an emergency like now, stuck here in the middle of nowhere, you're something else Jo you are. Don't worry, I'll pop back when I've sorted something, are you sure you'll be alright until then?"

"Yes I will, I'll be ok, you don't need to worry." And with that Stella quickly turns and takes the boggy path, back up to her car.

After Stella walks away and up the path, her words churn around inside of Jo's head. Maybe she is right, that she cannot live here and that she will be unable to manage cleaning the hut on her own. She was ok until Stella came and put doubts inside her mind. Looking around and seeing it from her perspective, she does have a point. But what choice have she got? She's here, this is her home and she must try and sort it out, she doesn't really have anyone else. She had felt, that maybe Anna would become a good friend whom she could trust and share things with, but what has happened to her? Maybe she has been flooded too. What ideas will Stella come up with, where has she dashed off to? Jo should have insisted that she will be ok and will sort things out on her own.

Does she really want Stella taking over and organising her life? She can still maintain the idea that she can manage on her own, if she does come back with plans for her to move elsewhere. It is a tempting thought, to be plucked, rescued and taken from here to comfort, away from this damp and dirty mess, but that would be giving up and giving in and this doesn't rest easily with her, she has come too far for that. Life's challenges meet us head on and we can crumble and die, or accept and move on from them. This has been her mantra and she doesn't want to change it now. 'So come on, keep on going, keep on trying to clean this place up and ride this storm out.'

Propelled by these thoughts, she begins again, dragging wet rugs and Jason's bed and dumps them outside in the continuous rain. When the weather picks up she can burn them, have a bonfire that will get rid of some of this rubbish. So she carries on working through the hours of the day, with purpose and commitment. She has always been self-reliant and has had to look after herself from an early age, and is used to struggling and managing on her own. Having had to do that, has given her belief and strength, to tackle whatever life throws up and somehow work her way through it, so she'll carry on and do it. She continues until the daylight begins to fade and puts a pan of water on the camping stove to boil. She cannot face another cold shower outside, so she fills the bowl up with hot water and washes her body as best that she can. And then refills the kettle and makes well-earned mugs of tea. She is so glad that she had the fish and chips earlier and is not so ravenous now; she makes a sandwich with the beef and has a piece of cake too.

After the food Jo goes upstairs to bed, she is so tired now and needs warmth and comfort and pulls the duvet over her head. This allows her to forget the mess downstairs as she snuggles, fairly contentedly, in a foetal position and softly drifts off into a deep, deep, sleep.

She is undisturbed by the rain and wind and sleeps through the night and wakes late the next morning. She has difficulty pulling herself out of the dozy state that the nights sleep has left her with. She doesn't want to leave the comfort of the bed, its warmth and safety wills her to stay. Eventually she gets up and quickly dresses in the dirty clothes and has breakfast and tea. Jason greets her with his tail wagging and bounces over to his food corner waiting to be fed. She gives him his dried food with hot water and makes another pot of tea. The tea stirs her and she looks around to decide what to do next. The small area of floor that she cleaned yesterday encourages her on, to scrape and brush some more and after letting Jason out into the garden she begins.

The rain is falling steadily, however the sky is not as dark and grey as the previous days, maybe the weather is breaking, she hopes so. There is no point in having a wash, so she brushes her teeth and makes a quick dash to the outside toilet and hurries back. In spite of the rain, she starts by shovelling the pile of mud inside the doorway and hurling it, on what was the vegetable patch, if she can reduce this down, she can work her way towards the door. Jason thinks this is a game and with each throw of the shovel he charges to where the heap lands and digs away with his front paws, at least he is happy. The pile is soon dispersed on the garden and Jo feels that progress has been made and takes a break. After washing her hands she makes another mug of tea; and eats the pasty and the last piece of the cake, sharing some with Jason, who sits and drools by her side. "We'll need to go shopping again Jase." She can eat the pasta and carrot salad tonight with bread and then tomorrow she will have to go into town.

Jo thinks of the plums and apples outside on the trees and has a sudden flash of inspiration, remembering her intention of jam making and preserving. She pictures the hot stove and bubbling preserving pan and thinks, 'why didn't I think of it earlier?' and chastises and berates herself – 'The stove. If I light it, the heat will dry the mud on the floor and the walls of the hut.' Sometimes she wonders how stupid she is, 'why didn't I think of it sooner?' and then quickly feels deflated, when she realises that she hasn't got any dry wood to put on it. 'Blast.' She's going to have to wait until the rain has stopped and the woodpile has dried out before she can light it. 'Plod on, just carry on, things will get better.' With these thoughts she takes up the shovel and continues.

Later on in the day, Jason's sudden barking startles Jo, breaking into her private world. There are footsteps approaching the hut. She puts down the spade and walks towards the doorway to see who is coming. The grey head and stout body of Charles, clad in a long brown coat and blue wellingtons, approaches the doorway.

"Charles to the rescue, Jo, Stella sent out an SOS and told me what has happened; she said we can't have you staying here in this, so I'm here to help." Charles takes in the sight of the hut and shouts. "Bloody hell, Jo, Stella wasn't kidding was she, she's absolutely right, you can't possibly stay here in this, you'll never clean this place up."
"I'll be ok, when the rain stops it will be easier to sort out then."
"Look you're not staying here, and that's that, I've got a flat in town that's empty, you'll be doing me a favour, so gather your things together and I'll take you, just look at the state of you, no strings attached come on."
Jo's argument and intention to stay, feels thwarted and no longer has credibility; she knows that in all honesty both Charles and Stella are right; she is fighting a losing battle here on her own.
"Are you sure, I will pay you, I'll stay until the weather takes up, and as soon as I've cleaned the hut I will come back."
"Look Jo I've made you the offer so take it, get your things together and I will drive you there." Charles insists.

Jo realises once more, that being around Charles and his powerful impact and pushy, rushed behaviour, doesn't allow oneself to think. 'Shall I go, what do I do, what do I take, and what do I need?'

"Come on, come on, just grab a few things." Charles orders.

She can't just leave without anything; she knows that she can come back for other things later. She dashes upstairs and takes clean jeans, a t-shirt and a pair of trainers. She hesitates and considers her journals and personal belongings, and decides to return later to collect them. Going back downstairs, she takes her money and bankcards and Jason's food.

"Come on Jo, you can come back later for the rest of your things." Charles speaks impatiently, he is ready to leave, he is already focusing on more important business matters that need his attention.

Charles waits outside whilst she puts her few belongings into the rucksack, along with Jason's food. She has a quick glance back across her shoulder and follows him out. How does this man have such a dominant impact and control? She wonders, as she walks behind him, feeling like a lost sheep and leaves her home behind.

Margaret returns to her bedroom and opens the vast
wardrobe to decide what to wear. After a futile search
across the hangers, she is unable to find suitable attire
for her morning outing. As her hand runs across the
fabrics, she is drawn to the comfortable and often worn,
linen suit. She removes it from its hanger and decides
she needs to add a few more garments to her collection.
Appearing smart and well turned out is most important
and she does not want to be seen in the same old thing
she has worn several times before, it is not the done
thing. Due to her various social functions and gatherings
and rare outings with Charles, means she has to change
her outfits and update her wardrobe on a regular basis.
Autumn is approaching and she needs to be ready and
ahead of the game.

She will drive on to Thornby after the mornings Towns
Women's Group meeting, and call at her favourite dress
shop Carol's and buy one or two things. She knows how
important it is to present herself well – as the wife of one
of Fenton's upper echelon she has to maintain her
position and project it for all to see. 'If only they knew,'
she thinks to herself – 'Charles, the great Charles, the
man himself, oh if only.'

Reaching inside her underwear drawer, she takes out a
pair of stockings and sits on the edge of the bed. She
tucks her toes into the rolled up stocking and pulls it up
her sleek right leg, she always maintains this softness
with regular waxing and allows plenty of time at the
beauticians for her treatments. She adores and has a
passion for French lingerie and always wears a matching
set. The lovely sensation and intimate touch of the fine
denier as it rises up her thigh warms her and as she clicks
the top onto the dangling suspender belt, it fulfils her.
She repeats the joy with her left leg and then slips on her
linen skirt – the pleasure and enjoyment she derives from
feeling the lining of the skirt, sliding up and down her
stocking legs, will take her through the day. Looking

again into the wardrobe, she picks a pair of navy mules from the shoe rack and steps into them.

Turning, she sees her reflection in the long full-length mirror, wearing her skin coloured, lacy bra and skirt, she pauses for a moment and then puts her hands through her hair and ruffles it slightly. 'If only Charles,' she thinks. She cups her breasts and holds them, pressing them close together, to emphasize her cleavage; she leans forward towards the mirror, holding her chin up as she does so. 'If only Charles,' she muses once again.

As her eyes stray back up from breasts to hair, she tilts her head and wonders if she requires a slight trim maybe even a re style. She must check her diary and make an appointment with Celia and ask her what she thinks, maybe a few bronze highlights, maybe just one or two to give it a lift. Celia would know, she always does, of how to add a little extra finesse to Margaret's hair. Margaret is fortunate to have strong hair with a natural curl that could be restyled and easily managed on a daily basis. She always books an extra appointment if she has a special evening engagement to attend. With a last lingering look, before she puts on the raspberry coloured blouse, she is secretly satisfied with her curvy and well-rounded body. 'Oh Charles,' she ponders as she puts her arms through the sleeves of the soft cotton blouse followed by the jacket. She takes a silk scarf from the array of scarves and folds it double and ties it around her neck. She opens the top tray of her jewellery box and chooses a pair of pearl earrings, leaning sideways she pops them on and takes her gold watch and checks its time against the bedroom clock, before slipping it around her wrist. She picks up her navy handbag and puts in her purse, checking it for cards and cash and then adds her mobile phone, a fresh handkerchief, lipstick and perfume. With a last look in the mirror to check herself and a quick comb of her hair, she is ready to go.

Looking out of the window – the day is rather grey and overcast; she hopes it won't rain again. She takes her umbrella and raincoat just in case.

Almost ready – she does her mental checks of everything, over and over again, to make absolutely sure she has prepared for every eventuality and then she leaves the house.

Anna now has a mixture of so many disturbed feelings, which have brought and hurried her back to the coast. Her son is one of them and the most pressing; she has had to rescue him yet again, from being lynched by a gang of angry young men and boys. This time he had come to her absolutely frantic and out of his head, saying he wanted money and needed to get away now, right away or he'd be killed. He had run into one of the members of the drug dealer, who he had double-crossed, and who was after him. "Your dead," the young man had told him and after delivering the message, Mark had head butted him. He had run back to his mother and she had managed to calm him down and not let him run away and contacted Mark's father.

It seems to Anna that her life has become one long endless round, a collection of crisis, which her two son's are involved in and which she has to somehow extract them from and try to bail them out of. When one of her son's appears to be making a little progress from one particular crisis or situation, then the other would find himself in another predicament. She realises, is aware that it never ends. That there isn't anytime really, when there isn't trouble or bother with either of her son's. Even Adam, for all his learning disabilities, would land in trouble if it weren't Mark, her eldest son.

She wants to step out of it all, away and start again but the never ending crisis, always bring her back to book, to answer for her sons in one way or another. Anna feels weary. Deep down, inside, she knows she will never be free from these troubles. Since the boys were young it had always been this way. In the early days, Anna hadn't been so aware or understood the signs of her son's disturbing behaviour. They were young, still adapting, growing up in a difficult world, her beautiful boys. Damaged children, from damaged families, who Anna and her husband had adopted, so many years ago. Mark first, Adam two years later. Not blood brothers but brothers by being adopted. Anna felt and held the guilt of letting her sons down. Of not being equal to them, or not being able to meet their endless needs.

Until Anna had spoken to the child psychologist, she hadn't understood why her son's behaved as they did, except to accept the responsibility that she had failed them. She had tried hard to give her son's the love, support and structure that they needed to live their lives. Anna had never been aware that she had put any expectations of hers onto either of them. She would and had and did support and defend her son's and lied, grovelled, begged and pleaded for them. Not once, or twice, or a thousand times, but always, never endingly, always.

She is worn out and exhausted, just racing through daily life, to keep standing still, not going anywhere, not flying off – her son's did that – just surviving daily life. This is where she put so much pressure on herself and son's –to live daily life, being normal. Her family life isn't normal but an individual collection, of damaged broken people, trying not to teeter and fall onto the periphery of life. To end up outcast and complete outsiders, sociably unacceptable members of society, but of course they are. Anna knows that her son's have become the children and young people that her mother would have kept her away from. She still can't accept after all she has done, to try to raise her son's up to be normal, decent people, that for the most part she has failed. Failed so utterly and completely and incomprehensibly. Her son's have grown up to become the young men they were born to be. For all her hopes, efforts and energy she hasn't done it, nature has taken over nurture. Her efforts haven't been enough. Her expectations have been too much, which means that she has not just failed her son's once but twice, because she has tried to raise them as she would have raised all children and that, couldn't work with damaged children.

It was an impossible expectation. She had peddled through treacle and it is only now, nearly seventeen years later that she realises and understands, that she's been banging her head against the proverbial brick wall. She hadn't believed in nature versus nurture, she believed she was strong enough, to mend any damage in her son's and to put diamonds on there heels, so that they would be able to sparkle and fly. Anna hadn't ever felt disappointed in her son's, only in herself and her failure to raise them, to belong and fit in to every day society. There is an element of irony, because as a childless, infertile woman, she had ached, longed to belong, to fit in and be accepted by society but her infertility and childlessness had left her on the periphery because she lacked the relevant qualifications to be an accepted member of society – children.

So here she is again with her son, trying to find yet another safe place for him, away from the hands of his would be murderers. Anna knows enough about the drug dealers who her son associates with and has worked for, to know what they are capable of. How they dragged people to answer to them, before they killed them, or battered them with baseball bats, or knifed them. They would wrap dog collars around their necks and attach dog chains and drag them to their chosen places of death or torture like frightened, quivering animals. She hadn't wanted to know about what these men did but her son had told her. He had taken part in this self-regulating efficiency, which had no formal courts or ever showed leniency or compassion, never. It was about money, power and control and her son had been intrigued, fascinated, weak and drawn in by these harsh, strong, violent men until he had trapped himself. He knew what the consequences of crossing them meant. He had been with them, whilst they metered out their punishment, to those foolish enough to double cross them. But it seemed no matter what happened Mark never learnt. No matter how close he ever came to the edge, it never seemed he was close enough to take the lessons, or be warned of what the consequences were. It was as if Mark felt himself invincible or he courted death. Anna felt it was a combination of the two elements, which fuelled her sons dangerous and chilling fascination and wish to touch fear and look at death, wide eyed, untouched, yet astonished. Yet Anna knew in the final analysis there was a tiny spark, which would flare up at the last moment when he chose life. It had happened when he had run into and head butted a member of the drug dealer's crew. It had ignited in him, the desperate urgency to leave the city behind and look for refuge and escape in this small seaside resort, so his mother had to leave her youngest son and daughter with their father whilst she ran away with him. The excitement gives Mark a buzz. The chase is on again they are after him. He has won; he has escaped from the thugs for now.

Anna is worn out by her son's endless exploits, is tired and has no desire to live her life on the edge. She is aware, she won't survive if she continues to exist in this way. There has to be an end to it. Anna owes it to her daughter, to live long enough to see her grown up and independent. She knows that the next few years Adam has at home, until he leaves high school for college, it will be difficult. She sometimes wonders, whether or not they will manage, until Adam reaches nineteen and moves into supported living. He can be abusive and threatening towards her, if she thwarts him or challenges him, or simply says no to what he wants. Adam's responses aren't just sulks or defiance, he also becomes verbally obscene and abusive, as well as threatening, to the point where she becomes afraid of further conflict with him and backs down for her own safety, because of the potential violence of his anger and temper. She hasn't allowed her son to be put on medication but knows if he can't control his temper, then this is an option she will have to consider. Again she feels the weight of guilt. If he goes on medication, he won't be the same child, the drug would define him and she would feel responsible for that too. Anna is also aware of the potential risk and threat her son is capable of posing but she wants to hold on to her beautiful boy.

Anna's daughter knows exactly how to handle her brother. She charms and babies him and scolds him and has him eating out of the palm of her hand. Anna isn't sure about how happy she feels, about her daughter having to humour her son, but is aware that it works.

Anna looks down now at Mark her sleeping son, the half bottle of cider by the side of his bed. He lay in the sleeping bag fully clothed. He has taken off his shoes. She feels exhausted after their dash from the city. The night has drawn in and the chill of early autumn creeps through and she decides to fill a hot water bottle and make a warm drink before getting into bed. The caravan is almost in darkness as she climbs under the bedcovers. The wind blows through the tree behind the caravan and moans beneath the door and in the cracks between the window frames. She snuggles further beneath the covers, reminding herself to put something behind the caravan door tomorrow night and to make sure the heavy, grey; valour curtains are drawn, to prevent the cold drafts from blowing through. She sips the remainder of her tea before settling down for the night. This is their second night and she doesn't know what tomorrow will bring. It depends upon what is going to happen with her son and if he is going to stay or move down along the coast to the next town, which is larger and has more openings for him.

Before she finally closes her eyes to sleep, she thinks about Jo. She hopes Jo's forgiven her and that she has managed to cope through the bad storms and floods, that she's seen on the news about the coast. Maybe if she gets the chance sometime, she can go and see how Jo is. Remembering the bench, Anna's heart somersaults. And then as she rolls on her side, her thoughts turn to the thicket and the warm feeling leaves her, as she tries to sleep.

When Anna surfaces from her fitful sleep, she hears the hiss of her son's cider bottle open. Lying quietly she listens to her son, taking his first drink of the day. Anna sighs. In the city, Mark had been involved in a drug abuse programme and although he still drank, his drinking had reduced as he received support. Here there wouldn't be the same help but there has to be something available. She would go with him to find what help there is. Is it her fault that he drinks? Is it because of how she had brought him up? Is it because he had ended up living alone? That's when the drinking began, when Mark lived alone and started mixing with the kinds of people who drank all day and smoked weed and did drugs, it all seems such a waste, a waste of what? Of life she believes, of life. Anna knows she hasn't taken care of him, as she should have. She knows that others would stick by their children no matter what, through thick and thin but she had let her son go, in order for her and her two younger children's survival. She now continues to be on call for her son because of the depth of her guilt, of letting him go, to become reduced to living in hostels, flats and bed sits.

How had it all happened? How had the dream of happy families, collapsed into such a complete broken down remnant of life? Anna feels the automatic switch inside her beginning to click. There is too much pain, disappointment, heartache and trauma. The psychologists called it secondary trauma that she and her other two children experienced when Mark started to go off the rails. Words. There were always the words, which explained the behaviour and how Anna felt. The psychologist had told her that she couldn't have changed things, regardless of the way Mark had been brought up. It would have been the same with whoever had adopted him. Mark was already damaged and traumatised when she and her husband took him into their hearts and lives. Anna hadn't understood about the paths of pain and loss, which ran through her baby's brain and heart, the early trauma of his loss, neglect and lack of bonding. He seemed to bond, when she held him close as a baby and toddler; he seemed to want to be with her. She knows now, that no matter what she gives her son and no matter what she does for him, it is never enough and he wants more, the next thing. His appetite is ravenous. She had always helped her son, when he put himself in danger and at risk but that too never ends, as he continuously sets himself up to be rescued. She knows, believes her sons behaviour isn't conscious or deliberate, it is just something he can't help, can't stop. Anna had tried to set up boundaries and give Mark structure and a framework to live his life by. She couldn't reach him. He needs her and that is the way things are for now.

With her son there is no order and structure and establishing a framework, where he is able to function and manage his life by. The structures that are set up around Mark's life, would usually be able to keep him going for between three weeks and two months, depending upon the level of support within the set up. He has had so many fresh starts and new beginnings that Anna has lost count of them all, so many new places to live and different introductory college courses. They all collapsed time after time after time. Somehow they had become life games. Games of proving but like love, there is never enough. Nothing is ever enough. She had felt so optimistic at each new start and then had stopped and turned on the automatic switch. So much hope and potential, so continuously sabotaged and still it isn't enough, still there has to be more. The next and the next and the next and still Mark is never satisfied. Anna knows now, she can never fill the empty space inside her son; she also knows that his birth mother cannot either. The space has become an empty void. A place that has left her son with an endless ache, that no one but he can forgive and give comfort to. For now he finds solace in the bottle, it distances him from himself so he can continue to function, to exist. She wonders if one day her son will find something that is enough.

Anna gets out of bed and fills the kettle from the water butt. "Do you want some toast? Anna asks her son. "No, no."

She knows he needs food down him if he is drinking. Anna takes her clothes into the kitchen and quickly changes out of her nightgown. Returning, her son is already pulling the duvet off her bed and lifting it, to store it away for the day. She draws back the curtains and opens the front window, to let fresh air through the caravan. Mark has already folded up the blankets and begins making tea and toast and Anna suppresses the urge, which is rising up inside her to say, 'Leave it alone, just leave things alone and stop trying to take over.' She knows she is being unreasonable and that her son isn't taking over but rather helping her. She should be grateful, but what happens is, it starts like this, with her son helping and then bit-by-bit he takes over and controls things and then would tell her what she could or couldn't do in the caravan. He would give the orders and she knows she would end up keeping quiet and just doing whatever her son wanted, or there would be trouble. In the end they would argue and he would yell and tell her, he was only trying to help, but she knows she is being taken over, at home, in the caravan and within herself.

Anna opens her clenched teeth and drops her shoulders. 'Relax,' she tells herself, as she eats the toast and drinks the tea her son has made. Mark sits drinking his cider and rolling a cigarette. How can she get out, get away, have some space for a while to clear her head? If she says she is going shopping, she knows he'll go with her.

No matter where she wanted to go he'd want to come, to
sit with her, to be with her. She waits now until he
finishes his cider. After finishing off his bottle, Mark
stretches out on the long seat beneath the window. He
has pulled the window too and only the net curtain
flutters, as the wind blows through the slight gap in the
window.

After collecting the spare key, Anna writes a brief note
for her son.

Gone to shops won't be long, love mum.

Slipping her bag and coat across her shoulder, she opens
the caravan door and pulls it too, until it clicks. Her son
will sleep for a few hours until lunchtime when she
returns. She puts on her coat and begins walking into the
town centre. The holidaymakers are gone now and the
small town returns to itself. Quiet and insular and
preparing for the autumn which is fast approaching, all
the leaves on the many trees have already gone on the
turn, some a dull green, others red and russets. Soon the
autumn colours will intensify and hold their own
captivating beauty, before falling after this their final
flush as they make way for the chilled, cold, rawness of
winter. To her surprise, Anna passes by all of the shops
and finds herself walking out of the town centre, towards
the lay-by to Jo's hut. 'So,' she thinks, 'that's where
you're off to then.'

As Anna pushes back the gate next to where the
hawthorn bushes grow, she is shocked at the amount of
force needed to open it up, enough for her to squeeze
through. This is strange. A cold chill runs through her as
she stands behind the gate. An overwhelming emptiness
fills her and instinctively, she feels that something isn't
right. She struggles through the once lush path, which
weaves its way towards Jo's hut. Today the ground is
deep in mud and Anna continuously catches her feet and

legs in the thick, tangled roots, of the long weeds and grasses and bushes that seem to have gone mad and have grown all over the place. As she draws closer, she realises what is missing. The dog would be barking, to let Jo know that someone is approaching but now there is nothing just the quietness, which is broken by Anna's own breathing and footsteps as she struggles through the muddied, tangled path. Her heart sinks as she finally catches sight of the hut. Where there had once been the busy organised home and garden, there now stands a dark, empty, derelict hut. The windows, gaping open and the door left ajar, wide open for all to see and walk in or out of. The garden gone, washed into a mud bath, even the window boxes, either fallen off or hanging from beneath the windows. She wants to keel down, to collapse and weep. It is all gone, all ruined. Such a life, so utterly destroyed. But, Anna tries to ask herself, 'how can this be so, surely not just with the rain?'

She walks into the open door of Jo's home and on seeing the utter devastation gasps. 'My God,' putting her hand across her mouth, to keep in her shock, fear and panic. The hut is empty. The entire floor is coated in thick black mud, set in some places solid. She doesn't know what to do. What can she do now? Jo has gone. 'Where?' Anna asks. 'Away,' is the only response that comes to her, in the dark, damp brooding place. 'My God what a mess, what can I do? What should I do?'

Carefully Anna makes her way to Jo's workroom. Here too the window is wide open. She begins to wonder if the door and windows have been deliberately left open, to try to dry out the hut but that doesn't seem logical, because it seems only to serve, to let more water in. One by one, Anna shuts the windows and puts the catches on them, with that action, calmness returns to the hut. She pulls off the hanging window box and finds a small, flat piece of wood, to use as a small spade, to dig up all the mud that has lodged around the door way and prevents it from closing. After beavering away for ten minutes, she has cleared enough to be able to pull the door too. She reasons, at least some of the wind and rain won't get in, to make the hut wetter. She pulls now, as hard as she can at the door, so there isn't such a huge gap. Anna looks again at her handiwork. It doesn't look good she admits but it does look and feel less open and exposed and for now that is the best she can do.

Returning to the town, she is aware of her muddy state but there is little she can do. Calling into and collecting only the basic things that she needs she makes her way back. Anna takes off her shoes and puts them beneath the caravan and slips her key in the lock and quietly enters. Her son is still stretched out along the seat.

Margaret checks her watch; it is 10.46 as she walks towards her vehicle – a silver, sports car, with black, leather seats. She opens the boot and carefully places her handbag, coat and umbrella in, and then opens the door and eases her leg across the foot well, as she holds the steering wheel, to glide over onto the seat. As her skirt rises up her legs she feels almost young again, she smiles and turns the ignition and slowly begins her drive into Fenton. The journey from home is hardly a walk really but Margaret considers the idea as unthinkable. How uncivilised, walking to the Town Hall, when she can just as easily drive in and park – after all she will be driving onto Thornby after the meeting anyhow.

The town's women's meeting today at eleven o'clock is a monthly affair and she has to attend, even though the idea of it fills her with boredom. She has to be seen, to be an active member, of the social women's activities that take place on a regular basis, even though she finds it trying and mundane. There is the Tuesday luncheon club, the Wednesday evening mah-jong, the fortnightly Towns Women's Club – today's venue and then the different charity events scattered throughout the year. And often a last minute phone call to work in one of the town's charity shops to help out. This last one Margaret tries her best to avoid if at all possible, she hates rummaging around other peoples used clothing and bric-a-brac, she cannot envisage anyone ever wanting to buy, the mere thought is abhorrent to her.

Whilst driving her car along the Main Road she hears the ringing of her mobile phone coming from the boot of her car. Turning into the car park at the rear of the Town Hall she considers herself to be early, as there are only a couple of cars parked up. She turns off the engine and retrieves her bag from the boot, to listen to the message on her phone. She is fully expecting it to be Abby, especially after the drama of this morning. As she presses her voicemail and listens, she is delighted to hear the voice of Giles wanting to speak with her. He never leaves a lengthy message; it is always the usual, 'hello M it's Giles here goodbye' and then ends the call. She checks around, to make sure there is no one in sight and sits back inside the car to wallow, whilst dialling Giles's number. He answers almost instantly.

"Oh hello, how are you today?"
"I'm fine, I have just parked up at the Town Hall for the meeting, how are you?"
"Look, I know it's not our usual day but I just wondered if we could meet say 1.30?"
"Oh Giles could we, how lovely, shall I bring lunch?"
"So you are rather hungry are you?"
"I'm sure I will be ravenous by then, how about I bring something along anyhow?"
"Sure I'll see you then, bye." Giles ends the conversation leaving Margaret excited and turned on by the thought of meeting him later.

Margaret steps out of the car with confidence, her inner barometer warmed by the promise of the afternoons encounter, she can hardly wait.
She can feel the moisture filling her cotton gusset and her breasts swelling and heaving against her balcony bra, as she strides head held high, into the Town Hall. The top of her stockings rub slightly against one another and the very thought of Giles's hand reaching up her skirt and slipping his finger inside her knickers, to find her clitoris and play with her, makes her want to come here and now. Oh how good life is, how lucky I am, she feels the flush on her face, as she makes her way along the wooden floor boards towards the kitchen.

The door to the kitchen is open and Joyce is placing cups on saucers as she walks through.

"Hello Joyce, I must say it feels rather warm this morning don't you agree?"

"Do you think so?" Joyce answers.

Margaret regains her composure and not one for domestic chores, tells Joyce that she will check the hall. She knows this amounts to doing nothing but at least it gives her another chance to fantasise about her afternoon with Giles.

During the talk she hardly listens, her mind wanders, reminiscing about her lover Giles, her body fills up again with anticipation. The affair is in its infancy, they have been seeing each other for sex the past two months and she no longer sees herself as dull, passive and past it. Giles has revitalised her, he has pushed and pulled his penis into her with such desire and pleasure that it has given re birth to the women she only half remembers, years and years ago.

'Oh Charles if only, poor Charles,' – this thought dashes through her consciousness and then disappears – pushed out of memory by the virulent Giles. Margaret has no doubt in her mind about her fling, she is a woman after all, and was born for it, sex is an important part of being a woman and if Charles cannot give it, her mind fills with distaste at this point, and Giles is willing to provide it – no strings attached – then she is all for it. Neither of them ever want this to come out into the open and are careful about their arrangements, always making sure it is safe to meet.

Margaret checks her watch and again to the hall clock, hoping that the hands will turn faster, each time she looks, they have hardly moved at all. This fuels her desire and when the speaker finally rounds off the talk and her companions give their salutary applause, she says a few quick goodbyes and leaves the room before anyone can pin her down with idle chitchat. Well Giles here I come.

She calls at the supermarket in Thornby and buys a bottle of rosé, fresh fruit, a piece of runny Brie and French toast for their lunch. She knows it might not get eaten and how often they have had to discard it, when taken over by each other. She is secretly amazed by her lack of inhibitions and how she can parade herself before him – Charles would never have thought it possible from her, this thought gives her a sense of power, albeit on her own and away from him, 'yes Charles,' she muses, 'you may like to talk down and belittle me and as always I comply, because it is easier that's why.'

She wonders about their evening meal but decides that 'The Sailors Arms' will probably be the end of Charles's day. He would no doubt arrive home tired and weary, he always does after being away for the night, and spending a good lunch hour at the pub.

Working away – well I found out the juicy truth of that from Giles early on – that was his discretion and one of our many secrets that bond us together. Yes, she concludes, the evening meal would amount to Charles's early to bed and foraging through the fridge and freezer for something for herself. Maybe here is the answer, she ponders – 'love-replacing food, no wonder my body is in good shape.'

Anna undoes the packaging from the pizza and places it on the baking tray and puts it in the oven. She fills the kettle with water to make tea. After putting her few groceries away, she takes the note from the sideboard she had made out for her son and tears it up. Wiping the splashes of mud from her legs, she is satisfied she has done all she needs to do. Putting the boiling water over the tea bag in the pot she waits for it to mash. Done. She sits quietly drinking her hot tea waiting for her son to wake up. It is 12.30 she will wake him up for 1 o'clock, when the pizza is ready. They will go shopping later.

Anna always feels torn about buying alcohol for her son, but she knows if she doesn't then he will merely get it himself, even if it means stealing or robbing someone for money to buy it. So she is dammed if she does and damned if she doesn't. She needs to get her son established with the usual 'Connexions', he'll need to function with after she leaves. She will only be able to stay for a few weeks with him. She has to return to the city to look after her other two children, because their father will only tolerate taking care of them for a limited period. It would mean him finishing work for an hour and a half earlier every day and working through his lunch break, losing an hour a day of his work. There is little else either of them can do, so that's how things are.

Mark begins to stir from his sleep. "Hi mum. What time is it?"
"Nearly 1 o'clock, we'll have some dinner soon. I've popped out for bread and milk and a pizza."
"Can we go for a walk later?"
"Yes, after dinner."
Anna knows the walk means alcohol and tobacco. Tomorrow is Sunday she reminds herself, as she lifts the hot baking tray from the oven and places it on the top of the cooker. It will be Monday before she is able to take him to Thornby, the larger town further down the coast.

Eating a piece of pizza, Anna begins to think of Jo. Where is she now, what is she doing? She feels lost and empty, not knowing what's happened to her. It fills her with such a profound sadness because of what might have been, with no hope of contact and no more touch.

She puts the two bottles of cider in her shopping bag, as Mark empties the trolley.
"We'll have a big tea tonight." Mark tells his mum as she finishes filling the shopping bags, with the provisions they need for the next few days. Mark has his supply of tobacco and booze to keep him going. The cheap cider is only for topping up his drinking, this means Anna tipping up more money. She would give him a fiver and with that he'd buy a couple of drinks and be able to tap a few more. He might or might not return home, it would depend on how the fancy takes him.

They have chicken pie with mashed potatoes and sweet corn for tea. She is pleased that her son manages to eat his food. The only thing is that after he's been drinking, he would be sick and all of the food would come back.

"Can I have the sink mam?" Mark asks as his mother fills the pan and kettle for water to boil.
"You'll have to refill the water butt." Anna answers as she collects the pots and leaves them on the table, waiting for her son to get ready to go out.
"Mam do I have a clean tee shirt and trousers?"
Anna unpacks the sack she's brought with clothes in for her son. There are Adam's knocking around clothes in the caravan but Mark wouldn't wear his brother's day-to-day rough clothes. She puts the clean trousers and t-shirt on the bunk bed as Mark prepares himself to go out. Whilst he gets ready, she pulls five pounds from her purse and takes it into the kitchen, where he is putting on his clean trousers.
"That's to go out with."
"Could you spare…?"

"No, that's all you can have." Anna snaps at him.

Why does she give it to him, if she feels so much
resentment? 'Why?' She asks herself. To please him, to
stop trouble, to get him out of her way, Anna no longer
knows, all these reasons and more probably.
"Love you mam." Mark says as he kisses Anna on the
cheek before leaving.
He smells of cheap aftershave and tobacco and as she
watches him walk away she calls out.
"You should take a coat, it'll get cold."
"No, I'll be fine, in a bit mama."
"In a bit Mark." Anna returns after watching him
disappear from her sight.

She fills the kettle and pan to heat water for the pots;
Mark had been too absorbed in the process of getting
himself ready to do the job. Whilst the water heats, she
re fills the butt and empties the slop bucket beneath the
caravan; it is over flowing. Then she sets to, tidying up
and making the beds. It is a cool, early autumn evening.
After her jobs are done, there is an hour or two, before it
grows dark, to sit on the seat beneath the window. It is
chilly now, as night begins to draw in, she sips her tea
wondering what to do, before she climbs into bed.

Anna rises and goes to the sideboard drawer and opens
it, she looks at her beautiful, blue, notebook. 'God.'
Anna laughs, 'I'd almost forgotten.' She takes the book,
'Now what about you, how have you been?' Anna opens
it and flicks through the written pages; it seems so long
ago now. Whilst she waits for the dark to approach, she
reads through what she has written.
It makes her feel sad. The escape route, of creating
imaginary people in their made-up worlds, is little better
than finding escape through the bottom of a bottle. They
are both attempts to flee. People believe imagination is
the better form of the two, because it involves intellect
and a bit of creativity, whilst the bottle demands only its

purchase and a steady hand. She has lost her clear sense of perspective, of what she now believes is honourable or not, what is of value or not. Anna has not managed to raise her son's to where she believes her family could be, but she has looked deeply into where they are and where she now is. The place where Anna is is very meagre, frugal, often grey, colourless and dreary, with little relief or need of imagination. The bottle is a quicker, easier, cheaper, escape route and she can see the truth and logic of that. Anna has succumbed to a deep weariness, a grey cover over her mind, thoughts and feelings, she has become deeply, sickeningly, numb, from the depths of her soul; unplugging and disconnection are the only ways she has survived. If she hadn't done that, she would have gone under, or found her own solace at the bottom of a bottle, as her son had. The values of life and its meaning, seem so pointless, looking at it from her point of view. Her life is on hold. Her life is the life of her children.

Her son's had in the end, not entered her life; it is she who had stepped into their world. At first she had tried so hard to engage them and share her world with them, but piece-by-piece, whatever they chose and decided upon, and those, which their father encouraged, had taken over and God help Anna if she thwarted them. She doesn't want to live in their world where everything spins, is dizzy and chaotic and has an overwhelming, never ending shower, of materialistic wants, needs and necessities. Their lives have become based on, getting the next and the next thing, so that nothing has enough value for them, because they know, that the next thing that their father gets them, gives to them, could be better than the last and the last and the last. She has no say. If she speaks, she is jealous, angry and a bitter woman and doesn't want them to have a good childhood. The boy's father can't get or do enough for them and they know it and Anna has been shut up. When Mark arrived, Anna's husband gave her up for his son. She had looked forward to becoming a family but it hadn't worked out like that. Mark and his father had bit by bit become a unit. She would be allowed to tag along with them, but fundamentally she was on the outside of their relationship. She wasn't allowed to make any comments that might be seen as critical. Anna had waited twenty years for her son and loves him as much as any mother could and she knows that her son loves her too in his own way and she accepts that. Anna feels stunned, wounded and hurt at the rejection of her husband. Their life as a couple and the possibility of being a family is over. Anna blames herself, for something she has done or failed to do, to make her husband change so utterly.

Over the years, Anna believed that she had to prove herself to her husband and her son's. In the end she knows, that she will never be worthy of them. This is a failure and a disappointment for her, accepting that in their eyes, she will never be good enough for them.

So now she will try to start again, to see if she can just be herself. Not prove herself, or measure up. Not have everything she tries to do twisted and thrown back in her face, year after year, after year. She is beginning to reconnect and get to know about herself, to be who she is and who she can be, not the useless baggage that her husband and son's value her as. She has freed another bond, which bound her. She accepts her failure and her role of worthless enemy.

There had been the hopes of love and beliefs of change, which had kept her there, bound to those who called her, regarded and treated her, as their enemy. Once she had accepted the stone, which she heard, clattering down the deep well of emptiness inside herself, she knew as she listened and understood what it was telling her, no matter what she gave, it would never be enough.

As Anna listens to the rain beating against the caravan, she wonders whether or not her son will return home, or go on somewhere with someone else. She falls to sleep, used to the uncertainty of her son's whereabouts; the worry has turned to acceptance. Anna understands now, that she has not lived her own life and realises she has never become herself, because she had become so completely over taken, in her pursuit of being whoever others wanted her to be. For the first time in her life, she understands with complete clarity, the name of the game she has been playing. She has never given herself the space before, to step aside and see what she had joined in on, because she had fallen so deeply into proving her value and worth; that she had lost the understanding of herself.

The experience has left Anna feeling worthless, useless and exhausted. She has lost her life, given it away to others, who have repeated through their endless mantras, 'you're worthless, prove to me that you're not….do this, do that……you see I was, I am right you're worthless.' 'No I'm not' Anna calls out. 'I'm me and I can be who ever I want to be, it's too late.' her inner voice whispers. 'No it's not, it's never too late, not until you're dead and only then is it too late.' She has been crushed and trapped and understanding who she has become, is only the beginning. She begins to feel afraid and wants to hide. 'Better the devil you know.' Anna thinks – at least she is a bit useful to them isn't she? She is afraid of herself. The game of life she has played, runs much deeper than she realises and the undercurrents, that direct the flow of her life, are more submerged than she can believe or understand. She can see what she has become but the reason why still lay silently, waiting to be discovered. Those who found Anna wanting in her life have tapped into a seam that is open to be mined.

It is light as Anna wakes. Her son isn't in his bed. She sighs and feels flat, defeated. Mark would be with a new

friend, sleeping it off somewhere. Anna isn't sure if he'll
return back today, or whether he will start another
drinking session and continue until the following day.
She knows if he returns, it will be well after dinner,
because that's how long it takes him, to surface after his
night and probably early morning session. He would
have found a lock in too; if anyone is be able to find one,
it's Mark.

There is a weak glow of autumn sunlight, splitting
through the cracks in the curtains. She decides to get up
and greet the day. Not sure what to do or where to go,
she finishes her few chores and sits on the seat under the
window. The campsite is quiet now, only a few regulars
sticking it out, until the season ends in October. Waiting
and unsure what to do, she decides to write again in her
blue book about the other Anna who is free and has a
life. Her husband would call her lazy, if he sees her idle,
whilst there is work to be found and jobs to do, but Anna
closes her thoughts and begins to write. Maybe she could
write herself into Fermanagh House and one day it
would all come true, like a fairy tale, or a story. It
doesn't hurt anyone, or do any one harm the writing, but
she still feels cautious. As a young girl, she had written a
story about watching her own funeral and hidden it,
under her pillow. Her mother had told her, that she and
her dad were very cross and upset about what she had
written and they had put it on the fire.

Opening the blue book she takes up her pen, it feels
strange but comfortable. She wants to go back into
Fermanagh House; she knows that, even if it is only for a
brief moment – to feel and to escape. Anna begins to
write.

*Anna awoke to a glorious autumn morning looking
forward to opening up her boxes of books and candles
and stones and crystals and angels and her family*

photos – it was exciting. Filling the kettle Anna could hardly wait to begin her journey of exploration into her belongings. Sipping her hot tea Anna started on the box where she had packed her family photographs……….

Anna's absorption in writing takes up most of the day, except to go outside to the toilets, or make a few drinks of tea. She is surprised as she finally takes a break, to see the sky darkening as the night approaches. Mark still hasn't returned. A pang of fear, as to what might have happened to him crosses her thoughts, but she let's it slip, she has to survive, reminding herself that this behaviour is normal for her son.

Going through the usual routine, she makes her bed and then a cheese sandwich, fills the hot water bottle and makes drinking chocolate, before the darkness falls. The night is chilly and she is grateful for the hot water bottle. She doesn't do one for Mark, because if it goes cold before he returns, it would be a miserable greeting for him.

Later after drifting off to sleep, she hears the caravan door open. A solid, dark figure, steps into the caravan and pulls the door too, Anna's heart is pounding so fast and loud, she feels sure it can be heard. She is afraid to call out her son's name, for fear of it not being him, but is so scared she must do something. At last she recognises his grunts and laboured breathing, as he leans forward to undo his shoes and take them off.

"Mark."
"It's ok mam it's me. Go back to sleep."
'Thank God' Anna whispers, as she burrows down into her bed, relaxing, now that he is back safely; finding peace she returns to sleep. Mark falls straight to sleep as soon as his head hits the pillow. Exhausted by his long walk and drinking sessions, he wants nothing more than

to sleep and rest. As he sinks deeply into a heavy sleep, he is oblivious to where he is, except to know that he is with her, his mother and whenever he is with her, wherever it is, he feels safe – he knows he is ok. So they sleep in safety together. No thugs or drug pushers will come to this place; Mark knows that, he is safe.

Anna's dreams are not safe, she returns to what happened in the thicket near the bench. Again she feels the oppressive weight of the man across her and she can't breathe. She feels as if she is suffocating. The reality of the dream terrifies her, waking her, she sits up in bed breathing heavily, sweating and cold. It's a dream, just a dream, it's not real, Mark is here, it's ok you're safe. Taking some deep breaths she feels her heart quicken as tears roll down her cheeks, shocking her. The pain rises from deep inside and hurts, until she releases it through her sobs. It is as if they have a will of their own and she has no control over them. The experience only lasts for a few moments and she is glad she hasn't woken her son. She doesn't want him to know what happened to her in the thicket. Lying back down, calmness returns and she slips back to sleep.

Out at sea the waves are high and wild, being swept up in the black cold air, by the fierce winds. The waves roll in along the coastline, smashing hard against the solid, dark rocks. It is a wild night full of frenzy, lashing against the rocks, relentless in its determination, to make itself felt as well as heard.

Anna decides she can't spend another day inside the caravan. Mark sleeps as she folds her blankets and lifts up her bed, and then makes a pot of tea and toast. She opens the kitchen blind and draws back the curtains in the dining area, but leaves those where her son is sleeping, closed.

After putting on her coat and collecting her bag she decides to go for a walk. The fresh air hits her as she opens the door, she wants to turn back and go inside but doesn't. Walking into the town centre through the streets, she remembers her dream. In the city she had put the experience behind her, whilst she got on with her daily life. Although knowing what had happened to her was wrong, she couldn't bring herself to tell anyone about it. She felt ashamed and fearful too. She knows that if someone told her about being raped, she would have made her go to the police and report it. So why hadn't she? She hadn't seen the man's face, he had worn a black balaclava, she hadn't seen his eyes, or looked into them, so she couldn't identify him. He had hissed obscenities and threats, as he suffocated and raped her. It feels a shameful thing. That she was somehow in the wrong, not him, the one who had done it. She hadn't asked for it, she didn't deserve it; she wasn't a bad person, so why had he done it? The experience makes Anna feel worthless. All she had wanted to do, after it happened, was hide, run away and wash him from herself.

She needs to return to the bench, to see again where it happened and to find some clue as to why? How it could have, when it is a path people walk through, it isn't a remote, deserted lonely spot. It is a footpath, which is used by everyone who walks to the park, the promenade, the beach and the town centre. Anna is uncertain, afraid to go back to the bench, it is such a lovely place to sit and look at the sea. But it didn't happen at the bench, it was the thicket just beyond it, but they are only a few steps away from each other.

This dilemma, leads her away towards the town centre; she decides to browse around the charity shops, before doing her little bit of shopping. The angel on the shelf in the charity shop, with her arms outstretched, holding a banner of 'Joy', makes Anna stop. She wants to buy it even before she looks at its price, £5 the women tells her. She gulps and mentally reckons, Mark would be able to go out on that, or she could pay for two bottles of cider and tobacco for him. But she decides the angel dressed in a red, flowing gown has to be hers. Anna doesn't covert much, but she really wants the angel. The woman wraps it in newspapers, before putting her into a carrier bag; Anna pays and leaves the shop, without looking at any of the other stuff. She decides to forego her stroll around the other charity shops in the town centre; she goes straight to the supermarket. After buying bread, milk and a pack of bacon, she walks steadily back, the rain in the air holds off, as the wind blows.

Glad to be back, she closes the door behind her. Whilst the kettle boils to make tea, Anna puts her groceries away. She checks once again to see if her son is still sleeping, before taking the angel from the plastic carrier bag, 'Now', she says lifting the angel out, 'You'll look after me won't you?' Unwrapping the layers of newspaper sheet by sheet, she finally uncovers her angel. Just holding it in her hands, makes Anna feel comfortable and safe. It is perfect, just what she wants. Turning it, she notices the price on the base. Immediately she peels it off, it wouldn't do for Mark to think she's spent £5 on an ornament. Looking at the angel, with outstretched arms of 'JOY' she smiles and sighs. Picking up the loose sheets of old newspaper, something in a headline strikes her. It is about the body of a man who had been found washed up on the beach, after the mud and debris from the storms and flooding had subsided. The body, Anna realises, had been found at the bottom of the cliff, near rocks, which were just below the bench. Reading this feels weird. Was it him, she wonders – had he fallen down the cliff, or been washed down with the flooding? I hope it's you, I hope it's fucking well you, you bastard. Anna gathers up the newspaper sheets and begins tearing them, ripping them and smashing them into the rubbish bag on the floor. 'I hate you. I hate you.'

Anna opens the door and puts the rubbish bag into the dustbin just behind the caravan. Taking the washing up liquid to the outside tap, she washes and washes her hands; until they are so cold she can hardly feel them. On an impulse, she returns to the caravan for the angel and takes it to the cold-water tap. For a second, she is tempted to bash the figure against the brick wall in front of her, but she doesn't. Instead she squirts washing up liquid all over her, to wash and rinse her, again and again, until the angel is clean. She holds the dripping angel against her breast, satisfied at last, that she has been cleansed of the filth from the contaminated newspaper. After turning off the tap and collecting the washing up liquid she goes back indoors. She gently wipes the base of the angel on her top and places her on the shelf above the window. Her pot of tea has almost gone cold, but she places her hands around it, to glean traces of its warmth and drinks the lukewarm tea.

It is well past dinnertime, so she decides to make a bacon sandwich; she'd fancied one in the town centre. So she lights the grill and opens the sealed packet of bacon. The bacon slices from the pack, feel soft, floppy and slimy and Anna is glad to see them arranged in the frying pan with a knob of butter and two quarters of a tomato. She places two pieces of bread underneath the grill to toast. The bacon soon oozes its heady aroma, which makes Anna hungry.

From the depths of the caravan her son calls out, "Do me a bacon butty mam."

Anna's anticipation drops, as she turns over the toast and bacon, after filling the kettle to make two pots of tea. She hands her son his sandwich and tea and notices the grazes and redness on his knuckles. He's been fighting

again then. Anna returns to the kitchen to put more toast
under the grill and two slices of bacon into the frying
pan for herself. "Tomorrow we've to go into town and
find out about what we can do for you and where to get
help."

"Yea, yea." Mark tells her, as he finishes eating his
sandwich and swallows the last of his tea.

After finishing his food, Mark places his plate on the
floor and puts his cup on top of it, before returning to
sleep for a few more hours.

"We'll go shopping later mam, if you like?" Anna's son
calls out to his mother, as she fills the kettle to make a
start on the dishes.

Charles strides on ahead, up the path, towards his parked
4 X 4 left in the lay-by at the roadside. He opens the rear
door and shouts out, "You can put the dog in the back."
Jo lifts Jason into the rear of the car and hopes that he
will be ok.
"Just throw your bag on the back seat and get in."
Charles orders whilst glancing quickly in the rear view
mirror, then thrusting the gears into first.
They lurch forward, before Jo has chance to fasten her
seat belt and off they shoot, towards the town centre.
"Good God, I don't know who smells the most, you or
the dog, I know you've been flooded out, but bloody hell
Jo, I don't know how you thought that you could stay
there, you can shower yourself and the dog where I'm
taking you." Charles steers the car towards the town hall.
Jo wonders where we they are going. "I'm sorry about
the smell and thank you for helping us out."
"I've just had the flat refurbished and it will be empty
until next spring, when I have a new tenant moving in on
a long let, so you're welcome to stay until the end of
February, providing you keep it clean and pay for the gas
and electric, and no rowdy all night parties." Charles
says with a laugh.
"Thanks for your offer, I'll go back to the hut when the
weather picks up and I've dried everything out."
"Look Jo, as much as I admire your spirit and all that,
there's no way that that hut will be fit to live in until next
year. It needs warm sunshine and plenty of it, so stop
being a bloody martyr and stay in the flat, do yourself a
favour and chill out, pamper yourself for a few months,
it's my pleasure and it's a done deal."
"Well that's kind of you, if you are sure, it's ok?"
"Man of my word Jo, Stella doesn't often ask for
favours, so when she called and said how worried she
was about you and could I help out, it was the least I
could do, she's a special lady our Stella, she must have a
soft spot for you, and anyway I'm sure I can find you a
job or two."

This insinuation of closeness and strong relationship with them surprises Jo, leaving her feeling baffled, she hardly knows these two people. Soon they are driving towards the museum and then take a left turn and stop outside a block of flats.

"Here we are then; it's the top flat, number 4." Charles gets out of the car and opens the door to let her out.

She has walked down this street many times, when visiting the charity shop further on, but until this moment she hadn't realised that it was once a chapel. Looking up to the top floor there are four original chapel windows. With the bold stone lettering, 'FISHERMAN'S CHAPEL c1870' painted black underneath them. The ground floor at street level was once occupied by retailers, and is now converted to flats. Charles opens the rear door and quickly lifts Jason down to the pavement and rubs his hands together, whilst Jo retrieves her bag from the back seat.

"Come on then?" Charles leads the way; the doorway opens into a large hallway with a staircase.

There are four letterboxes on the sidewall and a door to the right is numbered Flat 1.

"Yours it Flat 4 at the top, so up you go."

The staircase walls are painted white; and the steps are a matt black. The air is filled with the clean, fresh smell of paint, and their footsteps echo as they mount the staircase. Up and past Flats 2 and 3 and eventually they reach the doorway to Flat 4.

Charles puts the key into the Yale lock and pushes the door open. The hallway continues the theme of white paint and feels quite clinical and stark. This leads into a long corridor with a staircase at the far end.

"Go on take a look."

There are four rooms off the corridor, the kitchen the first, is a smallish square room, clean and fitted with white units and a small table and chairs. On the table is a brown paper bag with a card stuck on it.

"Stella's left you a welcome pack, she's working away now for a few weeks, so she sends her best wishes and hopes you will be ok here."

"That's really kind of both of you, thank you."

"Good girl our Stella, anyway make yourself at home and settle in, I'll have to leave now, work to do, must get on, so forget about that hut and clean yourself up, and I'll see you later." Charles finishes the last part of his sentence as he turns and goes back out through the door.

"Bye." Jo answers quietly, taking in the new surroundings.

Charles departs from the flat; he knows that he is needed back at the office. His secretary, Miriam, has left several urgent messages on his mobile, but he doesn't feel like returning phone calls and trawling through paper work, until he can clear his head. He will call at the office before 3 o'clock to sign the papers; he checks his watch this gives him a couple of hours at least.

He decides to drive up to the golf club for a coffee, he can park there and it will be fairly quiet at this time.

He pulls into the clubhouse and glances around to see if he recognises any of the parked cars. There are one or two familiar vehicles – their owners would be on the course – so he is in luck, there should be no one around for a chat. He orders a cafetiere and selects a newspaper from the rack and sits in a corner seat out of the way.

As he peruses the paper, his mind can't connect with today's headlines and he tosses it onto the table.

Whilst waiting for the coffee to arrive, his thoughts turn to his wife Margaret, and this girl Jo. He has definitely noticed a change in his wife's behaviour; she has an air about her. Almost serene and confident and it shows in her posture too, he thinks he knows why, but can't allow himself to acknowledge it. 'Don't kid yourself Charlie boy, you orchestrated it, so don't be surprised if it bites you on the arse!' And as for Jo, well she is another matter altogether. 'Dash Stella, why are you away when I need you?' He could always arrange a quickie over to France, to join her, 'no – too much to do at this end.' 'Well sod it, I won't be made a fool of, just you wait and see.'

The arrival of the coffee brings a change of heart to Charles, as he pushes down the filter with force. He pours it into the cup and drops a couple of brown sugar cubes in with purpose and stirs the coffee vigorously. 'Yes, you know how to stir things up.'

He lets his mobile ring again before answering, with venom in his voice. "All right I'll be back at the office before three and tell him from me, were not running a bloody circus, and it will get done."

Grabbing the newspaper, he shakes it open and then throws it back down. Taking a large gulp from his coffee cup he feels in his pocket for his car keys and reluctantly leaves the clubhouse.

Jo stands awhile taking in her new surroundings and then looks at the rest of the flat. There is a small bedroom with a double bed, a large fitted wardrobe and two chests of drawers. A living room with gas fire, three seater settee and a large armchair, a TV, bookshelves, a coffee table and a large rug, and a bathroom with a white suite, comprising of - bath with an overhead shower, a washbasin and a toilet. The whole flat having laminate flooring, white walls and doors, skirting and architraves, is so impersonal and completely lacking atmosphere, clinical and so unlike the hut. The chapel windows are also painted white with beautiful features and if the walls were painted with colour, the impact these would have upon the room would be terrific.

Jo takes the stairs at the end of the corridor, to see what's upstairs. Wow, this upper room is wonderful, absolutely gorgeous, it is a huge room full of light, with a beamed ceiling and four velux roof lights, and is completely empty without furniture, just laminated flooring like the rest of the flat. This would make a fantastic workroom. She imagines it full of art materials with finished and unfinished projects. Jason pads around tentatively; he is unused to the slippy, laminate flooring and is also wondering what they are doing here, and when they are going home.

She goes back downstairs to the kitchen and opens the brown paper bag, to find out what's in it. There is a box of chocolates, t bags, a loaf of bread, a bottle of red wine, a bottle of bubble bath and shampoo and a fluffy pink towel and an old one presumably for Jason. The card attached reads -

'Hi Jo, I hope Charles welcomed you with open arms, I'm working away from home for a few weeks, chill out, pamper yourself, see you when I get back, Stella x
P.S. You'll find a curry, milk etc in the fridge to put you on.'

She feels touched by Stella's thoughtfulness and
kindness.

"Come on then Jase, you first, you might not like it but it
has to be done." Jo beckons him into the bathroom and
lifts him into the bath. He looks stricken and unsure.

"It's ok Jase don't worry." She holds the showerhead
and turns on the water, adjusting the temperature until
it's warm but not too hot and begins to wet his coat,
grabbing his collar, to prevent him shaking the water off.
The water running in the bottom of the bath is grey and
murky.

"You're filthy Jase." Jo lathers his coat with shampoo
and rubs it all over, whilst trying to prevent him from
having a big shake by holding his collar tight. And then
rinses him. The water is grey and soapy and she
continues to shower and soap him until the water is clear
and clean. After turning off the water she lets his coat
drip, before wrapping him with the towel and then
vigorously rubs him all over. After lifting him out onto
the floor, she catches his collar, before he bolts away and
out of the room.

"Wait." She tells him and gives him another rub all over.
"That's better, you're all clean now Jase, does that feel
better eh? You smell like a woolly jumper."

When she releases his collar, he makes a wild, mad dash
and skids around the floors of the flat, shaking himself,
so glad that it's over.

When he finally settles down, she rinses out the bath and
fills it to the top and pours in some of the bubble bath
and steps in. She submerges herself beneath the foamy
surface and puts her head under, indulging in the
warmth, this feels exquisite and wonderful, and her body
welcomes the heat. After resurfacing she lays back and
soaks her aching body, to absorb the heat through to her
bones. After awhile, she squirts some shampoo and
massages it into her matted hair, then dips her head
under the water to rinse off the suds and does it again
until her hair feels squeaky clean. And then she takes the
bar of soap and washes herself all over. Her arms and

legs are covered in bruises and her finger and toenails need cutting, as does her hair. This bath is absolutely wonderful; when her fingers start to turn wrinkly and the water begins to cool, she stands up and gets out.

The clean fluffy towel is so luxurious, and exquisitely soft, she'd almost forgotten how things could be. Her internal voice reminds her to not get too used to this, as it's only temporary and life back at the hut will begin again. Another voice rises above this and tells her to forget that for now, just enjoy this and have a well-earned rest. Yes she needs to and is grateful for Charles's offer of staying here. She puts on the bathrobe hung on the back of the door and empties and cleans out the bath. The floor is covered in Jason's hairs, she will clean them up when they are dry; at least having the laminate flooring, means that she can keep the place clean. Jason is wandering from room to room trying to find his safe place to sleep or lie down.

"I'll buy you a new bean bag tomorrow Jase."

In the kitchen Jo opens the fridge, to see what food Stella has left. There is milk, butter, a pack of bacon and a ready meal of chicken jalfrezi and rice. Stella has thought of everything, Jo finds it easy to accept her generosity under the circumstances and after the trauma of the past few days, breaths a sigh of relief that it's over. She reads the instructions for the curry and rice and turns the oven on to preheat and fills the kettle to make a mug of tea. Jason signals his hunger by emitting a soft whine. He looks so different now that he's been shampooed; he is all fluffy and looks fatter than earlier in his filthy state.

"What then, what do you want?" She teases him. He looks up adoringly and continues his whining.

"In a minute, Jase."

She puts the meal into the oven and sets the timer for when it's ready and then makes Jason's meal. She will have to buy some dog bowls tomorrow from the £1 shop. Being here feels totally strange and disorienting, she can't believe she's here with the modern facilities on hand, the electric lights and modern bathroom and kitchen, it somehow feels unreal, that she might wake up from a dream and open her eyes and find herself back at the hut. Jason devours his food and awaits his usual scraps from hers. How lovely and easy to sit at the table and eat, without worrying or planning her next move or job.

She can hear passing cars and voices from the road below, the sound of the sea crashing against the shore in the background, reminding her she is still in Fenton. After the meal she puts on clean clothes and takes Jason out for a walk. Once down the stairs they are on the pavement in the centre of town. 'Gosh, Jase, everything's so handy, the shops are just minutes away.' She walks up through the gardens and beyond the centre to the Golf Club – this is a long walk and gives Jason a chance to burn some of his energy. On the way back she realises it has stopped raining and how pleasant it is to feel warm and dry.

Arriving back at the flat, she puts down a towel on the floor in the kitchen for Jason to sleep on, and then uncorks the wine and pours a large glass and takes it into the sitting room along with the box of chocolates.

This sudden life of luxury feels quite comical, the events and transition from life at the hut to here, she sips the wine and dives into the chocolates with reckless abandon. 'This is the life.' She knows also that when tomorrow comes and the novelty wears off, her attention will need satisfying, so that boredom doesn't set it. She can return to the hut to continue the clean up and then what? She'll contemplate that in due course.

Her eyes begin to feel heavy and tiredness sweeps over her, she says goodnight to Jason and goes to bed. The double bed with fresh clean sheets doesn't feel so inviting, when she remembers her own cosy bed. It is a sad reminder, as if she has left a part of herself behind and is unable to reach out to it. She tries to shut out her thoughts, she doesn't want to be tossing and turning all night long.

She transfers her mind from here, back to her ruffled up comfy bed, with its smelly sheets and begins to drift off into a deep sleep. Her body needs this rest and nourishment and she sleeps on and on.

The outside noises eventually wake her. The passing traffic and the muffled voices of people passing by on the street below, mixed in with the squawking sound of the seagulls and the sea cascading along the beach not far away, creates an instant picture of a bustling seaside town, and leaves her in no doubt as to where she is. The warm heat of the flat is gentle and soft as it wafts around the bedroom. Again so different from the hut, when her face was instantly cold on waking and her breath of steam billowed into the morning air as she pushed her head out from under the duvet. Here today it feels so warm, hot even and she wonders if the heating has been on during the night, so hot that she decides to open the window to let some cooler air inside. She touches the radiator and finds that it is actually cold.

She hears the tapping of Jason's footsteps along the hallway ready to greet her and puts on the bathrobe and makes her way towards the kitchen. "Well, well, Jase don't you look lovely and clean?"

She bends down and ruffles his thick, black coat and gives him a big hug. After filling the kettle to make tea she decides when she sees the electric toaster, to have toast for breakfast. Toast, what a treat, what a luxury, hot warm toast with butter on, she pops in two slices of bread and waits in eagerness. After their breakfasts she sits and wonders what to do today. She is so unused to sitting around and as she contemplates boredom and uncertainty she feels anxious and has to do something. She enjoys the pleasure of the bathroom and has a hot shower before getting dressed.

"Come on then Jase, let's go for a walk."

Glad to have a purpose, she takes his lead and her rucksack, some money and sets off. Entering the street outside, she walks through the town and up towards the

golf course. Jason is unused to being on the lead and
unable to dash off he starts to pull and she has to
continually call him to halt and snatches at his lead to
restrain him. He has to wait until they enter the edge of
the golf course and the public path that runs around the
perimeter, before she can let him off the leash. Now he
runs around enjoying the open space, it feels so good to
be out here catching snapshots of the open sea as they
meander along.

As they carry on walking along the path she spots one or
two golfers pulling their buggies intently, with their
heads bent down. When Jason slows down, she turns
around and walks back into town.
She heads in the direction of the pet shop, to buy Jason a
beanbag and his food, after tying him outside she enters
the shop, and goes to look at the beanbags. There are
three different sizes and various colours with comical
doggy prints on. She selects a large dark green bag, with
pictures of sleepy dogs on and then picks a pack of dog
biscuits and a 5lb bag of dried food. The young man rolls
the beanbag and sellotapes it tightly, to hold it together
for carrying. She pays for the items and puts the food
into the rucksack and carries the beanbag under her arm.
Jo chats to him about his new beanbag, as they walk
back to the flat. She remembers the bacon in the fridge
and looks forward to a bacon sandwich for lunch. Once
back at the flats, she hurries up the stairs, with Jason
scurrying up in front her to the top floor. She removes
the sellotape from the beanbag and unfurls it on the
kitchen floor.
"There you go Jase, your new bed, come on then, it's
yours Jase." Jason sniffs at it and strokes it with his paw
a few times and then grabs it with his teeth and pulls it
along the floor.
"No Jase, it's not a toy, it's your new bed, so leave it."
After repeating this a few times he begins to understand
and eventually lies down on it and drifts off to sleep. She
finds the frying pan and cooks the bacon. The novelty of

ease in cooking and making the sandwich is a joy and the speed at which it's accomplished surprises her. The hot, crisp, bacon butty is lovely with a mug of tea. After this lunch and washing up the pots and putting everything away she wonders what to do.

Her next priority is to buy new underwear, knickers and socks. The few pairs she left at the hut will have to be thrown away; she knows that not even the hottest wash will bring them clean.

So with this in mind, she leaves Jason to sleep and takes her bankcard to draw cash and goes back down the stairs into town. She makes her way towards the hole in the wall at the end of the road and takes out £50 in cash; this will keep her going for a while. She then wanders around aimlessly, wondering where the best place is to buy underwear, she discounts the cheaper shops and then remembers a small shop that she has passed whilst going through the town centre, specialising in underwear and although presenting itself as rather old fashioned should have what she needs, so she heads in that direction.

When she enters the shop, a bell rings and an elderly lady comes to the glass counter and asks her what she is looking for. She tells her that she wants to buy some socks and knickers. The lady then produces a wooden tray from underneath one of the counters with socks in. Jo realises that this shop is intended for older women and wonders what to say. Jo looks again at the tray of socks and picks up a woolly pair of green ones and asks how much they are.

"Those are £1.50 a pair, size 4-7 shoe size." The lady proudly says with a smile.

"I'll take three pairs of those thank you." They will be good quality and should last a long time; she decides to give the briefs a miss.

"Thank you love that's £4.50 all together." She wraps them into a brown paper bag.

Once out in the street again, Jo looks in Mad Mick's and the £1 shop, to see what they have in women's underwear. There doesn't seem to be much choice around here for new clothing. Jo has mainly picked things up from the charity shops and has bought underwear from the outdoor market, so if she doesn't have any luck, she can wait until the next market day. As her mind processes all of this, she turns down a side street towards the centre of town, arriving at the junction; her attention is caught by the headlines on a newspaper billboard. In bold black typesetting -

'MAN'S BODY FOUND FENTON'

Stares back at her and she stands still in her tracks, unable to move. Her feet stick and become locked to the pavement and as if by an unknown force, she feels a pulling and dragging of her body sideways. As she tries to hold on, try to dissuade this pressure from movement and hold herself upright, it becomes almost a battle of wills and she is no longer in charge. And then the woolly, sensation filling her head takes over and pulls her downwards and tips her and this is also something that is outside of her, external and in charge, and in control and is making this happen against her will. Her legs are no longer hers, her body a foreign entity to her mind and her mind too, an external being from afar and she is no longer herself.

"Love?" Somewhere from a distant world Jo hears the word again "Love?" And again. "Love?" only this time louder and more urgent. Through the muggy hazy distorted landscape above her, again comes the word "Love?" followed this time by the words, "Are you ok?" On the edge of her arm she feels a nudging, a prodding and a tugging, from a person from whom the words are being spoken. This intrusive action, ricochets and sends waves of incomprehension and despair and in her numbed out state, is being delivered from another planet, a foreign land, a world in which she in this moment does not belong and cannot understand. 'Leave me alone, just leave me alone, go away, stop talking, stop questioning and touching me.' And then these few words begin exploding and other voices; different questions and more bodies of people are hemming her inside of this dark space. Deep, dark, drifting, far away, detached and disconnected, here in this nothingness, empty and lifeless, in this solitary cocoon, shrinking in time, in an impenetrable space, unplugged from her vital force of energy. 'Just leave me, leave me alone……'

"Are you alright love? I think we should phone for an ambulance."

'An ambulance, no, no.' As Jo looks upwards and faces the dazzling bright light; she sees a face looking intently down.

"What happened did you fall?" Asks the person who now kneels down by her side and gently strokes her shoulder and turns to the other onlookers and signals them with a waft of her hand to move away.

She asks again, "Have you hurt yourself?"

As the edges of Jo's conscience slide back into place and the colours filter through and the darkness fades away she is able to say, "No."

"She's ok." Jo hears the woman's words clearer now and as her body re enters its skin, she tries several times to move without effect.

As the audience around her disperses and she refocuses again, she eventually, after an unknown passage of time, regains movement once more and shifts her body on the pavement. The temptation to recoil back inside remains strong and the anaesthetic pull sideward draws her away from herself and she knows somehow that she has to try and fight its powerful force. To sleep, to go into a deep, deep, sleep, away and far, far away, to switch off and forget everything, forget herself, not inside a place of peace but in an empty void stretching to infinity.

"Come on let's try and get you up."

The hand reaching down and taking hold of Jo's feels strong and sure and finding a seed of hope, she denies her captor and joins hands and enters the street once more. The process of getting up and standing, is one of relearning and feels unfamiliar and difficult – to become grounded and anchored to the pavement takes time. To assimilate language and movement is awkward and confusing and she steps carefully at first, taking care not to fall.

"Do you need a drink, would you like to go to a café for a drink?" The woman asks.

She stops and looks worried when Jo doesn't answer. Jo is unable to process thoughts, her mind has shut down and she is incapable of responding to the question.

They slowly walk along in the direction of the museum and a quieter part of town. With each step forward, Jo feels less sleepy and drugged and starts to wake up.

As they reach the museum garden and the empty seats, the woman asks, "Would you like to sit here and I will get you a drink, what would you like, tea, coffee, fruit juice?"

"Tea, thank you."

"Right you sit there and I'll go and get us some tea." The woman goes into the museum café for the drinks.

She returns with a tray carrying two mugs of tea, "How do you feel now, the colour is coming back into your cheeks, I'm glad?"

"Thanks, thank you for helping me."

They sip their tea in silence and Jo is thankful for its hot sweetness. "I put you some sugar in it for shock."

This is comforting and Jo is glad of its sweetness.

After finishing their drinks, the woman offers to walk Jo home.

"I'm ok; I can get home alright from here, thank you for offering."

"I would prefer it if you would let me walk back with you, to see you home safely." The woman insists.

"I'm sure I will be ok, but if you're walking back into the town centre, I will walk along with you."

"Yes I am going back through the town centre, so we can walk together, are you ok to set off?"

"Yes, thank you."

The pair begin walking back to the town, when they approach the road Jo tells her that she is not far from home and the flat. "It's the top flat in the old fisherman's chapel."

"I can walk that way with you, it's ok."

And with that they turn in the direction of the flat. When they reach the doorway at the bottom of the four flats, Jo turns and thanks the woman again.

"Are you sure you are ok now on your own?"

"Yes thank you I am ok now." Jo opens the entry door and says goodbye, ascending the staircase slowly.

Entering the safety of the flat, she says hello to Jason and gives him a couple of dog chews and then goes to the bedroom. She is overwhelmed by a sleepy sensation and has no option but to lie down and surrender to its demands. After removing her shoes and jacket, she tosses them onto the floor and crawls under the duvet fully clothed, she hasn't the strength to undress. She buries her head and shuts out the daylight and tries to find comfort in a curled up foetal position and pulls the duvet around her tight. Her breath deepens and becomes a circular heaving in and out; she wants to take in the deep breaths but restricts the exhalation, as this feels loaded with grief and hurt. She tries to hold on and tighten each revolving breath; the whole respiration cycle becomes an effort, a real challenge as if the mere action of breathing is a momentous thing. To give, to give into it is impossible; she doesn't want to go there, wherever that place is. This bed is unable to provide a nest of security and she feels trapped and again stuck in an uncomfortable space. This timeless holding position keeps her, for how long, she isn't sure. How does one make sense of the constriction and expansion of time when suffering, how does one measure it? Albeit it, eventually she leaves this prison and goes to the kettle, to fill it for a mug of tea.

Jo needs to hear music; she needs respite from this inner turmoil, and needs a gateway, a passage out into a place of heaven and beauty. She switches on the kitchen radio and tunes in to the classical station. The stirring sounds

of Claudio Monteverdi's Orfeo – 'Possente Spirito e
formindabil Nume' connects and pours its juices into
her. How apt like the words from the poem –

'Orpheus. Eurydice. Hermes.' – Rainer Maria Rilke
1875-1926
– All inwardness and fully clothed in her own death,
her treasure, she had become like a sweet fruit of
darkness: she was all crammed with death too huge
and recent for her understanding.

How resonant and true, she needs this music, this
vibration, to continue and drip feed her, to enter her
veins, to fill her bones with its purity and sanctity, to lift
her up and transcend this earthly fight and provide her a
place of rest, for enough moments of time to forget.

She leaves the boiling kettle and returns back to bed and
places her head down on the pillow, shutting her eyes
and returning like Eurydice to the underworld, awaiting
Orpheus with eyes closed, unopened, to lead her towards
the light.

The next day, late in the morning, she wakes and goes to
the kitchen to make breakfast and notices a small card on
the doormat. The business card with the picture of two
hands reaching out, reads –
Holistic Healing Centre
nestling in a quiet corner of Fenton
19 Larch Cottage
Harbour Road.
We have a team of skilled and friendly therapists and an
extensive range of therapies each designed to relax,
strengthen and bring harmony on physical, mental,
emotional and spiritual levels. For good health, well
being and personal fulfilment.
Tel No. 01839 267943 for more information
Client confidentially, comfort and care are our priority

On the reverse of the card, handwritten in blue ink, are the words –

Hope this card finds you well after yesterday,
if you need help or a guiding hand we are here.
Best wishes Simone.

Simone that must be the woman from yesterday, Jo remembers vaguely, a passing shadow of fogginess, with broken flashes of detail, her face lost in grey mist. She takes the card and between the palms of her hands, holds and strokes its soft surface, digesting and absorbing the gesture, the promise of a gift, a token, an Orpheus opening the heart of the gods and dangling a rope to lift her.
She puts the card on the worktop and props it up against the radio.
Then pours milk into a pan, to make porridge and boil the kettle for tea.

She wanders around listlessly nursing a headache, a dull throbbing and nagging ache, her head feels heavy and she doesn't have any painkillers to take. She contemplates going to the shops to buy tablets, but doesn't feel like going outside today. Jason is fidgeting and waiting for his walk and she knows that she doesn't have any choice.
"Come on then Jase, let's go."
She takes her jacket and rucksack and checks the gas ring to make sure that it is off and goes to the door. Her legs and feet feel leaden, as she steps down the stairs; at the bottom of the staircase they take the path towards the beach. It should be relatively quiet at this time of the year, as the weather today is windy and cool. They take the route through the streets, full of old cottages with tiny front doors that open directly onto the street. These date back to the 1700's when the livelihood of the townspeople was dependant on the fisherman and their catch, how different it must have been back then. Young

couples now occupy the old cottages and many are second homes and holiday lets.

It is good to be outside, even though the memory of yesterday, hangs around in the periphery of her mind and makes her feel uncertain and cautious. She knows that she cannot succumb to the temptation and hide away. The downward spiral that that would take, would make it more and more difficult to bring herself out of; 'one foot in front of the other,' she issues this mantra to herself. They reach the road leading down to the beach; the sight of the sand gladdens her. The sea is far out and the expanse of sand stretches to the Brigg and the cliffs at the other end. She cannot detect anyone walking along the beach and this propels her faster forward in anticipation. It's amazingly incredible, the positive and vibrant effect of breathing in the sea air from the breeze, as it whips up from the sea, it is intoxicating and sustenance for her body and soul, she is glad that she came.

"Go on then Jase, off you go." It is a lovely sight to see him bouncing along, sniffing with excitement.

Walking along she trawls the shells and pebbles left by the outgoing tide and picks up one or two. This connection with the gritty, salty, earth, allows another perspective to emerge, she can touch and see all of this wonderful reality and enjoys it, finding happiness. They walk the full length of the beach against the wind, it pushes and tries to prevent her forward movements and this continual challenge, as she fights her way across, is a positive and empowering kick up the backside that she needs. It is certainly blowing the cobwebs, blowing the negative debris and flushing it out of her mind.

Retracing their footsteps back along the coastline, her spirit lifts and her headache starts to ease. She feels so much more relaxed and skips and runs with Jason, playing catch up, as they approach the harbour landing. She feels reenergized and puts Jason on his lead and walks back to the flat.

She is ravenous and thirsty now and takes a digestive biscuit from the top of the packet, whilst deciding what to make to eat. Jason loves digestives and she puts one in his dog dish. She decides to cook pasta with pesto and pine nuts, this will be tasty and quick; she doesn't have any fresh bread, which is a shame, so she opens a packet of corn chips.

After the meal she takes her rucksack, coat and enough money to buy the shopping and leaves Jason to rest.

"I won't be long Jase, I'll see you soon."

She calls at the greengrocers for an onion, bananas and apples and then to the bakers for bread and a cherry pie. On the way to Martins butchers, she spots a poster in the window of the newsagents, it catches her eye, it's about Fenton art club, advertising their forthcoming show, at the town hall. At the bottom of the poster is a small paragraph, asking for anyone interested in exhibiting their art, to contact a Mr Andrews and his telephone number. She makes a mental note to take a look at the exhibition when it's on and then walks along to the shop. She buys mince and a couple of slices of roast ham and then hurries back.

Life is moving once again. The pace of living here, with its instant hot water and lighting, and the quick cooking facilities, soon opens up a huge amount of spare time. No longer is she chopping wood and toiling away in the garden, or making several trips back and forth into town, for supplies. She still hasn't returned to the hut. It's as though she can't bear to see it and doesn't want to acknowledge the severity of what happened. If she carries on ignoring it, then it will mend itself somehow. For a while at least she just wants to be oblivious, needs to take time out and switch off, from what needs doing there. So unsurprisingly, her creative juices soon latch on to new and fresh ideas.

One day whilst going around the shops, she sees the stacks of canvases, tubes of paints and brushes and picks them up. Several ideas spring to mind at once. In her minds eye she sees pictures of the seaside – sea, sand, boats, stripy deckchairs, beach huts, buckets and spades, a promenade of colour and happiness. She selects a few different sized canvases and brushes and a tin of acrylic paints and coloured crayons. With these tucked under her arm, she cheerily heads back to the flat and takes her treasures up to the top floor 'workroom'. The light coming in through the velux windows, floods the room with bright light, perfect for painting in. She will need a table of some sort, to work on and a chair. She will have to look around the market and shops, she doesn't want to buy anything from the junk shop – Charles might find second hand junk offensive – after all it isn't her flat. She should be able to find something that's not too expensive, if she searches around. In the meantime, she can work at the kitchen table. Jason lies happily in the corner of the kitchen, curled up on his new doggy beanbag.

Jo starts sketching out a few ideas on a piece of paper and finds herself writing lines of poems, drawing boats and ice cream huts and sandcastles. Then her hand draws the beach and the jagged cliffs and the bench looking out to sea, she transfers this to the canvas, pencilling in the outline, sketching lines of the beach, and the shrubs and vegetation growing out of the cliffs; such a simple scene, yet so strong and prominent in her mind – reaching out and connecting, linking, and joining, a meeting with a part of her soul – where did she go? Another disappearance – a past memory, begins to erase itself – to be forgotten and swallowed up by amnesia. She needs to paint this scene to mark it, to commit it to reality, to be able to see it, bring it back to consciousness, whenever it locks itself away inside a distant memory, erased or half forgotten.

Jo's first attempt fails to capture the scene so she tries again, rubbing out the first pencil lines. 'That's it, got it,' she has the effect she wants, of an empty bench, awaiting two people to sit down and share a moment of time together. The 'waiting', the vacant empty seat, the scene set, the view looking out to sea, blue sea, bluer sky across the horizon. The little rickety bench, with tufts of long grass around its posts, the bare gritty soil where people have shuffled their feet, leaves a shallow indentation in front. The surrounding thicket, bushy and dense and the little path leading through, and the warning notice of dangerous cliff erosion, a reminder to take care. Yes, this picture is gaining life and energy and she starts with the colourful paints. This experience – painting onto canvas, taking the brush steadily and carefully at first and then more liberally, dipping in and out of the colours, mixing and brushing it onto the white of the canvas, is satisfying once again.

The finished canvas, 'The Bench' has a naïve quality to it. Jo is really pleased with it. So much so, that she begins her second picture straight away, titled 'The Promenade', a mosaic tiled pavement, with iron hand rails above the beach, ice creams and cafes, lots of detail, lots of colour. She does a grand sketch first on paper, before starting the canvas; slightly larger than 'The Bench' this one is 18" wide x 14" long.

Jo's days become consumed with painting, the outside world, although directly outside the flat; unlike the hut, may as well be miles away. The TV down in the sitting room, has never been switched on since her arrival, it holds no interest, nor does lounging around on the settee. Her habits formed, whilst living in the hut, are lodged strongly in her day-to-day existence here.
As the days pass by, she is proud of her growing collection of finished canvases. Stood side by side along the wall, they reflect her view of this lovely, quaint harbour town. She manages to find a cheap folding table and chair at Mad Mick's, the table is easy to clean and the chair comfy with a cushion on it. The room upstairs has a magnetic quality and once she's there, she has difficulty drawing herself away.

Time slips by and merges, without definitive markers of hours, days, or weeks, as the brush strokes, the paint being the dictator, the time mechanism. She tends to wake early and take Jason down onto the beach, for a good brisk walk. The days are colder now and hardly anyone else is around. She still picks up pebbles and shells and keeps any interesting finds; she needs to take these to the hut, as she doesn't want to clutter up the flat, she has an obligation to Charles to keep it clean.

As of now she hasn't returned to the hut, she couldn't face it straight away and now with being engrossed here painting, she never seems to get around to it, but she must before too long. As for Charles and Stella, she wrote a thank you note and popped it in Stella's letterbox but she hasn't seen her around. She doesn't know where Charles lives, so unless he contacts her, which he hasn't yet, then she'll just have to wait until he does.

Jo had a haircut yesterday and feels stronger, sharper and less tired, than when she came. Jason has settled quickly, he sleeps a lot during the day on his beanbag, occasionally coming up to see her in the workroom. If the evening is dry and pleasant, they go for a walk down on the beach if the tide is out, or around the greener parts of the town. As autumn rolls on, the holiday shops close down and the town takes on a different identity, much quieter and takes time out to rest and sleep before the frenetic activities start all over again.

Having completed four canvases, 'The Bench', 'The Promenade', 'The Beach Hut' and 'The Harbour', she is pleased with these and has ruminated and wondered about entering them in the art exhibition, that she saw advertised in the newsagent's shop. And so after days of procrastination, she finally jots down the phone number and plucks up the courage to telephone Mr Andrews, about the exhibition at the town hall. He is a chatty man and tells her,

"I doubt if there are any Picasso's here in Fenton, it's for anyone in the town who wants to show their work and

were always glad of new people coming on board, so do
come along. You are allowed to enter six paintings but if
you only have one that's ok, so we would love to meet
you and see your work. Come along with your paintings,
the evening before the exhibition, so that they can be
hung up in the hall and what's your name, so I will know
you, when you come?"
"It's Jo."
"Right then Jo, I'll look forward to seeing you then,
goodbye."
After putting the phone down this inspires her and she
settles down to creating sketches for other canvases.

Although there are three more flats in this building, Jo
hardly ever bumps into the people living in them, and
wonders if they are all occupied. The walls are solid and
with working in the attic workroom most of the time, she
doesn't notice any noise coming from the flats below.
Occasionally she has heard doors closing and footsteps
on the staircase but that has been whilst she has been in
the kitchen or the bedroom. She doesn't spend much
time in the sitting room, maybe an odd hour here and
there, when she takes a break from painting and decides
to read a book, or just sit and think about things. Life
here is remarkably quiet and uninterrupted and the days
pass by, each day immersed in the palette of colours and
the brushing on of paint. Whilst sitting of an evening,
when the night draws in, she picks up a pen and paper
and plays around with words and sentences and creates
poems – words that wrap themselves around each of the
paintings. She takes each of these poems and writes them
onto pieces of coloured card and attaches them to their
respective pictures. This gives her an idea to make gift
cards for birthdays, or just blank ones for any occasion.

One day, a day just like any other here, she is startled
and her ears prick up, when she hears loud banging and
shouting, coming from downstairs. She waits and
wonders what has happened and is unsure if to go

downstairs to find out. She goes down from the
workroom and through the hallway to the door and
opens it. Looking out and down the staircase, she waits a
couple of minutes and then just as she is about to close
it, another shout and bang keeps her there. As the door to
the flat below opens, a young teenage girl with thick,
carrot coloured hair, carrying a rucksack strides out,
yelling back to whoever is in the room.

"I don't need your kindness, daddy, I don't need it," and
with that she stomps down the staircase, in a purposeful
hurry and slams the entry door.

From the inside of the room she has come from, a male
voice shouts to her retreating footsteps.

"That's what you think my darling, you'll be back to
daddy, just you wait and see."

Jo quickly shuts it and turns around with her back
pressed against it. She has to turn around to close the
catch and lock it, and then sinks to her knees, with her
back resting against the door. The incident leaves her
feeling shaky and small and she spends time fixed to the
spot and remains sitting, until the light in the hallway
starts to fade and the daylight has almost disappeared.
Jason comes to her side; he is disturbed and upset by her
motionless state and wants her to get up. He returns
again and starts to whine with worry. 'I must get up; I
must move and put on a light. Why has this happened,
what has put me here?' Jason darts back into the kitchen,
returning this time with his fluffy toy – a duck, with a
squeaker inside. He runs down the hallway, skidding,
this causes him to land with all his legs splayed apart,
still holding his duck between his teeth, his look of
horror and the long squawk emitting from the duck, is so
funny, that all at once the spell is broken and Jo can at
last stretch out and move.

"What are you like Jase?"

The relief that his world is back to normal sends him
giddy and he runs around in circles, tossing the duck into
the air and catching it as he slips and slides on the
laminate floor.

"It's my turn now. Give me the duck Jase."

Jo slides after him, trying to prize the duck from his jaw, without success. There is no way that he wants to let go. And on and on she tries, this is the game that Jason loves the best. They carry on until it is too dark and she has to stand up and turn on the lights. She makes a mug of hot chocolate and gives him a couple of chews. She is glad that he has had his afternoon walk and that they don't have to go out again today. She settles Jason down for the night and takes her mug to bed. She is glad of the duvet and the milky sweetness of the drink and sips it slowly and when it's finished she lies in silence awaiting sleep.

For the remainder of the week, Anna and her son, spend each day going down the coast, to the larger town of Thornby. There is a job centre and a 'Connexion' where he applies for emergency accommodation and puts in a new claim for benefit.

Mark explains to the agencies, the dangerous position he has been in and the urgency of his leaving his home city and consequently his need of support from them.

By the weekend he has made a successful claim and is given a place in a run down B & B, until there is a place in the hostel.

Anna is relieved now her son is safe and re-established. There is more talk about another college course being on the cards and Mark just needs a few more new clothes because he left so much behind. Anna buys the usual four tracksuit bottoms, four t-shirts, a jacket, socks and underpants.

Another set up Anna reminds herself, as she catches the bus back to Fenton. Mark promises to phone her daily, to keep her updated with how his life is progressing.

This time Anna feels weary as she returns, she's bought milk and bread to see her for that evening and the next morning. She will stay around for a while longer, before returning to the city.

This time Mark cannot return back to the city, he would be killed, he'd been told. Anna boils the kettle to make tea and picks up her son's discarded cigarette ends, from around the caravan. She locks the door and checks all the widows and makes up the bed before it gets dark. She reflects as she eats her toast and drinks her mug of tea. Because the site will be closing down at the end of the season, the caravan as a temporary home, is ruled out for Mark. She feels better, knowing he will be warm and safe during the cold winter months in his B & B and later on in his hostel place. He has re-established another support network. A part of her knows after six or eight weeks of this experience, her son will become bored and want to move on.

Anna fills her hot water bottle, she just wants to rest, she felt like a vagrant wandering through the streets, going from one office and building to the next. 'Sleep, after a good nights sleep, I'll feel better.' She is warm and comfortable under the duvet and is too tired; she's had enough and can't do it anymore.

Drifting off to sleep, she says goodnight to her three children.

'I wonder where Jo is?' Anna wonders as she finally surrenders to the warm darkness of the deep sleep.

In the morning she is relieved at the stillness and silence in the caravan. 'Poor old you, you weren't up to scratch, thank God.'

It is early, as Anna looks through a chink in the heavy closed curtains, it is just becoming light, another day and this one's mine. Tidy and clean around and then a walk to blow off these weeks of panic, fear and running around.

In the silence and stillness, her thoughts slowly return, to the bench and the rape. Since the experience she has turned off and not allowed it into her mind. Like her life, she has learnt to survive by cutting off and disconnecting herself.

Now the feelings, which she has pushed away, begin to drip back into her mind. The experience with the angel of joy and the newspaper pages, have brought back the pain inside herself, of what the man had done. 'Why? Was it random? She wants it to be random, because if it weren't, it would mean he had done it deliberately to her and that scares her. Who would want to do that? Who and why? She can't think of anyone who would want to do it. Who in her life would ever want her, in any shape or fashion?' No one wanted her, he had made that plain and she had cut herself off, closed herself up, to not allow anyone near her, or inside her. And this man, this total stranger had violated her and she had had no say. She couldn't, wasn't allowed any say, just the animal above her hurting her, why? Because he's a bastard. Something deep inside makes her think, is this what she is? Someone, something, who another person sees and thinks yes, she's game. Not a person, or a woman, or a human being but a thing to be used. What was it that he had seen in her, to make him feel he could use her to bang away on - to desecrate her body, which he had no right to do? People say, dogs know if you are afraid of them – they smell it and sense it. 'Does she smell of that fear?' Anna wonders. 'What fear? The fear that she doesn't matter, that she isn't important enough, not worth pissing on, a weak woman – a vessel and receptacle. A target, a victim to be victimised and abused.' That's how he had seen her. Not as anything but as something he could use.

The tears roll down her face now, she has space and doesn't want to stop them. Anna's whole life has been one of useful abuse and the man has shown her and made it a 100 percent clear that she can be abused. 'How has she become this pathetic, dribbling woman, with so little control over her life?' She believed if she kept herself separate from herself, then she could survive. 'But survive what? Survive, to be able to continue to be anaesthetised, from the use and abuse.' The cutting herself off had meant the abuse continued, because she hadn't actually stopped it. What she had done was make herself numb, so it could continue and she could absorb more and more of it, to the point where she had been wholly used and abused, by the man who raped her. The bottom of the bottle was no less destructive, than what she had spent the whole of her life doing.

Anna stops crying and gets out of bed. Collecting her towel and soap bag and a fifty pence from her purse, she locks the door and makes her way to the shower block. Putting her towel over the top of the door she begins to undress. Standing naked beneath the showerhead, she turns the dials before putting the money in the slot. There is a pause and then the mixture of scolding hot and cold water come gushing through, a bit of cold and a bit of hot, Anna decides. For a few moments she stands still whilst the water covers her and makes her skin tingle. Slowly pouring shampoo on her hair and soaping her body, as the hot water rinses away the suds. Words keep coming into her mind. She doesn't understand what they mean and listens as the hot water stops. 'You are worth it, worth what? Worth yourself, you don't have to be of use to be worthy. You just have to be you, to be yourself. You don't have to prove anything to anyone, not ever again it's over.' The steam rises from her body as she rubs herself dry and then slips back on her night dress, dressing gown and then wraps the towel around her hair to keep warm. Slipping on her shoes and taking her soap she leaves the showers.

Anna decides she will leave the cleaning for another time and go for a long walk and buy something good to eat and maybe even a bottle of wine. Inside she feels calm and more at peace with herself. She will complete her homeopathy course and not pack it in, as she had intended to, because it made her life so difficult. 'Fuck the difficulties – I will do it and I will become a homeopath, because that's what I want to do. What about the use bit? Yes that is one aspect of becoming a homeopath, but homeopathy is much more than being of use. It's a life transforming experience, which I share with patients. It's on my terms and I will receive a professional fee for a professional service.'

Getting dressed she thinks about her children and how much she loves them and how she wants the very best for each of them. She has her own measure and her children have theirs too, of what they want, as well as what she wants for them. She had let her husband and children define their own terms, rejecting Anna's input and that wasn't right or how it should have been. But there had been such a fight, a battle in the everyday simple things, which Anna had grown weary of, the endless rows, arguments and blaming from him and the

never-ending recriminations. It had been awful. He had
believed that Anna had to remain in her defined place
and fundamentally if she had beliefs, thoughts or ideas
about what would be best for their children, then he
would say she was full of anger and bitterness and didn't
want their children to have happy childhoods. If Anna
ever said anything, it would be a criticism against him
and his ways. She had grown tired of continually telling
him, that none of it was personal and it wasn't about him
but about their children. It had been an ongoing battle
about nothing, instead of a relationship based on mutual
respect and an understanding and acceptance of what
was the best for the whole family and each of their
individual children. Instead it was an angry, bitter,
bickering argument about completely nothing. Just
treading through treacle and damaging the family as a
whole, as well as each of its individual members. Her
children had no boundaries and as a consequence were
out of control. If her children were grounded for their
behaviour, he expected Anna to be the one to explain to
him why she had done so and not for him to ask, or for
his children to speak to him. He continuously questioned
her motives and would side with their children who
watched on, knowing it was a free for all and if played
right, they could and did rule the roost. They knew that
their father would undo, whatever their mother had done.
They would be rewarded for their negative behaviour
and all Anna could do, was run around like a headless
chicken, picking up the pieces of the fall out, which their
behaviour increasingly created. He plodded on, blinkered
by his own point of view, which didn't help their
children. Anna had tried to do her best for them, but it
was about picking up the pieces and repairing the
damage and not about building and moving forward as a
family or individually. They had ended up, as a
dysfunctional, group of individuals, with all the separate
and collective pain that brought. 'I should have left but I
wanted to play happy families and instead became more

unhappy and lost in a place I didn't create but lived in. I should have taken our children away.'

It is damp, cold autumn morning as Anna walks into town. There is a placard advertising an art exhibition in the Town Hall. Usually the artwork is displayed in the back of the Tourist Information building. It is held for and by local artists. She had gone in once and had even thought about buying a simple watercolour of three children but hadn't.
She might take a walk to the Town Hall later and have a look around the exhibition, after looking at the charity shops. She feels more optimistic about her day ahead, doing things, which give her pleasure and joy.
After looking around the shops she walks towards the Town Hall. The exhibition is more formal and better organised than it usually is. Walking around and looking at all the different pictures, takes Anna away from her thoughts about her children and daily life.
Anna suddenly stops in her tracks, as she is about to walk past, a small-unframed painting on one of the boards. 'It can't be, it's impossible.' Anna waits as her heart does summersaults whilst looking at the picture. It is called 'The Bench' and is the bench near the thicket. Scanning across the picture she notices it hasn't been signed, and near one of the bench legs, a bouquet of flowers has been placed. £15 is its price. Without thinking, she walks up to the desk and tells the woman she wants to buy it. The woman follows Anna to where the picture is and sticks a little red circle next to it, to show that it has been sold.
"You're in luck," the woman tells her, as she gets a £20 note from her purse to pay. "The artist who painted the picture is here somewhere."
"Really."
"The painting has to remain here, until the exhibitions over, I hope that's all right, I'll give you a receipt of course? You can collect it on the last day."

Anna puts the receipt in her purse, she knows the painting isn't expensive, but after paying out for her son, she hadn't expected to spend much money, '£20 - £20 on a picture and an angel.'

As Anna puts her purse back into her bag the woman says, "Look, there's the artist, she's just gone past the man in the red shirt."

Anna turns around and follows the man.

Saturday, the second day of the painting exhibition at the Town Hall, today unlike yesterday, when filled with nervous energy, and uncertainty Jo is happy. Her paintings definitely hold their own among the rest of the other artists. Her four pictures hang in different areas of the exhibition hall and as she stands proudly in front of 'The Promenade' she is pleased with its little red dot representing 'SOLD'. Her first sale of one of her paintings, with still another day to go, she remains hopeful that she will sell more and is enjoying being a part of the town's art scene.

Talking to the other artists, mostly older people from the town, feels like a huge hurdle and her body carries this nervous energy around in this unfamiliar space and she is determined to hold on to her privacy and not give too much of herself away. The general chitchat is ok, but when asked more personal questions, she excuses herself and moves on. She doesn't want to open and stretch her boundaries and prefers to keep people at a safe distance. She is enjoying discussing with other artists, their techniques, structures and ideas behind their paintings. The room today has a constant trickle of people looking around. She is fascinated, as she overhears their comments and watches how they linger and look at the paintings. There are fewer of the artists here today, the desk has two volunteers and Jo was in two minds as to whether or not to come today. Somehow she felt as if she was given a push from the universe and so here she is on day two of the exhibition. There is a table with wine and another selling tea and coffee and cakes provided by the local organisers. She decides to have a cup of tea and then walk back into town and shop for a few things.

As Anna reaches the man she hears a voice, which she recognises and remembers. She sees Jo talking to a woman who is at a stall making teas and coffees.

Jo discusses the visitor numbers of yesterday and her sale of 'The Promenade' as she chats to the tea lady, she stalls in her conversation, as she looks over her shoulder and sees Anna coming towards her. Jo is unable to say anything at first; unable to finish the conversation with the tea lady, her mind is blank.

"Hi." Anna greets Jo. It is wonderful to see her again; she looks so well in jeans and a pink t-shirt and at home in the exhibition.

"How are you, what are you doing here?"

As Anna talks Jo walks away with her from the table, towards the end of the hall. Jo has difficulty engaging with Anna, as she looks into her blue grey eyes, she detects a painful expression, before her eyes light up and her whole face beams into a smile.

"So, what are you doing here?"

"I've got some pictures here in the exhibition."

"So it is you, you have painted 'The Bench'?"

"Yes."

"I've just bought it, I looked at it and thought it was so lovely, and didn't realise you had painted it, why didn't you sign it?"

"Oh I haven't signed any of my paintings; it's lovely to see you again. But I will sign yours for you, so thanks for buying it."

The women stand gazing at each other in their pleasure at being reunited again.

"You didn't come back."

"No, I had to wait for Adam and we got caught in the rain and in the end, I thought you'd understand why I didn't come."

"I thought that was why. Look, let's go over there, get a glass of wine and catch up."

The women both pick up a glass of red wine and find seats.

"It reminds me of you, of us, of our meeting - the bench," here Anna pauses, "Which seems such an endless time ago."

"Yes it does, doesn't it?"

"I went to visit your hut to see if you were still there. It was a shock to see the place empty, the windows and door was open so I closed them, what happened, it looked a real mess?"

"I was flooded out and had to leave in a hurry."

"But where are you living now?"

"In a flat, in the town centre, it's not too far from here, but it's only temporary until the end of February until I can sort out my hut."

"That's going to be some job."

Reflecting on Anna's comment leaves Jo feeling suddenly downcast.

"Don't worry about the hut, I'm sorry I never called for the 'Purple Pearl', I couldn't something happened and I had to leave, so sorry about that."

"It's ok. I don't know if the 'Purple Pearl' is ok, as most of my stock was damaged by the flood and I haven't been back to see."

"Well if it has been damaged, don't worry about it, Adam isn't here with me now, so it's ok."

"Thank you for buying my picture, it's nice to see you, again."

"I've got a couple of weeks left on the coast if you're ready to sort out the hut I'll come and help you."

"Will you?"

"Of course. We can go and have a look sometime if you like."

"That would be great, is Monday ok for you?"

"Fine."

"I'll meet you on the corner where the junk shop is."

"What time?"

"How about 12 o'clock."

"Ok. That will be fine."

"So you're here by yourself? Where's Adam?"

"Adams back in the city at school, his dads taking care of him, I came back here with Mark, my eldest son. He got into a lot of trouble in the city with drug dealers, so I had to get him away. He's ok for the moment. He's staying in a B & B and starting a new college course soon, so I'm hoping."

Anna feels warm inside and relaxes.

"How's Jason?"

"Oh he's happy, he is back at the flat sleeping."

"How did you manage to find the flat?"

"Charles and Stella, do you remember Charles and Stella?"

"Yes, yes I do."

"They came to my rescue."

"Oh, that was lucky" Anna feels perplexed by their generosity.

"Come on, I'll show you the other pictures I have in the exhibition."

The women begin to make their way back to where the paintings are displayed.

After chatting and browsing the other artworks, they turn to each other.

"Would you like another glass of wine?"

"Yes, that would be nice."

Jo returns to the table for two more glasses and takes them back to Anna.

"Thanks."

After Anna walks away from the exhibition, Jo is happy that she has bought one of her paintings and has offered to help with cleaning up the hut. She has arranged to take 'The Bench' along with her on Monday, so that she doesn't have to make a special visit back to the exhibition to collect it.

Jo is glad to be going back to the hut to see it; to find out what condition it is in. And for Anna to come along with her is helpful, she really hadn't wanted to go back on her own and if Anna can help clean some of it, then that will be brilliant.

So Jo walks away from the exhibition with an inner glow, knowing that the weekend has brought about transformation – her art has proved successful and she can look positively in terms of the hut and hopefully to sorting it out.

However, life at the flat has shown her that she can have an existence feeling satisfied, without having to toil

away growing vegetables and living in the sometimes
harsh conditions in a hut.

She has found her ideal world in how she occupies her
time – she has other creative ideas too, that she would
like to have a go at.

It's too early to decide, or even think about selling the
hut and moving into a place in the town.

Anyway, she will see how it pans out and take it from
here and see what comes her way. Things are sent for a
reason, so maybe the flood at the hut was one of those
reasons to bring about change; she can only wait and see.
Nevertheless she is looking forward to spending time
with Anna and with her helping hands that can only be a
good thing.

Walking back through the streets of Fenton, after the
unexpected meeting with Jo, Anna feels she is in a
dream. The few glasses of wine have probably helped.
She decides to call off at the supermarket before
returning back to the caravan, to buy something she
would enjoy for tea. Picking up her basket on the way in,
she spots the advertisement. It is for wine, red wine,
'shall I shan't I?' Anna vacillates. 'Go on then.' she
picks up a bottle and puts it in her basket. She decides
she is in a decadent mood and on a roll, as she asks for
two slices of chicken from the delicatessen counter.
'This had better be it,' she reminds herself, in view of
the state of her finances at the moment.

Returning home she thinks about the meeting with Jo.
She looked well, different from how she'd seemed in the
hut. 'How?' Anna ponders as she unlocks the door. 'Not
so bohemian,' Anna reckons. She checks her phone;
there is a message from her son. She calls him back. No
answer just his voice mail. She leaves him a brief
message and tells him she loves him and then phones the
children's father and leaves him a message. She knows
he will call if there are any problems. 'I'm free now.'
Anna decides as she turns her phone off and puts it in the
drawer. A wave of frugality crosses her mind as she

makes a sandwich with the meat, because instead of using both slices, she uses one and puts the other away for the following day. She makes a pot of tea too instead of pouring herself a glass of wine. The wine will keep. The hot tea and food satisfy her. Soon it will begin to grow dark; there is only light for six to eight hours this time of year and by 4 o'clock it will be turning. She makes up her bed and fills a hot water bottle to air off the mattress.

The caravan is clean and tidy but sparse and frugal. Anna had washed all the walls down with sugar soap on the inside. The wood veneer of the wardrobes, sideboard, table and bits and pieces around the caravan have had a good clean and polish. All the cupboards and drawers have been organised, as had the food and store cupboard. Tomorrow she will tackle inside the wardrobes and have a go at sorting out the black sacks with clothes in. All she needs to keep at the caravan are clothes and shoes, which would fit the children for the following spring and summer, any that are going to be too small, she will take down to the charity shops. 'Good, I'm almost up to date with work in the caravan.' She re checks her store cupboard, to see if she needs to stock up on tins of beans, spaghetti, tomatoes, dried pasta or rice. Staples needed to spin out her food or provide meals, when she hadn't managed to shop. Long life milk and oats she also needs. No more today, tomorrow she would sort the clothes and take them into the centre on Monday, the day she has arranged to meet up with Jo. She would stock up for her store cupboard when she returned.

Anna suddenly has a brain wave. She would leave the wine and take it with her to Jo's and they could share it at the hut and toast their futures. This idea pleases her. The only jobs left to do are cleaning the outside of the caravan and the front patch to turn over and the outside shed to sort. These would be jobs for next spring. What would be the point of cleaning the caravan down for the autumn and winter, when it would receive the strong winds, the rain and snow and be splashed with mud?

Already underfoot the mud is starting to set and become firmer when walking on the grass. The rains have been particularly bad but that isn't usual, they had been flash floods and not at all like the usual coastal weather.

A soft wind blows around the caravan as darkness falls. Sinking into her bed she remembers her son's call. 'I'll phone him tomorrow, I can't give him any more money at the moment so it'll have to wait.' Her son is street wise enough to find the local youths who hang around the streets. He would have a set of new friends before the week's out. After finishing her drink she settles for the night.

When she returns to the city she will be in her fourth and final year of her homeopathy course. When it's finished, she will be a qualified homeopath, trained by a recognised college in classical homeopathy. Then when she has completed her training, she can register with the society of homeopaths. Homeopathy had come into her life at the right time. In time to stop her from falling to pieces and dying, literally and metaphorically, she knows she would not have survived without it. It had thrown her a lifeline. It had begun to haul her out of the abyss she had seeped into, bit by bit over the years. Now she can see a way out of the nightmare. It would take time and effort, but she has an understanding now, deep beneath the surface of herself where she intends her life to be. She would make it, she has no real alternative. Meeting up with Jo has reawakened Anna's physical self, another part she has disconnected herself from, submerged beneath the surface. It felt so nice to meet up again with Jo. She had been afraid she wouldn't see her again, after what had happened with the hut. It would dry out if this low wind, which chased around the caravan, kept up. It would need a lot of work to tackle it, to bring it up to something like, but it could be done.

As she falls asleep, the sea charges up to the shore and throws itself, in its chilly, cold, abandonment against the rocks and cliff face. What does it want? What does it seek to make itself complete? To become one with the land, to consume it and absorb it and to conquer it perhaps? But this endless task is still not done, not even after the billions of years and eons of time. The land can bear much, but the seas have much to give and both continue this cycle, to see which one could consume, or be absorbed by the other. Neither relenting willingly. Each night the sea creeps up to the land, to throw itself upon it, to beat itself upon it, to ravage and savage the land, but as the moon turns on her cycle and morning arrives, it retreats back into itself. To become restless and swell, as it waits for the deep undercurrents that run through it, to turn it again and again and again, for it to return to the shore, relentlessly it returns, unappeased, unfulfilled, savage, raw and hungry, ready to devour, with its unrelenting, insatiable appetite, slated but never satisfied, again and again and again.

The campsite is still and silent. The only sound that can be heard are the bangs, wraps and flaps that the wind creates, as it chases along the passages and corridors of the dark, cold caravans. The trees have been blown almost bare, with just odd leaves hanging on the branches.

She dreams again of the male character, John Doherty; she had begun to create in Fermanagh House. Again he holds his head close to Anna's and again she feels the anticipation of his touch and again she sees the astonishingly, ice blue eyes looking at her, absorbing her, washing over her and she feels as if she is drowning. The face then transforms into the black, hooded face and head of the man who had raped her and she wakes up gasping, trying to catch her breath and takes deep breaths, to regain her calmness and quieten her heart.

'It's a dream.'

The caravan is filled with darkness; shadows are cast all around her, where chinks of light from the few lamps around the campsite, split through the gaps in the curtains. Anna wishes one of her children is here with her, she feels so alone and puts her head back beneath the covers and fretfully returns to sleep.

Dawn breaks and the low wind turns into stronger gusts, which whoosh in and around and through and blow the few leaves left on the trees right off.

Anna sleeps on.

When she wakes she isn't sure what the time is, it remains dry in spite of the heaviness of the sky. She lights the small gas fire and fills the kettle. Whilst it boils, she folds up the blankets and puts the bed away, then she lights the grill to make toast for breakfast. The caravan begins to warm up, so she turns the gas fire onto the lowest setting. Outside it is dull, grey and not at all inviting. It looks as cold and bleak as it is. The few jobs she sets herself, will take about an hour or so, so they can keep a little. Having no children to do for, feels quite strange for Anna. She isn't used to, or comfortable about having, so much time on her hands. It feels decadent, almost a waste of time, not being busy or occupied. She needs to be doing something, even as she sits, otherwise she can't rest. The book, Fermanagh House, 'No,' she tells herself, recalling the disturbing dream she had during the night. 'But, I'm in control, not a character an unreal person.'

So she opens the blue book and tries to reconnect herself, to the words inside it and to the people and their lives and world. To be a proper writer would mean she needed to do it every day, otherwise she would just lose the threads, which hold it all together. Anyhow, this is just messing, just having a go, to see what happens, what comes up.

Anna thinks about what to write – We're going for the meal Anna reminds herself. Were going to Maya and Michael's for a meal. It's Sunday and she's meeting the people and they're going to vet her probably. So get her up, dressed and ready, she has two bottles of wine in the carrier bag, who's collecting her? Not Maya, she'll be busy cooking. Who? Him! OK. Go on then, Anna prompts herself.

So, Anna knew she needed to be ready before her lift came to take her to Fermanagh House. She had some tea and toast and then after opening all her blinds and curtains went up to her bedroom to look again at her choice of clothes. Had she made the right decision she began to wonder. Was she being too informal? Ok ok ok she told herself shut up, enough. After making her bed Anna laid full length across it. Soon her quiet and peace of mind returned to her. The clothes were right. Soft and warm and gentle and feminine. Pink for universal love. No axes to grind, no points to make no need to power dress no one to impress be yourself. Anna had had her fair haircut to shoulder length. She had worn it tied for so long. She was glad now she'd changed it. She'd had a body perm put in it too so it looked quite thick and healthy. She knew if she wanted she could also tie it back. Sitting on the floor Anna brushed and brushed her hair until she could run her fingers through it. She liked how it felt, soft but thick, full of life and body. Anna dressed. When she'd slipped on her shoes she fastened her rose quartz necklace on.

Anna puts her pen and blue book back into the drawer, 'well, that went better than I thought it would.'
She begins to look forward to her meeting with Jo. What does she need to take she wonders, besides the bottle of wine? Should she take a shovel to help lift the mud, or some bin liners, a bucket? She puts the shovel; the wine and few sacks into the tin bucket and puts it into a black bag ready to carry to their meeting. Finding an old t-shirt and old tracksuit bottoms she adds these to the black sack. She would go in her wellingtons and take her day shoes to change into.
Taking her jacket she decides to go for a walk. The wind is wild and Anna can hear the roar of the sea. The sea will be turning a darker colour now, almost brown because of the sand it disturbs, as it rises and carries it along, as well as washing more land into itself from the cliffs.

Anna doesn't go to the beach or the bench; she isn't
ready to do that yet. She stops before the donkey track,
turning around to retrace her tracks back to the caravan.
The light is disappearing as the autumn evening draws in
deeper, it will soon be pitch black dark. The lamps
scattered around the site, help people make their way to
their caravans and in the pitch-blackness of night, she is
so grateful for those glimmers of light amongst the dark
shadows.
Anna locks up. As the kettle boils for her drink and hot
water bottle she makes her sandwich. She hasn't done
the clothes, but knows she can catch up later with them,
as well as her food store cupboard. After putting her
plate in the sink, she closes the kitchen blind and draws
the curtains too. Unwrapping her nightgown from around
her hot water bottle, she changes into her nightclothes
and gets into bed. She finishes off the few mouthfuls of
tea that are left and gets comfortable beneath the covers.
They are to meet tomorrow on the corner, next to the old
junk shop. Anna will be ready.
In the morning she'd speak to her son and phone up to
see if her two younger children are safe.
Darkness creeps around the caravan, filling all the empty
spaces just as it does outside. Anna wonders where Jo is
now. 'In her bright, smart, warm flat working.'
Sleep comes softly and gently. Tonight she doesn't
dream of John Doherty, or the man who had raped her.
Waking briefly she thinks about the headlines she'd read
from the newspaper, after unwrapping her angel of joy.
The body of a man had been washed up; it had been
trapped amongst the rocks and buried by the massive
mudslide. She hoped it had been him. It should have
been him. Anna believes he deserved to die he should
die. She wonders about his spirit, if it still wanders
around the thicket and the bench and if he fell, or if he
slipped, or was he pushed. She hopes he had been
pushed, because she wanted him to feel afraid, as he'd
made her feel – as he fell into the black shadows and
darkness of death.

These thoughts are brief, fragmentary and slip back into the darkness and quiet of her memory and thoughts. Tonight the crest of waves race wildly, madly, passionately, to reach the shore, as in its frenzy of energy and excitement, it pushes harder and harder against the earth, eager to feel its solid reality again, to feel its deep containment and embrace, as it fights to cover and control it, to draw it into itself.

Anna sleeps soundly as dawn begins to break.

The sky has streaks of orange and grey, the day promises to be good with no rain. Monday should be fine, for the women to work on the hut.

What a weekend, what a few days its been – Jo has managed to sell all four of her canvases and has earned the princely sum of £70 all together, she is pleased and happy with that. Also she has two orders, she was asked to paint 'The Promenade' and 'The Harbour' again, when an interested lady found out that they had already been sold. She will make them slightly different, so that they are also unique. So that will be another £40 on top of the £70 making a grand total of £110. If she can carry on painting and find other outlets for her work and also attend more exhibitions in the town, she can foresee a regular income from her artwork. Maybe making more boats and pebbles to display with the paintings, this should work well together.

Back at the flat she is raring to go, fuelled by the interest and rushes up to the workroom to decide what to do next. The best plan really, is to begin the two paintings for the lady, before starting on any completely new ideas. Having already painted the two pictures before, it will be quite easy to do these. The largest canvas she has used so far has been 14" x 18" and she would like to do some bigger ones. Maybe paint the town centre and the beach and the surrounding area, stretching out to the main road and down to the hut. It will take quite a bit of sketching and planning but she has the design of it already in her mind.

So with this idea, she takes some A3 sheets of plain paper and sellotapes them together, to make a large working sheet. She begins by pencilling the main roads and the coastline and then starts sections of the plan. And bit-by-bit with lots of rubbing outs and changes, the map of the town and its surrounding area begins to emerge. This is only the beginning; she will have to transfer this outline onto a canvas. She must go and find out on Tuesday, what the largest canvas is to buy and build the plan around it; she remembers seeing some very large ones in Mad Mick's shop.

As time speeds along, she is oblivious to the evening drawing in and the nighttime encroaching, she is alive and captured by the vivid colours and pictures that are chasing through her imagination.

When Jason nudges and intrudes into this space and reminds her of food and drink, she reluctantly breaks off. Outside it is dark and quiet and they have not had their evening meal or walk. She doesn't feel like starting to make a meal from scratch and desires instant feeding, without any effort attached. So she pops a couple of slices of bread into the toaster and spreads it with peanut butter and mashed banana on the top. Jason looks up wondering what he is going to get and she fills his bowl and adds the remains of the pasta left from lunch. Jo takes the toast and a mug of tea back up to the workroom and munches away, whilst looking at the map. With toast in one hand and pencil in the other, she sets too with fresh ideas and scribbles notes and fills other areas of the plan in.

After what seems only a short while, Jason is nudging her to take him for a walk.

"Come on then, let's go out."

Reluctantly, Jo collects his lead and her coat. Outside the pavements and roads are empty, there are no late night stragglers about and it feels like a ghost town. She takes the route through the tiny alleyways, out towards the museum and the golf club. Jason has plenty of energy and is glad to be out for a walk. They soon arrive at the top entrance to the public path and she lets Jason have a few minutes walk on the grass. His biggest enjoyment is sniffing and burying his head in long grass, so even in the darkness he is happy and could stay out here all night long. She realises she should have brought a torch with her and turns back towards the pavements.

"Come on Jase, we can come back tomorrow."

Jason is not easily persuaded by these words and she has to be assertive, with a forceful tug of his lead, to drag him in the direction of the town again. She has no idea of the time but it must be late, as she looks down to the bottom of the hill towards The Harbour Bar pub and sees that there are no cars parked outside and the lights are on in the upstairs living quarters.

"Come on Jase, it's bedtime."

Jason looks in disgust because she has spoiled his chance of fun. Their walk back is a slow one, with Jason stopping and sniffing at every opportunity, unwilling to return.

Inside the flat, Jo settles him down on his doggy bed for the night and returns to the workroom to take a last look at the map. 'Wow, it's going to be amazing,' if she can achieve what she hopes to do, with the ideas rushing around in her head and finds herself again picking up the pencil but this time her eyes feel gritty and heavy and it is time to stop and sleep.

So she switches off the lights and chastises herself for being late to bed, because tomorrow she will need to feel fresh, to meet up with Anna, to go and clean the hut.

Part 3

THE BODY

Anna returns home to her caravan, feeling deeply warm and content. She realises that when she is with Jo she is happy, released from her burdens of daily life, a woman who does for others, a woman disconnected from herself in order to survive. She has become and allowed herself to be turned into a woman of stone. Jo isn't like that. With Jo she becomes human, a woman who has feelings and emotions, surfacing from the deep shadows, where she has hidden, not just from him and her family but also from herself. She begins to realise and understand why she feels she is a nobody and accordingly treated this way. Why she has allowed herself to become such a woman and who these people are in her life, her world, who willingly and constantly use and abuse her?

It began at the beginning as a child, her parents had controlled her, if she challenged or contradicted what they told her, and she was chastised and punished. Still she had something left inside her, that wouldn't let her mother, father, older sister and teachers destroy completely, and her soul lived deep inside.

They dented, rubbished and knocked it down, if it ever dared to stand up for itself. She had been used and abused, but never allowed, or given her autonomy to grow, into a person in her own right. She had been an extension of her family and not a person or an individual. She had been a child who had been knocked into shape. Anna's shape had been on her knees, with her head down and her mouth shut. If she dared to get up then there would be consequences. When she got to know what the consequences were, she had forgotten the plot and was so submerged in the drama of her daily life and world, that for most of the time, she lived within its confines, because she had nowhere else to go and nothing else to do. She probably wouldn't have wanted to go anywhere or do anything anyhow, because she had a fierce sense of loyalty and devotion to her family. They were her world, literally and metaphorically. Anna felt safe inside her world. Her father and the men who peopled her world, were themselves the children of late Victorians and predominantly patriarchal, in their approaches to life. With the look, the hand, the belt, or the ruler, being their final levellers of those who threatened, challenged, or frightened them.

Her mother ruled, when her father was not present, but would defer to him when he was. Anna's mothers world was built upon poverty, fear, babies, nappies and making do and mending, stretching herself and her resources so she could get by day to day. She adored her mother and would do anything for her, as her mother knew. It was always Anna who would do the begging and borrowing. Sometimes Anna's sister Nettie would go with her, but it was always Anna who had to ask, "Can you......?" She hated the asking, the begging. Seeing the look on their faces when they opened her mother's notes and when she asked, "Me mam said can you lend her...." That look, which for the most part said, "Fucking hell, not again." It was so humiliating to stand as her mother's proxy and whether they lent or turned her away, empty handed, made little difference. The looks given should have been for her mother, but she could never ask or beg herself, not even from her own mother or sisters. It was too much for her; she couldn't cope with the shame first hand, so sent Anna instead.

If she returned empty handed from her begging trips her mother would send her back out again, "You'll have to go and get something, so get out again we need...." Anna would trawl around the regulars until at last she would receive something to appease her mother and then she could return home. She had learnt then too, to cut off, in order to cope and survive the experiences of begging and borrowing, which she had spent so many years of her childhood occupied in for her mother. At home Anna worked hard to keep her mother happy. Her mother's anger and disapproval hurt as much as her fathers. She could do little to appease her father, except clean the house and do jobs and run errands, but Anna knew if she helped her mother by being on hand and on call, she could gain her approval and maybe win a smile.

The stigma and shame of the asking and begging remains with Anna, she still can't ask people for help or support. Sometimes she needs to, but those feelings she felt as a child, the shame and humiliation always return no matter what. It makes her feel uncomfortable and humble again. She would watch people's responses as she had learnt to as a child and could tell by reading their eyes what they were feeling.

So Anna reflects, it's hardly surprising that I have become the woman I am. What woman am I? A willing doormat, a plain, dull, squat woman, who's only use or purpose is to be used and to be of use.
The pleasure she experienced whilst being with Jo begins to fade. Turning to her books, she begins reading about different models for analysing her homeopathic cases. Chakras interest her. Anna lives in her base chakra, her root chakra that deals with the basics of life, the day-to-day struggle about survival. She wants to be more than this but realises she isn't and wouldn't be unless she does something about it. What can she do? Let go of the past she decides, but I can't because I'm still living in it, still functioning as I did, still trapped in the same space and time. Almost as if time has stood still, or is it herself who has stood still, trapped in the past, whilst time moves on, goes forward and she is left behind in some kind of time warp. This disorientates Anna and makes her feel disconnected from reality. 'Of course I've moved out of the fucking base chakra,' Anna tells the voice inside herself. 'No, actually you haven't,' the response comes back. As a child Anna struggled for survival, literally. One out of eight children, born into an Anglo Irish, catholic, labouring class family, 'get real, you struggled, but I knew who I was,' Anna returns.

'Did you? Well I knew where I came from then. Did you? Fuck off,' Anna decides. She is still in the same place that she had been born into. She has never really left the daily struggle of life and as such, her issues are all firmly rooted in survival. She mistook her academic and intellectual achievements as advancement. They were meteocratic rises and advances, but still very much based in the base chakra, because she pursued them from that space in her life. She has internalised and intellectualised the theories, ideologies and knowledge she has studied, but yet she still lives and remains within her base chakra.

Anna's daily life is still a struggle, being a poor intellectual doesn't change that, it merely gives her the mental capacity and tools to understand and verbalise it. Anna and her husband have bought their house and car, travelled abroad and can afford to pay for entertainment. They have risen meteorically from low working class, to low middle class, but they are still in the base chakra, still struggling with day-to-day survival.

To move beyond the base chakra, she needs to be rooted in herself. To own her identity, however unformed it is. To acknowledge her right to be worthy, by the simple perfect inheritance, given from the universe of life. The only justification needed for her existence, is to be alive and she continuously misses the vital point of life, which is fundamentally life. She has remained the same, for all her frantic trying to catch up, with what she should or shouldn't be in order to fit in, to belong and prove herself worthy. She has stepped into the mirror and cannot see the image of herself because she is inside it. She had tried to prove herself worthy and a worthwhile person, but to who? Forever wanting to please and be found worthy to everyone, her mother, father, her children, her tutors, even his approval Anna sought. But she never asks herself the most important question, what about you? Do you think you're worthy? She possibly wouldn't be able to answer that question anyhow, because she would be too busy doing the next thing, to

try and rise herself up from her base chakra, to prove
herself worthy. This effort she realises now, amounts to
nothing. It haunts her like a corpse that can't be buried,
rising up every time it is laid to rest. Her past stays with
her, because it lives inside her and will not leave. The
past seeks location, within the disorientation in which it
travels, from one decade to the next, trawling its
memories around each cycle of life. It wants, seeks
resolution, but can't find any.

Anna sips the hot tea. Clouds gather across the sky. The
beauty of early autumn has almost disappeared. Leaving
behind, the skeleton, black frames of trees and the heavy,
uncertainty of the dark winter, which lay ahead. In the
air there is the cold chill of the approaching winter. The
ground is settling and growing harder, sealing itself up
for the months ahead. The wind blows a little stronger
now as it whooshes along, or else it whips through low
and thin and sharp, with a hint of things to come. All
around the land is preparing for its long rest. To
conserve and renew itself, so that in spring the earth will
be ready and fertile to bear fruit again and supply the
world with its harvest. The sea is sharp and cold and as it
smashes against the earth, it senses its change. No longer
is the earth open and welcoming, warm and inviting, but
cold, hard, closed and impenetrable. The sea heaves and
swells, ready to crash again against the rocks and land,
but wave after wave it falls back upon itself, filled with
emptiness and disappointment, the sea desolate now in
its loneliness.

Jo struggles to remember where she is, as Jason nudges and licks her face, poking out from under the duvet and at first she doesn't want to let on to him that she is awake, she wants to come around slowly, out of the nights sleep. Jason prods her again, harder this time and she has to open her eyes. Happy now that she is awake, he bounces up and down continuously, whining for his food. "All right then Jase, I'm coming."

Reluctantly she draws her legs out of bed and goes to the kitchen to feed him. Whilst filling his dish she realises she must have overslept, because of the bright light streaming in through the window. She is accustomed to beginning the morning in darkness and has to switch on the light. After filling the kettle, she remembers her meeting today with Anna, to go and clean out the hut. She dashes upstairs to the workroom and on tiptoes looks out through the velux window, to see what the time is on the Town Hall clock – 10.45, gosh she has overslept.

She hurries back down the stairs to eat breakfast and get ready. 'What did I say that I would take along with me, was it bread and cheese, or was Anna taking that?' She cannot bring their conversation to mind as she crunches the cereal. After breakfast, she showers and gets dressed and puts on a pair of jeans, a t-shirt and a hoody, reminding herself to bring more clothes back with her. It's amazing what you can manage on when you have to, She has washed the few clothes she has here, over and over and worn them all the time since she's been at the flat. She bought six pairs of knickers and a couple of t-shirts from the outdoor market, but apart from that nothing else. After dressing, she pops upstairs again to check the time, 11.10 – she will make the junk shop on time. She grabs the rucksack some money, Jason's lead and her coat and sets off.

Jo calls at the bakers and collects a bag of crusty rolls and two pieces of flapjack and then goes to the supermarket for a large carton of cranberry juice and a piece of crumbly cheese. Even if Anna brings something, it won't get wasted after a hard afternoons work. She is so glad that today is a fine one, although there is a complete blue sky and sunshine, there is a sharp cold, nip in the air. At least they will be able to work and hopefully the hut will have dried out since she left, her hut and home of not too long ago, how strange to be returning. The comfortable, easy life at the flat has spoiled her and the old familiarity of life at the hut has been tainted and no longer fills her with the idea of comfort, warmth and safety. As she walks along, she tries to reconnect with the life she had there and each time the memory is buried under a flood of water and as hard as she tries, she cannot hold it, cannot see it in her minds eye to cherish and bring back the holding place for her that it once was. Maybe when they get there, maybe when they've cleaned the place up, maybe when the sun shines in and the stove is lit and she turns it back into a home it will feel ok. She hopes so.

Walking past the housing estate towards the junk shop, the aftermath of the flood is evident for all to see. In the front gardens there are fridges and furniture and carpets piled up, there are skips in some of the drives. Looking through the front windows, she can see empty rooms, ruined by the floodwater. They will have to be re-plastered; it will be weeks before these houses are habitable again. Jo wonders what they will be faced with today, she is so glad for Anna's offer of help, at least this eases the burden. Jo remembers how it was when she first arrived and how hard she worked to make it liveable. Right now, it feels like starting all over again and with that she lets out a big sigh, as if travelling the edge of a circle and ending up where she set off from, well maybe not, maybe it will not be as bad as she fears.

Anna realises, as she stands waiting for Jo outside the
junk shop, that she's forgotten the black plastic bag,
which she'd put the shovel and plastic bags in. Luckily
she put her shoes, the wine and food into a separate
shopping bag, which she's brought. Her old clothes
however she's also left. 'Oh well it can't be helped.' She
glances briefly into the junk shop window, it is yellow
and dusty and makes her feel nauseous. It is weighed
down with peoples faded past and she turns away. As
she does so, she sees Jo approaching.

Approaching the path to the junk shop, Jo looks up to
see if she can spot Anna waiting, it must be around about
12 o'clock by now. As she gets nearer the corner, she
notices her by the wall and feels happy and heartened to
see her.
Jo looks well Anna thinks and smiles.
"Hi."
"Sorry if I am late."
 "No, you're not, I have only been here a few minutes,
you're ok."
Jo notices her carrier bag with the baguette sticking out.
"Oh, I couldn't remember who was bringing what to eat,
so I've been and bought some food on the way here."
"It's ok, we can share what we have and take the rest
home with us, it won't get wasted."
"Let's go then."
They walk away from the town centre.
"It's a good day for it."
"I'm so glad you're here and I don't have to go on my
own. I don't know what to expect, that's why I haven't
been before now, I'm scared of what we might find."
"It's ok, I'm sure it won't be as bad as you think, anyway
we can start to sort it today, so that's good."

They walk along the cycle track and see the lay-by
ahead, Jo is filled with trepidation at the prospect of
what they will discover. In her minds eye, she can see it,
as if it was yesterday, the black water, the deep thick

mud and debris and sitting on the bottom step, looking into the bleak and frightening nightmare. Anna senses Jo's unease and turns towards her, Jo's pace has slowed to almost a standstill and she feels as if I can't go on. "What's wrong Jo?"
"I'm scared of going down to the hut, scared of what we might find, remembering how it was, what it was like when I left it."
"It will be ok, I'm with you, I can help you, it's not as if you have to stay here tonight, were just making a start today."
"Yes you're right, I have to do it sometime."

Anna reaches out her hand and gently pushes Jo's side to help her move forward. And so they begin the journey down to the hut. Before they can even take the path through the hedges, they have to remove an entangled, mass of branches, leaves and rubbish that has woven itself around, the almost invisible gate. Eventually they manage to push it open and then have the job of clearing the path, as they wind their way down. The torrent of floodwater has rushed through the gap between the hedges and taken with it all the debris collected in its wake. The path ahead is strewn with all kinds of rubbish and sticks and broken branches are banked up, as they trudge through the once reasonable path. Now it's messy and everything is caked in mud. The best they can do for the moment is to clear it to the side – this is going to be another big job in itself, never mind what needs doing to the hut.

Approaching the bottom of the path they see it, the sight in front of them, takes the women by surprise. The hut looks battered and forsaken, whilst the garden and vegetable plots and herbs are ruined. The only things, which haven't been washed away, are the fruit trees further down the garden. Strangely, they stand with ripe fruit still hanging, but even so much must have been lost, washed away, by the force of the rain and wind.

The shock between them is almost palpable and it is a
few moments of complete stillness and silence before
either of them speaks.
"Gosh." Anna murmurs.
"Oh my God."
"Come on, we will have to look inside." Anna quietly
suggests.

The hut – the homely place with clean windows, bright
blue windows and doors, with window boxes filled with
fresh herbs – the flourishing garden and vegetable patch
have disappeared, beneath a covering of mud and dead
foliage, a brown skin burying it and projecting outwards,
a place of death and destruction. Jo almost cannot bear to
look and wants to run away and back to the life of the
town centre and the bright lights and shop windows – a
town alive and well and the flat with its workroom, full
of works in progress, and forget and move away from
this eerie, deathly habitat.

Anna takes charge and moves forward and puts her bag
down on the ground and begins to move the boulder and
scrape away the earth that is backed up around the door.
Jo too finds a place to put down her rucksack and the
spell is broken and she begins to think of practical ways
of tackling what's before them.
"I'll go and find a shovel."
Anna is scraping away the mud with her boots.
Jo goes around to the back of the hut and finds the spade,
standing upright, in a pit of dried mud. She returns and
quickly clears the entrance and pulls at the door. The
door is swollen, she will have to plane some off the edge
later, in order for it to close properly and make it secure
again.

Once inside the hut, they force the windows open on to
their catches to let some fresh air inside. The musty,
cloying, damp smell is strong and the odour of decay

mixed in, is thick and makes both of them catch their breath and cough.

"Let's go outside and wait for the air to go through."

Looking inside, they can see the massive clean up that's ahead. However, now Jo is able to be constructive and detach herself from the events that took place and get on with the work.

"Are you sure you're alright to help, it's going to be dirty work once we get started?"

"Yes of course I am what shall we do first?"

Jo decides they need to remove the mound of earth that is by the entrance and then carry on and clear the rest of the floor. The mud has dried to a thick reddish, consistency and can be shovelled out onto the garden.

"If we shovel the mud and throw it onto the garden, we can clean up the floor inside and then tackle the outside later."

"It will take some getting back to a working, productive garden."

"Yes it will be another years work to turn the ground over and replant it and I'll have to build a bonfire, to get rid of things which can't be salvaged, or used as fuel for the stove."

Returning inside they pick up books and papers that are ruined. The wooden kitchen chairs and table will clean up, when they have dried out, but the armchair and rugs and other things need to be put outside. They carry out the wet damaged things, to give them a chance to dry, before they can be burnt. With the door and windows fully open, the stench, of murky, musty, damp and fowl air begins to lessen.

Then they begin the slow process of taking it in turns to shovel and move the mound of earth in a bucket and chuck it out onto the garden. The work is heavy and makes Anna sweat, but they carry on steadily. The air inside becomes much more bearable now and Jason is back from his excursion around the land and is keen to do his bit of digging and join in, it is his way of trying to help.

In amongst the mound of earth and unrecognisable in the drying mud around the floor, are more of Jo's books and cardboard packets and paper bags and foodstuffs and odd bits and pieces. Neither of them mentions the fact, as they continue the cleaning up, conscious of the painful acceptance of what's been lost. When they have shifted and cleared the mud from the entrance, Jo suggests that they stop and have a break. The day is still full of blue sky and sunshine and even though it is cloudless and cold, they feel quite hot with the energetic work. Anna has brought a couple of plastic mugs and she fills them with the cranberry juice. Jo suggests they stop to eat, but Anna is keen to carry on for a while. After another session of shovelling and shifting, they stop work.
"Come on let's take a break, I'm hungry."
"Good idea, I'm knackered but at least it looks like we've done something." Anna gasps and struggles to straighten herself up.

They are both pretty grubby now after the work, and looking at the state of each other they break into laughter. The sight before them now looks promising and they wash their hands under the kitchen tap.
"I've brought bread rolls, cheese and flapjacks."
"I've brought a baguette, cheese and two apples, so whose shall we eat?"
"Let's eat yours first, because the rolls are in a plastic bag and will keep longer."
They break off chunks of bread and lumps of cheese and eat, whilst chatting about the progress they have made.
"We can stop now if you've had enough." Jo tells Anna, conscious of her depleting energy and lack of fitness.
"It's ok. I'll be ok for a bit longer, I hope anyway." Anna says with a grin.

Again they work away, Jo makes sure she does the longest shifts with the shovelling. Now they are able to scrape more of the floor area, it is good to see the flags underneath drying, as they brush away the final dirt. It is brilliant now to see the rewards for their efforts and Jo is glad that they came, and happy that the hut is going to be all right eventually. Jo praises Anna as they work, it is lovely to be together again in each other's company. Jo is filled with warmth towards her and looks at her intent on the work and feels privileged by how she wants to help. She is a kind person and Jo is happy that they have found each other again. When they have cleared the area to the stove, Jo suggests that they stop and take another break. They eat the flapjacks and have another mug of juice.

"If I clean out the stove I can light it when I come again and that will help to dry the walls of the hut."

The stove has a build up of rust on the outside but that will easily brush off and it will be ok.

"That will be nice to light it, can't we do it now?"

"I think it will be better to clean it and let it dry out first, and I need to find pieces of dry wood to burn on it."

"How about if you collect the wood and bring it in here to dry out and I will clean out the stove for you?"

"Yes that's a good idea, we'll do that."

The connection they have between them is almost telepathic and doesn't warrant small talk and their silences are ok and they get on. Anna cleans out the stove and Jo finds a handful of dead branches and logs from the wood store and brings them inside to dry. When they have finished, Jo suggests they stop for today, they have achieved a lot.

"I can come again and help you if you like."

"That would be great, thanks." Jo feels pleased and actually looks forward to working together again.

They shut the windows and push the door to, as best they can and Jo makes a mental note, to buy a plane for the next time they come.
"I can't wait to have a shower."

Jo is so aware now of the crude facilities here and the outside shower and how it felt so natural and easy to use whilst living here. And at the same time, she wonders if she can return to this life, after staying at the flat, with the luxury of the instant, hot water and carefree living. Looking at each other, they both laugh at the sight of their dirty clothes and faces and a sensation of pure relief permeates around them, as if the hut has risen from the underworld of death and announced its life and is testament for them both to see. The hut is going to be all right after all.

"Thank you for helping, I don't know if I could have come here or done it on my own, so thanks Anna."
"That's fine, I'm glad I've been here to come and help you, I'm going to go back now to the caravan and have a wash, but if you want me to help again I will do."
"Do you have a shower?"
"No but I can boil water, I'll be fine."
"Come back with me to the flat if you like and you can have a shower there. I can put your clothes in the washer, you're welcome to stay the night if you want."
Anna stops and becomes deep in thought. "No, I'll be fine."
"Come back, go on, we can eat the rest of the bread and cheese and open the bottle of wine."
Anna looks and again is deep in thought and unsure what to do. A hot shower in a warm place, would be better than a stripped down, body wash, in the caravan. But staying over Anna isn't sure. It would give them time to talk, to get to know one another a little more. Working in the hut, they'd just managed to snatch bits of conversation, but to be able to sit down would be lovely, a relaxing pleasure.

"If you're sure it's not going to be any trouble?"
"Yes, sure I'm sure, come on."
Jo closes the hut door as best she can; the wood is still
swollen and the door won't lock.
"Come on Jase."
Jason is busy sniffing around the garden.

Walking back through the muddy, strewn path, quiet and
thoughtful, after their tiring day, Anna wonders about
leaving her caravan overnight. It would be fine, the net
curtains would keep it private and there was no food to
go off. She would return in the morning and could phone
her family then and make sure everything is all right.
There aren't any serious problems, or reasons, why she
can't have a hot shower and relax and enjoy Jo's
company.

Making their journey back to the flat, the daylight
quickly begins to wane, as the autumn, darkness,
descends the town. As they walk along the cycle track, a
car drives at speed with full headlights on and makes
them both step aside, into the grass verge. They are glad
to reach the safety of the pavement and hurry, until they
have the protection of the streetlights.
"The next time we come, we would be better to leave by
the beach path, it will be safer away from the traffic and
we can take the torch with us."
"Yes I think we would, that was scary walking along
there."
"My back and legs feel stiff, do yours?"
"Yes they are just a bit."
Approaching the flat, Jo looks forward to the prospect of
a hot shower and wonders how on earth she managed,
living the way she did.
"Go on up."
Jason is keen to be first up the steps and pushes in front
of Anna. At the top, they take of their dirty trainers and
Jo unlocks the door, they remove their coats and hang
them on the hooks on the wall. Jason is first into the

kitchen and goes straight to his dog dish, "Wait a minute Jase."

Jo fills the kettle with water to make a pot of tea.

"Would you like to have a shower, whilst I make us some tea?"

"Are your sure, don't you want one first?"

"No, you're ok, you can have one whilst I make Jason his meal."

"Well that will be lovely, thanks."

"Thank you for helping, I'm so glad that you did, it has made all the difference, so thanks."

Jo shows Anna to the bathroom and gives her, her own dressing gown to put on.

"If you pass me your clothes, I can stick them in the washer and then put them over the radiator to dry."

"Oh it's all right I can wash them back at the caravan."

"No, it's no trouble, I'm putting my clothes in, so yours will make up the load and it will be easier for you than at the caravan."

"I'll leave them outside the bathroom on the floor, if that's ok then?"

"Yes of course it is, I'll go and make the tea and feed Jason."

Jo mashes the tea and gives Jason his meal. The mug of hot tea is lovely and Jason devours his food in seconds and then drops down on his doggy bed and releases a deep and satisfied sigh, all is complete in his world.

She looks up as Anna enters the kitchen, her long blonde hair ruffled by the towel and her fresh, pink complexion and grey blue eyes, meet hers, she smiles, happily wrapped in Jo's dressing gown.

"Thanks Jo that was lovely thank you."

"Help yourself to a mug of tea, I'll just go and have a shower, I won't be long."

The hot water, streaming over Jo's hair and body, full of bubbles and froth, from the shower gel and shampoo, is wonderful and she lingers until the water runs clear and clean and then wraps a large towel around herself. She goes to the bedroom to dress and remonstrates herself for not bringing more clothes back, and also for not checking the bedroom. She picks up Anna's pile of dirty clothes and her own and takes them back to the kitchen to wash.

"I've just realised I should have brought some of my clothes back with me from the hut, I've been living in the same few things since coming here."

"Oh Jo, what are you going to do?"

"These jeans will dry overnight on the radiator and I can wear them tomorrow."

After refilling their mugs of tea they go into the sitting room. Jo turns up the thermostat in the hallway and they settle down in the comfy seats.

"Well Jo it's a lovely flat."

"Yes it is, I've been doubtful after living here of going back to the hut. But after today, well I don't feel as worried I must admit."

"You need to make sure it's all clean Jo before you go back."

"Yes well, I don't have to rush, that's a relief."

"Did you sell any more paintings?"

"Yes I sold them all, it couldn't have been better really. Oh and I got a couple of extra orders too, that reminds me, I need to give you yours Anna, come on upstairs, I'll show you what I'm working on at the moment and I can give you yours."

They go upstairs.

"Wow Jo you have been busy."

"I'm working on a map of the town, it's not the exact layout obviously, but it shows the places that I relate to and that I find interesting and picturesque, I just like the different colours and the seaside, touristy feel."

"It's brilliant Jo, are you going to make a large painting of it?"

"I don't know, its taken a long time to get this far, it would be an enormous project to paint it, I quite like the coloured crayon effect, and I still have a lot of work to do on it."

Anna walks around the room, staring intently on different pieces of the map, that Jo has stuck around the walls.

"I like this bit." Anna points her finger at a section of the map that shows the town centre and the Town Hall clock.

"Yes I do, it took me ages, it has lots of detail and I'm pleased with it."

Jo hands Anna her painting, 'The Bench'.

"This is a lovely painting, will you sign it for me?"

"Sure, I'll sign it for you now."

Jo takes the canvas from her and with a blue, ink pen, writes, 'For Anna – Samantha x' on the wooden frame on the back.

"Is that ok?"

"Yes thanks, it is special and I will treasure it – Samantha, I don't understand."

"I changed my name to Jo when I came to live here, it's a long story, maybe one day I will tell you about it – but not now."

Jo diverts her attention on to another canvas, to quash Anna's curiosity. They continue to talk about Jo's artwork and discuss various ideas for future projects.

"I'm hungry are you?"

Jo suggests they make a meal. They share the crusty rolls and cheese, with tomatoes and pickle, along with the wine.

They raise their glasses.

"Cheers and thank you."

"Cheers to you too."

"Tuck in, let's eat, I'm starving."

They help themselves to the food.

After eating they go into the sitting room. Anna asks again about the map.

"No more about me, what about you Anna what do you like to do?"

"I'm training to be a homeopath."

"Really, that's interesting, how long have you been doing it?"
"It's taken four years; I'm in the final year now and hope to qualify at the end of this year."
"That's brilliant, so are you going to set up a practise?"
"I hope to, but I have to qualify first and then decide what to do."
"Oh you will if you have managed to get this far, you will get to the end, surely?"
"It's been difficult and a really hard course, harder than doing my degree course, but I hope to qualify, I have a lot of work to do before that though."
"You've surprised me Anna, your life seems full on with the kids and everything."
"I know I don't know how I've managed it really."
"Would you like some chocolate?"
"Ooh yes please."
Jo returns to the kitchen, whilst Anna fills the wine glasses, she comes back with a large bar of quality chocolate and a box of medjool dates.
"Here help yourself."
Jo places the dates and chocolate onto the coffee table.
"The best way I find, is to have a piece of chocolate and a date together, it's a great combination, try it."
They each take a lump of chocolate and a date and push it into their mouths.
"What do you think?" Jo questions Anna through a mouthful of chocolate and sticky date.
"Mmmm, I see what you mean, lovely." Anna munches and sighs.

As they move into the nighttime, they continue dipping in and out of the slightly forbidden sweetness, the sensuous tactile tasting, the sharing and exchanging of themselves, as the warm, red wine, leaves a purple stain, around their tongues and mouths.

The next morning.

"Jo." Jo hears the loud booming voice of Charles as she steps out of the shower.

He enters the room and fixes his eyes upon her, completely ignores her privacy, as she stands on the bathmat totally naked.

"Jo, look I'm in a bit of a fix and need you, so there's no time for messing about, you're going to have to help me out here with this I'm afraid. Look, I'll give you chance to get up and I'll call back in an hour, so be ready – and by the way, who was that coming to greet me half dressed in the hallway, the agreement was that this flat is for your purpose and not a half way house, for all and bloody sundry, so make sure she's not here when I come back, and be ready."

Charles grabs the bath towel from the rail and flings it at Jo, as she catches it to cover herself, he turns and slams the door behind him.

Jo stands still holding the towel, as if someone has thrown a bucket of cold water over her and feels a cold shiver, running through her body.

"Jo."

This time the voice she hears is Anna's. Jo wraps the towel around herself and opens the door.

"What the hell was all that about, what did he want?"

"He wants me to help him out with something, I don't know what, he just wants me to be ready and in an hour he is coming back for me. Bloody hell."

"What have you got yourself into with him; he's not a nice man."

"He helped me out with this flat; I suppose I owe him really."

"He's obviously got his own motives for helping you by the sound of it."

"I'm sorry Anna but he doesn't want you here when he comes back, I'm sorry it has nothing to do with me, sorry."

"It's not your fault Jo, be careful, he's out for something that's for sure, I'll get myself ready to leave."

Anna turns and hurries to the radiator and takes her clean dry clothes and goes through to the bedroom to put them on.

"Look Anna you still have time for breakfast, there's cereal or toast help yourself."

Jo calls after her, whilst quickly drying herself off.

"It's ok Jo, I can eat when I get to the caravan, I'll be fine."

Before Jo has finished in the bathroom, Anna returns fully dressed, ready to leave.

"I'll be going now Jo, thanks for a lovely day yesterday." Anna calls from behind the door.

Jo opens it, wishing Charles hadn't chosen this moment to charge back into her life.

"Ok, thanks for yesterday, if you would like to help me again, I'd be more than grateful?"

"Of course I will, you'll have to let me know when."

"Do you have a phone number, or if you tell me where your caravan is, I can get in touch that way."

"I have a mobile phone, I can write my number down for you if you like."

"Yes that would be good and then I can phone you from the phone box in town."

Jo finds a pen and paper.

"Here if you write it down I'll call you."

Anna quickly jots her number down and says a quick goodbye, puts her shoes and coat on and leaves Jo alone to gather her thoughts.

An hour - Jo hasn't got long to have a quick breakfast and take Jason for his morning walk. She quickly returns to the kitchen and pours a large glass, of fresh orange juice and pops two slices of bread into the toaster. She takes her t-shirt and jeans off the radiator and puts them on. The t-shirt and jeans are creased but at least they are clean. Back in the kitchen, she spreads the toast with jam and takes a bite; her appetite leaves her as she thinks about Charles. She gives Jason the second slice and he wolfs it down.

"Come on then Jason we have to be quick today."
Jo puts on her trainers, takes her coat and they stride out
towards the golf course, Jason is eager to reach the
greens and she lets him off his lead and gives him what
she thinks is about ten minutes and then returns to the
flat. At least Jason will be all right left alone for a few
hours. She dashes upstairs to the work room, to check on
the town hall clock – it's 9.45, however she doesn't
know what time Charles called, so it's rather silly of her
to look. So she sits down and waits.

After calling to the supermarket for bread and milk, Anna makes her way through the tiny back streets, to reach her caravan. The older school children fall, or are pushed out of doors onto the pavements and scurry off to catch their school bus, wearing dark uniforms with white shirts poking out.
Their bags are big and heavy enough for a week away, let alone a day at school, but she knows with her own children this is how it has become.
She crosses the road to reach the fields and takes the donkey track way home. There are only people using it to walk their dogs, so the remainder of the journey is quiet.

'Why had Charles so much sway over Jo?' Anna wonders as she walks along the tarmac path.

Back at the caravan, she opens the kitchen blind and surveys the site from the window. Everything is quiet, a few people walk passed with their dogs, but most folk have packed up for the season and left. There remain one or two stragglers like her, hanging on until the end of the season. If it hadn't been for her son she wouldn't be here. She would have packed and locked up until spring, when the campsite re opens, instead of hanging around, to see him sorted and settled and being honest with herself she remains here because of Jo.

After making a pot of tea, she sits on the seat beneath the window. The heavy curtains are all open, as she hadn't returned the night before. No beds to make, or jobs to do. 'I'll phone Mark and the city to check on the other two, but really that's about it.'
Anna had felt decadent with Jo, drinking wine and eating chocolate and dates. Had she honestly learnt much more about Jo's life, no, but she had learnt about her, when Charles came pounding on her door and marching in as if he owned it? Of course he does own it, but that isn't the point, he could still behave civilised, instead of

roaring like a wounded bear. She'd noticed too, the filthy look he'd shot at her, as he walked past, trying not to look, or acknowledge her existence, but his need to strut had got the better of him and he'd been forced to make eye contact with Anna. She read the look of anger and mortification, which flashed across his face, when she was apparently in his way, as she stood holding the door back, cramping his style, his entrance. He burst through Jo's flat and Anna couldn't fully understand, why he would barge into Jo's bathroom, without even knocking. She hadn't stood by the door, waiting for him to leave, but she could tell his impact had shaken Jo. She appeared to lose her sense of self and be at his brusque and ill-mannered, beck and call.

She concludes there is more to Jo and Charles than meets the eye and more than renting a flat from him. Yesterday, she had worked hard with Jo on the hut, they really did seem to be making head way, good progress in fact. In comparison to how it was when she had first gone back to see it, she wouldn't have believed, that they could have cleaned up and cleared all the mud and rubbish out. Most of the books and soft furnishings would have to be burnt on the bonfire. The hut would dry out and it could be set up again as a home. Jo could get sandbags, in case of the possibility of any more flooding. It wouldn't stop things completely but it would certainly reduce the water level. Anna had promised Jo she would return to the hut with her to do more work on it. Underneath, she has a sense that Jo seems so settled in the flat. The obvious benefits of instant hot water and a shower and toilet she can understand. And of course Jo has the large attic room above the flat, which she has set up as a studio. A busy studio too, she remembers seeing all the various pieces of work she has in progress.

Anna now gets up and from the plastic carrier bag; she takes out the painting of 'The Bench'. Putting the painting carefully on the opposite seat, she sits down and looks at it. 'Why had she bought it? I mean why, really?' Anna wonders. She had no idea Jo had painted it, until much later after she'd paid for it, so she couldn't say because it was a piece of Jo's work. 'So why?' She stares at the picture. 'Because, because,' and then she stops. 'No,' she tells herself. As she struggles with the idea, she recognises now, what 'The Bench' represents for her. She had bought it because of her, because of Jo and their meeting and the magic and the sea and the dawn bang, which had seemed to split time and bring them together. They shared the experience of the dawn, a tender, fragile, innocent experience kissed by the elements and held in the delicate web of touch and sense and time.

As Anna continues looking at the painting, her eyes leave 'The Bench' and stray off towards the outline of the thicket, her heart somersaults in the memory of what had happened when she had strayed from that spot. All the light and beautiful softness and tenderness of the earth had been cast with a shadow of darkness and evil and in place of tenderness and touch. There had been violence, brutality, terror, pain and shame, a spoiling, a smashing savagely through time. Anna's tears fall, as she looks up again at the picture and sees the flowers at the feet of 'The Bench'. 'For you, to say sorry.' She returns the painting into the carrier bag and opens the wardrobe door. Moving the clothes to one side, she places the bag with the painting at the back, facing the wall. Allowing the clothes to fall back into place. After putting on the kettle, she selects sheets of cheap drawing paper. Taking the angel from the shelf, she carefully wraps her up and sticks a few pieces of sellotape on, to hold the sheets together and puts her in two carrier bags and places her on the shelf, in the wardrobe alongside the picture. Anna closes the door and turns the key. She will now make the phone calls.

Thud, thud, his heavy footsteps stomp up the staircase,
'Are you really here, or am I dreaming? It's been so
long, I can hardly remember your face anymore.
Refocus; remember where you are and who it is coming
up the steps.'
"Jo." Charles shouts with impatience as Jo opens the
door.
"Come on I've been waiting in the car for you, I don't
have time for hanging around, so let's be off, I've wasted
enough time today already, and don't bring that bloody
dog with you, I still haven't got rid of the smell from the
last time."
His face is red and his eyes piercing.
Jo reassures Jason, that she will be back soon.
"Look, let's not mess about, come on."

They hurry down the steps. Charles's 4 X 4 is parked on
the pavement; with the hazard lights flashing he means
business. Charles puts his foot on the accelerator as Jo
fastens her seat belt, the car lurches forward in the
direction of the railway station and then on to the main
road to Thornby.
"I'm so pleased you were up for helping, I have
everything in the back that you'll need, it's not great that
we are late, so we'll have to crack on."
Jo doesn't know how to answer his presumptive manner
and with Charles she feels she has missed out on a
valuable piece of conversation. He turns on the CD
player and the sound of violins, fills the ensuing silence
in the car. His erratic driving and cursing of other
drivers, occasionally breaks through the music and keeps
Jo on edge. As they approach Thornby, Charles takes the
road to the marina and drives past the harbour filled with
boats, and then further along the sea front, passing the
fairground and amusement arcades, towards the railway
station. Jo sits enjoying the scene unravelling in front of
them; her attention is brought back sharply.
"Wake up, were nearly here, just around the next
corner."

And like a rerun of before, with a turn of the wheel and foot on the brake, Charles brings the car to a standstill and parks it up on the pavement.

Anna sits on the seat beneath the window, gazing out at the remains of her day. She phones home to make sure her son Adam and daughter Georgina are ok and speaks to Mark. He has a job on the fairground in Thornby, working on the dodgems. Anna isn't sure how she feels about her son working with gypsies and travelling people. He tells her the gypsies are hard and at night they let their dogs run wild, to protect themselves. "Be careful," Anna cautions her son but inwardly she knows that he won't be. He would run wild with the youths and gypsies before getting into trouble again and then his world would fall apart.

It had been so good to see Jo and spend time with her. It had been a shame about the hut, but maybe providential in the long run. Jo set herself up in the flat and has really got into the swing of her art and painting. It wouldn't be easy or practical, to continue to do that, within the confines of her hut. A studio would be more practical. There is the Charles element too, which increasingly makes Anna feel uneasy and uncomfortable about the whole situation.

For dinner she decides to make herself some soup. Being in Jo's company has lifted her spirits and she is more optimistic about life. She still has a little more time at the coast before her return to the city. She will phone Mark again in the morning and arrange a day, to go over to visit him. The soup is from a can, not organic or home made. She knows a basic potato or onion soup is easy enough to make, but she wants to relax and keep things simple. Dipping her bread into the soup, she bites into the soggy hot mush and for all its processing, it is tasty and fills the empty spot in her stomach. Anna had noticed how respectful and special Jo treated her food and feeding herself. Anna's was a daily function to be got through, whilst Jo's was a ritual, almost a celebration of the food and the occasion, which honours and respects the food and its role as sustainers and source of nourishment. The whole process is important to Jo and Anna tells herself, one day it would be like that for her, not a perfunctory obligation she had to do.

Feeling tired she decides to make up her bed and put water on to boil for her hot water bottle. She wants to rest. After putting the small bag of rubbish in the bin outside, she shudders it has become much colder. She locks up the caravan and fills her hot water bottle and makes a pot of tea. Sitting down, Anna looks around the caravan. 'What a fucking life, what a life, what the fuck am I doing here, running around again?' The only positive thing to come out of the experience is Jo. This makes the dreary experience of spending her time alone at the coast, in the cold caravan, worthwhile. She pulls off her clothes and puts on her nightdress. The pleasure of being with Jo has begun to wear off, as she sits alone. She will feel better after a sleep she always does. Sleep is an ally, a comfort, and an escape for her, which she welcomes as she curls up in bed. Sleep will shake off these flat, negative feelings.

The wind blows through the gap beneath the door and windows, it is cold. Anna sleeps, warm, oblivious to the coldness, seeping through the cracks and crevices of the caravan. The cold is raw, but not yet with the sharp, icy, harshness of the winter to come. That will be much later on in the season, long after the campsite closes down for the winter months, when all the caravans stand, freezing cold and empty, until the spring sunshine comes and warms them up.

Anna wakes a few times, during the course of late afternoon and early evening, before she decides to get up. Somewhere in the top of the kitchen cupboard there are candles. A box of twelve she had bought at the £1 shop. She keeps them hidden for emergencies; because she doesn't want Adam or Mark to find them, fearing that they might start a fire. It is better that they don't

know. Taking one of the candles from the box she lights
it and drops its wax into an old saucer, to stick it down
securely. The candle spreads a gentle soft glow around
the caravan. She puts the saucer and lighter on the buffet
by her bedside. Later she will sleep. She fills the kettle
and makes a fresh pot of tea and re-fills the hot water
bottle, before climbing back into bed. She kicks the long
cotton, stuffed sausage, against the gap behind the door.
She takes her blue notebook and pen and begins to read
through what she has written about Fermanagh House.
She doesn't want to return to sleep, or remember, or be
in her own world, she wants to step into a different place
and time. So where has she left off? Yes, with Anna in
bed before her first day in practise. 'Right,' Anna tells
herself as she sips her tea, 'let's begin and get on with
this woman's life.' She doesn't want to leave her stuck
in the void of uncertainty, marking out time as she does -
she wants this woman to move, to roll, to fly, anything
but this endless waiting, which is never relieved.

*Anna's alarm clock rang out 6.30 am and from deep
beneath the warmth of her bed Anna heard it and
acknowledged it. It was too warm and too cosy and
Anna had no wish to rise. In this state Anna drifted
back off to sleep again only to wake up with a jolt.
Fuck he's coming Anna remembered. Anna threw her
duvet back and checked her clock for the time 6.37.*

Anna is pleased when Jo asks her to meet up again to go to the hut. Her voice sounds safe and comforting, as she listens to Jo on the phone.

She calls off at the supermarket before meeting up with Jo, because she'd said she would bring wine and crusty bread, if Jo takes a chilli she's made up in her flat.

It is a clear day. The sky is blue and there is a gentle breeze. The town is settling down into its autumn pace, as she leaves the supermarket and makes her way towards the junk shop, which has become their meeting place. As Anna turns the corner, she sees Jo waiting for her. This time Jo isn't so apprehensive, her mood is much lighter as Anna meets up with her.
"I've brought the bread and wine." Anna says holding up her supermarket carrier bags.
Jo holds up her sack, "Homemade chilli."
Their eyes meet and they both smile, pleased to be in each other's presence again.
Making their way towards the hut for the second time, Jo's mood now is buoyant and upbeat. How strange to be with Anna and hide the source of her underlying turmoil with Charles from their conversation and to shelve, put it out of her mind, out of the way and replace it with freedom and playful joy, to be in the moment, just the two of them here in this world, not forgetting Jason tagging along.
They definitely made progress during the first clean up and she hopes with the help of Anna, that the hut will become habitable again.

Chatting together they walk down through the bushes towards the hut.
"I think it's a good idea to light the stove first, to help dry out the walls. Once it's lit I can put the chilli into a cooking pot and leave it to heat through for lunch."
The prospect of working together and enjoying a well-earned meal, fills them with contentment and happiness.

The day again is dry and perfect for working. As they round the last of the hedge, the grubby, blue door is waiting for them to enter. Jo remembers her life here, its pleasures, its hardships and the sunshine and fleetingly, the nightmare of the flood. Anna asks Jo if she'll need to get a machine in, to turn the ground over, to replant next spring.

"I'm not sure yet, it's too soon to tell, I can't think about the garden just yet."

"It'll be back breaking work to try and turn all that lot over."

"Yes, I know." Jo agrees, at the same time putting those thoughts out of her mind.

"I need to sort out the hut first."

Jo puts down her rucksack by the doorway and pulls the door towards them; it opens easier this time. For a few moments they both stand and stare inside, on the floor there is a bright, white A4 envelope. Bending down Jo picks it up; it has been slipped beneath the door. The underneath is dirty and she brushes it with her hands, to dust off the dried earth. There is no writing on the outside. Jo pokes her finger into the corner of the envelope and tears it open and pulls out a solitary sheet of paper from inside. She sees words, shouting out at her from the page.

"What is it?" Anna asks feeling alarmed.

Jo's heart stops and misses a beat, she hears the loud thumping of a drum, banging away inside her ears and her head, she wants to walk back away from here, back to the footpath, up to the road and return to the town and safety of the flat.

"Oh no."

"What's wrong, what is it Jo?"

She passes Anna the letter to read. In large, black, capital letters, cut out from a newspaper and stuck down on the sheet of paper, emitting an angry message, are the words.

I KNOW WHERE YOU ARE
I KNOW YOU
YOU THOUGHT YOU COULD HIDE
BUT I HAVE FOUND YOU
GUESS WHO?
DO YOU REMEMBER ME???
I DIDN'T MEAN TO HURT YOU
WHY DID YOU DO IT?
I HAVE TO GO NOW
DON'T FORGET
IF I NEVER SEE YOU AGAIN
FOREVER NO GOODBYE

Tumbling through her mind like an avalanche, a torrent of thoughts, are waves of incomprehension, popping questions, firing across her conscience, darting and waiting for answers. 'It can't be. He can't have. How? But is it him? Who is it? Why?' On and on more questions, blurring and merging leaving a fog, a tired out sleepy feeling, shutting out Anna's words as she stands by her side.

Anna's hand shakes, as she holds the white sheet in her right hand. She sees the huge letters, stark against the white page and can't shake off the idea; it could be the man who had attacked her. It feels for the first time since the attack, the rape that he might still be hanging around, waiting, watching. Maybe the man believes the beach hut is Anna's home not Jo's. Anna stands for a moment silent and still and then asks.

"Is it meant for you?" Jo nods her head.

"Do you think it could be for me?" Anna asks.

"Why, why do you think that?"

"It might be." Anna says quietly.

They look at each other, their eyes filled with despair and anguish, both of them wondering about each other, and ourselves, nothing really making much sense.

"Come on, let's light the stove." Jo suggests.

Quietly and slowly, they go through the motions, of
knotting sheets of newspaper and pushing them into the
large, round, fat belly of the stove and breaking dry
twigs to put on top. Jo takes a match from the box and
strikes it, holding it under an edge of newspaper and
feels glad when it bursts into flame. When the twigs
crackle and flare up, she adds larger pieces of dry wood
and when they begin to burn, she closes the door to.
"I'll fill the kettle and we can make some tea."
It is difficult for either of them to talk, both lost in their
own fears, as their eyes fix on the orange flames in the
centre of the stove, as they wait for the kettle to boil. Jo
thinks to herself, how much comfort can be gained from
simple chores, like the adding of a log to a fire and the
mashing of a pot of tea. They gladly drink the tea and
then decide to leave the hut. Jo adds more logs and puts
the stove on to a light draw, so that it will burn slowly, to
help the hut dry out.
Gathering Jason's lead they begin walking in the
direction of the bench. At first, Anna isn't sure if she can
cope with going past the thicket again.
As they walk along Jo asks Anna, "Why did you think
the letter might be for you?" Anna is unsure and quiet
and doesn't know if she can answer. She feels ashamed
of what had happened to her. But as she spots the bench
in the distance she can't hold back.
"I was attacked, raped here."
Jo stands and stares at Anna in shock and waits for a
moment silent.
"You were raped here?" Jo quietly ask her, not wanting
what she has just said, to be true. Anna's painful
expression shows the truth.
"God, I'm so sorry."
Anna is unused to compassion from anyone, and drops
her head and tears begin rolling down her cheeks but she
doesn't cry. Jo puts her arms gently around her.
"Come on let's walk."
They walk slowly beyond the bench and down the steps
and along the promenade.

"The Sailors Arms is fairly close by, let's call for a drink."

Entering the pub in silence, Jo is stunned by what Anna has just told her and Anna is in shock. They decide to go into the snug. Its large fire roars and the battered, soft sofas and armchairs are inviting. Jo goes to the bar first and Jason follows.

"No Jase, stay."

He returns and lies down on the rug in front of the fire next to Anna. 'It's done now,' Anna tells herself, 'I can't unsay what I've said.' Anna sits back, happier now, to be away from the hut, the letter, the thicket and the bench. Passing Anna her pint Jo explains.

"I think the letter is probably for me. There was someone prowling around the hut, before the flood. I let Jason out because he was going mad and I think I saw someone."

"But why would someone do that? And why would they send this letter?"

They both sip deeply into their drinks, puzzled and confused, not knowing what to say. Not knowing what makes sense. Listening in silence to the crackle and spitting of the coal fire, they finish their drinks and Anna goes to the bar and orders two more.

"Did you hear about the body?" Anna asks as she puts the beers onto the table.

"It was in the papers. Near the bench, close by really to the hut too. It was the body of a man, which was found washed up, in between the rocks at the bottom of the cliffs. I thought it could have been him, the rapist, but now I'm not sure."

Jo takes a long drink from her glass and then another and before Jo responds, Anna's phone rings.

"Yes." Anna answers.

"Mam it's me." Anna hears her son's voice.

"What is it?" She asks, hearing the urgency and anxiety in his tone.

"Is it the gypsies?"

"No, no, it's not that, it's this girl's dad."

"Tell me what's happened Mark?"

"Johnnie's been told, to give me a warning, to get away from Thornby, or else I'll get sorted."

"What do you mean Mark?"

"Johnnie's not after me, but he's been told by this girl's dad, he's to give me a warning."

Anna listens as her son explains about another situation he is in; she is never sure, how much is pressure from him and how much comes from those her son tells her about.

"Johnnie's got his fair on this blokes land, so he's got to do what he tells him, or he'll get booted off and he'll have to pack up, Johnnie said you don't mess with this bloke, cos if you do, he has you battered or gets rid of you."

"Mark."

"I need some money mam."

Anna looks at the time on her mobile; she would have time to go catch the bus into Thornby, to give him some.

"Where are you going to be?"

"Here, mam, working on the dodgems."

"Give me an hour or two then." She turns off her phone.

"I'm sorry Jo, but I've to go into Thornby to see Mark, he's in a bit of bother, because he's hanging around with a girl, who's father doesn't want him to."

"I'll come with you."

"It'll be boring." Anna says, not wanting to drag Jo into another one of her son's dramas.

"That's ok, I'll come with you, but I just need to sort and settle Jason."

"Ok then, we can check the bus times at the bus stop on the road back into the town centre, so we know when the buses are due".

In the town Anna collects £30 from the cash machine and follows Jo back to the flat to feed Jason and fill up his water bowl.

"Are we ready then?" Anna asks and they say goodbye to Jason.

The bus journey into Thornby runs along the coastline and the views of the wide-open bays are beautiful. Anna sits back happy and content to have Jo as a companion on her journey. Anna knows the issue of the letter and the rape haven't been dealt with, but she feels relieved now they had been spoken of. She is also glad that, at the moment, Jo is living in a flat in the centre of Fenton. Away from the hut and prowlers and a rapist who she hopes is now the battered body, washed up between the rocks. She is safer in the flat, than the hut.

As we approach Thornby, Anna tells Jo. "We need to stay on the bus until it reaches the terminus, that's near where the funfair is."

The bus skirts around the town centre and goes down the hill towards the marina and stops just before the fairground and they get off.

The two pints of beer, they drank at 'The Sailors Arms', gives smiles to their faces, as they leave the bus and walk in the direction of the fairground. Underneath this facade of glee, is a cover for both of them - anxiety and concern for Anna, regarding Mark and more especially the rape. As Jo walks here beside her, she wants to reach out and take away what happened, to hold and reassure her and tell her that it was not her fault. Jo feels that she has not given her time to say more, however they have the future ahead of them and they will have space for that. As for Mark, Jo knows little of him and doesn't know what to expect when she meets him, she hopes it will work out and Anna doesn't have the weight of his situation preying on her mind, she doesn't need it. Jo is glad to be a support for Anna and to be with her; especially after the help she has provided her.

They pass the marina, with its bustle of activity and hardly speak, both occupied in their own thoughts. Jo doesn't want to think; she doesn't want to dwell on anything in particular, let alone the mention of the body. She is relieved to get away from Fenton and connect with Anna's situation and Mark's cry for help. Jo needs this distraction and how timely his phone call was at the pub and they made the decision to come here together and she didn't have to return home on her own.
Jo stumbles on the edge of a kerbstone and trips and lurches forward and Anna reaches out and prevents her from falling, headlong in a heap on the pavement. Jo laughs loudly, and Anna joins in when she realises that Jo is ok.

Approaching the fairground, the daylight is receding now and giving way to darkness, it is situated just passed the marina wall, where fishing and cargo boats are moored up. Looking out to sea, the breaking waves glint, with flashing lights, as they crash towards the land. Entering the fairground Jo senses Anna's unease as she searches for Mark amongst the few people milling around.

There is a kaleidoscopic flash of lights whizzing past, brilliant red ones, bright blues, greens and yellow ones too, far too fast for their eyes to hold. There is loud music, screeching and screaming and the sound of an organ, with its halting breath, is an intermittent intrusion amongst the rest. The fairgrounds last gasp, before closing for the winter. The summer heat is long gone, the people around, no longer with sun blest faces and traces of oil on their cheeks and lips, lingering around, tasting the sea salt.

Now the atmosphere is so much different, there is a lost longing for what has been - trying to recapture the magic, in this cold and darker place, a place much emptier and heavier now, less frenetic and giddy. The hunger and excitement is no longer around, the crests of the waves crash and leave the one armed bandit, bereft and empty, the punters are now long gone. Through the springiness underfoot of the wooden pier comes the racing tide, swishing and foaming, bubbling and twinkling, through the cracks of light. The cacophonies of noises ring out; in hope of attracting a few final stragglers, wanting to have another go. Even at the end of the season, the fairground stays, whilst ever there are customers to part with their money and weekend day-trippers coming for a day out.

Still there are the savoury, hot dog sausages and onions frying and burgers too. There's the sweet aroma, of the pink, fluffy, sticky candyfloss and the red toffee apples, waiting on sticks. The dodgem cars, bumping and turning, twisting and twirling as the sparks fly, cracking up above, now mainly empty, without frantic voices, shouting to be heard, as the lights flash and flicker off and on. The old tunes playing over and over again. The big wheel, with its genteel lift, pauses and turns up and around is empty. The seats are no longer rocking with passengers, squealing and screaming, in terrified delight, tipping and hoping that they won't fall out.

Anna looks around for Mark. "He's not here," Anna shouts as she tries to make herself heard through the music blasting out.
"Let's have a walk around for a bit and see if he turns up."

The waltzers loud speakers, try to drum up customers, as it gathers speed and the carriages spin and twist, they too are empty, with no young girls and boys, with heads jolting backwards and their hands holding tight. Now the lone tattooed worker walks the boards, with hands in his pockets wishing the night away, the fairground, full of circles, turning round and around. What goes around, comes around, many people say. Life is a carousel. Anna tries to phone Mark a second time and his phone is switched off.
"I don't think he's here Jo."
They search the fairground again. Jo doesn't know what he looks like. "We can walk around again, you might have missed him."
Making their way around the fairground a second time, they pass the coconut sties and kiddie's rides and Anna looks in every direction hoping to spot her son. Although they have had drinks at the pub, they haven't managed to have anything to eat. The chilli is still in the hut and Anna begins to feel hungry.
The light begins to fade further into darkness and the women begin another search for Mark and to look for the hot dog stall, they can smell its heady, cheap aroma, drifting across and Anna leads them towards it.
Stopping at the haunted house ride, they watch the seats moving slowly, eerily empty and they walk on and pass a notice board outside a small booth.
"It's a fortune teller." Anna reads the sign out loud.
"Gertie the fortune teller, have your future read for only £5. Let's go in."

"Oh, no but you can."

"Come on we'll both go in, it's something to do whilst we wait for Mark to turn up." Anna fancies the idea of looking into her future.

With the boldness, still sloshing around from the beer, Jo agrees.

"Oh go on then."

Anna pulls the curtain doorway apart and goes inside and Jo follows. Anna doesn't really believe in fortune telling, but sometimes to have someone else tell her about herself, gives Anna back the reality of her life. It is a smallish space, with heavy, paisley walls and an old red and black carpet on the floor. In the centre of the room, is a table, covered in a green damask cloth and a dark blue, velvet throw hanging over it, with red tassels dangling down.

Gertie hears their voices and appears from behind the curtain at the back, which must connect, to a caravan of some sort. She asks them if they want to see her together. Jo is about to say no, that it's ok for Anna to stay and that she won't bother after all, when Anna speaks up and tells Gertie.

"Yes that will be ok, I will go first."

Gertie is a large, plump woman, in her middle years, wearing a kaftan of purple, blues and reds and strings of large, multicoloured beads, wound around her neck. She has long, heavy, curly hair that has been dyed black, with a shockingly bright, floral bandana tied around it. On her small and middle finger are large gold rings and a number of jangly bangles, hang from her wrists. Gertie sits, almost majestically swathed, in her swinging 60's eclectic costume, of eastern mystic gypsy. Gertie puts out her hand.

"That will be £5 each."

Gertie asks for the money first and they find their own and put it on the table. She swiftly reaches across the table and picks up the five-pound note and coins and puts them into her kaftan pocket.

"Who wants to go first?"

"I'll go first." Anna offers.

"Your friend can wait outside."

"It's all right she can stay, we don't mind being seen together."

Gertie nods her acceptance of this arrangement and begins to shuffle her cards.

"Do you want the tarot or the crystal ball?"

"The cards."

Gertie continues to shuffle, as if she already knows which method Anna would choose. She asks Anna to sit down.

As Gertie shuffles the pack of cards Jo looks on and senses a change of energy inside this, heavy airless booth. The deck of cards are well used and have rough, worn edges; the backs of each one, have a picture of stars and moons, on a dark blue background. Anna sits on and waits whilst Gertie looks at her intently and for a long time and then asks her to cut the cards and Anna does so.

"Right."

Gertie deals Anna's fate out on the table in front of her. Gertie's bangles jingle as she picks up the two piles of cards from the cloth and joins them together in her hands. She looks at Anna and she waits in silence.

From behind Gertie's head, Jo sees the crystal ball in the background, on top of the cupboard and her attention drifts towards it. Her eyes become fixed and taken by the round glass dome. There is a glint of light shining from the right hand side of it and as Jo continues to look at it, the lightness grows and spreads outwards. Jo is fixated by it and is only aware now of the murmur of voices, the exchange of conversation between Gertie and Anna is fading away. The ball appears to be getting larger and Jo feels her footsteps adjusting, stepping forward to come closer to it. Her eyes are stretching wider and wider apart and the ball becomes the only thing in the room. Jo has moved away from the table and these other two people and she is deep down inside the sphere and it is becoming alive.

Inside the ball that Jo enters and is now travelling around is a landscape; from the blue, grey, sky up above, Jo looks down. She can see buildings and places that she recognises as Fenton. She knows this for definite, as it is a replica of a map – her map. She notices the tiny streets and the harbour with its cobbled landing. She passes over the roof of the flat and then down across the full length of the promenade and back up and over caravans and then at last to the beach hut. How fantastic this is, to travel over – up above. Jo is a bird now, flying and soaring and being swept along in the thermals, dipping and diving. And then swooping down with such speed towards the bench, she screeches and hovers over it and the edge of the cliffs. The magnificent, white tipped, terracotta jagged cliffs, topped with tufts of thick grass, are immense and awesome and Jo hovers and drifts and circles around.

Jo dives down towards the beach and the sand and rocks, her wings flutter and flap with ferocious energy, she is unable now, to swoop and soar upwards towards the sky. She is veering head long into a crash landing and cannot stop. As Jo hurtles towards the rocks below, she can see something lying on the sand and gathers speed, she can see clearly now – **the body**. Jo cannot close her eyes, they are fixed wide open and she can see him lying there motionless. It is him. He is dead. And now only a few feet away, she can hear him groan, a most agonising and tortured wail and then another groan, only louder this time and then just as she is about to close in on him and land beside him, he raises his head slowly to one side and his distorted face with dead eyes, looks directly into hers. No. No. No. Jo gasps now as his mouth gapes open and thick, red blood trickles out and with a long, slow, drawn out movement, he mouths 'YOU', followed by a weak sounding 'you' and then his head drops back to the sand and he is still.

Gertie reveals the cards. She peels the top card from the pack in her left hand and turns it facing upwards, towards Anna on the table. On doing so, she notices that there are two cards stuck together. She slides the top card – The Ace of Cups forwards to reveal – The Ace of Swords underneath. Pushing these two cards to her right side, she then takes the next card – Judgement and places it facing upwards adjacent to the Ace's. She continues this with – The World card - The Lovers card and finally – The Hermit card. Anna looks across the spread of cards lined up on the cloth. The two Aces'. The four major arcana cards. Judgement – A picture of an angel in a golden gown, blowing her trumpet. The World – A figure encircled by a green wreath. The Lovers – A young woman offering a flower to her partner, as they stand in a field full of flowers. The last card in the row – The Hermit – A bearded man dressed in a long green cloak, holding a lantern in one hand and a stick in the other, curled around the stick is a snake. Gertie begins to speak as she grasps the two Aces' and pulls them to her side of the table.

"The Ace of Cups is showing us a mirror to your emotions. This card tells us that you are seeing yourself for who you are and that your feelings are coming to the surface, however." Gertie pauses and looks at Anna and carries on.

"As we have The Ace of Swords stuck to this card, it also tells us, that there is a struggle for you with all of this. The Swords tells us that you are trying to reason everything and that you can't accept that things happened the way it did and that's it. Yes, you have difficulty letting go, it's like you have to keep on and on. What I need to say to you now is this – accept things for what they were, you can't change the past."

Gertie slides the two Aces's across to the edge of the table and takes The Judgement card and contemplates her thoughts looking directly at Anna.

"This card is giving you a second chance, so heeding what I have just said, think wisely."

Gertie looks intently at Anna, "You can have a different future for yourself."

Taking the next card – The World – Gertie continues. "You are beginning a new life for yourself with this card. One chapter of your life is closing and another one beginning. This could mean in terms of your lifestyle, or moving and living in a different place. Like I said to you, it is all down to you and how you manage yourself. What you accept and let go of in terms of the past, if you are able to move away from it too!"

Gertie looks up from the cards and smiles at Anna.

"You must allow your heart and not your head to guide you. If you do this, and there is every reason to believe that you can, with having this card today – The Lovers – you will encounter, a new world of people and places – for you this will be like starting your life again."

Gertie takes the final card – The Hermit and looks at Anna again this time in deep thought.

"I'm concerned by this card. It tells us that what has become your reality, any changes that you make, will determine how you live your life. This card is asking you to return inside yourself and come to terms with what has happened. This could be in a matter of months or years. I'm unable to see the time span of this card. It does show however, that you may seek out help from another person at this time. Yes that's it. You have learnt things the hard way. It's time to stop compromising."

Gertie glances behind her to look at Jo.

"You have a choice, which ever way you want to go. You can choose how you want to live."

Gertie finishes and gathers the cards up from the table and once again begins to shuffle the pack and looks beyond Anna towards Jo. Anna stands up.

"Jo, Jo it's your turn now." Anna repeats a second time.

From inside the ball, Jo hears another voice in the far distance behind her. She is desperate to turn and answer, to look away from his body, this monster beside her. Jo must avert her eyes and shut out this sight, turn and switch it off. The voice she hears is louder now and penetrates the crystal and as the ball shatters around her, she returns to the room. She tiptoes around the splinters and shards of glass carefully, for safe and solid ground, as she refocuses and adjusts to the foggy darkness around her. Jo is aware now of Anna and a woman sitting looking up at her. The woman is gathering cards from the table and shuffling them, her hands tossing cards across, from one fat hand to the other, Jo notices her large gold rings as they work up and down. As Gertie slows down her action, she takes another long look at Jo and stops and puts the pack of cards in a pile at the edge of the table. Anna tries to remember all the things, which Gertie has just told her. 'Which cards were they?' Anna can't remember now as she looks across at Gertie. Something is happening. Gertie is pulling her gown to one side and raising herself up from her chair and turning to the cupboard to reach the crystal ball. She stretches out her hands, to take the ball and then she stops suddenly. The ball no longer shines, it is much smaller now and darker, a dense black that almost merges and disappears into the curtain behind. Gertie reaches into her kaftan pocket and pulls out a black cloth and shakes it, before placing it on top of the ball, and turns around towards the women with her arms outstretched, her palms facing forwards, she ushers them outside. She looks at Jo and says.

"No more today, it is done."

Anna pauses and hesitates.

"Why, what do you mean?" Anna asks.

Jo makes her way outside, away from this stifling, eerie place and then Anna does too. As they walk away, Gertie follows them.

"You go now, go now please." Gertie takes in her board and pulls the curtain across behind her.

Anna watches Gertie take her sign in and close the curtain of the booth.

"Hang on." Anna catches up with Jo.

"You didn't get your reading."

"It doesn't matter."

"It does, she charged you a fiver and she hasn't given you a reading."

"It's alright." Jo walks on.

"You should get your money back."

They walk away from Gertie's booth and past the haunted house.

"Come on, she didn't give you a reading, so let's get your money back, come on Jo."

Jo keeps on walking away. Anna tries to insist and berates Jo for not going back. Jo doesn't know what has just happened and she is filled with a heavy, dark feeling and has to move on.

It seems the matter is closed.

"I'm hungry. Let's get something to eat from the stall. Look." Anna points. "It's over there."

"What do you fancy?" Anna asks.

"Chips, burger or hot dog? Jo." Anna repeats, "What do you want to eat?"

Anna goes over to the food van. Jo tries to shed this weight, this heavy burden, to cast it aside, she doesn't understand. Did she see him; has what just happened, really happened? This world she is in right now, is a blur and its edges are no longer sharp and clear, she feels the dark spirit of the ball following behind her.

There are two people queuing at the chip van and Anna joins them to wait.

The large grey ball looms and engulfs and wraps itself around the wavy edges of Jo's space. –

'I am a person without a voice to be heard, to whisper, scream or shout. I am an essence of energy, a shifting fog. Cold and lifeless, I leave behind an unusual, pungent, sweet aroma. I know that you can smell me. I shouldn't be here at all, in this half way heaven where I flit, to follow you around. My days were laid to rest, yet I cannot reside in peace. With growing unease, ghostly outlines I will form, to make my presence felt. The all-embracing doors of afterlife, I chose not to enter, I

*fought their final suck, of white, bright light. How can I
rest in peace, eternal and forever after? You hold me
back. I was your bone and your flesh. I am now in the
terror of the shadows of death. I beckon you to join me,
to hold hands once again and enter into paradise, in
unity. I see and watch you having fun and filled with life
and know that you're not ready. In my haunting, I want
to snatch you away from your earthly life; you see my
time is running out. Come back to me come to me.
Remember how it was our union, my obsession and
possession of you. I had to do it, can't you see? Why
can't you forgive me? I loved you. I see you now happy
without me, how can that be. Your smiling happy face, I
knew that face, I saw that love, and it was mine, all for
me. How can that hand of yours be now tied with
another? Come back to me, my one time love. You have
to come to me. – '*

"Jo are you sure you don't want anything?" Anna's
voice breaks through.
Jo shakes her head looking on as she waits.
"Look." Anna shouts. "There's a seat over there. You go
and sit down whilst I queue."
Jo follows her instructions and sits on the bench.

Joining the queue Anna decides, Jo doesn't seem herself.
Maybe it's the letter that's upset her, or worrying her. A
hot dog and a cup of tea will bring her round. Anna is
aware of the time. It is almost dark and Mark hasn't
turned up yet, nor has she been able to reach him on his
mobile. She needs to decide what to do. The last bus
back to Fenton will be at 7 o'clock. Time is getting on
and they will have to think about getting back into the
centre, to catch the bus home. Anna had bought day
return tickets too and this is annoying her, because if
they miss the last bus back, it will mean catching the
train and then the bus tickets will be wasted. 'Come on
Mark,' Anna says to herself, as her place in the queue
gets closer to the man selling the hot dogs. 'Why does he

look fat and grubby?' Anna asks herself, 'what an
advertisement for the stuff he is selling.'
"Two hot dogs."
"Onions and sauce?"
"Yes." Anna replies taking her money from her purse to
pay.

At the stall, Jo watches the sizzling onions as they're
placed in a long bun, with a sausage on top. Anna
squeezes out the red sauce, it sucks out its long thin line.
Jo feels a sensation, as if someone has run a finger down
her spine and recoils and stands up from the seat. The
smell she inhales is cloying and sweet and drifts like a
tidal wave, it returns and then is gone. Flashback, death,
connection red sauce, red blood. A quick turn, the
presence felt, the cold chill running down her back.
Recollections. In the bubble, that arrives in her head, like
a comic strip unfolding, the reel turns. She hears the roar
of laughter, but there isn't a joke, what comes next is not
funny. She didn't write the script, yet she was the
protagonist of the drama. Jo acted the part she didn't
have a choice. Or didn't think so. Blood red, dripping,
the cut deep. The comic strip is advancing forwards, then
backwards, and then jumping further forward again. The
knife like a sword fixed at her head. Accusations, a
madness that doesn't make sense. 'What, stop it, please,
no, stop.' Panic setting in, she freezes. The reel skips on
again. A groan and a thud, the body falls to the floor,
blood pumping, leaking and spreading, staining. The
blotting paper clothes, sucking like a sponge and going
pink and then a deeper red. The reel retracts. 'It's me
you love, tell me you love me, go on tell me!' the mouth
said. 'Please no, drop the knife, please stop. What has
she done?' The reel fast-forwards once again. The
bleeding body looks near to death. She panics. Too much
blood spurting and pumping leaks out. Looking into the
face now, she sees as if into a mirror, a reflection of a
monster, the reel rewinds and Jo remembers.
Hot dog sausage with red sauce on top.

Anna holds her hand out.

Taste buds adjusting, converting the blood to tomatoes, closing eyes and biting into the sausage, to find the onions. Switching off the projector, closing down the cinematic screen. Nose to hot dog, nostrils inhaling and filling the senses, Jo takes another bite.

Anna's mobile rings and she rummages around in her pocket to find it. She passes her hotdog for Jo to hold.

"Hello."

"Mam it's me."

"Mark."

"Mam I've been held up, I'll meet you at the station, I'll wait for you."

"Mark." is all Anna manages to say, before her son turns his phone off.

"Mark's been held up, he's been drinking, he's a bit tipsy by the sound of it."

Anna takes back her hot dog sausage and puts the phone back into her pocket.

"He wants to meet me at the station, that's where he is. That means walking back up through the town to get to the railway station."

The women begin the climb back up the hill, away from the harbour into the town centre and from there, across to the railway station.

"We've missed the last bus Jo." Anna explains as she looks at the clock in the station. "Look, there's a train in about 25 minutes back to Fenton and it's the last one, so you need to catch it."

Anna explains not wanting to be responsible for Jo being stuck in Thornby, when there is still a chance of her returning home. Mark has been drinking and is probably still drinking, so he could turn up at any time or not at all. That's how it is with him.

"I'll wait with you."

They go into the waiting room, where it's warmer to wait for him. It is empty, apart from an elderly man sitting on his own and they sit away from him, together in silence. As the last train comes in, Anna tries to contact Mark again, but his phone is switched off.

"I can't get him to answer, you had better get on this train."

Anna looks out through the plate glass window; she sees the shape of a man she recognises coming into the station.

"So you're here."

Her son walks into the waiting room. Anna can smell the alcohol on him, he reeks of it, she is annoyed as the train behind her pulls away. Rocking slightly, Mark looks down at his mother.

"We've missed our bus and train back Mark."

Anna says to her son, accusing him of the responsibility, because she has waited for him.

"I was with Freddie."

"So, what are we supposed to do now Mark?"

"Don't worry, I've got a place where you can stay for tonight."

"Have you?"

Anna is angry and sceptical.

"Come on mam."

"Where are we going Mark?" Anna asks, as her son takes off, skipping through traffic and walking determinedly in front of them.

"Well, at least we'll have somewhere to sleep." 'I hope,' Anna says under her breath.

"How far is it Mark?"

"Not far mam."

Approaching a block of flats, Mark takes keys from his pocket and unlocks the outside door.

"Mark."

Anna says to him, unsure if he is breaking in, or if he really does have the use of one of the flats. Mark stops and taps on one of the flat doors. 'Oh god,' Anna thinks 'what next?' Jo is even quieter now, than she was after leaving Gertie's booth. Anna hopes a good night's sleep will bring her round. Footsteps approach the door and a voice calls out.

"Who is it?"

"It's me Abbs, Mark."

The door opens and a red haired girl stands framed in the doorway.

"Mark, you bastard." the girl greets him.

"I know sorry Abbs but...."

Anna doesn't hear the explanation her son gives 'Abbs', as he leaves her and Jo on the doorstep and goes inside with the girl. A few moments later Mark returns.

"It's alright mam you can come in."

'Thank god,' Anna thinks as they step inside and close the door behind them. 'All we need now,' Anna tells herself, 'is the girl's mother or father banging on the door.' With Mark, this is more than possible. The flat is warm, clean and bright and Anna is thankful for its sanctuary.

"It's good of you to let us stay tonight." Anna says to the girl, adding. "I'm Mark's mam and this is Jo, my friend." Abby looks at Mark, as he puts his arm around her waist and pulls her towards him, squeezing her. Abby smiles and says.

"Mark please show your mother and her friend where the spare bedroom is and then you can make them a cup of tea."

"Sure, this way mam."

They follow him down the short hallway and stop next to a door. He opens it and turns on the light.

"This is it mam, the spare room, the bathrooms next door."

Anna walks into the bedroom. It has two single beds and is clean and warm and she just wants to sink into one. Mark leaves and returns with mugs of tea and hot buttered toast.

As Anna and Jo settle down for the night, Anna can hear the deep, low tones of her son's voice and Abby's scolding and then giggling, as she drifts off to sleep.

Charles knows that if he doesn't go to see Abby in Thornby, he won't rest. He has given warnings to the little runt who she has been seeing and hopes that Johnnie has made a good enough job at sorting him out, 'or else,' Charles thinks.

Selecting the key, Charles enters the block of flats. He considers the idea of letting himself into her flat and decides it is not a good one and rings the bell and knocks on the door.

It is early, but Margaret had told him how upset Abby had been on the phone yesterday, after Mark told her he was leaving.

'He bloody well better have left,' Charles thinks, as he bangs on the door again.

'A few days back at home and plenty of goodies will set Abby back on her feet and life will be back to......'

Charles doesn't have time to finish his train of thought, because the door opens.

Drawing in his breath, to prepare himself for Abby, Charles is floored when he sees the fat bitch at the other side of the door – looking at him bleary eyed.

"This is starting to become a habit." Charles says brushing past Anna and walking down the hallway to find Abby.

'I'll have something done soon to that woman,' Charles notes mentally to himself, as he begins to look around the flat for his daughter.

Hearing her father's voice, Abby manages to slip out of bed and pull some clothes on, before he comes bursting in.

"Oh darling, mummy was so worried about you after your phone call. How are you feeling now, are you alright?" Charles asks, ignoring Anna as she walks past the pair.

'God it's her father,' Anna says to herself, 'I'd better get Mark up as soon as I can. Take him into the sitting room,' – Anna pleads to Abby in her head. They are heading for the kitchen, so that will give her a few minutes.

"Come on get up, get up." Anna shakes her sleeping son. He is hung over and has no intentions of moving from his warm and comfortable bed.

"Mark." Anna pushes him; he wakes up swearing and angry.

"He's here." She says between her teeth.

"Get up, before he comes in and finds you in her bed."

"What?" Mark musters.

Anna pulls off the covers and wishes she hadn't.

"Get up." she persists.

"Fuck's sake."

"Right Mark, that's it I'm going."

"What?" Mark wakes from his doped state and tries to focus on what his mother is saying, because she sounds worried and in a panic, so it must be important.

"Put your clothes on." Anna repeats and is relieved as eventually he bends down and begins to haul up a pair of trousers.

Pushing him off the bed, Anna begins to straighten it.

"Her fathers here Mark." He begins to understand his mothers panic and urgency.

"Fuck him what can he do."

"Have you beaten up, or maybe killed."

"Put your shoes on." Anna tells him and then goes to the door. She can hear Abby and her father talking in the kitchen.

Grabbing a hold of her son by his t-shirt, she pulls him out of Abby's bedroom and into the sitting room.

"No, no, I'm going outside for a smoke."

Anna panics, but then thinks; perhaps this is a good idea.

"Ok." she says, checking to see if the coast is clear.

Anna returns to Abby's room and finishes making the bed and picking up the used condoms with a tissue and puts them in the wastebasket.

Anna returns to their bedroom, Jo is already up and dressed.

"Charles is in the kitchen."

"Charles?"

"Yes, he's Abby's father. Let's go into the sitting room, Abby's talking to him in the kitchen, Mark has gone outside for a smoke. God knows what's going to happen."

The two women sit down in the sitting room, listening as Abby and her father argue. Abby tells Charles that Anna is Mark's mother and that they had missed their train last night back to Fenton and Mark had brought her and her friend to stay. "Her friend?"

"Yes, her friend who came with her, Jo".

"Jo?" Charles nearly chokes on the name.

"Where are they all?" Charles demands.

"Daddy."

Abby calls after Charles as she follows him through the hall towards the sitting room.

Charles stands in the doorway glaring at Anna and looking at Jo.

"What's all this then?"

Charles throws the question open, to anyone who might care to answer it. Anna looks at Charles, thinking he might explode, he looks so angry, waving his arms in the air. She watches his hands return to his sides, clenched into fists.

"Oh, come on daddy." Abby upgrades him.

Just as Charles looks a little calmer, Mark opens the front door of the flat and saunters into the sitting room. Charles looks mortified but remains silent, looking at the people in the sitting room slowly and deliberately he begins.

"Right then sweetie, when you're ready, we'll get off."

"Daddy." Abby begins, but Mark chips in.

"We've to get off now Abbs."

Abby turns towards Mark and the two look at each other. Charles wants to fell the boy here and now but he can't. 'Ok,' he says to himself, 'get them all out.' Looking at Jo, he tells himself, 'I'll deal with you later.'

"Mark."

Mark turns to face Charles. He is full of himself Charles can see that.

"Can I have a word?" Charles controls his tone.

"Yea, sure."

"Darling, please get ready." Charles tells Abby.

"Mummy's worried."

Mark turns to Abby and says, "In a bit." as Abby walks out into the hall.

"I mean it Daddy." Abby warns Charles.

Charles smiles charmingly.

"Now Mark." Charles begins eyeing up the young man in front of him.

"I thought I had a message delivered to you."

Charles looks into Mark's face for a response, a wince or a flicker but he is deadpan. "Johnnie, remember."

"Oh, yea." Mark replies, deliberately obtuse and uncommunicative.

"Yea, yea." Mark says to Charles looking straight into his face

"I remember, but the thing is, I don't have any money to fuck off with."

Charles stops himself from punching the boy. Instead he takes his wallet out from the inside of his jacket pocket and draws three £20 notes. Giving Mark the notes, Charles looks him in the face.

"Last warning Mark, if you see my daughter again, if you touch her again, well, you know don't you?"

Charles looks as Mark slips the money into his pocket, fighting again the urge to deck him right here. Charles tries to stop Mark from returning back into the sitting room to speak to Abby, but Mark pushes past his outstretched arm and says,

"In a bit."

"In a bit."

Charles repeats under his breath, as he watches Mark go into Abby's room and walk back out with his jacket.

Abby returns to the hall and the men face each other again.

"In a bit then Abbs."

Mark takes her by the shoulder and gives her a kiss on the mouth.

"Just wait."
Charles says as he walks away from the couple and
begins to round Anna and Jo up.
"I think you're leaving now," he says standing in the
doorway.
"I'll get our coats."
Jo waits for Anna to return.
"Small world isn't it?" Charles says to Jo.
"Yes."
"Here we are." Anna gives Jo her coat.
Turning to go, Anna stops briefly in the doorway to look
at Charles as Jo mutters her goodbyes to him. He turns
around and Anna stops him.
"Charles." she recognises the loathing in his look.
"Yes."
Anna stands still before him.
"If you touch, or hurt my son, I'll kill you."
Charles almost chokes, at what the little fat bitch has the
affront to say to him.
"I know what you're up to, I know your games and now
I'm warning you, leave my son alone."
Charles laughs at the ridiculous, preposterous, rubbish
she has dared say to him.
"Oh you do, do you, well I know yours too my dear and
for all concerned, I think it's worth pointing out, that for
all your illicit entertainment, you look marginally better
with clothes on. So I would be careful what you say in
future and bear one thing in mind – no one messes with
me, do you hear that, no one."
Charles finishes and turns away, letting out a loud
guffaw as he leaves.
She has upset his day; he will deal with her son later.
Abby he can handle and Jo too, but this fat bitch Anna
has to go, she is too full of herself, just like her son.
'They had both better fuck off,' Charles says to himself
mortified, as Mark, Abby and Anna walk out of the flat
with Jo.

Outside, Mark gives Abbs another kiss and a squeeze as Charles watches on. Charles looks at Jo and nods his goodbyes to her and glares briefly at Anna.

"In a bit then." Mark tells Abby, as she climbs into Charles's 4 X 4.

"Definitely Mark." Charles repeats "Definitely in a bit."

"Right Mark." Anna says to her son. "Where are you going to go now?"

"I'll go and chill out with Freddie for a bit and then either go to York, or move down the coast".

"Well I think you should for your own sake, we have to get off now."

"Be careful Mark, keep out of that lunatics way, he'll hurt you, he's a mad man."

"I know."

"Phone me, so I know you're safe."

"Yea, yea."

"Where are you going now?"

"Back into Abbs flat for a kip." Anna shakes her head.

"Mark." she puts her arms around him and gives him a hug and kisses him goodbye.

Anna watches as he slowly walks back to the flat, stopping and starting and bending over to roll himself a cigarette. Anna knows too, that when he gets inside, he will smoke it. Abby doesn't seem to mind, but Charles does. Anna saw clearly that Charles minds a great deal about his daughter and Mark.

"Let's go and find somewhere to have a cup of tea and a bit of breakfast," Anna suggests.

Anna feels glad to be going back to Fenton and something, which resembles normality, she is thirsty and peckish after having left Abby's, without even a cup of tea. 'Be careful,' Anna thinks to herself, Charles is not a good man and she feels worried now, as she remembers the look he gave her and his comments haunt her. For all his attempts at charm and swagger and superficial conviviality and despite his blustering bravado, deep beneath the surface he is a disturbed and damaged man. As a damaged person herself, she can always see beneath the veneer of other people. She sees their chips and dents underneath their surface. Anna knows that her son should keep well away from him, because he is a powerful and dangerous person. He isn't a big pussycat, although his daughter treats him like one. Anna concludes, he is not a man to become involved with, or underestimate what he is capable of doing; otherwise you could end up in trouble.

Anna's eyes widen, above the mug of steaming coffee that she nurses in her hands and looks at Jo.
"You look exhausted." she comments and takes another sip of her drink.
The coffee bar, a greasy spoon, has steamed up windows and nicotine yellow walls and Formica tables and chairs, most of which are occupied by noisy men, eating full English breakfasts and reading the mornings papers. The air is thick and filled with fat frying.
The scraping legs of a chair, being pulled away from the table behind her, accentuates Jo's edgy disposition, as if its leg has hooked her own raw nerve and twanged it and Jo compensates, with a reflex jump of her feet from the floor – and then scrunches her whole body, as she awaits the next scrape and screech.
"Eat your toasted t cake, you must be hungry – we've hardly had anything since yesterday, I'm so sorry that I got you into all of that with Mark."
"It's ok." Jo pushes the toast around the plate, before taking a small bite.
"Look I'll tell you what we can do." Anna continues, "We could go back to the hut and heat up the chilli and I can help you again with the cleaning."
Jo churns the swelling piece of bread around her mouth in dread, as it wrestles with her tightening throat, she is in fear of gagging and retching this soggy mass, this almost human morsel back onto the plate. She continues to move, contain and shrink it with her tongue and finds help with the mug of tea, as she takes some of the hot liquid into her mouth. She now struggles, with the even

greater difficulty, of controlling the volume of liquid mush and opens the back of her throat, in hope that it can take it and waits.

The flush of heat rises, filling her cheeks and forehead with hot blood; she is released now she has swallowed it down. The panic is over. Jo lifts up the mug again and takes a longer swig of the hot tea and tests her throat again with success. She feels glad now the panic is over and she can breathe and swallow. She takes another bite of the toast and this time it is light and free and tasty and her tongue is gladdened as it bursts open a sultana, she accepts its juicy sweetness and eats and drinks on.

"Your colour's coming back a bit Jo, you look better." Jo tells Anna.

"I'm worried about Jason, I shouldn't have left him alone all night."

"We can call at the flat first."

"What time is the next train?"

Anna looks at the clock on the cafe's wall.

"There's a train back to Fenton in half an hour, so we can catch it."

"Ok then, if you don't mind helping again with the work."

"No Jo, I don't mind and anyway you helped yesterday with Mark."

Jo tries to recall the events of the previous day; she remembers flashing lights, a fairground and vaguely Anna's son Mark and his girlfriend – Charles's daughter Abby. The girl is the same person she heard arguing at the flat below hers in Fenton. And Abby's flat here is the same one that she cleaned up after workmen for Charles.

"I hope for his sake that he moves down the coast and forgets Abby, Charles is a dangerous man, don't you think?" Anna asks.

"Do you mean about Mark?"

"Did you not hear what he said to me?"

"No, what was it?"

"He must have seen us down on the beach that day, swimming in the sea."

"Why, what did he say?"

"He said to me, when I tried to warn him off Mark, something about my illicit behaviour and looking better with clothes on."

"No, he couldn't have, you mean he saw us that day?"

"He must have, he must have seen us. He is not a man to be involved with, Mark needs to realise, he means his warnings and he is not to be messed with and I think it's something you should think about, staying in his flat, you don't know what he is up to do you?"

"No you're right, but I am only going to be there until February and then I am on my own again back at the hut, I shall have to keep out of his way though I know that."

"Come on then, shall we do that, go and do some more cleaning?"

"Ok then I need to collect Jason, he will be desperate to go out and have his breakfast."

It is good to leave the cafe and feel the cool, early morning, sea breeze on their faces. The day should stay dry again and aid their work at the hut. Jo's thoughts are easier now, her mind feels safer and more in touch and aware of the surroundings and protected in the company of Anna. With each forward footstep, her concern is for Jason now; she has left him too long alone in the flat. She needs to get to him and feed and take him outside for his walk. How stupid she has been to leave him alone last night, to not be thinking straight, she should have gone back and left Anna with Mark. Oh the constant recriminations pounding around her head. 'Be ok Jase; be ok when we get to you.'

Charles and Abby hardly exchange words on the journey
back to Fenton, he knows that if he unleashes his anger
on her, it could backfire and the consequences would be
interminable.

Abby has incomprehensible feelings clashing through
her mind. She knows that as far as the flat in Thornby is
concerned, she wouldn't be returning. Charles would
certainly make sure of that, in spite of his quiet
demeanour sitting next to her, he is seething inside and
would lay the law down, in his controlled way, back at
home. She knows that she will have no say over the
matter. As for Mark she probably wouldn't see him
again, he had told her he would be moving on soon, but
if she does go to York Uni, she can call him to meet up.
She likes the idea of that, Mark is good fun, he messes
around and she enjoys his risk taking and living life on
the edge; being with him is thrilling and always has an
element of not knowing what might happen. He is so
unlike the Fenton crowd, ok they like a good time, but
they know when to draw the line, and when to stop. With
Mark there are no boundaries, he just does whatever he
wants and sticks two fingers up at anything or anyone
who stop him. With him by her side she feels safe and if
Mark likes her, then she must be something special. One
thing is certain; she must make sure that her application
for York is successful, so that she can get away from
home and Fenton. She has enjoyed her short time of
independence living in Thornby and the thought of
returning home fills her with dread. She has revelled in
her freedom and space and remembering last nights sex
with Mark, she wants more. She would have to bite her
tongue and wait until things settle down and then win
Charles over, yes, she knows in a few days she will get
exactly what she wants.

Abby jumps out of the car, as soon as Charles parks it at
the rear of the house and grabs her bag from the back
seat and makes her way to the door. Charles's leather

soled shoes, scrunch on the driveway, as he follows her
into the house.

Entering he shouts, "Margaret," and then disappears into
his office.

Abby slings her bag on the hall floor and takes the
staircase to her room.

Margaret is aware of their arrival and knows she should
acknowledge him, but she cannot detach herself from
organising her suitcase. She has packed and unpacked
the case several times, going through her mental
checklist, to make absolutely sure that she has got
everything she needs for her trip. Her special lingerie set
that she has just bought, the knickers and bra, a soft, silk,
powder blue, with a skin coloured, lace trim and tiny
white forget-me-nots, sewn across the edge. Also tucked
underneath these in the case, a black set with red lace
and purple nylon bows, along with her stockings and
matching suspender belt, spare knickers and toiletries.
She has been to her beauticians and purchased day and
evening moisturisers, several hair shampoos and one or
two extras for her make up bag and also a wonderful,
sexy, body cream. Yesterday she spent most of the day
pampering herself, she had had a full body wax and
pedicure and facial and this morning she had her hair
conditioned and a trim to maintain its style. Lifting the
layers of clothing, she strokes and gently folds the
garments meticulously in the case.

Her mind wanders and her body fills with excitement, in
anticipation of the next few days away with Giles. She
imagines removing her outer clothing in front of him,
stripping and parading and taunting and teasing him. 'Oh
Giles, I can't wait.' Her hand stops as it touches the
parcel – the small, gift wrapped box, a pair of cufflinks
that she has bought for her lover – a thank you for a
wonderful time, she would give him them on their last
night away. She had asked the goldsmith to engrave the
initials G. G. on each one. She smiles softly at the

thought of him, her G. G., she wants to keep and hold the contentment of this feeling forever.

Sitting on the edge of her bed, her mind traverses her daily rituals – morning – toothpaste, dental floss, shower gel, hair shampoo, deodorant, hairbrush, make up. Stockings, knickers, suspender belt, bra, skirts, blouse, jumpers, shoes, and coat. 'Oh Giles,' she can't wait for him to mount and ride her, she imagines herself straddled and rocking, looking into his concentrated eyes, as his strong hands dictate their rhythm.

"Margaret where the bloody hell are you?" Charles shouts out from the hallway.
Charles's loud intrusion breaks her train of thought and annoys her; she will have to start all over again.
Toothpaste, floss, shower gel, hair.
"Margaret will you come down here now."
Margaret reluctantly leaves her suitcase and goes to the landing and leans over the banister rail to talk to him.
"There you are, what's all this bloody hide and seek about, come down here I need to talk to you, now."
Margaret exudes a deep sigh and steps serenely down the stairs.
Charles satisfied with Margaret's obedience, strides off into the kitchen and immediately feels out of place and turns around towards the snug.

"Well?" Charles asks as she enters the snug with a look of impropriety on her face.
"I'm going to visit mummy for a few days."
"Your mother?"
"Yes she needs me, for a few days, until Tuesday."
"Well, well, well, you are are you, well what about me, the house, didn't you give that a damn thought?"
"There is food in the fridge and freezer and I have asked Susan to come in everyday." "Well that's all I need on top of everything else, is sodding Susan interfering around here, I've told you, I don't like her snooping

around and if she steps foot in my office again, then
that's the end she's down the road, I just won't have it,
anyway if your determined that you are going. Are you?
Then I shall have my meals out, so you can tell that
ruddy Susan to stay clear until you're back, now if that's
settled I have work to do. And if you have any thought
for anyone other than yourself, you might like to know
that your daughter is home again. That idiot Mark was at
her flat this morning and I've given him his marching
orders, so you can tell her from me, that she has some
making up to do. I instilled it into her, not to see him.
And so this is all I need, you going away, just when
things become difficult. And more to the point what has
your mother ever done for you? Women, bloody
women, I've had enough."
Charles leaves the snug and goes to his office.

Margaret could have done without the unexpected issue
of Abby coming home and thinks 'of all the days, why
does she have to cause a drama today?' she knew
Charles wouldn't be too pleased about her going away,
however it would have been simpler if Abby was out of
the way at the Thornby flat. Let's hope Giles handles his
side of things; Margaret returns to her bedroom to re
check her suitcase. She will have to check it through, at
least another six times, before she is sure she has packed
everything, now that Charles has disrupted her
concentration. Oh Giles, oh, G. G., I can't wait to get
away, away from all this, from Charles, from this house
and even from my own daughter Abby.

Jo and Anna arrive at the flat greeted by Jason's nervous barking, he is obviously distressed and Jo takes the stairs two at a time to reach him. She opens the door and he bounds towards her, nearly knocking her over in his excitement.

"Oh Jase I'm here, it's ok, I'm here now."

He leaps up on his hind legs, trying to kiss her.

Jo enters the flat carefully, looking around to check for pools of urine or worse. Jason's doggy bed has been dragged through to the hallway and his food and water bowls are empty. Apart from that, the floors look clean and dry and she praises him for being good. Anna follows them through to the kitchen; Jo fills his water bowl and sets it on the floor for him to take a drink.

"He's ok Anna, he's all right, I'm so glad."

"What do you want to do?"

"If you don't mind putting the kettle on, I'll just take him out for a quick walk first."

"Ok I'll do that."

Quickly, Jo takes Jason out to relieve himself and returns.

Jason wolfs his food as they drink their tea.

"Do you mind calling at the DIY shop on the way, to buy disinfectant? If we finish cleaning the floor today, we can scrub the walls and flags with it, we can call for a crusty loaf at the shops on the way there."

"Yes, we will have more time if we set off now."

"I'll nip to the loo and then we can get off."

Jason is happy now they are on their way, through the town centre, heading in the direction of the DIY shop, calling at the bread shop for a walnut loaf and two vegetable pasties. They peruse the shelves of cleaning fluids at the DIY shop; Jo is uncertain which is best to use, to clean the walls of the hut and also the stone floor. Whilst reading the labels of the different products, a young man interrupts their conversation.

"Is there anything I can help you with?" he asks smiling.

"I'm looking for a cleaning fluid, to disinfect and clean wood and stone."

"Is it for inside our outside use?"

"It's for inside a wooden hut for the walls and the flag floor, it was flooded and the water has left a dirty tide mark on the walls and the floor was covered in filthy water."

"Well let's have a look".

On the front of his green dungarees, is a badge with Gary printed on. He is stocky built, with ruddy red cheeks and shoulder length, blonde hair, with a middle parting. As he bends down to look along the bottom shelving, he wraps his fingers around his wavy hair and tucks it behind his ear. He selects a plastic container and lifts it off the rack and reads the label.

"This one should do the job – what size is the hut and how large is the floor?"

"Oh it's about 25 foot by 25 with two smaller areas of about another 10 foot by 10 foot – that's the floor area and then there are the walls that I need to clean."

"Well you're going to need a couple of these, you will have to dilute it in a bucket and then use it as a wash, this will clean it and disinfect it at the same time."

Jo contemplates the idea of carrying two, gallon plastic containers and Anna reads her thoughts.

"We can carry one each."

Before Jo has chance to reply, Gary interrupts.

"Where are you taking it? We can deliver it for you, if you live in Fenton."

"Oh can you, that's good, but when can you deliver it?"

"If you decide now, we are taking out deliveries this afternoon."

"All right then, it will save us carrying it, that's great."

"Shall I take them to the checkout for you?"

"Yes please, if I buy a few more things, can I have them delivered with the cleaner?"

"Yes anything else you want, we can deliver it all together, just tell them at the checkout."

Jo thanks Gary and turns to Anna.

"Can you think of anything else we might need?"
"Buckets, cloths."
"Good idea."
They go off in search of these. At the checkout Jo gives
the delivery address and pays for the cleaner, two large
black buckets, a scrubbing brush and a roll of cloth.
It is good to be on their way again. The day is crisp and
dry and to have this sense of purpose fills Jo with
optimism and promise.

They decide upon arrival, to light the stove and open the
windows and door. The progress they have made is
obvious now – most of the floor area is cleaned of the
thick mud and the stone flags have almost dried out.
Once the stove is lit Jo fills the kettle and pops it on to
make tea.
"I'm hungry now Anna, are you?"
"Yes I am, shall we eat the pasties before we start?"
"Yes and then we can put the chilli on to cook through."
The pasties are tasty, made with short crust pastry and
plenty of vegetable filling.

Between them, they decide upon an area of the vegetable
plot to build a bonfire, to burn the soiled rugs and
Jason's bed and the armchair, plus the other detritus
from the hut. They turn the rugs to dry out and then
remove the soiled books and packets from the shelves
and the curtain beneath the sink and then tackle the
workroom. Jo has no choice, other than to discard her
sunken boats, soiled and wrecked by the flood and add
them to the bonfire. She is sad to lose her work and art
books, but as she flicks through their smelly curled up
pages, she realises they cannot be saved and tosses them
outside to the growing heap on the ground. Her few
prized possessions are no more and with a shrug, she
reminds herself that she can start again. Once the shelves
and fridge are checked and cleared of contaminated
items, they begin sweeping the floor. The job this time is
so much easier and the results are instant. When they are

nearing the end of the sweep up, they are notified of
someone's arrival by Jason's barking.
"It must be the delivery van."
Making their way outside, Jo calls Jason, to prevent him
scaring off whoever it is, coming down the path. Gary
appears and makes his way over.
"Hi you two, how's it going?"
"Ok"
"Where do you want this lot?"
"You can leave it outside thanks."
"I never knew this place existed, it's great isn't it?"
When he sees the bonfire he looks at them and asks,
"Have you lost all that lot?"
"Yes."
"You're not the only one, there's plenty in the town too
and some of them aren't even insured. I don't suppose
it's as bad for you, but all the same you could do without
it." Gary continues.
"Let's have a look at what you need this cleaning stuff
for."
He goes inside the hut to look around. Anna and Jo
follow him, he brushes his feet on the flags and then
goes to the wall of the hut and rubs the tidemark with his
hand. "Yes this stuff should do it, if you mix it fairly
strong, it will clean and disinfect it and the flags as
well."
"Great, we'll get started then."
"Well I'll be getting off, I'll leave you two to get
cracking." he turns and leaves them to start work.

Anna volunteers to mix the solution in the bucket and
start cleaning the walls of the hut, leaving Jo with the job
of cleaning the shelves, windows and the workroom. Jo
decides to tackle the workroom first and clear the
workbench and floor area of damaged materials and take
them out, to add to the bonfire. With cloth, cleaning fluid
and bucket she washes the workbench and makes a
mental note to have some shelving installed for future
work, this will provide a place for works in progress to

be kept away from the floor area and enable her to have more space on the workbench itself. If she continues working on canvases, she will need as much table space as she can find. The 'Purple Pearl' leaning on its side reminds her of the summer and a very different time, when life was clean and free and easy and she remembers Adams, wide-eyed innocence and his enthusiasm for his boat, which has luckily survived. Jo calls out to Anna.

"Come and look, here's Adams boat the 'Purple Pearl' it's ok, it's survived, would you like to take it for him?"

"Gosh it has, how amazing, it would be nice if he could come for it, can you keep it until Adam comes back to the caravan?"

"Yes sure, it should be safe here now, I think I need to put some shelving in here, to give me more space for painting canvases, I could do them in the kitchen on the table I suppose but in here would be better."

"Have a look at the walls now that I've cleaned them, you will be surprised."

Jo puts the 'Purple Pearl' back on the bench and when she see Anna's work, she almost can't believe it, the cleaner has removed years of ingrained dirt and the wood is lighter and looks absolutely fantastic.

"Wow, that's brilliant, amazing."

"I have had to wash right up to the top, to clean all of the wall, because it would have looked silly otherwise, a clean bit and a dirty bit at the top."

"Oh it's going to look so different when its all finished, I can't believe how dirty the walls were, even before the flood, gosh."

"I'll go and mix another bucket full and carry on."
Anna tells Jo on her way to the tap.

The stove is sending out lots of heat and the hut feels warm and cosy. Jo fills the kettle to make another pot of tea and puts the chilli pot on the stove to heat. She glances around and imagines how the place will look when it is finally finished and breathes a sigh of relief and carries on, cleaning the workroom, breaking off to make the tea. When she has finished, she gives the chilli a stir and decides to help Anna with cleaning the walls. With the two of them tackling the job, it is not long before they have finished three walls and break off for lunch.

The flavour of the chilli has intensified after leaving it for a day and it is richly nutty and spicily hot. They are hungry now and take huge chunks of crusty bread, to dip into it and eat their way through the whole pot.

"Mmmm that was delicious, really lovely thank you." Anna says.

Jo leans back from the empty bowl satisfied with a full stomach, she looks around at the progress they have made and in all honesty would never have believed that it would look as good as it does now.

"Right then," Anna continues "There is only the other wall to do and then the floor to clean."

Anna looks tired, although peaceful and content and Jo wonders if she has done enough for today.

"You look tired, are you sure you are ok to carry on doing some more?"

"I am but I'm fine, I'll be ok, come on let's start or we shan't begin."

Anna takes hold of the bucket to fill it again.

"If I take a look upstairs and see what needs doing up there, are you ok to carry on on your own?"

"Yes you do that, I'll be ok doing this."

Jo finds a few dog chews for Jason who is at her side, waiting for a titbit. "Here you go Jase."

Then she goes up stairs, her priority has been downstairs and now she can focus her attention on the bedroom. She takes hold of the duvet and smells it and decides that she shall have to burn it – the cover is dirty and it has a musty odour - she will buy a cheap duvet, pillow and bed linen from the market. After pulling off the sheet from the bed she sniffs the mattress, thankfully this doesn't smell too bad, so she chucks the bedding downstairs and returns back down with the rug from the floor.

"I'm going to have to burn the bedding Anna, it stinks and I don't think it will wash out, if I put the rug outside in the fresh air and give it a good shake it might be ok."
"It might be worth trying to wash the bedding and the rug, if you put it on a hot wash, they should be alright, I would try washing them anyway."
"Do you think so?"
"Yes I would give it a go."
Jo puts it all into a plastic bag, to take back to the flat to wash them. She then fills a bucket with fresh water, adding hot, from the never-ending boiling kettle and adds a couple of logs to the stove. She takes the bucket upstairs and washes the bedside cabinet, bed head, drawers and the top of the trunk and the chair and then sweeps the floor. And then on hands and knees, she uses the water to clean the whole floor, she is surprised by how much grit and dirt there is. She waits until the floor starts to dry out and then takes off her trainers and stands on the bed and unhooks the curtains from the window, she will take these to the flat also to wash through. Returning downstairs Jo tells Anna.
"That's the bedroom finished, it was really dirty, it looks great now a different room altogether."
"Good, I'm glad, I have nearly finished this wall now, so all there is to do really is the floor."
"We can both do the floor, I will put another pan of water on to boil, if we just get the thick of the dirt off, it will be easier next time."
"Yes it will need a few goings over."
They begin by giving the floor a good sweep, to get rid of the dust and then begin the slow process of boiling water and washing over the floor. By the time they have finished, it certainly looks cleaner and the air inside is much fresher. They stand by the doorway watching the flags dry out; Jo acknowledges their efforts and wishes they had somewhere comfy to sit down.
"I shall have to look around for chairs and rugs and bookshelves, the kitchen table and chairs are drying out, they are ok."

"You could try the auction and see if they have anything."

"That's a good idea I'll do that, I think that's it for today, don't you, so thanks again, you have been a great help."

"I'm happy to help, I have enjoyed it really."

After empting the buckets of dirty water, they swill them out and Jo puts another couple of logs onto the stove and closes the air vent slightly, so that it will slowly burn out and continue to dry the floor.

Jo closes the windows and takes the black bags of laundry and reminds herself to take some clothes next time, to wash. They close the door and leave.

The next day.

Now that the work on the hut is virtually finished and complete and although Jo still needs to buy armchairs and a few other things, her mind is more settled and she begins the day early. Although it is dark and cold, she feels driven with enthusiasm to get up and get on. She decides to eat a cooked breakfast, so that she won't have to break off at lunchtime to make something. She turns on the oven and washes a couple of tomatoes and a handful of mushrooms and slices them. She puts these into a baking tray, along with two rashers of bacon and a couple of sausages and pops it into the oven and then has a shower. After dressing, she returns to the kitchen and turns the bacon and sausages in the tray. She then boils the kettle for a pot of tea, pours out a glass of fresh orange juice and puts two slices of bread into the toaster. Jason is hungrily sniffing around and she tells him to wait. When the toast is ready, she opens the oven door and cracks open two eggs and empties them next to the bacon and sausage. The smell oozing out around the kitchen is wonderful and deepens her appetite. She sets the table with a glass of orange, a small plate, cutlery and mug. And then mashes a teapot of tea and puts that alongside the mug, as well as milk from the fridge, and butter and marmalade for the toast. By the time she has put the toast onto the small plate the breakfast is ready. Jo serves the food and leaves a sausage and an egg for Jason. The tang of the orange, complements the savoury bacon and sausage and she eats the meal with relish. The toast with butter and marmalade is the perfect finish with the hot tea. When she has eaten the last of the toast, she pours Jason's dried food into his dog dish and slices up the sausage and egg and adds that on top with a drop of boiled water.

"There you go Jase, sausage and egg on top, how's that?"

Jason drools in readiness and quickly attacks the dish the moment it touches the ground. Whilst Jason enjoys his breakfast, Jo begins the task of washing up.

Afterwards, she gathers her coat and Jason's lead, and sets off for their morning walk. There are lots of cars setting off to places of work out of town; the pavements are relatively empty, as the shops aren't open yet. She heads down towards the beach and out of curiosity makes her way to find the Holistic Healing Centre on Old Harbour Road. She has never come across this place during her walks around the town and wonders where it is. Jason pulls with eagerness to reach the beach and she has to regularly bring him to heel. She is pleased to see that the tide is far out and he can have a good run on the sand.

The sea is unusually calm and dark and merges with the grey dusky morning, there is an eerie stillness and emptiness and not even any sounds from the seagulls calling out. Jason is unperturbed and thrilled to be at the beach, he leaps forward once off his lead and races around on the sand. Jo follows him and picks up his dog poo, puts it into a plastic bag to drop into the dog waste bin. It is difficult to scan the sand for pebbles and interesting objects, so she runs along with Jason to the far end of the beach.

They return and retrace their only footsteps in the sand, back to where they came from, there are now flickers of light amongst the shadows of the sea. The dividing line of the sea and sky is changing and daylight is pushing through.
"Come on then Jase, let's go." Jo clips on his lead.
To find the Healing Centre she needs to walk along Old Harbour Road, which is above the slipway to the fishing boats. On reaching the road, she is surprised to note that this road is actually Harbour Road, no wonder she hasn't passed the centre before. She must never have walked along the old road. Walking along, she hopes to find a sign indicating the Old Road; on reaching the top, she is baffled to have not found a sign for it.

She makes her way back to the town hall and takes a look at the map that is displayed for tourists. The shops are beginning to open and the town is waking up with people walking by. Outside the Town all, she looks through the glass case at the map. The glass has been etched with a sharp instrument and graffiti covers the frame, making the map difficult to see. Not a welcoming sight for tourists, visiting this lovely seaside town, how can kids gain pleasure out of damaging something, which should bring them pride and joy by living here? The typeset is tiny and the street names are difficult to read, after a long time searching, she manages to spot the road. It is a small road after the turn off for the museum; it must have years ago been the main Harbour Road.

Leaving the Town Hall, she walks back past her flat and towards the road to the museum. The small road after the turning for the museum, is signed access only to - Old Harbour Road, it is a road she has never walked down. The road is narrow and cobbled. Years ago, this road must have continued down to the harbour, possibly where the steps are now to the Harbour Bar from the slipway. There are five, old, detached stone cottages along the road, the end one, a large, double fronted house, with the sign 'Holistic Healing Centre' at the gate. It is tucked away and is in a lovely setting with sea views all around. The house has a large garden area at the front and sides and is well kept. The paintwork and windows look clean and fresh and the place has a positive energy. At the side of the sign is a holder containing leaflets for the centre and she picks one up and turns around for home.

Nearing the town centre, Jo is happy to return to the flat, she cannot wait to get started again, on her own town map.

The next morning, Jo hears the shoppers vaguely in the background, down below on the pavement and the traffic as it clogs the street - noticeable by the slow drone of the car engines. She has two jobs in mind to do today. The first one, is to make two pairs of curtains for the hut, she never bothered to put any up before, except in the bedroom, however, it seems imperative now, especially after 'the letter' to do so. She's bought a length of material from the market at the weekend and also needles and cotton. The fabric is heavy cotton; a lovely sunshine yellow with limes printed on and will look fresh and cheerful and prevent anyone peering in, especially at night. The two windows are different widths, although both are the same length, so she intends to make the largest ones first.

The second thing she would like to do today and which now takes precedence on thinking about it, is to go back to the hut and collect fruit from the trees and plane off the swollen edge of the door, as she forgot to take a rasp when she was with Anna the last time. And again because of 'the letter' it seems a most urgent thing to do, the door needs closing properly and locking tight.

So without further ado, she puts on her coat and takes the rucksack containing the freshly washed sheets, pillowcase and duvet cover and a small amount of money. Anna was right, the bedding after a hot machine wash, cleaned up like new and she only has to buy a new pillow. She carries the duvet also in a plastic bag and walks along to the local hardware store to buy a rasp and a couple of sheets of sandpaper, that should do the job on the door. She then walks down to the promenade and up the steps, towards the path along the cliff top.

At this time of year there are relatively few people walking the cliff tops and she is glad of Jason's company and protection. It's good to be outside in the fresh sea air, the wind today is gusty and below the waves are fierce and crash noisily against the rocks. Turning off the public path towards the hut, she picks up her pace and feels warm and sticky by the time they arrive. Around the apple and plum trees there are lots of windfalls going rotten on the ground. She hunts the dropping branches for the best fruit and puts them into a plastic bag, apples first and the plums on the top. She will make fruit pies and crumbles and freeze them at the flat. It seems such a waste, looking around at the pounds of fruit still left on the trees. She can only eat and freeze a tiny portion of the amount there is here and it seems pretty pointless setting a stall up – the time and effort, toeing and fro in from the flat, would not be worth it. She will come back later and store the best apples in newspaper.

At the hut, Jo experiences an enormous relief, when there is no evidence of an intruder- 'no letter'. She takes one of the large logs from the fuel store and uses it to block the door from the jamb and begins the job of taking the edge off. The wood has dried out and she is able to shave off the swollen edge and after rasping and sanding it, the door closes easily. She tries the key in the door, yes job done, the door locks once again, she is happy and shouts Jason from the garden. After a couple of whistles, he comes running with his tail wagging.

The odour inside is sweeter than before and as Jo looks around at the empty space, she feels much more positive about the idea of living back here again. There is still work to be done, to clean and disinfect the floor again and buy furniture etc, but it can be achieved and the worst is now done, thanks to the help from Anna. She climbs up the steps to the bedroom, noticing how dirty these are, but at least the floors are clear of the thick mud. As she places the clean bedding onto the bed, she looks sideways and notices something is wrong – the padlock on the trunk is open – that should not be. Surely it was locked; she knows it was, so why is it open? She surfs through her actions and tries hard to remember when she last locked it, to confirm to herself that she's right. That it was definitely locked. She lifts the lid of

the trunk, hoping and praying that everything is just how she left it. Inside she sees the plastic bag, with her journals scattered all around it. Oh no, did she leave them like that, she can't remember, she thinks she left them inside the bag but she is unsure, has someone been in here nosing around, she doesn't know. Jo sits down on the edge of the bed, cursing herself for leaving the key to the trunk on the bedside cupboard. 'What was the point in locking it, you idiot, when the key is here to open it? But why the hell should she have to hide it, it's her place and not for anyone to come inside and take a good look around. 'But the door wasn't locked you fool,' the hut isn't secure; it is an easy target for anyone who dares to trespass and look inside. Has someone been in? Have they taken any of her journals? Will they come back? Who wrote 'the letter'? Has he found her, and if so will he come back? It seems an impossible idea. Is he alive? This thought forces her to take stock and she gathers her journals and quickly shoves them back into the plastic bag and takes them downstairs and puts the bag into the bottom of her rucksack and the fruit on the top.
"Come on Jase, were going now." She calls out and closes and locks the door behind her. Then takes the path up to the roadside, without looking back.

At the flat she takes out the fruit and makes a drink. As she sits, sipping her hot steaming tea, she hears a knocking and with Jason's accompanying barking, it pierces through her mental trance and alerts her. After several knocks and Jason's continuous barking, her hope of whoever it is, to go away recedes, the person is not giving up and she goes to the door.
She opens it a fraction to see who it is, giving her the option of shutting it quickly and locking it.

It is Stella standing, wondering what an earth is going on.
"Hello Jo, is everything alright, are you alright, is there something wrong?"

"Sorry, no, do come in, I wasn't expecting anyone that's all."

Jo wishes Stella hadn't chosen this moment to pay her a visit.

"I've just made some tea would you like some?"

"Oh yes that will be lovely, thank you."

Stella follows her, filling the flat with her buoyant presence.

"Gosh it seems ages since I last saw you."

"Yes it must be a few weeks ago now."

Jo answers whilst making the tea.

"I've been away on business, to France. I've been to look at a residential venture. If all goes well, which it looks likely, then we will be building six houses, with a rolling programme for expansion, if the demand is high. So that explains my sudden disappearance and Charles offering you the use of this flat. Sorry I couldn't organise it myself, but Charles and I work hand in hand on lots of things, so it worked out for you in the end ok, didn't it. It's better than the hut and you couldn't have stayed there could you, how is it by the way, have you been back?"

Stella asks whilst taking a seat at the kitchen table.

"I've been back to the hut a few times with a friend, we have cleaned up a lot of the mess from the inside, and it should be ok. But I will take Charles's offer of staying here until the end of February, so thanks again Stella, I don't know how I would have coped without your help."

"Oh it's nothing, how have you been, what have you been doing here, anything much?"

"I've been painting canvases and sold a few at the art exhibition at the Town Hall recently and now I'm working on a map of the town, come on up, I'll show you if you like."

"I just knew it, I'd love to take a look at what you've done."

Stella follows Jo upstairs.

"Oh wow Jo, it's amazing, I just love how you've drawn this."

Stella announces whist leaning over the table and looking at the map laid out before her.

"I haven't quite linked it all together yet, there are sections of it that I have still to decide on and what is going to go in it, but yes I'm pleased with it so far."

"It is so colourful and playful, it would make great advertising posters for the town. I know it's not the exact layout, but that doesn't really matter, it's the seaside image that it's portraying, it's spot on, I'm sure the town would go for it, if you showed them. If you are interested Jo, I can see what I can do."

"Really, well I would be, I just thought that the map would transfer well onto canvas – create small pictures from it – you know for the next exhibition. But yes it would be a nice idea, to paint posters for the town."

"I can visualise it now – a blown up version, at the roadside coming into the town, or picture postcards, well lots of ideas really, anyway leave it with me. The reason I called, apart from seeing you of course, is to give you the money for the boat, I never paid you did I, how much was it, I can't remember now?"

"Oh never mind, let's say it's a thank you for helping me out, you don't need to pay me."

"No of course I do, business is business, I know that too well, that's the way to get on believe me, so how much and don't say nothing."

"Well I'm not too sure myself now, but if I say £15, how does that sound?"

"Brilliant, £15 it is then."

Stella reaches into her handbag for her purse and picks out a ten and a five-pound note and gives them to Jo.

"Thank you, thanks ever so much."

With the business done, Stella begins a virtual one-way conversation, talking about her trip to France and her aspirations and ideas, she clearly loves her job and her success shines through her excited and ambitious dialogue.

"There's definitely a market, there are so many people getting fed up with life here in Britain and France has

certainly got the sought after lifestyle and who can
blame them, I must admit its got me thinking, but I'm
sure I'd miss the surfing, that would be hard to give up.
But I can have the best of both worlds, what with the
business there and here, life's pretty good at the moment
and I can't complain."
Stella's conversation tails off and she stops for breath.
Before Jo has chance to find something to say to her, she
begins again, telling her about the properties she's seen
and the people she's met, until she has emptied herself
out.
"I love this room, the canvases and colours everywhere,
it's great. Well Jo I must be off, it's good to catch up, I
need to dash, I have a business engagement this evening
and don't want to be late. I'll be glad when I can fit some
surfing in and settle down for a few weeks, I seem to be
up and off these days with work, but that's good, anyway
lovely seeing you again, we'll have to have another get
together one evening, I'll be in touch, so cheerio then."
They go downstairs and Stella leaves the flat with the
same flourish that she entered.

It's developing into rather a strange day – as days go - a
day that stretches like elastic, of time being added on, the
day becoming almost eternal and everlasting and time
itself expanding.

After Stella leaves, Jo measures, cuts pins and stitches
the edges of the material for the curtains and thinks back
to this morning at the hut. It seems so weird to be
weaving the needle in and out of the cotton, whilst
sitting in this clean and well lit room on a comfortable
settee, listening to the noise of the town outside, whilst at
the same time remembering rasping and sanding the
edge of the swollen door of the hut earlier today.

Like living a parallel life almost, sneaking and slipping
in and out of each one, having a fleeting glimpse of the
other world that she's visited. Two spaces in tangent,

having a foot in each one – on the cusp – in the middle
and just waiting to see, in which one her whole body will
land. Like the game of hopscotch, leaping sideways or
forwards on one leg, hopping, jumping and hanging in
the air and landing, teetering with a wobble, trying to
land correctly in the square and staying clear of the white
line. And yet knowing that there really isn't a clear
white line, there isn't a finite divide, an absolute clarity
of either or, if there was it would be easy, like yes or no.

Sometimes life is a guessing game, looking for clues and
answers along the way and waiting for a blue sky at the
end of the fog. At others, too busy engaging with the
vast clear horizon, oblivious to life on the ground.

To live the waiting game, to see what happens and then
decide, inept, unsure and putting life on hold, so how can
life on hold be life, how can it be living? Jo feels like
that right now, today. The scales are tipping; they are up,
they are down, what does she need to do, to balance
them. Is life weighed out, can it be level, do we get back
what we give out? Does it amount to our 'treasure map'
and what we put on it – what we imagine and create with
our visualization, what we want it to be?
She knows sitting here that she wants hers to be simple,
she wants to be healthy and to enjoy creative pleasures –
to feel fulfilled and to be recognised for her
achievements, not in a flash with bright lights, but in an
affirmative and knowing assured way. So as her feet hop
and leap in the air – she needs to decide – it is her life
and she must give it the direction she needs and not wait
for it to happen, she must grasp it, trust and take it where
it feels right.

Life is a journey that is for sure and she knows today,
she has found out that this cul-de-sac she is in, is a
holding space that she doesn't control – as if she has
relinquished her own inner guide to that of another and
she has to take it back for herself and lead the way.

Why has her mind taken on this route, why are her thoughts delving and diving this way? As she sits and closes her eyes and stops the threading of the needle, she is back upstairs in the bedroom of the hut, looking sideways again at the trunk and her journals. That's it, this is the straddle of her ruminations – the unlocked trunk, the diaries and writings, her notebooks and photos from another world, travelling towards her now from two habitats and hooking in and not letting go.

She owes these mishmash of thousands of words a place - and like an angel that has been dropped down from the heavens to guide her, she realises what it is she is showing her now – in this stretched space in time – a book, her book, she needs to construct and weave it, stitch it all together as a testimony to her life.

She has tested and left it alone and adrift and it is still here beside her and so she no longer feels she is walking in opposite directions – she has found a junction and knows the road ahead.

She needs to pack up her belongings from here and thank this place, for it has given her a healing space to warm her from the cold. And although she knows also, this direction she is taking, will have its twists and diversions and stopping places, it will be her own space in which to be herself.

Part 4

CONNECTIONS AND SEPARATIONS

Jo sleeps deeply throughout the night, without dreams or waking and emerges refreshed knowing what she is about to do; she is filled with intention and purpose. She needs to gather her belongings together, transport them and start over her life again back at the hut. Taking stock of her possessions, she realises whilst munching on a bowl of cereal that she will have difficulty taking the larger canvases back home. The small ones are no problem at all, but the bigger ones are bulky and she will have to take them one at a time. She crunches and munches away and thinks about what she can do to help herself. There is also the folding table and chair, Jason's bed, her foodstuffs and few clothes and journals. Sipping her tea and eating toast, her thoughts turn to Gary and she wonders about asking, if he would take them in his van. There is only one thing for her to do and that is to ask him.

With breakfast finished and Jason ready, they set off to the DIY shop. This is not Jason's favourite walk through the town centre, so he stops and stalls and pulls on his lead and tries to yank her in the direction of the golf course.
"Come on Jase this way."
Arriving at the shop, she ties his lead around a metal railing by the entry to the door.
"I won't be long Jase."
Inside she goes in search of Gary. When she reaches the wood section of the store, she notices stacks of racking for shelving, these would be great for the workroom and maybe in the living area too, the price is reasonable also. They would be handy to store her canvases and paints and beach finds and create more space. When a young girl in a green overall passes by, she asks her if Gary is in the shop today.
"Yes he is, I think he is outside in the garden section."
Jo thanks her and makes her way through the sliding glass doors, where stacks of plant pots and garden furniture are displayed. Looking around, she eventually

spot him driving a small truck, piled high with grow
bags on. She waits until he stops and jumps off the
vehicle and walk towards him. Whilst doing so, a
thought flashes through her mind - will he remember
her? Before she has chance to walk away and leave, he
looks at her.
"Hi."
"Hello."
"What is it today then?" He asks.
"No, well yes, it's just I have come to ask you a favour
actually." Jo blurts out.
"What's that then?"
"I have one or two things that I need to move to the hut
and I wondered if you could take them in your van, I will
pay you obviously, I have some large painting canvases
and other things that are a bit too big to carry far. It's ok
if you can't, it was just a thought."
"Well it would have to be after work, after five o'clock if
that's any good?"
"Yes that would be great, I am living at a flat in town
and I want to move back to the hut now that it's clean
again."
"I suppose I could take it this afternoon on my rounds, at
say 3 o'clock – if it will all fit in one trip? But if not
tomorrow after work, just after 5 o'clock."
"Oh yes, it should all fit in one journey, if you're sure
you don't mind, today would be brilliant."
"No sure, today's fine, where is your flat by the way?"
"It's Flat 4, Fisherman's Chapel on the high street."
"Yes I know the ones, I'll see you later then about three,
I have to get on now, so see you then."
He jumps back on the truck.
Jo leaves the shop delighted.

Back at the flat Jo takes off the sheets, duvet cover and
pillowcase and puts them into the washer with the tea
towel and dressing gown and then cleans through the
floors of the flat. It doesn't take long to pack her clothes
into a bag and then remove her foodstuffs from the

cupboards. She decides to cook a good meal whilst she has the last use of the cooker and throws all her unused veg and a chicken leg that she bought yesterday, into a casserole dish and pops it into the oven. That leaves a small amount of dried foods and there is milk, cheese, butter, yoghurt and fruit juice in the fridge. She will put these into a bag just before Gary comes. So with the meal in the oven, she nips upstairs to the workroom and soon doubts her decision to move back home.

Stepping into the huge, airy, well-lit room, with her art works scattered around, she knows she is going to miss this space. Hearing the wind whipping up on the roof tiles above, she takes a moment and shivers, knowing that it is going to be, much colder tomorrow in the hut. 'Am I stupid, mad?' She asks herself. The decision made yesterday, seems crazy now in the clear light of today. Should she change her mind? It would be easy to cancel Gary's help, but she knows that she won't, so stop thinking about it, she chastises herself and gathers everything together to leave.

She rolls up the sections of the town map carefully and puts a rubber band around them and puts all the crayons and the rest of the materials into a box. She then stacks the canvases on top of each other and then carries everything downstairs into the hallway, as well as the table and chair. One last check upstairs and a quick clean up of the floor and it is done.

Back downstairs again, she looks at the bowl of apples and plums and quickly washes and peels one or two and puts them into an ovenproof dish with brown sugar and puts it into the oven above the casserole. The earthy aroma coming out of the oven is lovely; she will enjoy the food later. Looking at the pile of belongings in the hallway, she is happy and pleased, knowing the flat is nearly all clean and tidy. She goes to the bathroom and cleans it and then has a shower – a long, last, lingering hot shower. She puts the wet towel into the washer and turns it on, she can leave the washing on the clothes airer before she goes and the place will be as she found it. She needs to inform Charles of her leaving and writes out a note for him.

Dear Charles,

Thank you so much for your generosity and kindness in letting me stay in your flat. I am writing to let you know that as of today I am leaving, so thanks once again.

Regards Jo.

She still doesn't know where Charles lives, so she will drop the note, together with the key into Stella's letterbox, for her to give to him.

"Well that's it Jase all done."

Jason is wondering what is happening and is pacing around the flat looking distraught.

"It's ok, were going back to the hut, you'll like it there won't you?"

When the meal is ready, Jo empties the casserole into a large bowl and saves a small portion for Jason and puts the fruit dish on the worktop to cool. The chicken is moist and tender and the vegetables are cooked to perfection. To finish the meal, she uses the last of the plain yoghurt from the fridge and spoons it onto the baked fruit and savours each mouthful. She gives Jason his dinner, topped with the chicken and veg and then washes up, giving the oven and fridge a last clean.

"There Jase all done." He licks the empty bowl again and again.

Jo bobs upstairs to check the town hall clock, it is 2 o'clock and not long now to wait, before Gary comes with the van.

When Jason barks to Gary's knock on the door, Jo leaves the kitchen to greet him.

"Hi is everything ready then?"

"Yes it's all here, not a lot of stuff, but some of it is too big for me to carry far."

"Right then, I'll take this lot, if you want to bring the rest."

They soon have the van loaded.

"If I put Jason in the van, do you want to have a quick check around, to make sure you've got everything and then we'll get off."

"Yes, good idea, I'll be quick."

Jo rushes back up the stairs to check the flat over.

Dashing through the rooms and out via the hallway, she has a fleeting feeling of having never lived here at all, there's no evidence of her existence, now that everything is cleaned and clear. 'Well goodbye flat,' She mutters, as she puts the key in her pocket and pushes the door, to check that it's locked then turns and leaves.

The journey with Gary is so different to her previous one with Charles; Gary is happy and chatty and makes a big fuss of Jason as they drive along. He parks the van in the lay by and they take relays to ferry her belongings to the hut. The hut is cold and dark compared to the flat and they soon have everything inside.

"Right then are you ok?"

Gary asks as he brushes his clothes down with his hands.

"Yes thank you so much, how much do I owe you?"

"Call it a fiver. How's that?"

"Yes thanks that's fine." Jo rummages in her pocket for a £5 note.

"If you need the van again you know where I am, well I have to be off now so good luck." he turns around and is gone.

"Bye thanks." Jo calls after his disappearing figure and closes the door.

"Well Jase were back again aren't we?"

He is excited to be back and charges around the room. Jo opens the door of the stove and rakes out the cinders and ash and puts in some knotted newspaper, dried twigs and lights it and then adds smaller pieces of wood to get it going, before putting on a larger log. Waiting for the heat to come she feels chilly and puts on her Peruvian jumper for warmth. She fills up the kettle and in doing so, reacquaints herself with the primitive aspects of living here and then puts away her food items onto the shelves and into the fridge. After taking her art materials into the workroom and stacking the canvases onto the workbench, the kettle has boiled and she makes a pot of tea. Sipping the tea, she stands and feels the quiet solitude and connects again with this timeless, spacious way of living.

She is back again to what feels right. She is happy now, to take Jason for a long walk through the garden and down towards the cliff top, overlooking the sea. To be part of this remoteness here is good for her soul, 'it is going to be ok,' she says to herself over and over again.

Making their way back to the hut, the daylight is fading and it is getting dark. Inside, the stove has warmed the room and she locks the door behind them. After making a sandwich and another drink she feeds Jason and adds more logs to the fire.
"We'll have an early night tonight Jase and then tomorrow we can start again."

The next morning, Jo pulls on her clothes quickly after stepping out of bed it is a chilly morning. She had woken a few times in the night feeling cold – she will have to buy another duvet from Mad Mick's today. She had forgotten how cold it is here, she has been spoiled with sleeping in the warm flat and it will take awhile to accustom herself again.
After putting a couple of small logs onto the stove, to bring it back to life she fills a small pan with milk and

porridge oats for breakfast. As she stirs the milk and oats, she thinks about her plans for the day. She decides to go into town and take a look at the auctioneer's salerooms, to see if there are any armchairs for sale. It is important to have a comfy chair to sit on, after a hard day and she doesn't fancy sitting on the kitchen chairs. They have dried out now and need sanding down and painting – she looks forward to doing that and adds another item to her mental list of things to buy, paint. And then after lunch she will light the bonfire, to burn the pile of damaged stuff from the hut, as the weather might change. It is another dry and bright day, but days like these will be few and far between now and she doesn't want to have to stare in the face of the flood, every time she looks out of the windows.

After breakfast she hangs the new curtains up. She is pleased with what she has made and as she ruffles them together, the bright material gives light to the room and they look good. Once all the curtains are up, she admires her handiwork; they certainly make the room look cheerful and private when drawn together.

Outside she turns over the bonfire pile, to let the underneath dry out, it will be ok to light it later. Returning inside, she fills the bowl with hot water and has a wash, how easy it is to slip back to the ways of living here, remembering the luxury of the shower of only yesterday and now to managing a body wash from a bowl.
With clothes back on and ready, she takes Jason's lead and rucksack, some money and the note for Charles and the flat key, to drop off at Stella's and sets off via the cliff path into town. The view is astonishingly beautiful, looking out towards the horizon, the charging, crashing waves, bashing against the rocks look superb and one could be fooled in to thinking that it is a summer's day. The sky above is an intense, vivid, deep blue and yet the

cold wind, whipping up into her face, burns on contact and makes her eyes water.

Reaching the promenade with its boarded up beach shops and empty walkway, she reflects on what the universe sent her way, after those long, hazy, sun filled days of the summer. And how as much as we'd like, we cannot control nature and its impact upon us. Somehow we have to go with the flow and bend with the times, otherwise if we try to stay straight and rigid, we will snap and break.

Further along, she crosses over and takes the pavement towards Stella's house. After knocking a couple of times the house remains silent – she must be out at work. So Jo takes the note and wraps it around the key and pushes it through the letterbox and listens for it to drop inside. Closing the gate, they walk up the hill into town and make their way to the auctioneers on the far edge of Fenton.

She looks inside the window, there is nothing much to see and she ties Jason outside and goes into the saleroom. This is the first time that she has been in here and she is taken by surprise – it is a huge place. There is an array of old furniture and modern pieces, packed into several different rooms and she scans her eyes across the jumbled display, looking for a comfortable armchair. Most of the items have a numbered ticket stuck on and when she enters the next room there are two men writing and checking and tearing the numbers and sticking them onto the pieces. On a table by the doorway is a pile of forms for bidders to register their details on and she picks one up. When one of the men briefly looks across at her, Jo asks him when the auction is. It is tomorrow at 12 o'clock. Jo thanks him and goes into the next huge room, where tall, farmhouse dressers, wardrobes, beds and cast iron fireplaces are on show. There are some fabulous pieces that would look lovely in an old farmhouse or cottage. After taking another look around she can't see anything that would be useful for the hut,

except for a large, enamel coalscuttle – number 116 on the ticket.
So she leaves and walks to Mad Mick's for the duvet. She buys the cheapest one with the highest tog rating for £7.99 and a pack of ballpoint pens and a large pad of writing paper, and then calls at the shops for bread and one or two other things and returns home.
She will visit the auction tomorrow, just to see how much things go for and maybe make a bid for the scuttle and call for a tin of paint at the D I Y shop.

Back at the hut she puts more logs onto the stove and has lunch; and afterwards prepares a sausage and bean hotpot, to cook slowly on the stove for her evening meal. With that done and her new duvet put inside with the other in the cover, she can start on the bonfire.

Charles has only one thing on his mind – please let Stella
be at home.

He had left his own house, because he couldn't contain
himself any longer. After pacing around his study trying
to think things out, he couldn't make sense of himself or
anything. He had returned upstairs to face Margaret,
wanting to end their constant fighting. He knows he is
the culprit and it seems that everything is going beyond
and out of his control. Why? What happened is what he
thought he had wanted to happen, so why does he feel
that his whole world is falling apart? He had entered
their bedroom and seen the suitcase and clothing laid out
on the bed and heard the sound of splashing water
coming from the en suite shower. He had stood for a
moment, not knowing how or what to say to her and
given up on the idea, defeated by himself; he had never
felt so dispirited and lacking.

As he was about to turn and leave, he'd spotted the gift-
wrapped box, left for him by Margaret, placed on his
side of the bed by his pillow. This was too much; he
popped it in his pocket, whilst looking sideways at the
bras and suspender belts, left in a neat pile by the
suitcase. His eyes had filled as he thought, 'oh Margaret,
what's going on?' He had turned on his heel and left, he
couldn't stay and face her.

Stella might have some answers, Stella – well at least
she would talk and hold a conversation and not just go
along with everything he said. Unlike Margaret, with her
sweet and inattentive demeanour, yes he had wanted to
shock her, wanted to shock himself and now he had. The
whole idea had backfired, oh yes he wanted to bring
alive his fantasy. The fantasies of his mind are incredible
and thrilling; he was running the whole show and had
complete control of all the action and the stage it was set
on. He had cajoled and pushed and engineered it in real
life and it had begun to play out in front of him, he had
chosen the actors, the protagonists of his game. But now
the game is being acted out away from him and he no

longer has the script, he no longer holds the camera and zooms in on the action. It is turning out, to be one, whole, bloody, disastrous mess and he feels helpless and doesn't know what to do.

He shouts out "Stella."
As he walks through the doorway into the hall and again when there is no answer from her. She must be home if the door is unlocked, so he heads for the kitchen to find a drink.
The kitchen is empty, so he assumes she is upstairs and shouts her again. He glances around the worktops for a bottle of red and is disappointed, this fuels his agitation and he shouts.
"Stella." once more.

From the top of the staircase he hears her reply, although intelligible, as she speaks with a toothbrush in her mouth.
"There you are." he calls whilst looking up to her from the kitchen doorway.
Stella opens her lips and the toothpaste foam, bubbles around her mouth.
"Be down in a minute." She then disappears into the bathroom.
Charles paces around the sitting room and then back through the hall to the kitchen, waiting for her to come, before returning to the sitting room and slumping down onto the settee.
Stella comes down the staircase, assuming he has left, as the place is silent. She enters the sitting room and becomes concerned, seeing Charles with his head in his hands. "Charles."
"Charles what's happened?"
He raises his head and allows his body to rest back on the sofa and lifts his arms into the air, as if in surrender. She has seen Charles many times, after consuming large amounts of alcohol, full of remorse and sorry for himself, however he doesn't appear drunk. She goes

forward to check and still she can't smell or detect signs
of him having been drinking. The fact that he is sitting
quietly disturbs her and she is puzzled by his posture,
normally boisterous and strong, he now looks feeble and
weak, he has an air of dejection and sorrow. She feels
sorry for him. She almost expects him to cry, to give in
to himself and weep, something that she would never
expect to come from him. In his drunken states she is
acquainted with his sometimes morose and childish
manner, however this is different.

"Charles what's happened?" she implores again, quietly
this time.

His arms fall and rest by his side and he looks sideways
avoiding eye contact with her. "It's Maggie, I think she's
actually gone and done it."

"Done what?"

"I never thought she had it in her, it's all my bloody
fault."

"What, what has she done?"

"She's going away and I bet you any money it's with
Giles."

"Giles, what, Margaret, are you saying she has left you
for Giles?"

"It has all the hallmarks, she says she's going to stay
with her mother, her bloody mother for God's sake."
Charles slumps down again with his head in his hands.

"What makes you think that?"

Charles startles Stella by leaping off the settee and
shouts from deep inside of himself. "Because she's being
like I want her to be with me, only I can't have her can I,
I'm just a complete bloody failure, I thought if she could
do it, it would make it easier for me, that I could get the
fucking thing up and I know that I can't."

Charles stands still, speechless now after his outburst.
Stella's thoughts course through her, as she tries to make
sense and understand what he has said.

"I'm sorry Charles." is all she can bring herself to say.

She feels uncomfortable and wary of what he might say next and decides the best thing to do, is leave him be and wait.

The tension fills the room and the slightest sounds amplify, the dripping of the tap echoes around the house, becoming louder and louder, waiting to be taken out by a human voice. She feels the urge to comfort him and take his head into her arms and stroke away his distress and fear; she wants her Charles, not this broken down man in front of her. She adores his joviality and brusque and voracious nature, not this darkness; she has glimpsed this side of him through drink but never sober, willingly offering up his fragile, truthful self.

"Oh Charles."

Going to the kitchen, she takes the kettle to the dripping tap, fills it and pushes in the switch, to make coffee, instant, she is glad to occupy herself. Eventually he follows her and sits upon a bar stool, the storm has passed and relief seeps through her, as she offers him coffee, which he takes.

As they sit opposite each other drinking they both know that what has just happened can never be taken away.

Margaret knocks lightly on Abby's bedroom door, waiting for her to respond. She's unable to predict her mood at the moment, her daughter is up and down like a yoyo, ever since she became involved with Mark. The more Margaret hears about him from Charles, the less happy she feels about their relationship and hopes beyond anything that something will come between them. He sounded totally the wrong sort for Abby to be going out with. She knows Charles's habit of exaggerating but instinctively senses that on this occasion, he isn't far out on his judgement. She draws this conclusion from her daughter's behaviour, her erratic and sometimes, outrageous tantrums – if Mark were an upstanding young man, he would bring out the best in her, not these recent outbursts.

Life before Mark had been joyous, they had enjoyed relaxing, happy days, spent shopping and chatting – taking Charles out of the equation of course. They had an unspoken understanding regarding him, to ignore his rants and humour him as much as possible. This policy had worked fine in the early days of their marriage; Margaret had blossomed under the strong protective shield of Charles – she felt safe and totally secure. For a moment, thoughts flash through her mind, she is taken back to the beginning when it was all fresh, new and exciting; she looks at her gold wedding ring as a reminder.

Margaret knocks again.

"Is it you mummy?"

Abby's voice gives away her hurt, as the words can barely be heard.

"Yes darling, it is."

"Come in then."

Abby's face has black streaks, down her puffy, red cheeks, hot from crying. Margaret sits on the soft bed next to her.

"Why does he always have to interfere, it's my life and I can see who I want to see, I can't stand it any longer mummy."

Abby stutters, fuelled by a bubbling anger, remembering earlier today at the flat, when Charles had come crashing in.

"Darling you know Charles, he only wants the best for you as do I and really this Mark character, is he really good enough for you, I mean from what Charles has told me."

"There you go mummy, you always take his side, what does he know anyway, he doesn't know everything," Abby retorts.

"Look darling, let's not let this develop into yet another heated argument, we have had too many just lately and maybe Charles is right, if you gave Mark up, it might settle you down. Remember darling, we haven't spent much time together you and I, maybe when I get back from visiting grandma, we can have a shopping spree – I know how you always like that."

Margaret tries to appease Abby.

"Oh yes that's it, that's always your answer to everything isn't it mummy, to spend money, as if that's going to change things and make it go away."

"Look darling this isn't getting us anywhere is it? I'm trying to help and all I get is another backlash from you and that's very unfair don't you think?"

"Charles has made Mark go away, so I won't see him ever again, so that's it mummy, I've had enough, I'm applying to York Uni and then I'll be away from Fenton and then I can do just what I like, without either of you interfering and I'm sure you'll both be better off here without me."

"Abby darling you know that's not true, I want the very best for you and on this occasion I do think Charles is right, Mark is not good for you, we can all see that. I mean darling look at you, you have never been as unhappy as you have these past few months, since you have been seeing him. You are up and down and we have to tiptoe around you, as if we are walking on eggshells, never knowing what sort of mood you might be in. It really isn't on darling, if he is making you so happy, then why are you crying and being so argumentative all the time?"

Margaret knows that whatever she says, it isn't going to bring Abby round to her way of seeing things.

Abby falls back on her pillow in defiance and Margaret waits through the silence. Looking down at her daughter her heart flutters and somersaults for a moment, as she notices the strong, striking resemblance of her first husband and father to Abby, Anthony. She has the same thick hair and fierce angry look about her eyes, just like him, on the rare occasion when he had been mad about something. 'Oh sweetheart,' Margaret thinks as she remembers Anthony, 'we both miss you in our hearts.' Charles has filled his shoes, not in a way that she expected or thought he would but he has and we have to make the best of it. The image of Giles enters Margaret's thoughts as Abby looks up.

"Mummy are you really going to Grandma's?" Sensing Margaret's forthcoming disloyalty.

"Oh darling, try not to make matters worse for yourself, let's get you something to drink shall we, how about your favourite – a hot chocolate with hazelnut sauce and a marshmallow on the top."

Margaret hopes this will change the subject.

"Mummy I'm not a little girl anymore, you can't speak to me as if I don't know anything, I've seen and heard you and Charles, he doesn't fool me anymore and I know your not happy like you were. So even if you don't tell me I know, anyway I'm alright mummy and you don't have to worry."

Abby says in her adult voice – aware of her mothers neediness, as she wraps the edge of the quilt around her fingers and conscious of her grieving mothers past disposition, after her father died.

"Yes mummy we'll have hot chocolate, come on, let's go to the kitchen and have blueberry muffins with it." Abby leaps off the bed.

Stella has time to think as she sits opposite Charles, who is bent over, staring into his cup of dark, black coffee – he has the appearance now of a broken, dishevelled and destroyed man, his drink is going cold and he is silent. Stella takes a deep mouthful of the strong liquid and rises from her seat and goes to her office.

As hard as she tries, she cannot detach herself from what has just happened. The mental picture that plays inside her, of a strong and powerful man, is no longer and all she sees now is his weakness and vulnerability. In the past she had been aware of his self-pity that often emerged from the bottom of an empty glass but in the cold light of day, he is a tough and strong man. She wishes above all else, that she hadn't been here for him, hadn't witnessed this break down and the fact that she has, has shattered forever the image of the man she clings to, as her protector and this makes her feel less strong and sure of herself.

He has been a rock for her over the recent years and shielded and protected her and given her fabulous contacts for her work. This business arena is where she first met him, she was new to the town and eager to meet and work her way into the local hierarchy. She recognised at once, when she had spotted him across a room, that he had a powerful and charismatic aura; by the way people were drawn towards him. She knew he was definitely worth getting to know. And by the end of the evening, she had introduced herself to him and it was apparent to both of them that they shared the same chemistry in business and pleasure. She needed success and wanted the rewards that came with it, as did he, and for sure she has certainly climbed the ladder of opportunity and promotion muck quicker with the support from him. He has helped, encouraged and directed her; she owes him now in his time of need.

She knows that whatever happens, she has to help
Charles regain himself and quickly. 'Why Charles,
why?' If he had just been satisfied with what he has,
without having to have everything and more, maybe this
wouldn't have happened. But it has and there is no going
back for him, what can she possibly do to get him away
from some of this mess, before it escalates and he
becomes swallowed up inside the hole that he has dug
himself. He always has to test everything to the limits –
almost trying to find the something that he can never
have.
She isn't at all surprised by Margaret's actions, after all
Charles doesn't play the role of devoted husband, he is
always far too busy for that. And knowing about some of
his antics and how he lives his life, nothing about him
could ever surprise her. So what now? What can she do
to help his situation? After all, the impact of his
breakdown is all too evident and she believes it will
ricochet out of control, if she doesn't do something.

Sitting down in her office chair, she presses the power
button on her laptop, waiting for the screen to colour up,
with a panoramic view, of fields of bright, yellow,
sunflowers. This lovely picture, reminds her so much of
France, a place where she can relax and switch off from
the stress and speed of life in England. France runs at a
much slower pace – they enjoy hours spent eating and
drinking and make sure work is arranged around this
quality time and she has no choice, to adapt herself to it.
After a few days of living there, she always notices the
difference in herself, how she slows down and her nerves
are less on edge and jumpy.

This is what Charles needs, to get away from here and
spend some time in France. She logs onto the Internet
and from her favourites, she selects the website of a
cheap airline and enters tomorrows date for the outgoing
flight, travelling from Newcastle airport to Limoges. The
first one she selects doesn't fly out, so she puts in the

same date on the next airline and again finds that there are no flights. Becoming frustrated by her lack of success, she decides to try Manchester airport, there is a flight early the next morning at 7.20 to Limoges, with available seats for the outgoing and return flights the following Wednesday. This would give Charles five days to regain his equilibrium and with sunshine, good wine and great food, it could be the answer to his problems. She makes the selection for two people without checked in luggage, leaves the screen waiting for payment and their details and returns to the kitchen.

Charles is in the same sitting position, still staring into the full cup of black coffee. "Charles I have an idea, what do you think about taking a break from here and flying out to France for a few days?"
Charles doesn't look up, or appear to have heard her question; he just continues to fix his eyes on to the coffee cup.
"Charles, come on for God's sake, you can't do this to yourself, what do you say, I've checked on flights and we can fly out tomorrow morning and we'll be eating at an Auberge this time tomorrow, what do you think?"
"It's no good, I can't Stell, I've had it."
Charles looks up his eyes filled with sorrow.
"Right that's it, enough, I'm going to book it, I can't bear to see you like this, Charles drink up your coffee and try and get a grip on yourself."
Stella walks away from the kitchen, back to her office.
"Stell, I'm sorry." Charles mutters as she leaves the room.

Back at the laptop, she realises that she needs Charles's passport details and curses the air, as she turns towards the kitchen again.
"Charles I need your passport details to book the flights, come on you need to do this, we'll have a good time when we get there."
"I can't face Giles, my passport's at the office."

 "Look I will call and collect it and anyway if what you said about Giles is correct, then he won't be at the office will he."

Stella instantly wishes she hasn't said the last comment, as Charles's head drops once more.

"Oh Stella what am I going to do?"

Charles sinks down further, full of self-pity.

"I am going to go to your office and collect your passport, and then I shall book the flights and we will set off tonight and stay over in a hotel near the airport and fly out tomorrow."

Stella leaves and hopes Charles will regain himself. His office isn't far from her house and it doesn't take her long to arrive. Miriam his secretary is at her desk and smiles as she enters. After a brief exchange of friendly banter she asks for Charles's passport, adding the reason – an urgent business trip to France that she is booking for the two of them. Miriam knows not to ask questions and hands over Charles's passport and wishes her a good trip. Miriam has a list of things she needs to check with Charles and knows she is going to have to make excuses whilst he is away, damn him.

Stella jogs back to her house and is pleased to find the kitchen empty.

"Charles."

"I'm in here Stell."

His voice is coming from the sitting room and she goes to find him.

"Your right Stell, I need to get away, book it, just bloody book it."

Stella breathes a sigh of relief at finding this change in him.

"Ok, there's a flight from Manchester at 7.20 in the morning to Limoges and a return flight next Wednesday, so that will give us five days to cheer you up."

"Good, book it."

Stella strides back to her office and enters their details and makes payment with her credit card she holds with the airline. She prints off the booking form and the boarding cards. It is so much easier flying without luggage, they can take hand baggage each and buy anything they need in France.

Charles has enough items of clothing that he keeps here, which will have to suffice; she knows he wouldn't want to return home.

Back in the sitting room she informs him of the arrangements and leaves to pack a few things for herself. Charles follows and flings a couple of shirts and a pair of trousers and underwear from his bedside drawer onto Stella's bed.

He tells her that he will have to phone Abby, to say he won't be going home.

"Ok I'll get the bags ready and be down shortly". Stella tells him.

Margaret sinks down at last into the leather driver's seat, relieved to be on her way, how inconvenient and unlucky to have her preparations interrupted by Charles and Abby earlier. She almost curses as she checks the digits on the dashboard; she needs to hurry now after being delayed. It is seventeen minutes later than she had planned to set off. However she always added fifteen minutes extra to her journeys, to allow for unforeseen circumstances impinging on her plans.

Wrapping the seat belt around her, her thoughts turn to earlier, to both Charles and Abby. She wants to erase Charles out of her mind; he is becoming hellish to live with. His dissatisfaction with life, attaches itself to everything at present and this thought endorses her sneaking away for a few days. How can he expect anything else, he seems to be pushing her further and further away, with his acerbic attitude and subservient treatment of her.

'Oh how people change,' she ponders now, thinking of Abby as she turns on the engine. Her daughter, no longer steady but volatile and too knowing, too understanding, too intuitive, she picks up on everything and no doubt, has a fair inkling as to what I'm about to do.

Margaret is torn, has she forgotten anything, has she managed to check her bags without being interrupted? She stalls now, trapped in a moment of paralysis, fighting within her mind, of giving herself permission to go ahead. Fuelled by an anxiety and dread, scared for fear of making a mistake, which amounted to forgetfulness, of omitting any one of a number of items, in her meticulously planned luggage.

She glances once again at the clock, it is now twenty minutes past eleven o'clock. Three minutes have elapsed since she sat down in the car. Whatever transpires later to be her errors, she has to set off – somehow she has to push to the back of her mind, her huge fear and doubts within herself and go.

Revving the car engine, she begins to regain control. She allows her thoughts to turn away from Charles and his sterile effect on her and engage herself with the prospect of the next few days with Giles.

She slides her thighs effortlessly against each other in anticipation of their opening and undoing – this is exactly what she needs right now.

Speeding through a speed camera, she revels in the thought of Charles's reproach and limp excuse she would give him, when the fine landed in the post. At least it gives her chance to make up time; so she is there to meet Giles, a little before their allotted arrangement of twelve o'clock.

They are to meet at one of Giles's apartments, five miles outside of Thornby. She has visited the place only once before, Giles has a large portfolio of houses, apartments and commercial properties that he owns and rents out. For convenience sake, they spend their time together, in his flat in the centre of Thornby.

Today however, they arranged to meet and park up Margaret's car and travel to their destination in Giles's vehicle, left there it would be out of sight and undiscovered by Charles.

Pulling up to the block of flats, she drives into the space marked G2 – Giles's space. He hasn't arrived yet, so she is pleased and has a few moments to add a touch of lipstick and regain her composure and equilibrium.

Leaving Fenton behind, she has edged away from Charles's influence and found her sense of control and serenity, excited now at the anticipation of the days ahead. With Giles, life would not be frantic and tense; it would be alive and full of thrills and fun.

Waiting, her mind harks back to her early relationship with Charles, at the time she was thankful for the security he brought her and as a surrogate father figure for Abby she thought she had done well. She had thought that Charles, six years older than her would take care of her and make her feel safe, strong and protected. Initially he had, but when his issue of erectile dysfunction came between them, his temperament towards her changed and five years down the line at the age of forty seven, Margaret realises the impact of his domineering, destructive behaviour, is loosening her insecurities. She has kept them well hidden but little by little as she watches herself checking and re checking everything from the dripping of a tap, to the exact contents of her bag, she is just holding on. She is being drawn back down, to a dark place that she thought she had left behind, after the death of Anthony, her husband. The timing of Giles's flirtatious approach, at then end of an evening of the Fenton and Thornby annual business dinner, earlier this year, couldn't have been better. She had tearfully bumped into him in the corridor, on the way to the ladies, with Charles's comments ringing in her ears. She gave herself permission to say yes to his advances. He was renowned for being a ladies man and she knew that she would be playing with fire but she was flattered that he was interested in an older woman, as he touched her gently on the shoulder and whispered into her ear.

"Well Maggie, I think you look fabulous tonight, don't listen to that old man of yours, he doesn't know what he's talking about."

He slid his hand down the back of her dress and pulled her towards him, brushing his lips gently across her cheek, kissing her on her earlobe. Margaret had relaxed her body and allowed herself to lean into his touch, oblivious to her surroundings, she didn't care, already

Giles had the capacity to excite and sexually arouse her, to such an extent, that she wanted to have him right there and then.

Giles at the age of thirty-eight, had had enough experience of women, to know that Margaret wanted him, that she wouldn't refuse, and say no. He couldn't believe how easily she slipped into him and how ready she seemed. He wanted to take her down on the carpet and put himself inside her, to push and pull and satisfy her longing that he judged she had not had for a long time.
"Meet me, call me tomorrow."
He managed to say, as he reluctantly gave her back to herself and fished his business card from his jacket pocket.
"Call this mobile Maggie." He smiled and walked along to the bar.
Margaret had wanted to follow him, to feel his touch and hear his whisper again. Her large breasts, heavy and trapped inside her balcony bra wanted releasing, her erect nipples needed gently tugging and her pulsing vagina ached for his penetration.

She had taken herself to the ladies and chose the end cubicle, once inside; she had quickly slid her hand up her dress and into the crotch of her knickers. With her head held back she'd found her erect clitoris and stroked it. She longed for time but had to hurry. The women's voices outside couldn't distract her, as she gave herself the climax, that Charles, nor Giles on this occasion was able to give her.

Charles's burning comment had left her as she returned to the table, she felt flushed and knew that whatever he said to her from now on, it wouldn't matter, it couldn't hurt her. She realised that Charles's dysfunction was not her fault. Looking back to that evening, she wonders if he had deliberately set her up; this is an odd idea,

however she remembers the look he exchanged with
Giles, when he returned to his seat shortly after her, it
intimated that they were both in on something.

Charles returns to the kitchen, to phone Abby from his mobile phone.

"Hello sweetie, do you need me for anything, it's just I'm sorry darling but I have to pop over to France for a few days on business, something's cropped up and I know mummy's away, so will you be ok on your own?" Abby's face lights up, as she hears about Charles's trip away, her thoughts already filling up with the knowledge of the house to herself for a few days and she is unable to answer straight away.

"Abby are you there?"

Charles's voice breaks into her vision of days and nights of excitement and sex with Mark.

"Yes, I'll be fine daddy."

"If you need Susan to come in and help out."

"No, no I'll manage, it will give me chance to study, read up on a few things."

Abby quickly chips in, to stop him arranging for Susan to foil her plans with Mark. "Ok then darling, I will be back on Wednesday, be good, if you need to buy any extra food or anything you want, just pop it on your card and I'll sort it out when I get back, so bye sweetheart." Abby grins to herself.

"Bye have a good trip." and ends the phone call.

She can't press Mark's phone number quick enough and is disappointed when her call goes onto his voicemail, so she leaves him the message.

"Hi Mark it's me Abb's, hope you haven't set off from Thornby yet, great news if you're up for it, I've got the house to myself for a few days if you want to stay, can't wait, hurry up and ring back, hope you can come, bye, bye, kisses, kisses, kisses Abs."

She presses the end call button and puts the phone to her breast and wishes with all her heart that he hasn't left just yet.

Giles arrives shortly after 12 o'clock, Maggie's car is parked in his space, so he checks himself quickly in the rear view mirror, sweeping his fingers through his course, thick, hay coloured hair.

He keeps the engine running, lifts the handbrake and steps out of his car.

Margaret opens her door and Giles greets her with a kiss. "Hello darling, you look wonderful."

Margaret loves the way Giles welcomes her, he is always pleased to see her and makes her feel special. Her body responds to his words, heightening her sensations – he knows how to excite her, already she begins to connect with her own skin, conscious of her actions and movements, as if uncoiling before him and connecting with her limbs, herself as a woman. Margaret exclaims as she always does in silence to herself, 'God he is handsome.'

He is dressed in a lightweight, navy, linen suit, with a pale blue, pin checked shirt, open at the collar, always meticulously clean and yet he has a natural way of appearing slightly unkempt. Margaret loves his cheeky, shabby roughness. He removes his jacket and hangs it in the rear of his car. Margaret opens her car boot and before she has chance, he reaches in and picks up her bag and places it next to his, soft leather case in the boot. After locking her car, Giles opens his passenger door for her to step in.

Before pulling away he leans over and picks a strand of hair away from her face and winds it around his finger, then gives her a kiss.

"Let's go."

Letting go of her, he pushes the gear stick into reverse and takes control of the car.

"Where are we going G?"

Margaret asks, looking across, as he steers the car into the flow of traffic.

"My surprise, just you wait and see."

He smiles as he drives along, lifting his hand from the gear stick now and then, to stroke her stocking leg. Margaret's eyes widen with adoration, she can't wait to arrive at their destination, to be alone with him. Giles lifts his hand to switch on the CD player and as Neil Diamond begins to sing he returns his hand to her leg. At every given opportunity, He gently rests his hand and runs his fingers across the silk covering of her skin. Giles prides himself on booking a country hotel, a distance away from Fenton; it allows him the opportunity of quietly fantasizing about what he would do with her, when they finally arrive.

He runs the sequence of their pleasures through his mind and once or twice he has to adjust his position in his seat next to her, to assuage his erection and let his hand return to the gear stick.

Margaret is turned on by his attention and cannot wait to reach their hotel room and wonders how much longer it will be before they finally arrive.

"Oh Maggie, this is so good, I'm glad you could make it my darling, although I have to say I don't know if I can wait until we get there."

Giles struggles now to tame himself, to put off the inevitable, the more he fights it, tries to remove his hand and the fantasies growing in his mind, the more he wants to come.

"Shall we pull over darling?"

Giles battles with his self as he drives on, looking out for a lay-by or a quiet turn off in the road. He will have to stop the car it is no good, he can't wait, he can't shrink down his erection again, he has to have her now.

Up ahead, he knows there is a country park with a place to park, and he adjusts himself once more.

"Oh yes, Giles."

Margaret manages to say, as she too fights with the waves of pleasure that surge through her body.

The hundred or so yards before the turn off into the parking area are tense, as both of them ready themselves for their own climax, just hanging on.

"Oh God."

Giles utters, as he steers the car, to find an enclosed space out of the way.

Before he has time to turn off the engine, Margaret leans across and unzips his trousers.

"Oh Maggi."

He removes his safety belt and yanks down his trousers and underpants to expose his erection, it is bulging and throbbing as he undoes Margaret's safety belt.

Giles is happy now that he can control himself, his erection has space, he loves seeing it lengthen and swell between his legs, he is bursting to come, he knows it won't take much, but he wants to tend to Margaret first, he lifts his bottom to allow himself more freedom.

He looks outside of the car they are parked alone.

"Come on?"

He decides on instinct to take her outside, it would be easier than in the confines of the car.

He pulls up his pants and trousers and gets out, helping Margaret and pulling her towards the trees.

The lines of conifers on the edge of the wood enclose them, as he leads her inside the dense foliage.

Margaret discovers a new place inside herself, as Giles leans her against the trunk of a tree.

He puts his hands around her to raise her onto him; the hollow in the ground helps him, as he stands beneath her.

She is moist and ready for him, he pushes his firm erection inside of her and gasps, he is happy now as he begins the rhythmic, pulling and pushing in and out of her, careful as he does so, to shield her back from the bark of the tree.

Margaret holds him tightly, her arms wrapped around him – she raises her hips and spreads her legs, up and down faster and faster, it doesn't take her long to quicken and come, as she slides and weakens and gives herself above him.

Her juices are a joy as they run from her, he mounts his final thrusts and he too is done.

"Oh Giles."

"Oh Maggie, Maggie."

Anna receives a phone call from her son Mark. He is fine. He's decided to move a little way down along the coast, to do some work with a different traveller's gang, who he had met in a pub in Thornby, he would be leaving in a few days time. He could earn about £30 or £40 a day and live in a trailer. He fancies the idea and it would keep him out of Abby's father's way for a bit. He is a mad bastard Mark tells his mum, a real pervert according to Abby. Anna asks how things are going with her.

"Fuck em and chuck em." her son replies.

"She'll be useful when I need somewhere to stay in Thornby and York so that's good."

She doesn't asks him what Abby means about her father being a pervert and really she doesn't want to know. Life is difficult enough, without adding further complications to it and becoming involved in Charles's life.

Anna feels that there is little more she can do by staying on at the coast and she misses her children and wants to be back home with them. Soon too her course will be starting up again, so she needs to be thinking about making tracks back home to the city, to get on with her life. Mark is all right for the present. What about Jo? I wonder how she will feel, when we meet up next time and I tell her I have to return to the city in a few days. The prospect of leaving makes Anna feel sad, but happy too, to be returning home to see her children.

There isn't too much left to do in the caravan and spring would come before she could turn around. Anna sorts her store cupboard out and makes a list of supplies she needs to buy in town, to top them up for her return. She would leave washing the outside of the caravan until the springtime and would spend an hour before leaving Fenton, cutting down any long weeds, or tall grasses, that have grown around the edge of the flags.

Anna has three large carrier bags of her children's
clothes, two of which she fits into her pull along trolley
and the third she carries. After struggling into the town
centre with the bags of clothes, she drops them off at the
charity shop, and then calls into the supermarket to buy
the tins of beans, spaghetti, tomatoes and rice to fill her
store cupboard with. Two cartons of long life milk also
go into the trolley as she saunters around the shops.

Once back in the caravan she unpacks her supplies and
puts them away. Her work in the caravan is up to date
and finished. Before closing it up, all she has to do is bag
up her bedding in the thick plastic bags and store them
beneath the seats in the huge boxes. She would leave the
heavy curtains up and take the nets down and put in a
bag until spring, when she would wash them in the
washhouse. What bits she has left to do can wait, until
the morning of her departure. She would phone him, to
let him know that she would soon be returning back to
the city, now that Mark is settled. She would call
tomorrow to tell Jo that she is leaving. Perhaps they
could have a meal together, before Anna's return. She
knows she will miss Jo, when the time comes for her to
leave, but knows too, her children and their father are
waiting for her return.

The late autumn sky is beginning to draw in, by 4
o'clock it would be too dark to work. She makes up her
bed in preparation for the darkness and fills her kettle to
make fresh tea and a hot water bottle to air off her bed,
before it is time to go to sleep.

It has certainly been a busy time during her visit. Anna
takes her blue, notebook, out of the sideboard drawer.
'Now, what am I going to do with you? Shall I leave you
here unfinished or take you back to the city? I'm not
sure,' Anna admits, and opens the book where she has
left off. Perhaps I could write a little more. I have today
and perhaps tomorrow. She places the hot water bottle in

bed and puts her nightgown over it and pulls the duvet up, covering them both. She collects the candles, saucer and lighter, and is ready to begin writing a little more about Anna and Fermanagh House.

Anna's life had begun to fall into a pattern as she was collected each morning by John Doherty to work as a homeopath in Fermanagh House. The post menopausal women still made up the bulk of Anna's cases, but bit by bit different patients began to appear.

Stella takes her car keys from their hook above the
kitchen worktop and tells Charles that she will drive
them both to the hotel. She doesn't fancy, sitting
alongside him, throughout the four-hour journey, finding
her nerves jangling, every time he put his foot down on
the accelerator and steered into the fast lane. And
besides, she has booked the car park, for her car
registration, so she can drive safely and steadily to
Manchester. They would arrive in plenty of time, giving
them chance to have an evening meal before going to
bed.

She has a quick check around the house, picks up her
bag and locks the door, whilst mentally going through
her hand luggage, making sure that she has her passport,
boarding cards and personal items with her.

Charles stands by the car waiting, like a lost sheep, with
his holdall in his hand. She doesn't feel comfortable
around this mute side of his persona, and is too tired to
offer up small talk as they drive off. She knows her idea
of an early flight would deprive them both of sleep and
they would be tetchy when they arrive, however they are
on their way now and will be able to sleep on the plane.
Thinking about this relaxes her slightly, knowing that
she would be able to close her eyes and forget Charles
sitting beside her.

She leans forward and turns on the car radio to Classic
FM and takes the turning towards the main road. The
roads are busy and as she looks sideways, Charles is
resting back with his eyes closed. Good. Thinking ahead
to France, she looks forward to arriving and settling in to
their stay. She would phone her contacts from Limoges
airport, to find out what accommodation is available. She
prefers The Argentor – a rustic, family run hotel, with
comfortable rooms and quiet location by a river, in a
picturesque village not far from the airport. Failing that,
it would be a bed and breakfast 'La Pinsoniere', in the

small town of Ruffec. Both places are about an hours drive from the airport. As this isn't intending to be a business trip for either of them, they can chill out and enjoy themselves, she hopes. Charles begins to snore softly; she concentrates on the road ahead, listening to the music. She loves driving; she enjoys the power and thrust when she touches the accelerator pedal as the car shifts forward. Cruise control now, she pushes the gear stick into fifth and the miles flash by. She reminds herself to stay alert as the hours pass by.

Mark is sitting in 'The Castle' pub in Thornby,
surrounded by his newly found mates, with a pint in his
hand having a good time, he is drinking his way through
Charles's money and this thought gives him added
satisfaction. The travellers he has tagged himself onto,
are rough and streetwise but they work hard and drink
most of their earnings, which suits Mark, he belongs. He
knows how to graft and put his body into hard labour, if
at the end of it, he has enough money in his pocket for
fags and booze. He has proved himself to these men and
is happy to be going with them, further down the coast to
work in a few days time. He always enjoys a fresh scene,
he is looking forward to tasting new beers in different
pubs and meeting plenty of young birds, life is good.

As he feels in his pocket for money, for the next round
of drinks, he picks out his phone and notices he has a
missed call. At the bar he asks for four pints, one for
himself and one each for his mates. Whilst he is waiting,
he listens to his message – it is from Abby. Mark can't
believe his luck as he hears her voice and knows straight
away, that he would go and spend the few days with her.
He couldn't pass up the offer of a few days of shagging
and there would be free drink, life doesn't get much
better than that.

He has to find an excuse to meet up with the gang later
and as he takes the beer to the table, he thinks of a
reason.
"Cheers."
Mark says, as he pushes the drinks across and watches
the cream from the top spill down the edges of the pint
glasses.
"I need to sort something out." He tells the men.
They pick up their beer and each of them takes a long
swig from their glass, leaving a white moustache above
their top lips.
"Cheers Mark."

They say in unity, appearing to have not heard his last comment. As they take another swig and lick the foam from their mouths, they look at Mark waiting for what he has to say.

"Something I need to sort, I'll have to come down later."

"D'ya need help?" One of the men asks.

"No I just need to sort it, but I'll be down in a few days."

"As long as that's all it is, or else the jobs off Mark." Another of the men chip in. "Cheers lads, thanks."

Mark finishes and then holding his full pint, pours it down his throat.

"Right then, see you then."

Outside the pub he phones Abby, who answers almost straight away.

"Hi Abb's, is it still on then babe?"

"Yes, can you come?"

"Sure, be there in a bit Abb's." Mark answers and ends the call.

Anna lights the new white candle and sticks it to the saucer and once again the room is filled with light. She pulls back the duvet and climbs back into her warm bed to continue writing.

Anna saved what money she could from the salary Fermanagh House paid, but she realised it would probably be in the New Year before she could begin to think about looking for a decent second hand car. She needed something, which was reliable, and not forever breaking down, so she ended up just paying out money, until she gave up on it all together...................................

Giles and Margaret rearrange their clothing as they return laughing to the car. Luckily no one else has parked alongside their vehicle, as Giles opens the door to help her in. Her dress is creased and her stockings torn from leaning against the tree, but she is happy and intoxicated with what has just happened.

Giles feels relieved now to drive on in comfort, towards their destination, an award winning country hotel and spa. He knows Maggie will love the place, it offers everything for a romantic getaway and well worth the drive. He hadn't anticipated the stop along the way, he can't keep his hands off her, and she turns him on like no other woman ever has. He has had plenty of woman around his age or younger, but Maggie is the only woman older than himself.

He had often fantasized about an imaginary, older woman but these haven't measured up to the reality of how Maggie responds and matches his own desires. 'Five whole days,' he thinks to himself, 'five whole days of unhurried and passionate love making, yes, it doesn't get better than that.'

Margaret removes her shoes as they drive off, back onto the main road of traffic and then gently peels off her stockings, revealing her smooth legs. Giles changes gears and puts his foot down on the pedal, glancing at her movements. Watching her, he wonders why everything about her is sensuous and as she leans forwards to remove the last of her stockings, he can see down the centre of her cleavage and wants to cup her breasts in his hands. He can feel again the stirrings in his pants; he feels sticky and longs for a hot shower.
He will have to concentrate now on the driving and wait until they reach the hotel, before he touches her again.

Margaret too feels her body's waves of pleasure mounting, as she remembers herself by the tree, she has

their shared fluids moistening her crotch and she wants
him inside her once more.

Somehow they don't need small talk or deep
conversation as they drive along, each of them tied to
what has just happened, that is enough.

Giles starts the CD once again and when they turn off
into the winding, hilly country roads, Margaret imagines
that they must be almost there.

Anna masturbates until she reaches an orgasm. It is clear and defined and the surge opens her heart and she is breathless for a few moments, what comes out of the breathlessness are sighs and tears and such sadness. 'I still don't want you back,' Anna whispers into her pillow. It is just the writing about the act of sexuality that reminds her of what she and he once had. Not now, not for so many years, has Anna shared that union and connection.

Her characters have ignited the remembrance of how their intimacy felt – how special and remarkable it had been. Anna feels bereft of the loss of that intimacy. 'I'm not angry with you anymore,' she says, in the emptiness of the caravan. 'I just feel sad, empty, and lost.'

Anna recognised long, long, ago, that it wasn't just the sex, the fucking that had gone, it was much more intimate than that. Anna had been afraid, scared. She wanted, craved, ached, needed, desired sex, the drive was still there. She can console her urges and feel the sexual release through masturbation but in the end it is sad and lonely and Anna wants, craves, the physical touch and intimacy and trust and connection, which comes within a close relationship, which they had lost, such a long time ago.

Her characters remind Anna of what she has lost, and what she aches for and now, what she is recreating in fiction. But like her character, Anna doesn't want fiction; she wants the touch of reality.

She falls asleep unhappy and sad, whilst her characters lives move on, forwards.

The large welcoming sign for 'The Red Lion Country Hotel and Spa' greets them as Giles drives past it, following the car park sign. Margaret looks at the old stone, former coaching inn, with delight; it couldn't be more perfect. Giles opens her door to step out and collects their bags from the boot. The huge oak entrance door opens into a large hallway, with parquet flooring, leading to the reception desk.

A young man stands to receive them.

Giles offers his name "Giles Gantry."

The man checks the computer screen.

"Yes sir, you are booked into room 27 on the second floor, I hope you have had a pleasant journey. If you require anything, we are here to assist. Would you like help with your bags sir?"

"No thank you I can manage."

"Do enjoy your stay with us, I will show you to your room, please follow me."

He signals them towards the staircase, leading them up the stairs and along to the end of the corridor and unlocks the door and shows them into their huge room. Giles is eager to dismiss the clerk.

"It looks absolutely fine, thank you, if I need anything I know where to come."

The young man asks if he should uncork the wine, and quietly dismisses himself when Giles replies.

"No, thank you."

The clerk leaves the room, handing Giles the key, Giles waits a moment and then hangs the do not disturb sign on the outside of the door.

"What do you think Maggie?"

Margaret is standing at the window looking out.

"Oh Giles it's wonderful, look at the view from here, you can see the river, it is so pretty."

Giles stands alongside her and slides his hand down her back.

"I'm so pleased that you like it, we are going to have a wonderful time."

The room consists of a king size bed, with crisp white linen, two comfy armchairs and a table by the window, other pieces of quality furniture and a large bathroom with a corner bath, shower, bidet, toilet and two hand basins side by side. Complete with lots of white towels and dressing gowns.

Giles uncorks the bottle of red wine to let it breathe and joins Margaret to unpack his case. He soon has his clothes hanging up in the wardrobe and pushes his case on top, leaving Margaret to attend to hers.

He enters the ensuite and turns on the hot tap in the bath and fills it to the top. As he undresses he turns sideways and looks at himself in the full length mirror, flexing his stomach muscles and rotating his arms, thinking he needs to spend more time at the gym, he doesn't want to loose his shape.

Margaret's reflection appears behind him in the mirror and he watches her, waiting. Again his desire for her mounts as she peels off her dress slowly, dropping it to the floor. The curve of her neck as she tips it sideways, her wide eyes meet his full on and step into his senses, as she pulls her camisole above her head.

He waits, wanting to see the next image in the reel, her full breasts, round and curved, held firm and tight, trapped inside a lacy black bra, he wants her to reveal them to him. As she reaches behind her back to unhook and unleash them, he gasps as they bounce out. He wants to hold them in the palms of his hands and bury his face between them, take them inside his mouth and pinch and suck each nipple and stroke his tongue along the length and divide of her cleavage, 'oh God Maggi.' He drops his head to continue the journey, as her hands slide down each side of her breasts and across the curve of her belly and then on down to her knickers. He watches as she puts one finger into the lace elastic, pulling it and pushing it, sliding it towards the centre and as she tugs it, he can see the dark curly hairs hidden beneath. Margaret turns to show him her firm, round bottom, he swings around and catches her, putting his fingers inside the black knickers, pulling frantically to get them off.

The bath behind him is filling quickly and he turns off the tap and pulls her to the floor. They lay side by side on the soft rug and Giles turns and guides her above him as he lay on his back. He takes her hips in his hands and straddles her onto him.
Margaret brushes her breasts across his chest as she rides him, teasing him with her tongue as he tries to catch it. He transfers his hands, from hips to breasts, cupping and stroking and back again, to lifting and rocking, he waits for her pleasure as she quickens her ride, he asks her to bite his nipples to stave off his climax. They continue their lifting and rocking, biting and stroking and it becomes their rhythm, timed to perfection and it is quite sometime before she let's our her joyous relief and he too is ready to come.

Stella's dry eyes are glad to see the turn off sign for their hotel, she finds a parking space at the rear of the building and Charles stirs when she turns off the engine and there is silence in the car.

"Come on Charles we're here."

He seems genuinely surprised to find himself at the hotel and looks heavy eyed and fatigued.

"What, what?"

"Yes Charles we're here, come on let's check in and find ourselves a coffee." They make their way to the desk inside and give their names to the clerk who hands them the key to their room. It is a typical overnight place to stay, no frills and basic accommodation but suitable for one night. They would hardly be in bed, before getting up again at 4.00am for the airport.

Charles asks the directions for the coffee lounge and the clerk informs him, that it is in another building away from the hotel. Stella is aware of Charles's dissatisfaction with this arrangement.

"Charles, you go and order the coffee's and I'll drop the bags off at our room and meet you over there."

"Just coffee?"

"Yes that's fine."

Stella takes their bags along to the room.

Charles soon finds his way to the coffee lounge and restaurant – it is outside, to the left of the car park. He orders two coffees and sits down at a table by the window. He feels slightly better now that he has left Fenton, his doze in the car has done him good, he decides to forget about life back home. Stella is great company she knows how to enjoy herself; so they would have a good time in France.

He is pleased to see her, with a smile on her face, looking around the lounge to find him. He raises his hand and calls out.

"Here Stell."

She is relieved to find him back to his usual self.

"I've ordered the coffee's Stell."

"Were on the second floor Charles."

"Not bad, not bad at all, I've stayed in worse, the menu isn't Michelin star but we can make up for it in France."
"It's only for one night Charles and it's close to the airport."
"That's my girl."
"Let's plan what we are going to do Charles."
Stella is happy now, she knows that this will be good for him, to get away from Fenton; they would have a wonderful few days together. The coffee is surprisingly rather good and they order a refill.
Between them they come up with several ideas of how to fill their days in France. They are both regular visitors and each have their own favourite places. So they draw up a list for when they get there.
Stella thinks it best to engage Charles straight away so that he can detach himself from thoughts about Margaret and Giles back home.
The main tourist attractions will be closed at this time of the year in rural France, it generally opens its doors throughout the months of July and August, for the rest of the year it goes to sleep. So they prioritise Saintes and Angouleme for window-shopping, both within an hour or so from Ruffec and a longer trip down to Aubeterre son Dronne – a lovely place where Stella has previously visited, it is home to lots of unusual artists and craftspeople.
Already their enthusiasm begins to rub off on each other, as they look forward to their arrival and the days ahead.

Giles carries the bottle of wine and two glasses and
places them on the edge of the bath; Margaret is
submerged beneath the water, soaping herself, creating
bubbles on top. He steps in and joins her and leans over
to pour the wine.
"Cheers Maggie."
"Cheers."
The wine tastes of berries and deep black cherries and
smells of summer fruits.
"Not too much darling, we have the rest of the evening
ahead."
It would spoil everything, if they were too sloshed to
enjoy their time together.
"Of course."
Margaret lifts her leg from under the water and presses
her toes against his chest. Giles puts down his glass and
holds her foot and pops her big toe into his mouth and
sucks it, his tongue explores the hard varnished nail and
the soft skin around it. Margaret giggles. He takes each
toe in turn and does the same and then looks up at her
and pops her big toe back in his mouth.
"This one is my favourite."
Margaret is in heaven, so much attention, so much
affirmation of her womanliness, she raises her other leg
for him to do the same. As she does so, she slides the
former leg up and down Giles's inside leg, being careful,
as she touches his balls floating up and down around his
penis. She strokes his penis gently with her toes, such
soft skin, softer than her own, undemanding now, resting
and limp.
Giles gives the same attention to her breasts, Margaret
almost wants to weep, oh how long she has waited for
this. She cannot bring Anthony back, nor can she have
this with Charles, so she thinks herself lucky now that
Giles has come into her life.
"What are you thinking, sweetheart?" Giles asks.
Margaret waits a moment choosing her words carefully.
"I needed you, needed this, I never thought it possible I
suppose, so thank you."

Giles pulls her closer to him and slides her around, so
that her back is against his chest, he wraps his arms
around her and holds her breasts.

"I've got you now, I can give you this anytime."

He says not quite believing his words, he knows this is
what she needs to hear, so not one for disappointing, or
spoiling the days ahead, he too wants more, he is
enjoying himself, rather more than he could have
imagined.

"Again, darling, are you ready for more?"

He laughingly whispers into her ear and slips his hands
down to the mound of hair and strokes her with his
fingers.

"Oh G. G. yes, yes."

"Well then my sweet, come here."

Giles holds her breast in one hand and continues stroking
her clitoris.

"Take your time darling, we have all night."

Margaret rests her back against him and allows herself to
take it slowly, after all there is no rush.

Later after dressing, they go down to the hotel brasserie;
Margaret is taken by surprise at the contemporary style
of the room. They have left it too late to dine in the
restaurant, it is now 8.30 and the restaurant is full, they
would take a table there another evening. The brasserie
is a riot of rich colour, with seated diners, exuding a
convivial buzz, the white seats are covered in a bright
array of cushions and original pieces of contemporary art
hang along the walls.

They take one of the few remaining tables in the
conservatory and sit down. Giles tells her he has chosen
the hotel for its reputation, of offering the finest dining
for miles around and is known for being one of
England's elite restaurants. It has several awards,
including 4 AA rosettes. Tonight they decide to have a
light meal. They select sharp, refreshing tonic and lemon
to drink. The have the remainder of the bottle of wine
upstairs in the room, left for their return. They both

choose salmon escalopes with watercress, sugar-snap
peas and avocado. Afterwards, Giles asks her if she
would like a dessert, he is instantly surprised after
having eaten all of her main course that she is interested,
he is so used to women leaving most of their food and
looking aghast at the mention of a pudding.
"Let joy be unconfined." Margaret says adding.
"I'll have chocolate pear pudding, how about you?"
Giles gives this idea some thought, he would normally
refuse – like his women he watches his figure and prides
himself on his toned physique. Margaret has the ability
to offer him freedom and be unrestrained.
"Love to."
The sweet, sticky, pudding, runny with chocolate sauce
is heaven and Margaret eats every mouthful and Giles
tucks in too. He is starting to enjoy this sweetness of her
and the food; he can work it off at the gym when he
returns to Fenton.
This is part and parcel of Maggie, this voluptuousness,
this needy greed for the good things in life, of sex, and
food also, he now realises.
It encapsulates her and in her he has found his addiction,
and this weakness for her would probably never go
away. This he hadn't expected, he prides himself on his
ability to stand by his boundaries, of knowing how far to
go, and already before their first night is over, he has
stepped over the line, his marker for staying in control.
He is hooked, physically especially and emotionally he
isn't now sure. As he watches her tongue licking the last
drop of dark sauce from the spoon, he wants it inside his
mouth, 'oh my God again,' he can feel himself wanting
her and as his foot reaches out to rub up and down her
legs, he knows he won't have to wait much longer.

Returning to their room, Charles and Stella decide to each have a shower to freshen up and then return to the restaurant to enjoy a late dinner.

They share a bottle of house red and choose the ravioli with basil and pine nut sauce, which turns out to be a decent choice and Stella finishes with ice cream.

After coffee and mints, Charles thinks better of himself and decides against a brandy or whisky to finish.

This leaves them both in good spirits as they turn in for the night.

As Margaret lay gently sleeping beside him, Giles's thoughts turn for the first time since setting off, about Arabella, his fiancé. He thinks to himself, 'how crazy, what is this all about?' Sex with Arabella is physically satisfying, but compared to Maggie; well there is no comparison. Arabella is tall and thin, the typical sought after size 10 figure. He realises now how he takes care, when on top of her to steady himself, fearful of breaking her bones, but this is a small price to pay for having her by his side. He knows how he is envied by his contemporaries, his male friends who are married to larger women, this is how it is to look good, to have a blonde, tall, skinny girl by ones side. It is society's measure of doing well, after all, who wants to parade around the circles with a plump, squat female.

His thoughts turn to Margaret nuzzled next to him, exhaling softly by his side. Looking at her his heart fills, remembering from only a few minutes earlier, how her full, rounded, womanly body felt beneath him, he didn't have to fear, she willingly wanted to take him, devour him, to swallow him up inside of her. 'And Oh God, how she has.' He wants her again, what is this? She is going against everything he thought he believed in. Dear Arabella, a lady from the right breeding stock, and how his family were so proud when he had introduced them to her, she fitted the bill exactly and how his father had puffed out his chest at the mention of her family name – 'The Ackroyd-Faulks's', he had almost began to preen the invisible feathers on his chest.

Maggie, he looks at her curled up, with her head settled contentedly on the feather pillow, you were to be a plaything, a distraction, someone who could be used for satisfaction as and when the mood struck. To fulfil his needs, the space where Arabella cannot fill. 'You fool, you idiot,' Giles taunts himself. But there is no going back, he can't retract the wedding plans, the future with Arabella is cast in stone, his parents have taken care of that. He would lose everything if he did so, his parents, his inheritance would be annulled and his brother would gain everything. He had had the ideal bachelor life, the education, the fast car, the flat and all at the expense of his parent's generosity. This had the unsaid proviso, of carrying on the family name in grand style, oh yes; marrying Arabella would certainly give them that. Their investments in him would pay off, that would never be in question. Already they had stepped into the world of the Ackroyd-Faulks's, the mutual consent was active, in that their paths were connecting.

In the hierarchy of Fenton and Thornby it would raise their position, to the likes of Charles Harcourt his business partner and it couldn't get better than that.
In his minds eye, he sees his mother and father gleaming on the wedding photographs, no, he can't take that away from them, especially his mother, the wedding has to go ahead.
His eyes still settled on Maggie, he wonders how much she knows about him and Arabella, she must know, she leads her life in the same circles, it must have been talked about.
'So what am I for you?' he muses, still looking at her, 'are you my Mrs Robinson, is that it?' Giles is experiencing feelings and emotions now, that he has never had before in his life, Maggie is coursing around his veins, she has wound herself around his heart and it is impossible for him to let go. He notices, a feeling of contentment and relaxation within himself and he rests his arm and snuggles in beside her and closes his eyes, he wants the night to never end.

Charles snores beside Stella as she lay awake unable to sleep, she wishes she had her own room and could get up or read a book. She battles with her thoughts, to keep at bay anxieties and worries that jump back into her mind, as often as she tries to shut them out.

When the alarm on her mobile shrills out, she feels as though she has just dropped off to sleep.

Her legs mobilize themselves, fighting her desire to sleep as they step out of bed. She fills the kettle to make coffee and on doing so Charles wakes up.

"What time is it?" he asks.

"It's four o'clock time to get up, I've put the kettle on, we've got half an hour before we leave, I'll go and have a quick shower."

Charles loves her energy, her ability to switch herself on, as and when required, he struggles now at his age, she reminds him of himself in his younger years.

He is glad of the extra minutes in bed before he has to get up.

Stella is back and dressed in no time and as she sips her hot coffee, she presses Charles to hurry up.

He uses the excuse of having no luggage to check in, as his reason for taking his time.

They leave the hotel fifteen minutes later than Stella wanted to but the roads are relatively quiet and they arrive on time at the airport.

She loves flying and especially this easy transfer through to the boarding gate, without having to queue and check in, it makes the journey much more relaxing. They have time to buy a morning paper and a coffee before stepping on board the plane.

Her favourite part – the taking off – when the injection of speed and thrust of the engines press into the small of her back, always gives her a pleasant, sexual sensation.

As Charles sits beside her, leafing noisily through the pages of his paper, she secretly enjoys her pleasure.

The flight is steady and short, they manage a coffee and muffin each and they exchange papers until the seatbelt signs light up for their arrival.

Anna wakes early and after surfacing, picks up her book
and pen to write down her thoughts that had been on her
mind before she fell asleep.
Her fingers turn over the pages to where she had left off,
she is surprised that her book has only a couple of empty
pages left.
Anna hunts around for spare A4 paper to continue.
She manages to find a few dog-eared sheets and begins
to write.

Later Anna breaks off her writing to reflect on how she
would continue with the remainder of Fermanagh House,
she feels uneasy and perplexed as she gets up to make
herself a pot of tea and to think.

Anna realises she has only a few more pages left to write
of Fermanagh House. She also knows exactly what they
will be about. It's not going to be so much a novel, but
more like a little novella. Anna now knows, through
what she has written, that she doesn't want to write
anymore. She has certainly written herself into the
novella.
The rain patters now upon the roof and sides of the
caravan and falls heavier and heavier. She surrounds
herself with her duvet, to keep the cold, wet, damp
morning out.
Reflecting now on how Fermanagh House has ended,
brings her back to the time, when she swam in the early
morning sea with Jo.
And another time, long before Jo, when she had briefly
stood, beneath an astonishingly, amazing, waterfall, the
water falling so hard and heavily upon their heads and
pounding onto every inch of their bodies, it had been
such an exhilarating experience. She had been so
completely absorbed by the total sensation of life, every
sense stirred, every thought clear and every view vivid.
So incredibly, astonishingly, alive, and the embrace, one
of innocence and affirmation, the pounding splashing,
crashing powerful waterfall, more than enough for both

of them then, to be satisfied. No thoughts of sexuality, they were each experiencing their own sensuality that was enough, it had filled her senses up to the brim and she needed nothing more. Anna brings back the woman into her mind; so long ago now, so much time and space had separated them and what they had. Déjà vu, knowing me, knowing you.

That relationship had been based on a game of seduction, but only when it had ended, had she realised how the game had been played and the rules. Only later she found out about what the rules were and weren't. She had been drawn in willingly, guiltily, by the woman's seduction. By her ways and willingness to explore and be explored. As Anna's starved senses were opened by the gentle seduction, she began to feel again, how it was to be wanted, and connected to another, to be touched and to be allowed to touch another. This gave her the sense and feel, the reality of herself. The experiences of being allowed to pursue, to touch and fumble the breasts and share embraces. Anna wanted to be free inside, to be able to have a complete relationship with the woman, but her guilt and fear held her back. The guilt and fear was that which belonged and was attached to Anna, not the woman. She had appeared to want to have, a sexual relationship with Anna. In the end, Anna understood that she had failed the game. It turned out that she had not been a part of an adult awakening, but a predator. To a woman who it seemed could give herself and her sexuality, to see if like all the other predators in her life, Anna too took the bait. She had taken the bait, too late in the end to change anything, too late to fit into the role of a caring, person. Anna didn't want the role of protector, friend perhaps had she known sooner. She had believed the woman had offered herself freely in their attempts at a relationship, but it seemed in the end she hadn't. Anna had accepted the persistent seduction.

So what now? Nothing, she has failed yet another proving – of course she has – she accepts that. The thing is, when does she know when she is being tested and what are the rules and when are people being level with her. Instead of Anna feeling like a woman who's had an adult awakening and sensual experience and connection with another adult, she's ended up being a predator. It has been a lie, and now it is over and yet here, Anna is in her starved, hungry state, almost walking, literally and metaphorically into the same situation again.

Anna decides that she won't do that; she will step back and not allow herself to be tested again. She would find in herself, what she has looked for in others, because it is only through her feeding her own hunger, that she can appease it.

She has walked herself into Fermanagh House but she will close this now, end it and walk away. She doesn't need to continue to repeat the same story again and again and again without learning the lesson the universe is trying to show and help her understand. And as for the woman? Anna can't change the past but she can learn by it and not repeat it in real life now, or in the future with Jo or anyone else. She decides this will not happen; she is master and mistress of herself. For now that is enough.

It is time to get up and make hot tea and toast and marmalade, to warm her.

Anna watches the rain splash off the glass panes; she wonders why she's stayed so long with him and why she hadn't left him sooner. It would have been a normal, almost acceptable response. She would have been forgiven and understood. And the sexuality, what is it all about and where does it belong in her life? Looking at her, no one would ever think or guess, that raw, sexual energy runs and still surges through her body, she knows how she feels, when the force comes crashing and charging inside her. She has learnt to suppress and control it, but it is still a profound force, which drives her on and on and on. Its energy has propelled and forced her, to go beyond her limits, much more than she would have, had she not had it. If she had spent her energy on desire and its satisfaction alone, then she would have dissipated, spent her resource and not done the things in her life she had felt she needed too. Things she cannot think about or analyse. The energy inside, supplies her with the resources to sustain her efforts and keep them going, until she has done the things she needs to do. Had she not had the source, she would have given up, given in on her endless efforts for her family and the family of childhood before she married. And then afterward for twenty years and more, as she went in and out and around and around in hoops and circles, in her search of founding her own family, she had pursued her efforts, until her children appeared, so much time and energy, so much of herself given in that pursuit. When her mother died, she remembers her father talking about why he needed to marry again. He had said he knew he was too old and shouldn't but he still needed to have a sexual relationship with a woman. Anna considers this now and finds her father's statement, honest and profound.

Anna knows she must have had reasons for staying with him, when she should have gone long ago. Children had been one of the reasons, she had hung on, in the hope that one day they would come and as the prospect grew further and further away from her, after the cycles and years of treatment and clinics and doctors and tests grew constant, she stayed on because she had come too far not to. She had to continue, pursue her dream, her hope and search for her unborn children.

The disturbing journey through the days had haunted her and at night, the restless ghost of her unborn babies gave her no peace. She could not accept either infertility, or childlessness, they were unacceptable, she could not live with either states, even after twenty years she continued, until in the end her children came and the ghosts and hauntings stopped and she held her children in her arms and belly and no longer in her heart and head.

So she stayed, because she needed him and his support to pursue her dream of babies and happy families. She had used him. He had complained and grumbled but in the end had accepted it and gone along with her. It had seemed such a simple thing – to want children – to expect children to come along but they hadn't and in the end she had needed his support in the process. It was too late to do any other. She did not regret what she had done. Had she not done it, she would not have rested. Her soul would have found no peace in the grave. She had found her family after so long a search and then another story had began with them. Her children had their own stories, which they brought with them, but at first Anna didn't see that or understand. She had thought that once her family had been found, then that story was done, only of course it wasn't, it had only just begun.

So she stayed because she had to. An infertile, childless woman would understand, but probably no one else, except a mother, sister, lover, or a friend perhaps. Having done what she had done, she then had to take the responsibility and live with it, because she had created it. Only when it is finished and the job she had started is done can it end, legal responsibility is only one thing, while moral responsibility is another.

She now understands the whole picture, sees it more fully than before. Anna knows that everything has a beginning, middle and an end and that the cycle she is now in will end. Obligation comes to mind and love, for she loves her children. She cannot change the past, no matter what she thinks or feels, she can only plan her future and live in the present and accept it.

Anna's journeys usually take her a long time, probably longer than most people, but in the end she usually gets there. Her mother had once said of her.
"Our Anna does things, but she does them in her own time."
She knew me, she didn't judge me, she just knew me.

It depends how we measure time Anna considers. Some people might feel twenty-five years to have a first baby is crazy, but then that's because they would be using their own measure of time to make that judgement, as if time could be only measured by its length. Time has depths and space, different dimensions and it seems unrealistic to think, it is lived all the time, every day, in exactly the same state or way, when it isn't, it just isn't. Such a prospect would be dull and tedious. And what pressure, having to do everything you ever wanted to do, squashed up into one space, in one lifetime. The prospect makes Anna's head reel.

Stella and Charles arrive on time at Limoges Airport,
they are first in the queue for their car hire and are given
a blue Renault Clio.
Stella switches on her mobile and dials Cecily to arrange
their accommodation. Before they have found their
parked car on the tarmac, Cecily returns the call.
"I have managed to book you a room at The Argentor,
you can pay for it when you arrive, is that ok?" she asks.
"Lovely, thank you Cecily, I will call you again later,
bye."
She informs Charles where they will be staying. He
begins singing and dancing, delighted at this
arrangement as they continue looking for their car.
Stella smiles as she calls out to Charles that she has
found it.
Stella drives away from the airport, happy to be in
France.
They journey through the quiet roads, empty of life and
people, except for solitary figures, carrying baguettes in
their hands, it offers up and emphasises a complete
change in pace and lifestyle. Even sedentary Fenton by
comparison is hectic, busy and thriving – in these
hamlets and villages, life stands still, nothing has
changed for many years.
The battered, rustic, double fronted French houses, with
glass canopies over the entrance doors and flaking paint,
look untouched, as if the clock has been turned back
generations.
It's good to be here, to be home Stella acknowledges to
herself silently. She knows this road like the back of her
hand; she has driven along it many times. Nothing ever
changes.
Turning right towards their village, across the old stone
bridge and past the derelict, cobweb filled joiners shop
they arrive. Stella parks in the public car park, opposite
The Argentor and they both get out.

Giles is the first to wake up the following morning; he leaves Maggie asleep and chooses to have a shave and a long shower; he notices the tiny red bite marks along his chest and smiles inwardly. Afterwards, feeling refreshed and clean, he picks up the hotel's brochure and runs through the breakfast menu, as he does so Maggie begins to stir, he looks at her fondly, her hair ruffled and her face full of the nights sleep.

"Good morning darling."

Giles slides across the top of the eiderdown and gives her a kiss, firstly on her nose and then her sleepy eyes and lips.

"Hello."

Maggie whispers as she comes out of her deep sleep. Margaret adores sleeping, she loves to nestle herself down beneath the covers and hide away from herself and the world. Last night had been easy to snuggle down with Giles, she had anticipated a nervy time, of becoming accustomed to each other, before falling asleep. They had bonded together like two spoons and the safety of his arms around her, allowed her to slip into the night without thoughts or fears.

At home, especially after a fraught time with Charles, she was often unable to switch off her internal monitor, her continuous checks, that during times of stress, churned around her mind and the harder she tried to turn them off, the more they billowed and grew.

She feels comfortable and happy here with Giles.

"Would you like breakfast downstairs or here in the room?"

"What time is it?"

"It is just before ten."

"Up here would be nice."

"What would you like?"

"Fruits, yoghurt and French pastries and tea would be lovely."

Margaret tells him, savouring the idea of the food.

"Ok, are you ready for it now, or a little later?"

"Now, if that's fine with you."

Margaret notices his damp hair.

"Unless I take a quick shower first?"

"Ok then, I'll order it whilst you take a shower."

Margaret slips out off the bed. Seeing her naked body again, reminds Giles of his thoughts last night regarding Arabella. He doesn't want her interfering in this space with Maggie; he doesn't want the spell between them broken. He leaves her to shower and picks up the hotel phone and places their breakfast order. He draws back the covers of the bed to let it air and waits.

Margaret carefully soaps herself, she feels slight bruising in places, there are no obvious marks on her skin, she is just not used to this amount of physical contact.

Especially in between the tops of her legs, she feels sore. As she steps out of the shower, Giles is waiting for her with a large bath towel in his hands and he wraps it around her.

"Thank you."

He begins to rub her softly with the towel and she pulls back and winces.

"What is it?"

Giles's eyes are filled with concern.

"I am a little sore, I'm not used to this."

She tells him feeling rather embarrassed.

"Oh sweetheart, come here."

Giles gently pulls her out of the bathroom and onto the top of the bed.

"Let me dry you."

He takes a corner of the towel and dabs softly all over her skin.

"I'll have to leave you alone then, won't I?"

"Maybe just a little, until later."

Margaret says with mischief written across her face.

The knock on the door startles him and he gets up. He turns around to make sure Margaret has put on her gown, before allowing the breakfast trays to be brought through.

Tucking into their food, Giles asks Maggie if she would like to spend time in the hotel spa facilities, take a sauna, a massage or a swim, or maybe go for a walk along the riverbank.

Margaret munches on her croissant, oozing with jam and thinks for a moment.

"How about we attempt doing all of it, I would love a walk outside and the spa idea sounds terrific."

"Tonight there is a tango evening down in the bar, can you dance the tango?"

He asks, watching her as she struggles with the leaking jam.

"Years ago, I tried it, can you?"

"Well I wouldn't mind giving it a go, it could be fun, so how about we try the lot, a walk this morning and lunch, followed by the spa and then the dancing tonight?"

"Yes, why not."

Margaret concludes as she wipes her mouth with the serviette and walks across to her wardrobe. They both choose casual trousers and sweaters and Giles selects his waxed leather shoes and Margaret her boots.

"I just need to make a couple of business calls before we set off."

Giles explains as he laces up his shoes.

"Ok I'll wait downstairs in the lounge, is that ok?"

Giles relieved at the opportunity to contact Arabella, dials her number as Maggie leaves the room, he loves the way she trusts him, or seems to, unlike Arabellla with her never ending questions. If he speaks to her now, he can appease her for a day or two.

"Hi are you ok?" he asks her.

"I was expecting your call last night, is everything alright?"

Arabella asks him.

"Sorry, I got rather dragged into the fold so to speak, and were having meetings during the day and you know how it is when men get together, so anyway, I'll have to go now. I'm pleased your ok."

"But Giles darling, we have so much to talk about
regarding the wedding, we need to discuss and decide on
certain things."
Arabella doesn't want to end the conversation.
"Look we can sort it all out when I return next week, I
am sure it can wait and business is business – so leave it
until I return and then were not making any rash
decisions are we, because we don't want to do the wrong
thing, do we, so bye for now, kisses, love you."
Giles ends quickly. Before he has chance to switch his
phone off, it rings – he knows that it will be Arabella
calling him back, dissatisfied with his brief conversation
and so he quickly turns it off and hides it in his bedside
cabinet drawer. She will have to wait, he doesn't want
her to jeopardise his time here with Maggie, he has a
vague sense of his world slipping and turning itself
upside down, but needs to step aside from it for now.

Maggie waiting for him in the lounge looks radiant with
rosy cheeks and a beaming smile on her face.
"Right let's go."
They walk towards the doorway. The day is crisp and
beautiful; the autumnal leaves float gently in the breeze,
to their resting place on the earth's floor. They walk in
the direction of the river, following the footpath signs
along the way. The air is so different from Fenton, earthy
and deep, it has been a long time since she has been
away from the sea, the changes around her seep in and
forms their days ahead. She feels rooted and anchored
and yet at the same time free, if this is life – she is happy
to live it.

Pierre dashes across, as Stella enters The Argentor, he kisses her on both cheeks.

"Stella." he exults and greets Charles by shaking his hand.

There is the usual atmosphere of music playing, coffee cups clinking, and locals sitting propped up against the bar drinking and turning around saying.

"Bonjour Monsieur dame."

Pierre hands them the key for their room and they take their bags upstairs to settle in.

Charles slings his bag down on top of the bed and starts to do a jig around the room, trying his best to wiggle his hips as he does so, singing and humming with his movements.

Charles's is back on form, Stella thinks as she joins in for a quick moment.

The aroma from the kitchens below permeates up to the room and she is hungry.

"I'm starving Charles, are you hungry?"

Stella's question interrupts his frivolities.

"For you my darling, of course I'm hungry."

He gleefully takes her by the arm and pulls her towards him and kisses her quickly on the end of her nose.

Stella brims with happiness; they are going to have a thrilling time.

Downstairs in the restaurant Pierre finds them a table for two and suggests a bottle of St Emillion grand crux, which Charles doesn't hesitate to accept.

"Let's blow the bloody budget Stell."

They settle for the plat de jour and begin with chicken consommé followed by the main course -beefsteak served with French fries and carrots and a selection of cheeses to finish.

The meal comes to a glorious conclusion two hours later with a dark coffee.

They are both happy and complete and thank Pierre, before going for a stroll around the village towards the arboretum. The day is a memorable one and Fenton now seems a long time ago, forgotten and cast aside for the moment. Their moods are heightened by the added ingredient of a clear sky, the weather almost balmy for the time of year.

Keeping their conversation light, they steer around the outskirts of the village, noticing any minor changes as they pass by. The odd for sale sign, of interest to both of them as they peer through windows to check the places out, eventually arriving back at The Argentor where they enter by the side door and go straight up to their room. Charles flops down on the bed and Stella removes her shoes and jacket and takes herself to the armchair by the window to read her book.

All in all, it's been a good start, Stella acknowledges as she settles down to read and Charles dozes on the bed. Day one and all is going well.

Back at The Red Lion Country Hotel, Margaret lay on a
soft mattress, under the skilled hands of the proficient
masseur at the hotel spa, reliving the day in her mind,
knowing that it has been one of the most perfect she has
ever had. They had found a lovely old pub, serving home
made food and had stopped for lunch, the butternut
squash and sweet potato soup with warm crusty bread
was hearty and filling. And the walk back after was
highlighted, when they spotted a heron standing at the
edge of the riverbank. The dappling sunlight, filtering
down through the trees, cast its crystal light on the
standing stones, as they stood looking through the gentle
current for fish.

And now here having her body tended too another treat,
she secretly wonders if the masseur picks up on the
fragility of her aching body, however she doesn't care.
Tonight she will be dancing, another dream come true,
'Charles oh if only.'

Meeting up with Giles after their pampering sessions,
they both decide against taking a swim, it would keep
until another day here; they need to return to the comfort
of their room.

Only this time he doesn't take her roughly and greedily,
he touches her slowly and gently and with his breath like
a wafting feather, he explores every crevice of her
wanting body.

"Oh Giles."

Maggie murmurs, she can't take anymore, she wants him
firmly and deeply inside of her, she wants the deep roar
of him above her, she wants to hear his groan as he
finishes deep, deep inside of her.

"What Maggie?"

He whispers in her ear.

"Oh Giles I want you."

"I don't want to hurt you."

"I don't care."

Giles eases her legs apart and lifts himself on top,
entering her carefully, watching her face. Oh yes, she

needs him; he pushes slowly, in and out again and again. He rests himself on his elbows and brushes his chest across her cushion of flesh.

He has the full length of his penis inside her now.

"Is this ok Maggi?"

"Yes, darling, take it slowly."

He feels the increase of blood engorging his penis and he fights the urge, to thrust and pull, thrust and push and pull.

"Oh Maggi."

He pulls himself partly from her, his penis heavy and hard, erect and ready to drive into her.

"Oh Maggi."

He pushes back gently, in and out, softly and gently. His actions slow and careful, holding back from deeper thrusts, he is amazed by his control.

Margaret is entranced by his movements, his gently taking of her. She falls into the rhythmic patience and is ready now. She begins to lift her buttocks off the bed and oppose his movements, pulling away as he pushes and trying to meet his withdrawing.

"Oh Maggi you are driving me wild. What do you want?"

"Faster, Giles, faster."

"Oh my God, Maggi."

He needs and wants to hear her orgasm, for her to cry out her pleasure. He pushes again as he buries his head on the soft warm pillows of her and this time she digs her nails into his bottom, forcing him deep inside. Pushing and pulling and forcing, demanding him, he hears her at last and finishes and exhales his breath.

"Oh Maggie, I love you."

He cannot stop himself as the words gush out.

"I love you too." She simply says.

Whilst Giles showers, to prepare himself for their evening meal and later dancing, Margaret searches through her belongings, she remembers arriving and hanging her garments onto the coat hangers and putting them into the wardrobe, her lingerie, make up and accessories she had placed in the set of drawers at the side. But she can't find the little parcel containing the cufflinks that she had bought for Giles. She looks inside every pocket and takes out the contents of the drawers but it isn't there. She can't understand where it might be, after another search she concludes that she must have left it at home, probably on the bed. If that were the case, there is every possibility that Charles had found it and then what, she dare not think.

'Damn.'

She is immensely disappointed, it means that she can't give them to Giles tonight after dinner like she wanted to and at the same time she is rather anxious as to the outcome, if Charles had found it and opened the box. She doesn't think it a good idea to phone Charles at home, just in case he has the cufflinks.

She decides to phone Abby to sound her out, she would inform her of Charles's mood whilst she has been away and after all it has only been one day.

After putting the last of the contents back into the drawer, Giles comes out of the bathroom.

"I would like to phone Abby before we go down for dinner."

"Sure I'll dress and bob down and find a table, whilst you finish dressing and it will give you time to phone her, is that ok?"

"Yes I'll be down in fifteen minutes."

Margaret checks her gold watch.

Giles dresses himself quickly, putting on a black pair of trousers and a clean shirt; his shoes and leaves the room. Margaret selects a pearl necklace and puts it around her neck and dials Abby's mobile phone. Margaret is preparing to leave a message, when her daughter answers.

"Hi."

Abby speaks seeming a little out of breath.

"Hi darling, is everything alright?"

"Yes mummy, yes I'm fine."

"Are the two of you managing ok?"

"The two of us?"

Abby falters before continuing.

"Oh no mummy there is just me, Charles has gone away on a business trip to France?" Margaret thinks for a moment not knowing exactly how to answer.

"France?"

"Yes I haven't seen him since you left, he just phoned to say that he would be gone for a few days and that he had business to sort out. So don't worry mummy, I am ok here on my own, it is giving me chance to sort out a few things, how's grandma and granddad by the way?"

"Look darling, Charles hasn't been in touch, I had no idea he was going to France, it must have been an urgent last minute thing, anyway you know how he is these days don't you and as long as you are all right that's fine. Could you do me a favour darling?"

Margaret asks quickly, steering her daughter away from discussions of grandma and granddad.

"What mummy?"

"Would you take a look in my bedroom and see if there is a small gift wrapped box on the bed or on the dresser, anywhere in the room. It was a little thank you gift and I seem to have left it behind."

"Sure mummy I'll just go and check."

Margaret waits a couple of minutes.

"Well mummy, I've looked everywhere and I can't find it, did you put it in a drawer or did you leave it downstairs somewhere?"

"No darling, never mind, I'm sure I'll find it here in my bag somewhere, I've probably overlooked it. Do you need money darling and how about food, should I ask Susan to pop in?"

"No, no mummy I'm fine, I don't need Susan, please don't ask her to come in, she will only disrupt my concentration and if I need anything Charles told me to put it on my card, so I'm fine mummy honestly."

"Well if you're absolutely sure, darling?"

"Yes, mummy I am fine, so don't worry I will see you when you get back next week." Abby replies giving Margaret chance to say a quick goodbye before ending the call.

Margaret pushes away the thought of Charles and the cufflinks and turns off her phone. 'Well, well, France,' she ponders for a second whilst slipping on her heels and heading for the door.

The atmosphere is alive and buzzing down in the dining room, the music from the dance floor can be heard and everyone seems happy and as the cutlery clinks as the diners eat, Margaret and Giles chat.

They discuss their choice of food and bottle of wine, Giles admires Margaret's appetite and passion for eating and it is an absolute pleasure to share this with her. They have grilled wild mushroom risotto to start, followed by pan-fried partridge, with a pearl barley, pea and lettuce stew and Margaret's choice of orchard eve's pudding, with whisky jersey cream to share.

The whole meal is historic with delicate portions, enabling them to complete the meal, without feeling bloated and gorged out. They take their last glass of wine and find two comfy armchairs at the edge of the dance floor and sit down.

The live musicians belt out the rhythm of the tango, as the accompanying dancers step out to the beat across the floor, they can't hear themselves speak and turn their attention to the people on the dance floor. Some couples are obviously trying to copy the professionals, laughing and stepping out of synch. Margaret signals Giles to join in; he has reservations of impending embarrassment but steps up to the floor, holding out his hand for Margaret. In the convivial anonymity of the dancers, what does it matter if their dance is out of step. He pulls her towards him with ease and ungraciously they begin to tango, going left instead of right and heads colliding at the wrong moment, adding to their fumbled contact. He is holding her and this is enough, the beating rhythm rising

from the floor, gives momentum to their feet as they keep going. Plenty more couples come and go as the night progresses and when the music stops for a break Margaret pulls Giles's hand to sit down. They are soaking wet with perspiration and their faces glisten. "Thank you that was wonderful." Margaret tells him. "Unbelievable that was hot."
Giles exclaims, wiping his forehead as he sits back in the chair. Their glasses are nearly empty and they ask the bar attendant for cool mineral water. As they sip the drink, the band plays on. It has been a night to remember, one of the best Giles decides.

Anna decides to walk into town, to buy some provisions for her last few days in Fenton. Calling into the cake shop, she buy's some bakewell tarts to take to Jo's, they can have them with a cup of tea.

She would visit the supermarket later. She makes her way through the quiet streets, towards the converted chapel, where Jo has a flat. Anna is in luck, because as she arrives, a man holds open the entry door for her to go in.

'Great, I hope she's in,' Anna feels uncertain now about turning up on speck, she might have gone out, or be taking Jason for a walk.

What strikes Anna, as she stands waiting at Jo's door is the silence. No barking from Jason. 'She's not in,' Anna sighs deeply and makes her way back down the stairs and out of the flats. She is disappointed, standing on the pavement outside the old chapel building.
She could go and get on with her shopping, or she could go by the lay by to the hut and see if Jo has gone there to do more work.
There is still flood damage left all around the town and she is saddened when she sees a huge landslide, which has blocked and still hasn't been cleared from the path, which leads to the beach.
As she gets nearer the hut, she hears the familiar barking of Jason. Her spirits rise. 'She is here then,' Anna says to herself.

Jo can't decide, whether or not to break off from work in the garden and go into town to check out the auction. She realises that she will have to be quick if she wants to get there on time, her internal clock tells her it must be around lunchtime as she is beginning to feel hungry. She had a bowl of porridge this morning for breakfast and with working hard, adding more rubbish to the bonfire; she is ready to eat again.

She breaks off from the work and turns around to admire what she has achieved today, and is pulled out of her thoughts, hearing Jason running up towards the path barking, to meet whoever it is coming down. Jo knows when his barking stops, that it is someone he knows.

Anna smiles as she sees Jo following Jason to greet her. Jo looks less polished in her appearance than she has seen her for a long time, much more how she used to be when she lived here.

When Anna appears Jo's heart lifts as she walks over to greet her.

"Hi."

"Hi, I called at the flat but you weren't there, so I thought you might have come here."

"Oh, sorry, I should have phoned you but its all been a bit of a rush, I've moved back here."

"Really, that was quick, I thought you were still clearing and sorting it out."

"I know, but I decided now would be a good time to return. To be honest, I didn't want to stay any longer in Charles's flat. It felt."

Jo gathers her thoughts as she gazes across to the hut.

"I felt as if I was trapped at the flat by Charles, like he was controlling me. I decided I needed to be in charge of my own destiny and not be beholden to him any longer, and the place is clean and dry now, so the hut is ok to live in."

Anna is thankful at last that Jo has finally seen the light as far as Charles is concerned and feels happy now and less anxious about her safety.

"I'm glad you're back here, it's a good place. I can always feel that when I come here. How have you managed to bring all your stuff?"

"I called and asked Gary at the DIY shop, luckily he said that he would bring it in his van, so were back now aren't we Jase?"

"That's good, I'm pleased for you, you look happy."

Anna continues as her eyes spot the growing bonfire.

"Gosh you have been busy."

"Yes I have, it's been good for me to work."

Jo smiles and asks Anna if she would like a pot of tea.

"That'd be great and I've got these to go with it."

Anna holds up the bag with the bakewell tarts in.

"Oh lovely, thanks."

"The curtains look brilliant."

Anna tells Jo as she walks around the hut.

"Yes they do don't they, I plan to buy some things from the sale rooms and make sure I'm prepared for the winter and I'll have to sort out the workroom before I can continue with my crafts and art work."

"You'll miss the big loft space in the flat, will you be able to paint here?"

"Yes, eventually, the canvasses I paint will be smaller, but I can do big ones outside during the summer and store them in the workroom and keep all my materials in there. I'm hoping to get some plans worked out for having the workroom made larger, so I can do bigger pieces in there all year round."

"A lot of brilliant ideas."

"Yes, it will be great if they work out."

Anna looks around the hut thinking to herself, it looks much more how it used to, even though there are no longer the cosy chair and rugs and books.

Inside the hut it is warm and cosy from the heat of the stove and Jo fills the kettle to boil.

"I'm sorry you will have to sit on the kitchen chairs for now, I called at the auction to see if they had any armchairs but they didn't, I was thinking of going to the sale today but I won't bother now that you're here."

"Don't stay for my sake, if you want to go."

"No it's alright I can go again any time, it's nice to see you, I was going to have a go at tackling the path from here up to the lay by. There's so much rubbish, stones and branches that really need to be cleared before the winter sets in."

"Ok, that's what we'll do, I'll help you."

Anna turns and looks around the hut, there doesn't seem to be much for them to do indoors, but outside they can tidy up and gather the best of the wood for Jo's fuel store and just clear things and pile up rubbish onto the large bonfire, which is mounting up on the vegetable patch.

"Do you fancy staying for lunch, we can make some soup for later."

"Are you sure, I'm not putting you out?"

"No of course you're not and if you fancy helping me afterwards I would appreciate it."

"Yes I'll help you and it will be lovely to share the soup."

Jo puts the basket containing the vegetables onto the kitchen table.

"Jo?"

Anna asks as she stands helping to scrape the vegetables for the soup.

"What?"

"In a day or so I have to begin making my way back to the city. Mark's as settled as he's going to be for now and I have the children to go back and see to."

Jo puts the scraper down.

"I'm going to miss you, when will you be back?"

Jo feels less happy inside as her heart acknowledges the forthcoming loss of their friendship.

"I will miss you too, I will be leaving in a couple of days but I will be back to catch up with Mark again in the spring, you have my phone number if you ever want to give me a ring and I can give you my address and perhaps we can write until then?"

"I don't know what I would have done without your help you know and I will phone and write when you're gone, it will be a nice thing to do when I'm here on my own."
"Well if I can help you a bit more before I go, I'll be happy to."
Jo makes a teapot of tea and pours milk into two mugs and gives the pot a stir. Filling the mugs she marks out this moment in her mind, to treasure it and save it, to recapture later when Anna is gone. She will miss her, Anna her gentle friend. Jo wonders to herself, where is she heading back to and who is it that awaits her. She knows little about her life away from here and can't imagine her other world and how she manages her time in it. She hasn't mentioned her partner; presumably the father of her children and that makes me think – is she happy with him. Whenever Jo observes her, when she is not looking, it is of someone who is carrying the weight of others on her shoulders, not someone who is light and free and easy with herself and the world. In those moments, Jo has wanted to reach across and lift off this pressure and give her wings to fly and enjoy a space in time that is hers alone and not at the mercy of others.
"What are you thinking?" Anna asks.
"About you."
"Why what about me?"
Anna has a worried look on her face.
"Sometimes when I look at you, when you have been busy working here with me, you look light and free and happy, and other times you seem weighed down, as if you are carrying others and your life is not your own."
"I have enjoyed being here helping you and yes it is a break for me, from having to be responsible for Adam and my family back at home."
"Come back then and stay here for a break, whenever you get the chance."
"I'll see, I can't promise anything."
Anna replies with the appearance again of having the whole world on her shoulders. "Just turn up, it will be ok, if you can."

"What would you like me to help you with?"
Anna asks, as they break from peeling, scraping and
scrubbing the vegetables, to eat the tarts and drink the
hot tea in peace and simple contentment. "I might be
able to get away in the Christmas holidays too."
Anna's voice enters into the silent preparations.
"That'd be great."
Jo is happier now.
"I could spend time with Mark and we could meet up."
Anna sighs now with contentment.
"Brilliant."
"Shall we get started then?"
The clearing work is dirty and heavy, with most of the
land spattered with the trodden in mud, but they work on
through early afternoon to get it finished.
Later Anna asks.
"The bonfire's magnificent, I bet it's a brilliant fire,
when are you going to light it? You'll have to do it fairly
soon whilst it's dry, otherwise you're going to have a
huge soggy pile."
"I hope tomorrow if it's dry, now most of the rubbish is
ready to burn. Do you fancy coming over to light it and
watch it burn, we can put some jacket potatoes in and
have beans and sausage with it?"
"Yes, that sounds a nice idea, what time are you thinking
of?"
"I thought it would be best in the morning and then have
the potatoes for lunch, if you fancy doing that."
"Yes I can come over then, I will bring a bottle of wine
if you like."
"Yes, it will be our final farewell before you leave."
Walking back up to the top of the path they pick out the
last bits of rubbish and dead wood from the hedge and
take it to the bonfire pile. They take out any pieces that
will do for the stove and put them inside the hut by the
doorway.
"At least I have plenty of wood to see me through the
winter, these small pieces are ideal for lighting the stove

and there is plenty more further down the garden by the fruit trees."

Now they have taken all the rubbish away, the path is clear and easy to walk down and as they stand admiring their work, Jason has a giddy moment and charges up and down it at speed.

"I think he knows that were here to stay don't you?"

"Yes he does."

"Come on let's go and have the soup."

"Lovely."

And with that they clean their shoes, wash their hands and ladle the soup into bowls and sit at the kitchen table to eat. Jo breaks the crusty bread into chunks.

"I will be so glad when all the rubbish is burned and I can think about growing vegetables again."

"Yes I will be too, it's not nice to see the pile of rubbish and everything you have lost in a heap. The soup is delicious."

Afterwards, Anna decides to leave before it gets too dark. She prefers to be back before nightfall. The hut is warm and cosy and Anna feels reluctant to go, but knows she must.

"I'm off. I'll bring eggs, bacon and mushrooms with me in the morning and we can share breakfast if you like."

"Yes that's a lovely idea. I'll see you in the morning then, thanks for helping me again."

"Oh that's fine, bye then."

Anna leaves the hut.

Returning along the path is a much more easier walk than when she had arrived, struggling through the fallen branches and stumbling over the stones and boulders which had been dislodged. Now the path is clear and the boulders and large stones are in a tidy pile in Jo's garden.

She calls off at the supermarket before returning to the campsite, to buy the fresh eggs, bacon and mushrooms and bread she needs to bring with her in the morning.

After Anna leaves, Jo reflects on her decision to leave
Fenton and goes upstairs and lies down on the bed. Part
of her is sad, knowing that she will miss her and their
times spent together and wishes that they had longer to
get to know each other. She looks back at the hours they
have shared and recognises that it has been a sensitive
and gentle space and although they have each been
through trying and painful experiences individually; their
joint connection has been special.

Lying here on the bed, resting her head on the pillow,
she remembers their first meeting of swimming in the
sea. They had been drawn to each other; it was destiny to
meet, on the early dawn of that summer morning.

Without many words, they knew and had felt the impact,
as their two souls bonded and coiled themselves around
their other half.

Jo knows that after reaching out and touching Anna she
felt whole, as if she had been waiting for her. It was a
validation and affirmation of herself as a human being
and yet it demanded and needed nothing from her, the
desire simple, to spend time with Anna's essence and
energy was, is wonderful and in itself undemanding. The
close proximity of her is in itself safe and unremarkable
and yet because of all of this, it is quite extraordinary to
have this shared affinity with each other.

In a non-sexual way, Jo holds Anna in her mind as a soft
cushion and hopes that in future times, they can support
one another and find paths that run a similar course and
swim through the rivers of life together.

Another part of Jo, knows that she can carry Anna with
her and draw from the well where she lives inside of her
and in that respect she will always be there – on tap – to
drink from.

Jo also knows that she is self-sufficient and has lots of
work and plans for the months ahead. And as time itself
has its own mysterious and inimitable way of surprising,
it will soon be Christmas and then spring.

So she looks forward to the days and weeks hence and
lay here not restless, sad or discontent but hopeful and

happy. What is ahead she believes, is filled with opportunity and promise and as her eyelids drop, she falls, fully clothed, into a deep and heavy and dreamless sleep.

Anna has what is left of the evening, to complete the writing she wants to do in Fermanagh House. Then she can spend an hour or so, finishing off the jobs she has left.

Sitting down with a cup of tea she looks forward to meeting up with Jo in the morning.

And the day after that, she would be leaving the coast on the early morning train, to arrive home by lunchtime.

'So where was I?' As she gazes out of the front window, around the campsite everything is still and quiet.

Anna takes a sip of her tea and begins writing on the last few sheets of the A4 paper.

Later putting down her pen, she has finished Fermanagh House.

She is ready now to light the bonfire with Jo. Only a few bits and pieces left to do in the caravan but they wouldn't take up too much of her time.

She has put a couple of things in a bag, to take to Jo's, to burn on the bonfire.

It has grown dark now and the wind is raw and battering against the caravan.

'Well,' Anna thinks as she curls up warm in her bed, 'at least if it doesn't rain and the wind continues, the bonfire will be dried out, when they come to light it tomorrow.'

The following morning after breakfast, Stella offers to drive down to Aubeterre son Dronne, an old medieval town she had visited once before and a place she promised herself she would call at again.

Charles delighted by the idea rallies himself and changes into his navy blue linen pants and short sleeved, sky blue shirt.

"Ready for off then Stell?"

Charles calls across to her as he ties the laces on his shoes, wishing that he had packed a pair of sneakers in his bag. Stella checks her shoulder bag and picks up her jacket and walks towards the door.

"Yes, let's go."

She drives the car slowly, meandering through the tiny hamlets and small villages of the French countryside. She always feels she is on the rooftop of the world here, the vast expanse of miles and miles of open space, green fields and woodlands reaching out as far as her eyes can see, meeting the edge, the blue sky horizon – the roof, the lid of the earth. She loves it.

Charles too, happy settled beside her in his seat, allows himself to appreciate the scenery and fights his urge to fidget and twiddle with the radio – he knows he has to make up to her, so for the moment he stills himself. He is appreciative of the calmness and harmony here with her and reflects that she had been absolutely correct; this trip is just the thing he needs. So he doesn't want to rattle or spoil anything, he is conscious of steering away thoughts that pop up into his mind, choosing to divert them and manages to stave them off.

Turning left towards a small hamlet, Stella spots a sign for a vide-grenier sale and as she drives past she notices the line of parked cars along the grass verge.

"Come on Charles, let's take a look."

She pulls the car into the side of the road and stops.

"It will be a load of bloody junk Stell."

"There are plenty of cars here, it's worth taking a look."

Stella gets out of the car. As they walk along, Charles follows, fighting the urge to say that it will be a ruddy waste of time.

"Oh look at that Charles."

Stella points ahead towards rows of tables filled with bric-a-brac and old vintage furniture and farming tools. There are lots of people milling around taking a look at the stalls. Charles thinks, 'what a load of old rubbish' and says nothing.

Walking along there are people coming towards them, carrying an array of old objects back to their cars. Stella stops at each stall in turn, picking bits and pieces up and reflecting. Charles spots the food and refreshment marquee up ahead and tells her he will go and have a glass of wine whilst she looks around.

Stella loves browsing and wishes she owned a place in France, where she could furnish it with unusual pieces, like the ones here. There are a couple of things she would like to buy, but she knows she won't be able to take them home on the plane. It seems silly not to have a home here when she visits on business and pleasure as much as she does. 'It is something I will have to get around to,' she decides, as she looks lovingly at a bureau, that with a little effort would make a beautiful office desk.

She reaches the end of the road and crosses over, to make her way down the opposite side, her mind works its way around ideas, of where she would like to have her holiday home. Several places come to mind; she likes Ruffec and the village where they are staying, it's lovely she thinks as her eyes fall onto a small object, covered in dust. It appears to be a clay tile with a religious icon set inside it. She asks the stallholder how much it is, "six euros." the man replies.

This seems such a small amount for a lovely thing. She finds her purse and tells him she will take it and offers a €10 note. The man wraps the tile in a sheet of old newspaper and gives her €4 change.

Stella walks away pleased with her purchase and goes in
search of Charles. She spots him chatting, with a wine
glass in his hand, he looks happy and she is pleased.
Charles looks up and their eyes meet, he finishes his
drink and makes his way through the throng of people
towards her.
"Do you fancy a hot dog Charles?"
The smell of the sausages and onions frying on the open
grills makes her feel hungry.
"No thank you."
"I'm going to get one, how about some fries?"
"Ok then."
She buys one hot dog, in a long French baguette and two
packets of French fries. They find a table and sit down;
they share the baguette and eat the fries.
"Good idea Stell."
Charles states as he brushes the crumbs of his shirt and
stands up.
Walking back to the car she shows him the tile and
Charles appears nonplussed.
"That's my girl, where are you going to put it?"
"It's beautiful Charles, I'm going to take it home and
hang it in the living room."
Stella wraps it back up in the paper.

The drive to Aubeterre son Dronne takes them through
tiny villages and by the time they arrive, they have
hardly seen anyone along the way. They park the car in
the centre and call for a coffee before wandering around.
They follow the signpost for the town's attraction - a
monolithic church, carved out of a rock underground.
Stella enters the rock face first.
"I think this place is amazing, don't' you? It always
makes me wonder how long it took and what the people
were like who carved it out of the rock."
"I wonder what went on? I can't imagine it was just
preaching and praying."
They walk up the steps and around the upper floor, along
the narrow corridor with carved out openings. Looking

through these open windows, there is a huge drop to the ground below.

Stella imagines bearded men, wearing long length hooded cloaks, made out of grey woollen cloth with a belt tied around their waists, heads bent, shuffling along the corridors and down below on the ground. It has a weird and peculiar energy, strange and not at all like how she feels when she ventures inside an old French church.

"Well, Stell it's not for me, I'll meet you outside."

Stella looks around to see if there are any other visitors and it appears that they are on their own.

"I'll come too Charles."

She follows him to the entrance door.

They are both glad to be back outside and head for the charming streets of the old town. Pausing outside a chocolate shop, with its display of hand made treats, Stella stops.

"Oh Charles, let's buy some."

Inside the shop, she selects a large box of the delicate chocolates to take home and a handful for them both to eat as they walk. 'Yes Charles,' Stella thinks as they stroll along feeding themselves with the sweets, 'you can be happy and content.' They weave and meander through the quaint cobbled streets looking in the shop windows.

The enamelled sign, sticking out above the doorway of a gift shop, impresses Stella and she peers inside the window and is enchanted by the intricate array of enamelled pieces. Charles watches her; he loves the way she hones in on things that she likes. She is taken by an enamelled brooch; it reminds her of the tile she has bought at the vide-grenier sale. Charles takes her hand and opens the door of the shop, when the artisan appears; he asks to buy the little brooch. Money is never an issue for Charles, he follows his impulses and this is one of them, he wants to buy her this gift and that's that. He takes the golden gift-wrapped box and puts it in his pocket.

Leaving the shop Stella is unsure if the brooch is for her and feels uncomfortable about asking him.

Returning to their parked car they sit down fulfilled, it has been another lovely day; she turns on the engine for their journey back.

Later back at The Argentor, Charles wakes from his sleep and looks around the room to find Stella; she isn't sitting in the seat by the window where she had been reading. Lifting himself up to the edge of the bed, he calls out for her. He assumes that she's gone out when there is no reply. He walks towards the window and looks out into the courtyard below but the tables and chairs have been taken inside and there is no one around. So he sits down on the chair and glances at the book on the floor. He would read the occasional best seller doing its rounds but Stella enjoys psychological and thought provoking novels and reference books.

She's obviously got fed up and taken herself off for a walk.

Charles wonders if she's gone downstairs to the bar to have a drink and debates whether he should go and find her, he wouldn't mind a drink himself.

He opens the wardrobe and looks at the feeble display of clothes, he curses himself for not bringing more changes of shirts and trousers and decides to buy a couple of each when they go out tomorrow.

He opens the top drawer where he has put his underwear and a polo shirt and decides to change into it and then go and look for her. Rifling through his socks and underpants, he catches sight of the gift-wrapped box, as it falls out from between two pairs of boxer shorts. He has forgotten about this little package, which Margaret had left for him. He pulls the edge of the sticky tape and undoes the wrapping paper, revealing, a square black leather box and lifts up the lid. Staring at him from two cufflinks, sitting upon a cushion of red velvet, are the initials G. G. For a moment, he does nothing as his eyes fix on the initials. He blinks, sure that he's misread them

and hopes to find C. H. on the shiny, silver heads when
he looks again. Charles opens his eyes, the initials
remain the same G. G. Snapping back the box lid; he
puts the cufflinks into the drawer and after screwing up
the wrapping paper, throws it in, then slams it shut.
Now he needs a drink.
Bending over, he slips on his shoes and grabs his jacket
and goes downstairs to the bar. Stella is sitting by the
fireplace with a cup of coffee.
"A large whisky." he tells the passing waiter.
Stella looks at him as he sits down, he looks furious.
"I thought I'd let you sleep."
Stella is unsure what has upset him.
"I've just opened my little pressy from Margaret."
"Present?"
"Cufflinks."
"Cufflinks for G. G."
Charles sits in stony silence.
When the waiter puts down his whisky in front of him,
he takes a long drink from the glass.
"What the bloody hells going on?"
"I don't know."
"Join me and have a bloody drink."
Charles demands as he finishes off his drink and orders
another one from the waiter. He has a look of total
dejection about him.
Stella looks about the room; it would be better if she
could get him back upstairs and out of the way before he
makes a scene.
"Let's take a bottle upstairs."
"I don't know what's going on anymore Stell."
Charles is full of self-pity.
"Oh come on Charles, we have come here to have a good
time, so don't spoil it please, let's take a bottle upstairs
to the room and chill out for god's sake."
Charles looks into the bottom of his glass, searching for
answers as he sips his whisky. She waits, hoping the
drink will calm him down; she doesn't want their break
ruined by a drunken session in public. At home and in

private is another thing, but here she feels responsible for
his behaviour.

Charles sits back in his chair now and puts his glass on
the table.

Trying to change the subject, she asks him how the
business deal with his new client in York is going.

"Good, but I'm a bit stuck because he wants to come
across to Fenton for a few days, so I'll have to put him
up in a hotel with all of the flats being let."

"But the one you let to Jo is empty."

"What?"

"I'm sorry Charles I should have told you, she's moved
out, she left me a note to give to you."

Charles calls to the waiter.

"I was trying to keep her sweet, because of the deal I'm
trying to negotiate with Fred at Wood End Farm, he's
thinking of selling up."

Stella listens as he tells her about his ideas for
developing Wood End Farm into holiday homes and how
Jo's land would lend itself to providing an access road to
the beach and a few log cabins.

It sounds a fantastic opportunity, a one off in Fenton and
a brilliant deal if it works out. She wonders how long he
has known about the farm, he has kept this one carefully
to himself. She is puzzled why he hasn't mentioned it,
and is unsure as to what might be Jo's reaction to his
ideas.

Charles orders a bottle of wine and when the waiter
arrives she watches him thank him and order another
whisky. 'Damn you Charles, why don't you ever learn,'
she will have to get him upstairs somehow.

Anna wakes early. It is still dark, so she remains in her warm bed, not wanting to uncover herself to the coldness of the early morning. The campsite is quiet. The following morning she would be leaving and she couldn't return until March when the site reopens. She waits for the dawn to break, when the seagulls fly in from the sea and do crash landings on the top of the caravan.

When she had first stayed and heard the noise of their heavy bodies and then their hard horny feet, scuttling across the top of the caravan, she had been alarmed but now they are another part of her early morning wake up call.

She isn't sure what to expect back in the city. She knows he will sulk to begin with and be grumpy, because of having the children to look after full time but Anna reasons, she can't cut herself in two, no matter what.

She is up to date with all her homeopathic course work and decides to work at it when she returns, so she can gain the pass marks she needs to complete the course. She has to continue to work on the clinical hours but if all her other material is up to date and she passes, she will be able to move on.

There would be no changes in her life in the city, unless she makes them. She has to be the one to change, Anna has become more and more aware of this. The other people in her life, wouldn't change, it is up to her. She is afraid of the thought of change. The prospect daunts her, the most frightening aspect, is that she can do it. She has all the capabilities and capacities to, 'but what?' Anna asks herself. 'It, the it,' started to seep into her head when she began to read up and understand about charkas. Charkas are about energy but behind Anna's dismissal of the concept, is the 'it'.

She has begun to understand that she isn't grounded in her base, her root chakra, but trapped in it, she realises that she has given up her physical self, to live within the safety of her head.

As Anna gathers the food for breakfast, she wonders about Jo and the bonfire.

Anna isn't surprised when she puts the broken clock and the 'Fermanagh House' blue note book, in her bag to take with her. The morning is dry and crisp and as she approaches the hut she begins to feel hungry. She has only had a pot of tea before leaving the caravan. The breakfast with Jo will be just the thing.

Jason's barking wakes Jo from sleep and groggily she opens her eyes to the day. Her head is full of cotton wool and it takes her awhile to register her whereabouts.
"OK Jase."
Jo shouts down to him at the bottom of the stairs as he continues to bark. She is surprised at being fully clothed and gets up from the bed and goes downstairs. Jason continues barking as she walks across and opens the door to find Anna standing and then her befuddled brain remembers.
"Hi come in, what time is it?"
"It's about 9 o'clock am I too early?"
"No you're ok, I've slept in."
"I've brought bacon and eggs and stuff for breakfast."
"Great, that's lovely, I'll just put a few logs onto the stove to get it going again, and then we can cook and make tea?"
"It's so much better walking down the path now that we have cleared it."
Jason whines for his food.
"Just a minute Jase and I'll get your breakfast."
Jo puts three logs into the stove and opens the air vent and fills the kettle and puts it on the top.
"It seems sad to be leaving – I'm going to miss this."
Jo makes Jason's breakfast and puts it on the floor for him.
"Yes so will I, we will have to have a nice day to day, I will be glad when I have some soft chairs to sit on, I

ended up going to bed after you left yesterday and fell asleep."

"You could always go into Thornby and have a look at the furniture shops there."

"Yes I might do that if I can't find any in Fenton."

Anna hands over the bag containing the bacon, eggs and a loaf of bread. Jo takes the frying pan from the hook on the wall and places it on top of the stove to heat up.

"I'll just go to the loo, if you wouldn't mind making a pot of tea."

"Sure I'll do that."

Anna looks about the room. It is a home again for all its sparseness. She can sense this. It has something to do with intention and Jo's presence, that's why she can feel the hut returning to itself. It is grounded, rooted and knows its purpose. Anna begins to understand now, how being trapped in the base chakra, isn't like being rooted in it. It isn't the same. It isn't about getting on, doing well, and bettering yourself in the meteoric or material sense. It has nothing to do with external influences; rather it is what comes from within. It is from her brain, her mind, that isn't grounded. It is Anna who is unbalanced, not her base or roots or meteoric risings. She has plucked a little of so many ideologies and tried to blend them together to make sense or herself and her place in the world. She believed, if she could perform, do what was expected from her and gain approval, then she would win and be successful and fit in. She understands now that she has done everything to prove herself and in the final analysis she has turned herself off, in order to live the lie.

Outside it is cold and the morning hits Jo full on, as she makes her way round the back of the hut to the toilet. Inside she pulls the door to and shivers as she sits on the wooden seat. She makes a mental note to find a way of making this place warmer and brighten it up with coloured paint.

Jo returns to Anna who is pouring out the boiling water into the teapot and Jo washes her hands under the cold tap.

"I'm going to have to sort something out for the toilet, it's freezing in there and it will get colder through the winter, I need to insulate it and paint it."

Anna stirs the teabags in the pot.

"Its been really cold using the toilet block on the caravan site."

"I might try sticking some insulation foam on the walls and ceiling to make it warmer. I'll have to go and have a look and see what they have at the DIY shop."

"Shall I put the bacon on, whilst you pour out the tea?"

"Yes, there's eggs and mushrooms too."

Anna finds two mugs and milk to make tea. Whilst the bacon sizzles in the pan, they chat together about Jo's ideas for making the hut warmer and Jo pours out two glasses of orange juice and gets the plates and cutlery ready for the breakfast. "How do you like your bacon?"

"As it comes." 'Of course you do,' Anna tells herself.

"And your egg?"

"Sunny side up please."

Jo pushes the crisp bacon and mushrooms to the side of the pan and cracks two eggs to fry. When they are both done she shares it onto the plates. She feels ravenous now and can't wait to dip a slice of bread into the egg and start eating. The breakfast is lovely and tasty and they soon devour the lot with slices of bread.

"Would you mind if I cook Jason an egg?"

"No of course you can, keep the rest anyway because I won't need them now."

Jo cracks an egg into the pan and turns if over to cook the other side and then puts it into Jason's dish.

"You'll have to wait Jase, until it cools."

Anna fills the kettle to wash the pots and make another pot of tea.

"That was lovely, thank you."

"Yes I enjoyed it too."

Jo draws back the curtains and looks outside at the pile
of rubbish waiting to be burnt.

"We are lucky that it has stayed dry for the fire."

"Yes it will be good to light it and get rid of your stuff
and then you can start afresh and forget about the flood."

"It's strange but now that I'm back here it feels like it
never happened, I know that my chair and rugs and
books have gone, but it is like remembering a bad
dream."

"Well that's good if you can see it that way, when do
you want to light it?"

"I'll just wash the pots first and then we can do it, do you
still fancy jacket potatoes for lunch?"

"Yes that will be nice, I've brought a bottle of red wine
to share."

Together they clear the table and wash the dishes and
then Jo scrubs two large potatoes and wraps them in foil
to bake in the bonfire.

"I've got a tin of baked beans and sausages to go with
the jacket potatoes."

"Lovely."

Jason wolfs his egg and licks his dish and walks away
and then returns to lick it all over again.

"Right then, matches."

Jo takes a box of matches and an old newspaper and they
go outside. Jason scurries off down the garden as they
take the sheets of paper and knot them and place them at
the edge of the pile. Jo strikes a match and lights a
corner of the paper. It soon flares up and they add tiny
twigs to begin with, before adding larger sticks so that it
doesn't go out. The fire billows out puffs of smoke,
when the flames lick the damper bits of wood and they
pull back, hoping that there is enough red-hot tinder
underneath to catch the pieces on top. It is a slow process
of creating a hot furnace and adding more of the bonfire
pile, taking care that this doesn't put out the fire beneath.
When they are confident that the bonfire is burning
properly, Jo returns for the potatoes and pushes them
inside the bonfire.

"I've put the kettle on again."

"We could bake some apples for pudding."

"Good idea, I'll go and find two big cooking apples and see what Jason is up to."

Jo walks down the garden to the fruit trees. Jason is sniffing around the bottom of the garden near the wall and comes running when he sees her. She selects two large apples hanging from the tree and takes them back to the hut to wash and wrap them in foil. Anna is in the kitchen pouring out two mugs of tea.

"Look at these they're lovely, I'll take the cores out and fill them with sultanas, brown sugar and nuts."

Jo washes the apples at the sink.

"They're massive."

Anna picks up her mug of tea and takes a sip. Jo removes the cores and squashes inside the fruit, sugar and nuts and wraps them in foil.

Returning outside, they tend the fire and place the apples inside the hot embers and sip their tea. After a while of watching the fire in silence, Anna takes the empty mugs inside and comes back with a bag in her hand.

"I've brought something's to burn on the bonfire."

Anna removes a blue book and a clock from a carrier bag.

"What is it?"

"It's a book that I have written called Fermanagh House, I've just finished it."

"Why do you want to burn it?"

"Because I wanted to write a beautiful book, about a woman who I wanted to be, but I ended up writing about who I am, instead of who I would like to be. A woman who would live her life for herself, be the woman that I only wish that I could be, only she didn't, she couldn't, she was just the same as I am really."

Anna has a look of sadness on her face.

"But I don't understand, how can you burn something that you have written."

"Because I don't want to be that person in the book, I don't want to be reminded of her, I want something different for myself, and I don't want another version of me by keeping the book, so I want to burn it, today is a good time to do it. I want to live my life, not give it away free, because I feel I don't have any value or worth or don't deserve it. I don't want to write about who I've been. I want to be myself, who I actually am, I understand now."

"It seems almost like a write of passage, as though by burning it, you are moving into a different place of being with yourself."

"Yes it does, it is a way of moving forward, acknowledging what I don't want for myself and hopefully then I can start the journey to what I do want."

"And the clock?"

"Time, it's for all the time in my life that I've wasted not being me."

"Good."

"I want to try and be me, not become me, I've spent so long doing that."

"I think this calls for a celebration, how about we have a glass of wine?"

"I've brought a bottle with me, I'll go and get it."

"It's ok, I have a bottle in the kitchen."

"No I'll open mine, save yours for later."

Anna disappears inside.

Jo stands and looks into the heat of the fire and reflects on what Anna has just told her. She thinks Anna seems full of self-realization and knows where she wants to go and what she needs to do. Anna comes back with the wine and two glasses, she hands one over to Jo.

"Are you sure about burning the book?"

"Yes it is a good thing for me to do, a necessary thing to do."

Anna opens the bottle and pours out the wine and stares intensely into the fire, deep in thought.

"Cheers Anna to you."

They clink their glasses together.

"Cheers Jo thanks."

Anna places her wine glass onto the ground and flicks
through the hand written pages of the blue book and
kisses the front cover and then without hesitation flings
it into the red-hot flames and picks up her glass.
They both watch as the book quickly catches alight and
the blue cover, curls into dark brown ash and then
flutters and flies off and the white pages, quickly wrinkle
and burn and blow away. Soon the book is gone and all
that is left are a few grey pieces that lift and drop back
into the fire.
"Wow, I've done it, I didn't think I would be able to, it
wasn't that bad either."
Anna drops the clock onto the red-hot flames and
continues staring into the fire. The clock still at dawn
melts and drops down through the blazing flames – gone,
as if it had never existed, like time itself.
"To you Anna, your future, whatever you want it to be."
Jo salutes Anna with her glass.
"Thanks and all the best to you too, I hope you are safe
and happy here."

Standing back from the heat of the bonfire, they watch as
the flames rise up, higher into the sky. Beyond the
bonfire and the hut, the tide turns and the sea draws back
from the shore as it returns into itself.
Sitting down on the dry ground, away from the heat of
the fire, they drink their wine in silence. After a length of
time that has no measure, Jo wants to share with Anna
something that she would like to do.
"I want to write about my past, it was something that I
decided when I left the flat. I have all of my journals
about my life before I came here to the coast and I want
to put them into a book."
"Do it Jo, you must if you feel that you need to."
"I will, when you have gone, it is something that I can do
during the winter, when I can't work outside, it will be
nice to buy a comfy armchair and sit writing away in
front of the stove."
"It sounds a lovely idea."

"I hope you can make your life how you want to live it for yourself Anna."

"It feels like it's a long journey that I have only just started."

"It doesn't matter how long the journey, what matters is that it is your journey for you and not for others and what they want it to be."

"I know and that is the hardest thing to be able to do, to live my life for me and not for others."

Anna sighs.

"I will support you in any way I can."

"Thanks Jo, thank you that's kind."

Silence settles upon them once again, they separate into their different worlds and then later they decide upon testing the potatoes for lunch. Jo goes and gets a fork and inserts it into the foil and it slides in easily.

"They're done, I will go and get the beans and fetch the sausages, we can cook them on the bonfire."

Jo returns with the sausages and long skewers and the beans and a pan and a couple of plates. They hold the skewered sausages, over the red-hot coals until they're well cooked and remembering the beans, heat them up in the pan. The potatoes are hearty, and the skins have burnt black in places and with salt and butter they are delicious and as a few grey ashes, float across from the fire and land on our plates, they both eat some of the chard remains of Fermanagh House. As they digest these ashen words between them, they each recognise as women, the impact of their message and the context for themselves and for all women, how necessary it is to live out their own lives. In the fanning of the fire and the scattering of the ashes, they hold up their glasses, in recognition of a rebirth of self and the turning of the tides.

Standing, a distance away, he forces the letter back down into his pocket. For now he will have to leave it.

With his back leaning against a tree he watches her. She is with the other woman. The bitches are standing close together now, as they watch the fire blaze, too close, too intimately close.

He continues to watch, the rage surges through him and he wants to split them into two and have the pair of them, to teach them.

He watches them sip their red wine, smiling into each other's faces, there is little he can do, so he pulls the hood from over his head and feels the coldness across his face, as it becomes exposed to the chill of the autumn air.

His fingers move down slowly to his zip as he continues to watch her and remember what she had felt like and imagine again what it was like when she had been beneath him.

When he has finished, he gives them a final look before turning away quietly and retracing his footsteps back along the path.

Another time he promises her, he would wait for another time when she is alone.

As the train leaves Fenton station, Anna settles back in her seat. She has said her good byes. Jo has Anna's phone number and Anna has Jo's post box address for Wood End Farm but still she is sad that it will be a while before they meet up again.

It has been an odd summer and early autumn and a part of Anna wants to stay in Fenton but the other half wants to be at home. She has spent most of her life trapped or caught within the spell of time. Always needing to be in more places, than her body would allow. Having said this, Anna knows that if she sliced herself into two parts, there would still not be enough of her.

Does she have loose boundaries, as her supervisor thinks? She probably does. The thing is, she is just going to do one more thing and then that is it, done, finished, but every time she reaches the end of one 'thing' another 'thing' needed to be done. So it never ends, or stops and she is trapped in the middle of time's span. So what is it that you really want? 'I don't know, I don't know what I really want.'

She wanted children, she loves her children and wants to see them grow and become adults. Grandchildren? Yes, that is one of the aspects of being a mother, but she also knows that her children in themselves are more than enough for her. So what else? 'Peace, I want to stop chasing around, on this endless treadmill and I want to step off it and sit quietly beneath the shade of a tree and just be still for a while and have space inside myself to live life. To experience the joy and mystery of ordinary day-to-day life, with no strings attached. No more of the next and the next and the next.' That pursuit has carried Anna along and she has ended up becoming a woman who performs tasks to prove things, to whom? To everyone except perhaps her self.

She has done the things that matter deeply and will continue to do those things, but now she needs time and space to discover and feel the existence of her self. No more hoops.

She has caught up with herself, but now even that sounds
sceptical and crass, like some demented sad woman.
Anna knows she isn't, but it feels like who she is.
Taking a few sips from her bottle of water and screwing
the cap back on, she looks out of the window. This bit of
her life is free, I don't have to do anything, or be
anything, or have to do things; I just have to be me
sitting on a train. This is simple. It feels good. Time to
stop chasing around, in the futile endless circles. This is
because you're weary and tired, I know I am, I'm worn
out. It's better to wear away than rust and she
immediately stops herself from finishing the rubbish she
is about to say. I'm jaded and faded around the edges
and I need to put my houses in order and stop running.
Yes Anna acknowledges and then I want to decide what
to do with my life.

Another year and she would be a qualified homeopath.
She knows she wants to be a homeopath doesn't she? It
is a good thing to be, a fine thing, and honourable thing,
helping people on their journey in life. When she's
finished the course, it will have taken her nearly five
years and then one more year, working towards
registration. She doesn't care at the moment about her
homeopathic crusade. She'd earned her G.C.S.E's and a
degree, and had wanted to round it off by gaining a
professional qualification. As a homeopath she would be
a well educated woman, with a professional, caring,
recognised qualification to finish things off, so why isn't
she whooping with delight and glee at her really
remarkable achievements? All done off her own back.
She'd gone from a child who had left school at fifteen,
failing the eleven plus, to a woman who held a degree
and a second masters degree, as a registered, qualified
homeopath, so why aren't bells ringing? Anna feels
dead inside herself. Numb, from keeping herself
disconnected, separated, physically as well as mentally
and emotionally. She doesn't connect anymore, or
register with herself. Somehow, somewhere, she has lost

her self. She has knowingly cut herself in two, in order to function and survive. 'You're burnt out,' Anna eventually decides. 'Nothing reaches you anymore.'

She gazes out of the train window, 'I have to somehow go back and find myself; it all has to stop, until I can find me. I don't want to live in this dead, dream world, anymore, I want to come back and live inside myself and start again. She feels like a broken doll, damaged and unwanted. 'Is this what happens when you're finished with? What's it all been about? A journey of discovery, of finding out about myself! Bollocks, you haven't found yourself; you've lost yourself trying to be someone else.' Anna closes her eyes and rests against the headrest of the train seat. She feels she's run a very long way and realises she's run around in a circle and is back in the same place where she started, but ripped in two by the process.
She had thought, that if she founded her family, became educated and held a professional, respected, qualification she'd cracked it. Only she hasn't. Are all these things what she wants, or are they what she thought she wanted, what she feels she 'should' want, to be, to become. Putting it intellectually, does acquiring the correct philosophical prescriptions and remedy, find fulfilment within her? 'No,' Anna has to admit, 'it doesn't.' Then why? Because I'm not happy, inside I'm not happy. So Anna finds the loose thread of connections, 'what is happiness? To 'feel' happiness, not to think or strive for it, but to feel it.'

The drive, the push to achieve and justify and prove had taken over, the means had become more important than the end. To do it, to be aware that she could, had become Anna's benchmark and somewhere along that road she had got lost and in the end stopped being. She had given herself up, to justify and to prove to herself and others that she could. Why? Because she had felt worthless and inadequate, not good enough and not up to scratch, and now? It is all a game of hoops and like a fool she still isn't happy inside and the hoops are not enough to prove herself worthy.

It makes her shake her head sometimes, when people speak to her the way they do and she would reply simply but succinctly and then watch as their expression turned from one of patronising condescension, to become sharp and clear and to the point like hers. When she wants, she can be as sharp as a knife but she could also disarm people, with her comfortable open smile and soft, blue grey, eyes but mostly she prefers to remain locked up inside herself, safe and guarded, hidden from everyone. He had helped to feed her insecurity, because of his own and she had believed him.

Writing in the blue note book, she had hoped to create a strong, prototype, functioning version of herself, but it hadn't turned out like that. Her character had turned out running around and being what others wanted her to be, fitting into their spaces, not be who Anna wanted her to be. This was inevitable, but she had not seen that. She ended up writing herself into Fermanagh House, because that's all she knew. Bit by bit, piece by piece, she had begun to filter through into the book, until it reached the point where Anna recognised her own self and ended it. Anna had wanted to re write Fermanagh House, create a second version with a different ending, where her character gained control over her life and where the patriarchs didn't rule, but how could she? How could she imagine something, which she knows nothing about?

She had tried to create a character, who was strong and determined and always lived her life in her own focused way, where people respected and accepted her, but it had collapsed into the messy, bodice ripping trash, which mirrored the emotional limitations of inner landscapes. Anna's reality inside her mind, for all her intellectually cleverness, is still ruled by patriarchs, because that is all she knows about. She can't imagine being free, being good enough, or really being anyone else but herself.

It is about balance and proportion and Anna is neither balanced, or in proportion. Her overcompensation of her intellect doesn't go beyond the surface of her brain. Inside her heart, she is a much different woman from the one in her head. If the two parts joined, then great things perhaps could be achieved, but as things are, they haven't, not yet anyhow.

The train stops in Thornby, before doubling back upon itself and continuing the journey. Anna looks around at the familiar station platforms, she had walked up and down with Jo, not so long ago and now she is going back to her life, whilst Jo gets on with hers in Fenton. She would be continuing now, with the enormous picture of the map she had begun of the town. Jo has found a new lease of life with her art, since she moved to the flat and now would continue doing the paintings and much more. Anna is glad for her.

For the moment Mark is stable and safe and for now this is the best that she can hope for. At this time in her life she isn't ready to rewrite Fermanagh House. She can't write the second version, where her character finds whatever it takes to be confident and self possessed. Anna doesn't feel that sense of certainty, so she is unable to write about it. So no second version, perhaps there never will be. When she had taken the book to burn on the bonfire, once the deed had been done, the moment had passed. She had really wanted to put her past on the bonfire and put it all behind her, but she knows it isn't finished yet. Her past is tied into who and what she is now. She couldn't burn it and pretend it is over and done with, because it haunts her as she lives in the present. Anna senses that when it is ready, her past will take its own leave and that will be the right time for it to go.

The train travels forwards and she makes the decision that she will take charge of her own life and world, in the only way she knows how. Her way, her own way and not how she thinks others will approve. This life, what is left of it, belongs to her. She will mould her destiny from now on. It wouldn't be about how it ought, or ought not to be, but about how she wants it to be. She wouldn't jump through any more hoops. She would complete her homeopathic course and would then work towards registration but nothing else. She will then make a decision when she qualifies, if she intends to practise but the decision will be hers. When she has finished the course, she wants to take time away from study. And whilst she works towards registration, she will spend time on herself and her family. Put back time into her life and children, that she has missed, since she began the course. She is sure that, for at least six months, or a year, she will do that. 'Right, that's a beginning and I'm decided upon that.'

Anna takes another drink from her water bottle. 'Good, I have begun to start something positive. I need to remain focused, on what I feel is right for me and not become side tracked; I need to tighten up my boundaries.'

As the train pulls into York, Anna feels excited, that in around an hour she will be back in the city and soon home to her children. She feels weary with self-analysis, basically she's analysed herself to death and yet there always seems to be more. 'That's because people keep on growing and developing and moving on.' This is probably true.

As a young girl she was awkward, innocent and gullible too. She remembers how, but not when, she had learnt to switch off. It was almost a process of desensitisation. Everything had been so vivid and extreme when she was younger, almost larger than life, like a dream. Her world had been crowded with people, such a large family and also her mam's massive, extensive, extended family. Now they are all gone, dead or dispersed. To see one or two of them is a rarity. That strong matriarchal group of women, that she spent her early years with, no longer exists. All finished. That shy, simple, innocent girl would not recognise her now.

Gazing out through the window, Anna isn't sure anymore, what she's really achieved or gained. The things which people put high stall by, don't move or impress her anymore. She has acquired them all and yet in truth, she knows that in the final analysis, they are not what really matter. Without the knowledge she has acquired, she would not have thought such thoughts, or grasped such concepts, or understood their undercurrents and meaning for herself. She accepts and understands and acknowledges the truth of this. 'You could go for a masters or a PHD,' Anna muses, but the voice inside her head says 'no, no more.' That would be just another layer, another target, and then what? What then when you've gained your masters and your PHD. Tell me where your degree certificate is now? Somewhere I expect! OK I need to look at this from a different angle, a new perspective. Forget doing and achieving, or acquiring, think on another level.
I have to try to stand still, to stop existing on the back foot. Why does it feel so scary not to be doing something? Because she wouldn't be able to run away from herself, it would mean she has to look at herself and she can't, either figuratively or literally. Like John Doherty in Fermanagh House, she couldn't look straight at him, or at herself, or at any one else if she is honest.

She usually looks at people when they are thinking about themselves and consequently their attention isn't focused on her, she can manage that. One-way relationships keep her safe; she can remain free from herself, whilst still being a part of the human race and not a hermit, or a recluse. What she has done is shut off, close down, because she thinks and feels deeply but knows if these two aspects of herself met it would be too much.

If Anna used her mind, her intellect, to communicate with her feelings, not the surface ones but those, which lay beneath the surface it would break her heart and she wouldn't be able to cope.

So Anna decides as she struggles with the weight of the entire luggage she has brought back from Fenton, that's what I have to do. Ask my heart and brain to have a conversation. We already have, when? When my heart told my brain that it wasn't happy. 'Oh, yes,' Anna thinks, as she climbs aboard the bus, dragging her luggage on with her, hoping she's left the conversation and analysis behind her, at the bus stop.

Awaking from his heavy session with Abb's, Mark
opens his eyes and draws in a breath. He can smell the
fresh, laundered sheets on Abby's parent's bed and
stretches out his legs, enjoying the comfort of it. He feels
and smells the wealth in the room it is loaded.
He decides not to wake her up now for more sex, so he
slides out of bed and leaves her sleeping. It is still dark,
so Mark guesses it must be early. He takes his trousers
and finds the bedroom door and goes across the landing
and downstairs.
The house is warm with the central heating and walking
downstairs naked, he feels light headed with having the
freedom of the house.
In the flats and digs and caravans he lives in, it is damp
and cold and he would sleep in his clothes and wake up
frozen to another day, cramped and hunched and rigid
with it, until he warmed up.
Now enveloped in this sensuality of warmth and comfort
and striding through this large open space, where he can
be free to be himself, he stops at the bottom of the stairs
and debates as to which room he will go into, from the
large hall.
He is like a child now, excited about which one to
choose. In the end he decides to go in for the kill. He
will find Charles's study and see what the tosser does.
After opening doors, he eventually finds the one, which
leads into the study; he halts momentarily, as the smell
of Charles meets him.
For a second he stands on the threshold unsure, but then
finds the light switch, he turns it on and walks inside. 'It
certainly is something,' Mark tells himself, as he walks
towards Charles's desk.
On his route to the desk, Mark spots the bottles of spirits
and crystal decanters arranged on a side table. Diverting
his direction, he lifts a bottle of southern comfort and
pours himself a half glass and continues his journey to
the desk.
Sitting in Charles's swivel chair, Mark holds up his
glass.

"Cheers mate."

He says into the air and sits back contented, as the warm, strong liquid, hits the back of his throat and slips down his guts warming him and lighting up the vast, empty space inside him with measured satisfaction. Mark shudders with pleasure at the strength of the drink. Putting the glass down, he looks around the room as he swivels in the chair. Like the master bedroom, it has the heavy hand of a man's touch. The dark, oak panels, that surround the walls and the door and the heavy bookcases are oppressive and their weight makes Mark take a deep breath. The room is suffocating but he hasn't finished with it yet.

Taking a smaller sip of his drink this time, he begins to open the drawers of the desk. They glide out quietly and smoothly on their expensive runners. Mark doesn't see much in the drawers that interest him but there is a remote control on the desk. 'Ok, where there is a remote control, there is a telly, so where's yours Charlie boy?' Standing up, Mark looks around the room to find where Charles has his TV. It isn't visible. There are books, rows upon rows of them and two, large leather armchairs and a filing cabinet. This looks interesting. Going to it, Mark decides to see if the drawers open. 'No,' he pulls each one; the bastard's locked them. Doesn't trust his family obviously, or he's got something he doesn't want them to see.

Mark knows that Charles would carry the key for the file with him but he also knows that somewhere there will be a spare one hidden for safekeeping. 'So Charlie boy, where do you keep it eh?' Looking around the room again he sees the large potted plants. Feeling inside and around them, he is disappointed not to find the key. His mother used to hide things in her potted plants and he could always find what she hid. It became a challenge, a game. The more things she tried to hide from him, the bigger the buzz he got from finding them.

Again Mark scans Charles's study. 'Got you,' he walks up to the ornate stone and oak fireplace and kneels down in front of it. He lifts the heavy brass fender and feels each side to check for the key. 'Fuck it,' he says, as he begins to let the fender down back into its place. As the fender touches the large stone slabs on the hearth, he notices a crack in one of the pieces of stone. Easing up the fender again, Mark looks at the small chip in the stone. As he rests the heavy fender up on his knee, he prises his fingers under the cracked piece of stone – it moves – 'Bingo.' Mark smiles as he picks up the key and returns the chip and fender back into their places.

Standing up and holding the key out in front of him Mark smiles, he smiles a lot. He needs a fag. Normally he would have just rolled one and lit up where he is but he decides he needs to be a little bit careful.

Picking up his trousers, he puts the key safely inside his pocket.

Hearing Abby moving about, he finishes his drink and turns off the light and leaves Charles's study. 'In a bit mate,' Mark tells himself.

The filing cabinet would keep – Abb's and a fag wouldn't.

In the kitchen Mark slips on his trousers and begins making his roll up. Lighting it, he sits down on one of the high breakfast bar stools to have his smoke and wait for her. He feels content and strokes his pocket, the key is safe, he glides his hand across to the inside of his leg in anticipation for Abb's.

She walks into the kitchen and smiles at him.

"Hiya."

She looks sleepy eyed.

Mark finishes his smoke and puts it out in the saucer in front of him.

"Hiya."

Abby puts her arms around him and kisses him, as she does so he slips his hands underneath her top and grabs hold of her breasts in his hands and pulls at her nipples and lets them go. She smiles as he guides her hands down to his crotch, to find him ready and waiting to have another quickie. Mark can do so many quickies; he

amazes Abby. As he pushes down his pants, she lifts up
her top ready to climb up on him for a shag, before they
have breakfast.

"No, no."
Mark tells her, as she begins getting eggs and
mushrooms from the fridge.
"Too early for me, just juice please."
"Orange?"
"Yea."
Mark rolls himself another smoke. Later he intends to go
out and buy some more backy. He'll have to be careful,
he doesn't want to walk into his mother, she'll go loopy
if she sees him and Abb's together, after he'd told her he
was moving away down the coast. He had intended to
but how could he give up Abb's offer of spending a
couple of nights at her house, whilst both her parents are
away. He can go back down the coast in a day or two, no
problems. He might get a couple of quid off Abb's too,
before he leaves. She is an easy touch and can afford it.
She is enjoying herself too and is getting a good deal
from him.
It's as well he can keep up with her; she is dirty and
greedy and can't get enough of him – which suits Mark
for now. He knows he can perform to order, no
problems, except when he is stoned but then if she still
wants more, she takes matters into her own hands and
still has what she wants. It works for both of them. When
he moves along the coast there will be more girls. There
are always more, they always want the same, always
wanting him to want them, to fuck them, for them to feel
good. Mark knows he makes girls feel good but
sometimes they bored him, pissed him off but there are
benefits as well, so he takes what's on offer.

He had once thought a lot about a girl. A girl he hadn't
even touched. She had meant more to him, than all the
other girls he'd ever had. He knew he had lost her,
because she wouldn't become what he had needed her to

be – to be a part of him. He had wanted her to be absorbed by him, she had not allowed him to consume her and in the end he had gone wild with rage at her rejection of his totality and it had ended. Now he gives girls what they want and takes what he can in return. He never gives himself anymore; he had begun to close that down.

"Let's go into town Abb's."
"What, like this?"
They both go upstairs and return into her parent's room. The bed is huge, king size, the sheets are silk and the bed ends oak. They'd have a bath together Abby tells Mark.
"Yea, whatever."
"You stink."
"Fuck off, bitch."
Mark pulls Abby down onto the floor. Taking off his trousers, he pulls up her top and she squeals with delight at the prospect of him fucking her again.
"Where do I stink then?"
Mark asks sucking hard on Abb's tits.
"Come on, tell me bitch."
"Your dick."
Abby says laughing.
Mark kneels in front of her.
"You mean this?"
He holds up his hard dick in front of her and she opens her mouth and licks her lips and opens her legs even wider.
"Yes, yes I mean that."

Lunch at the Sailor's Arms, Abb's treat, goes down well for Mark. He's forgotten about buying more backy and keeping a low profile from his mother. He's had four pints and doesn't give a fuck. Everyone in the pub is happy and Abb's has bought cigarettes from the landlord, which he now keeps in his storeroom since the smoking ban.

Life is good as they climb back up to The Manor and undress to finish off another session before resting and sleeping. Mark sleeps as Abby showers.

Massaging the shower gel into her breasts, she feels full of herself and her sexuality. Abby knows that Mark isn't the right man for her but he knows how to really fuck her and make every inch of her body feel alive and on fire. He satisfies her body completely and she likes him. There would never be any way that they would be allowed to take things further but Abby needs this single minded determination of hedonistic pleasure which he gives her. The boys she knows pale into insignificance in comparison to Mark. He is so alive, so wild and on fire. He is burning with energy and life and Abby wants it from him.

Tomorrow night they are going down to Thornby to an all night party, so Mark will be on a roll there and she wouldn't see much of him, except for the odd time when they would be able to get together and he would back her into a corner, or against a wall to have a quick shag. She looks forward to those moments when the party is in full swing and he would grab her from wherever she is and as she opens her legs, he is inside like a dog on a bitch in heat. And she loves it and wants it. She wouldn't wear knickers or trousers for the party, just one of her long skirts, to make things easier. Abby isn't sure how many other girls he's had but she has seen him a few times sneak off with different girls. When she could she would follow him and hide, as he takes the other girls and grabs their breasts. She would watch excited, seeing him perform, wanting to go up to him so he could have her too but she knew he wouldn't like it. She accepts and enjoys Mark's infidelities.

Abby steps out of the shower and dries herself. She feels liberated by her naked body, as she moves about unfettered by the confines of clothing. She decides to make them a snack and have booze and then they can spend the rest of their day in bed.

How would she manage when he has gone and her life returns to normal with her mother and Charles back? How could she focus on even the thoughts of study, when she knows her body would ache for him and this feeling, which devours her is never enough, the more she gets, the more she wants, until she is full and her desire is slated, only to be rekindled again, time after time. What her parents are up to, she doesn't know or care. It is just Mark and her that is enough for now.

After their food, drink and sex they rest.

Mark hasn't drunk as much as usual, when free booze is on offer but he has a reason for staying sober and the booze he will get later anyway. It has grown dark as Mark listens to her sleeping, the sea is wild and he can hear it roaring and crashing against the rocks. It is a wild, cold night and as Mark gets out of bed he waits to make sure Abb's is settled down for the night. He has made sure she has drunk enough to make her sleep. She can't take that much alcohol, so Mark is satisfied she will remain in bed and sleep. She might wake during the early hours but he will be back in bed by then, so he is ok for a bit.

Pulling on his trousers and taking his t-shirt with him, he makes his way back down stairs and into Charles's study. After turning on the light, he immediately takes the key from his pocket and goes towards the filing cabinet. The key fits the lock and turns perfectly.

'Yes,' one by one the file drawers slide open, papers, piles and piles of papers and A4 files, which mean little to Mark. There has to be something quick and easy and simple he can take. The dirty old bastard has a black leather wallet, half filled with unmarked DVD's. He takes the wallet into the large sitting room and turns on the TV and DVD recorder. Carefully and keeping them in order, Mark loads the DVD's in and watches with the volume turned down low. Charles's little collection of home movies. They are mostly pornographic, tame really, nothing in particular, nothing which either entertain or impress Mark. There are a couple with

women, that if he had time he might have watched.
Returning the DVD's back in their case, Mark decides to
try one more, before returning them back into the file.
As the DVD plays Mark actually sits down on the floor,
he realises he is watching a souvenir, of an adult
adventure fantasy. The DVD is called 'Adult Baby Day
Mementoes' – Mark nearly chokes when he sees a man
sitting in a big nappy, with a frilly bib wrapped around
his neck and a giant dummy stuck in his mouth. On his
head there is a frilly hat too. Mark laughs.
"What the fuck?"
And then he stops laughing and his stomach turns over.
"Fucking hell!"
Mark gasps, it can't be. Mark gets up and sits on the sofa
carefully now, as he continues to watch the big baby's
day. A large breasted woman is attending to 'baby' and
taking out the baby's dummy and then she let's the baby
suck on her nipples. Mark's eyes widen as baby
continues his functions of having his nappy changed and
his bottom washed. "Fucking hell," he watches the
woman who is dressed in a nurse's uniform, taking
cream from a jar and massaging it around Charles's limp
dick. As Charles sucks harder on the nurse's nipple,
Mark is shocked by his little dick. Afterwards she sits
him on a potty and feeds him in a huge high chair and
then rocks the 'baby' in an enormous pram.
"Fucking hell!"
Mark repeats.
"What the fuck?"
Mark takes the DVD out of the machine but doesn't put
it back into the wallet. He zips up the leather wallet and
returns it to the file and locks all the drawers. Checking
around the study Mark is satisfied it is all in order –
Abb's had washed the glass he'd used earlier and had
returned it to her father's drinks table.
Returning into the sitting room he switches off the telly
and finds a plastic wallet to put the DVD into. Turning
off the light, he closes the room door and gets two,
empty carrier bags from the kitchen cupboard. Putting

the DVD inside one and then the other, before wrapping
it up carefully and sellotaping it. He turns off the alarm
and unlocks the back door and slips on his trainers.
Pulling the door to, Mark pockets the keys and runs
across the damp cold grass until he reaches the footpath,
which leads to his mam's caravan site.
"Don't be in mam."
Mark keeps repeating to himself.
"Yes."
Mark is euphoric when he reaches the caravan and sees
the slop bucket gone and the steps removed – she's gone,
locked up for the winter. He puts his hand underneath
the flagstone, where his mother places the steps and
finds the spare caravan keys. Opening the door he climbs
up and into the caravan. He is shaking with excitement
and fear. What he has in the plastic carrier bags would
make him rich he knows that. He also knows Charles
and if he doesn't work it out properly, he would have
him killed. The big baby in the DVD is Charles, and
what he can do now makes him feel sick, but also
absolutely triumphant. Lifting the mattress from the bed
in the kitchen, Mark pushes the DVD to the back of it.
"This'll make us rich mam."
Mark says as he catches his breath and jumps down, out
of the caravan. Locking the door, Mark returns the keys
to their hiding place. Everything is quiet and in order.
Mark's heart races as he runs back to The Manor House
and Abb's and the big warm bed and a fucking big, big
drink of southern comfort. Life is good and getting
better, an awful lot better.

Part 5

FESTIVITIES

Outside the rain is lashing hard against the hut, the sky is heavy and grey and Jo decides to remain inside for the day. The stove is burning fierce and hot and she looks around for something to do. There are cushions to make, using the thick curtain that she found at the charity shop, it is a vintage piece of fabric, with deep, rich autumn colours and she should be able to get four out of it. She brushes her hand along its dense, course texture – it feels warm and heavy as she lifts it onto the table. She opens the material out and spreads it across the surface and then folds it in half. She carefully cuts along the length and then does the same again.

Taking one of the off cuts, she begins the process of stitching the side seams, creating a pillowcase that will hold the stuffing without it falling out. Because the remnant is thick, it is rather difficult to pull the needle through to the other side and she has to go back over some of the stitches to ensure they are tight. Once the sewing is finished, she turns the cover inside out and puts her hand in and presses against the seams. Not bad, she thinks. Dashing upstairs, she finds a couple of old woolly jumpers that are well worn and takes them back downstairs. She cuts each one into shreds and packs this into the cushion cover, leaving a little left over for the next one. Turning the pillowcase end over, the first one is finished. Although it looks rather lumpy in places, she knows that after awhile it will find its own shape. She plumps it up and holds it against her, she is happy with its warmth pressed against her and then puts it down, to stitch the three remaining covers and then breaks off for lunch. She will need some more stuffing to fill these and makes a mental note to find something next time she walks into Fenton.

Enjoying a bowl of hot vegetable soup that she prepared earlier she looks around the hut; it is becoming a warm and cosy home once again with its collection of handmade and collected bits and pieces.

Later sipping a hot drink, Jo listens to the rain as it splashes on the windowpanes and remembers the flood – it is difficult not to. And then she thinks, however bad that day was, it pales into insignificance, compared to what drove her to live here.

Looking down at Jason beside her, she is grateful for his devotion and soft love as his attentive eyes watch hers, in wait of what comes next. She leans down and strokes his black coat and he rolls over onto his back with all four paws in the air. His underbelly is pink and she caresses it with her hand, as she speaks to him in doggy language of 'I love you Jason' over and over again. How adaptive he is to her actions, he knows and senses today that he can rest and sleep and so rolls over and takes himself to his bed.

'What now? What to do?' Jo's furrow of activity earlier has left her now feeling inert and still and she can't muster any energy to work.

Leaving Jason to sleep, she goes upstairs and rummages through the bedroom drawers, in search of more stuffing for the cushions. Her entire wardrobe is scant to say the least and after another look she finds nothing that is past wearing. She lifts the lid of the trunk, to see if there is an old blanket that might suffice; she takes out the pile of old, faded, bedding and presses them against her breasts. Although these would make excellent stuffing for the cushions, she decides against cutting them up, there is still plenty of wear in them, although they are a bit dog-eared.

Looking down into the bottom of the trunk, her bag of journals, with its contents poking out, stares back at her. She puts down the blankets on the edge of the bed and reaches inside the trunk for the old, split, black bag.

As she carefully handles the plastic and picks it up, some of its contents drop back down into the trunk. She places the bag alongside the blankets and returns for the rest of the papers. She sees a photo of him – slipping out from inside a letter – his eyes look directly into hers. 'Why did I never see what his eyes speak to me now? How could I have ever seen warmth and love in this man's face?' She sees terse and vindictive hatred, and uncompassionate cruelty in his stare. She sees a calculating menace that never relents and a man, whose only wish at the end of his life, his day, was to witness the destruction of her life. And for him to see a complete and total disintegration of every aspect of her world unfold before him, was his only reason for waking. In his obsession and possession of her, he destroyed and killed himself in his blindness.

She turns the photo over, she can't bear to look anymore and wonders now, 'is he dead or alive? Did he survive, did his warm blood run cold, did the red, robust, fiery heat of his body turn pale and give up his last breath?' She doesn't know. Will she ever know? She can't bear to look anymore. She picks up an A4 piece of paper and reads the page of writing that was once her own.

I am 36 years old and I find it hard to believe the age that I am. This makes me sad because I feel that I have spent years just hanging on to life rather than living my life and now as I grow older I sense the loss of opportunities and choices I otherwise might have had had I not been so trapped within myself. I've spent most of my life living it for other people and what I thought they wanted from me and through an intrinsic lack of knowledge of myself as a real person. I often felt alienated as if I had just landed from another planet. This experience seems indescribable and impossible to put into words for others to understand. I feel almost as if I have lost years of my life, this maybe due to a problem that I have had with continuity. I have never had a sense of relationships with people as ongoing with a history, a past, it's as if the memory gets lost and then I feel that I am starting all over again. I then have feelings of – does this person know me, what do they know about me, what have I spoken to them about me because I can't remember, can they remember? I feel now writing this as though, up until this point in my life, that I've been struggling and trying to get through without success 'can anyone notice me, I'm Samantha, I am a real person with an identity, why doesn't anyone want to know who I am? I have great difficulty recalling significant events and dates. I find it remarkable when I hear someone say such and such a thing happened in the year 19 whatever and then they explain in detail their recollections. Whilst writing and after re reading this writing, I experienced with such a complete surprise that I can't remember ever feeling before, of feeling alive and real and that I do actually exist as a person. The unreal quality of my outline, the image of my figure without real substance and connection to the world and with no continuity as a self or with others, an imaginary being, in danger of being killed off and losing another identity.

She lifts the page to her lips and kisses it tenderly and then lays it flat on the floor and sweeps her hand across the writing to smooth out the creases. She goes down the stairs and glances at Jason asleep in his bed and finds a strong carrier bag from the kitchen drawer and returns upstairs. Carefully she takes the documents out of the old plastic sack and puts them into the bag and places them back into the trunk along with the blankets.

She feels tired and sleepy now and takes off her jeans and pulls back the duvet and slides into bed. She is glad of this place of sanctuary as she snuggles inside for warmth, it is a long time since the sheets were washed

and they are infused with my own scent. She gives into
the tiredness that seeps through her and rests, drifting in
and out of sleep, turning away unwanted thoughts.
This dozing and sleeping during the day, has become a
habit since coming back to live here and she slips in and
out gently. This makes up for the nighttime, when her
eyes and ears stay awake and alert and ready for any
disturbance outside, tossing and turning, hunting the
darkness of night. Although she installed a set of locks to
all the windows and also rigged up a guard using a plank
of wood and metal brackets to the door, she still finds it
hard to settle in peace, even though here with Jason she
is safe and protected. But when the blackness of night
arrives, especially if it is raining outside, she is unable to
relax. Sometimes she hankers for the security of the flat
and also its hot shower and bathroom, but these thoughts
pale into insignificance when the daybreaks and she adds
logs to the stove. And her trip outside to the loo isn't as
daunting now that she has lined the ceiling and walls
with foam insulation boards.

She remembers Gary dropping off the boards and how
she cut them to size with a sharp blade and tacked them
into place. The day scrubbing the flags, leading from the
hut to the toilet, now they are clear of the thick mud she
no longer returns inside with muddy boots. She keeps a
clean pair and also dirty ones for the garden and going
for walks. She tends to leave an old towel, inside the
doorway for Jason and sweeps the floor occasionally
with a stiff brush to keep the dirt at bay.

She feels kind and caring towards herself, as she absorbs
the heat from the heavy duvet, it is a lovely sensation, as
if being touched by a soft feather of love that ekes out,
protecting and comforting her. She is privileged here on
her own, to have found this out for herself, how could
she have ever have thought or believed, that to love
oneself in such a deep way, is unprecedented in its
ability to heal and forgive. 'Yes I am ok, I am good

enough just the way that I am,' the only judge is actually myself and she is accepting of who she is. 'Yes my judge and inner voice, we are in union and harmony, as one together. Let's try to let go of the past and live for now and the future, be happy and hopeful and make each day count.'

Abby doesn't welcome the prospect of her parents return but after leaving the party, she knows she'll have to go back home and check through the house, to remove all traces of Mark's presence. As she says goodbye to him in Thornby, she knows she doesn't want to live with her mother and Charles at 'The Manor House' much longer.

Arriving home, she contacts Susan, to arrange for her to come in and clean for a couple of hours. She feels determined now, to re apply for a place on an art and design course at York University. Her grades are excellent and she is confident she will get a place. Unfortunately she has missed this year's entrance date and will have to wait until next autumn to begin. She would soon convince Charles of her idea of a 'brand new start', post Mark, and her plans of attaining a University degree. She knows this will go down well with him, meeting his ideas of education and building a strong foundation for her future. And hopefully she can persuade him, that in her year off she can move to York, find a job and live in one of his flats.

Abby wants to move after Christmas, because up until then, Mark will be based in Thornby and she would be able to snatch moments with him, providing she stays out of Charles's way. It is imperative that she keeps Mark a secret during this time– if Charles were to find out, then that would definitely be the end of the end, as far as getting help from him is concerned.

The day her parents are due back, Abby leaves 'The Manor House' and takes the train to York, to speak to admissions and hand in her details, and send off her UCAS form.

She had left Susan at the house, to give it a thorough clean and have things prepared and ready for when her parents return. She had mentioned to Susan about her mother's phone call regarding the gift and she said she'd keep a look out for it.

York is busy and vibrant and Abby likes the buzz, which the place gives her. She had thought about moving even further away, maybe as far as Leeds Uni but reasoned that York is far enough away from Fenton but near enough if she needed bailing out. The University of York is on the outskirts of the city and most students cycle in and around the flat roads of York. Abby doesn't fancy this idea and having a car to get around, seems the perfect thing. Her mother had promised to pay for driving lessons, if she furthered her education, so she could start the driving lessons straight away. She knows Charles would pay for her University fees and allow her to stay in one of his flats, providing she obeys his rules, but out of sight, out of Charles's mind – she could live her life how she wanted to in York and have a brilliant time away from him and her mother's hindrance about how she lived it. They would insist that she found a job until the course starts and she likes the idea of earning money of her own, to be able to spend it on whatever she wants. Knowing full well that she would get extra funds from them.

There are quite a few Starbucks around York and Abby goes in for a hot chocolate. Looking around, the idea of working in one of the café's seems a good idea. It would be a good place to start meeting fellow students and people who lived in York and she could build up a social life before she began Uni. Abby finishes her mug of chocolate and looks around. Mark wouldn't like Starbucks, or the kinds of people who come into it. But there would be more people to meet here and get to know, Abby decides as she looks outside and gazes up at the huge white stonewalls and the archway, which had once been a gate to keep the city safe. In summer there would be the river and the clubs, bars, restaurants and cafes, which would be a laugh and good fun to discover when she moved here. Life would be fantastic and learning to drive must be her next important move.

Abby returns home feeling excited. She has begun to plan her future and the thought of the driving lessons, thrills and scares her. Her life is starting to take shape. It is beginning to grow dark when she arrives back home. Opening the door she is pleased with herself and looks forward to telling her parents about her plans for York University, the driving lessons and asking about their ideas on a car. 'What kind?' Abby wonders. Not a huge 4 x 4, she fancies a mini maybe, something small that she could easily park and run around the city in. Yes – a dark red, sporty model with all the extras and a cute steering wheel would be ace she imagines.

Pulling back the curtains stirs and wakes Jo, it is dry and bright outside, the sky is clear and blue and she decides to work in the garden. She has had little chance to do much tidying since Anna left, so after a bowl of cereal and a mug of tea she pulls on her boots and Jason is soon alongside and raring to go. She walks around deciding what to do. There are plenty of jobs to tackle and she decides to prune the overgrown trees by the hedge and stock up the woodpile for the stove. Jason is soon bounding around, sniffing and exploring and helping with the wood. This is a good time of the year, to take out any dead branches and cut back hard the overgrown trees. She has found that if she does this, the garden is manageable and flourishes the next spring. It doesn't take long to build up the log pile and add the smaller branches to the fire lighting wood. It is a lovely day and soon she is working in just a t-shirt and jeans.

Breaking off for a glass of fruit juice, Jo assesses the condition of the paths, even though they had cleared the landslip, many of the flags and stone steps are still covered by mud and some have been hidden completely. She decides to leave the trees for another day and work on the stones. After scraping of the thick dirt with a shovel, she throws it into the barrow, pulling out any weeds as she goes. Looking back at her efforts, it is pleasing to see the flags drying out as she works. When she has cleaned them from the hut to the lay by, she starts work on the stone steps going down to the fruit trees.

Passing the site of the bonfire, she remembers her time with Anna, she can see the two of them holding their glasses of red wine and the hot flames licking out from the fire, it was a special celebration of themselves and she misses her. She wonders what she is doing right now, this moment, she hopes she is happy and her children are too. She tries to mark out the days since she was last here and struggles – the time merges in on itself and becomes just one expanse of time.

Jo decides to call at Woodend Farm tomorrow, to check her mailbox, maybe Anna has sent a letter; to hear from her would be a lovely treat. 'Will she remember me' Jo asks herself? 'Oh come on, don't go there' Jo continues and scrapes the steps, carrying on until she reaches the bottom. The wheelbarrow is heavy with the weight of the mud and she curses as she pushes it back up the slope to the top. After tipping the load onto the vegetable area she stands up to ease her back. The work has been hard but worth it, she takes the stiff brush and sweeps the drying flags and steps, to clear the remaining dirt. Wow, what a difference, the paths are better now than before the flood, the scraping has revealed more of the flags and stones and she can see the garden will become lovely once more.

Simone leaves her car parked in the yard of Wood End Farm. Collecting the cards and her bag from the boot she locks it and makes her way towards the kitchen door of the farmhouse. It has been a difficult time for Fred and his daughter Feebie since Florence's death two weeks ago. The funeral had been at the beautiful ancient church of St. Mary's in the old part of Fenton. As Florence battled with her illness which led to her death, Simone had become involved in her life and care as well as supporting her. The initial request for therapy had come from Florence's daughter Feebie but over the course of the remainder of months until she died, Simone had grown to have a sense of admiration and respect for Florence. Shortly after the funeral, Simone had been surprised at the unexpected donation she had received with a thank you note from Fred and Feebie to say that they had appreciated the care and support that she had given to Florence. The cheque was a donation to the centre and Simone wanted to thank the father and daughter for their generosity, as well as offer them whatever support they might need to cope with their loss.

Simone taps on the door, the dog barks and then footsteps approach. The dark green door opens and Simone is greeted with the soft, fair, open face of Feebie. Her eyes break into a smile as she recognises the caller. "Come in."
Feebie invites Simone into the old farmhouse. Feebie no longer lives at home but since the diagnosis of her mother's illness, she has spent a lot of time at the farm with her mother and now her father. She would stay on until after the Christmas holidays but then she would need to return to her life in London. Her partner would be joining her for the holidays and then they would return to London together. There has been little modernisation to the farm and although it has the basics of running water and electric, it doesn't have central heating or double-glazing and although clean and tidy it is fifty years behind the times.

"Dads in the front room, come through I'm just going to put the kettle on, can I get you a tea or a coffee?" Feebie asks.
"Tea will be fine."
Feebie stays behind in the kitchen to make the tea. Simone walks into the hall and taps softly on the front room door, before pushing it open. She has become well acquainted with Wood End Farm over the course of time she's visited it, whilst seeing Florence.
"Now then Fred, how are you today?"
"Mustn't grumble."
Simone notices the sadness and grief in his eyes.
"Sit down, sit down." Fred insists.
"I still expect to see her, I still expect to see her walking through that door and telling me the tea's ready or the hen's have fought again, or…"
Fred stops talking and gazes into the fire, which burns in the hearth.
"I can't get used to it, there's nothing left here for me anymore. We shared it all." Fred begins again.
"We shared all the work here, like we shared all our lives. It seemed forever."

Fred stops as Feebie enters the room carrying a tray with three mugs of tea and a saucer of ginger biscuits. Simone waits as Feebie passes their drinks before speaking to them both.
"I've come to say thank you, for your kind and thoughtful card and your generous donation to the centre. Thanks both of you."
Simone hands Feebie the two cards she has brought with her.
"There's a thank you card and a Christmas card."
"Thank you."
There is silence. It is Feebie who speaks next.
"Dads been thinking about the farm since mum died, he thinks it'll be too much for him now."
Feebie looks at Fred.

"Dad knows I can't come and take over, because Carmel and I are so busy with our own computer business and besides, as much as I love dad and would do anything for him, well, dad knows the farm just isn't me."

"So you're thinking of selling up then Fred?" Simone asks.

"Ay, it looks like it."

"You don't sound so sure, that's all."

Fred glances at Simone and then at his daughter.

"He wants to stay, he loves the farm."

"Yes I can understand that."

"I've been talking to a business man in town, he said he's interested and I think he was. I could tell by the look on his face."

Fred stops.

"Dad has been talking to Charles Harcourt and he's only interested in redevelopment and knocking down and clearing the farm away."

They remain silent for a few minutes.

Simone drinks her tea. A mad idea and scheme crosses her mind but she immediately dismisses it. Simone puts down her empty pot.

"I didn't just come with the cards, we shared a lot together with Florence. I want you both to know that if there's anything I can do, any help or support that might be useful you only have to say."

"That's kind of you."

Feebie tells Simone.

"Yes, that's good of you, Florence thought a lot of you and we're grateful for the help you gave her towards the end."

Fred falters.

"At least she went at peace, that's to be thankful for, not like Jack Wilson the poor old bugger."

"The old coastguard, yes I read about him in the papers. He slipped didn't he?"

"Found him on the beach, a terrible mess, he should have known better, walking along the cliff top at night in torrential rain."

After finishing her tea, Simone rises from her seat and tells Fred to call her if she can be of any help and although difficult she wishes him the greetings of the Christmas season.

"I'll see you out."

Feebie tells her.

As she walks through the house, Simone feels such a strong sensation in her stomach, such a pull, that however it looks until she has said it, she won't rest. Wood End Farm would make a fantastic Holistic Centre with Wood End Farm at its base. Simone could invite other healers to join her and they could build up a community and run retreats and hold courses. Wood End Farm could be such a remarkable place, Simone reasons. Florence is no longer her client, so there would be no clash of professional and private interests. She would have to look into the finances of course and see if it would be a viable proposition and speak to her bank manager.

Turning now to Feebie as they stand by the car, Simone looks at her.

"What is it?" Feebie asks.

"Has your father actually sold the farm to Mr Harcourt?"

"No"

"Do you know, Feebie, I think Wood End Farm would make a wonderful Holistic Centre and retreat."

Feebie's eyes widen.

"I don't know what made me say that."

Simone falters. For a long time Feebie looks at Simone and then beyond her to the farmhouse.

"I feel I am being rather impulsive Feebie, sorry."

"You've taken me by surprise Simone but do you know something, it would be a lovely idea, in fact, I can't think of anything I'd like better for the place."
Simone feels such a sense of relief and continues.
"I mean I don't know what figures we would be looking at, or whether it is way out of my league but the ideas just struck me and…"
"I'll speak to dad."
"Gosh I really don't know what to say now."
"Let's see, how about I work out the figures with dad and an agent and then call you?"
Feebie stops as she watches Simone's blank face.
"That was so unlike me, the idea popped out of nowhere Feebie."
"My concern here is for dad, whoever buys this place will have dad to think about, I want him to move into the small cottage. It won't be easy for him, but I know he wouldn't want to move away from Woodend, it's been his whole life."
"I can understand that completely Feebie, he belongs here."
"Leave it with me then, I'll phone you."
"Thank you."

Simone turns and gets into her car, as she drives off her head is full and brimming over with all the ideas that tumble through her mind.

Feebie draws a deep breath of the clean air. 'It might be a good idea,' she thinks to herself. It would enable her dad to stay here on the farm. A soft breeze slips across her cheek and touches her hair.
'Yes, it's ok mum, dad's going to be fine.'
Closing the door behind her, Feebie returns into the farmhouse. She would talk to her father later, after she has made her enquiries, there is plenty of time and he would take her advice as always.

Jo wakes later than usual and is undecided as to what to
do today. Her head feels groggy and her back and limbs
ache from the work in the garden. She has a bowl of
cereal for breakfast and a glass of fruit juice. Although
her preference is to sit and be still and become lost in
dream space, she rouses herself and puts on her outdoor
boots. "Come on Jase."
She calls Jason who has returned to his bed. He leaps up
with his tail wagging, ready and eager to come with her.
She grabs her rucksack and his lead and sets off.
Walking down the stone steps to the fruit trees is a
pleasure, now that the path is clean and clear of weeds
and mud. This thought pleases and shifts her mood – the
air too is refreshing, with a sharp wind, whipping
through the vegetation and trees. They make their way
towards the beach, at the top of the cliffs she looks down
to check the tide, they are in luck, it is on its way out.
She hasn't been down to the sea recently and it feels
good to return.

If she wanted to be organised and know in advance the
times of the tides, she could get a timetable from the
tourist information centre, but as she hasn't got a watch
and never seem to know the date, there is no point. She
remembers a day, not long after she first arrived here,
when she had set out for a walk along the beach. It was
before Jason came and she was on her own and realised
the tide was coming in. She had looked back to where
she had set off from, it was submerged under water and
she began to panic. She didn't know the area or where
the next exit was, so she hurried on, hoping that she
would reach a coastal path. By the time she found a way
off the sands, at what she now knows as Hunsby Gap,
her feet and legs were soaked and she was frightened.
She learnt a valuable lesson and has taken care ever
since.

Today the beach is empty apart from a couple walking
two dogs; she lets Jason run across to say hello and

carries on. The outgoing tide has left its usual debris and seaweed and she scours the sand for treasures. She picks up any sea glass and adds it to her bag, She hopes to find pieces of dark blue but these are few and far between. Further along she spots something white and goes to inspect it, to her delight it is a piece of ripped sail cloth – this is a brilliant find, it will make lots of sails for the boats and she shakes off the sand and puts it in her rucksack, along with yards of coloured fishing line and some interesting shells and stones. Jason is soaking wet now after swimming in the sea, he comes over giddy with delight and has a massive shake all over her. Pleased with her haul, she turns and makes her way back home.

Inside the hut is warm and cosy and she gives Jason a rub down with his towel and takes off her boots. She is hungry now and washes her hands and cuts a wedge of bread and cheese. As they share the food, Jo reflects on her findings and looks forward to making a few boats and wonders how she can make use of the glass. The pieces of broken sea glass would look good as some sort of mosaic, but she doesn't have the exact idea yet in her mind. In the meantime, they look lovely in a bowl on the kitchen table, so for now she will continue to gather and add them to the dish.

After lunch she goes to Woodend Farm to check her mailbox, she is conscious of her excitement and her disappointment both at the same time. To receive a letter from Anna will be wonderful, however if the box is empty, she will feel bereft. Walking up the pristine clear path, she notices the pile of stones that Anna had collected, after clearing between the hedges to the roadside, and wonders what she can use them for. The way through the hawthorn is easy now and soon they reach the lay-by.

Woodend Farm is further along the main road and her mailbox is just beside its old wooden gate. The farm comprises of a large, ramshackle farmhouse and a number of old, derelict outbuildings and barn, fields and a dense wood surround it. The buildings and land are in need of attention; Jo notices the neglect as she makes her way to the gate.

Looking ahead to the farmhouse, she sees a car pulling away. Jo lifts the lid of the box and is surprised to find a white envelope waiting for her. She takes it and looks at the hand written address; it is Anna's writing that's for sure. As she stares at the letter, the car pulls up to the gate. The driver appears familiar and at first Jo wonders where she has seen this woman before and then she remembers, it is the lady who helped her and took her to the museum, when she lived at the flat. She winds the car window down and speaks to Jo.
"Hello."
"Hi." Jo replies.
"It is so good to see you up and about, I was rather concerned, especially when I have not seen you around."
"Thank you, yes I am fine now, I'm ok."
"Would you like a lift, I am driving back into town?"
"No thanks, I am not far from home, I live in the beach hut now, just along the road, but thanks anyway."
"Oh right, would you mind opening the gate for me?"
"Sure."
Jo swings the gate to let the car out.
"Thank you, what's your name by the way?"
"It's Jo."
"Well thanks Jo, it is great to see you looking well, bye for now."
Simone then accelerates forward and drives down the main road.
Jo closes the gate and turns back for home, holding the letter eager with anticipation, to open and enjoy reading it.

Sitting down at the table she carefully opens the white envelope and unfolds the pages and reads the letter.

Dear Jo,

Well I'm back home and things are returning to something like normal.

It was lovely to see Adam and Georgina again and I'm just battling through all the housework and piles of washing, which has built up over the few weeks since I left. How's things in the hut? Have you sorted out your workroom yet? How's the beautiful map of Fenton coming along? I miss our times together they were so special.

I'm in the final year of my homeopathic course and I'm going to really get down to all the work I have to do, so I can finish on time and be ready to register and set up practise. I've started to look at brochures for cottages on the coast for Christmas. I've just received the Yorkshire tourist boards lists and they look pretty good and I'm going to do some phoning around after I've finished your letter.

I've been in touch with Mark and for the moment things seem to be working out for him.

How's Jason and the sea? I miss the smell of the coast and the clean air.

I've decided I'm going to join a homeopathic group in York with an experienced homeopath leading the group who's into meditation and provings and chakra work. She's an unusual woman and I like her fresh approach and I'm looking forward to the group beginning.

Another homeopathic student from my group will be going so she's said she's happy to take me in her car so I don't need to worry about transport. We'll share costs of course.

I'll write again soon and let you know how the cottage search is going. It will be brilliant to have that to look forward to at Christmas. If I can I'd like to book up to the New Year, we could celebrate it together. You know how much I would like you to come to the cottage. You're welcome to stay for the whole two weeks or as much as you feel you want to and I'll make sure Jason can come too.

Bye for now. Take care.

Anna.

Jo sits and re reads the letter, over and over again. As she looks across the words, Anna's presence is here with her. What strikes Jo is Anna's purpose and determination, regarding her homeopathy work. She is so pleased for her, that she has something entirely for herself to occupy her time. And the fact of her mentioning the cottage for Christmas and New Year is a bonus, she will be able to see her again and the children. This leaves Jo warm and contented and she immerses herself inside this feeling and lets it wrap itself around her. Hours later, as the darkness descends and the flicker of the red flame inside the stove becomes the only light, she stands up from the table and prepares an evening meal.

Abby hears the soft, violin strings of Vivaldi, coming from the downstairs snug and walks towards the room. Approaching the doorway she catches sight of Charles and her mother exchanging words. She stops and takes two steps backwards and listens.

"Yes Charles but never mind that, you didn't inform me of your trip to France either."

"Oh well that's precisely it, don't you think. Work. You know how things are and how at the drop of a hat I have to fly over there. Work Margaret, but what would you know about that. How was your mother by the way?"

"Charles we are becoming like strangers who pass in the night, we never seem to talk anymore."

"What the bloody hell do you think were doing now?"

"Beginning to argue Charles."

"Oh yes here we go, point the finger in my direction, blame me."

"You hardly resemble the man I married Charles, it seems such a long time ago. You thrived on work when I met you, but now everyone has to tiptoe around you, as if you are about to explode."

"That's because nothing is straight forward anymore. Things have changed; maybe I'm losing my knack. There was a time when a deal was a deal and all I had to do was count the money. Not anymore. Maybe I'm getting to old for this game. I used to be ahead of the rest but not anymore, I'm the one who loses out, it appears that someone is stabbing me in the back and I need to find out who."

"Oh Charles were hardly penniless."

"That's not the point Margaret, it's my name at stake, my reputation in this town."

Abby decides she has heard enough and stomps into the room.

Margaret turns around.

"Hello darling, it is lovely to see you."

"Thanks mummy and you too."

"Hello sweetheart, have you been alright here on your own?"

Charles asks.

"Of course silly, I've been to York today to sign my application for Uni and to check out places for part time work."

"Wonderful, that's my girl, back on track I'm pleased to hear."

"So daddy, I will need help to find some accommodation and maybe a car when I have passed my test."

"Absolutely darling, just say the word and we can work something out. Well seeing as we are all together for once, why don't we have a little celebration tonight? Margaret phone the Harbour Bar and book a table."

Abby smiles but inwardly finds herself wishing that she could just disappear up to her room, she doesn't fancy making a special effort but realises that this is the deal, if she wants their backing and financial support.

"I'll go and take a shower."

Abby turns to leave the room.

"Oh and by the way mummy, Susan looked everywhere but she didn't find the present that you left."

Abby's words cut through the room, as Charles's eyes fix on Margaret.

"Present?"

Charles asks.

"Oh it was nothing Charles, just a little something that I had bought for my father."

"How thoughtful of you, I hope Philip wasn't too disappointed."

Margaret stops herself before answering; the thought crosses her mind that he is aware of the cufflinks.

"Margaret what is going on?"

Margaret feels the heat rise within her as she touches her cheek with her hand.

"Margaret what are you thinking about? Sometimes I wonder if you should see a doctor. You are forever gazing into thin air and in dreamland. Is there something I should know?"

"No, no Charles. I am alright."

"Well you certainly don't act like it. Why bother, why do I bother. I was hoping that tonight we could all make an effort for each other."

"Yes, yes we can. I will go and phone to book the table."

"Tell them no later than 8.30 Margaret, we don't want to be sat around until nearly midnight. I've got an early start in the morning."

Margaret leaves the room and makes the reservation for 7.30 and then orders a taxi to collect them at 7.15. This allows her enough time to shower, dress and have a couple of glasses of wine before they leave. She needs to relax and hopes that the subject of the present will have been forgotten. Her mind is churning around and the more she fights it, the harder it becomes to erase it from her thoughts. The difficulty is, her inability to come up with a feasible answer to Charles's probing questions. She also knows that it will take her forever to shower and dress herself. The predicament exacerbates her need to check everything. From her toenails, fingernails, varnish, legs, underarms, eyebrows, teeth, flossing and hair. Every time the issue of the present enters her thoughts, she begins again her checks from the very beginning, toenails, fingernails, varnish......

Jason is laying in his bed with his head resting on his front paws, his eyes look directly at Jo's, as the cold blustery wind slaps itself against the sides of the hut, she is happy to be inside with him adding logs to the stove. Today seems so much colder than yesterday and she is wearing a thermal vest and leggings underneath her jeans and tops. She has taken to sleeping occasionally downstairs near the stove.

Her purchase of a huge, comfy sofa from Thornby last week has been brilliant, a soft place to sit during the day and at night with the thick duvet she can sleep without being frozen.

She turns her attention back to the letter that she's writing to Anna. This is her second attempt, the first one she screwed up and burnt on the stove.

Hi Anna,

Thank you so much for your letter, I picked it up yesterday from my post box at Wood End Farm, I couldn't wait to get back to the hut and read it with a pot of tea. It will be brilliant to share time with you all at Christmas, let me know when you have booked it and the dates.

I'm pleased that you are continuing with your homeopathic studies, it's the last hurdle and will be worth it.

I have missed you since you left, thanks again for helping with the clean up of the hut, I couldn't have done it without you!

Life here as you know is full especially with work. I have spent a lot of time in the garden when the days have been dry. Working on tidying up – sorting dead wood for the fire and digging over the vegetable patch. I hope to do more pruning of the trees and have another bonfire. I'll probably light it on bonfire night and join in with the town. Jason is happy to be back here and I am too but remember life at the flat when it is really cold. There are lots of jobs inside that I would like to tackle; I haven't done much since you left. I suppose they will keep for rainy days. We still have our walks down to the beach but have to take the long route because the path down to the bench is cut off, I think it's to do with the aftermath of the flood – the cliff eroding and the steep steps down to the beach have also been cordoned off.

I have picked the best of the cooking apples and wrapped them in newspaper and packed them into a wooden box. These will keep me going through the winter. I have a long list of things to do and so by the end of each day I am tired from trying to do the extra one more thing before it gets dark. I keep the stove burning and the hut is cosy and warm when I return inside.

I am conscious writing to you of how much I miss our togetherness, I don't suppose I have spoken to anyone other than in the shops for any length of time and that is a down side to being out here. I suppose I am more aware of it since I met you, prior to that it was just me and Jason getting along with life. The other day I needed to connect with the world and popped into the library for an hour or so, just to hear people around me. But mainly like I said, life is full and busy and before I know it, it's another day over and to bed. I love coming inside to a homemade soup or stew cooking on the stove and a wedge of crusty bread.

We had a particularly windy night a couple of days ago and Jason wouldn't settle, pacing around and barking, I am so glad he is here and looking after me.

As far as the workroom goes, I haven't done anything with it yet, nor work on the map, although I look forward to it when I get the chance. I was planning to start making wine but it will probably have to wait until next year. Now that the vegetable patch is cleared and dug over I can plan what I am going to grow and feel like I am getting somewhere.

I have found a solution to having a decent shower, because it's too cold outside to use mine, I fell upon the idea of going to the school's swimming pool after walking past it on my way home. There was a poster at the entrance advertising classes and times for public swimming. So I went along with my towel, soap, shampoo and cossie. Instead of taking a shower after the swim I had a glorious hot steaming shower before and a rinse after the swimming. The feeling of total cleanliness afterwards was brilliant and I almost danced on air the whole way home. So when I get too dirty and the idea of a body wash seems inadequate, I can now pop along to the school and have a swim also, ace!!

Life is good again now that I am getting sorted. Well Anna I will finish now and send this letter to you. I am so looking forward to Christmas, to share it and not be here on my own.

I will provide a share of the food and chip in to the cost of the rental, just let me know how much?

The speed of life at the moment is fast and slow but before we know it, we will be together again. Lovely!!!

Lots of love to you Anna
from
Jo and Jason XXX

Mark doesn't want his time with Abbs to end but her parents are returning home and he'd promised Paddy and the lads that he'd join them along the coast, to make up the gang, to do the jobs which Paddy and his wife Lily touted for beforehand. Mark likes the life of the travellers. He enjoys the male company and the work, which he is good at. He has started to get a name as a hard grafter and he likes that. The base site in Thornby, where the caravans park up until the spring, is where he will be living. After that, Paddy would pack up and take his gang and go across to Sweden to look for work. If the caravan site is full, Paddy puts them up in a hotel room along the coast. It is up to the lads, who gets a bed or who has the floor. They manage.

Mark meets up with the gang on the outskirts of Thornby in Balby. They have half a dozen new drives to put down, so that will keep them fairly local to Thornby, as Balby is only a couple of miles away. Mark has good reason to want to return back to Thornby from here, he needs to see Charles. Abby had told him that Charles goes to the Sailors Arms often, particularly for a pub lunch. Mark needs to throw in a sick day and get Paddy to let him off work. He is usually sick most mornings, especially after trying to eat the sausage sarnies Paddy brings them.

Mark's moment comes early on Friday morning, after the lads have eaten their sausage butties. Mark throws up and manages to get out of the caravan; otherwise he'd be made to clean it all up. Paddy isn't a soft touch.
Mark bends over.
"Me guts."
Mark moans and leans over again, as Lily comes round to give the men their money before they set off for work.
"What the hell's up with you?"
Lily asks.
"It's me guts Lily, I'm gonna have to lie down, tell Paddy."

"He won't like it Mark."
"He's not right."
Lily tells Paddy as she fills his flask.
"Give him a break for today."
She says screwing the cap securely onto his flask.
Paddy looks into Lily's eyes, he knows he can trust her.
"Tell the little runt he's in tomorrow and don't let him
bugger about today."
Paddy climbs up into his wagon to go to their work.

Mark watches as the two wagons set off in front with
Paddy and Keith and then the old car with the rest of the
lads in. He knows Lily will come and check all the
caravans. She'd dock money the following day, if any of
the lads left them dirty. All Mark has to do is lie down
and cover himself up with his duvet and turn around and
pretend to be asleep. So that she would leave him alone
and then set off in her car to take Paddy some dinner.
That's when Mark would nip off to the Sailors Arms, to
see if he could find Charles.
When he sees Lily close her caravan door, he jumps out
of bed and changes his clothes and washes and cleans
himself up for the pub.

After Lily has driven off, Mark goes to catch the bus to
make his way to the Sailors Arms. He has enough money
to buy a couple of pints but knows he has to be careful
because if Lily or Paddy sees him, he'll give him a
punch and dock his money.
The Sailors Arms isn't the kind of pub that Mark feels
comfortable in but needs must – he'd enjoyed his meal
there with Abbs, although it wouldn't be a place he
would choose. Mark buys himself a pint and sits down
and looks about him. He doesn't know anyone in the
pub. After draining his pint, he gets up to buy his second
drink, knowing he has time for one more before catching
the bus back and sneaking into his caravan before Paddy
returns.

Mark pays for his drink and thanks the barman, then glances in the bar mirror. He is shocked when he sees Charles walking into the dining area of the pub, where he'd been with Abbs. He is with another man; Mark follows them through into the dining area. Charles sits down with his friend and Mark goes across. The man sitting opposite Charles points Mark out. Charles turns in his seat and glowers at him. "What do you want?" Charles demands.

"A word."

"Give me a minute."

Charles tells his companion.

Charles follows Mark and directs him to a seat in a quiet corner of the pub. Mark sits down and takes a long drink from his glass.

"Well, what do you want?"

Charles asks again.

Mark glances briefly at Charles and then recalls his image in the DVD. It seems ridiculous that they are the same man. Charles looks smooth and sleek and in control now and yet in the DVD, well Mark thinks. Charles nudges him.

"I don't have all day."

"I've got something, I've seen something of yours."

"What the hell are you talking about?"

Charles demands wishing he had a drink in his hand.

"It's about a baby."

Mark pauses.

"A big baby."

Mark doesn't get a chance to say anything else because Charles hisses at him to be quiet.

"So you know what I'm talking about?"

Mark takes another long swig from his pint. The lager quietens his shaking but Charles's face is livid, like thunder. Mark leans back a little in his seat away from him.

"What is it, where is it?"

Charles asks not in any mood to play games.

"It's a DVD and it's safe."

Charles looks into Mark's face and lets his glance fall
beyond him. Charles is silent for a moment.
"How much?"
Mark gulps.
"A hundred."
He dares to ask, not expecting it.
"Not today."
Charles looks into Mark's eyes.
"Tomorrow."
 "No, no."
Mark begins.
"You'll have to come into Thornby at night and I'll meet
you."
"Where?"
"The fairground."
Mark takes another drink.
 "8 o'clock."
Charles says rising from his seat and returns back into
the dining area. He no longer has an appetite for food but
will have to go through the performance for his client's
sake.
"Sorry about that, he's part of a gang doing work for me.
You know what these bloody labourers are like, greedy
little bugger and forever spending all they earn."
Mark finishes off his lager. As he places his glass on the
table he can feel his hands trembling. He has to hurry
back to the caravan site before Paddy comes back. He
doesn't need trouble at the moment, not now, not how he
is feeling.

Mark feels so high; if his feet weren't firmly planted on
the ground, he could take off and literally fly.

After returning from town to post Anna's letter, Jo's thoughts turn to Christmas day and her list of things to do. She will spend today making presents for all of them. She has decided to finish off 'The Purple Pearl' for Adam. It needs another coat of black paint on the hull, the sails need another brushing of purple paint and a couple of the pieces of cork need gluing again. Remembering back to the flood and the huge loss of her other boats and belongings, Adam's ship has not done too badly after all. She collects the black boat from the workroom and places it on the kitchen table and on doing so one of the bullet cases slips out. As she fiddles and tries to push it back into its gun hole, she curses when part of the wood breaks off and the bullet case slips straight through. 'Damn,' she utters as she thinks about how she's going to fix it, she fills the hole with another piece of wood and drills a new space for the bullet, it fits tight now and she leaves it to dry. The cork glues down easily and she mixes a small pot of purple paint and brushes it on to the mildewed sails – 'The Purple Pearl' is looking fierce and strong once again. Jo is pleased with the result and looks forward to Adam opening his Christmas gift. He never saw it the first time and so it will be a total surprise for him.

Putting the boat to one side she starts work on Georgina's present. She has bought a length of thin, brown leather cord and bronze necklace fastenings and begins to make her necklace. She places the tiny shells collected from the beach and also a selection of vintage beads found at the charity shops on the table. She makes a small hole in the shells and threads the cord through, interspersed with beads. When all the pieces are strung along the necklace she lifts it up and admires it, she truly hopes that Georgina will like it, it is pretty. For Anna, she found a lovely old china bowl in the charity shop and has filled it with sea glass, and bought a large church candle from a craft stall held in Fenton, (this event would be perfect for her produce and something to think about for next year), and a box of medjool dates filled with chocolate from the health food shop. For Mark she's decided to give him a £5 note.

During the afternoon Jason's barking alerts Jo from sleep and she quickly fumbles around for her jeans. Pulling them on as she goes down the stairs, she hears a voice from outside.

"Jo, it's only me Gary."

Jo shouts that she's coming and goes to open the door. Gary is standing holding a pile of cork tiles.

"Sorry to disturb you Jo but I thought you might be able to use these, they were being thrown on the skip at work."

"Come on in, oh yes they would, thanks ever so much, they would be great for sticking onto the insulation boards that I put in the outside toilet."

Gary bends down and puts the tiles on the floor and makes a big fuss of Jason. Jason bounds around with glee and goes to find a toy to offer Gary to play with.

"That's what I thought, I've got plenty more in the van, some of them are a bit stained that's why they are being chucked out, any chance of a cuppa?"

"Yes sure, I'll fill the kettle."

Jason drops his rubber duck from his jaw and nudges it towards Gary's feet. Gary tries to pick it up but Jason grabs it and teases, wanting him to play at tug of war. Gary waits for his moment and then pulls at the duck, Jason is too quick again and the two of them carry on the game whilst the kettle boils.

Jo makes two mugs of tea and takes them to the kitchen table.

"Did you manage to do the insulation?"

Gary asks.

"Yes it was quite easy really, it makes such a difference when it's freezing outside, what will I need to stick these on with?"

"PVA glue should do it, if you want me to drop you a container off I will, thanks for the tea. How are you doing now that you are back here?"

"Were doing ok, it suits us living here, the flat was only temporary and this is our home, so we have to make the best of it."

"Don't you get lonely with no one to chat to?"

"Sometimes when I don't go into Fenton for a few days and the weather is bleak and grey like today."

"If ever you fancy a night out at 'The Jolly Sailor' I play guitar most Wednesday's, it's who ever turns up really, sometimes there are only one or two, other times everyone does, or I could bring my guitar here and play for you."

"Well thanks, but I don't go out at night when it's dark."

"So only one thing for it, I'll have to come here then."

Gary looks up from his mug and smiles. Jo acknowledges his attention and returns his smile without comment.

"Right then, how many of these do you want?"

"If it's ok, I'll take the lot, I can use them in the workroom if there are any left over." Gary stands up from the chair and goes to the door.

"I'll give you a hand to carry them."

"It's ok, you stay here, it won't take long."

After a few trips to the van and back, a corner of the hut is piled high with cork tiles. "Look this is all that's wrong with them."

Gary holds one of the tiles to show Jo the staining.

"That's nothing, they will be great for finishing off the outside toilet and there will be plenty left to put some into the workroom, or even upstairs, so thanks."

"Great, well I'll be getting off, I've a couple more deliveries in Thornby to do, so if you want the adhesive, pop into the shop and I'll drop it off for you."

"Thanks again, I'll call in and pay for some adhesive and one or two other things that I need, sometime next week probably."

"OK see you then, bye Jason."

Gary turns and leaves with a wave and another goodbye.
"Thanks, bye."
Jo calls out.

A few days later Jo spends the morning tidying up the
workroom, she will insulate it and put in more shelves
higher up the walls. After lunch Gary calls with the PVA
adhesive for the tiles and a few more bits and pieces.
This time he breezes in and out, saying that he has a lot
of deliveries to make and has to get on.
His last words are left hanging in the air, as he dashes
off.
"So I'll come down one night with the guitar, don't
forget."
Jo's mind begins its somersaults of anxiety and to deter
it, she channels herself into hard work. She opens the
outside toilet and begins cutting and sticking on the cork
tiles. With her new Stanley knife blade they are easy to
cut and she soon has one wall completed – the end result
is impressive and this spurs her on. When she has
finished the walls and the floor she counts up the
remaining tiles, there are plenty left and she puts some
on the inside of the door. The day is drawing in as she
clears her tools away and before going inside to make a
meal, she lights the storm lantern and closes the door.
Sitting down on the loo seat, she admires her efforts, it
should make it much warmer.
The next day she takes it easy and calls for some food
shopping in town; on the way back she carries on to
Woodend Farm and checks for Anna's letter. Sure
enough there is a letter waiting and she rushes home to
read it. This time she opens it readily, without putting the
shopping away.

Dear Jo,
    Good news I've found a cottage, which I
think, will suit all of us. Dogs are welcomed so
Jason will be fine. It's called Thorn Cottage

and it's just beyond the Brig at Nabb's End. I'm really pleased and can't wait.

You sound busy with all the work you're doing in the hut. Keep yourself warm because I can imagine how cold it will get so close to the sea at night. Even in early spring in the caravan it can be freezing. How's Jason? Give him a pat from us.

The children are fine getting back into their routines again and life is busy and we keep going getting on with daily life.

I'm working hard on my course and to be honest it is so complicated and takes up such a large part of my life. I'll be glad when the actual course work is finished.

Maybe if you get a chance you'll be able to take a walk over to the Nabb with Jason and have a look at the cottage. Just an idea.

How's your artwork going? Are you still going down to the beach to collect your driftwood and shells and stones? It seems such a different life here in the city, when I remember what it's like in Fenton. In the city it feels like I'm on this wheel and once on it, it just turns and turns and life just runs out of control. It really does go on and on. It's like a trap when I think about it, that keeps me moving not getting anywhere but it keeps going so I don't stop. It's a really strange experience compared to Fenton, when I stop off the wheel to some extent and have a more balanced experience of life. At least I can step off the wheel and stop for a while at Christmas.

I loved our time together and can't wait until Christmas, we'll have a great time and I know it will be here soon.

Take care.

Love, Anna.

Today couldn't come quick enough, after reading Anna's letter yesterday, Jo wanted to take a look at the cottage straight away. She hasn't walked as far along the coast as Nabb's End and is really looking forward to exploring it. She packs a sandwich and a bottle of water and a few chews for Jason and sets off early. She doesn't know how long it will take to walk the distance and is pleased the weather is fine. They walk down towards the beach and then across the promenade, there is hardly a soul about and the sands are deserted. It is a cold day but soon she feels hot with walking and takes of her cagoule. The shops and café's and beach huts along the front are closed, and the kiddie's rides are all covered up. She walks to the far end to the harbour and then takes the steep flight of steps up and past the harbour bar towards the golf course. Jason is happy when they reach the top and are walking on the grass.

From this point on she is not too sure of the directions and hopes that there will be a signpost, somewhere along the course. She notices only one or two playing today, as she works her way around the public path. Eventually they reach a small signpost giving directions; there are two places on the post, the first is a circular route ending back in Fenton, the other is to the Nabb. The views along this path are spectacular, the enormous white cliffs stretching out to sea are awesome, and the drop to the sea with its crashing, pounding waves below is frightening. Looking back to where she came from, she can see the brig away from the harbour out to sea. She calls Jason several times, to keep him away from the edge. The noise from the sea and spray rising up is like a light rain, being carried in the air. It is a long way before she sees the cottages at Nabb's End – it is a pretty and quaint sight. There are relatively few houses and they are nestled together, almost perched on an incline inland from the sea. Further along before she reaches the Nabb, she passes a steep set of steps, cut out of the cliffs that lead to the beach. The tide is in today and she's unable to go down.

Not much longer now and they reach the cottages – Thorn Cottage is the one she is looking for. There are a few farm cottages at the end of the road and she soon spots the one she is looking for. She is pleased with the sight of it and looks inside the windows, it is a large house and has a fireplace and comfy furniture, and it should be ideal for Christmas for all of them. Jo is hungry now and sits on a wooden bench outside one of the cottages to rest and eat. She assumes it has taken a good hour and a half to reach this place and would be a good walk along the road back into Fenton. She thinks Anna will probably need to use a taxi to get here. After sitting awhile, she begins to feel a chill and puts on her coat, it is time to set off back. Choosing the way they came rather than the road, they set off in the same direction, the views are as panoramic and it is a beautiful stroll home.

Back in the hut, it is good to add a few logs to the stove and sit down; Jo has thoroughly enjoyed the walk and reminds herself to do it again. Picking up paper and a pen she composes a letter to Anna.

Dear Anna,

Jason and I have just returned from a long walk to the Nabb to look at Thorn Cottage. The walk along the cliffs was amazing and the views were stunning. The house looks brilliant and is quite large, it is on the end of the Nabb and one of a few farm cottages - so it's remote and you will probably have to take a taxi to get there. But I think you will like it, I think it's perfect for a Christmas, wintry holiday. There is a walk along the edge of the cliffs that takes you back into Fenton, this is the route I took with Jason, however it is rather tricky in places and although there is a steep set of steps down to the beach these are not ideal, especially for the kids. There is a rough farm road that you could use to walk into Fenton, however a taxi wouldn't cost much as it is only a short car ride into the town, so I think it would be a perfect place to rent. By the looks of it, it has an open fire – I took a look through the windows – no one seems to be staying in it at present. It has comfy furniture and looks clean and tidy and also well equipped so it should be ideal. I can give you some money towards the rent, if you let me know how much. And also how long you would like me to stay, you might like some time with the kids on your own, I don't want to intrude on your space. Anyway I hope it works out and that we get together over the holiday.

I have done lots more work here at the hut. My hands are red raw, sore and chapped now with all the washing and cleaning. The flag floors were filthy again after working and coming in and out of the garden so I had to clean them once more. They look amazing now that I have gone over them a few times with a scrubbing brush. I called at the D I Y shop and spoke to Gary again and he recommended I treat the flags with a protector so that they would be easy to keep clean. So he dropped me some off at the hut, along with several lengths of shelf racking for the workroom. I have given the floor two coats and it really does make a difference, it has a waxy appearance and I am so pleased with it. It is easy to sweep clean now. I haven't begun the work in the workroom yet, I need to give my hands a break, so I enjoyed the extra long walk to the Nabb. It is a wonderful walk on a good day and it took a good couple of hours to get there. I called in Fenton on the way back for fish and chips so that was an incentive also.

It has been freezing here at times so pack plenty of woollies, coats and boots.

Sometimes Anna I think to myself I must have been mad to give up the flat but I did the right thing, we have the place cosy and aired out now and apart from icy cold mornings going to the loo!! It isn't too bad. Having Jason here to chat to makes all the difference. It's hard to imagine you living in a busy city Anna, I can't see you there somehow. All I know is I look forward to seeing you again at Christmas.

So I await your plans for the holidays and look forward to sharing time with you again.

Lots of love

from

Jo and Jason XXX

Several days later Gary arrives in the afternoon with some more of the damaged cork tiles, Jo shows him the outside toilet now that it is finished and he is impressed with the result. She will have enough now, to do the same with the work room and this should make it warm enough to work in, with the door open through to the living room even in winter. Gary announces as he leaves that he will come down this evening to play his guitar, he cheekily says that she deserves a night off.

Since his departure, Jo reflects on his desire to spend time here with her. This prospect heralds a moment, a moment of trust, a moment of change, a moment that she never believed would ever come, to trust her heart, her soul once again, to allow her instincts to guide her and lead her into a safe haven and not into dangerous games. As often happens, like with Jason and Anna coming into her life, things are sometimes meant to be, inevitable fate that divides ones reality and shapes it anew. Unlike Anna and Jason, both of whose sudden impact on her world were instant and life changing, Gary's presence in the ether floated around the edges of her world in wait for the moment, this moment. And yet looking back to the first time their energies met, it was unremarkable, safe and yes on the edge of her sphere, her world. The gradual and intermittent flitting in and out of her space, has been a protection and meant that she has remained without guard in his company. Today, this evening, tonight, entails a crossing over of the line, the line that she marks out, so that others cannot tread or climb across. With Anna and Jason there was no time for attempts at manoeuvring, of distancing, of placing them here or there, they just existed and found an empty void waiting in readiness just for them.

Time has allowed a choice to be made about Gary and it seems that somewhere within her, she has reasoned and found out that he is ok and she can allow him a place to meet with her. He is coming here to play his guitar, this is in itself straightforward and yet for Jo it feels an extraordinary stepping-stone to jump across. There will be no fervent action and passionate fire between them she can vouch for that, she is assured enough to know, that her mending heart is shielded and almost senses that Gary is aware and has been from the moment they first met. So she is quietly looking forward to being with him, listening to the strumming of his guitar.

With Charles's sudden, impetuous, controlling demeanour, Jo begat inside his spell, without aids to disembark his perilous actions and unable to make sure of her boundaries and limitations – he acquired his expectations, with greed and without joy. Oh how glad she feels, to be out and away from his demands and clutches. He was and is a mirror of her past and she must stay clear, detached and away from him, she knows that now. She should have known that then, 'oh but I did and I do.' This is the dilemma, how often what we feel and

know is wrong, becomes right, because it is in our genes
and courses our veins, time and time again.

Gary hasn't travelled before in her cells and therefore
she knows that it will be all right, he will be ok. He has
no tried and tested map, with which she knows how to
follow, but here lies the affirmation – the rugged,
treacherous territory, the precipice, the caverns, the
bottomless rock pools, the edges of the cliffs – all and
more of which she knows, are not drawn out on Gary's
map, therefore, it is safe, he is safe – with undulating
hills and flat plains and a calm sea lapping at the shore.
And yes, how sure she is to acknowledge the loss, the
gaping chasm and ache for the excitement, the chartered
terrain, of the land beyond the mountain top, but she
knows the cost, knows the result, of treading on loose
rocks and falling down into a heap on the ground with no
life line, no hand reaching out to hang on to and not
knowing if her climbing partner is alive or dead.
"Come on Jason let's go for a walk."
Jo grabs his lead and puts on her jacket, it is windy
outside, she needs to get out of the hut and away from
her inner turmoil of reflections. They take the path to the
cliff top and then walk along the rough track that leads to
Hunsby Gap, it is not a walk that she often chooses,
looking out across the turbulent sea, the view is amazing,
the sheer cliffs jutting out around the coastline are
dramatic and soon distract her thoughts. When they
reach Hunsby, they pass the hut with its shutters boarded
up; this is a café in summer and opens when the tide is
out. Today the place looks drab and forlorn, empty of
people and asleep for the winter. They walk on past tiny
rows of cottages, the local shop and The Sandpiper Pub.
Soon reaching the main road and make their way along
the cycle track and past Woodend Farm. Jo checks the
mailbox and is surprised to find another letter from
Anna. Jo hurries back to the hut and sits down to read it.

Dear Jo,

I was really pleased that you and Jason liked the cottage, it sounds amazing and the views spectacular, I can't wait to see it and for Christmas to arrive.

Your poor hands, have you thought about using some calendula cream from the chemist, it might be worth going in to have a chat with them? When I come across at Christmas I'll bring you some, which I can make up for you.

I will pack up plenty of warm clothes for the cold biting winds on the coast.

Make sure you stay warm and cosy in your hut and give Jason a hug from me.

Take care of yourself.

Bye for now. Anna

P.S. I'll meet you on the 23rd at the railway station about 11.30 ish – I've to check times yet but the notice board in the station will tell you what time were due in exactly.

It is early evening when Jo hears Gary's footsteps
coming down the path, this puts an end to her anxiety
and worries, as if the preceding hours of doubts and
stress were all for nothing, as her heart steadies itself and
calmness fills her.

"Hiya."

Gary shouts out as he opens the door. He has his guitar
slung across his back and under his arm he is carrying a
pack of lager.

"Hi."

Jo acknowledges him as Jason bounds forward, making a
huge fuss.

Gary puts the bottles down on the table and stands his
guitar against the sofa and bends down to play with him.

"I envy you this place."

Gary says looking up.

"Why, where do you live?"

"I have an ex council house on the Eastfield estate, it's
ok but I like this, it's quiet and the large garden is great.
You could do all sorts with this place, I know it's only a
beach hut but with the stove lit, it feels lovely and
warm."

"I'm glad that I'm back, the flat was ok but I like the self
sufficiency of living here, sometimes it's hard when the
weather is freezing cold but it's a lot better than when I
first moved in."

"I've brought a few lagers, I wasn't sure what to bring."

"I don't usually drink much but thanks the lager will be
nice."

"Have you eaten? I could order a pizza or something."

"No I haven't actually."

Jo tells him and then blurts out without thinking.

"I was a bit nervous about you coming."

"Well that's sorted then, what would you like, a Chinese
an Indian or a pizza?"

"Any of them would be a treat for me; I don't buy
takeouts living here."

"Right then, how about a Chinese, do you prefer chicken
or beef or are you vegetarian?"

"Chicken would be nice, I'll pay half towards it."
"No it's ok, you can pay next time. Shall I order, it will
be at least half an hour before it comes?"
"Yes, you choose."
Gary takes his mobile phone from his jacket pocket and
calls the takeaway.
He is wearing jeans, a checked shirt and dealer boots on
his feet. He has a well-scrubbed appearance, his hair
freshly washed and clean-shaven. His body is lean and
strong and Jo feels as if she's noticing him for the first
time. She is unused to him standing before her, without
his work clothes on.
"Would you like a lager?"
Gary asks intruding on Jo's observations.
"Yes, I'll get some glasses."
"I'll drink it out of the bottle Jo."
"Ok then, I will too."
Gary removes his coat and places it on the back of the
kitchen chair and then takes two bottles from the box.
"Have you got a bottle opener?"
"Oh no, I haven't."
Gary looks around the hut for something else to use. He
spots the metal boot scraper in the doorway and takes the
bottles across. With a quick hand and wrist action he
flicks off the tops and the foamy froth pours out of the
top. He takes a swig from one and walks over and hands
her the other.
"Cheers."
Gary says as he clinks his bottle against Jo's.
"Cheers."
She takes a sip of the fizzy liquid and enjoys the
sensation, as her mouth fills with the icy cold bubbles.
After chatting about his suggestions for improving the
hut, Gary leans down and picks up his guitar and sits
down on the sofa, placing his bottle on the floor. He
looks intently at the strings and plucks his fingers and
brushes his hand across them. Jo sits in the chair
opposite.
"Would you like me to play?"

"Yes, sure I'd like that."

After a few attempts at tuning he begins to play. The sound is delicate and gentle and he looks up occasionally to check her response, Jo smiles back and watches as his fingers quicken. He exudes a look of total contentment as he plays and then as he starts to sing his whole face lights up. Later when his mobile phone rings he stops and places the guitar on the floor.

"Cheers mate, I'll be just a sec."

"The delivery van is up at the lay-by, get the plates ready and I'll nip up and get it."

Jo takes the plates from the rack and holds them in front of the stove to warm them and adds another couple of logs to the fire. When Gary returns he puts the paper bag down and takes out the containers.

"That was lovely hearing you playing, thanks."

"Great, let's get stuck in to this."

He takes the lids off, exposing the contents.

Jason plods across from his bed, wondering what this new smell is all about. They take turns in filling their plates with the food. There is chicken with peppers and a black bean sauce, fried rice, noodles and a portion of filo parcels and a dipping sauce. It smells wonderful.

Gary eats greedily and Jo quickly relaxes, he is totally at ease as he drops a forkful of noodles and laughs. The sauce is deep and tasty and Jo savours every mouthful, as her taste buds come alive to the flavours. She pushes a couple of pieces of chicken to the side of her plate for Jason, who sits waiting for his share. Gary watches and instinctively does the same.

"That was gorgeous, thank you."

"I thought it would make a change for you, what do you normally cook?"

"In the summer I eat lots of salads and fruit grown in the garden and in the autumn and winter, I cook on top of the stove and just put vegetables and meat into a pot."

"Such a simple existence, you have a rare place here Jo, remember that. Would you like another lager?"

"Would you like a mug of tea first?"

"Yes, why not."

Jo fills the kettle and puts it on top of the stove to boil.

"Shall I give Jason the leftovers?"

"Yes the chicken and rice but not too much of the sauce."

Gary scrapes the scraps into Jason's bowl and then takes the plates to the sink.

"Shall I wash up?"

"No it's ok, I'll do them later."

"No, I'll do it, I'm used to washing up."

"OK then."

"How's your friend?"

"Anna, oh she's returned home, she doesn't live in Fenton, she was staying at her caravan on holiday."

"Oh I see she was just helping you out then?"

"Yes, she is coming here for Christmas though, she's renting a cottage at Nabb's End and I am staying with her for the holiday."

"Great, that will be nice for you, I'll be playing at The Station pub on Boxing Day night if you fancy coming along, I'll buy you both a drink."

"Thanks, I'll remember that and tell Anna when she comes."

After the mugs of tea, Gary opens two more bottles and reaches again for his guitar.

"Would you like me to play again?"

"Yes, definitely."

This time the rhythm is faster with more intent, Gary appears to be inside the music and as he taps the instrument like a drum, his voice wells up with emotion as he sings.

'FROM THE SURFACE OF THE SEA
 TO THE BOTTOM OF MY HEART
I DON'T FORGET THE YEARS, OR OUR
LAUGHTER

IT IS 16 MONTHS AND COUNTING
AND MY SONG FOR YOU'S THE SAME
NO MORE HELLO'S, NO MORE GOODBYE'S
IT IS 16 MONTHS AND COUNTING
AND MY SONG FOR YOU'S THE SAME'

After the song, Gary puts down his guitar and takes a last
swig from his bottle.
"Sorry Jo, I shouldn't have sung that, I don't know what
made me." Gary stands up.
"It's ok."
"Well I'll be getting off now."
"Thanks for coming and playing, I've enjoyed listening
and the food."
"Another time then?"
Gary picks up his jacket and swings his guitar across his
back and then kneels down to give Jason a last pat before
leaving. He turns around before opening the door; his
face shows a soft smile with sadness in his eyes, he gives
a wave of his hand and leaves.
The evening with Gary leaves Jo feeling both perturbed
and happy, this man, whom she thought to be a happy,
go lucky type, has surprised her with his song. She
doesn't feel tired and ready for bed just yet, so she picks
up a pen and paper and composes a letter to send to
Anna.

Dear Anna,

Thanks for your letter. I am so, so looking forward
to the holiday with all of you. I have been gathering a
few food things together to bring along to share. I took
your advice and bought the cream you recommended
for my sore hands and it has helped a lot, they are less
red and chapped, so thanks.

I will meet you all at the station and we can take a
taxi to the cottage, hopefully we should all squeeze in
together.

It will certainly feel like a 'holiday' for me, away from the ongoing work here, to rest and eat good food and have company will be Christmas in itself, I don't desire much more than that. These past couple of weeks have been the coldest since living here, I've worn more layers than an onion, to try and keep warm!

The thoughts of turkey and all the trimmings and Christmas pudding, well – pure and utter bliss for me and Jason, he will think he has landed in heaven I'm sure!!

So it won't be long now until you're all here. I think you know how much I am looking forward to it, so see you soon.

Love from Jo and Jason X

P.S. Gary is playing at The Station Pub over the holiday and he's asked us to go along – it would be a nice thing to do if you fancy?

South London.

The clock on the shelf behind him ticks noisily; there are moments when it falls silent, only to return with much more purpose to tick, tick, tick. This ticking induces in him a concentrated effort to focus; he cannot allow its persistent reminder of time running out to deter him. He sighs and draws in a long deep breath and fixes his eyes once more. He likes the idea of the random letters spread out in front of him on the desk; he enjoys shuffling his hands as he rearranges them. The cutting out he has finished; the absorption with scissors and paper is over. This time he has used several magazines and different papers, resulting in an array of coloured fonts in many sizes.

He particularly likes the red. The image he holds in his mind is of liquid; deep rich red blood dripping, it arouses him. To the ticking of the clock, the blood forms into droplets and falls to the floor. He remembers the warmth, remembers how he had felt, gripping his right side as the blood trickled out. And too, how the strange, satisfying calm, infused and comforted him on its release. He pulls his shirt from inside his trousers to check the scar; it still has a raised welt along its length. He smiles as he runs his finger where the stitches had once been and presses it, until he can feel the heat, the hurt. The inflamed cut is now fiery and red as he returns his hand to the desk. He needs to select each letter carefully and place them on the white A4 paper, before sticking them down. The pleasure he derives from composing the few words satisfies him and he reselects once again. As he thinks of her, he wills his sexual desire to come, for his penis to enlarge and feel heavy, to pulse and throb but there is nothing, no stirring, no tightness, no urgent hand needed to work up and down to release his orgasm – he feels bereft and adrift. If only, if only he had this, one hungry urgent erection that couldn't wait, that had to be assuaged before anything else.

He peruses the alphabetic collection, with precise and intent intention, it consumes him, until he is satisfied enough to rise from his chair, knowing that this selection will carry him through the day.

Passing the kitchen, he notices the table set, with the half eaten remnants of his breakfast, the toast rack with piece of cold toast, the eggcup on a plate with a mound of salt, toast crumbs and broken eggshell. The matching teapot, milk jug and sugar bowl lay also on the tablecloth. He carries on to the hallway and selects a warm coat from the stand and with a brief glance in the mirror he locks the door.

His quick footsteps belie his age and he soon turns the corner, making his way to the shop. He collects a copy of the Times newspaper and continues his brisk walk, leaving the estate behind, heading towards open countryside. His decision to collect the paper at the onset of his stroll fills him now with irritation, the grey sky hangs menacingly over the trees, it is bound to rain. He will have to tuck the paper inside his coat if the heavens open. His stout shoes are adequate, as is his coat and with a brisk shake on his return, they would dry out in a day. He prefers a bright and sunny morning, when the sky is full of birdsong and the plethora of rabbits are out at play. He loves to stand and observe the red kites soaring and the spotting of a deer, darting through the woods lower down the bank thrills him.

Today however it is cold, quiet and empty of the sounds of nature at its best and he hurries stepping aside the molehills, rocks and rabbit holes. He slips and lumbers forward, his breath quickening as he regains his footing and the memory of the day he had twisted his ankle in a divot comes flooding back. He had limped slowly home and vowed to be more careful ever since. His chest heaves with the physical exertion against the dankness and he has to stop to draw in a lungful of air as he climbs the last mound, before descending down towards the woods. Continuing warily down the slope, he adjusts his footing as the heavy raindrops begin to fall. He curses, slipping the paper inside his overcoat. A momentary pang of contentment follows as he presses his only ally and friend close against his chest. It is the promise of spending a good few hours of the day immersed between its pages, reading and doing the crossword that pushes his footsteps into the driving rain. He revels in the challenge, revels in the day when the clue evades him, when his whole preoccupation is attached in search of its answer, contemplating the conundrum of completing the puzzle. The day when it is too easy, when his pen races through filling in the empty boxes and it is over for the day, always shrouds him with it's offering of space and time, time to dwell, time to think. It has the reverse effect of satisfaction and leaves a nagging, impatient willing of an end to the day. He demands a complex, succinct and arduous challenge, and a task that would carry him through the hours until evening, darkness and the blackness of night. Time is a double-edged sword; he needs it, but feels contempt for it all the same. On days where he has the generosity of space to think inside of his own mind, he is ravaged by his spiteful assignation, he detests his mission that he set himself, the unprecedented, dogmatic, vengeful and relentless pursuit of her.

The rumbling thunder and the flashing cracks of lightening, light up the menacing steel sky, as he braces himself against the wind, that whips through the air and surges through the branches of the trees, bending them towards the ground.
At last he turns down the avenue that leads to his house. Standing beneath the porch, he waits for a minute before removing his coat. His heart sinks as he watches the paper drop with a thud onto the tiled floor, it is wringing wet through – it is beyond rescuing. His resolve is set as he attempts to pick it up, it is a soggy mush and any

attempt at drying it out would fail, he has to return to the
shop and purchase another issue.

Later as he strips off his wet clothes and rubs himself
with a towel, he is determined that for the remainder of
the day he will stay inside. His pattern and orderly
routine has been disordered with the second visit to the
shop and he cannot afford himself a chill. This decision
to render his lunchtime pint and general shopping to
another day festers, leaches and stirs, resulting in an
impatient irritation, that gives him no satisfaction with
any task and impacts throughout the day.
His usual appetite, post pint is generally hearty – he
would tuck into an assortment of savoury delights, select
cuts of meat or fish accompanied with fresh vegetables
or salads and a strong cheese followed by fruit. He
always dines at the table, which he sets out meticulously,
and he prides himself on being an accomplished cook.
Now however, he looks with distaste at the mess from
the breakfast earlier and turns to check the food cabinet.
The tins of store cupboard standbys are in military
alignment, row upon row of tuna, corned beef, salmon,
ham, crabmeat and jars of pickles. He selects the nearest
and a packet of crackers and slams them on a plate. The
meal is dry and tasteless and he loses interest,
disregarding the leftovers and pushes the plate away.
The table now is unpleasing to look at and his dejected
spirit forces him to snatch The Times and take it to the
sitting room.

His mood lifts slightly as he sits in his armchair, he slips
on his reading glasses from the coffee table and picks up
his ballpoint pen and rolls it between his fingers. He
turns to the crossword page and snaps the paper, laying it
carefully across his lap and smoothing it with his hands.
He fixes his eyes on the clues, across and down and
searches his mind for an answer. Although his eyes stay
glued to the page his attention is elsewhere, he cannot
settle. He whips the paper and drops it onto the table and

gets up from the chair. The rain hitting the window irritates him and he moves across to the drinks cabinet, picks up a wine goblet and runs his finger along the bottles and selects a burgundy red, one of his favourites. He rips the foil from the top and pierces the cork, the turning of the screw pleases him and the resulting pop, having just the right note delights him momentarily. He knows the wine should be served at room temperature to be at its best, it would be an insult to its vintage and its astronomical price not to wait. He takes the bottle and glass back to his seat, determined to let the wine breathe and come to room temperature and then leans forward to light the gas fire.

Stella's eyes open slowly and close again as her head lay softly on the plump, duck down, feather pillow. Christmas day is only a couple of weeks away and she knows she would have it to herself, that she would be on her own in seclusion – no family gathering, no well orchestrated Christmas day turkey lunch to prepare and eat with close relatives or friends. Not even any carefully wrapped presents waiting for her to open with delight and enjoy their contents for the rest of the day.

'I've told a lie,' she instantly says to herself, there is Charles's gift with its gold ribbon tied around it, waiting for her downstairs. A present – no surprise either, no anticipation and wonder, she knows its contents, she had pointed it out herself to Charles during their trip to France. Yet she eagerly looks forward to opening it, it is beautiful. She had spotted it in a tiny shop window, as they had walked around her favourite village one afternoon. She remembers the day fondly, it was the day after they had arrived – the one-day that Charles was completely sober and detached from his angst about Margaret back home in Fenton. The little shop with its enamelled sign was open and she had pointed her finger at an unusual, coloured, hand made, enamelled brooch in the window, saying how much she loved it. The price tag was hidden out of view but she knew instantly that she needed to have it. The brooch was only one of many unusual pieces displayed inside the shop, its owner – a young man, had been delighted to show off his different handmade items. He had enamelled jewellery boxes, mirrors, bracelets and large wall hangings, lots and lots of fascinating, original and distinctive gifts. As she held the brooch in her hands and turned it over and looked at it closely, she was amazed how he had achieved so much depth and beauty in the texture and colour of the piece. It had intense blues, reds and greens and appeared to have golden threads pulled through resting on the base. She had told Charles how beautiful and unusual it was.

She had been surprised by Charles, as he picked up on her curiosity about the brooch and had actually agreed with her about its uniqueness and didn't hesitate in handing over the €150 from his wallet to buy it. The craftsman had covered the dark green, gift box, proudly and studiously in gold paper.

Later that day back at The Argentor, they had shared a steaming hot bowl of garlicky, moules mariniere with crusty bread, followed by slices of rare roast beef with squashed, herby potatoes and green beans. They had taken their time eating through the courses and sipping their way through the carafe of rough red wine and Stella had felt the tension of the past few days gently float away from her. The sticky, chocolate tart with crème anglais and to the two, runny, local cheeses with bread were sublime, finished off with a tiny cup of dark, rich coffee. Charles was in his element there, eating his evening meal served on the outside terrace, talking about French property and she had thought that he had found himself again and had begun to lift himself out of his self-pity. Charles had ordered another carafe of wine and afterwards, strolling arm in arm, they had walked around the village.

'Why am I thinking about Christmas? Why am I thinking about Charles and France?' Stella ponders. 'Because you need to decide what and who you want in life – Christmas is a time of celebration and here you are weeks before deciding to opt out.' Stella remembers Charles's conversation of yesterday and his invitation to spend the day with his family and how she had made her excuses of 'wanting to chill out on her own'.
'Oh for God's sake get a grip.' she remonstrates. The problem is she doesn't know what she wants and with this thought she gets out of bed.

Anna hopes, as the train pulls into the station, that Jo and
Mark will be there. Adam and Georgina are excited and
can't wait to see the cottage at Nabb's End. Anna has
brought clothes and gifts and a home made Christmas
cake but once settled and a cup of tea and toast they will
have to be back into the town centre to do the shopping
to see them through the Christmas holiday. The cottage
isn't that far away from the centre and Anna knows that
they could walk it but with their entire luggage it would
make life easier to take a taxi. Adam had nattered non-
stop on the train and before they left the city to 'Please.'
call off at the caravan to get his mobile phone, which his
friend had given him, when he was last at the coast.
Anna had hoped with the excitement of the holiday and
seeing his brother and Jo again, that he would have let it
go and given up on it but he still wants his phone.
"It doesn't work."
Anna had told him repeatedly. Adam got through mobile
phones quicker than anyone. He lost them, or swapped
them, or gave them away and she has had enough of the
mobile phone saga.
"Please mam, I can buy a new sim card from the pound
shop."
Adam asks again as they stand on the station platform
waiting, on a cold late morning the day before Christmas
Eve.
"Ok, we'll see what we can do."
She promises her son.
"Mark will be able to make it work."
Adam beams as he saunters down the platform while
Anna and her daughter struggle with the trolley and the
pull along suitcase and bags.
"Adam."
Anna calls after her son.
"Come on."
Anna and her children make their way into the station
waiting room where they are to meet Mark and Jo.
"Come on now sit down, we won't be waiting long."
'Come on Mark.' Anna says to herself, 'be here, come.'

Sitting down with crisps and juice, Adam and Georgina
settle for a few minutes.

"Hiya Jo."

Adam calls out. Turning around Anna sees Jo walking
towards them with Jason and loaded up to the brim.

"Jo."

Anna calls and catching sight of her, Jo smiles and
waves.

"It's good to see you again."

Excited at their reunion Anna tells Georgina.

"This is Jo."

Georgina smiles.

"How's things, how are you?"

"We're fine, look Jo, Mark isn't here yet. You remember
what he's like about being on time I'm sure, but I think
he will come."

"That's ok, we can wait and catch up a bit."

Georgina and Adam stroke and pet Jason; he is
obviously enjoying the attention.

"Jo, would you mind if I nipped off for ten minutes up to
the caravan. Adam has nattered me to death since we
returned home from the coast, at the end of the summer,
about an old mobile phone he left behind. I won't be
long, I'll nip off quickly and be back straight away."

"Yes that's fine, I'll stay here and wait for Mark to turn
up."

"Good, I'll go up there by taxi and when I come back we
can all go to the cottage in it."

Anna tells her children what she plans to do and says she
won't be more than ten, fifteen minutes and they have to
wait with Jo and watch out for Mark. Georgina doesn't
look happy about being left, so she tells Jo she will take
her daughter with her.

Climbing out of the taxi, on the cold deserted campsite,
Anna asks the driver to give her five minutes.

"I just have something I need to collect."

Unlocking the caravan door, Anna climbs in and holds out her hand to help her daughter up.

"Right, you empty the toy box and book box out and I'll look under all of the seats."

Anna searches, she can't find the phone under any of the seats. Lifting one of the large cushions near her bed she picks up a handful of A4 crumpled sheets. 'These can go in a rubbish bag,' Anna tells herself as she briefly unravels one and realises that they are actually the loose sheets of Fermanagh House. They had obviously got stuck under the back of the cushions and she had forgotten them. She'd meant to put them on the bonfire with the blue note book but what with one thing and another she'd left them behind. She stuffs the sheets into her bag, to burn on the cottage fire.

"Come on Gina, let's try and find Adam's phone, or we won't get any peace all the holiday."

Anna goes into the kitchen and opens the cupboards and drawers but the phone is nowhere to be found. After searching through the top of the mattress, on the bunk bed in the kitchen, she lifts it up. There is nothing except for some plastic carrier bags. She pulls them out to see if the phone is underneath. Feeling a solid object inside the carrier bags, she opens them and finds a CD in a plastic wallet.

'What's this?' Anna asks herself as she calls through to her daughter to say they will have to go in a minute. She puts the CD in her bag and returns into the living room area. Georgina stands up smiling she is holding an old, black, cracked mobile phone in her hand.

"Is this it mum?"

"It must be, come on Gina, let's put this lot back and get into the taxi."

Together they pile all the toys and books back in their boxes and Anna puts the phone in her bag and looks around her caravan.

"Come on love, let's get back in the taxi and see if Mark's here."

Anna helps her daughter down and locks the caravan, she is glad to see the taxi still waiting for them.
At the train station Mark has arrived.
"Hi mam."
He smiles after their greeting. They put all the luggage into the taxi and somehow Anna, Jo, Mark, Jason, Georgina and Adam all fit in and they are on their brief journey to Nabb's End and Thorn Cottage for their Christmas holidays.

The drive across town doesn't take long and soon the taxi is coming off the cobbled section of road to take the rough track on to Nabb's End, it begins to climb and weave gently until they can see the sea and the Brig.
"Were near the sea."
Georgina and Adam cry squealing with pleasure.
 "Which one is it?"
The taxi driver asks as they begin to approach the first farmhouse on the Nabb.
"Thorn Cottage."
Anna tells him.
"A bit further then."
Pulling up outside a large, stone, double fronted house, the taxi driver says.
"This is it love, Thorn Cottage."

There is a car parked outside the cottage and as Anna pays the taxi driver, the front door of the cottage opens and a small, dark haired, middle-aged woman steps out, she is smiling.
"Hello, hello, I'm Mrs Thompson."
Anna introduces herself and her family and Jo and Jason and with everyone's help, all their things are taken into the large hallway.
Leading Anna into the large kitchen, Mrs Thompson begins her tour of Thorn Cottage.
"This is obviously the kitchen; we have a dish washer and washing machine and the cookers gas. I'll make a pot of tea, so please help yourselves."

On the large scrubbed pine table there is a tray of mugs, milk and sugar and a plate of biscuits. After mashing the tea she puts the huge brown teapot alongside.

"Do you have dishes for the dog?"

Mrs Thompson asks.

"Yes."

"That's fine, I'm happy for the dog to have the run of the house. The cottage has stained and polished oak floorboards, so there are no carpets to soil and the rugs can all be cleaned and the settee covers are washable. I don't allow dogs to sleep on the beds and you must collect their business outside."

Mrs Thompson adds.

"That's fine, I will make sure that we don't leave any mess."

"What's his name?"

"Jason."

Anna and Jo continue their tour around Thorn Cottage; they are both happy with the two downstairs sitting rooms. The open fire in the large sitting room is lit, making the room warm and cosy.

Mrs Thompson tells the women.

"If you have any problems we're not far away and we can help you out if you need it."

Anna loves the huge roaring fire, which lights up the large comfortable room – she knows that they are going to have a wonderful time here. The other smaller room has an electric fire and TV with a VHS/DVD player attached, as well as a large radio and CD player. The kids will be happy. All across the mantles of both rooms are delicate fairy lights, which have been turned on, and the window cills have holly and tiny Santa Claus candles and miniature Christmas trees on. The bathroom is big enough for all the family and there are four bedrooms, two with double beds and two with single beds in. Upstairs there is an attic with a large comfy bed in. Anna notices that Mark has already bagged this room for himself, seeing his rucksack and carrier bags on the floor. She has agreed to Abby coming to the cottage to

spend a few nights here but in a way she hoped he would
not have chosen a room with a double bed in, but that's
unrealistic she realises. She also feels a touch of concern
too about her son. Since she'd returned back to her life in
the city, he never wrote or called asking for money and
was forever telling her what he had bought, or what he
was going to buy. She hoped it was money from doing
the work with the travellers, doing driveways and odd
jobs but he seemed never to be short. She also wondered
whether or not he'd been tapping Abby for money or
else stealing. Mark seems full of himself, confident and
fine but Anna has a sense of unease with her sons newly
found wealth. She'd find out in the end, she always does,
'where he is getting it all from?' she only hopes it is
reasonably legal and safe. Drugs come to mind, but she
pushes these thoughts away as Mark and Adam argues
about who has a right to the attic bedroom.
Mrs Thompson decides to leave, after having shown
them around and leaves her phone number on the kitchen
table. Anna tells Georgina to take her things into one of
the twin rooms and she and Jo have one of the double
bedrooms each. After Anna put her things into her room
she finds the old mobile phone in her bag.
"Adam."
Anna calls her son.
"Is this your mobile?"
Adam comes straight away, followed shortly after by
Mark. Adam picks up the mobile from the bedside
cabinet between the two single beds.
"Bring his sack in and help him to get his mobile
working."
Anna tells Mark.
"I'll buy him a new one for Christmas."
Mark tells her, as she turns to check on her daughter,
before going downstairs to the kitchen for a cup of tea.
Jo is filling up Jason's water dish and arranging a corner
in the kitchen, out of the way, where Jason can have his
bed.
"I've made a fresh brew."

"Lovely, after this, shall we walk into town and finish our Christmas shopping, so that we have Christmas Eve free?"

"Yes, that's a good idea, it will give Jason a walk and the fresh air will be good."

"Yes, it's not too far and once I've emptied this trolley, we can use if for the shopping and we can take a rucksack each to carry what other things we need."

Jo pours the tea whilst Anna unpacks her trolley.

"Christmas cake and a few tins of tuna."

Anna says.

"I think it might be a good idea if we make a list of what we need, once we've sorted out what we have."

"Good idea."

Jo has already unpacked Jason's sack of dog food and biscuits and chews and has begun to unpack her groceries.

"It's all from the farmers market."

Jo tells her as she puts the large bag of potatoes, the parsnips, carrots, sprouts, mushrooms and tomatoes on the large kitchen table.

"God that must have weighed a ton."

"I'm used to carrying heavy things."

"So."

Anna begins as Jo gets a pen and her notebook.

"What do we want?"

Anna thinks.

"Turkey, sausages, bacon and eggs. Stand pie, Christmas pudding, stuffing, crisps, snacks."

Jo writes it down.

"Baking ingredients for mince pies."

Anna adds.

"Yes, we could also make a couple of quiches with the cheese and bacon and tomatoes to stretch our food."

"Good idea."

"Wine."

Jo reminds Anna.

"And pop and juice and sweets for the children."

"Fruit, we have to have oranges and apples, satsuma's and shelled nuts and dates."
"That's enough for a few days, let's finish our tea, I'll check the cupboards for baking tins."
Anna puts away what foods they have and clears the table.
"A pizza for tea and yoghurts to finish."
Going upstairs Anna checks on the children. They are all up in the attic with Mark 'chilling' and listening to music.
"Mark."
Anna smells the cigarette smoke.
"Smoking isn't allowed in the cottage, I told you, smoke outside."
She begins walking downstairs.
"And don't give Adam cigarettes."
Anna hears her youngest sons guffaws, at what she's said and the 'as if' makes her more sure Mark has given him a smoke.
Anna unpacks her own clothes and is amazed when one of the wardrobes turns out to be a small bathroom. It's amazing, 'I won't tell the kids or I'll never get a chance to use it for myself.'
She puts away her children's clothes and leaves their personal belongings on the floor in neat piles for them to sort out; she puts the empty sacks and suitcases on top of the wardrobes out of the way.
'Done.' She leaves Georgina and Adam's pyjamas on top of their beds.
She puts the pages of Fermanagh House with the CD in her bedside drawer to look at later.
"Come on now."
Anna shouts up the attic stairs.
"Were going shopping."
"Do we have to?"
Adam asks.
"Yes you do, so all of you come on."
"I'm hungry."
Georgina moans.

"Well come down and get a jam sandwich, come on."
Anna calls as she returns down stairs.
"We could buy a pasty."
Jo says putting on her coat.
"Yes, we can but I'll just do jam sarnis to keep them
going, Mark says he will come too because he still has a
couple of presents left to buy."
Anna wants to tell Mark to be careful. There is
something, which she can sense about her son, which
makes her feel uneasy but she doesn't know what it is.
The sea is so near to the cottage, it sounds wild and
chaotic. Although the cottage is high up on the road and
the sea is much lower, they can feel its immense energy
and power as they all walk into the town to shop. The
group are excited at the prospect of a happy holiday.

As they walk into the town centre, it seems life within
Fenton has woken up to the festive season. Fairy lights
are in the shop windows, as well as decorations and as
they all walk down one of the main streets, there are
swags of Christmas lights swung across the shops all the
way down.
"We'll have to come back into the town centre."
Anna says to Jo.
"And see the lights when they're turned on."
There is excitement now in the air; it is almost tangible
as they walk.
"Mam."
Mark catches up with Anna.
"I've got some bits and pieces I still have to do and
collect and if I can, I want to phone Abbs and see if we
can meet up."
Anna looks into her son's face.
"Don't be long Mark, be careful."
She adds.
"Pizza for tea."
"In a bit mam, I'll get Abbs to drop me off at the
cottage."

Mark crosses the road. To the pub Anna thinks, as she watches him disappear around the corner. Looking back she sees Adam and Georgina with Jo looking in the Military shop window. She will have to go and move Adam on; otherwise he'll spend all day looking in, or else going in the shop itself.
"Can we go in and look, just once?"
Adam pleads.
The women look at one another and smile. Georgina protests and Anna tells her.
"Just a minute."
In the shop, the man who had sold them the bullet cases is talking to a middle aged man. When the group walk in he glances briefly at them and then looks away.

Malcolm's stomach turns over. So she is still here in Fenton. He can feel his heart racing and fluttering. When he has finished serving the man he returns to his counter and Adam immediately asks him if he can look at the big red and white bullet in the glass case.
"It's a shell."
Malcolm corrects him but still slides the glass back and lifts the 30 mm GAV Avenger and lets him hold it.
"It's brilliant, what's it called?"
Adam asks.
Malcolm tells him.
"It's an Avenger."
"We bought our cannons from you."
Adam reminds Malcolm.
"Yes, I remember."
"Right, we need to give the shell case back don't we?"
Adam holds onto the case but Anna opens out her hand for him to return it.
"Thank you."
Anna turns to Malcolm and puts the shell into his hand.
"Say thank you, Adam, for the man letting you look at the shell."
"Thanks."
"Ok, thank you very much and have a happy Christmas."

Anna tells Malcolm and smiles gently at him.
Malcolm feels her touch and her words leave him unable
to respond and it is awhile after they have all left before
he gets himself together.

As Mildred sees the happy group leave the shop, she
watches them. 'It isn't natural,' she tells herself, for
these kinds of things to be going on. 'These lesbians.'
Albert would have known what to do about them. He
would have sorted them out and given them what's what.
There are children too. Mildred watches them smiling
into each other's faces and the children hanging on to
their arms.

"Let's go to the butchers first."
"We can get the turkey there and buy our stand pie and
sausages and bacon, it's nicer than the supermarket."
Anna agrees, so their first stop is the butchers.

Stella hates the crowded supermarket, its aisles crammed full of tetchy people scrambling for their Christmas indulgence of food shopping. Anyone would think the shops would never open again, by the way the trolleys are piled high and nearly spilling over their metal cages. She particularly dislikes the close proximity of human flesh next to hers, especially when they brush against her, jostling to overtake. She wishes she could forget the shopping and leave this overbearing and frantic place to these people who seem to want it all for themselves, as if there isn't enough to go round. However, she knows she hasn't sufficient food to keep her throughout the Christmas break and so she has no option but to push her virtually empty trolley and put in the things she needs. She can hardly concentrate, or think what to buy; she is fatigued and exhausted. All she really wants to do is undress and flop onto her soft bed, pull up the duvet and switch herself from the world and Christmas and sleep and wake up when it's all over.

If this were a normal working week, she could have popped in here, or into the local shops in Fenton and bought what she fancied for that day and be in and out in a few minutes. Today, the day before Christmas Eve is unbelievably horrendous, she can't decide on anything and the queues at the checkouts are spilling into the food aisles, it will take forever to get out. Stella appreciates good food and likes to cook; she normally chooses fresh ingredients, fish, meats, chicken and lots of fruit and vegetables to create her own recipes with herbs and spices. Today she is unable to think, her mind is so frazzled by the pressure of the last working week, trying to catch up and finalise last minute contracts, before the office closed down for Christmas. And being a part of Charles's roller coaster, of the last few weeks, she had stepped in and helped out, whilst he sank further into despair and self-pity and right now she just wants space to opt out.

And so without a food list of things to buy, she is pushed along and at intervals, throws into the trolley an array of items. There is no way she will be cooking a turkey and all its trimmings, she wants to step away from this ordeal of Christmas; she had flatly refused Charles's invite and had phoned Margaret to make sure that she knew, Charles would carry on in earnest, insisting that she couldn't possible be on her own. She also knows that she would be there for his benefit and she doesn't fancy another drunken display in front of Margaret and the rest of their family.

She needs nurturing and pampering and this part of her grabs at comfort food and finishes off with a selection of wines, at the end of the shop. 'This should do it,' she thinks as she heads for the queue at the checkout, she struggles to separate herself and switch off from the shrieking kids, the bickering parents and the complaining golden oldies. There are few unattached people like her; they have escaped this ordeal somehow. As she waits for her turn and the long line of people in front of her to pay, she wishes that she could be anywhere but here, where the seasons greetings are blaring and glaring at her. She doesn't want to hear Noddy Holder belting out merry Christmas – everybody's having fun, one more time, or see the red hooded Santa with a present in his hands. She just wants out, out of here and out of Christmas altogether.

Mark saunters away from his mother, Jo and his brother and sister and smiles to himself, in anticipation of another meeting with Charles. Their arrangements have changed, from Mark turning up randomly, to a regular meeting at The Station pub. Mark isn't greedy; he only gets £20's and £50's and £100's. He needs to ask for £100 this time because it is Christmas and he would be seeing Abbs and his family, he wants to give them decent gifts. He's spent the last lot of money that Charles gave him; the money just spills through his fingers. He still works on the driveway's with Paddy and the lads but he needs to think about what he intends to do come February when Paddy takes the gang across to Sweden to find work.

Mark and Abbs have met up on a number of occasions. They'd spent a couple of nights together in Mark's mums caravan, but it was freezing cold and Abbs wasn't impressed with no toilet facilities but they both warmed up after awhile and his mother's large pull down bed, with duvets and sleeping bag, gave them a place to be together. She would be meeting him later on, after he's seen Charles and done the last of his shopping. Abbs has a new car since passing her driving test, a smart mini cooper it goes like a bomb. Mark has chosen the attic at Thorn Cottage for good reason. His mother had said that Abbs could stay. Mark isn't sure if his mother meant Abbs would sleep on the large sofa, or have Georgina's room, whilst she moved in with their mum for a couple of nights but Mark has different ideas. They'd probably have to be a bit more careful and quiet but he looks forward to having a good holiday with all of them.

Mark enters the short passage, which leads to the back entrance of The Station Pub; he looks forward to downing his first pint. He can almost taste it; Mark slips his tongue in and out slowly, as he anticipates the first swig of his drink.

The two men have been waiting in the dark shadows of
the closed doors and as Mark draws level with them they
step out, one stands in front of him and the other behind.
Both men are wearing balaclavas and gloves.
"Come on lads."
Mark says, stunned at their appearance, whilst trying to
get out of the trap and angry with his own stupidity at
not being aware of them, because of his preoccupation of
spending his time and money.

He knows he is in for a beating, he can feel the hairs on
the back of his neck bristle and a chill runs through him,
he also knows he can't take on these two big bastards by
himself. If Paddy was with him, they could fight together
back to back, no problems. Paddy had been a bare-
knuckle fighter back in Ireland and could hold his own
against anyone.
The first punch in the guts stings Mark. The punches are
hard and push him against the wall with their force.
Mark tries to fight back but is too winded to stop the
massive punch, which knocks him senseless. As Mark
falls backwards he reaches out with his arms and hands
trying to hold on. He is falling now and keeps on falling
further and further, until there is nowhere else to fall and
he can't feel the walls or the ground, it's like falling into
a deep sea. He can't see anymore and there is a quiet
slow stillness and then the darkness washes over him, as
wave after wave of blackness covers and consumes him
utterly and completely, until at last finally there is
nothing.

The butchers have beautiful, plump, free-range turkeys hanging up in rows, which Anna and Jo agree to buy, as well as bacon, sausage and a stand pie.

"That'll keep us going for a good bit of the holidays."

"Right, where next?"

Anna pulls the trolley through the white, tiled, sawdust floor of the butcher's shop, which leaves a strange smell in her nostrils, of blood and death, which is the stock and trade of the butchers business.

Walking through the streets, there is a buzz of excitement and anticipation about the spirit of the season. As the group walk around the shops to finish off their Christmas shopping, Anna looks forward to returning back to the cottage. Eating their tea and getting the children to bed and relaxing with Jo, in front of the fire with a glass of wine and spending a cosy evening indoors.

Pulling the trolley loads of food and carrying heavy bags back to the cottage is a more difficult journey, than when they had set out. They want to get back before it grows dark because although the road to the cottage is well lit, there are no streetlights on the Nabb itself. As they approach Thorn Cottage, the light gradually slips into darkness and Adam and Georgina try to scare each other, hiding behind trees and bushes.

Inside the cottage they unpack the shopping, Jason races around euphoric, as he smells the fresh turkey and stand pie. The kitchen turns into a busy, chaotic place, filled with noise, light, warmth and fun, as the groceries are all put away and the pizza is in the oven, the kettle is filled and switched on for tea, coffee and drinking chocolate.

Quietness fills the house as Georgina and Adam take their drinks and biscuits into the family room to watch TV, whilst Anna and Jo sit down to enjoy their drinks, waiting for the pizza to bake. The kitchen smells of baking dough, melting cheese and basil.

"I'd better just check and see if Mark has left me a message."
Anna says.
"He might be staying out all night, or he might be coming back."
Anna adds, switching on her phone. She sees she has a voicemail; and presses 123, waiting to hear the message.

Anna listens and is stunned into silence. The call is from the hospital. Her phone number has been retrieved from a young man's mobile, his body was found lying on the beach.
"What's the matter, what's happened?"
Jo asks worried.
"I have to phone the hospital, it's Mark."
Anna phones the hospital and the description fits her son, she tells them she will come straight away. Turning her phone off, she isn't sure what to do.
"I have to go to the hospital, I don't know what's happened to him."
Anna is shocked.
"Oh no, what did they say?"
"He's been found on the beach, something must have happened to him, oh God. He had my number in his phone, that's why they've rung me, oh Jo, what shall I do, I need to go and see him, I don't want Adam and Georgina to know, not yet anyway, I need to find out how he is."
"Of course, you need to see if he's alright. Don't worry, I'll look after the kids, so don't worry about them."

Anna phones for a taxi and collects her bag and jacket and looks around, not sure if she should take anything.
"Oh Jo, I knew there was something, I just knew it."
"Try not to worry, take as long as you need, the kids will be fine."

It seems a long time before the headlights flash across the kitchen window. Anna hovers in wait at the door.

"Right I'm off, don't tell them what's happened, just say I had to go into the town, don't say anything until I'm sure."
"OK."

Climbing in, Anna tells the driver where she wants to go.
"Thornby Hospital please."
The pizza, Anna remembers as the car turns around to go back into town. The road is in darkness as they travel, only the headlights from the taxi shine in front to light up the way. Inside she sits back, as the car makes the short distance to the hospital. The taxi is stuffy and smells of air freshener. She feels impatient to get there, yet dreads her arrival.

Finding the reception and admissions desk, Anna gives her name and that of her son to the clerk. Yes, Mark has been admitted into accident and emergencies and is now under observation. Getting direction from the desk clerk she makes her way along the corridor to the lifts and presses floor 'B'. Mark is in ward 2.
Anna opens the doors to the ward and spots a nurse; she has a tray in one hand and is locking a door with her free hand.
"It's not visiting time I'm afraid."
The nurse tells Anna; as she lets the key attached to a chain, drop down by her side.
 "I have just had a phone call about my son, Mark, Mark Stubley."
"Oh, yes, he's just been admitted for observation."
 "Can I see him please?"
"If you can just wait in here for a moment."
The nurse leads her down the corridor into a small waiting room. Anna sits down on one of the chairs.
"Help yourself to tea or coffee, I'll see what I can do about you seeing your son."
The nurse leaves and closes the door behind her and Anna is left alone in the stuffy, quiet room. She can hear the muffled activity of the ward, as it goes about its daily

business and Anna wants to get up and ask, 'Please can I see my son.' Standing up she looks about her, the phone call has been such a shock and yet in the back of her mind there has been the silent nagging that something wasn't right. As Anna reflects on these thoughts, the waiting room door opens and a man walks in. He's wearing a pale blue top with a nametag on.

"Hello, I'm David Malloy, charge nurse. Mark has been beaten up and was found unconscious. But he's now regained consciousness and we've done all the preliminary tests, he is battered and bruised but there's no serious harm."

"Thank God, can I see him?"

"Yes but we've sedated him and given him pain killers after the tests and examination, so you won't get much out of him but he'll know you're there."

He leads Anna towards an open bay where there are six beds. The charge nurse stops at the first bed.

Mark's face is a mess, his swollen eyes are closed and his bruised chin and cut mouth look painful and sore, he is still and in a calm repose.

"Mark."

Anna whispers. Taking the chair offered by the charge nurse, she sits down and touches her son's hands gently.

"Thank God you're safe."

Anna says quietly.

"Mark, it's me, mam, I'm here."

"Make sure you take those dinners out of the freezer?" Malcolm's mother, Mildred, shouts through to the kitchen, from her spot in front of the small sitting room window.

"Do you hear me Malcolm?"

"Yes, mother."

Malcolm lifts the lid up from the Christmas dinners he'd bought at the frozen food shop. The packaging shows a foil tray with some appetizing looking roast potatoes and turkey with sausage, stuffing, carrots and sprouts, arranged in little compartments.

The food when it has been defrosted and put into the oven to heat wouldn't be as good as it looks. After scraping the remains of the ready-made meal of lasagne into the bin, he fills the kettle, to make his mother and himself a cup of tea. Malcolm sighs as he pours the scolding hot water over the tea bags, as he looks around for some milk and biscuits. 'So, that's our tea done and Christmas dinner sorted out for tomorrow.' Putting the usual, two spoonfuls of sugar into his mother's tea, Malcolm carefully carries both cups into the sitting room.

"So, you've remembered have you?"

Malcolm's mother questions him.

"I thought you'd forgotten about me again, like you did last week."

"Come on now mother, you know I couldn't do that, no matter what."

Dipping the two ginger nut biscuits into her tea, Mildred sits contented for a while. The sitting room hasn't changed much in all the years Malcolm can remember. Above the mantle, the large oval mirror, which has the scene of an English country garden of flowers, with a bird bath in the middle, beneath an archway of colourful flowers and the crinoline lady in yellow in the corner. Malcolm has spent many times gazing up at this scene inside the mirror and imagining himself talking to the crinoline lady.

The old tiled fireplace and brass fender are no longer the focal point of the room, not since the colour television had taken over. Inside the empty hearth of the fireplace, there is the two bar electric fire, which his mother switches on when she decides. It is rare for her to tell Malcolm to put two bars on; it would have to be very cold for that. There is just the one bar on now. In the middle of the room, the large heavy table stands with four chairs tucked in around it. His mother keeps it covered in all kinds of tablecloths and he isn't allowed to use it. At the back of the room is the small sideboard, with the little glass mirror. Dusty and gloomy now, because his mother can't do since the accident, she's been confined to her chair for much of the time and it is up to Malcolm to clean their upstairs accommodation.

He always dusts his father's photograph, which takes pride of place, not just on the sideboard but also in the whole room. Malcolm is proud of his father. His picture shows him in full military gear – a sergeant in the Yorkshire Fusiliers, a proud fine man, a man to look up to and respect. Malcolm aspires to be like his father, but he is aware he falls short. He knows that. He knows it because his mother has told him so, for as long as he can remember.
"You'll never be like your father Malcolm, no matter what."
There are two Christmas cards and a faded red plastic Santa Claus on the sideboard. The only signs of the season and the only way Malcolm can feel it will be Christmas day in the morning.

His mother sits beside the window; it gives her something to do, to pass time she says, whilst he is gallivanting about downstairs in the shop. His mother watches the customers who come and go, up and down the street, as well as checks who comes in and out of the shop. There is a crystal fruit bowl on the sideboard, but it is empty except for the dust, which has accumulated inside it. The sofa and armchairs in front of the fire are salmon cut maket and covered, to keep the dirt from ruining them. Malcolm always disturbs the antimacassars on the arms, which infuriates Mildred. Next to her chair, there is a little occasional table with a wobbly leg, where she keeps some of her medication, but the majority of that is kept on the tin trolley, where she keeps her teeth, glasses and bottle of sherry. The walls are a mixed flora design, fading now, after hanging for so long, but Mildred says they would serve so they would have to. If Malcolm had a say, he would have them painted but he doesn't, so that is the end of that.

"Have you locked up properly downstairs?"
"Yes mother."
"And you've put the lights out haven't you?"
"Yes."
"Good."
She can settle now and have a snooze before the news comes on. Tomorrow there will be the speech to look forward to. Mildred's head begins to nod.
Malcolm finishes his tea and then takes their pots into the little kitchen to wash up, whilst his mother sleeps. The kitchen is painted bottle green, at least the mould doesn't show as much, so in spite of its gloominess there is something to be said for it. The sherry trifle is in the fridge, as is the box of mince pies and the lump of cheese and slab of Christmas cake. Malcolm had just remembered to buy a stand pie before the shops had shut – his life wouldn't have been worth living without the trifle and stand pie. He is satisfied he's done the best he can. Switching the light out in the kitchen, he returns into the sitting room. His mother is well on, so taking the rug from her armchair next to the fire; he covers her up so she won't get cold. 'Right mother, that's me done.' He puts the box of dairy box chocolates, on to the sideboard for Mildred and in the morning she would say he could have something from the shop.

Malcolm slips on his coat, goes into the hall and down the back steps and opens the living accommodation door, to the cold, frosty evening air; he will be back later to help his mother into bed. He shivers, before finding his footsteps leading him in the direction of the promenade, towards The Sailors Arms.

Margaret has her Christmas itinerary laid out before her on the kitchen worktop. This step-by-step plan has evolved over the years and she sticks to it to the letter. It consists of five A4 sheets that she has laminated to ensure that she is able to use them year on year and can wipe them and file them away after the Christmas period. The sheets kick in two weeks prior to Christmas and consist of shopping lists for gifts, cards and party invitations. The food ordering is a task in itself, as all her recipes consist of local produce with delivery dates and reminders for last minute items that she needed to purchase from the best supermarket in Thornby. Also wines, spirits, aperitifs, champagnes, ports and sherry order lists to stock up the cellar.

She had taken care of her hairdresser appointments in October to make sure that she had several treatments booked throughout December and the beginning of the New Year. She had also bought several outfits for evening wear, party gowns, plus casual wear for day to day running around and a couple of skirts, jumpers and pairs of boots and day and evening shoes.

It is now Christmas Eve and she has worked her way meticulously through the first two sheets for this evening and preens herself in the knowledge that she has everything under control for the big day tomorrow. This attention to detail distances her from Charles and she can live in her inner world of Giles.

She allows her mind to digress away from the instructions in front of her and remembers their few days spent together, she enters a beautiful dream, their sessions of lovemaking playing over and over as her body fills with the arousal Giles gave her. As much as she should, she can't compel these thoughts out of her conscience, it has been a long time ago now and she wants him again. As her thighs rub together and her arms brush the sides of her breasts she is ready again, 'oh

Giles, I need you now.' Her eyes flash back down to the checklist, she wants to throw it into the air and run, she wants to shout out for him, to come and find her and love her once more. 'Oh Giles, how much longer do I have to wait for you?' she asks as she reads the instructions before her and double-checks the sheet for the umpteenth time, to ensure she hasn't missed anything. She prides herself on her regimented articulation of the proceedings for Christmas and if she sticks to the plan before her, it runs like clockwork.

Her mind digresses once more and she lets it flow, she imagines a different day to the one in front of her. A special day with Giles, whereby nothing is planned or organized, a day by themselves, with the phone off the hook and meals being secondary to their explorations and joining of each other. Yes to have wine ready in the chiller and tasty ingredients to help themselves too, as and when the mood dictated, but as for grand, elaborate and time consuming cooking – that would not be necessary or thought of. However, she reminds herself this is only a dream, a fantasy and the reality is she has Charles, Abby and her parents tomorrow and she begins checking sheet three again. The countdown is on and as time is running out, she has to engage her full attention and proceed. Charles is out in Fenton, taking refreshments either at the golf club, or at one of the pubs in town so he isn't around to disturb her. He knows better than to invade her kitchen space this evening and having only ever done it on the eve of their first year together as a couple, she decided from then on, never again – he is better out of her way.

And so, with the evening to herself she starts once more her preparations for tomorrow. She has her cookbooks to hand and her fresh ingredients in the fridge. Her parents are due to arrive in an hour, so she has plenty of time. Margaret turns over the laminated sheet, there is just the table left to dress with the special Christmas cloth, to polish the silver cutlery and glasses, lay the serviettes and place the luxury crackers on the table mats. The next instructions are for Christmas morning. 'So all done,' she thinks to herself and decides she will have time to make a few stilton and walnut tartlets, for Abby in case her daughter decides against the turkey. Margaret isn't sure if she is in her vegetarian diet phase or eating meat, Abby changes her dietary habits like she changes her clothes. She will make the tarts and then have a relaxing soak in the bath with a glass of red wine, before her parents arrive. As she rolls out the pastry, her heart sinks as the doorway opens and her mother and father breeze in to greet her.

"Hello dear, merry Christmas."

Her mother attempts to hug her and pulls away scolded and quickly pecks her daughter's cheek.

"Oh dear, what's all this, you are still cooking, you knew we were arriving at 8 o'clock."

Her father Philip chips in.

"Let's take the luggage to our room and get out of Margaret's way."

"If we must."

Monica turns and leaves the room.

Margaret doesn't like to rush and begins to panic, why did they have to turn up early, she checks the time on the kitchen clock, 7.30. Before she has chance to put the little tartlets into the oven, her mother reappears in the doorway.

"Margaret dear are you sure you can manage yourself these days, it appears that you need an extra pair of hands around the house. The guest bedroom is looking rather tired. One has a standard to live up to you know, are you feeling all right dear? Maybe you need to reorganise your priorities, Charles is a busy man and his standards are impeccable, you knew that when you married him. We don't want to let standards slip do we dear? Maybe you need to stop dashing around so much and give up on some of those ghastly charity shops, I know they're for a good cause, but really Margaret one must be organized at home, that comes first. I think Charles is right about Susan, I'm sure you could employ someone much better than her. And where is Abby, surely she should be here to greet her Grandparents?"

"Oh mother really."

"Shall your father pour his own drink?"

Margaret gives up on the pastry and asks her mother what they would care to drink. Monica seems pleased now as she turns away.

"Oh it's all right dear I will get it myself, just remember, do allow yourself more time in future so that your guests aren't kept waiting."

Monica leaves the room.

Margaret allows herself a few minutes to calm down and waits for the tartlets to bake. She longs to phone Giles to hear his voice, for him to say, 'Come on Maggie let's go,' and for them to disappear off somewhere and return after Christmas when the festivities are over.

After loading the dishwasher and putting away her unused ingredients and cleaning the work surfaces she makes her way to the sitting room to face her parents. When she opens the door her mother is sitting stony faced and her father is asleep with his head bent over, still holding the whisky glass in his right hand.

"Well Margaret, I think your father and I will retire to bed, we've had a long day and had hoped to spend time with you and Abby this evening. I think good manners are in short supply with the young these days but really dear, yours, my own daughter, I would never have believed that they could ever be questioned and really Margaret it is a quarter to nine and we have been sat here entertaining ourselves since we arrived."

Margaret thinks to herself, 'That is why mother, I asked you to arrive at 8.30, so that I had finished in the kitchen and could sit with you both when you arrived.'

She remembers the first Christmas when she had invited her parents on Christmas Eve, she had tried to entertain them and do the cooking – and with her mother flapping about it, had reduced her to a nervous wreck and the meals were disappointing. Her mother had chastised her saying she believed her daughter, like herself, to be an excellent cook and hostess, so what on earth had gone wrong. Margaret declared after that, that she would make sure it never happened again, she would plan everything to the last second, hence the written sheets, she couldn't cut herself in two, therefore the arrangements were for her parents to arrive at 8.30 when she had finished.

Margaret doesn't argue with her mother, she is relieved to hear her say that they would go up to bed, she could have the rest of the evening to herself, to drink a couple of glasses of red wine and relax.

Pouring the ruby wine into a crystal glass she raises her arm, 'Merry Christmas Maggie,' and sits down in the three-seater settee.

Anna stands waiting for her taxi; she is surprised to see
Abby walking towards the doors.
"Is he alright?"
Abby asks.
 "Yes."
Anna says relieved her son is going to be all right this
time.
"Yes, he's going to be fine. He's been beaten up and
they've sedated him but he's ok."
Abby looks pale but relieved.
"The hospital phoned me, they had my number on
Mark's mobile."
Anna watches behind Abby, as her return taxi
approaches the hospital entrance.
"I have to go Abby, back to the cottage."
"Can I have your number?"
After exchanging their numbers, Anna tells Abby where
her son is and they say goodbye.
Sitting back in the taxi she feels tired. Thank God, Jo
was there for the children. Tomorrow she would go
again to visit Mark. 'Maybe, if Abby is going, then they
could go together.'

After paying the taxi, Anna enters the cottage. It is quiet
and warm; the aroma of the pizza and baking still lingers
through the hall. Jason barks as she takes off her coat
and Jo opens the sitting room door.
"How is he?"
"Is he alright?"
"He's been beaten up but he's going to be fine."
"That's a relief, I'll put the kettle on; there is a slice of
cold pizza left if you'd like it."
"Sounds lovely."
Anna says, weary now after her long day.
"The kids?"
"In bed asleep."
"The mince pies smell nice."

Anna looks at the cooling pies on the tray and the jam tarts. Jason leaves his bed to see if there is any more pizza for him.

"No Jason, you've had yours."

"I'll save you a bit. What a long day, I'm worried Jo about Mark, what he's got himself into, I knew there was something."

"At least he is ok, that's the main thing."

"Yes you're right, it's never easy with him though."

After finishing her pizza Anna gives Jason a mouthful, which he wolfs down. Satisfied that there is no more, he goes to his bowl to take a drink.

"How about a mince pie and a glass of wine, there is nothing else that you can do tonight?"

"Yes that would be nice, they smell lovely."

Sure enough the mince pies are delicious.

"Did the kids help you?"

"Yes they did, although there wasn't much jam left for the tarts as Adam ate every other spoonful."

"Oh he would."

Jo fills the glasses up with more wine, happy now that Anna's mood has lifted.

"It is lovely to be here with you and the kids, I appreciate the invite Anna."

"Oh it was, is going to be a great Christmas. At least in the hospital Mark can't get into anymore bother, so it should be ok."

Anna continues.

"Adam is difficult at times, but Mark always lands me with the unexpected, I never know from week to week with him, what he's doing."

"Do they know who's beaten him up?"

"No, I'll hopefully find out more tomorrow when I see him and he can talk."

"Surely the police are going to look into it."

"I don't know I dread to think, what mess he has got himself into."

"Let's hope they find whose done it, whatever he has done he doesn't deserve that."

"No Jo but it's not the first time, so."

"Well see what tomorrow brings then, there's nothing we can do tonight."

"No you're right."

"Adam's been asking about getting his mobile working, he wanted to phone you."

"Well he might have to wait now until Mark comes back."

Anna remembers the saga with the mobile.

"That reminds me Jo, when I went to the caravan to search for Adam's phone I found a CD under the seat. I'm not sure where it came from but can we just check it out whilst we've got a minute."

"Yes sure."

"Let's go in the other room, we can switch the fire on and listen to it in there."

Anna goes upstairs and takes the CD from her drawer and then checks on her children. Georgina is fast asleep so she turns off her bedside light and puts the book her daughter has been reading on the bedside table. Kissing her daughter she leaves and closes the door but not shut. Adam is listening to music with his headphones on. Anna kissed him goodnight.

"Where did you go mam?"

"Just to get some bits, I'm coming to bed soon so settle down now."

Anna returns downstairs with the CD.

"I don't want to throw it away if it's any good."

"This is a DVD, not a CD, I'll switch the telly on and we can see what it is."

Anna takes a sip from the wine. It is fruity and explodes in her mouth with a tingly sensation.

"That is good."

"Right, let's see what it is, it might be a good film – I can't remember the last time I watched a film."

As the women sip their wine the DVD begins to play.

Anna watches and then puts her glass down on the coffee table she is unable to drink. The image on the screen in front of her is bizarre, unreal. The women turn and look at one another.

"My God it is isn't it?"

They both watch, as bit-by-bit the 'big baby' film plays. The women watch – fascinated, appalled at the image, which is playing in front of them.

"My God, it is, it's Charles? Oh of course, I understand now."

Anna says.

Anna realises now what her son, Mark, has been up to. The how's and why's Anna doesn't know or understand but she is certain the DVD belongs to her son and that he's been getting money from Charles.

"Mark's mixed up in this somehow, Charles must know he's got it, that's where Mark's been getting his money from. From Charles, that's why he's been beaten up."

Anna sits back in her seat and briefly glances at the screen. It is appalling and slightly scary, as several thoughts and ideas flash through her mind.

"You had better turn it off?"

Anna is worried that Adam might come into the room.

"What are you going to do?"

"I'm not sure yet, I need to think first."

Jo takes out the DVD and gives it to Anna.

"We'd better keep this out of the way. And safe."

This is how Mark is getting all his money, from Charles but how, where had he got his hands on such a thing? Anna is aware that the DVD is an important weapon against Charles. Mark has used it against him and must have been warned about it. Anna needs to think and to consider what she intends to do with the DVD.

"This would be funny Anna, if it wasn't for Mark, let's have another glass of wine."

"What did I say about Charles, I wasn't wrong about him was I?"

"No, it doesn't bear thinking about, I'm so glad I am out of his flat, that's for sure."

"Gosh I'm tired."

"I'm just going to take Jason out."

"I'll come with you."

"We can leave the door unlocked, if we just go within sight of the cottage we'll be fine."

The women put on their coats and slip quietly outside. Jason enjoys his late stroll and after sniffing around they manage to put him back on his lead and return indoors.

Anna settles in bed trying to make sense of what has happened to her son. If Mark had somehow got hold of the DVD it would explain how he acquired the money for all the things he's been buying. The cash hadn't just come from working with Paddy, he always spent that as soon as he got it, so it must have come from somewhere else. She couldn't be sure but feels the beating had come through Charles. She would find out more when she speaks to her son.

It is Christmas Eve in the morning and Anna would telephone Abby about their hospital visit and decide if she'd speak to her about the DVD and the contents of it. She needs to know if Abby is behind it all. She can't understand how Mark could have got hold of it without Abby knowing. Anna is unable to think anymore she is too tired.

When Anna wakes it is still dark. She looks at the clock radio it is 6.15am. 'Ten more minutes,' she tucks her head beneath the duvet. She must have dropped back off to sleep because as she surfaces she hears Jason's barking, 'Time to get up.' The bed is warm and comfortable and Anna wants to stay curled up in the warmth longer but knows she can't.

Downstairs she switches the kettle on to make coffee and then tidies and washes up the few things that have been left from last night. When the children come down she will make them porridge and toast to keep them going until lunchtime. They could then have the rest of Christmas Eve and Christmas day free to share and enjoy.

The women prepare breakfast together whilst Adam, Georgina and Jason explore around the cottage. The place is warm and comfortable and once the excitement has settled, Anna knows they will have a happy and enjoyable time. She hopes Mark will be on the mend and she can give herself up to their break. She decides to speak to Adam and Georgina about what has happened to Mark when she returns. She has told them he is spending time with friends.

They decide on sausage and mash for dinner with mince pies and jam tarts to finish.
"Shall we explore outside for a bit, before dinner."
Jo suggests.
"Yes."
The children cheer.
"Right go and get your hats, coats and gloves."
They race across the hallway.
"Would you mind looking after the kids again later?"
"Yes, sure it's the least I can do."
"I'll just go and call Abby."
Abby answers straight away.
"I'll collect you at 2 o'clock and we can go to the hospital to see Mark together."
Anna is pleased with the arrangement and tells Abby the directions to the cottage and says goodbye.
The kids return ready for the walk.
Outside it is cold, such a contrast from indoors.
"Come on we'd better keep moving."
Jason begins to sniff and rummage along the path and hedgerows as the little group set out on their adventure.
"Can we go down to the beach?"
Georgina asks.
"There's a footpath further down the Nabb, but I'm not sure if it's safe enough for us to get down at this time of year."
"Let's walk that far, it'll give us an appetite for dinner and we can check out the path."
Walking along the Nabb, Anna and Jo walk together, whilst Adam and Georgina go on a little way ahead exploring. Georgina has a small camera and stops to look at the bushes and plants, happily snapping away at anything that is alive and moving. Scolding Adam and Jason, if they come up to her whilst she clicks away.

"No, Jason."
Georgina shouts as he plods up to see what she has
found so interesting in the bushes, he has already sniffed
out.
Anna feels relaxed now as they walk down the rough
path. Forking off at varying intervals are the signs to the
small farms, which run along the Nabb, 'White Swan'
and 'Silver Lake Farm'. The last one is 'Nabb End' and
when they arrive Jo checks out the footpath with Jason
whilst Anna and the children find a huge old oak tree to
hug and listen to what it says to them.
"It's granddad."
Georgina tells her mum, whilst Adam turns to follow
Jason.
"No, the path's not safe so let Jo check it first."
Adam shrugs his shoulders and walks off.
Jo reappears with Jason.
"The tides in and it doesn't look safe either, I wouldn't
like to risk it, even when the tides out, it's steep and
looks slippery."
"Come on then, we're going to make our way back."
"But I thought we could go on the beach."
Adam sulks.
"Not here, Jo's says it's not safe."
Reluctantly Adam walks away.
"Who's for bangers and mash?"
Jo asks changing the subject.
"Me, me."
Everyone cheers.

After dinner the women drive off in the car, Anna
doesn't feel it is the right time to tell Abby about the
DVD but trusts she can't have been involved with Mark
taking the money. They remain silent throughout the
journey to the hospital. When they pull into the car park
Anna turns to her and says.
"Wait a minute."
Anna notices Abby's eyes red and puffy from the
previous days crying.

"Abby, I know how you feel about Mark."
She takes Abby's hands.
"Abby I think I know why Mark has been beaten up."
"Why?"
"Mark has something which belongs to your father, I have it now."
"What is it?"
"I think Mark has used it to blackmail him."
"But what is it?"
"If you come back to the cottage with me when we've visited Mark, I'll lend it to you and you'll understand and."
Anna looks at Abby intently now.
"Abby would Mark have had the chance to take something from your father?"
Abby thinks for a moment.
"Yes, I suppose he could have."
The pieces fall into place now for Anna, she understands and only needs confirmation from Mark.

When they walk into Mark's ward he is sitting up in bed. In spite of his sore and painful face Mark smiles when he sees them enter. There is just one chair by the side of Mark's bed so Abby goes to find a spare one.
"Mark."
Anna needs to know from her son what has been going on.
"You've been taking money from Charles, haven't you?"
"What?"
"I've seen the DVD."
Mark's smile vanishes.
"That's why you got beaten up isn't it?"
Mark looks away.
"Don't tell Abbs."
As Abby returns with a plastic chair to sit on, Mark looks at his mother. After sitting with the pair in silence, Anna rises from her seat.

"I need to get back to the cottage Mark, I've left Adam and Georgina with Jo and it's not fair to leave them too long."

Anna opens her bag and takes a Christmas card from it and gives it to her son.

"I've put you some of your things in this carrier bag, there are some of Adam's pyjamas and some toiletries, a towel and some chocolate."

Anna kisses her son and wishes him a happy Christmas and says she will call the hospital after Boxing Day to see when he is due to leave.

"Abby will bring you to the cottage."

Anna looks at them.

"If you wait for me, I will give you a lift back to the cottage."

"Thanks, I'll be in the corridor outside, don't be too long."

"In a bit mam."

Mark tells his mother as she walks out of the ward.

"In a bit Mark."

Anna walks down the corridor to reach the lifts.

Back at the cottage.
"Come in and have a drink of tea."
Anna asks Abby as she parks up outside Thorn Cottage.
"Thank you, I would like that."
We make tea, coffee and chocolate to drink and open a
packet of oat biscuits for everyone to share.
"How's things been?"
Anna asks as they sit with Abby and the children
drinking their tea and coffee.
"OK, the kids have been fine, I thought we could have
baked potatoes and some quiche we made yesterday for
tea."
"That sounds lovely."
"Where've you been mam?"
Adam asks as he finishes his second biscuit.
"I've been to see Mark, he's in hospital, but he's going
to be alright."
Anna tries to reassure him.
"Why, what's happened?"
Georgina asks this time.
"He has been beaten up, but he is ok, so there's no need
to worry."
"Right, who's ready to help me in the kitchen?"
Jo asks hoping to direct their attention away from Mark
and the hospital.
"Me, me."
Both children shout.
"Adam and Gina are going to prepare the potatoes and
help."
"Yes, scrub them and prick them and put them in the
oven to bake."
Adam and Georgina say in unison.
"Why don't you stay and join us?"
Anna asks Abby.
"Are you sure that will be ok?"
"Of course it is, Mark did say you would be coming to
spend time over the holidays. So you're welcome."
"Thank you very much."
Abby says as she finishes her hot chocolate.

"Right let's get organized then."
"I do appreciate your watching Adam and Gina. It would have been difficult taking them."
"It's been fine and Mark's going to be ok now, so come on kids."
In the kitchen Jo supervises with the baked potatoes, quiche and salad and Anna begins to prepare the vegetables for Christmas day lunch. Abby asks if she can take Jason for a walk.
"Sure, his lead is at the back of the door."

They will have roast and boiled potatoes as well as carrots and sprouts. The turkey would go in the oven first thing in the morning and they'd have eggs, bacon and sausages for breakfast, which would keep them going until early afternoon.

In spite of Mark, Anna enjoys the meal – it is simple and tasty, looking around the table she is content and satisfied, glad that they are all together.

Later in the evening after the Christmas day preparation are finished, the children leave a carrot and a mince pie on a plate, along with a thimble full of red wine in a small glass, for Santa Claus and his reindeer.

In the morning Anna would phone the hospital to wish her son a happy Christmas, as well as calling the children's father, to wish each other seasons greetings.
"I have to go home now." Abby announces although she seems settled.
"My grandparents are visiting this evening."
Whilst Abby collects her things, Anna goes upstairs to her room to get the DVD for her.
"Here Abby this DVD will explain everything, for Mark's sake I would like you to give me it back."
"You don't have to worry I will keep it safe."
Abby says her goodbyes to everyone and Anna walks to the door with her.

"Abby."

Anna calls out before she climbs into her car.

"The DVD is about Charles and when you see it, it might upset you but it explains why Mark was beaten up."

"What do you mean?"

"You'll understand when you see it, Mark has asked me not to let you know what's been happening, but I believe you need to understand about Mark, as well as your father."

Turning on the car engine Abby pulls her seatbelt across her and clicks it into place. Looking at Anna, Abby says.

"Well, goodbye then."

"Merry Christmas."

"Merry Christmas."

"By the way Abby, you're welcome to stay here with us, you know that don't you?"

"Thank you, that's kind of you."

Anna watches until the lights of Abby's car have vanished into the blackness of night. "My God."

Anna says quietly as she turns to go back into the cottage. Closing the door behind her, she can hear the TV in the family room. Anna sits down and they watch The Snowman together. Outside the wind is blustery and a shower begins to beat against the cottage. The sea roars and smashes itself against the rocks and the warm glow of light from Thorn Cottage, makes a welcoming sight from the outside.

The tide is in as Malcolm walks towards the pub, he is aware of the sea's power as it pounds hard against the boulders and concrete slabs, as he looks across the bay – all he can see is darkness, pitch black darkness and hear the loud roar of the sea, as it continues to smash and beat itself against the hardness of the wall.

He opens the door of The Sailors Arms; the lights, the warmth, the noise and sounds of people and music draw him in. He makes his way through the noisy crowded pub and people hello him.

"Now then Tommy, how you doing?"

He winces slightly, as the name Tommy is called, instead of his given name Malcolm. But he knows that's what most of the locals call him.

"Tommy."

It has been Tommy since Malcolm was a young boy and started school and Tommy because his dad owned a military shop and had once been a soldier in the Yorkshire regiment.

"Now then Malcolm."

Alan the pub landlord asks.

"How's things, how's your mother?"

"Just the same."

"Usual?"

The landlord asks, Malcolm nods and watches, as Alan pulls him a pint of bitter. Malcolm sinks his first pint feeling better, relieved temporarily of his usual responsibilities. Taking his second pint he sits down with it, Malcolm leans back in his usual seat, to sip his drink more slowly.

The trimmings are up and when a breeze wafts the strands of coloured tinsel they quiver, catching the light and glitter. Malcolm looks about him. Many of the faces are familiar and as they pass his little table out of the way in the corner, they nod their acknowledgement towards him and he returns it.

Sipping his pint, Malcolm can feel all the other people's energy and excitement of it being the festive season. He doesn't feel any himself, Christmas being not much different for him, from one day to the next, but he is aware of the change in the pubs atmosphere of excited anticipation. He tries to make his second pint last him, but before long he can see the bottom of his empty glass. He is tempted to stay and get another one, but he knows she'll be waking up and he has to be there to help her prepare for bed.

Slowly, reluctantly, Malcolm rises from his seat, with his empty glass in his hand. The crowd's part for him to approach the bar and leave his glass and after doing so he manages to catch the landlord's eye to give him a nod goodnight.

"Goodnight Malcolm."

The black, cold air engulfs him, as he steps out of the pub, to make his journey home to his mother and 'Mountcross & Son'. The streets are deserted, as he walks home slowly, with his head bent against the bitingly cold wind.

Entering into the small hallway of his home, Malcolm closes his eyes before he locks and bolts the door. Christmas Eve and here he is alone with his mother, in this cold, empty place. In bed Malcolm knows there will be little warmth for him, the thoughts of spending another night in his cold, hard bed, almost makes him want to fling the door open and run away.

Malcolm makes his way upstairs in the dark. When he reaches the landing, he can hear the television playing to itself. The loud noise of happy, excited chattering resonates as he hangs up his coat and enters the sitting room. The TV flashing its coloured pictures as his mother sleeps. The room is just warm, so Malcolm walks across to the fire and puts the second bar on. He stands in front of the fire to warm himself and gazes at the television and his sleeping mother. She'll be awake soon and want her cocoa and would ask him if he's put her blanket on.

Going along the passage to his mother's room, Malcolm
draws her curtains and switches on her electric blanket.
Pulling back the bedclothes, he puts her winceyette
nightgown on the sheet to warm up. 'Right kettle,'
Malcolm decides, after switching it on, he returns to the
sitting room and quietly turns off one of the bars on the
fire. He watches as the red glow of the bar fades and
turns its usual dull, dusty black. Satisfied, he goes back
to the kitchen to start making a warm drink to have
before going to bed. He carries the piping hot cocoa into
the room.
"Come on mother."
Malcolm calls, as he puts his cocoa on the shelf.
Walking into his mother's bedroom, he places her cocoa
on the bedside cabinet and turns on the light.
"Come on now mother."
Malcolm repeats wanting to wake her and help her from
the chair.
"I'm starved."
Mildred moans to her son, as he eases his mother up
from the chair. She is dry, so that gives him hope that his
job will be a bit easier.
"Your blankets on mother, you'll be as warm as toast
once you're in bed."
Malcolm steers his mother towards the bathroom.
"Do you need to go?"
Malcolm tries to hold his mother steady as she shuffles
towards the bathroom. He prizes her claw like grip from
his arm, which begins to dig into his skin.
"Don't cling so tight mother."
"I'll fall."
"No mother I won't let you fall, I have you, just put your
weight on me mother."
"You've been drinking haven't you Malcolm?"
As Mildred hovers over the toilet seat, Malcolm looks
away into the darkness of the unlit hallway. She huffs
and puffs as she arranges her clothes, to sit down on the
toilet.
"I'm ready Malcolm."

"Have you got them down properly mother, you know
what happened last time, we don't want any more
accidents do we?"
Malcolm takes his mother's weight, as she eases herself
down onto the seat.
"I'll give you a few minutes mother."
Mildred lets out a massive fart, which turns his stomach.
He walks into the sitting room and turns off the fire. He
looks at his mug of cocoa but can't face it now, so he lets
it stand. Looking about the room, he switches off the
light and closes the door. Returning to the bathroom
doorway, Malcolm calls to his mother.
"Are you done mother, are you ready now?"
"Yes."
"Have you cleaned yourself and pulled up your pants
mother?"
"Of course I have, what do you take me for?"
Malcolm clenches his teeth, as he tries to stop the stench
from entering his mouth and nostrils. As he hauls her up,
he automatically flushes the toilet and tries to check that
she has pulled her pants up. Her dress has been tucked
into the back of her knickers but Malcolm can't touch it
now, she'll have to manage. Leading his mother into her
bedroom, he helps her to sit down on the bed.
"Come on now mother, I'll help you with your slippers."
Malcolm carefully releases his mother's foot from each
of her slippers and rolls down her stockings.
"Do you want your stockings leaving on, or taking off
mother?"
"Leave them on, I'm starved."
"Right mother you've got everything. Your nightgowns
here."
Malcolm says lifting back her covers and giving her, her
warmed nightgown.

Malcolm has had enough; he has to get away now.
"Call me if you need anything mother."
"Have you done my drink and tablets?"
"Yes, there's everything on your bedside table."

Malcolm walks away, pulling the door closed behind him.

"Malcolm?"

He hears his mother whine but ignores her and goes into his own room closing the door, so that he is unable to hear her. He sits down on his bed, tired, sick and fed up but this is how his life is and he has to cope. She is his mother, he can't walk out and leave her and besides where could he go he has no one else now just his mother. Helping her, as he has to now turns his stomach, he cannot stand it but he has to try.

Anna tries to settle Adam knowing it will be Christmas in the morning.

"If you don't go to bed and sleep, Santa Claus won't come and leave you presents."

"But I can't mam."

Anna gives him one of his favourite books on guns to thumb through, to keep him absorbed until he becomes tired and would eventually drop off to sleep. Georgina is reading her book Horse and Cart when Anna enters her room to kiss her goodnight.

'Done,' Anna goes into her own bedroom to collect the two carrier bags of gifts she's brought to the coast with her. She has some of her children's Christmas gifts and Jo's presents, a selection of paints, brushes, and dark chocolate and dates, a reminder of the evening spent at Jo's flat.

Making her way downstairs she enters the larger sitting room and arranges the gifts around the tree.

Hearing Anna's movements Jo finds her in the sitting room.

"Do you fancy sitting in here for the rest of the evening. We could share a bottle of wine?"

"That would be great."

"It will make a nice change having a bit of peace and quiet together after what's happened."

Sitting in front of the fire, sipping the red wine they relax. Jo tells Anna about the work she wants to do at the beach hut.

"If I can remove the back wall of the workroom and extend the sides, it will give me a lot more space and then I can produce larger pieces, which is what I'd like to do."

"It sounds a good idea, will you have enough space behind your workroom to expand?"

"Yes there should be and I've got ideas too about making jewellery, using vintage pieces, to make necklaces and brooches but that's for later when I've got the room sorted."

"It sounds interesting and exciting."

"Yes it will be."

Jo puts another log onto the embers of the fire.

"I'll just go check on the kids."

Georgina is sleeping, so Anna switches off her bedside lamp and goes into Adam's room. 'Thank God, he's fallen asleep.'

Anna covers her son and kisses him.

'Santa Claus will definitely come to you my lad, he certainly will.'

Closing the door Anna feels ready for her bed but wants to enjoy the company of Jo downstairs. Knowing the children are settled down now, she can make the most of the evening.

As Anna sits opposite Jo drinking her wine, she wonders about Jo's family and friends, where they are, or even if they exist. To have reached this point in life, without any connections with people puzzles her. Especially now at Christmas time, to find Jo here with her and not to have any of her own family or friends to visit seems rather strange. Anna is tempted to ask her but she doesn't want to spoil the evening and she also realises, she too doesn't want penetrating questions about her own life back in the city. She acknowledges that there is a similarity, a resonance; after all she is here too - although with the children, apart and distant from her own family and friends. Knowing Jo's harsh and reclusive existence of life at the hut she wants this holiday time to be special and hopes there won't be anymore unexpected dramas cropping up via Mark.

Later walking with Jo and Jason in the cold, windy, wintry night, Anna feels alive and connected and in touch with herself and the elements around her. The sea roars out its presence, Anna welcomes and embraces its strength, power and force as the evening draws to a close.

Undressing in the dim light, coming through the window from the street lamp, Malcolm is cold and weary. The warm glow from the pub is fading as he pulls his trousers off. Tomorrow he would have to put the uniform on, an hour before the speech.

He clenches his teeth, as his warm body comes into contact with the cold, cotton sheets, on his single bed. Gradually his flesh becomes accustomed to the assault and little by little he lets his body relax and hides his head under the covers, up to the top of his lips. His door is closed, so he can't hear her if she calls, he doesn't want to hear anything else now, just sleep until morning.

Mildred manages to drop off eventually, but how she does it God only knows, after calling and calling for Malcolm to come and pass her cocoa. In the end, she had to manage it herself but because of him, she spilt it on her covers and nightgown – she'd speak to him in the morning, she reminds herself as she surrenders to the warmth of her electric blanket and the comfort of her large double bed.

The double bed is a luxury that Mildred had not enjoyed with her late husband, Albert Mountcross. They'd had single beds all their married life. She had been taken aback when Albert had said no to the double bed idea, after their marriage.

"Not healthy."

He had told her.

"It makes you weak and lazy, a couple can get along well enough, without all that lovey duvey stuff and after all, it keeps a man keen and ready, on the alert and less chance of distraction if he has his own bed."

When Albert had passed away, Mildred had given Malcolm one of the single beds, the other she had put in the storeroom for when Malcolm wore his out. The double bed was Mildred's little treat to herself, a comfort to her when Albert had gone. She'd earned it, Mildred acknowledged.

Malcolm turns over and the old springs of his bed
squeak, his mother would no doubt tell him about it in
the morning. He could do with another pee now – he
would wait a few more minutes, before he leans over the
side of his bed for the bottle – he doesn't want the
springs to give again.
"You'll jigger that bed up Malcolm, I heard you last
night jumping up and down on it, you think I don't hear
you Malcolm but I do."
He hears her words ringing in his head, as he holds back
his bursting bladder for a bit longer.

"He's been mam, he's been."
Adam cries excitedly.
"Look mam, look at what he's left me."
Anna squeezes her eyes and tries to open them to focus
on her son.
"What time is it Adam?"
"Don't know."
Anna manages to make out the time on her bedside
clock, 4.55. 'It's going to be a long day,' Anna decides
as she climbs out of bed and begins to dress before going
downstairs. Adam is in the large sitting room. Torn
Christmas wrapping paper is scattered all over the floor,
as well as sweet and chocolate wrappers. Jason has
joined in Adam's fun and is shredding pieces of paper
and flicking them up into the air. Anna checks to make
sure that Georgina's and Jo's gifts haven't been opened
and encourages Adam to gather his gifts and take them
into the smaller room to play with, whilst she makes tea
and toast for them both. She knows that if she leaves the
two much longer, there won't be any presents left to
open.

After eating her toast, Anna puts the prepared turkey in
the oven and then goes to check on her son. Jason and
Adam are having a tug of war with a sock; the gifts for
now are left strewn across the floor.
"Let's go get Gina."
Adam shouts and runs out of the room with Jason in hot
pursuit.
Anna calls to stop them but it is too late, they are already
chasing each other up the stairs.
She gives up, knowing that Georgina and Jo will be
awake by now, so she goes back to the kitchen to fill the
kettle.
Georgina races into the room with a parcel in her hand.
"He's been, come and look."

Hearing the rumpus around the cottage Jo decides to get
up, looking sleepy and bedraggled she enters the kitchen.

"Sorry Jo, I know it's early but Adam is always up at the crack of dawn at Christmas."

"Don't worry, it's ok, Merry Christmas Anna."

"And to you too, Merry Christmas."

"Come on Jo, mam you've got some presents to open."

Adam calls excitedly.

The sitting room is covered in pieces of torn wrapping paper, it is difficult to ascertain which presents belong to whom and what is unopened.

"Right."

Anna shouts.

"Let's calm down and tidy this up first."

Jason has a furry Santa Claus toy between his teeth and he is entertaining Georgina with its loud squeak as she tries to tug it from his mouth.

"Adam put the used paper into this bag."

Adam is reluctant to do as he is told and joins in with Georgina and Jason.

"Right who wants to open another present?"

Jo tries to intercede.

"Me, me, me."

"OK then let's clear away the rubbish first."

After a half-hearted effort of clearing the floor, Jo opens the cupboard beside the fireplace and Adam dives in, grabbing the gifts and pulling them out onto the floor.

"Adam calm down let Jo get them out."

Anna calls out.

"This ones yours Gina."

Adam tears at the parcel and rips a hole in the paper.

"Look Adam back off now."

Anna leans across and tugs Adam's arm.

"It's mine."

Georgina squeals.

"There's no need to rush, come on now both of you."

Jo tries to calm the situation.

Georgina opens her gift and lifts the delicate necklace and shows it off to Adam.

"It's beautiful, look mum."

"Oh mam, it's The Pirate Ship, look it's got the bullets in
it, can we go and sail it mam?"
"We'll see, thank you Jo, your gifts are lovely."
Anna sighs and reflects.

It seems such a long time ago, the flooded hut, the
cleanup and the night spent with Jo at the flat. The
summer is past and gone and future times would always
be different and yet Anna acknowledges deep inside of
herself, the impact of this last one and how it has begun
a process of transformation and evaluation of her
existence and life.
Her world and time spent in it, would from now on travel
another course, not one predetermined from birth that
she understands and knows how to follow, but a richer
journey, of un-chartered terrain, that she would have to
stumble along and find her way.

Christmas morning 7 o'clock.

She will want to go to the toilet soon, Malcolm looks about him. It is Christmas day and there are no presents at the foot of his bed, no stockings filled with chocolate coins, no apples or oranges. Malcolm is warm in his bed. When he lifts his head from beneath the covers, his breath rises up in a wave of mist, before it disperses in the room. It isn't light yet but Malcolm can see every bit of his room.

He both hates it and loves it. He hates it because it is filled with old, worn out furniture, that he's had all his life. Even the floral carpet he can remember when he was a boy and the dark green brocade curtains, which he no longer closes. Love? Malcolm loves his room because it is his. It has always been his and he can come in to it and escape. Escape his mother and his father when he was alive and the lads who called him names and chased him and the girls. The girls who looked at him and then at one another and then giggled back at him. Malcolm puts his head underneath his covers and squeezes up his eyes; he doesn't want to see their silly, stupid, laughing faces anymore. She hadn't laughed at him; he'd made sure of that.

"Malcolm."

His mother shouts.

"Malcolm."

She continues, until at last he has to get up.

He pulls his jumper over his t-shirt and then puts on his trousers. He feels how hard he is but expects it will go down after he's had a pee.

"Malcolm."

Mildred continues to call, as he fastens his shoes up and goes to the toilet. He stands with his hands planted on the walls and calls out to her.

"In a minute mother."

After flushing the toilet he makes his way into Mildred's bedroom.

"Right mother are you ready?"

"I shall be going now, if you don't frame yourself Malcolm."

Gripping hold of her sons arm as he leads her towards the bathroom.

"Lift your nightgown up mother, or you'll wet yourself."

"Oh, Malcolm."

'Not again mother, not again,' Malcolm says to himself as he walks out of the bathroom.

'Fuck off; fuck off.' He screams under his breath as he finds her a clean nightgown. Returning into the bathroom, Malcolm asks her if she is done.

"You've cleaned yourself haven't you mother?"

"Yes."

Mildred replies more meekly than usual.

"You've got your vest still on haven't you mother?"

"Of course I have."

Malcolm undoes the buttons on the clean nightgown, as he waits for her to unfasten the ones on the nightgown she is wearing.

"Right up."

Malcolm orders. Mildred rises and as he hitches his mothers dripping wet nightgown up to her stomach, he focuses his gaze above her head.

"Can you manage now mother?"

"Yes."

"All right mother, I'll go and put the fire on and the kettle while you're getting done and put the old one in the bath."

Malcolm calls out as he switches on the sitting room light and both bars of the electric fire.

"It's Christmas day."

Malcolm calls out to himself, his mother and to the flat. After he's drawn the curtains and put the tea bags in the pots and the bread in the toaster, he returns to his mother's room and gets her blue nylon, floral dressing gown.

"Come on mother let's put this on or you'll freeze."

Christmas morning has begun for them both. After giving his mother her tea, he leaves her to sit whilst he gets on. After turning off her electric blanket, he checks to see if she's wet the bed. It is dry but for the few dribbles she's left on the end as she sat putting her slippers on. 'It'll save,' Malcolm pulls over the blankets on his mother's bed and picks up her dirty clothes and draws the curtains. Later when he remembers, he will get some shake and vac for the carpet, where it smells of pee.

Before their dinner he would take her back into her bedroom, to dress. In his own bedroom, he throws his covers across his bed and picks his dirty socks up. He collects the nightgown from the bath and puts the dirty clothes into the washer and switches it on.

Back in the sitting room he takes the box of chocolates and Christmas card from the sideboard and gives it to her.

"Here mother."

"What's this for?"

"It's Christmas day mother, it's a present and a card from me."

"For me, me?"

"Yes mother."

"Well then Malcolm, when you've time, you'd better go down into the shop and choose something for yourself."

"Yes, mother, thank you, I will a bit later on, do you want a nice bacon butty mother? It's Christmas day, so I thought we could splash out a bit, now what do you say?"

"That would be nice Malcolm, will you have one too?"

"Finish taking your tablets mother, then I'll make a fresh cup of tea and we can have one with our bacon butties whilst we listen to the carols for a bit."

Malcolm returns to the kitchen to trim the bacon and put the toast and tea on. Once it is done, he takes the bacon sandwiches into the sitting room, with their pots of tea on the tray.

After the egg, bacon and sausages for breakfast and once they've cleared away, Anna and her children make their phone calls to friends and family. After wishing everyone a merry Christmas, she is free.

"I need to take Jason out for a walk." Jo tells Anna.

"We will all come with you."

"Come on let's get shoes and coats on, we are going to take Jason for a walk."

Outside it is cold and breezy and as the wind blows, Georgina and Jason take the lead and walk up the steep hill. The footpath passes a farm, where dogs yap at them through mesh fencing and Jason decides against introducing his usual friendly self to the farm dogs. When they get to the very top of the path, it levels off to a field. They all climb over the stile, where in front of them is the view of the sea. The sound increases as they get nearer to the end of the cliffs and Anna calls to her children to stay away from the edge.

"It's brilliant mam."

Georgina yells, thrilled at the sound and power of the sea.

"Right," Anna calls. "I think we've gone far enough for the minute."

"But you said we could go down to the sea mam."
Adam grumbles.

"We will, but we can't get down this way can we, so come on for now."

Anna walks up to her children and takes each one by the hand.

"But it's amazing."

Georgina tells Anna.

"I know, but after dinner we can go for a proper walk on the beach and go on the Brig, so come on now."

"Yes the tide will be out later and we'll be able to run on the beach."

"Yes."

The children shout.

After their sandwiches, Malcolm switches the main lights on and goes down the steps, which lead directly into the shop. It is cold because the electric heaters are off, now the shop is shut.

Tomorrow he'd have a break from his mother. The women from the church are coming, to take her to their get together and Boxing Day lunch. She would enjoy the fuss and they'd pick her up and drop her off and if she takes her stick she will manage.

He might go for a long walk if it stays fine. The coastal path is one of his favourite walks; he used to walk a lot when he was younger but as his mother began to need him more and more, it is difficult for him to slip away for longer than an hour or so, without her nattering the life out of him when he returned.

'Now,' Malcolm says to himself, as he screws the top back on his flask after having a good swig of the brandy, 'What shall I have?'

Malcolm is torn. Since his father's death, year-by-year, he has built up a nice collection of postcards, badges and his own little wardrobe of army clothing, as well as the memorabilia. Of course he had chosen the usual things, which he'd shown Mildred over the years. The bottle green, British Mark Assault helmet and the cartridge belts, but some of his favourites things, like his WW2 German Naval Officers cap, he could only wear that when he'd shut up the shop. It is black, with the gold eagle and plumes beneath it. That hadn't cost the usual £10 or £15 quid she allowed him to spend, it had been closer to £40. He also has a navy blue, German air force uniform, with its smart silver buttons and wings. The canary yellow trim on the hat really set it off. Malcolm keeps it in his wardrobe upstairs and doesn't let his mother see it. He feels good when he dresses up in it but he knows his father would have beaten the living daylights out of him, if he had ever seen Malcolm wearing it. But with the boots and stick, it makes him feel like a man. She wouldn't know it isn't a British uniform, but he couldn't risk ever letting Mildred see him wearing it. Malcolm has two of the Masonic badges so far and this year he is torn between the £12.95 British Army Northern Ireland Gloves or should he go for the 30mil GAV Avenger shell, the one the boy had looked at and the one she had touched and held. It certainly is striking in red and white and would look good on his bedroom mantle shelf, with his 20mil Vulcan's. Malcolm chooses the Avenger and reasons he could have the gloves for his birthday.

Replacing the gloves, Malcolm selects his shell from the case and then slides back the glass. It feels cold and hard in his hand and he likes the sensation of its weight, as he remembers her touch, he can almost feel her hand as she'd held it between her fingers, another one for his collection. This one would go right in the middle of the others. In a few years, his mantle would be full.

Taking a final swig from his flask, he returns it to its drawer and makes his way back upstairs into the flat. The break has bucked him up no end and he feels better, happier now, than when he'd gone down stairs. Turning off the lights, Malcolm pulls the door too, locks it and slides the bolt across.

Later he turns the oven on, 'Christmas dinners in,' after that they would have to start getting dressed for the speech.
"Won't be long now mother, dinners on."
"I'm hungry."
Mildred complains.
"Won't be long mother."
As the Christmas dinners cook in their foil trays, he puts the Christmas pudding in the microwave and switches the kettle on, to boil water to mix for the powdered custard. Things are going well. Malcolm puts the Christmas dinners on separate trays and with knives,

forks and spoons for the pudding he proudly carries his mother's tray into the sitting room.

"Here we go then mother."

He lays a towel across her knees and puts the tray with the Christmas dinner and pudding in front of her, pleased with his efforts.

"I can't eat all that Malcolm."

"Just do your best mother."

Malcolm encourages her, pleased that the food hasn't turned out as bad as he thought it would – you can eat it and that's something. Sitting down in his armchair, Malcolm sets about tackling his own dinner.

"I can't eat all this Malcolm."

Malcolm eats his Christmas dinner and ignores her. When he's finished, he is bloated and belches satisfied with how he is feeling.

"You're just playing with that mother."

He walks passed her, taking his tray into the kitchen. Filling the sink with hot water and a squirt of washing up liquid, Malcolm washes the pots and cutlery. After putting the kettle back on for a cup of tea, he takes his mother's tray of half eaten food and throws it into the bin.

"Right mother, we'll have a cup of tea before we get changed and then we can get out the sherry and glasses, to toast Her Majesty after the speech."

"We'll have time shan't we?"

"Yes, mother we're on schedule, there's Christmas cake for tea, with cheese and enough for your ladies tomorrow, if they want a piece and there's the mince pies which we haven't touched and we've the stand pie and trifle for later."

Malcolm is in control.

"Right mother, what is it going to be then today?"

"The blue."

"Come on then."

Malcolm coaxes his mother through to her bedroom. Leaving her to sit on the end of the bed, he collects clean knickers and nylon stockings for his mother.

"Come on put them on mother."
He opens one of his mother's large oak double wardrobe
doors and selects the sky blue, crimpolene dress and
jacket that is hung up.
"I want my white sandals Malcolm."
Mildred says, as he takes the two-piece off its hanger for
his mother to put on.
"Come on Malcolm, you need to frame yourself as well
and get yourself ready, instead of telling others."
Malcolm opens the opposite wardrobe door, where his
mother has saved and hung all of her husbands clothes,
including his Yorkshire Fusiliers uniform. Lifting the
heavy hanger with the uniform and cap on, Malcolm
closes the doors and goes into his own room to change.
He lays his father's old uniform on his bed and opens his
own wardrobe door and takes out the Yorkshire Fusiliers
uniform he will wear. He had grown out of his father's
uniform years ago, but it makes her happy – to think he
is wearing his father's. Piece by piece, Malcolm dresses
himself up as a soldier – as Tommy. The black lace up
patrol boots are more comfortable than the heavy leather
boots that don't fit him and she never notices what he
has on his feet. Next to his Christmas gift of the Vulcan,
Malcolm looks at the old photograph of his father.
Above the photograph is a small mirror on the faded
yellow wall. Peering into the mirror he salutes. 'Dad,
Merry Christmas, Dad.'

Looking down now, Malcolm turns away from his
father's picture and the mirror. He swallows down hard
what he is feeling. From the bedroom, he hears his
mother call, "Were going to miss it all Malcolm."
"No we won't mother."
Malcolm walks through to collect her. She smiles and
even manages to pull herself up from her bed.
"You look nice mother."
Mildred puts her arm through his and totters slowly and
proudly into the sitting room. Getting ready, Malcolm
turns the telly on and goes to the sideboard for the

glasses and puts them on his mother's table next to the
bottle of sherry.

"Malcolm don't forget."

Going back to the sideboard, he takes out two boxes.
One holds his father's medals and the other his forces
revolver, he places them carefully in front of his father's
photograph and Malcolm stands to attention.

"Malcolm."

Mildred yells.

She is pointing to her head.

"The cap Malcolm, take off the cap, show some respect."
Her Majesty's face appears on the screen and Mildred
sits upright in her armchair, whilst Malcolm stands to
attention, with his cap held properly beneath his arm, as
they wait to hear the Queen's speech on Christmas Day.

Stella wakes to the silence of the house, she is warm and cosy, hidden beneath the warm feather duvet. It is Christmas day she remembers, as she pushes her nose from under the bedclothes and breathes in. She inhales the cold air and disappears again underneath the covers. She enjoys the lack of pressure, the need to leap out of bed and rush around and ready herself for a working day, it's Christmas, 'I don't need to do anything; I can stay in bed all day if I want to.' This injection of inertia induces a floppy, soft sensation and an inability to move or shift her. So she drowsily, drifts in and out of dream states, neither awake, nor fully asleep, the places she travels around are peculiar and unnerving and leave her feeling tired and lifeless. She glances across at the alarm clock; it displays 11.15 on its face. She turns over and her body feels uncomfortable and stiff, this is no good she decides, she must get up.

She lifts herself out of the hot, sticky bed and draws her dressing gown around her and stands in front of the full-length mirror. She sees a tousled head, popping out above the blue, towelled robe, staring back intently. 'Who are you?' she asks herself, as she ruffles her hair with her hands and moves closer to her own reflection, the unblinking, staring, wide eyes, wanting more answers, as they scrutinize the glassy image, in the mirror. 'You are Stella, but who are you?' the eyes question once again. 'Who are you beneath the skin and surface, who are you underneath this outer image, upright and facing, breathing and alive before me?'

Stepping back she withdraws, a feeling of betrayal fills her as she moves away from the mirror. She tightens the dressing gown belt and knots it and slips on her flip-flops and goes into the bathroom.

This is not the start to the day she envisaged or wants and as she begins her regime of teeth cleaning, flossing, rinsing and brushing, she tries to freshen her thoughts and decide how to spend it. She would take a shower, or a long soak later in the bath but now she needs to eat. The lie in has thrown her routine and she can't decide upon breakfast or brunch, if she has breakfast she can make a decent lunch and eat early evening, rather than later. She opens the fridge door for inspiration and sees the pack of bacon and eggs, her hand reaches for the milk, she will have a bowl of cereal and a mug of hot coffee.

Taking the breakfast into the living room, she eats the crunchy, milk soaked flakes. After putting down the empty bowl, she spots the solitary, golden box and the festive scenes on the few Christmas cards, dotted around the edge of the coffee table. She takes a long sip of the coffee and slides her hand to pick up the gift. She enjoys the process of unwrapping the little package and lifting the lid of the green box. As her fingers pull away the soft deep blue tissue paper, to reveal the enamel brooch, she draws in her breath as she touches the cold metal. Lifting it from the box, she marvels at the intensity of its colours and the rough texture, underneath the smooth glossy finish, as she runs her finger across. It really is something special, she acknowledges as she looks at it closer and turns it towards the light from the window. The brooch glistens as it meets the light and then becomes dark and deep as she places it back on the table. She would keep the box and the tissue paper. Charles hasn't written a card or put in a note, which is a shame, however, it is a reminder of the wonderful day she shared with him in France.

Her thoughts turn to Charles and she wonders how his Christmas day is going, she knows it will be a rather grand occasion, the traditional lunch, the day functioning like clock work and in an orderly fashion, the opening of the presents, the impressive lunch with turkey, trimmings and crackers, with plenty of wine and champagne no doubt. Probably taking a glass of port,

with a dainty mince pie, into the lounge to rest off their
hearty lunch and tuning into the Queen's speech. She
hopes the day would pan out ok for Charles and
Margaret. She pushes away these thoughts as she looks
around her room and at the pictures displayed on the
walls – she loves this house, she has put her heart and
soul into it.

Sitting here, sipping coffee in solitary silence disturbs
her, so she tries to plan what to do. She is unused to
flopping and chilling and having an open expanse of
time to waste, she chastises herself for staying in bed. If
she had risen at an earlier time she could have taken
herself off for a walk on the beach before the rest of
Fenton were up and about. She imagines visitors to the
town, revelling in a beach walk as part of their stay with
friends and family and this deters her from dressing and
going outside for a brisk walk. She would stand out on
her own, presuming everyone else to be in family
groups, chatting, happily wearing their Christmas day
outfits. It would highlight her isolation, her lack of
closely formed relationships, of family, yes especially
family.
 She doesn't want to dwell or think about this any longer,
she has had her chance to join others for the day and
chosen not to.
She hadn't envisaged the day, to be a day of
contemplation and reflection and battling hidden away,
deep feelings of insecurity and loneliness. Nor does she
want to think any more as to why this is; it is Christmas
day after all. So she rises from her seat and takes her
pots into the kitchen and returns to the living room, to
watch a DVD. She scans the line of films stacked on the
shelf and runs her finger across, hoping that one of them
will ignite her imagination, so that she can escape and
disappear into another world. There are several that she
has watched umpteen times and they always have the
knack of giving her a different perspective on life and
inspiration. Today she struggles to find one to do this, so

she selects a film that she bought on a whim months ago but never watched.

It is a Spanish film, located on an island; about a writer who's created world begins to mirror his own reality. She pushes it into the DVD player. Before she settles herself down to watch it, she opens a bottle of red wine and places it on the table, alongside a wine glass and a tub of roasted mixed nuts with black olives. She stretches out along the soft settee and presses the play button.
The sound of waves spilling across the rocks and the sun glinting across the sand, as if it where diamonds and the intense blue of the sea, clear and deep, as the shadows of the fish shoal across the sand, grabs her attention and she becomes fixated as she watches.

During the film she uncorks the wine and pours herself a glass and rips back the tab on the nuts and enjoys their salty, course and earthy flavour. She finds the film difficult to fully understand, especially with it having the subtitles to keep up with, she would have to watch it again another time and this fact satisfies her. She pauses it a couple of times, to make coffee and cut herself a thick wedge of date and walnut loaf. When the credits of the film roll, she turns of the player and looks down at the wine bottle, she has drank more than half of it and wishes that she hadn't.

She stands up and goes across to the window and looks out at the grey, brooding sea, so different from the sunny, Spanish island on the film. 'How is it, that we think what is in front of us is everlasting and will never change?' the summer here in Fenton seems a million miles away and hard to imagine that it will come back, she tries to console herself that it would.
Surfing in the cold sea during the autumn and winter is hard and tough and often uninviting, unlike the long days of the summer.

She recognises she needs to re-establish an exercise routine, somehow it has fallen by the way side under the pressure of work and she is beginning to feel heavy and stiff. 'My new year's resolution, well one of them,' she declares to herself, 'is to do the coastal walks and start cycling again. And what others?' She asks as she catches her reflection in the side pane of glass. 'Find out what you want, who you are, stop running away from yourself. Just look at you, here, Christmas day for god's sake, pretending that it's ok, that you prefer it like this, on your own, stop kidding yourself.' Turning quickly away from the window she sits down again and pours another glass of wine from the bottle and picks up the remote for the TV and turns it on. She doesn't want to hear her own thoughts; she needs something to drown them out.

Malcolm and Mildred's House.

"Look we've missed a bit."
Mildred tells Malcolm, as they wait for the Queen's speech.
"No we haven't mother, they're just introducing her, if you listen now mother you'll hear it. Look."
Malcolm nudges her.
"She's talking now."
"This year I'm speaking to you from the Household Cavalry Barracks in Windsor because I want to draw attention to the many servicemen and women...."
As the speech begins Malcolm relaxes because his mother is engrossed in it.
"I think we all have very good reasons for feeling proud of their achievements both in war and...."
Malcolm allows himself to think about the woman now and how her hand had slipped across his palm and touched him.
"These individual servicemen and women are our neighbours and come from our own towns and villages, from every part of the country and from every background."
Malcolm can smell her, her hair as she leant towards him.
"The process of training within the Navy, the Army and Air Force has moulded them together into disciplined teams."
Malcolm glances briefly across at Mildred; she is starting to nod off. If he switched off the TV, she would wake up and moan about him, not having any respect and God alone knows what. The speech continues.
"As we think of them and of our servicemen and women far from home at this Christmas time, I hope we all, whatever our faith can draw inspiration."

She had held the red and white Avenger Vulcan in her hand, touched it, so really in the end he'd had no choice, other than to choose it.

"Teach us Good Lord to serve Thee as Thou deservest......"

Malcolm stops listening now to the speech, he wants to go back into his room, change his clothes and touch the Avenger.

"Malcolm, Malcolm."

Returning to himself, Malcolm turns to look at his mother.

"Yes, what is it?"

He asks absentmindedly.

"You're not listening properly Malcolm, come on now, show some respect, what would your father say?"

"I am listening mother."

"To labour and not to ask for any reward, save that of knowing that we do Thy will."

Stella's House.

Stella sits directly opposite the Queen, her perfectly controlled, English words, ring out intent and personal, it is a one-way conversation and Stella listens.

"Joy and sadness are part of all our lives. Indeed, the poet William Blake tells us that:

'Joy and woe are woven fine,
A clothing for the soul divine,
Under every grief and pine
Runs a joy with silken twine.'

In October, 51 representatives of Commonwealth governments met in Edinburgh, very much in the spirit of a family gathering. We all enjoy meeting old friends and making new ones, but there was

also important business to be done. The world
saw that the Commonwealth can make a major
contribution to international relations and
prosperity.

For most of us this is a happy family day. But I
am well aware that there are many of you who
are alone, bereaved, or suffering. My heart goes
out to you, and I pray that we, the more
fortunate ones, can unite to lend a helping hand
wherever it is needed, and not pass by on the
other side.
I'm sure that most of you will be celebrating
Christmas at home in the company of your
families and friends.
But I know that some of you will not be so lucky."

'How do you know, how can you?' Stella's transfixed
state snaps with anger as she picks up the remote and
flings it across the floor. The Queen carries on talking as
she dashes upstairs away from the room. She runs up the
staircase, taking the steps two at a time and comes to a
sharp standstill in her chill out room, and plonks herself
down in the armchair. Her mind is spinning, her thoughts
spiralling out of control, she has to hold on, and she has
to stop herself from letting go. 'Oh what a fucking
Christmas day,' the mantra repeats over and over in her
head, until she slumps down and waits for the words to
go away.

The Manor House.

Christmas day is going like clockwork, Margaret has
managed to continue her preparations for lunch and cook
the meal to her stringent plans. Charles has done the
onerous thing and taken Philip and Monica out for a
short stroll along the promenade and a drink at the golf
club, leaving Abby upstairs in her room.

The dinner is set for the pre arranged hour of 1 o'clock precisely and duly they return with Monica's insistence at 12.45.

Charles pours them all a glass of sherry from the decanter before sitting down to eat. Margaret still immersed in the kitchen is oblivious to the fact that Abby is still in her room.

"Margaret, have you seen Abby?"

Charles shouts through to the kitchen.

"No darling I haven't, she must be upstairs in her room."

Charles storms to the bottom of the hall staircase.

"Abby."

He hollers, waiting for a response from her bedroom. Charles becomes incensed when there is no reply and he charges up the steps. Before he reaches the landing, the door to Abby's room opens and her head peeps out.

"Abby, do you realise what day it is? It is Christmas day and your grandparents are downstairs and you my girl haven't had the decency last night, or this morning to greet them and I am sure your mother is most embarrassed about your discourteous behaviour, so I think you had better get dressed and make amends because you have some making up to do young lady."

"I am coming."

"That is what I need to hear and don't be long."

Charles turns and descends the stairs.

Abby battles with the feeling of sickness and pulls on her boots. She pushes the bedside drawer, hiding the carton containing the pregnancy test; she decides to leave it until later. She knows she has been careful, but with all the sex she's had with Mark – they could have slipped up. The fact that she could be pregnant would have to be dealt with later, for now she doesn't want to think about it, she has enough on her mind.

Monica's mood is more relaxed after the couple of sherries she has drunk and when Abby comes into the dining room she greets her amiably.

"Merry Christmas darling, let's take a look at you, give your grandmother a kiss." Monica leans forward with

her eyes closed, waiting for Abby to hug and kiss her.
Abby quickly pecks the offered cheek and draws back.
Margaret comes into the room to announce dinner and
asks Abby to help bringing through the tureens.
Monica mutters to Charles, whilst helping Philip to his
chair and shames Charles into assisting. When they are
all seated, Charles stands at the end of the table to
propose a toast and make his usual pre dinner speech.
The heat of the room and the smell of the hot food makes
Abby's stomach turn.
"You look rather peaky dear."
Monica speaks as she dips her spoon into the fresh
melon balls covered in lemon sauce.
Abby waits and then in an effort to avert their gazes she
takes a single ball into her mouth. The refreshing sweet,
sharpness of the fruit lands and fights inside her gurgling
stomach and she doesn't know whether it will stir or
settle the motion.
Charles helping himself to another large glass of red
wine is in full flow and his spirits are high as he picks up
a cracker to pull with Philip.
"Merry Christmas to all of you, cheers and all the best of
the season."
Philip lacks the strength to pull his end of the cracker
and Charles grabs it from him and places it in Margaret's
hand to Philip's surprise. Margaret follows suit with
Monica and the atmosphere becomes more relaxed. After
waiting for Philip to finish his starter, Margaret clears
the dishes and then removes the lids off the tureens,
whilst Charles carves the turkey.
"Abby darling are you alright, there's no need to worry
yourself about the turkey, I have made stilton and walnut
tartlets specially for you."
Margaret stands up from her seat and leaves the room.
Charles contains his urge to raise the subject about
vegetarianism and helps himself to a large wedge of the
turkey breast and places it on his plate.
Margaret returns with the tartlets.

"Sometimes Margaret it doesn't do to indulge, this vegetarian fad is so unhealthy, no wonder Abby looks so peaky, do try the turkey darling, I'm sure it can't be so difficult."
Monica appeals to Abby.
Abby sits in silence and then Charles decides to join in.
"Yes Abby I think you have taken things far enough, what you need is a good dinner with plenty of meat, no wonder you can't get up on a morning, sleeping in till all hours, you haven't got enough energy and that comes from eating a decent diet. Not this messing about with one fad after another."
"Oh Charles, really darling do you have to, it's Christmas day."
Margaret interrupts trying to stop Charles's flow.
"The stuffing Abby, would you mind, it's in the top oven."
Margaret asks.
"What a pantomime, sometimes this house is like a bloody circus."
Charles spouts.
"I remember the circus, Billy Smart's."
Philip says paying attention.
"Come on dear, let's help ourselves before it gets cold."
Monica begins to spoon small portions of the vegetables onto Philip's plate.
Abby returns from the kitchen and sits down but as the smell wafts from the unleashed sprouts across the table she springs up from her seat and dashes from the room.
"Oh that's it, another drama – like walking on eggshells, well I've had enough, pass me the stuffing Margaret, let's not have all this good food going to waste. There's plenty Monica, if that girl wants to starve then let her."
Charles helps himself to the roast potatoes and vegetables.
"The gravy Margaret."
Charles asks looking around the table for the gravy boat.
"Oh dear."
Margaret says dejectedly.

Monica looks at her daughter.

"It must be in the kitchen."

Margaret walks out of the room.

"The food is going to be cold Margaret, at this rate we would have been better booking a table at The Hunter's Inn in Thornby."

Charles remarks.

When Margaret is out of earshot Monica chips in.

"Margaret's isn't coping very well Charles, she seems at sixes and sevens, preoccupied and flustered, last night I told her she is letting her standards slip and that she needs to prioritise, do you think Susan needs a word Charles?"

Margaret picks up the gravy boat from the worktop and notices the green light on her mobile flashing; she puts the dish down and unlocks the phone. She has received a voicemail. Pressing the number she places the phone to her ear and listens. It is Giles, for a moment she stands transfixed and hears his message.

"Happy Christmas Maggie, wish I was with you, take care Giles."

For a moment she is back in his embrace, back in the safety and comfort of his strong arms, she feels her body soften and fill with desire for him. As she dials his mobile number, her mother pauses by the doorway to listen.

"Happy Christmas to you too, I need you and wish I,"

"Margaret."

Her mother snaps.

Margaret puts the phone down and turns towards her mother.

"Oh I see, so this is what it's all about, we'll talk about it later dear."

Monica says with disgust.

Margaret picks up the gravy boat and walks past her mother as if nothing has happened, she is unsure how much of the conversation she has heard and is still caught inside Giles's spell, protected and safe.

Entering the dining room, Philip's head is bent over, his party hat lay across his plate and Charles is filling his own wine glass to the brim. If it was physically possible, there would be steam rising from the top of Charles's head, his red face looks ready to burst. Monica and Margaret sense the volatile atmosphere and say nothing. Charles takes the gravy boat and tips it over his plate and begins to attack his food with his knife and fork. Monica nudges Philip and he wakes with a start. The rest of the meal is eaten in silence, concluding with the traditional Christmas pudding and white sauce. Charles continues drinking and topping up their glasses and the mood around the table becomes less stifled as Monica's speech starts to slur.

"Let's retire to the sitting room."

Charles announces.

"Yesh Charles, that wash very nice, washnt it Philip?" Monica slurs.

Margaret aids Monica and then Philip into the sitting room.

"Anyone for a port?"

Charles asks.

"Yesh just a teeny weeny shlittle one."

Monica begins to laugh.

Charles does the honours and fills their glasses and passes them round.

"Whoops a daisy."

Monica laughs as she spills her drink.

"Save a toast for her majesty the Queen."

Charles says lifting his glass.

"To the Queen."

Monica cheers.

Charles takes the remote and turns on the television.

The Queen is issuing her speech to the nation.

'Ever since the first Christmas when the three wise men brought their presents, Christians all over the world have kept up this kindly custom.

Even if the presents we give each other at Christmas-time may only be intended to give momentary pleasure, they do also reflect one all important lesson. Society cannot hope for a just and peaceful civilisation unless each individual feels the need to be concerned about his fellows. All the great works of charity and all humanitarian legislation have always been inspired by a flame of compassion, which has burnt brightly in the hearts of men and women. Mankind has many blemishes, but deep down in every human soul there is a store of goodwill waiting to be called upon.'

At this moment Abby enters the room and picks up the DVD remote from the table and presses play.

"Come and sit here shdarling."

Monica taps her hand on the cushion in between her and Philip on the settee. Abby wiggles her way into the middle. The whirring sound of the DVD player displaces the voice from the TV screen and the 'Big baby day mementoes' film begins to play. Margaret looks on in shock and Monica starts to laugh. Charles can't believe his eyes as the DVD plays on.
The nurse on the screen is holding out a big dummy for Charles, who is dressed in a frilly baby suit. The women sit watching agog, speechless as Charles takes the dummy into his mouth. Suddenly Philip slumps down, dropping his glass of port, whilst Abby stands up and leaves the room.
"Daddy."
Margaret rushes across to her father who gives out no response.
"Charles, daddy."
Margaret calls out.
"Phillip, Phillip."

Charles shakes him.
Philip doesn't respond, his mouth appears to have
drooped and he is unable to talk.
"An ambulance, phone for an ambulance Charles."
Margaret cries.
Charles fumbles around for the DVD remote, as the
nurse on the screen offers her generous breast for
Charles to feed, as he sucks purposefully on his dummy.
The TV screen returns to the Queen's speech as Charles
picks up the phone.

*I am sure the custom of giving presents at
Christmas will never die out, but I hope it will
never overshadow the far more important
presents we can give for the benefit of the future
of the world.*

*People of goodwill everywhere are working to
build a world that will be a happier and more
peaceful place in which to live. Let our prayers be
for a personal strength and conviction to play our
own small part to bring that day nearer.*

*Being united - that is, feeling a unity of purpose -
is the glue that bonds together the members of a
family, a country, a Commonwealth. Without it,
the parts are only fragments of a whole; with it,
we can be much more than the sum of those
fragments.*

*St Paul spoke of the first Christmas as the
kindness of God dawning upon the world. The
world needs that kindness now more than ever -
the kindness and consideration for others that
disarms malice and allows us to get on with one
another with respect and affection.*

Christmas reassures us that God is with us today. But, as I have discovered afresh for myself this year, he is always present in the kindness shown by our neighbours and the love of our friends and family.

God bless you all and Happy Christmas

At the cottage.

The Christmas dinner is lovely but they can't face the pudding.
"We can eat it another day."
"Yes, we've plenty of time left to eat puddings and cakes and I think everyone's full up for now."
Anna agrees as they begin to clear the table and put the dishes into the dishwasher, as Jason lays full and content on his bed. The children are in the smaller sitting room watching TV.
"Let's finish the bottle of wine we began last night."
Jo suggests to Anna.
"Yes, why not."
Anna collects two clean glasses from the cupboard and shares the wine between them. "Would you mind if I listened to the Queen's speech for a few minutes?"
Anna asks.
"No, is it on now?"
"It should be coming on soon."
"Right kids, your programme will be going off soon and I'd like to listen to at least some of the Queen's speech."
"Oh no, you do this every year."
"Just listen for a bit."
Anna takes hold of the remote and switches the channel. The voice of the Queen in mid speech, meets the loud groans from her children. Anna sits down and begins to listen.
"This year I should like to speak especially to women. In many countries custom has decreed

that women should play a minor part in public affairs."

Anna takes a sip from her glass.

"This is boring."

Adam whines.

"In a bit."

Anna tells him.

"Yet in spite of these disabilities, it has been women who have breathed gentleness and care into the harsh progress of mankind. The struggles against inhuman prejudice, against squalor, ignorance, and disease, have always owed a great deal to the determination and tenacity of women. The devotion of".

"How long is this going to last mam?"

Georgina sulks.

"the care of mothers and wives."

"In a minute love."

"and the conviction of reformers are the real and enduring presents which women have always given. In the modern world of opportunities for women to give something of value to the human family are greater than ever, because, through their own efforts"

Jason now expresses his boredom by whining to go out.

"We know so much more about what can be achieved; we know that the tyranny of ignorance can be broken"

"Jo can I take Jason for a walk?"

Adam asks as he rolls around on the floor teasing Jason with his sock.

"We know all these things are important in our own homes, but it needs a very active concern by women everywhere if this knowledge is to be used where it is most needed."

"When this is finished we can all go for a walk."

"The meeting also showed that unity and diversity can go hand in hand.""Mam."
Adam calls.
"Alright shoes, socks Adam and coats and gloves on."
Anna shouts.
"As proof that the kingdom can still enjoy all the benefits of remaining united. In this country"
"Come on Adam, put your coat on."
Georgina tells him.
The children leave the room, with Jason following behind them, eager to be out. Anna and Jo listen for a few moments.
"There are groups of people who are giving their time generously to make a difference to the lives of others."
"Oh come on then."
Anna presses the off button on the remote, thinking to herself, she had at least done her bit, listening to the Queen.
"Mam."
They switch off the TV and put on their outdoor shoes and coats, ready to go out for a long walk on the beach with Jason. The long walk will be good for the children and help them use up some of their energy.
"Are you alright?"
Jo asks Anna as they walk away from the Nab.
"Yea."
"You don't mind about missing the end of the speech?"
"No."
Anna says honestly. She welcomes the huge open expanse of the sea. To be in physical touch with its source and not just looking at it and hearing it from a distance. The children and Jason run on ahead laughing, as the two women follow.

Stella's fury finally subsides and she pulls the telescope
towards her, for the sake of something to do, she looks
through the lens and catches sight of the icy, cold waves,
tossing and foaming their white froth, over the grim,
grey sea. She points the scope down towards the beach,
there are only a few people walking across the sand. One
or two groups huddle together in their winter coats and
high boots, bracing against the wind. She pushes the
eyepiece towards the cobble landing and the harbour; she
can see the colours of the flashing Christmas lights and
the fishing boats leaning on their sides. She is about to
let go of the telescope when something catches her
attention. Adjusting her hold on the scope she presses
her eye against the glass, to find out what it is. At first
she can't see anything and then zooming in she
recognises who they are, it is Jo with the other women,
she had seen swimming with Jo, at the beginning of the
summer. Following the two women are a boy, girl and
the dog. The dog is chasing a ball and the two children
are running after it, towards the cobble landing.

The children stop to play in the rock pools until the dog
joins in, digging and splashing in the water. Stella
notices as the children leap up and run across the sands
that they have left a dark object in one of the pools.
Zooming in closer, it looks like a piece of dark, wet
cloth. She continues to watch them, walking towards the
landing, the whole impact of her own loneliness and
inner emptiness shakes her. She lets the telescope drop
from her hand, she doesn't want to see anymore, she
doesn't want others to have what she hasn't.

She sits until darkness falls upon the room, and then
raises herself up from the chair and creeps back
downstairs. She hears the noise coming from the TV and
goes into the living room. The flashing light from the
television is the only brightness in the house and as she
reaches behind her to switch on the wall lights, her ears
tune into the cheery voices coming from the screen,

singing carols. Stella searches for the remote to turn off the happy voices and when silence returns she picks up her glass and fills it and takes a large sip of the red wine, 'Merry fucking Christmas.'

She takes her glass and another handful of nuts and goes into the office and switches on her laptop, cursing as she nearly tips her wine onto the keyboard. She decides to browse through her favourite art website, to find and treat herself to a Christmas present, a painting. She enjoys looking at the pictures as they pass along the top of the screen; she fast-forwards them and stops when something catches her eye. There are hundreds of paintings to browse through; she often spends hours looking at these when she cannot sleep. She bought about twenty from the site when it first opened, then they were value for money and relatively inexpensive.

Now with the popularity of the website they have increased considerably in price, except for the unknown artists. When she finds a painting that she likes she checks out the artists other works and then moves on. With bleary eyes the pictures speed past the top of the screen and she hits the button to playback the order again. With wine fuelled fingers she taps forwards and backwards in vain trying to find her favourites. When she has filled her shopping cart with ten paintings she makes her final choice. She clicks and enters the artist's page; there are six painting by – Bradley. All of them are interesting and unusual oil paintings. It is the small one titled – The Paper Doll that appeals to Stella as she looks at it closely. It reminds her of her childhood, when she spent hours cutting out outfits for her magazine paper doll. She had created worlds in her imagination of how her doll lived its life, so different and much more exciting than her own.

She had several dolls, each with a different name, their own personality and family life. She could entertain herself by conjuring up their worlds and friends, and how they would spend their days.

The price of the painting is £75, a lovely present from Santa Claus, a little late maybe, but so what, she thinks to herself. She presses the back button to double check on her selection and reads the small printed statement at the bottom of her chosen picture. It reads – This painting is an image used in the book – The Paper Doll by Bradley, to buy a copy...........This is definitely her final choice and intrigued by the book she decides to find out about it later. She checks out and purchases the painting and pays with her credit card. She shuts down her laptop and feeling peckish now, goes to find food. She will take a look at the book tomorrow.

Abby sits holding Mark's hand, she is content to be in
Thornby hospital, spending late Christmas afternoon
with him. She is glad to be anywhere except The Manor
House. There is a lot of activity going on around the bed
next to Mark's, the curtains have been pulled around.
"An old kid."
Mark tells her.
Abby listens carefully to a commotion beginning along
the corridor. She dismisses what she thinks she can hear
as Mark begins to stroke her hand.
'You deserve it you pig.' Abby thinks, as she looks at
the mess her father's thugs have done to him.
After she had watched the DVD, it became obvious to
her, what Charles had been up to. She hadn't hung
around to see what happened, after she put the copy of
the DVD in the player. She had left her family dumb
founded no doubt, at what was playing.
She has the original and her own copy, in her bag by the
side of the chair. After the hospital, she would take up
the offer, of spending some of the Christmas holiday
with Mark's family. She has no wish to return home to
her mother, Charles and grandparents and be asked to
explain. She has worked out that Mark must have taken
the DVD whilst he was staying with her but she doesn't
care; not now, it doesn't matter anymore.
Abby shakes her head and stands up, she is sure she can
hear the sounds of her mother's voice and Charles's
unmistakable booming, along way off.
The patient in the bed next to Mark's is quiet and the
nurses are talking to him in subdued tones. Abby walks
to the entrance of the ward. She has to lean against a
wall to stop herself from falling, when she sees Charles
followed by her mother and grandmother charging up the
corridor towards her. What do they want?
"So you've come to say you are sorry."
Abby's words stop Charles in his tracks.
"How did you know?"
Charles manages to splutter.
"So you've come to see what you have done?"

Abby accuses Charles.

"What the bloody hell are you talking about?"
Charles hisses as Margaret and her grandmother step
behind the curtain, to the next bed. Abby looks beyond
her mother, through the curtain and sees her grandfather,
pale and hooked up and attached to various wires and
tubes. Her mother and grandmother sit down in the seats
at the side of Philip's bed.

"This is what your bloody tricks have done young lady."
Charles tells Abby furious at the girl and what has
happened to Maggie's father because of her ridiculous
attempts of teenage bravado. This is the result, a whole
bloody mess that he could have done without.

It isn't too far removed from the truth for Charles, to
have felt something like a sense of relief when the poor
old sod had taken Margaret's and her mother's attention
away from him, when he had slumped down. This matter
had thrown the women from gaining the opportunity of
pinning Charles down and making him answer.

"There, there."
Charles forces himself to sooth the crying Margaret. It is
unusual to see her show so much emotion openly but he
intends to capitalize on what is going on, realizing it has
to be every man for himself!

Abby goes into the cubicle and puts her arms around her
grandfather.

"Oh, grandpa," she sobs.

"It wasn't aimed at you, but him."

'What the fuck's going on?' Mark asks himself as he
listens to the goings on in the bed next to his. Mark
assumes that Abbs has gone off for a piss and a drink.
He hopes she'll come back with one for him from the
cooler. A nice cold coke, Mark thinks, licking his sore
lips. 'The noisy fuckers next door had better keep it
down,' Mark says to himself, leaning back into his firm
pillows. As he waits for Abbs to return, he hears the
women whining in the next cubicle. 'What the fuck?'
Mark says opening and closing his eyes. 'This lot had

better not be carrying on for much longer or I'll never get a wink of sleep.'

Mark's swollen eyelids close now as he manages to nod off once again.

Stella sets her alarm clock for 6.00am the next morning, Boxing Day. She intends to have a determined start, filled with intent and purpose, unlike today wallowing in self-pity. Now that Christmas day is almost over her mood begins to lift. She will have an early swim, to invigorate her; the physical exercise is just what she needs.

Before turning off the lights downstairs, she opens the freezer and takes out a piece of fillet steak, she intends to cook herself a decent meal the following evening. Climbing the stairs she wrestles with the temptation to enter her chill out room to observe the night sky, knowing that if she does she will end up falling asleep in the chair and walking up in the early hours cold and stiff. She makes her choice and opens the bedroom door and turns on the table lamp. After removing her clothes she turns back the duvet and slides into the king-size bed. She spreads out her legs to check the space around her and sighs then reaches out to turn off the light.

In the darkness, she allows her mind the freedom to explore its multi faceted cavities, to peruse, to verify, to backtrack, to unearth its contents, as if witnessing as an outside observer, its layers – to stretch and pull them apart, to read between their expanse and fantasize, twist and re fabricate them into a new and altered real life drama. Her ruminations leap about at random and then fall upon the evening spent with Charles and Jo.

She can almost taste the soap filled bubbles as she submerges herself beneath the water, she feels the tingling of the froth upon her skin, the gentle warmth of the water. The deep, richness of the dark red wine as she takes another sip from the glass beside her, conscious always of Jo next to her, silent and naked beneath the water.

Her mind traverses its options and she sees her hand reaching out to Jo and allowing it freedom, she tentatively touches her face and feels the heat beneath her fingertips. And then she sees Charles entering the room carrying a tray filled with fresh fruit, marshmallows and chocolates. Then Charles too in the bathtub offering his fare, the whole scene like a Bacchanalian feast – with the passing around of the sweet delicasies, the juices running and the sticky mouths filled with promise, from the gorging of the soft pink marshmallows. And then Jo giggling and slipping, trying to stand up and then falling back against the side of the tub, creating a wave of water as she slips and tries again. And then Charles grabbing at her as she rises once more. And then Stella's mind tracks back to the feel of her, as her hand explores the curves, mounds, the depths of her. And as she leans across and kisses her she inhales the sweetness, she tastes the tiny traces of sugar around Jo's lips.

She holds onto this thought, this recreation and allows it space to stretch and open up inside her mind.

In between the sheets of her bed now, Jo lays beside her. She feels the smooth length of her limbs against her own. Her mind fights to retain this, to continue its enchantment, its desire to fulfill, to consume her, to abandon all inhibitions and satisfy all longings, not rushed or forced but with total mutual acceptance. As she stretches her arm across the sheet she finds the cold, empty place of her. She strives once more, to find her presence, to locate her, to plant her inside the memories, to build a world about her that is accesible, not one that is generated out of wistful, transient longings but one that is lifelike, real and true.

As the excitement of Christmas day begins to fade in Adams memory, Thorn Cottage settles down and relaxes. Anna doesn't need to rise at the crack of dawn as Adam sleeps longer.

Awhile-later Anna slips out of bed and puts on a jumper to keep herself warm. Downstairs Jason stretches himself out as Anna wakes him from sleep. The kitchen is chilly and Anna appreciates her warm jumper.

"Well Jason, let's warm this place up, I'll set the fire and start on breakfast."

Outside it is crisp, frosty and still dark.

"I'll let you out soon, once the fire is lit."

Anna takes pleasure as she lights the scrunched up paper in the grate and the tinder wood catches fire.

"Come on boy."

Anna encourages Jason and slips on her coat and takes his lead to let him out. The cold chill blows across Anna's face and makes her shudder.

"Not too far it's freezing."

Jason pulls on his lead wanting to be off.

She lets him pee and then coaxes him back into the cottage.

The cold air fills the room as Anna opens the door.

"Gosh it feels cold out there, there was no need to take Jason out, he would have been ok for a bit longer."

Jason bounds across to nuzzle and play as Jo switches the kettle on.

"It's ok Jo, I thought seeing as I was first up."

"Well thanks, anyway, that's kind of you."

"Shall we have porridge for breakfast?"

"Yes it will warm everybody up."

"The heating is on, so it should warm up soon."

Breakfast is a happy time and the entire household including Jason, eat their bowls full of satisfying porridge with honey and toasted nuts.

"Come on, let's play hide and seek."

Adam yells after finishing his food.

Jason keen to be involved in any action leaps up from the floor with his tail wagging.

"You hide, I'll count to ten and then we'll find you."

"Alright but wait until I'm ready before you start counting."

"One, two, three, four."

"Wait, I'm not ready yet."

"Five, six, seven, eight."

"Right I'm not playing."

"I'll hide first then."

"Oh all right, one, two, three, four."

"Now you're counting before I'm ready."

"Serves you right."

Adam picks up a cushion from the sofa and hurls it at Georgina. Jason quick to join in the fun intervenes and grabs it between his teeth and begins tossing it into the air and wrestling with it.

At this point Jo enters the room.

"Jason drop it now."

Jo runs after Jason who dodges the group, dashing into the kitchen with the cushion in his mouth.

"Now drop it."

Jason heeds the severity of Jo's warning and sheepishly lets the cushion fall and gives a hopeful wag of his tail.

"Good boy."

Jo strokes lovingly the length of his back and Jason wags his tail with delight.

"Right then who fancies a walk to the hut?"

Jo shouts, hoping to settle the kids down and prevent them from charging around the cottage.

"Yes."

"You need to get wrapped up it's cold outside."

"Can we look for the Purple Pearl?"

Adam asks.

"Why where is it?"

"I lost it."

"Lost it where?"

"Georgina left it in the rock pool."

"No I did not."

"Oh Adam."

"So can we go and look for it?"

"We can if the tides out when we go down."

"I did not Adam, so don't say I did."

Adam launches at Georgina.

"Right come on hats and coats, or are you both staying here?"

"Well I'll stay here and wash the pots and do a bit of washing and prepare the dinner."

Anna declines.

"We could finish off the turkey and have salad and baked potatoes."

"That sounds great I'll get it ready."

"We could have soup to start if you like."

"Yes, it'll warm us up."

Anna closes the door behind the well wrapped up children and excited dog, she clears the table first and then washes the pots.

Finding dirty clothing in the children's room and a few bits of her own, she takes them downstairs to wash in the sink. There is a washing machine as well as a dishwasher but for so few things, it is quicker to wash them through and peg them outside. Anna makes up the salad and puts it into the fridge, tidies up the downstairs room and puts another log on the fire. It will be good to go and sit in front of it later with a mug of hot tea. Anna straightens the beds and then finds the loose notes of Fermanagh House in her bedroom. She can read through them whilst she has a little free time on her own. Anna returns downstairs and rinses the clothes in clean water and rings them out and puts each article onto the drainer. After drying her hands she begins to read the last pages of Fermanagh House.

John awoke after he'd dozed off he hadn't intended to sleep. If someone saw the car parked on the verge at the end of the cottages people might talk and he didn't want that. John felt loathed to leave the warmth of the bed and the softness of Anna but he withdrew his arm from underneath her and inched his way out of bed so as not to awaken her. Downstairs he dressed in the sitting room and turned the gas fire down low before leaving. Opening the outside door the early morning chill brushed over him and he shuddered. All was quiet, no lights on in the other cottages to draw attention to him. Starting up the car as quietly as he could he was soon away driving along the dark, frosty country lanes on his way home. After parking up John put his key in the lock and entered his house. The hall was warm and smelt of polished wood. John drew in a deep breath of satisfaction and exhaled. The atmosphere of his large, airy, warm home filled him with peace. He liked the fine heights of the ceilings and the vast space within his house always freed him of his cares and soothed his tired body and gave him space to think. A hot shower and coffee to set him up. Amy, his cleaner wouldn't be in with it being the Christmas holidays. After his shower he would catch up on reading his newspapers and then rest before starting again on this new day. Later there would be the meal at Fermanagh House with Maya and Michael and Mary. She, Anna had not been invited to this particular intimate family meal. Christmas dinner. It had always being special to them and not for strangers or outsiders. Mary had earned her place after her personal loyalty to him and the practise. As he showered John knew it was now time to deal with Anna. She had begun to talk to Maya about things that Maya would be better forgetting. He didn't want the past to be raked up, brought back with all the utter misery it had brought up whilst she was alive. When she had found out their lives as a couple had totally changed. She had been an extraordinarily beautiful woman and keeping away from her had been almost impossible. But he had found consolations on his travels and no one knew. That's what mattered the most now. Maya had forgotten. She was a beautiful talented woman and she was a good doctor. He wouldn't allow her to interfere with her remedies. Maya had been happy until Anna had arrived but now he sensed her unsettled, restless dissatisfaction. He knew she was desperate to have a baby and already he had arranged for her to see a fertility consultant in Dublin in the New Year. He was a good man and got most of his patients pregnant. That's what had to happen now for Maya but it also meant getting rid of her. He knew Anna and he knew what she wanted and he knew she would trust him. The rest he would deal with. Paul had been only too happy when Maya had asked about hypnosis to oblige John and not actually hypnotise Maya during their session. He'd lied about an early trauma he hadn't wanted Maya to be put through again. But she, she was digging too deep for comfort. He had managed to change the remedy Anna had prescribed for Maya to a sac lac no one had been any the wiser but he needed to do more. Mary had always kept him up to date with Anna's prescribing as she posted them. John had decided he would give Anna something she would remember but there would always be the element of uncertainty women like her always fell down on that. Fundamentally for all her knowledge and education and new age ideas she was a basic working class insecure woman who had gotten out of her depth believing herself to be liberated and independent and on a crusade. John had known as soon as he'd touched her who and what she was and as she devoured him and yielded to him like a whimpering bitch in the end he had her measure. He'd felt glad in the end at the kiss in Fermanagh House beneath the mistletoe. A boozy, wet sloppy kiss but unmistakably one loaded with her need and desire. Back at the cottage he'd been unsure but then everything had fallen into place. A half decent slob and a half dozen children would have kept her in her place and settled her but who ever she'd had he either hadn't kept the lead tight enough or didn't want her. As a consequence she'd believed she'd found herself and was now going to help Maya to find herself. Maya would settle for a pregnancy he knew and Anna would settle for whatever he chose to give her. Really she'd been easy, too easy really; no real challenge just another frustrated, highly-strung middle-aged woman. More than common enough in his practise and surgery. Those he put on tranquillisers he would leave another one to do that job for her but he had noted her symptoms and would accordingly prescribe for her. Driving back to Fermanagh House John at last began to settle and gain some pleasure from the festive season and looked forward to joining his family. His gifts were already perfectly chosen and wrapped by Mary; Maya had chosen and wrapped Mary's. Life felt better all round and a good shag always set him up for the day so he was away.

Stella hears the obtrusive ringing of the alarm and reaches out to turn it off. She has been inside the cocoon of deep sleep and it takes her a few moments to rouse herself. Remembering her commitment for the day ahead, she reluctantly steps out of bed. Whilst going through the familiar motions of readying herself for the beach she detects a change within her. If she were pressed to discern it, she would probably describe it as something soft and even now she has difficulty articulating this sense within her. Her immediate thought of being stroked by a feather, tickles her and she smiles almost with disbelief by this – it is certainly not how she perceives herself to be. Casting the idea aside, she locks the door and strides towards the cobble landing – this route is at odds with her regular habit of choosing the opposite end of the beach and she walks on. Arriving at the point where she had witnessed the two women and children, she retraces their footsteps along the rocks.

The beach is empty, apart from a lone jogger running the other way. The seagulls squawking and competing with each other, cry out against the roaring, rushing tide. Looking down to her right she spots it, she knows instantly that this is what the young boy had left behind. Lolling on its side, meshed in strands of fishing line and limp sailcloth is one of Jo's boats – it has her signature, of that she is sure. The hull, painted black, with a plank sticking out, with what appears to be purple sails, knotted by the line, looks like an old shipwreck in the deep rock pool. Lifting it out of the water carefully, Stella begins unravelling the mess. She decides she needs a pair of scissors to untangle it and places it into her bag.
Removing her tracksuit she shivers and dashes into the sea – the water although cold, feels warmer than the outside temperature as she plunges forward and swims. She has difficulty catching her breath at times, especially when her arms push through the colder, deeper stretches

of water. After several laps, she locates her belongings on the shore and crawls her way back.

Back at home Stella has a hot shower and breakfast. She is pleased that today has got off to a better start and with a fresh mug of coffee she enters her office. Determined now she decides to check out several flights to France and book one or two for the New Year. Looking through her emails she reads again the order from yesterday and clicks on the website. The painting she purchased reminds her of the book and she accesses the link to a bookstore. The Paper Doll by Bradley is now on the screen. Stella reads the introduction............
The Paper Doll is a book for self-development. The book leads you into parts and places within yourself and allows you to discover your identity – who you are and who you would like to be......
She decides to buy herself a copy. After checking out her order, she returns her thoughts to France and with her diary at hand; she books three flights for the coming year. Satisfied now, she turns her attention to catching up with some paper work.
Hours later whilst eating her evening meal she pronounces the day a success – she has managed to live in its 'time' and not battle, bemoan and resent its offering of space as something to skirt around, avoid or detach herself from. She feels triumphant with the knowledge that 'time' is what you put into it and make of it – it is not predetermined and specific to everyone – it is what you can want it and make it to be. The dripping tap of thoughts, break through, as she heralds the 'Christmas day' exemption from her preceding ideas. 'Don't,' she reprimands herself as she stands up from the table to clear her dishes and wash up.

Malcolm closes his eyes and momentarily rests his head on the outer door – she's gone, he sighs to himself as he plods up the back stairs to sort himself out. Mildred had smiled at the other women as they put a rug over her and then turned and lost her temper with him, shouting out that he'd lost her bag when all the time Mrs Hardwick was holding onto it, whilst she settled Mildred on the minibus.

"Here it is."

The woman had squealed to his mother, as she handed over the beige vinyl bag, that his mother always kept by her side. She'd smiled again at the woman and then gave Malcolm a sharp dismissive look. That had meant for him to go, he knew that look and had seen it often enough all through his life.

Malcolm had gone as his mother had ordered, muttering his goodbyes to her as he backed away.

"Well enjoy your day mother."

He'd said and all the women in the bus had clucked back at him that she would. They'd make sure of course, that she did enjoy the usual trip, along the coast road to Thornby. The windows would be steamed up and the sea fret would probably cover the view in any case but she insisted she enjoyed it. Then the inevitable toilet stops and cups of tea in the church hall and sandwiches left over from the turkey, the mince pies and Christmas cake and then the slow drive home back to Fenton. Mildred said she looked forward to it.

"It's a day out, sum ut to do, to stop me getting stalled." He'd had to go to the chemist to buy the special pads for her before the shop closed for the holidays. Just in case she wet herself before the toilet stop, so it wouldn't show. She'd given him no peace until he'd gone out and brought them back to give to her. She'd put two spare ones in her bag.

"Just in case, to be on the safe side."

Malcolm switches on the second bar of the electric fire. She wouldn't find out. As he warms himself through, the idea begins to grow slowly inside his head. He knows he has time. He'd been to the hut to look for her. He'd thought it was hers, where she lived but it wasn't. It is the other woman who lives there. Malcolm still can't fathom out where she had stayed during the summer months. It must have been somewhere close by, local, for her to be about as much as she had been. This time he knows where she is, the boy had let that slip when he'd called at the shop just before Christmas and she and the others had followed him in a few moments later.

He knows the Nab well enough and the few cottages that are there, he knows the whole area like the back of his hand. He could go up and around the cottages just to see, to find out which one they are staying in and to have a look at what they're doing. He could wear his German Army uniform, with his Mac on top, so no one would know or be able to see it. It would make him feel good if he wore it, proud. He could wear the boots too but he hadn't broken them in properly. His old trainers wouldn't look as good as the boots but in the trainers he could walk faster and they'd help him not to slip about on the bits of ice.

Turning one of the bars off, he stands for a moment undecided. No, he will leave the other bar on all day, even when he goes out. She wouldn't have allowed it but as Malcolm turns to go into his room, he reasons that if he closes the door, it will keep warm for when he and later on his mother returns. He'll be back before her naturally, there is no question whatsoever about that. He opens his wardrobe door and puts his hand to the back and feels for his German uniform. Lifting it out he hangs it on the door. He smiles slightly, feeling the excitement beginning to rise up in him. The hat, no, no, not the hat, he can't wear that. He wants to, he is torn but knows that outside it would be impossible, if anyone saw him wearing it. He could fold it and put it in his raincoat pocket but that would completely spoil it. No, he couldn't do that. Instead he takes one of his black balaclavas, yes that's what he decides on, the balaclava.

As he undresses to change into the uniform, Malcolm glances again at the mantle shelf. He has quite a good collection now. Stepping out of his trousers, Malcolm is a bit taken aback, to see how much his privates are sticking out. He looks down, to see it sneaking out of his baggy underpants. He can't put his uniform trousers on over it. The longer Malcolm stands in his freezing cold bedroom, the bigger it is getting, it feels heavy, it aches so much and he knows he'll have to sort it out before he starts to get dressed. He lifts one of the bullet cases from his mantle and blows the dust off it. As he touches the case with his fat fingers, it feels cold and hard and he begins to slowly grasp his fist around it and move it up and down. As his movements quicken, Malcolm slips his free hand down into his underpants. The coldness of his hand startles him at first but he quickly falls into the rhythm he had started on the bullet. He'd always been too well endowed. His father had told him that.
"It doesn't do Malcolm to have so much."
Malcolm had felt ashamed then and hadn't been able to look at his father. He had been doing exercises with his father at the time and things had got a bit out of hand. His father had told his mother that she needed to buy the boy bigger shorts to cover himself up with. Mildred had said she couldn't keep track of the way he was growing out of things but the next day Malcolm had found two new pairs of underpants and shorts on his bed.
He needs to change his underpants now or his uniform would end up smelling. He wipes himself on his pants and dries his hand before getting a fresh pair.

He will have to get a move on, or she'll be back before he's even set off. He decides to take his flask with him. Malcolm carefully avoids the picture of his father and the mirror, as he pulls the clean underpants on. He puts a vest on; he is freezing with the coldness of the flat.

After locking the door, Malcolm pushes his black balaclava, gloves and mobile phone into his raincoat pockets and puts his key back on to the dog tag he has around his neck. He pulls his collar up against the winter chill and makes his way to the familiar coastal footpath that would lead him past the town and towards Nabb's End. A bit of weak sunshine spills through the heavy sky. It is going to turn out to be a good day – well a decent day - better than the one he thought it looked like being, when he had seen his mother off. People can't see underneath his Mac, that he is wearing something special; if they could it would surprise them. He closes his mouth more in satisfaction than a smirk and continues to walk briskly in the direction of the Nab and Thorn Cottage.

Malcolm manages to miss Jo and the children and dog by a few moments. He spots them as they round the brig; the dog is racing into the sea with the boy following him. He stands and watches, he can't see her; she is not on the beach with the others. In two minds as to whether or not to continue to the Nab, he checks once more. No she isn't with the other three. He stalls and then decides to carry on, in the hope that she might be there. The thought of her being at the cottage on her own fuels his footsteps and stirs him. He is desperate now, more than ready, his earlier action of sorting himself out, means nothing now. His erection this time is hard and strong and would not be satisfied with such ease as before. His thoughts turn towards his childhood beatings as he takes in a lungful of breath. Walking on now, he sticks his hands in his trouser pockets to rearrange himself and curses his wet trainers, as the moisture from the ground soaks through their membrane and wets his feet. 'She had better be there.'

As he reaches the cottages he makes his way along the backs of the hedges, so that he won't be seen but has a good view inside the houses. He knows the occupants who live in the first cottage, so he moves on to the next. He sees a couple seated by their coal fire and continues. Looking down below the next two cottages he sees the path veering off to the right and the large overhanging trees. Before he has chance to check the next house he sees her. It is her, she is carrying a washing up bowl as she walks past the trees. Malcolm creeps along the hedges and stops.

He manages to hide behind a fairly solid tree trunk, which keeps him out of view. A lot of the bushes and trees around the hedge are bare but if he remains here he will be safe.
There she is. He sees her walking around the side of the cottage, carrying an armful of wet washing. Piece by piece, she stretches up, to peg the things she's draped at intervals, along the line. The dampness of the wet washing has seeped into her top, which clings and outlines her breasts.
Malcolm takes his raincoat off and feels powerful, as he stands erect and ready. He can hardly hold himself back now. He knows it is what she wants, he is certain, he can tell. As she continues to bend over, Malcolm begins to undo his buttons. His fingers are trembling with the anticipation and he keeps loosing his grip, he can't hold back.

The ringing telephone startles Malcolm. He stands stock still, shocked out of his skin unable to move. Coming back to himself Malcolm bends down and picks up his Mac and pulls out the ringing phone.
"What the fuck."
Malcolm cries.
"I beg your pardon."
A stern voice responds.
"No, not you, not you, I'm sorry, sorry ...."
"Is that Malcolm Mountcross?"
"Yes, yes."

"Well Mr Mountcross we have your mother Mildred, she is very upset and is sitting in our bus unable to get in to her home."

"Yes, yes."

Malcolm says apologetically.

"You said she'd be back for 2 o'clock."

Malcolm adds by way of an explanation.

"It's almost that now Mr Mountcross."

"No, it's not."

Malcolm mutters under his breath.

"It's half past one."

"Your mother is very distressed."

"Yes, yes I see."

Malcolm tries to pick his raincoat up and put it back on. He can hear a dog from a short distance away barking. They are coming back. Malcolm begins to trot.

"I'll be back in twenty minutes."

"I'll tell your mother."

The woman concedes.

"Tell her I'm sorry and I'll be home shortly."

Malcolm jogs and trots away from the back of Thorn Cottage. He feels odd and has to stop and see what is wrong with him. Looking down, all his private parts are dangling in the gap in his open fly. He feeds his parts back into his trousers and underpants and manages to fasten one of his buttons and button up his Mac. He runs home as best he can. He feels frustrated, angry and disappointed with how things have turned out and apprehensive as to what will happen when he arrives home to the awaiting Mildred.

Anna returns indoors, thinking the phone she has heard is coming from inside the cottage. Indoors it is quiet and there is no ringing phone.

From where the detective is standing he watches
Malcolm and his antics. He is a buffoon an imbecile. He
is slow and stupid and has lost his chance, missed his
opportunity.

Watching the dog foraging along the hedgerow, he
knows it is time for him to leave too, before the dog
spots him and gives him away.
He walks steadily but purposefully, back into the small
town of Fenton, to collect his car where he has parked it.

Opening his car door, he is happy to be returning to his
hotel.

There will be other times, other opportunities. He can
wait. He wouldn't miss them or waste them when they
came up, not in the way Malcolm had.

Turning his key in his ignition he puts his car into first.
Looking in his mirror he signals his intention to pull out
and in doing so drives off, as flurries of snow flakes start
to fall.

Inside the cottage, Anna glances at the last remaining sheets of Fermanagh House, still spread out on the kitchen table and sits down and begins to read through them.

*When she thought about it Anna realised she had
never spent Christmas day alone before. She tried
to look back across her life but knew she had
always spent the day with her family and friends.
It felt strange now being alone in the cottage. The
party at Maya's and Michaels had been lovely.
And then, later with John Anna felt both pleased
and sheepish at what had happened between them.
Anna had believed and felt that that part of her life
had ended and it was over. What had happened
had surprised her because it had been so
unexpected yet once it had begun it felt so easy
and right? Anna knew, could sense he had enjoyed
the experience as much as she had. What now
Anna wondered as she switched the electric kettle
on to begin making her breakfast? Christmas day
Anna said aloud, announced it to herself and her
kitchen, who would have thought it she finished.
Her daughter hadn't been able to come because
she had already accepted an invitation from her
father and a group of her old friends. She would
spend Christmas with them. That was alright Anna
thought. She would manage, be alright. Later in
the day she would telephone her daughter and
wish her a happy Christmas and him too, there
was no reason not to now. Her sons she had sent
cards and money for as well as sending a small gift
for Mathew and Georgina to their father's house.
He would pass them on Anna knew. Anna took her
tea into the sitting room and sat down on her large
comfortable sofa. Gazing into her fire as she
drank her tea Anna accepted the thoughts now
that had been chasing around her head since she
got up. I'm lonely, I'm lonely she told herself. I
know she answered. Let's do something different
Anna said. What? Finish your tea, get dressed in*

warm clothes and just go for a very, very long walk. Shake off all the cobwebs and do some thinking. Yes Anna thought. I'll put the chicken and roast potatoes and onions in the oven on a gentle setting and I'll take myself off and then when I come back to the warm glorious aroma of chicken cooking and onions and roast potatoes. I'll phone Georgina what then Anna asked herself? Then she said I'll eat some of my delicious food and change back into my night clothes and lock up the cottage and get pissed! Good Anna told herself that sounds a plan for survival. Once her food was on a low light and the timer on to turn the oven off Anna went upstairs to dress. Pulling on her warm jumper and track suit bottoms Anna went down stairs to put on her walking boots and top coat. She had already posted Christmas cards in all her neighbours' letter boxes and had given Bridget a small gift at the beginning of the week. Pulling her cottage door too Anna put her key safely in her inside pocket so she wouldn't lose it. A dog would have been lovely Anna said as she walked down the quiet winter lane. So many Christmas's filled with family and friends and this one she had to spend alone. Come on she told herself there's worse things. It's only one day really. What was at the heart of Anna's rumination and reflection she was aware of? People she knew didn't spend Christmas alone. That was for unwanted and unloved people, for loners, for losers, not for happy successful people like she was! All her plans, her dreams, felt as if they had become nothing in the end because no one really wanted her, they never had. Anna began to climb now away from the road and up a steep incline. There were no houses or farms just *trees and bushes. Eventually the path Anna took began to level off and the climb became easier. Over a small ridge Anna looked down on to a beautiful wood. Scrambling down Anna could see how the frost clung to the trees, like icing sugar, the scene was so lovely. Like a Christmas card Anna thought. She wished she'd taken her camera or even her mobile then she could have used that to take a picture. Anna didn't see the tangled roots she stumbled over. She had caught her foot in the twisted strong roots and the fall and pull on her ankle made her feel sick. Anna fainted with the pain. She was in shock and couldn't move she was trapped with her foot caught tight, wedged, between the roots of the trees. Waves of nausea came across Anna and she pleaded to God to let the pain stop and to set her free. Anna must have passed out again because when she came around she saw a tall dark shadow standing close by. Thank God someone had come someone had found her trapped and in pain. They would help her now. As the man leant down next to her Anna's heart felt as if it had done a somersault. The man lowered his head and looked into Anna's face. As he leant across her she felt his breath on her face and against her ear. "You fucking bitch" he spat into her ear. This time Anna could hear and understand all the obscenities that the man called her and hissed into her face. Anna tried to fall back now away from him and out of the nightmare but the oppressive weight of his body upon her as she lay unable to move trapped her.*

After reading, she takes the sheets upstairs and returns them to her bedroom drawer. The ending of Fermanagh House is not what she wants anymore. She has changed since writing herself into the role of a victim. The transition has been slow, letting go of the woman she was, to become the woman she wants to be isn't an overnight change, it takes time and it is up to her – the how's and when. She has begun to reclaim the parts of her life that she has given away, piece by piece.

She makes a mug of tea and then sets the table for their return.
Right, just a basket of logs to collect and then the potatoes to put in the oven to bake.

The pages of Fermanagh House she has read through, don't please her, they disturb her. Why would she opt for such a role – she has changed from the women who wrote the story.

Bending over by the side of the log pile Anna picks up the logs and places them into the basket.

Giles sets off, his excuse and reason for leaving the family huddle, late afternoon on Boxing day is work related –'I need to go to the flat and check up on one or two things. I won't be long, I'm going to walk it, I could do with some fresh air.' He realises how limp and feeble his excuse, as soon as he sets off on the thirty-minute jaunt. 'It's Christmas and you're talking about work' he admonishes himself. Work is the last thing on his mind. His preoccupations are all about Maggie, he has left messages on her mobile and she has not returned any of them, this is so unlike her. All day this has disturbed him, and time appears to standstill as he checks again his mobile for her reply.

Pacing forward on the pavement, he barely notices the snow falling, covering the ground, he wants to push time away beneath his footsteps, the quicker he walks he hopes that time too is marching on. He has no measure of it, of time as he pushes ahead – if he slows his pace, would time pass by with lethargy, or if his feet stretch out with longer, faster strides would this have the desired effect and hurry time along. This juxtaposition irritates him, as his thoughts turn once more to Maggie; when he is with her, he just wants time to stall and stand still. He wishes that he were able to cast a spell upon their shared space and halt times' progress, to suspend and slow it down so that seconds became hours. If his Christmas gift had been a magic wand, or an ounce of magic dust, he would use it now and travel backwards to their time together at the hotel and be with her.
Giles can't believe the strength of feeling he has within him, of how caught inside Margaret's sphere he is. This was never meant to happen, it had just been a fling, a bit of fun before settling down.
Walking the pavements his thoughts turn to yesterday and the festive meal, it had been a grand affair and he felt he had earned one or two points by spending time with his parents. They adore Arabella, she fulfils the role of future daughter in law superbly in their eyes, and their

gift of a pearl necklace delighted her. He knows that the day should have been filled with happiness, especially looking forward to their future lives being spent together – their marriage would take place in a couple of months time and right now as his heart skips a beat, he experiences total apprehension and is unable to shake it off.

With each and every footstep, his misgivings amplify and as he enters the flat he kicks the junk mail to one side and collapses on the leather settee. Looking around his bachelor pad, he seeks gratification in its empty space. He remembers the partying, the boozy nights and hangover days, the rugby weekends and the many stag does – as his mind flicks through these events, what strikes him more than anything, is the fact of how inconsequential the women were. Most of the girls had enjoyed the one-night stands, the sex and the partying, the frivolity, the laughter with his mates – yes it had been one long party. And now on the verge of settling down, marrying Arabella, the idea grips him with fear. 'What the hell am I doing?' The idea of marriage he realises now has not been born out of unconditional love but rather going with the flow. His contemporaries have married one after the other and now it is his turn – one of the last of his gang to settle down. Arabella had always been on the perimeter of their crowd, looking on yet not participating fully with whatever was going on, holding herself back as if in wait for him. They had slipped together in order to stay with the crowd; the gang, who were mostly couples and they wanted the partying to go on. He had been swept along at first and now the full impact of the wedding strikes him, as he stares once more into his phone. There is still no text or voicemail message from Maggie and he presses his mobile to call her. This time her phone is switched off and feeling disappointed he leans back and wonders what he can do. With adolescent yearnings coursing through his veins, he is filled with jealousy; he experiences a level of contempt towards Charles because he is with her now. And knowing Charles as well as he does, he will probably be totally oblivious to her, he imagines him strutting around giving out his orders unmercifully throughout the holiday. Maybe, this is the reason why she hasn't been in touch, she has been unable to escape his demands and hasn't had time for herself. He breathes more easily now, feeling there is an explanation for her distance.

Charles alone at last, sits down in his office chair. He takes his whisky glass and curses; his sticky fingers tell him that Susan hasn't been to clean the house. Realising it is still only Boxing Day, he opens his mouth to call out for Margaret and rescinding pushes the tumbler away. He needs to be on his own, to think.

The past few weeks and the epic drama of yesterday have drained him completely. 'What the bloody hell has gone wrong'? He looks at the glass once more, desperate to fill it to the brim and down it in one go. 'What dam use is that?' He is still nursing a bad head from last night's excess. 'What the hell.' Charles stands up to find a clean tumbler and pours a generous measure and returns to his chair and looks intently into the brown liquid. 'The answers not in there you bloody fool.' he thinks, fighting with his conscience. 'All your life's been one long battle and just when you thought you had it all, you've buggered it up. You idiot, you bloody fool.' Margaret so far has said nothing. 'Margaret, I am one of life's cock ups.' He lifts the glass to his lips and slams it back down. 'Cock ups, cock up, the chance of that would be a fine thing.' This time he draws a mouthful of the whisky and then pushes the glass away.

It had started out as a bit of fun. He recalls the moment, the banter, the laughter and the joking when Stuart had arrived at the clubhouse. He had been doing a survey at a warehouse unit and returned with a brochure entitled 'Sexperiences for Adults.' He told them all about the place and of the extra space the company required due to its growing success.

"Look we could all go – call it managerial team building or how about corporate entertainment."
Stuart had joked.
Derek read out from the brochure.
"Amsterdam fetish hotel adventure."
James roared with laughter at the idea of body casting him and then suggested another drink and the topic of conversation changed.

After leaving the clubhouse later, Charles's fascination grew.

Believing the organisers discretion and that it would be doing no harm if he kept it secret, he had made a call for a session. He had enjoyed the experience, had felt for the first time in his life to be accepted, adequate and cared for. He had let his guard down and shown a part of himself, the part that was hungry and needy – not the strong, confidant business man – the baby inside of him who longed to suckle and feed from its mother. After the initial session, he continued and his attachment grew, he had found someone to bond with and he couldn't let go. The DVD helped with that – watching quietly in the early hours of the night in his office. Yesterday's revelation had tarnished, tainted and spoiled this. It had been shown to make it all seem sordid and dirty – this he had never felt. He hadn't experienced it as doing wrong. How could he explain, how could he make them understand.

He had told Stella, he could tell her anything – she never judged him, she accepted him and always seemed to understand. From first meeting her, their roles had reversed, he had been her supporter, guru, mentor in a way – leading her and showing her the ropes. It didn't take her long to take the baton and run with it. He fills up now with fondness for her. The temptation to turn to her now beckons but he needs to work this one out by himself, or try to. 'You're not all bad, you old bugger.'

His thoughts turn to Mark and his beating. Maybe that was taking things too far. He would be ok, he is alive and he'd had no choice, he had to stop the handouts, shut the little sod up. It could have been a lot worse.

Margaret and Monica are both in the lounge. He can't face seeing them, not now; one of them is bad enough, but not the two of them together. Monica is bound to say something; if there is a pot to stir, she is always the one to put the spoon in.

A walk, he asks himself. Now would be the ideal time to have a dog, a purpose for going out in the dark. He stands up and decides to get his coat.

He pokes his head through the lounge doorway and tells Margaret he is going to stretch his legs and get some fresh air.

He takes the path towards the cliffs leading down to the beach, he is surprised by the snow as it lifts in the air and wafts in his face. The way is strewn with pebbles and tufts of course grass, impeding his footsteps as he stumbles along. If the snow continues this path will become treacherous to walk along. The sea below him, invisible, yet sending out its powerful message, as it crashes against the shore. The darkness of the night makes the decision to turn back appealing; the idea of returning to Monica however makes up his mind and propels him forward. He will walk to the pub and have a couple of pints. The women would be in bed by the time of his return.

These moments spent alone steady him, he has found a small measure of peace and feels agreeable with himself. The lights from the promenade below greet him and he can see the sign of the pub further along. He smiles as his feet take to the pavement and thinks, 'life is not all bad.' Opening the door of the Sailors Arms he has found a haven and can leave his reflections for now.

"Margaret dear, would you like to tell me what's going on? I know Charles is not an easy man but the embarrassment; what on earth was that all about for heaven's sake? You don't need me to tell you, that that sort of behaviour comes from someone who is satisfied with their lot. And as for you, well I've seen this all before, look at you dear. Your distracted, your minds elsewhere, floating off. Who is he, who is it this time?"

"Oh mother must you?"

"You know you can tell me dear, I am your mother after all."

Margaret stands up from the settee.

"I'll go and put the kettle on mother."

"Oh that's it, here we go, another cup of tea, were almost drowning in it."

"I'm worried mother, worried about daddy, one thing at a time."

"It's no good trying to change tack darling, Philip will be fine, he is in good hands – the doctor said he's had a minor stroke and will have to take it easy. Charles's escapade is the last thing he needed don't you think?"

"Oh mummy."

"Well Margaret if it is money that's the problem, if you really want to leave Charles, then you have our total support, after all he has let you down, what on earth can he have been thinking of. A baby Margaret for goodness sake and who on earth was she, the nurse? A gin sweetheart, I think we both need a gin."

Margaret knows her mother has only just begun and that this is only the start.

"Would you like tonic water and ice mother?"

"Yes darling, I'll have a large one."

Margaret pours out the two gin and tonics, making sure the glass for her mother is mostly filled with the spirit. After their second refill Monica loosens up and Margaret wishes she had insisted on having a cup of tea, the idea of getting her mother a bit tipsy is about to backfire.

"Margaret shall we take another little look?"

"A look at what mother?"

Whispering Monica begins.

"The DVD, where did you put it?"

Starting to laugh Monica carries on.

"I do wonder darling, where they got the big dummy from and the frilly hat."

Monica bends over in stitches.

"Stop it mother, stop it, it just isn't funny in the slightest."

Monica contorts with a fit of giggles and can't stop herself.

"I'm going to bed mother, I will see you in the morning."

Margaret stands up, leaving Monica in tears, draped along the arm of the settee.

"I'll just check the kids before we settle down."
Anna says.
The room looks cosy and inviting. The logs are well
caught on in the hearth, crackling and spluttering out tiny
sparks.
"I'll open the bottle of wine."
Anna enters Adam's room first. The lamp is on at the
side of the bed; she has let Georgina sleep in her bed
because Adam needs longer to settle down. Seeing his
mum, Adam slips the earphones out.
"Do you think we'll find it mam?"
Anna knows this will become another saga, if it isn't
sorted out or settled before they leave the coast, just like
the mobile phone left at the caravan.
He would natter on now endlessly, about loosing the
boat.
"We'll have another look for it tomorrow."
Anna puts his duvet straight and places his action man
on the floor by the side of his bed.
"I want it back."
"I know you do love."
"We'll go out again tomorrow to look for it, so stop
worrying."
Anna passes him his new book on cars.
"Jo said."
Anna tells her son.
"That if we can't find this 'Purple Pearl' she'll make you
another one for next summer, so you see, things will
work out, if this 'Purple Pearl' has gone."
"Gone where?"
"Gone on a dangerous voyage across the sea with a band
of tiny seahorse pirates."
"Do you think it has?"
Adam asks, warming to the prospects of his boat having
its own adventure.
"Of course, you've heard of sea dogs haven't you?"
Adam nods his head.

"Well, these are similar things to sea dogs, only they're seahorses but they're as bad and as dangerous as sea dogs."
This explanation seems to be sinking in and taking a hold of her son's imagination.
"They'll bring it back you know."
Anna warms to her theme.
"And then Jo will do it all up again for you, so you have all the summer to play with it."
Adam puts his earphones back in. He is satisfied now and would settle. Later when she comes to bed she will turn his bedside light out if he hasn't switched it off.
Anna pulls the door too but doesn't close it properly, so it is very slightly ajar.

Thinking about the 'Purple Pearl', reminds Anna about the papers she slipped back into her bedside drawer. Opening the drawer, she watches her sleeping child and takes out the small bundle of papers and kisses her daughter on the forehead and turns off the bedside lamp. Georgina is in the middle of the bed, which means that when Anna comes up, she'll have to sleep on the edge unless she feels ruthless enough to push her sleeping daughter to one side.
Taking the bundle of papers downstairs, she is glad to be able to sit down at last and relax.
Anna takes the glass of red wine and closes her eyes and takes a sip, it is smooth and fruity and she licks her lips to absorb and savour the moment.
"Mmmm, this is good."
Anna puts her wine down and sits back on the large comfy sofa. This is good Anna decides, 'This is where I wants to be.'
"Penny for them?"
Sitting up Anna begins.
"I was thinking. It's been a long time but for the first time in ages, I feel that this is where I want to be. I am where I want to be."
"That's good."

Anna picks up her bundle of papers. The last scraps she has left of the book she began in the summer.

"Do you remember the blue notebook that I brought to your hut to burn on the bonfire?"

"Yes."

"Well, I found these pages, when I had to go back to the caravan to look for Adam's mobile phone, and today whilst you were out I've read them and know that this isn't the ending I want for my character, nor do I want to write this kind of book."

Anna stops and explains what she is going to do.

"I'm going to burn these, just like I burnt the book. That was the right thing to do for the book and I'm even more certain that it's as important for the ending that I've written."

"Are you sure?"

"Absolutely certain, what I have been thinking about and what's been going round and round my head since I read these pages, is that I created the people in the book and the awful ending is as much about me. If I am the creator of the book and have chosen to give it a crap ending that's up to me and if I can create something with an unhappy and sad ending, then I can also create something which can have a positive and hopeful ending or beginning. So in some ways."

Anna lifts her glass from the table and takes a sip.

"It's up to me and that's big."

"Yes it is."

"The abuse and rape have happened, I can't change that, nor can I make honest sense from it."

Anna takes another sip from her wine before continuing.

"I want to write another story and create a different ending, a good ending."

Anna drains her glass and places it on the table.

Picking up the pages she places the sheets of paper onto the fire to burn. Standing up she turns and looks at Jo.

"It's time to write a new story now with a better ending – one that shows me who I want to be, or who I can be – not someone who I was. I'm not that same person anymore. I realise now that I can create another version because really it's up to me how I write the story of my life."

Anna turns again to look at the charcoaled sheets of words, as flames devour them. "All those words of how time stood still and consumed her life, time so much lost time."

Margaret checks around the kitchen for the umpteenth
time – the cooker, the taps, the coffee maker and then
finally she switches of the lights.

Entering her bedroom she removes her slippers and sits
on the dressing table stool and looks into the mirror. Her
mother's laughter has been the final straw. Right now
she doesn't even want to speak with Giles, she cannot
face him. The overwhelming sense of ridicule and
embarrassment envelops her and she is unable to
summon Giles to her mind. She wants more than
anything to erase yesterday, to turn back the clock, to
delete it from ever having happened. She hopes with all
her heart that this revelation never gets out. That it will
remain inside this house. She feels deflated and rejected
and not even her thoughts about Giles can lift her. As
desperate as she feels and struggles, she is at a loss as to
what to do. Giles has been her lifeline recently and as
hard as she tries, she can't summon him to her.

She decides a long hot soak in the bath might wash some
of her troubles away. This only helps to stir other
emotions of her times with Giles and she quickly pulls
out the plug and dries herself. Sitting before the mirror
again Margaret combs through her hair. As she looks
again and beyond her own reflection she hears a knock at
the bedroom door. She waits, fearing the worst that her
mother has decided to continue her dissection of her
world, her life, to belittle her.

"Margaret."

Charles knocks again.

Margaret is tempted to ignore the call; she has had plenty
for one evening. Standing she goes across to the door
and opens it. She can smell the beer fumes as Charles
steps into the room. Margaret sits back down on the edge
of the bed and Charles bends down before her.

"I'm sorry Margaret, sorry I've embarrassed you. I never
intended you to know, I never intended to hurt you. I am
so sorry."

Charles offers with genuine regret.

"I know, I'm sorry too."

Charles sits at Margaret's side and their arms touch each other's.

"How's Philip?"

"The doctors say that he has had a minor stroke."

"Well he's always been a tough old bugger."

"He's ninety three Charles."

"Yes I know, he's in the best place Margaret."

"I'm tired Charles, tired – I've had my mother acting as if its been a huge piece of entertainment. It's her way of detaching herself from daddy. I think she is suffering from shock."

"Your mother has always been capable of turning other peoples troubles into entertainment for her own ends. It prevents her from looking at herself, would you like a drink?"

"No thank you."

"Shall we have an early night then?"

"Yes."

Charles watches as Margaret takes off her dressing gown and slips into bed beneath the sheets. He removes his clothing and goes into the bathroom to take a quick shower.

Returning he climbs into bed and feels the heat of her body as he nestles in beside her. Charles moves closer and holds her. He inhales the scent of her as he draws her towards him, protecting her.

Why Margaret thinks, 'has it taken all of this for you to come back to me?' She thought that this caring side of him had disappeared forever. And now here tonight of all nights, he lay holding and reassuring her, breathing softly against her neck comfort and love. As his hand cups her breasts she feels safe, secure and protected by him. She has wanted this for such a long time.

Forgiveness of him comes easily for her. About herself she is unsure, about her hidden secret. With Giles it is different, a driven passion never fully satisfied and always wanting more. 'This is enough for us Charles'; Margaret answers the question rising within her. Giles is a different relationship entirely, sexually frantic, a hunting out of each other to satisfy their needs. 'Can I carry on? Should I stop seeing him? Is it now time to confess – to own up?' She knows if she does, this closeness between them now, would be again corrupted, it would probably be the end.

She hears the gentle, peaceful and steady snoring of Charles and closes her eyes. For now, this moment is all that matters; of this she is absolutely sure.

Anna's words echo through Jo's whole being as if she
has set fire to her soul – however much Anna's thoughts
are true to her, Jo very much doubts she could
comprehend her missing years. Etched in memory now,
as a faded background of fleeting transient moments. Jo
has stepped out of the world of her past and begun again.
Running away has challenged her existence and
somehow she has survived. This juxtaposition in their
lives is the same for both of them. For Anna a portent
dwelling in her family history and fictitious playing out,
a repetitious remake of the same, heralds a realisation
and transition to pave a new map for her life.
Jo is pleased for her, yet she drinks the wine greedily as
if to douse the flames inside herself, to flood her mind
and body, to slake its vehement words, to drown out his
presence.

Anna leaves the room and Jo begins to shake and sob,
it's as if the returning wave of grief cannot be assuaged
or stopped. And strangely she welcomes it. For such a
long time she has held it back, held it inside, and closed
off these feelings with belief, that if allowed, they would
leave her alone and bereft in a deep, dark place, a
sinking ship and that she would never return, that she
would be lost and gone forever.

The red-hot tears running down her cheeks burn her face.
Jo's whole being yearns to purge itself and empty out
this unbearable, toxic waste that has consumed her for so
long.
As her torso heaves with each increasing wave of
emotion, she lets go and allows the surge of motion to
eke itself out.

"What's wrong Jo?"
Anna puts down the bottle of wine, the nuts and the
chocolates and sits by Jo's side.
"What is it, what's the matter?"

As her body subsides Jo looks up to Anna.
"He's not dead, I didn't kill him."
"What do you mean, who, I don't understand."
Jo wipes her face and blow her nose and takes out the
crumpled sheet from her pocket.
"Here."
She hands Anna the piece of paper to read.

I AM   ALIVE NOT DEAD

YOU DID **NOT KILL** ME
MY *HEART* STILL   *BE*ATS

LIKE *YOU* SAID **IT** NEVER   WOULD

SO NOW YOU KNOW

I *AM* **HERE**

YOUR CLUE **FOR** TODAY

SO YOU BELIEVE ME!!!

I HAVE *STILL* **GO** *T* THE **RABBIT'S** FOOT

"Where did you get this?"
"Today at the hut, it's from the same person as before,
you know the other letter we found."
"But how do you know, who sent it?"
"It's a man that I ran away from, I thought I had killed
him and now I know that I didn't, he must be still alive."
They both sit in silence, watching the flames on the logs
in the fireplace.
"Are you certain that it's from him?"
"Yes only he would have put about the rabbit's foot, I
gave it to him as a present."
Fresh tears pour down Jo's face as Anna sits quietly
aside.

"Do you want to talk about it?"

"I don't know where to start."

"What happened Jo?"

"I really thought I'd killed him."

"But you didn't."

"No, I can't have done. I left everything, I couldn't take anymore, oh Anna."

"It's ok."

"That's why I came to Fenton, bought the hut. I ran away from him."

"Gosh."

"I left myself behind, I had to and became Jo."

"You haven't left yourself behind."

How could she discard and reject her psyche, the reality of herself, just close the door behind her persona and lock it, as if walking away for a day.

"I understand now, why you've changed your name."

"Yes I had to. I can't go back."

"You have a choice."

"No I could never go back."

"He must have really hurt you."

"Yes but he can't now, even if he is alive. I'm free, my life's here and I'm not hiding in the shadows anymore."

"No and that's true for both of us, do you still want me to call you Jo?"

"Yes, I am Jo now and I know why this hurts so much, remembering what happened and finding a part of myself that I thought was lost for ever."

"I'm sorry and glad Jo, glad that I found you."

"Yes me too, it's been good to share this Christmas and ourselves, let's not lose what we have together."

"No Jo, let's not."

South London, 4 p.m. - New Years Eve.

It is time. His eyes check the hands of the clock once again; it is time to set off. This habitual ritual weighs heavy, against his desire to remain seated in front of the gas fire, he is compelled to move, to heave himself up from the chair and put on his hat and coat. He would feel a failure, if he allowed his idle temptation of ineptness, to dictate the course of his day. In all his later years, he has maintained his regime of sharing in the celebratory festivities of New Years evening. His predilections prevent him, from joining in with the hoards of people in the pubs, waiting for the countdown to twelve o'clock. He prefers to go to his local mid afternoon and have a couple of pints in relative solitude before the revellers descend en masse.

He decides to leave the fire on for his return. The stack of papers and envelopes set out meticulously on his desk remind him of his actions and he drops his head momentarily. He sighs. Knowing that no matter what time of day, his first thoughts belong to her. The prolific costs, spiralling at the very notion of his continued pursuit and the letters he had sent, but for what purpose? And the detective, he can feel his hackles raised knowing this man has seen her, watched her and waited, reporting back to him. He realises now, why he deferred writing the cheque, why he protracted his last payment, filled with resentment he decides the detective will have to wait.

In the hallway he laces his shoes, takes a woollen scarf, wraps it around his neck and pulls on his coat and hat. Opening the door he is surprised by the thick covering of snow on the ground as he locks it behind him. The wind whips the snow in the distance, creating swirls of flakes to spin and dance around the lamps and car headlights coming his way.

Had it been any other day he would have turned around, retreated back to the warm comfort of his home. He presses on. Passing the avenues with fairy light adorned

trees, the Santa's pulling their sleighs, the whole
Christmas theme in massive exaggeration.
Eventually he turns the corner and joins the main road
into town. Pursuing his cause, he maintains his efforts
and enters The Royal Oak, cold, stiff and his feet
sodden. After removing his coat he makes his way to the
bar and orders a pint of best bitter. There are several
hardened drinkers who acknowledge his entry as he sits
down near the roaring coal fire. It is too early for the
partygoers and the place is waiting in readiness for the
evening to come. His frozen hands clasp the glass as he
lifts it to his icy lips, the beer is cold and he finds no
affinity as he drinks. A red wine at room temperature is
his preference and he places the glass down with disdain.
However he is happy with his attempt at marking out the
evening of the coming year. As the glow from the fire
warms him, he rubs his hands together and occasionally
he shudders when the cold draft wafts across from the
opening door.
After his prerequisite of two pints, he stands and for a
fleeting moment allows the heat of the fire to warm his
back. He can go home now.

With his coat collar turned up, he nods to the few
stalwarts as he leaves the pub.

The snow is heavy now, lying thickly on the frozen
ground. On the pavement opposite there is a huddle of
girls, leaving a restaurant, laughing and holding onto
each other, as they slip and slide in their high heels in the
snow.

It all happens in slow motion and at the same time, so
very fast, as an onlooker and then a victim, the car spins
out of control, the laughter ceases, the car veers
sideways and hits him.

The complete blackness and the residual bang are left
hanging in the air.

www.ingramcontent.com/pod-product-compliance
Lightning Source LLC
Chambersburg PA
CBHW020241030726
47499CB00001B/9

* 9 7 8 0 9 5 5 9 9 0 5 5 7 *